French Tales of
Cataclysms

FROM THE SAME PUBLISHER

Jean-Marc & Randy Lofficier. *The French Fantasy Treasury* (3 volumes)
Jean-Marc & Randy Lofficier. *French Tales of Alien Contacts*
Jean-Marc & Randy Lofficier. *Shadowmen: Heroes & Villains of French Pulp Fiction*
Jean-Marc & Randy Lofficier. *Shadowmen 2: Heroes & Villains of French Comics*
Brian Stableford. *Automata: The Imaginative Legacy of Jacques de Vaucanson*
Brian Stableford. *The Plurality of Imaginary Worlds: The Evolution of French* Roman Scientifique
Brian Stableford. *Tales of Enchantment and Disenchantment: A History of Faerie, with an Exemplary Anthology of Tales*
Brian Stableford. *Weird Fiction in France: A Showcase Anthology of its Origins and Development*

French Tales of Cataclysms

by
**Georges Bethuys, Raoul Bigot,
Camille Debans, Henri Falk,
Alfred Franklin, Louis Gallet,
Maurice Leblanc, Eugène Mouton,
René Pujol, J.-H. Rosny Aîné,
Colonel Royet** and **Pierre Véron**

translated, annotated and introduced by
Brian Stableford
(with the exception of *The Tremendous Event*)

A Black Coat Press Book

ISBN 978-1-64932-110-7. First Printing. June 2022. Published by Black Coat Press, an imprint of Hollywood Comics.com, LLC, P.O. Box 17270, Encino, CA 91416. All rights reserved. Except for review purposes, no part of this book may be reproduced or transmitted in any form or by any means, electronic or mechanical, including photocopying, recording, or by any information storage and retrieval system, without permission in writing from the publisher. The stories and characters depicted in this novel are entirely fictional. Printed in the United States of America.

TABLE OF CONTENTS

Introduction 7
Pierre Véron: *The Paris Deluge* 13
Eugène Mouton: *The End of the World* 19
Alfred Franklin: *The Ruins of Paris in 4875* 27
J.-H. Rosny *Aîné*: *The Cataclysm* 48
Camille Debans: *The Story of an Earthquake* 61
Louis Gallet: *The Death of Paris* 76
Georges Bethuys: *Cataclysm* 82
Raoul Bigot: *The Iron That Died* 99
Henri Falk: *The Age of Lead* 113
Maurice Leblanc: *The Tremendous Event* 143
    Part One: William the Conqueror 145
    Part Two: No Man's Land 205
René Pujol: *The Black Sun* 263
Colonel Royet: *On the Brink of the World's End* 313

henri Falk

L'Age de Plomb

1 fr.

A L'ŒUVRE, 25, Rue Royale, PARIS

Introduction

The term "cataclysm" is defined as a large-scale and violent event in the natural world., or a sudden and equally violent political or social upheaval. Such concepts are common in the French *roman scientifique*—a genre that some might call proto-sf—from its origins in the 18th century through today.

This thematic collection gathers ten remarkable short stories, published between 1802 and 1928, plus two full-length novels, including one by Maurice Leblanc—the father of Arsène Lupin, published respectively in 1920 and 1928. But there are other, equally remarkable, but longer works which deserve to be mentioned in this introduction for the benefit of those wishing to further study the amazing range of ideas and styles in which this theme was handled by French writers in past centuries.

A number of these works have already been translated and published by Black Coat Press (as indicated in **bold**) and are available on paper or as eBooks on our site, *www.blackcoatpress.com*, on Amazon, Barnes & Noble, and wherever books are sold online.

Not surprisingly, the pioneer of "cataclysmic fiction" was Nicolas-Edmé Restif de la Bretonne, a prolific author of semi-autobiographic and somewhat pornographic novels. His many proto-science fictional works were virtually "resurrected" by noted researcher Pierre Versins, who devoted a full eight pages to them in his *Encyclopédie de l'Utopie, des Voyages Extraordinaires et de la Science Fiction*, and called him a "master of conjecture, utopia, and science fiction." In the trilogy *Les Posthumes* [**Posthumous Correspondence**] (1802) (Black Coat Press, ISBNs 978-1-61227-513-0, 978-1-61227-514-7 & 978-1-61227-515-4), the Duke of Multipliandre masters the ability to free his mind from his body, embarks on a vast journey through space and time, eventually watching the Earth plummeting towards the Sun—the final and ultimate cataclysm—some three million years in the future.

Despite its excesses, the French Revolution succeeded in imposing the values of scientific progress and so-called Cartesian thinking on French society, thus setting the stage for the Industrial Revolution. The 19th century was also a period of colonial expansion, with fierce competition between European powers. Literature being the mirror of society, some of these notions were bound to be reflected in the novels of the times.

The earliest and most notable novel in the ever-popular theme of "The Last Man on Earth" was *Le Dernier Homme* [The Last Man] (1805) by Jean-Baptiste Cousin de Grainville. In it, we meet the eponymous Omegare in a bleak vision of the future when a dying Earth has become sterile. The god-like Ormus tries to manipulate him into fathering a new race of cannibals doomed to live in eternal darkness, but Omegare instead chooses death.

The notion of a future apocalypse was again forecasted and explored in greater details by Antoine-François-Marius Rey-Dussueil in *La Fin du Monde* [The End of the World] (1830). In it, a comet pushes Earth off its axis, causing the ice to melt and the world to be flooded. Fortunately, a man and three women (!) survived at the top of the Mont-Blanc. While Rey-Dussueil failed to fully exploit the theme of a cosmic cataclysm bringing about the end of the world, he earned the right to be considered the first serious "cataclysmic" author of the 19th century.

Of passing interest is *Histoire de la Fin du Monde, ou La Comète de 1904* [*Story of the End of the World, or The Comet of 1904*] (1882) by a Swiss author signing "Verniculus" in which the comet threatened to turn Earth's atmosphere into a flammable gas. Jules Verne himself appears as a character in the novel.

The most notable cataclysmic fiction of the time was penned by astronomer-writer Camille Flammarion, who penned many brilliant, ground-breaking science fiction stories collected in *Récits de l'Infini* [*Stories of Infinity*] (1872), revised as *Lumen* (1887). His masterpiece is *La Fin du Monde* [*The End of the World*] (1893), loosely adapted into an eponymous 1930 film by Abel Gance. The book exposes in great details the history of Man in the 25th century, and the eventual disappearance of Earth's atmosphere. Perhaps not surprisingly for someone so well versed in the history of the genre, Flammarion's "last man on Earth" is also named "Omegar."

Félicien Champsaur came up with a rather original cataclysm in his novella *Le Dernier Homme* [*The Last Man*]) (1907), in which a passing comet increases the amount of oxygen in Earth's atmosphere and causes the forests to take over Paris and man to revert to an ape-like condition.

J.-H. Rosny Aîné's novella, *La Mort de la Terre* [*The Death of the Earth*] (1910) (included in the Black Coat Press collection, **The Navigators of Space**, ISBN 978-1-935558-35-4) also takes place in the far future, when Earth has all but dried out. In it, the last descendants of mankind became aware of the emergence of a new species, the metal based "Ferromagnetals" who are destined to replace humanity.

In *La Force Mystérieuse* [**The Mysterious Force**] (1913) (Black Coat Press, ISBN 978-1-935558-46-0), Rosny tells of the destruction of a portion of the light spectrum by the "force," possibly aliens who, for a brief moment, share our physical existence. This causes panic, then a progressive and deadly cooling of the world. Social upheaval follows before order is eventually restored.[1]

---

[1] *La Force Mystérieuse* is, coincidentally, similar to Doyle's *The Poisoned Sky*, published at the same time.

World War I with its 2.3 million dead and maimed, sapped the confidence of French society, despite the chauvinistic pride and xenophobic arrogance it created. This schizophrenic conflict between the illusion of superiority and the desire to preserve old values on the one hand, and the emergence of a new world on the other, played out, with dramatic results in science fiction.

The years following the end of the Great War bought forth a glut of catastrophist fantasies, partly as a reaction against the fact that virtually all fiction published during the war was obliged to be relentlessly upbeat, as a calculated instrument of maintaining morale, and partly because of the realization, rammed home in no uncertain terms by the experience of the war, of exactly how vulnerable civilization was to complete collapse, and how people might genuinely be expected to react and behave under tremendous stress and the threat of imminent annihilation.

In addition to the stories assembled in this collection, we should also single out the following:

In Colonel Royet's *La Tempête Universelle de l'An 2000* [*The Global Storm of the Year 2000*] (1921), solar flares kill all life on Earth, except for an American man and a French woman; this new Adam and Eve must then fight giant worms for possession of our planet.

Henri-Jeanne Magog, the author of numerous popular adventure novels mostly forgotten today, penned the pulp-like *Extraordinaire Aventures de Deux Fiancés à travers le Monde* [*Extraordinary Adventures of Two Fiancés Across the World*] (1922), which takes place in 2050, when a mad scientist uses heat from the Earth's core to cause the oceans to dry up. In *L'Île Tombée du Ciel* [*The Island That Fell from the Sky*] (1923), a chunk of a wandering planet falls on Australia; explorers discover that it is inhabited by invisible aliens who turn out to be benevolent.

Perhaps the first professional female author in science fiction, Swiss writer Noëlle Roger (nom-de-plume of Hélène Pittard penned *Le Nouveau Déluge* [*The New Flood*] (1922) in which the entire European continent is sinking. The ensuing exodus and fight for survival are narrated with uncharacteristic sobriety and subtlety, anticipating the British novels of John Wyndham and Edmund Cooper.

In a more sensational vein, Aslan's *Adieu, Britannia!* (1923) showed the British Isles submerged by a giant tide.

Another female author of the period, Renée Dunan, wrote *La Dernière Jouissance* [**The Ultimate Pleasure**] (1925) (Black Coat Press, ISBN 978-1-61227-406-5) about the future of the human race after it has been decimated by a deadly underground gas called "necron."

The most visionary novel of the decade on the theme is undoubtedly José Moselli's *La Fin d'Illa* [***The End of Illa***] (1925) (Black Coat Press, ISBN 978-1-61227-031-9) which begins with the emergence of a new island in the Pacific, on which is found a cache of ancient documents and a small fragment of something called "zero-stone." A scientist manages to decipher the documents, which tell the tale of the final, apocalyptic clash between the ancient Gondwanan cities of Illa and Nour. Later, his servant unwittingly throws the fragment of zerostone into the fireplace, causing the famous 1906 earthquake. In *La Fin d'Illa*, Moselli not only anticipated the technological horrors of World War II, but he was the first to equate nuclear conflict—even one won by one side—with mutual destruction.

That same year, Ernest Pérochon, a winner of the prestigious Goncourt Award, penned an equally remarkable scientific anticipation, *Les Hommes Frénétiques* [**The Frenetic Men**] (1925) (Black Coat Press, ISBN 978-1-61227-118-7). The novel took place in the 30th century, following a global war. Energy is now provided by the controlled disintegration of potassium salts, and cities, stretched like wires along the meridians, form a planet-wide grid. When another war starts, new, even more horrible weapons are used, which mutate humanity, and the novel ends with yet another Adam and a new Eve.

Pierre Dominique's *Le Feu du Ciel* [*Fire from the Sky*] (1926) was the description of a fiery apocalypse.

In 1927, Claude Farrère, the first recipient of the prestigious Goncourt Award, wrote *Fin de Planète* [*End of a Planet*] (1927) in which a disgruntled chemist, unable to marry the girl he loves, causes the disintegration of his world, which is revealed at the end to be the missing fifth planet of our solar system.

As early as 1913, Henri Allorge had predicted the dire consequences of the disappearance of iron in *La Famine de Fer* [*The Iron Famine*]. His more elaborate *Le Grand Cataclysme* [**The Great Cataclysm**] (1927) (Black Coat Press, ISBN 978-1-61227-026-5) features a world suddenly without electricity.

The disappearance of iron was a popular theme that had also been explored in Raoul Bigot's *Le Fer qui Meurt* [*The Iron That Died*] (1918) (included in this volume) and Serge Held's *La Mort du Fer* [*The Death of Iron*] (1931), in which alien spores carried to Earth by a meteorite destroy all iron.

André Armandy's *Le Grand Crépuscule* [*The Great Twilight*] (1929) prophetically dealt with the exhaustion of our petroleum resources.

Georges Lebas who, in *Jean Arlog, Le Premier Surhomme* [*Jean Arlog, The First Superman*] (1921), had written about a telekinetic mutant who had tried, but failed, to stop the rotation of the Earth, described how our planet is captured by a wandering star in *L'Heure Perdue* [*The Lost Hour*] (1930).

In 1930, Théo Varlet wrote *La Grande Panne* [*The Great Breakdown;* tr. as **The Xenobiotic Invasion**] (Black Coat Press, ISBN 978-1-61227-054-8), in which Aurore Lescure, the first fictional female astronaut, unknowingly brings back to Earth a virus which nullifies electricity.

In Charles de L'Andelyn's *Les Derniers Jours du Monde* [*The Last Days of the World*] (1931), it is a new ice age that threatens mankind's survival.

In *Tréponème* (1931) by Dr. Marc La Marche, it was a new virus that spells out the death of humanity, leaving behind a new race of mutants.

Pierre de Nolhac's *Saison en Auvergne* [*Season in Auvergne*] (1932) imagines an earthquake which creates an inland sea in the center of France.

In Jean Quatremarre's *Alors la Terre s'arrêta... [Then The Earth Stood Still]* (1934), an asteroid crashes into the Moon, which then falls to Earth, killing everyone except for a couple of humans.

In 1935, Jacques Spitz, a dark and pessimistic writer influenced by the Surrealists, wrote his first novel, *L'Agonie du Globe* [*The Agony of the Globe*], in which Earth becomes bisected into two hemispheres, one of which eventually crashes into the Moon.

René Barjavel, the last major author of the period, and the first to emerge after World War II, was equally pessimistic and stood against scientific progress and science. His first novel, Ravage (1943), also deals with the mysterious disappearance of electricity and portrays a post-holocaust France turning away from the evils of technology and returning to an agrarian, utopian setting.

Finally, B.-R. Bruss' (a pseudonym of René Bonnefay) first genre novel, *Et la Planète Sauta... [And The Planet Exploded...]* (1946), told of the self-destruction of the fifth planet when a nuclear scientist ultimately chooses death over enslavement by a tyrant with mind-control powers.

Later works, including recent ones, deserve to be mentioned here, but we chose to stop just after World War II, because French science fiction then began to reflect and incorporate the growing influence of American science fiction. We are pleased to refer readers who would like to have a more detailed study of the field to Brian Stableford's **The Plurality of Imaginary Worlds** (Black Coat Press, ISBN 978-1-61227-503-1) and our own *French Science Fiction, Fantasy, Horror & Pulp Fiction* (McFarland, 2000, ISBN 0-7864-0596-1), now out of print but still available online.

Jean-Marc & Randy Lofficier

LE N° MENSUEL, PRIX PROVISOIRE : QUATRE FRANCS.   15 OCTOBRE 1920

JE SAIS TOUT

LIRE DANS CE NUMÉRO :

LE FORMIDABLE ÉVÉNEMENT

ROMAN INÉDIT, PAR MAURICE LEBLANC

Éditions Pierre Lafitte

Pierre Véron: *The Paris Deluge*
(1859)

"Le Déluge en Paris" (tr. as "The Paris Deluge") was published in the collection Les Marionettes de Paris *in 1862, but if it follows the common convention of setting futuristic fantasies a precise number of centuries in the future after the date of writing, it must have been written in 1859.*

When he began to carve out a successful career as a journalist in the early 1860s, Pierre Véron (1833-1900) swiftly became a frequent contributor to two of the most popular Parisian humorous papers, both founded by Charles Philipon, Le Charivari—*the satirical magazine which served as the model for the English magazine* Punch—*and the more broadly humorous* Journal Amusant. *Most of his contributions were made during the editorial reign of Charles' son and heir, Eugène Philipon, which began in 1862, and Véron succeeded Eugène in his turn as editor-in-chief of both periodicals in 1874, retaining that position until his retirement, only a few months before his death.*

Once he had taken over the editorial chairs, his own contributions to the magazines became considerably less prolific, and somewhat less mordant. It is arguable that he did his best satirical work in the early 1860s, and that his work became steadily more relaxed and amiable thereafter, as his sarcasm gradually smoothed out the aggressive edge typically contained in this novella.

Apart from an early collection of poetry and the published versions of some of his plays (which were mostly written in collaboration with Edmond Gondinet), the contents of Véron's many books, including his patchwork novellas, were derived from his writings from those humorous periodicals, almost all of which was done in the form of vignettes that rarely ran to much more than a thousand words. Almost all of his prose pieces, whether fictional or nonfictional, were ironic reflections on Parisian life, and his work for the theater, including librettos for operettas with music by Robert Planquette, is in the same vein. All of his speculative works were stimulated by his interest in the manner in which Paris was evolving, both physically and socially.

Véron's speculative fiction is mostly contemporary with the birth and early development of Vernian roman scientifique, *reacting to the same social stimuli, albeit in a markedly different fashion. Life in Paris during the Second Empire was dominated by the metamorphosis of the city directed by the Prefect of the Seine, Baron Haussmann, who supervised the total demolition of many of the old and cramped districts, and the planning of the network of boulevards and squares, complemented by parks, fountains and an elaborate system of sewers. Details of the work were always controversial, and even those sympathetic to the overall plan, often wondered whether the Baron's demolitions might not be a little too extreme, and his reconstructions more than a little too "vulgar." The social changes represented and embodied by the physical alterations were bound to occasion satirical reaction, and also to stimulate curiosity as to where the city, and the society to which it played host, were headed in response to scientific and technological advance and the inexorable forces of commercialization.*

B.S.

The newspapers, large and small, have all recently made a meal of the certainty of a new Deluge resulting from a rupture of equilibrium between the various seas.

The due date of that scheduled inundation is, in truth, distant by a number of years that guarantees our generation against any non-Duval *bouillon*.[2] However, a day will come—*dies irae*—when the impotent Parisians will see themselves submerged beneath the umbrellas of the *Medusa*. It is that day and its consequences that we ask your permission to envisage, transporting ourselves in anticipation into the remote future.

Before

The year 4859 is reaching its end, but for ten years already the most alarming news has been circulating. Every day, in fact, the seas have been gaining ground in the north and retreating in the south; a scientist beloved by Parisians, Monsieur Babinet LXIV,[3] charged with monitoring the scourge, has declared that the equilibrium will be broken within a week. That was six days ago.

Thus, the physiognomy of the great city is unrecognizable; the theaters have stopped opening, the boulevard cafes are devoid of customers.

All the vices have suddenly disappeared; all the good qualities are the order of the day. Everywhere fees are being offered to agents who can procure some poor individual with whom a rich one can share his fortune. Shopkeepers are advertising their merchandise at below cost price. Proprietors are stopping passers-by in the street and begging them to accept gratuitous hospitality.

---

[2] The new restaurant chain created by Pierre-Louis Duval and vastly expanded by his son Alexandre, the largest of which was *La Belle Bouille* [Lovely Stew], the rest becoming known as *Bouillons Duval* in consequence, seemed to many observers to be a key feature of the New Paris in the process of creation by Baron Haussmann.

[3] Undoubtedly a descendant of the physicist and meteorologist Jacques Babinet (1794-1872), whose public lectures were famous for wit and accessibility; one of them might well have been the stimulus for this piece.

The columns of all the critics are devoted to defaming their own works and praising those of their colleagues. Three novelists have taken abnegation so far as to returning to all the purchasers the money from three novels which, they admit in a circular, is not worth two sous.

Such is the enthusiasm for virtue that has gripped the population that the Académie has been obliged to renounce judging the Prix Montyon, seventeen million, nine hundred and seventy-seven thousand people having been deemed worthy *ex aequo*.

On the site formerly occupied by the Bréda quarter, three gigantic houses of retreat have been built; each of them contains three thousand penitents and is directed by a former dancer at the Opéra.

After virtue, the unique occupation of Parisians is constructing balloons, dirigible or otherwise, in order to escape the scourge. Monsieur Godard CXI[4] has made a profit in that operation of twenty-three millions, which he has generously donated to the Association of Ruined Stockbrokers.

During

The great cup has overflowed.

The swell is camped where Tortoni was. All the balloons, torn apart by the atmospheric convulsions, have burst unanimously. Vengeful waves have taken up residence where the innocent cascades of the Palais-Royal once reigned. Unlike Vatel, Paris is complaining that the fish have arrived too soon,[5] for myriads of them have spread out in the streets, along the boulevards and in the squares.

Two oysters (opening their shells as they pass the Institut): Say, what if we were to go inside?

First oyster: It would be original.

Second oyster: Not half!

First oyster: Ha ha, Messieurs les Parisiens, you made our name into a term of scorn. Our turn has come to take our revenge. Wouldn't you like to be oysters today!

Second oyster. Let's go back out—there's no lack of room.

---

[4] The Godard family, headed by Louis Godard and his brother Jules, although their fame was exceeded by one of Louis' three sons, the daring aeronaut Eugène Godard (1827-1890), were the entrepreneurs who made a successful business of the manufacture and sale of aerostats from the 1850s onwards, to the extent that balloons became popularly known for a while as "Godards."

[5] François Vatel (1631-1671) was Nicolas Fouquet's butler, who famously committed suicide when a delivery from the fishmonger was delayed before an important dinner to be held in honor of Louis XIV. The fish arrived mere moments after he had literally fallen on his sword.

A sole (strayed into the kitchen of a restaurant on the Boulevard du Crime,[6] and perceiving a colleague): Heavens! My daughter! My progeniture, that a sweep of the net stole away from me the other day! Child, do you recognize your mother? No response. Dead! Dead! They've killed my child!

A turbot (on hearing these exclamations): Hey you, outside, when you've quite finished your tirade! Take your exclamations to the vicinity of the ex-theaters!

A lobster (caught on the tip of a lightning-conductor): Help! Rescue me! Help!

A whale (having just entered the Panthéon): So these are the monuments of which humans were so proud. A nice carcass! To be able to turn around, I'd need to smash a window with my tail.

At that moment, a de-masted ship entered at great speed what had formerly been the Place de l'Hôtel de Ville.

The last of the Prudhommes (having taken refuge on the summit of the Tour Saint-Jacques) A ship! Paris seaport! All my wishes are granted, and I can die![7]

The increasing tumult drowns out his voice; the waves are still rising.

After

Three thousand years have gone by. The waters have quit the place once occupied by Paris, having deposited a calcareous stratum there several meters thick. A new city has risen up, populated by new humans.

These new humans, endowed with new defects, have founded a new Académie des Science, where new deliberations often lead to nothing new.

Today, however, the day's schedule promises a curious report by a geologist on the debris of the antediluvian world that he has discovered.

The seats are occupied by an elegant crowd. The journalists are at their post.

At two o'clock in the afternoon, the famous geologist goes up to the podium in the midst of the most profound silence, unrolls a manuscript, and begins to read:

"Messieurs,

---

[6] The familiar term for the Boulevard du Temple, so-called for a clutch of theatres specializing in lurid melodramas of the kind likely to contains speeches akin to the sole's.

[7] The dream of making the Seine navigable to ships, popularly known as "Paris seaport" was almost as popular throughout the 19th century as the idea of building a channel tunnel, and schemes were continually produced, all of which languished on the drawing-board.

"Science, the indefatigable searcher, endows humankind with a new benefit every day, even in her infancy.

"Because, Messieurs, only three thousand years have gone by since a deluge destroyed a creation anterior and inferior to ours.

"It is precisely that deluge and that creation about which I want to talk to you." (*Attentive shuffling.*)

"Was the Earth before the deluge inhabited by human beings or not? Such is the grave question that immediately presents itself to the scientist.

Some of my colleagues say yes; others say no. Personally, I do not say either yes or no." (*Violent marks of approval.*)

"But from my excavations, Messieurs, I have extracted one certainty. That is that the Earth, prior to us, was covered by a gigantic creation, and I shall prove it.

"By digging in the ground in all directions, I have discovered for items of fossil debris of the greatest importance. The difficulty, however, was not finding them; it is necessary to recognize their nature, and, if you will forgive the expression, stealing from destruction the secrets of the past. I have done that!" (Unanimous bravos.)

"The first item of debris discovered by me is a perfectly conserved skeleton. Its form represents a truncated sphere; the bones are disposed in squares, and, bizarrely enough, the action of time has metalized them. The skeleton must be that of an animal having some analogy with the toys known to our children as bobo dolls. That animal, extinct today, must have been acephalous, moved by crawling and lived a vegetable existence.

"The second item of debris is a skull, which, given its restricted form, must evidently have belonged to a species of colossal bird of the family of our domestic canaries.

"The third item of debris, one of the most curious, is about a hundred feet long and is completely petrified. That debris, I have become convinced, is the dorsal spine of a gigantic fish run aground in these parts during the deluge. To judge by the extent of the backbone in question—it is still broken at its extremity—the monster that it ornamented was the monarch of the antediluvian seas and belonged to the species of which today's whales are the diminutives.

"As for the fourth item of debris, we have found specimens in fairly large quantities. It affects the same form, the same flatness and the same hardness everywhere. That hardness is such that it has resisted all efforts to break it down into fragments with blows of a hammer. It will be the subject of a special report.

"From now on, however, three capital facts have been acquired by science, to wit: the existence of enormous reptiles, birds and fish prior to the last deluge.

"Glad to have been able to play my small part in that retrospective progress, I leave to the Académie the honor of being the godmother of my discoveries and giving a name to each of the races that I have, by dint of patience, been able to resuscitate."

That reading was followed by a salvo of frantic applause. All the newspapers were filled with details of and praise for the marvelous discoveries for a month.

A pension for life of two thousand francs a year was granted by the Académie to the author s a sign of gratitude.

Moral

In all deluges and all cataclysms, only one thing will always rise to the surface without the help of any Noah's Ark, and that is the ridiculous.

Translator's note:
This story is an early inclusion in what was eventually to become a long series of tales, by various hands, in which future archeologists dig in the ruins of long-dead Paris discover artifacts mysterious to them, which they routinely misinterpret in an ironic fashion. The convention that eventually developed in the series was to leave the discovered items unidentified, while planting sufficiently clues to allow an alert reader to work out what they really are, but Véron, working within an unusually tight word-limit, did not have the space to elaborate his descriptions to that extent. Instead, he inserted four curt footnotes identifying the four items discovered by the unenlightened scientist as a frame for displaying skirts, the head of a dandy, the Obelisk and a "32-sou beefsteak."

Eugène Mouton: *The End of the World*
(1872)

Eugène Mouton (1823-1905) was the son of a military officer who spent his childhood in Guadeloupe. He embarked upon a career as a lawyer, which culminated in an appointment as a prosecutor in Rodez. He began writing humorous short stories on the side, using the pseudonym Mérinos [Merino sheep or wool], making his debut in Le Figaro *in 1857, and gave up his legal career ten years later to become a full-time writer.*

He remained best known for his humorous short fiction, much of which was fantastic in a vein somewhat akin to the "nonsense literature" produced in England by Edward Lear, Lewis Carroll and W. S. Gilbert, but he also wrote various non-fiction books, including one on French penal law and of the first ever guide-books for would-be authors. Partly inspired by the example of Mouton's professionalism, his nephew by marriage, Paul Duval, went on to become one of the leading lights of the fin-de-siècle Decadent Movement as Jean Lorrain.

Mouton produced a number of items directly inspired by reading contemporary popularizations of science, of which "La Fin du Monde" (here translated as "The End of the World") was the first. It was initially published in book form in Nouvelles et fantasies humoristiques *(1872, by-lined Mérinos), but it had probably been published previously in a periodical.*

Like Mouton's other exploits in this vein, "The End of the World" exemplifies the perennial problem that early writers of scientific romance had in finding appropriate narrative forms for their speculative excursions, being as much an essay as a story. It also provides a graphic illustration of the license that the adoption a humorous tone gave to a laconically casual imaginative extravagance that might have seemed inappropriate in more earnest work. It is, of course, an exercise in absurdity, but it demonstrates very clearly that in 1870 or thereabouts, it was only by reaching into the utmost extremes of absurdity that a writer could have any chance of imagining the prospects that would be visible on the horizons of possibility established in the 21st century.

Mouton thus became the first writer to imagine an ecocatastrophe precipitated by global warming generated by human industrial activity, and the first to imagine some potential effects of applying a sophisticated biotechnology to agricultural production. Although Mouton's jesting exercises in scientific romance helped to lay groundwork for the more elaborate and sophisticated speculative works of Alphonse Allais, Alfred Jarry and Gaston de Pawlowski, only the las came remotely close to duplicating the imaginative reach of Mouton's story.

B.S.

19

And the world will end by fire.

Of all the questions that interest humankind, none is more worthy of research than that of the destiny of the planet we inhabit. Geology and history have taught us many things about the Earth's past; we know the age of our world, within a few hundred million years or so; we know the order of development in which life progressively manifest itself and propagated over its surface; we know in which epoch humans finally arrived to sit down at the banquet that life had prepared for them, and for which it had taken several thousand years to set the table.

We know all that, or at least think we know it, which comes down to exactly the same thing—but if we are sure of our past, we are not of our future.

Humankind scarcely knows and more about the probable duration of its existence than each one of us knows about the number of years that he has yet to live:

> The table is laid,
> The exquisite parade,
> That gives us cheer!
> A toast, my dear!

All well and good—but are we on the soup, or the dessert? Who can tell us, alas, that the coffee will not be served very soon?

We go on and on, heedless of the future of the world, without ever asking ourselves whether, by chance, this frail boat that is carrying us across the ocean of infinity is not at risk of capsizing suddenly, or whether its old hull, worn away by time and impaired by the agitations of the voyage, does not have some leak though which death is filtering into its carcass—which is, of course, the very carcass of humankind—one drop at a time.

The world—which is to say, our terrestrial globe—has not always existed. It had begun, so it will end. The question is, when?

First of all, let us ask ourselves whether the world might end by virtue of an accident, a perturbation of present laws.

We cannot admit that. Such a hypothesis would, in fact, be in absolute contradiction with the opinion that we intend to sustain in this work. It is obvious, therefore, that we cannot adopt it. Any discussion is impossible if one admits the opinion that one is setting out to combat.

Thus, one point is definitely established: the Earth will not be destroyed by accident; it will end as a consequence of the continued action of the laws of its present existence. It will die, as they say, its appropriate death.

But will it die of old age? Will it die of a disease?

I have no hesitation in replying: no, it will not die of old age; yes, it will die of a disease—in consequence of excess.

I have said that the world will end as a consequence of the continued action of the laws of its present existence. It is now a matter of figuring out which, of all the agents functioning for the maintenance of the life of the terraqueous globe, is the one that will have the responsibility of destroying it someday.

I say this without hesitation: that agent is the same one to which the Earth owed is existence in the first place: heat. Heat will drink the sea; heat will eat the Earth—and this is how it will happen.

One day, with regard to the functioning of locomotives, the illustrious Stephenson asked a great English chemist what the force was that moved such machines. The chemist replied: "It's the Sun."

And, indeed, all the heat that we liberate when we burn combustible vegetable matter-wood or coal—has been stored there by the Sun; a piece of wood or coal is therefore, fundamentally, nothing but a preserve of solar radiation. The more vegetable life develops, the greater the accumulation of these preserves becomes. If a great deal is burned and a great deal created—that is to say, if cultivation and industry evolve, the storage the solar radiation absorbed by the Earth on one the hand and its liberation on the other will increase incessantly, and the Earth will become warmer in a continuous manner.

What would happen if the animal population, and the human population in its turn, followed the same progress? What would happen if considerable transformations, born of the very development of animal life on the surface of the globe, were to modify the structure of terrains, displace the basins of the seas, and reassemble humankind on continents that are both more fertile and more permeable to solar heat?

Now, that is exactly what will happen.

When one compares the world with what it once was, one is immediately struck by one fact that leaps to the eyes: the worldwide evolution of organic life. From the most elevated summits of mountains to the most profound gulfs of the sea, millions of billions of animalcules, animals, cryptogams and superior plants, have been working day and night for centuries, as have the foraminifera on which half our continents are built.

That work was going rapidly enough before the epoch when humans appeared on the Earth, but since the appearance of man it has developed with a rapidity that is accelerating every day. As long as humankind remained restricted to two or three parts of Asia, Europe and Africa, it was not noticeable, because, save for a few focal points of concentration, life in general still found it easy to pour into empty space the surplus accumulated at certain points of the civilized world; it was thus that colonization increasingly populated previously uninhabited countries innocent of all cultivation. Then commenced the first phase of the progress of life by human action: the agricultural phase.

Things moved in this direction for about six centuries, but large deposits of oil were developed, and, almost at the same time, chemistry and steam-power. The Earth then entered its industrial phase—which is only just beginning, since that was not much more than 60 years ago. But where this movement will lead us, and with what velocity we shall arrive, it is easy to presume, given that which has already happened before our eyes.

It is evident, for anyone with eyes to see, that for half a century, animals and people alike have tended to multiply, to proliferate, to pullulate in a truly disquieting proportion. More is eaten, more is drunk, silkworms are cultivated, poultry fed and cattle fattened. At the same time, planning is going on everywhere; ground has been cleared; fecund crop rotations and intensive cultures have been invented, which double the soil's yields; not content with what the earth produces, salmon at five francs a side have been sown in our rivers, and oysters at 24 *sous* a dozen in our gulfs.

In the meantime, enormous quantities of wine, beer and cider have been fermented; veritable rivers of *eau-de-vie* have been distilled, and millions of tons of oil burned—not to mention that heating equipment is improving incessantly, that more and more houses are being rendered draught-proof, and that the linen and cotton fabrics that humans employ to keep themselves warm are being fabricated more cheaply with every passing day.

To this already-sufficiently-somber picture it is necessary to add the insane developments of public education, which one can consider as a source of light and heat, for, if it does not emit them itself, it multiplies their production by giving humans the means of improving and extending their impact on nature.

This is where we are now; this is where a mere half-century of industrialism has brought us; obviously, there are, in all of this, manifest symptoms of an imminent exuberance, and one can conclude that within 100 years from now, the Earth will have developed a paunch.

Then will commence the redoubtable period in which the excess of production will lead to an excess of consumption, the excess of consumption to an excess of heat, *and the excess of heat to the spontaneous combustion of the Earth and all its inhabitants.*

It is not difficult to anticipate the series of phenomena that will lead the globe, by degrees, to that final catastrophe. Distressing as the depiction of these phenomena might be, I shall not hesitate to map them out, because the prevision of these facts, by enlightening future generations as to the dangers of the excesses of civilization, might perhaps serve to moderate the abuse of life and postpone the fatal final accounting by a few thousand years, or at least a few months.

This, therefore, is what will happen.

For ten centuries, everything will go progressively faster. Industry, above all, will make giant strides. To begin with, all the oil deposits will be exhausted, then all the sources of kerosene; then all the forests will be cut down; then the oxygen in the air and the hydrogen in the water will be burned directly. By that time, there will be something like a million steam-engines on the surface of the globe, averaging 1000 horse-power—the equivalent of a billion horse-power—functioning night and day.

All physical work is done by machines or animals; humans no longer do any, except for skillful gymnastics practiced solely for hygienic reasons. But while their machines incessantly vomit out torrents of manufactured products, an ever-denser host of sheep, chickens, turkeys, pigs, ducks, cows and geese emerges from their agricultural factories, all oozing fat, bleating, lowing, gobbling, quacking, bellowing, whistling and demanding consumers with loud cries!

Now, under the influence of ever more abundant and ever more succulent nutrition, the fecundity of the human and animal species is increasing from day to day. Houses rise up one floor at a time; first gardens are done away with, then courtyards. Cities, then villages, gradually begin to project lines of suburbs in every direction; soon, transversal lines connect these radii.

Movement progresses; neighboring cities begin to connect with one another. Paris annexes Saint-Germain, Versailles and then Beauvais, then Châlons, then Orléans, then Tours; Marseilles annexes Toulon, Draguignan, Nice, Carpentras, Nîmes and Montpellier; Bordeaux, Lyon and Lille share out the rest, and Paris ends up annexing Marseilles, Lyon, Lille and Bordeaux. And the same thing is happening throughout Europe, and the other four continents of the world.

But at the same time, the animal population is increasing. All useless species have disappeared; all that now remain are cattle sheep, horses and poultry. Now, to nourish all that, empty space is required for cultivation, and room is getting short.

A few terrains are then reserved for cultivation, fertilizer is piled herein, and there, lying amid grass six feet high, unprecedented species of sheep and cattle, devoid of hair, tails, feet and bones are seen rolling around, reduced by the art of husbandry to be nothing more than monstrous steaks alimented by four insatiable stomachs.

In the meantime, in the southern hemisphere, a formidable revolution is about to take place. What am I saying? Scarcely 50,000 years have gone by, and here it is, complete!

The polypers have joined all the continents together, and all the islands of the Pacific Ocean and the southern seas. America, Europe and Africa have disappeared beneath the waters of the ocean; nothing remains of them but a few islands formed by the last summits of the Alps, the Pyrenees, the buttes Montmartre, the Carpathians, the Atlas Mountains and the Cordilleras.

The human race, retreating gradually from the sea, has expanded over the incommensurable plains that the sea has abandoned, bringing its overwhelming civilization with it; already space is beginning to run out on the former continents. Here it is the final entrenchments: it is here that it will battle against the invasion of animal life. Here is where it will perish!

It is on a calcareous terrain; an enormous mass of animalized materials is incessantly converted into a chalky state; this mass, exposed to the rays of a torrid Sun, incessantly stores up new concentrations of heat, while the functioning of machines, the combustion of hearths and the development of animal heat cause the ambient temperature to rise incessantly.

And in the meantime, animal production continues to increase; there comes a time when the equilibrium breaks down; it becomes manifest that production will outstrip consumption.

Then, in the Earth's crust, a sort kind of rind begins to form at first, and subsequently, an appreciable layer of irreducible detritus; the Earth is saturated with life.

Fermentation begins.

The thermometer rises, the barometer falls, the hygrometer marches toward zero. Flowers wither, leaves turn yellow, parchments curl up; everything dries out and becomes brittle.

Animals shrink by virtue of the effects of heat and evaporation. Humans, in their turn, grow thin and desiccated; all temperaments melt into one—the bilious—and the last of the lymphatics[8] offers his daughter and 100 millions in dowry to the last of the scrofulous, who has not a *sou* to his name, and who refuses out of pride.

The heat increases and the wells dry up. Water-carriers are elevated to the rank of capitalists, then millionaires, to the extent that the prince's Great Water-Carrier becomes one of the principal dignitaries of state. All the crimes and infamies that one sees committed today for a gold piece are committed for a glass of water, and Cupid himself, abandoning his quiver and arrows, replaces them with a carafe of ice-water.

In this torrid atmosphere, a lump of ice is worth 20 times its weight in diamonds. The Emperor of Australia, in a fit of mental aberration, orders a *tutti frutti* that cost an entire year's civil list. A scientist makes a colossal fortune by obtaining a hectoliter of fresh water at 45 degrees.

Streams dry up; crayfish, jostling one another tumultuously to run after the trickles of warm water that are abandoning them, change color as they go along, turning scarlet. Fish, their hearts weakening and their swim-bladders distended, let themselves drift on the currents, bellies up and fins inert.

And the human species begins to go visibly mad. Strange passions, unexpected angers, overwhelming infatuations and insane pleasures make life into a series of furious detonations—or, rather, one continuous explosion, which begins at birth and concludes with death. In a world cooked by an implacable combustion, everything is scorched, crackled, grilled and roasted, and after the water, which has evaporated, one senses the air diminishing as it becomes more rarefied.

---

[8] The lymphatic temperament, associated with one of the four humors of ancient medicine, is better known as the sanguine; it is associated with sociability and compassion, among other traits.

A terrible calamity! The rivers, great and small, have disappeared; the seas re beginning to warm up, then to heat up; now they are already simmering as if over a gentle fire.

First the little fish, asphyxiated, show their bellies at the surface; then come the algae, detached from the seabed by the heat; finally, cooked in red wine and rendering up their fat in large stains, the sharks, whales and giant squid rise up, along with the fabulous kraken and the much-contested sea serpent; and with all this fat, vegetation and fish cooked together, the steaming ocean becomes an incommensurable bouillabaisse.

A nauseating odor of cooking expands over the entire inhabited earth; it reigns there for barely a century; the ocean evaporates and leaves no other trace of its existence than fish bones scattered over desert plains...

It is the beginning of the end.

Under the triple influence of heat, asphyxia and desiccation, the human species is gradually annihilated; humans crumble and peel, falling into pieces at the slightest shock. Nothing any longer remains, to replace vegetables, but a few metallic plants that have been made to grow by irrigating them in vitriol. To slake devouring thirst, to reanimate calcined nervous systems, and to liquefy coagulating albumin, there are no liquids left but sulphuric and nitric acids.

Vain efforts.

With every breath of wind that agitates the anhydrous atmosphere, thousands of human creatures are instantaneously desiccated; the rider of his horse, the advocate at the bar, the judge on his bench, the acrobat on his rope, the seamstress at her window and the king on his throne all come to a stop, mummified.

Then comes the final day.

They are no more than 37, wandering like tinder specters in the midst of a frightful population of mummies, which gaze at them with eyes reminiscent of Corinthian grapes.

And they take one another by the hand, and commence a furious round-dance, and with each rotation one of the dancers stumbles and falls down dead, with a dry sound. And when the 26th cycle is over, the survivor remains alone in front of the miserable heap in which the last debris of the human race is assembled.

He darts one last glance at the Earth; he says goodbye to it on behalf of all of us, and a tear falls from his poor scorched eyes—humankind's last tear. He catches it in his hand, drinks it, and dies, gazing at the Heavens.

Pouff!

A little blue flame rises up tremulously, then two, then three, then 1000. The entire globe catches fire, burns momentarily, and goes out.

It is all over; the Earth is dead.

Bleak and icy. It rolls sadly through the silent deserts of space; and of so much beauty, so much glory, so much joy, so much love, nothing any longer remains but a little charred stone, wandering miserably through the luminous spheres of new worlds.

Goodbye, Earth! Goodbye, touching memories of our history, of our genius, of our pains and our loves! Goodbye, Nature, whose gentle and serene majesty consoled us so effectively in our suffering! Goodbye, cool and somber woods, where, during the beautiful nights of summer, by the silvery light of the Moon, the song of the nightingale was heard. Goodbye, terrible and charming creatures that guided the world with a tear or a smile, whom we called by such sweet names! Ah, since nothing more remains of you, all is truly finished: THE EARTH IS DEAD.

Alfred Franklin: *The Ruins of Paris in 4875*
(1875)

A crucial literary watershed was reached in the late 1880s, when H. G. Wells, in order to facilitate the endeavors of his brief exploratory phase, invented a time machine for the use of "The Chronic Argonauts" (1889; revised as The Time Machine, *1895): a facilitating device that could shift a narrative viewpoint into the future "bodily," in such a way as seemingly to evade the inherent unreliability of visionary experience.*

Relatively few subsequent narrative excursions into the future employed an explicit time machine, but the device itself became unnecessary almost as soon as it was invented, having done the essential work of establishing that the future could be regarded as a habitable narrative space, into which a writer could stop without having to issue a preliminary potential defense of sanity, effectively denying ridiculousness by admitting it. On the way to that watershed, however, and in the years that followed it, there was unsteady process of evolution, illustrated by the sequence of stories mentioned below.

Théophile Gautier's "Paris futur," first published in Le Pays *in December 1851 and reprinted in 1852 in* Caprices et zigzags,[9] *was not the first essay-cum-fiction to bear that title, as Gautier's friend Joseph Méry had published one several years earlier, but Méry's was far less interesting, and is best seen as a tentative preliminary to two far more extravagant adventures in futuristic fiction, "Ce qu'on verra" and "Les Ruines de Paris", both dating from the mid-1840s.[10] Gautier's piece was, however, the direct inspiration of Arsène Houssaye's "Paris futur" (1856; revised 1889 as "En 3789"), and probably of Victor Fournel's "Paris futur" (1865).[11] The side-branch of the sequence begun by Méry's tale eventually became prolific in its own right, provoking Alfred Bonnardot's "Archaeopolis" (1857),[12] which in turn provoked Alfred Franklin's "Les Ruines de Paris en 4875" (1875), here translated as "The Ruins of Paris in 4875."*

The rhetorical strategies of the earlier items in this group of stories are relatively straightforward, although Gautier's shows the relative sophistication one would expect of a writer of his genius, but Franklin's, extrapolating and capitalizing on the extra twists introduced by Méry and Bonnardot, is noticeably

---

[9] Available in *Investigations of the Future*, Black Coat press, ISBN 978-1-61227-106-4.

[10] Both available in *The Tower of Destiny*, Black Coat press, ISBN 978-1-61227-101-9.

[11] Both available in *Investigations of the Future*, q.v.

[12] Available in *Nemoville*, Black Coat press, ISBN 978-1-61227-070-8.

more convoluted in its exploitation of the moral and political stance adopted by the various signatories of the letters sent by the explorers of ruined Paris to their base in New Caledonia.

The essence of the joke is that those notional narrators are in earnest, although the true narrator, Franklin, is a committed satirist who expects his readers to see the unstated truth shadowing their errors. The story deliberately opens up a considerable "distance of stance" between the actual and notional narrators, and it is the reader's appreciation of the width and depth of the gap in question that gives the work its particular appeal. The strategy is in some ways demanding, requiring the reader to keep in mind two distinct narrative threads—that of the story's surface and that of its buried core—as well as to draw inferences from hints of varying delicacy, but it is correspondingly rewarding, augmenting the conventional double bluff of the humoristic contemplation of the future in such a way that it become, in effect, a triple bluff.

B.S.

I

To His Excellency the Minister of the Navy and Colonies, at Noumea (Caledonia)[13]
Within sight of Paris, 20 May 4875

Monsieur le Ministre,

The exploration fleet of which Your Excellency placed me in command has completed the first part of its task.

If, as tradition says, Noumea owes its origin to a Parisian colony, I have found the cradle of our ancestors. I have found the most beautiful, wealthiest, most famous and most sumptuous city of the old world, for it is within sight of the ruins of Paris that I am writing this dispatch. It will be delivered to Your Excellency by Lieutenant Inveniès, who had the glory of being the first to set foot on the land for which we were searching.

On 10 May, the winds had suddenly turned from south-south-east to south-south-west, the sea became very heavy, the barometer dropped below eighty millimeters and a furious tempest dispersed the ships of the squadron. My fears

---

[13] Noumea was, and still is, the capital of the French territory of New Caledonia in the south-west Pacific. Between 1860 and 1897, New Caledonia was a penal colony, to which many of the Communards of 1870 were transported; Franklin could not know when he wrote the story that most of its political prisoners would be allowed to return to France in 1879, when they were granted amnesty. Nor could he know that there would be a native rebellion on the island in 1878, which commenced a long guerrilla war.

28

were all the greater because the region in which I was sailing is unknown, and my frigate was being driven the wind with a speed of twenty-five knots. Soon, the water penetrated below decks, broke through the wall of the engine-room and threatened to put out the fire.

At midday, our position being 34° 37' 47" north latitude and 42° 24' 40" east longitude, the wind suddenly dropped and a rapid current carried me eastwards, where we perceived land. Two of my ships, the *Répertrix* and the *Eruo*, were then able to rejoin me, and we advanced with extreme caution. Sounding only indicated a depth of six fathoms, and we were surrounded by a prodigious quantity of rats, which it was necessary to disperse with rifle fire.

Finally, at about two o'clock, we dropped anchor on a good bed of fine sand, in an immense and safe harbor. A large river was slowly emptying its waters there, and on the coast, as far as the eye could see, a dense curtain of trees concealed the horizon from us. I gave orders to gather the flotilla and decided to spend a little time there. My crew needed rest; we had not had any fresh meat for a fortnight, and the corvette *Eureka*, which I am sending you, required urgent repairs.

I admit that at that moment we had no idea that we were so close to the objective of our search. Kortambert, in fact, in the geographical fragments so expertly restored by Monsieur Dartieu, says in a positive manner that Paris is situated about two hundred kilometers from the sea.[14] It is necessary to recognize, however, that our scholars and geologists, even in their most boldest hypotheses, are far from having exaggerated the incredible violence of the cataclysm that wrecked the entire old world, and which only our little island had the privilege of escaping.

At about five o'clock, while the crew was at table, our eyes were attracted landwards by flames and clouds of smoke, which were rising a short distance away behind the trees. I immediately sent out a launch with a dozen men, commanded by Lieutenant Inveniès, to investigate.

They came back in the evening, at nine eighteen, bringing news that caused hope to leap in our hearts.

Three or four kilometers from the coast, our men had found a town of rather wretched appearance, the inhabitants of which, numbering approximately

---

[14] The notional author inserts a reference: "Kortambert, *Fragments*, Dartieu edition, liv. I, ch. 7, p.5.—Conf. Meissas et Michelot, IV, 9, 11; Expilly, IX, 5, 3, and Malte-Vran, VI, 4, 7." Franklin probably had Eugène Cortambert's *Leçons de géographie* [Lessons in Geography] (1846) in mind when improvising this reference. The confirmatory references are presumably to Achille Meissas and Auguste Michelot's *Nouvelle géographie méthodique* [New Methodical Geography] (1827), Jean-Joseph Expilly's *Manuel de Géographie* [Handbook of Geography] (1757) and Conrad Malte-Brun's *Géographie universelle* [World Geography] (1870).

two thousand, appeared to be prey to a great agitation. The flames that we had seen from afar were completing their work, and three or four dwellings had been reduced to a pile of rubble. It was easy to see that the conflagration had selected the least constricted and the least poor, and, as they were not adjacent to one another, it was easy to deduce that criminal intent had designated them for the ravages in question.

The natives ran to our sailors and pressed around them, all speaking and shouting at the same time, fighting to get closer to them and studying them with a child-like avidity. Five minutes after its arrival, the little troop was surrounded by a compact crowd, whose curious gazes and frankly indiscreet attitude was not at all threatening. A few words pronounced by Lieutenant Inveniès were immediately understood, and they replied to him in a language that has, like ours, striking analogies with French.

The mores of this population, with which we have since been able to familiarize ourselves, offer strange contrasts. In the bosom of this savage tribe, which seems to have sprung from the ground in these uninhabited regions, among these barbarians clad in animal skins, one observes virtues, vices, tastes, defects and aspirations that are usually the product of refined civilizations.

Their great preoccupation is the quest for pleasure. Everything is an occasion for celebration; on the slightest pretext, they assemble outside or gather in one another's homes to sing, eat, drink, dance and talk. Any event occupies and amuses them, any spectacle delights them. Noisy, talkative, restless and impressionable, they become enthusiastic without reflection, and become weary just as rapidly. Self-regard is the most obvious of their faults. Everything that glitters and everything that gleams attracts and impassions them: the sight of plumes and braid excites them madly. They are also good, frank, hospitable, generous, brave, intelligent, delicate, even full common sense, so long as it is not a matter of governing their little city.

Unfortunately, that is the habitual subject of their conversations, and the only one on which they permit no mockery; they are, however, wont to assure themselves, by the periodic overthrow of their leaders, of distractions that are dear to them and the pretext for glorious anniversaries. Sacrificing everything to form, they are more preoccupied with the title that their leader will bear than the manner in which he will rule them.

There are, in any case, many other difficulties to resolve in organizing authority in a population in which everyone yearns to command and no one consents to obey. The most modest individuals dream of a public function that will give them at least a few subalterns to govern, but all of them, even the poorest and most ignorant, believe themselves to be perfectly capable of ruling the tribe; they talk incoherently about the city's affairs, emitting ideas, theories and principles as insensate as they are disparate, and, when they do not see them adopted, experience an imperious desire to revolt. The clever lie in wait for a opportunity, seizing it when the moment comes, and in a trice, the leader is overthrown. Then there are cries of triumph, public rejoicing and endless parades through the town; they congratulate one another, compliment on another and embrace one another.

When our men arrived, it was the evening of one of these great days, and the flames we had observed came from a few huts that had been set on fire in the riot. In consequence, the dethroned chief and his two principal ministers found themselves homeless.

The lieutenant also learned that these improvised revolutions took place twice or three times a year. However, he was told that this one would certainly be the last, and that an indefinite era of calm and concord was about to commence for the population. It had, in fact, just adopted a form of government that limited the exercise of power to thirty days, and determined that a new leader had to be chosen every month; every citizen would thus have his turn, and would live in peace, nurtured by that sweet hope.

That ingenious expedient, which might seem bound to content everyone, is not, it seems, as sure a remedy as one might be led to believe, and it has already been tried more than once without success. Everything goes smoothly for a month, apparently, but the head of state often refuses to stand down to the end of his term of office, and it always requires a revolution to reclaim the throne from him.

Women greatly envy men the privilege of governing and making revolutions; for want of anything better they strive to dominate in the hut, and often find a latent but incontestable despotism there. Impressionable, passionate and nervous, they alternate between behavior that is good, gentle, affectionate, sharp, nagging or cruel, according to atmospheric conditions. They are witty and refined, but thoughtless, futile, frivolous and frenetically flirtatious. Gracious, frail and delicate, but avid for pleasure, they support fatigue with an inconceivable energy. Pleasure has an instinctive attraction for all of them, which the most reasonable are sometimes impotent to combat, and they express irresistible needs corollary to the state of mind in question by means of a term that does not exist in our language, the reflexive verb "to amuse oneself." When a woman speaks of "amusing herself," wise husbands lower their heads and wait for the fit to pass.

The population is strongly attached to the territory that it has occupied since time immemorial, and very proud of its petty city. They fought for the honor of showing our sailors around, who were obliged to visit every part of it, and received the most cordial welcome everywhere. People also boasted to them about the beauty of the surroundings, and above all, the imposing spectacle presented by the ruins of an immense city situated half a league away. The day was too far advanced, however, to permit an immediate excursion, so the lieutenant brought his men back to the ship, where their stories filled us with surprise and joy.

The next day, I sent word that I would pay my compliments to the new leader that the natives had chosen. I reached land at about three o'clock, accompanied by my senior officers. Indigenes sent to meet me cleared a passage for us through the tightly-packed crowd and led us to the leader's hut, where everything had been arranged for a solemn reception. Guards with a stern appearance defended the vicinity, and the ephemeral sovereign awaited us there surrounded by his ministers.

He was clad in an ample wolf-skin constellated with variously colored seashells, glass trinkets and small objects in polished metal: buckles, rings, nails, paper clips, collar-studs, buttons and bells. His head-dress, composed of feathers of various sorts, was augmented by an oyster-shell, whose nacreous surface gleamed in the sunlight. I strove to seem dazzled by so much wealth, which pleased the leader greatly without surprising him. His manners, however, were not lacking in dignity or grace and he responded without the slightest embarrassment to the compliment that I addressed to him.

We set out on foot, followed—or, rather, escorted—by the entire town, men, women and children alike. No one had wanted to miss the party, and the ill and infirm were seated in crude carts. The chief noticed my surprise, doubtless mistook it for fear, and sought to reassure me, confessing to me, besides, that no human power was capable of retaining his subjects in their homes on such an occasion. By way of reply I took off my sword and ordered my officers to do the same. Our gesture was immediately understood and saluted with enthusiastic cheers by the joyful crowd, whose members, breathless with curiosity, admired the gilded ornaments of our uniforms, commented on our slightest gestures and pressed around us, competing for our glances.

For about half an hour we followed the verdant banks of the river, whose breadth appeared to be at least double what it had been in the times of the French, if one can rely on the estimations of Du Laure and Joanne.[15] Finally, we climbed a small hill and arrived at the summit, and an exclamation escaped all our throats.

---

[15] The notional author adds another reference: "Du Laure, Fragments, I, 3, 26; Joanne, Extracts, VI, 9, 12.—Conf. Varbertet et Magin, IX, 2, 16; Mentelle, III, 7, 21; Max du Camp, II, 27, 9." The primary references must be to Jacques-Antoine Dulaure's *Histoire physique, civil et morale de Paris* [The Physical, Social and Moral History of Paris] (1839) and to the regularly updated guide to Paris compiled by Adolphe Laurent Joanne and Paul Joanne, which was current when Franklin wrote the story. The confirmatory references are presumably to Charles Barberet and Alfred Magin's *Précis de géographie historique universelle* [A Historical Summary of World Geography] (1841), Edmé Mentelle's *Choix de lectures géographiques et historiques* [Selected Lectures on Geography and History] (1783) and Maxime du Camp's *Paris: ses organes, ses fonctions et sa vie* [Paris: its anatomy, its functioning and its life] (1870).

In front of us unfolded the most impressive scene that can ever have been offered to human contemplation. It was really Paris, none of us had any doubt about it; those grandiose ruins really were the tomb of the queen of the Old World. Her proud head still floats above those desolate spaces.

In a valley whose extent our eyes could scarcely embrace, domes, columns, porticos, slender steeples, immense heaps of rubble, frontons, statues, capitals, entablatures, ridges and cornices projected pell-mell. To our left we could see, boldly and proudly outlined against the dark sky, the crown of the triumphal arch elevated by one of the last Poleons of France to the glory of her armies. No earthquake had, therefore, obliterated the great city, and it ought to be possible to rediscover today what it was three thousand years ago, when the gigantic avalanche of earth, ash and sand under which it is buried descended upon it.

We stood there pensively for some time, absorbed in mute contemplation. Silence had fallen around us, as if, habituated as they were to the view, its grandeur still induced and indefinable effect of terror and vertigo in them. They did not know, however, what riches, marvels and memories lay beneath those heaps of sand, beneath that arid plain, where only a few sickly and jaundiced grasses grew. They say that it never rains there, and that the sky is always veiled; a superstitious dread prevents them from bringing their flocks to graze there, and even the bravest dare not venture there by night.

People recount that on certain stormy nights, life seems to reveal itself within those abysses. Myriads of phosphorescent glimmers skim the ground, and confused sounds resound in the bowels of the earth. Hammers fall on anvils, machines hiss, workmen shout, horses whinny, carriages roll heavily over paved roads. Outbursts of laughter mingle with stifled sobs, dolorous plaints with mocking sniggers, blasphemies with chaste prayers. One can hear the clamor of orgies and the sighs of virgins, imprecations and sacred canticles, the gnashing of teeth and joyful songs, dull groans, desperate cries and the murmur of amorous voices, the rattle of chains and the sound of kisses, the collapse of stacks of gold coins and the croaks of hunger. Then, suddenly, the strident call of the clarion resounds, and, over the tumult, causing all heads to bow, the grave voice of thousands of organs rises up, launching funereal symphonies into space, which seem to be announcing the funeral of an entire world. Then, gradually, the fires go out, silence is reborn, and death resumes possession of its empire.

It depends on you, Monsieur le Ministre, whether a part of these dreams will become realities. You understand, however, and the great intelligence of the Emperor cannot fail to agree with you, that in order for a rapid and complete result to be obtained, it will be necessary for the means at my disposal to correspond to the importance of the objective prescribed for us.

I have the honor of being, with respect to Your Excellency, Monsieur le Ministre, your very humble, very devoted and very obedient servant,

Admiral Baron Quésitor.

To Admiral Baron Quésitor, Commandant of the Caledonian Naval forces in the French Seas
Noumea, 30 June 1875
Minister of the Navy and the Colonies
Office of the Minister No. 8717
(n.b. Note this number in the margin of the reply)

Monsieur l'Amiral

I have had the honor of communicating to the Emperor the dispatch from Paris that you addressed to me on 20 May last.

His Majesty has instructed me to transmit his congratulations to you, and deigned to sign yesterday a decree that, on my suggestion, confers upon you the Grand Cross of the Imperial Order of the Green Falcon.

His majesty desires that the clearance of the ruins of Paris be commenced without delay and be carried out with all possible rapidity. With that intention, He is placing under your command two infantry regiments and three regiments of military engineers, forming a total of 5,122 men, who will be embarked in the early days of next month.

The administration is putting at your disposal, in addition: 10,321 pickaxes, 9,814 spades, 2,503 sets of pincers, 1,001 mattocks, 6,062 birch brooms, 3,603 heather brooms, 1,025 horsehair brooms, 6,206 wheelbarrows, 1,409 tumbrils, 807 watchmen's cabins, 1,206 skips, 301,837 kilos of rails, 12,004 sleepers, 203,128 rail-chairs, 711,902 rivets, 127 spirit levels, 142 surveyor's poles, 59 rotating plates, 24 steam-cranes, 19 mechanical sweepers, 201 portable engines, 99 locomotives, 3,001 horses, 603 mules and 13 photographers.

It has been decided that a scientific commission will be attached to the expedition. It is composed of three members of the Académie des Beaux-Arts, three members of the Académie des Inscriptions et Belle-Lettres and three members of the Académie des Sciences. You will, I have no doubt, treat these venerable scholars with all the respect that is their due, and you will obtain inspiration from their experience and advice.

Receive, Monsieur l'Amiral, the assurance of my most distinguished consideration.

Minister of the Navy and the Colonies.
Comte A. Statarie

III

To His Excellency the Minister of Public Education in
Religion and the Fine Arts in Noumea (Caledonia)
Paris, 30 November 4875

Monsieur le Ministre,

The scientific commission charged by Your Excellency with exploring the ruins of Paris has remained silent for some time, leaving it to Admiral Quésitor to keep the ministry up to date with all the details of the expedition. We did not want to send out our first report until the results obtained would not only be of a nature to satisfy public curiosity but also to focus the attention of archeologists.

The moment has now come, and it is to me that the honor of representing the commission with regard to Your Excellency has fallen.

No incident troubled our crossing, which was too rapid to allow us to make many significant observations *en route*. On 21 August we came into harbor, and less than three weeks thereafter, a double railway line having linked the ruins to the sea, all the equipment was disembarked, an immense camp extended around Paris, and the clearance commenced.

The geological agglomeration that covers Paris is far from presenting a uniform surface; soundings carried out at intervals have permitted us to establish that although, at certain points, it rises thirty-six meters above the original ground level, it is sometimes only thirteen or fourteen meters deep. It is formed by successive layers, which were certainly superimposed on one another with prodigious rapidity. The origin and nature of the upheaval will remain, according all appearances, permanently insoluble problems; however, the form that the debris of organized bodies has assumed and the direction that the mineralogical deposits have affected reveal to the most inexperienced eye a great irruption that arrived from the south-east.

The entire mass can be divided into two quite distinct parts.

The upper stratum, which nowhere exceeds five meters, is composed of earth, ash and sand, forming three beds of various thickness.

The second stratum reveals the most varied elements. On proceeding from top to bottom, one first encounters two thick banks, one of quartz and the other of marl; they rest on a thin deposit of chalk, which is succeeded by two considerable foundations of oysterous schist and lobsterous clay. The latter system is characterized by the presence of an immeasurable quantity of oyster-shells and fossil fish, all of which are known to our ichthyologists. We have found, among other debris, the remains of *Anguilla tartarea, Astacus burdigalensis* and *Goujo friturius*.[16]

The flora is equally rich, and offers us, especially in the inferior layers, a few interesting subjects of observation. The most abundant species are the laurel (*Laurus militaria*) and the camellia (*Camellia feminea*), very often accompanied

---

[16] All the Latin names in this passage and subsequent ones are jokes, mostly easily penetrable; *Anguilla* is a genus of eels and *Astacus* a genus off crayfish but *Goujo* is an improvisation based on "goujons" [of fried fish].

35

by petrifactions, among which one can make our leaves of tobacco (*Nicotiana cigaretica*) and absinthe (*Ductaria charantonia*).

The fauna has not furnished us with the opportunity for any important discovery. However, the bones of *Canis canichus* and those of *Felis gouttierius* are numerous, and we have discovered a complete head of *Lepus civeticus*—but these animals are already described in our treatises of paleontology.

I am limiting myself to listing here the most salient facts that have emerged from our observations; this brief summary will shortly be completed by a detailed memoir that my colleague Monsieur E. de Beaupré intends to address to the Académie des Sciences. The conclusions are explicit; they undermine a few historical data admitted previously and provide a definitive solution to the chronological quarrel that has divided archeologists for such a long time. In fact, M. de Beaupré has demonstrated, with evidence, that the great geological revolution in which France was destroyed occurred toward the middle of the seventeenth century, no later than the year 1700 of the Christian Era. One must therefore, unhesitatingly, regard as falsified or interpolated in the surviving fragments of French authors, al the passages that seem to accord Paris a longer existence.

The Emperor's orders instructed us to clear, before anything else, the triumphal arch erected on the right bank of the Seine. Three days sufficed for that work, and the glorious monument emerged intact from the shroud that had enveloped it for thirty centuries. It was then permitted to us to admire at our leisure that masterpiece of ancient architecture, to which, without any doubt, these beautiful lines from the *Anthologie Française* are addressed:

> *Rise up toward the skies,* [gate of][17] *victory*
> *So that the giant of our glory*
> *Might pass through without bending down!*

All the faces of the monument are covered with perfectly preserved sculptures. Beneath the arch, twenty meters high, a multitude of names engraved in the stone were designed to conserve the memory of the principal victories won by the French, and on thirty shields placed around the attic one can read the names of their most illustrious generals. We have established that important dis-

---

[17] The notional author inserts a footnote: "These words are missing from the original and have been thus restored by Monsieur Walken. One recalls the long debate that he sustained with Monsieur Laignes, who preferred "portico of victory." On this issue, consult: *Lettre de M. Walken à M. Laignes, au sujet d'une épigramme attribuée à Victor Hugo et insérée dans le troisième volume de l'Anthologie française*, Noumea, 3860, octavo." At the end of the verse, he adds a second footnote giving the reference: "*Anthologie française*, t. iii, ch. Ix, p.281." The quotation is from Victor Hugo's "À l'Arc de Triomphe de l'Étoile" in *Odes et ballades* (1837).

tinction without difficulty. A fragment of Duruy includes a list, unfortunately incomplete, of the principal French leaders,[18] and in that number feature the Ducs de Valmy, Montebello and Castiglione, whose three names we have found inscribed on the shields. The effects of time have, however, rendered the majority of these inscriptions illegible, and we are far from having succeeded in deciphering all of them. We can, however, cite among the battles those of Kellermann, Lannes, Augereau, Ney, Masséna, Lafayette, Kléber, Dumouriez and Murat. We have similarly gleaned the names of generals Valmy, Montebello, Castiglione, Elchingen, Austerlitz,[19] Marengo, Wagram and Aboukir.

This triumphal arch and the immense avenue that precedes it comprise the most grandiose entrance to a capital of which the imagination has ever been able to dream; reality here exceeds the fantastic tales in which the marvels of Babylon and Nineveh are celebrated.

Twenty meters wide, ornamented with flower beds and fountains, shaded by centuries-old trees whose roots we have found transformed into lignite, the avenue extends as far as the eye can see, bordered along its entire length by constructions lavished with marble and gold.

Here, however, a difficulty arises. How can such a considerable number of princely dwellings gathered in the same place be explained? We have contrived to resolve this question triumphantly.

Garnier and Cassignac relate, in fact, that one of the last sovereigns of France, having been obliged to reconquer his throne by force of arms, rewarded the zeal of the leaders who had helped him in that struggle with the gift of sumptuous habitations.[20] Is it not natural to presume that they were built in the vicinity of the monument consecrated to the glory of French warriors, and that they became a kind of addendum to it? We hesitated to admit this hypothesis, however, in spite of its plausibility, until an interesting epigraphic discovery dispelled all our doubts.

In the course of the excavations at the extremity of the avenue, an engineer discovered an indicative plaque similar to those placed at the corners of our streets. It bore the words:

AVENUE DES CH... ...ES.

---

[18] The notional author includes a reference: "Recueil général des historiens français t. VIII, p. 117."

[19] The notional author notes: "Joanne (*Extraits*, V, IV, 109) informs us that the name of this general was given to one of the bridges of Paris."

[20] The notional author gives the reference: "*Fragments de l'histoire dite du 2 décembre*, in the *Recueil général des historiens français*, t. IX, p. 314." The mangled reference is to Adolphe Granier de Cassagnac's *Histoire du Directoire* (1851-55).

Enlightenment was there and did not take long to illuminate our eyes. A brief discussion sufficed for us to restore the letters erased by time and complete the inscription, which must obviously have been:

AVENUE DES CHEFS-ILLUSTRES.

The Avenue des Chefs-Illustres terminated in a vast square, once magnificently decorated, but only one of its ornaments survives intact: an immense needle formed by a single stone, twenty-five meters high and entirely covered by characters that we have been unable to decipher. We think that it ought to be recognized as an *ex-voto*, probably a religious monument erected to the memory of the ancient sailors who inaugurated river commerce, always so active on the Seine. In fact, the situation of the square on the bank of the river, a fragment of an inscription—ERE DE LA MARINE—and the debris of numerous rostral columns all concur in demonstrating that the interests and services of river navigation were centralized in that location.

A precious discovery results from these observations and the impossibility of comprehending a single word of the symbolic writing with which the monument is covered. We see there the proof that among the French, as among many other peoples of antiquity, the priests had a special language, known only to initiates and unintelligible to laymen. I will add—a fact whose great importance will not escape Your Excellency—that Monsieur Nairan believes that he recognizes in these mysterious characters a vague resemblance to the hieratic script of the primitive Egyptians.

I have the honor of being, with respect to Your Excellency, Monsieur le Ministre, your most humble, most devoted and most obedient servant,

L. Le Rouge,
Membre de l'Institut,
Académie des Inscriptions et Belles-Lettres.

IV

To His Excellency the Minister of Public Education in
Religion and the Fine Arts in Noumea (Caledonia)
Paris, 28 December 4875

Monsieur le Ministre,

Since the date of its last report, the scientific commission to the ruins of Paris has continued its work actively, but the ice and snow have recently created a fairly serious obstacle for us, and ten days have been spent installing our workers—previously lodged in tents—in the cleared buildings, as best we could.

However, in spite of the relative slowness with which we are now advancing, the progress made in the month of December has yielded precious secrets, and also embarrassing problems.

On leaving the Place de la Navigation one encounters an important road to the right, bordered on one side by houses preceded by covered arcades and on the other by a very extensive garden, the extremity of which we have not yet reached.

We know from Max du Camp[21] that gardens were very rare within the perimeter of Paris. Our first thought was, therefore, that the immense space must have served as a cemetery, and partial excavations carried out a trifle haphazardly at various points have confirmed this supposition.

Several tombs still exist. In those that we have opened all traces of organic matter have disappeared under the effects of the centuries, but the group and the statue that surmounted two of them were still in a perfect state of conservation.

The group is composed of three individuals: a vigorous man and two young people, doubtless his sons; all three are engaged in a desperate struggle with snakes that have them in their coils. We have no information about the terrible accident that cost the family members their lives, and the geographical location of Paris scarcely permits the supposition that snakes of those dimensions can ever have lived wild there; these must therefore have escaped from a menagerie, and only been recaptured after immolating three innocent victims.[22]

The statue, similarly sculpted in marble, represents a knife-grinder busy sharpening a blade on a stone. The head is beautiful ad expressive, but we have no way of knowing by virtue of what exceptional circumstance a tomb of white marble was build for a man of such humble status, and who seems to have hardly possessed enough to enable him to buy clothes. Perhaps it is necessary to see him as the hero of one of the popular insurrections so dear to Parisians.[23]

On the other side of the street, the clearing of the buildings has only furnished us with one discovery worthy of inclusion in this report.

In the middle of a small quadrangular square lay a fallen equestrian statue in bronze. The horse, massive in form, supports a thin young woman, frail, delicate, dressed in iron armor and wearing a crown of laurels. She is standing upright in her stirrups and her right hand is waving a flag. On the front of the granite pedestal, a very brief inscription has become illegible.

---

[21] The notional author adds a reference: "*Fragments*, I, 19, 37."

[22] The statue presumably depicts the myth of Lacöon; Napoléon I had looted the original of the most famous Classical statue representing the story but it had been returned to the Vatican after his fall; numerous copies and castings can still be found in Paris and elsewhere.

[23] The original of this statue is similarly antique; again, numerous copies exist, including one by Fognini designed for the gardens at Versailles.

This singular monument constitutes an enigma, of which we have given up attempting to penetrate the meaning.

In order to study the woman more closely, we have separated her from the horse, and in the cavity thus opened, we have found the following words traced in chalk: *République française. Pucelle d'Orléans*: an inexplicable phrase, which complicates the problem instead of clarifying it.

We have had several discussions on this subject. Many hypotheses, sometimes very ingenious, were proposed, discussed and set aside, then taken up again re-examined, modified, and finally rejected. Despairing of arriving at a satisfactory solution, we have taken the decision to pack the statue up and send it to Noumea, in the desire that it be submitted to the examination of our colleagues at the Institut.

I have the honor of being, with respect to Your Excellency, Monsieur le Ministre, your most humble, most devoted and most obedient servant,

J. Lepère

Membre de l'Institut, Académie des Beaux-Arts

V

Imperial Institute of Caledonia (Fine Arts Section)
Account of the Session of 17 March 4786, M. Duparc Presiding

The President. The floor is given to the reporter of the committee charged with examining the equestrian statue found in the ruins of Paris.

M. Legendre, reporter. Before making known to you the conclusions that the committee has reached, I think I ought to summarize briefly for you the three hypotheses that remained standing at the time the closure of the debate was declared.

According to some of our colleagues, the statue that you have before your eyes represents one of those warrior women known in antiquity by the name of Amazons. The adversaries of that opinion, however, respond that the statue is armored in iron, while the costume of the Amazons consisted solely of a short breastplate. In another respect too, the statue is too complete, for everyone knows that the Amazons had their right breast excised because it hampered the use of a bow. Finally, none of the words inscribed inside the monument are able to lend any support to it.

That inscription, they add, ought to be our principal guide, and, in fact, includes everything that we seek. If one brings together three passages contained in the fragments of Thiers, Michelet and L. Blanc,[24] one cannot doubt that the

---

[24] The notion author gives the reference: "*Recueil général des historiens français,* IV, 9, 11; V, 7. 8; VII, 12, 3." Jules Michelet devoted an entire volume of

French were governed for some years by a woman named République. Is it not quite natural that a statue of her was erected, and that she should be represented on horseback, clad in armor and crowned with laurels?

That second opinion rallied more partisans than the first—without, however, yet being able to satisfy the majority.

Even admitting the reality of the historical fact, it was objected, perhaps the first part of the inscription only indicates that the statue was erected under the reign of that République, in which case it is the second part that ought to furnish the solution to the problem.

Minerva, the goddess of war, is more often represented fully armored, with a shield on one arm and a spear in the other. The helmet is undoubtedly lacking, but let us not forget that Minerva disputed the golden apple with Juno and Venus on Mount Ida; the French, whose gallantry became proverbial, did not want to hide that charming face under a helmet; they left uncovered the only beauty that was ever shown to humans by the chaste goddess who punished the indiscreet gaze of Tiresias by depriving him of sight, and who always conserved her virginity.

This third hypothesis, based on a literal translation of the two lines doubtless traced by the artist himself, is also in accordance with the most incontestable scientific, historical and artistic data; it is the one that has prevailed in the bosom of the committee.

The committee thinks, therefore, that the statue sent from Paris represents Minerva, and that it was founded in the city of Orléans under the government of Queen République. In consequence, it expresses the desire that a request be addressed to His Excellency the Minister of Public Education, soliciting the gift of this ancient Minerva, to replace the modern bust that ornaments our meeting hall.

These conclusions were adopted unanimously.

VII

To His Excellency the Minister of Public Education in
Religion and the Fine Arts in Noumea (Caledonia)
Paris, 2 March 4876

---

his mammoth *Histoire de France* (vol. 7, 1835) to Jeanne d'Arc, effectively formulating the now-familiar mythical version of her exploits. Adolphe Thiers produced an *Histoire de la Révolution française* (1824-27) in his early days, before becoming President of the Third Republic in 1871. The fervent radical socialist Louis Blanc, long a thorn in Thiers' side, was one of the leading participants of the Revolution of 1848.

Monsieur le Ministre,

We began the year rather sadly, awaiting the arrival of the *Scrutatrix*, which did not dock until 8 January, but the day after, our venerable senior member told us in solemn session about the distinctions accorded to us. It is, therefore, with the expression of our very sincere thanks that our report will commence on this occasion, and we beg Your Excellency to transmit to the Emperor the homage of our respectful gratitude.

The decorations accorded to the army have been distributed to it by Admiral Quésitor, after a grand review during which the name of His Majesty was cheered enthusiastically several times. The tribe established on the banks of the Seine made haste to enjoy the spectacle, and those last representatives of the Old World mingled their cries loudly with those of our soldiers.

The intelligence of these still-half-savage people cannot be praised too much. Incessantly in contact with us, they are trying to discover the secrets of our civilization, and are appropriating them, one by one, with a prodigious rapidity. Several of our methods have already been improved by them, and our country is in their debt for numerous inventions that we have hastened to adopt.

They now know about our political institutions in the smallest detail and criticize them loudly. Strangely enough, as soon as they broach the subject, passion carries them away and reason seems to abandon them. These barbarians, totally unfamiliar a few months ago with our social organization, gladly propose improvements to us in this matter too. They have already offered us two or three complete systems, each more unreasonable than the last, which overturn all received ideas on the subjects of taxation, public education, religion, municipal elections, etc., etc. They would be particularly delighted to see us adopt the fundamental principal of their government, which consists of changing their leader as often as possible.

In spite of these aberrations and the scant success they obtain with our soldiers, the little tribe still manifests a very real sympathy toward us and seems to be following the progress of our endeavors with keen interest.

The latter are continuing actively, and we have discovered the imposing necropolis in which, since the origin of the monarchy, the mortal remains of French sovereigns were deposited. It is an immense palace situated at the extremity of the cemetery described in our last report. The upper floors have collapsed, but the ground floor had supported their weight almost everywhere without weakening, and its vas halls have conserved incomparable historical treasures for us.

Two of them enclose stone coffins, large, massive and charged with inscriptions in hieratic characters. We observe there that the sacerdotal language of the French varied through the centuries, for several inscriptions differ from the kind employed on the monolith in the Place de la Navigation. The script is heavy regular, literal rather than symbolic, but just as indecipherable.

The connecting rooms are full of statues and busts representing the kings and queens of France, whose bodies doubtless rest in the subterranean pats of the edifice. There are also groups representing the principal events of their reigns.

Some of these sovereigns wear the costume of Roman emperors, but it is not necessary to conclude therefrom that the French sometimes adopted it. Only four or five kings, H. Martin[25] tells us, had the innocent mania of having themselves represented thus. Others are almost nude; the latter preferred to imitate certain gods of primitive religions. Even the queens did not escape this defect. We already knew by way of Jehan de Sismondi[26] that one of them, named Diana, had posed more than once for status of that goddess, and we have discovered here the marbles to which the veridical history makes allusion.

Venuses are equally numerous, and there is one among them that surpasses all the rest by the boldness and delicacy of its execution. She is nude to the waist, and her left knee, slightly raised, seems to be retaining unaided the thousand pleats of a garment ready to fall. The torso is supple and lively. The breast recalls those pretty lines from the *Anthologie*:

Do you see those azure veins,
Light, delicate and polished
Running over those rounded breasts,
In the whiteness of pure marble?[27]

The head, noble and proud, expresses a power conscious of itself and always sure of victory. The two arms are missing, unfortunately, and we have searched for them in vain. Monsieur Chevalier thinks that the masterpiece in question ought to be attributed to the sculptor Karpeau,[28] who flourished toward the end of the sixteenth century.

While our photographers took possession of the necropolis, we pursued the course of our research, and we found ourselves in the presence of two churches

---

[25] The notional author's reference: "*Recueil général des historiens français.* XII, 17, 12." The reference is presumably to H.-Marie Martin's *L'Empire et la Révolution* (1861)

[26] The notional author's reference: "*Fragments de l'histoire de Henri II.*" The reference is to J.-C.-L. Simonde de Sismondi's *Histoire des français* (1821-44)

[27] The notional author's reference and note: "*A. de Musset, Anthologie française,* II, 4, 9. These lines demonstrate the gross error into which those scholars have fallen who claim that the French poets always alternated masculine and feminine rhymes." The original, which uses an ABBA rhyme-scheme, contains three adjectives accompanying feminine nouns and one a masculine noun (ironically, *sein* [breast]). The poem cited is "*Sur trois marches de marbre rose.*"

[28] The garbled reference is presumably to Jean-Baptiste Carpeaux (1827-1875).

constructed in the same plan and inked together by an octagonal tower. We have only cleared the façades, which are very elegant, and we have learned therefrom that one of these temples was consecrated to Saint Marie du Louvre. Indeed, an inscription engraved in the stone, and doubtless incomplete, includes the words MAIRIE DU LOUVRE and all philologists are aware that in old French, the etymologic A that bore an accent was reinforced and became the diphthong AL; thus Bretagne was written Bretaigne, Champagne Champaigne and Marie Mairie, etc., etc. Your Excellency is not unaware that philology has become, in our day, an exact science of the same kind as algebra.

The combination of all the data, the text of this inscription having confirmed the data furnished by architectural examination, has demonstrated with mathematical rigor that the monument in question was built before the sixteenth century of the Christian Era.

While digging in the ground in front of this church, an engineer discovered two bottles of white glass, taller than they are broad, cut at right angles, whose purpose we do not know. Nearby was found a small lead medallion, which seems to us to merit profound study.

Approximately twelve millimeters across, it has the form of a regular hexagon and is traversed in the direction of its thickness by a fairly strong wire. On one of its faces three interlinked capital letters are depicted, which we believe to be a J, a V and a B. The other face presents the mutilated inscription:

VIN ??? ?? B LL

The two letters making up the second line are illegible and there is only room for a single letter at the end of the third line.

I can make a firm declaration on this issue. In the discussions held to search for the meaning of this numismatic enigma, Monsieur Pinson made the initial suggestion that perhaps we had in our hands a specimen of the military medal instituted by one of the last Poleons of France.[29] I recalled in my turn that Latin was frequently employed at that time in inscriptions. That was a flash of enlightenment, and Monsieur de Lonpont immediately proclaimed that it must have read: *VINCIT IN BELLO*. No more doubt was permissible.[30]

This medal must therefore have shone on the breast of a soldier, a French warrior to whom the fatherland rendered this solemn testimony: *Brave in War!*

---

[29] The notional author's footnote: "*Voy. Les Pharaons, les Sésostris et les Poléons, rapprochements historiques. p.209.*" i.e., See *The Pharaohs: Historical parallels between the Sesostrises and the Poleons.*

[30] One hesitates to disagree with such a brilliant deduction, but is it possible that the three letters were actually SVP and the half-erased name Vincent de Paul?

I am gripped by emotion as I write these lines, and it is with them that I wish to terminate. Our next report will tell you about the new direction we adopted several days ago, and all the hopes that it promises us for the future.

I have the honor of being, with respect to Your Excellency, Monsieur le Ministre, your most humble, most devoted and most obedient servant,

L. Valfleury
Membre de l'Institut,
Académie des Inscriptions et Belles-Lettres.

VIII

To His Excellency the Minister of the Navy and Colonies, at Noumea (Caledonia)
Paris, 6 April 4876

Monsieur le Ministre,

It is with despair in my heart that I take up my pen to write this report, doubtless the last that Your Excellency will receive from Paris. I do not wish, however, to attempt any justification of my conduct here, and I do not wish to devote myself to any recrimination against the men you have given me as auxiliaries and have betrayed the Caledonian flag in such a cowardly fashion; I owe Your Excellency a sincere and impartial account of the facts, and here it is.

Since the beginning of the month of April, I had noticed certain mutinous tendencies among our soldiers; the repression was prompt and energetic, but ineffective. Soon, murmurs, and even threats, reached my ears. I interrogated the officers but their embarrassed, evasive replies told me nothing. Resolved to put an end to it, I announced that I would review the troops the following day.

I slept on board, and toward midday I arrived in the Avenue des Chefs-Illustres, where all the troops were in battle formation.

A sickening spectacle met my eyes. Most of the men had refused to put on their dress uniforms and were wearing their working clothes. Mingling with the indigenes, they were laughing, sinking, smoking their pipes and passing bottles from hand to hand, which, once emptied, they threw away. When I arrived, the officers took up their positions but they remained mute and impassive. As soon as I set foot in the avenue I was greeted by hurrahs, acclamations and confused cries whose meaning I could not make out. It seemed that the wretches had been suddenly afflicted with vertigo. I tried to speak, but the cries redoubled, and I was able to make out the following phrases: *Long live the Republic! Freedom of the Press! Right of Association! Down with Capital! Organized labor! No more exploitation of human by humans!*

I understood everything.

I understood the error I had made by allowing my troops to associate with the indigenes—but the political fantasies of those barbarians were so irrational

45

that the contagion of such follies seemed impossible. Alas, I am now convinced that the scholars who affirm that Noumea was once a French colony are not mistaken; the voice of the blood has made itself heard; it only required a spark to awaken instincts dormant for nearly thirty centuries!

I did not know what decision to make, when a man emerged from the ranks and came straight toward me.

By his insignia and the nacreous seashell resplendent in his head-dress, I recognized the present leader of the indigenes.

"Monsieur l'Amiral," he said to me cheerfully, "you can see that all resistance is futile. We have eight thousand well-armed men, and no foreigner can any longer set foot on this territory, which belongs to us; bow down to the inevitable and join us. The reign of tyranny is over; you can read on our flag the three words: *Liberty, Equality, Fraternity*; they will go with us around the world." He smiled, and added: "For that, one admiral is not too many; accept my offer, therefore, and you can retain your title, your functions and your brilliant uniform."

Indignant at this proposition, I turned to the venerable scholars that Your Excellency gave me as advisers and interrogated them with my gaze.

They all bowed their heads.

The chief went over to them. "Monsieur Syssel," he said to one of them, extending his hand to him, the position you have solicited in the new government is granted to you. By a decree signed ten minutes ago, you are appointed the curator of the monolith of the Place de la Navigation..."

7 April.

Yesterday's dispatch was interrupted by a visit from our new leader. He explained to me the political ideas that will serve as a basis for his government, and the social reforms he is considering. Some of them seem to me, in reality, very sensible, even urgent, for in many respects, the foundations on which modern society rests are barbaric, unjust and fortunately decrepit. I therefore decided that I ought not to refuse him my collaboration and the support of my long experience.

At any rate, unless I can swim all the way back to Noumea, I am compelled to remain here, since all my mariners have abandoned me and my fleet has been confiscated. I shall, in consequence, enclose this dispatch in a securely-sealed bottle, and will then throw it into the sea, and hazard will deliver it to you, Citizen Minister, when it wishes.

Farewell and Fraternity,
Admiral Quésitor.

Vanitas vanitatum, vanitas vanitarum et omnia vanitas. Non est priorum memoria; sed nec eorum quidam quae postea future sunt erit recorrdinato apud eos qui future sunt in novissimo. Vidi cuncta quae fiunt sub sole, and ece unversa vanitas.

(Ecclesiastes)[31]

---

[31] Vanity of vanities, vanity of vanities; all is vanity. There is no remembrance of former things; neither shall there be any remembrance of things that are to come with those that shall come after. I have seen all the works that are done under the sun; and behold, all is vanity and vexation of spirit. *Ecclesiastes* [1: 1, 11 & 14].

J.-H. Rosny *Aîné*: *The Cataclysm*
(1888)

"Le Cataclysme" was initially published in 1888 as "Tornadres" and re-printed until the more familiar title in a volume with "Les Xipéhuz" (1887) by the press associated with the Mercure de France in 1896. The latter volume might well have been produced as a direct response to the success in England of H.G. Wells's early scientific romances—Henry Davray, Wells's French transla-tor, was on the editorial staff of the Mercure—and certainly had the effect of ini-tiating J.-H. Rosny's reputation as a French anticipator of Wells, although it was issued at a time when Rosny had abandoned such work, and was not to re-sume his experiments in speculative fiction for more than a decade.

Like its companion-piece, "Le Cataclysme" can now be seen as spinoff from the speculations that Rosny dramatized in a less conventional fashion in "La Légende sceptique" (1889), featuring a temporary interaction between dif-ferent kinds of matter, initiated by virtue of a cosmic incident. When Rosny re-turned to the writing of scientific romance, under the influence of Maurice Re-nard's propagandizing in favor of "scientific marvel fiction," he picked up the theme of "Le Cataclysme" for much more elaborate development in La Force mystérieuse, *which was serialized in* Je Sais Tout *in 1913 before being reprinted in book form by Plon in the following year. Rosny subsequently produced an abridged version of the latter story for publication alongside "Les Xipéhuz" and "La Mort de la Terre" in the collection* Les Autres vies et les autres mondes *(1924), but I have reproduced the fuller earlier version here.[32]*

B.S.

I. Symptoms

On the Tornadre plateau, for several weeks, nature palpitated and equivo-cated in anguish, the whole of its delicate vegetable organism shot through by intermittent electricity, symbolic signs of a great material event. The free beasts

---

[32] A collection of J.-H. Rosny *Aîné*'s works including the titles mentioned in this introduction is available from Black Coat Press in *The Navigators of Space* (ISBN 978-1-935558-35-4), *The World of the Variants* (ISBN 978-1-935558-36-1), *The Mysterious Force* (ISBN 978-1-935558-37-8), *Vamireh* (ISBN 978-1-935558-38-5), *The Givreuse Enigma* (ISBN 978-1-935558-39-2), *The Young Vampire* (ISBN 978-1-935558-40-8), *Helgvor of the Blue River* (ISBN 978-1-935558-46-0) and *Pan's Flute* (ISBN 978-1-61227-755-4).

on the farms and in the chestnut plantations were not as quick to flee quotidian perils; they seemed to want to get closer to human beings, wandering around the tenancies. Then they came to an extraordinary decision, sounding an alarm: they emigrated, going deep into the valley of the Iaraze.

As the nights fell, in the gloom of forests and thickets, there was a drama of nervous animals furtively quitting their lairs with hesitant steps, often pausing and stopping, melancholy to be fleeing their native land. The somber and languid howling of wolves alternated with the muffled grunts of wild boars and the sobbing of ruminants. Ashy silhouettes were gliding everywhere, generally toward the south-west, over cultivated ground beneath the open sky: great antlered skulls, heavy tapir-like bodies with short legs, and slimmer beasts, carnivores and herbivores alike—hares, moles, rabbits, foxes and squirrels. The batrachians followed, the reptiles and the wingless insects, and a week ensued in which the south-western direction was flooded with inferior organisms, a frightful vermicular population, from the hopping silhouettes of frogs to slugs and snails, through the marvelous wing-cases of carabid beetles and horrible crustaceans that live under stones in eternal darkness, to worms, leeches and larvae.

Soon, nothing remained but winged creatures. Then the birds, filled with unease, increasingly clinging on to branches, fearful of flying, saluted the twilights with more subdued songs, often leaving the locality for a large part of the day. The crows and the owls held great assemblies; the swifts gathered together as if for their autumnal migration; the magpies became agitated, cawing all day long.

The mysterious terror spread to the slaves: the sheep, the cattle, the horses, even the dogs. Resigned, in the confidence of their humble serfdom, all expecting salvation from humankind, they stayed on the Tornadre plateau—except for the cats, which had fled in the early days, returning to savage liberty.

As the evenings went by, a confused sadness, an asphyxia of the soul, took possession of the inhabitants of the tenancies and the proprietors of the estate known as the Corne: the confused anticipation of a cataclysm—which, however, the topography of Tornadre belied. Being distant from volcanic regions and the ocean, insubmersible—having only a few streams—and compact in texture, what form could the threat possibly take?

It was felt nevertheless, electrically, in the rigidity of small branches and blades of grass at certain morning hours, in the singular attitudes of foliage, in subtle and suffocating effluvia, unusual phosphorescences and the prickling of flesh by night, which caused the eyelids to rise, condemning the individual to insomnia, in the extraordinary behavior of livestock, often stiffening, their nostrils open and tremulous, and *turning their heads toward the north.*

II. The Astral Downpour

One evening, at the Corne, Sévère and his wife were finishing dinner next to the half-closed window. A crescent moon was wandering near the zenith, pale and full of grace, above the vast perspectives, and rising mists decorated the western frontier. A troubling spell—an ardor of the nervous system, a suddenly awakened obscure commotion—kept them silent, impregnating them with a particular aesthetic sensibility, a profound wonderment relative to the nocturnal splendors.

A harmonious tremor welled up from the trees in the garden; at the rear, visible through the gate to the avenue, there was an enchantment of confused objects, the crop-fields of the Tornadre, the blanched farmhouses, the friendly mystery of human lights and the vague slate-covered steeple of the rustic church. The masters of the Corne were moved by that, troubled by the vibration of their nerves. The commotion being keener along the spinal column, however, the wife dropped the bunch of grapes that she was plucking, her lip trembling.

"My God! Is it going to go on forever?"

Sévère looked at her, with a strong desire to give her courage—but his own soul was in a stupor, obscured by an imponderable force.

Sévère Lestang was one of those grave intellectuals slowly seeking the secret of things, studying nature without impatience, disinterested in glory—but he was a man as well as an intellectual; his eyes were gentle and courageous, and he had a desire to *live his life* as well as developing his faculties. His wife, Luce, was a nervous mountain Celt, delicately graceful, amorous and captivating, but a trifle somber. Under the calm and attentive protection of her husband, she was like certain infinitely frail flowers that live in the inlets of great rivers, between large shady leaves.

"If you want," said Sévère, "we can leave tomorrow."

"Yes, please!"

She came closer to him, seeking refuge, murmuring: "They say that one can't keep a foothold any longer, you know, especially in the evening…that something takes hold of you and carries you away! Well, I don't dare walk quickly any longer, my steps draw me on so…and one climbs stairs effortlessly, but with a constant fear of falling…"

"You're mistaken, Luce. It's a nervous illusion." He smiled, pressing her to him—but he too, with a terrible malaise, had perceived that incomprehensible lightness. Sometimes, before dusk, had he not wanted to walk more rapidly, to get back to the Corne, and found his stride lengthening, transformed into bounds, launching him forward with frightening speed? With his equilibrium lost, having difficulty in remaining vertical, experiencing a sensation of ataxia at each footfall, he had reverted to a slow pace, clinging to the ground, solidly, seeking large patches of sticky ground.

"You think it's an illusion?" she said.

"I'm sure of it, Luce!"

She looked at him, while he stroked the fringe of her hair, and she suddenly realized that he was as nervous as she was, electrified by a profound anguish: no longer a refuge for her, but a poor frail creature confronted by enigmatic powers.

Then she went paler, her teeth chattering.

"The coffee will settle you," he said.

"Perhaps."

But they sensed the deceit in their words, the poverty of any tonic, or any human remedy against the approaching Unknowable—against that vast metamorphosis of phenomena, in which terrestrial life no longer participated, which had been troubling the flora and fauna, the animals and the plants, for weeks already.

They sensed the deceit. They did not dare look at one another, instinctively afraid of communicating their presentiments, of doubling their distress by nervous induction. And for long minutes, they listened inwardly, in their flesh, to the dull and confused echo of Mystery.

A fearful housemaid brought the coffee; they watched her leave, unsteadily, not daring to question that anxiety, similar to their own.

"Did you see how Marthe was walking?" asked Luce.

He did not reply, looking in surprise at the little silver spoon that he had just picked up. Perceiving his fixed stare, she looked at it in her turn, and exclaimed: "It's green!"

The little spoon was, indeed, green, with a pale emerald gleam—and they suddenly noticed the same tint on the other spoons, and all of the silverware.

"Oh, my God!" cried the young woman. Raising her finger, she began to recite, in a low voice, whispering painfully:

"*When the Silver goes green,*
"*The* Roge Aigue *will come*
"*Devouring the Moon and stars...*"[33]

These words, an ancient and vague prophecy that the peasants of the Tornadre plateau had handed down through the ages, made Sévère shudder. They both had an impression of darkness and fatality, colorless and soundless, beyond all anthropomorphism. Where had the poor rustics obtained that oracle, now so

---

[33] I have left the key words unaltered, because they are deliberately misrendered in such way as to conserve a certain ambiguity. *Roge* is only one letter away from *rouge* [red] or *rogue* [arrogant], while *aigue* is subtly distinct from both the masculine and feminine forms of *aigu/aiguë*, whose usual meaning is "pointed" or "sharp," although the term is also used as a noun to signify a diamond, referring to its "water" rather than its facets, by analogy with *aigu-marine* [aquamarine]. The readiest inference to be drawn, therefore, might be reckoned as "red gem"—but the other possible implications should not be left out of account.

serious? What science, what observations of remote eras, what cataclysmic memories, did it symbolize?

Sévère had an immense desire to be far away from Tornadre, remorseful at not having obeyed the sure instincts of the animals, at having dared to follow poor cerebral logic rather than the warning of Nature. "Do you want to leave this evening?" he asked Luce, ardently.

"I'd never dare leave the house before morning returns!"

He thought that it might be as perilous to venture out by night as to stay at the Corne; he resigned himself to it, thoughtfully. A great lamentation interrupted his thoughts: feverish whinnying, the dull banging of horses struggling against the stable door. The dog howled, and the clamor spread along the length of the Tornadre plateau, echoed by other animals, terrified ruminants and braying donkeys. At the same time, there was a greenish glow in the sky, and a shooting star passed over, huge, with a resplendent tail.

"Look!" said Luce.

Other meteors welled up, isolated at first, then in small groups, all with bright nuclei and leaving long trails, miraculously beautiful.

"It's the night of August 10," said Sévère, "and the star-showers will increase... there's nothing abnormal about it."[34]

"Why, then, are our lamps growing dimmer?"

The Lamps were, in fact, lowering their flames; a superior electrical density enveloped everything, a terror, not of death, but of exasperated life, of supernatural dilatation—so that Sévère and Luce clung on to the furniture in order to *weigh more*, in order to *perceive contact with solid material*. A strange pressure lifted them up, robbing them of their sense of balance. They felt that they were in a new atmosphere, in which the ether acted with a *living* power, in which something organic—extra-terrestrially organic—was disturbing every drop of blood, orientating every molecule, intruding into the very marrow of their bones, and gradually stiffening every hair on their bodies.

In addition, as Sévère had predicted, the stellar downpour accelerated, the entire concavity of the firmament filling with bolides. By degrees, it was mingled with an unknown phenomenon, persistent and increasing: voices. Faint, distant, musical voices, a symphony of tiny strings in the celestial depths, a sometimes almost human whisper, reminiscent of the ancient Pythagorean harmony of the spheres.

"They're souls!" she murmured.

"No," he said. "No, they're Forces!"

---

[34] August 10 is the usual peak of the Perseid meteor shower, consisting of particles left behind by Comet Swift-Tuttle; the shower has been observed for the last 2000 years, and is sometimes known as "St. Lawrence's tears" because August 10 was the day of his martyrdom.

Souls or forces, however, it was the same Unknown, the same hermetic threat, the pressure of a prodigious event, the blackest of human fears: the Shapeless and the Unforeseeable. And the voices went on, above the murmur of things, frightfully gentle, essential and subtle, taking Luce back to the Humility of childhood, to Worship, to Prayer:

"*Our Father, who art in Heaven...*"

He did not dare smile, the beating of his heart increasing as if to burst his arteries, while his masculine mind—more curious about causation than his wife's—tried to imagine what magnetism, what extraterrestrial polarities, were working upon this corner of the globe, and whether it was the same in the valley of the Iaraze.

Outside the plateau, however, since the commencement of the phenomenon—and Sévère had gone down to the river again that very day—no one had perceived the unfamiliar symptoms. The animals and people there were living tranquilly. Life preserved its normal form there. Why, though? What correlation was there between the sky and the plateau, what cycle of phenomena—for the prophecy of the peasants of Tornadre implied a cycle—regulated this great Drama?

A misfortune occurred: a triumphant assault by the animals against the old stable door. The Corne's three horses appeared, bucking and foaming at the mouth beneath the pale rays of the sinking Moon,

"Here, Clairon!" called Sévère.

One of the horses approached, the others following. Never had there been a scene as phantasmagoric as the three long heads hollowed out in the light and shadow, in front of the window, their large eyes bulging, sniffing Luce and Sévère, visibly questioning, with a return of vague confidence in the master, a troubled idea of the power of the person who fed them. Then, for no obvious reason—perhaps an increase in the meteor shower—with absolute terror in the depths of their large eyes, their nostrils more cavernous, the mad panic of their race took hold, and they tore themselves away from the window whinnying, and fled.

"Oh, how they're leaping!" said Luce.

They were, in truth, running with an amazing gait, in enormous bounds. Suddenly, at the far end of the garden, confronted by the iron gate, the most impetuous rose up like a winged creature, and cleared the obstacle.

"You see! You see!" cried Luce. "He too has no more weight!"

"Nor the two others," he added, involuntarily.

Indeed the other two black shadows, rising up, without even brushing the bars, leapt more than four meters high. Their agile silhouettes, carried vertiginously across the fields, diminished, evaporated and disappeared. At the same time, a manservant appeared outside, alone and timid, hardly daring to come forward with the fearful step of a little child.

Sévère felt an infinite pity for the poor devil, realizing that everyone else at the Corne must have shut themselves up in their rooms, prey to the same increase in terror as the Masters.

"Let them go, Victor!" he called. "We'll find them later."

Victor came closer, holding on to trees, then the wall, and the shutter. "Is it true, Master," he asked, "that the *roge aigue* has come back?"

Sévère hesitated, preserving the modesty of his intelligence and his doubt in the midst of the sinister events, but Luce could not be silent.

"Yes, Victor."

A bleak silence fell, the three individuals equalized by the sensation of the supernatural—but Sévère was still examining, questioning himself about the connection between the phenomenon and the meteorites. He studied the increasing rain of stars, the stream of supreme beauty from the depths of the Imponderable. A new observation alarmed him: that the sad fragment of the Moon sinking toward the horizon could not be providing the light that persisted over the landscape. Looking westwards, he watched the satellite disappearing, its convexity ready to collapse, adjacent to the western horizon.

A few minutes more, and then it was gone—but the light over the Tornadre plateau persisted, as if emanating from the zenith: only a few degrees to the north, according to the indication of its shadow. Was it from the zenith, then, that the phenomenon was coming? He turned his face to it, slowly. There, an amethyst glow, a lenticular glimmer, was thinly displayed like a slender cloud, with a maximum radiance toward the north.

Sévère thought that these things would have been a delight to behold, without the creeping of the flesh, the sepulchral threat and the presentiment of death falling from the Heavens upon the Earth.

III. The Appearance of the Aigue

"Look!" said Luce. She had perceived the light in her turn; more affected than Lestang, she was pointing at it.

Victor, clinging to the window on the outside, was shivering with fever, as if he were drunk, occasionally coming round with a sigh, and ever-increasing horror.

Up above, the light was increasing. As it did so, the whispering voices of the firmament faded away, and an enormous silence weighed upon the Tornadre plateau. Then, faint at first, a light from below appeared to reply to the other, light fringes floating over the treetops and over all the plants. It was delicately and wildly heart-rending. On the three people, so dissimilar, it made an almost identical impression, of funerary lamps or a pyre, an immense conflagration that was about to engulf Tornadre and all its inhabitants.

Luce moaned, almost unconsciously, and uttered a desperate plaint: "Oh, I'm thirsty!"

Sévère turned toward her; the tenderness of his heart, his love for the Celtic mountain woman, gave him strength. He fought against his desire not to move, to end his existence there, at the window, with the bottom frame in his clenched hands. Swaying, he went to fetch a glass of water—but he continued questioning himself, astonished that the atmosphere was cool, almost cold, in spite of all the subtle fire in the heavens and on Earth.

He had great difficulty bringing back the water; the glass in his hand was so light that he had no sensation of holding anything, and had to grip its base with all his might. He lost half the liquid *en route*.

Luce took a gulp, and spat it out, nauseated. "It tastes like iron filings... like rust!"

Sévère sipped the water, and had to spit it out in his turn; it was metallic and powdery. They both looked at one another for a long time, desperately. The veils of memory lifted, across so many charming years, on the moment when they had glimpsed one another for the first time in the Real World, the appeal of their nervous systems, amorous thereafter. Delicate and indefatigable periods of adoration. (Oh, what long, elevated, immense hours, woven of divinity, revive beneath the nebulous portico of the past!) And their gazes embraced, in an infinite pity for one another. Was this truly the death-agony? Would they have to leave their young lives behind like this, dying of asphyxia, thirst and that hideous impression of antigravity, that *non-contact* with matter. Oh Lord!

Personally, Sévère, so full of vital force, did not want to admit it, in spite of everything. Curiosity subsisted in his skull through the knell, making it attentive to the exterior again. The marvelous and lamentable drama continued to evolve; an opera of subtle fires, colossal corposants, lit up the distant landscape; at the summits of the tall trees, slender and flickering at first, and displaying the infinite scale of the spectrum, flames multiplied, trembling on every twig and the tip of every leaf, and then spread to the lower vegetation, the bushes, the grass, the stubble.

Every protrusion of vegetation thus had its glow, directed upwards at the sky.

Above the dream-like glimmers of that fiery landscape, birds were flying in flocks. They had finally decided to flee. Super-electric creatures, they had initially resisted these phenomena, which were doubtless less antipathetic to their organisms than those of terrestrial animals. Crows, with somber cries; sparse but infinite flocks of sparrows, goldfinches, chaffinches and warblers; intelligent groups of magpies, swifts, swallows, in traveling formation; and raptors in ones or twos, all headed southwards with an excited chirping and twittering that was almost speech.

Again, Sévère concentrated on the innumerable flames, which were neither fusing with one another nor giving out any appreciable heat; they were also, as he looked at them so directly, elongating into fine strips, building towers and Gothic monuments with billions of dazzling spires.

He was interrupted by a raucous cry, emitted by Luce.

"Hold me down! Hold me down…I'm being carried away!"

He saw his companion delirious, livid and cramped, her breast rising in a pitiful attempt to breathe. His own heart became weak; he was overcome by an absolute and infinite desperation, while he held on to Luce with a mechanical gesture. Shivering, she gazed at the shining plateau, and spoke confusedly:

"It's the other world, Sévère—it's the immaterial world…the Earth is about to die…"

"No, no," he whispered, aware of the vanity of his words, "it's a Force…a magnetism…a transformation of movement."

A lower voice made him start: that of the hypnotized Victor, who had woken up: "the *Roge Aigue*!"

Sévère leaned out. Less than 20 degrees from the north he saw a large rectangle the color of rust, with an irregular border, as if excavated from abysms of sulfur. Gradually, it became brighter, as transparent as a wave, a veritable lake extended over the north, over which ran wrinkles of a paler red, similar to waves. And around the red lake, over the entire sky, a green darkness appeared, which turned blue and darkened, casting a profound jade shadow over the southern extremity.

The stars had died away. Nothing remained by that sky of red water and green water, of green gem and jade darkness.

What was it? Where had it come from? And why this enormous influence on the Tornadre? What power of special induction, and what affinities, were prowling around the firmament? These questions racked Sévère's brain, but did not spare him at all from the stupor that had taken hold of Luce and Victor on seeing the peasant prophecy fulfilled. He no longer doubted that death would come swiftly, that the heart which was galloping so terribly in his breast was about to burst and shut down forever…

Meanwhile, her dying face raised toward the heavens, Luce began to recite, with a poignant solemnity:

"When the Silver goes green,

"The *Roge Aigue* will come

"Devouring the Moon and stars…"

Releasing a heavy sigh, she collapsed against the windowsill, rigid, with her eyes closed.

IV. Toward the Iaraze

Motionless at first, devoid of strength, Sévère drew his wife toward him. Was she dead? Had she vanished forever? Black laughter—the laughter of unavoidable destiny—rose to his lips, and the word "forever" circulated in his skull in an ironic manner—that "forever" which, so far as his own existence was concerned, might not extend beyond the next hour.

His grip on Luce grew tighter then, becoming unhealthy. He lifted the poor woman up, holding her across his chest...

Then, suddenly, bizarrely and delightfully, a kind of relief overwhelmed his entire body: *firmness on the ground, weight, had returned!*

What! Chance must have told him to do it; he had not arrived theoretically at the idea of combining someone else's weight with his in order to recover a sense of material security.

Reanimated and solidified, in spite of the oppression in his breast, a flood of courage and hope ran through him now, which further augmented the consequences of the event, including the singular ease with which he was holding Luce in his arms like a little child. Then, his heart skipping a beat, his memory reverted to the catastrophe, forgotten in the shock of glad emotion. Was Luce dead?

He listened carefully, with his ear upon the young woman's breast; the inconvenient sound of his own arteries prevented him from hearing anything. She was not stiff, though—but she was so pale! Her eyelids opened upon unmoving eyes.

"Luce! My darling Luce!"

A sigh; a slight movement of the head. He discerned a very faint breath—of life! His willpower was reinforced; he resolved to make every effort to save her.

He stood there for a few minutes, thinking, then shrugged his shoulders. What good was calculation? It was necessary to act like a brute, the least of organized beings, and flee straight ahead until he reached the banks of the Iazare. And with no further hesitation, taking the shortest route, he climbed on to the window and leapt through it nimbly, shouting to Victor:

"Get hold of something heavy. Release the dog and go to warn your comrades. See how I'm carrying my burden. That's how anyone might save himself. Do you understand?"

"Yes, Monsieur."

And Sévère ran off at a trot, his tread steady but oppressed, his breath whistling, troubled by the electricity, which was livelier and more debilitating outside. He went out of the garden gate and found himself in open country. In its prodigious majesty, the red lake seemed to magnify the stellar abysses even further. Its glory, at its palpitating edges, with the softness of stained glass, delicate and resplendent, terminating in lace, orange cinders and dendrites, almost overwhelmed the zenith. No other stars could be seen any longer. Here and there, a fine serpentine line—a streak of fire—ran from the extreme north to the extreme south. On the ground, on the flat surface of the Tornadre plateau, the fires persevered everywhere, a taciturn inferno: an inferno without heat, or even consumption.

The colossal candles of large trees and the torches—infinite in number—of the short grass, the steep ascensions, the great never-ending polychromatic bows devoured by the neutralization of forces and indefatigably recomposed, filled Space with a terrible and beautiful life. Sévère marched on, going through it, closing his eyes periodically when he had to cross excessively flamboyant zones. Luce's hair emitted a torrent of sparks which dazzled and blinded Sévère. Instinct guided him south-westwards.

Every few minutes, a farm appeared, which served him as a landmark, but one in which he had no great confidence, so uncertain were appearances rendered by the infernal transfiguration.

A moment came when he thought he had gone astray; in front of him there was a pool, with reeds rising up like avenging blades, and willows with pale emerald leaves. Fireflies were moving continually over the surface. There was a suffocating odor of phosphorus and ozone. He felt the soft ground beneath his feet, the confused attraction of hidden water. He tried to get his bearings, but in vain. He knew, however, that it was Cilleuses pond, less than 500 meters from the edge of the plateau. He went around it and marched for ten minutes—and found himself back at his point of departure.

If he remained there miserably, his great effort would be wasted.

"Come on, Sévère!"

He gets under way again, striving to recognize some landmark, some familiar sight, but weakening in that research, convinced that he will fall unconscious within an hour, to die in the open countryside.

Suddenly, he makes a discovery: a sharp little promontory, the only one on the pond, from which he can deduce which direction to take. From then on, it seems that he has wings, progressing in a straight line, and ending up finding a little path that he knows well, which he never leaves thereafter. He cannot estimate the duration of the journey—perhaps half an hour, perhaps ten minutes, or even five—but he has come to a halt, overwhelmed amazement, before a black gulf parallel with the blazing Tornadre: an abyss of darkness beneath his feet, which something separates from the phosphorescent outpouring flooding the plateau.

"The slope! The slope!" He repeats the word; full of strength, he begins to go down a sinuous path at a run.

Already, he feels a physical well-being; the induction is decreasing, the lights are becoming steadily sparser, as gentle as will-o'-the-wisps, and the moist and tepid air is more breathable. On the other hand, Luce's weight is becoming harder to bear. It is breaking his arms and slowing him down.

He falls down, collapsing on the slope without the interposition of any root or branch. Then, as he resumes his course, out of breath, indomitable instinct masters his nerves.

Eventually, to his immense joy, he hears the running of the Iazare, and perceives imminent salvation through his every pore. Only a few more steps! Already, the peril can scarcely reach him in this environment, where, the mysterious influence having been reduced to a minimum, there is already the healthy, vital terrestrial nature of old, hospitable to humankind.

He does not stop, sweating and haggard but full of strength. Finally, the vale arrives, with the river sobbing in the darkness. With a loud cry, a violent and dolorous delight, he lets himself go.

Luce is lying across his knees. Momentarily, he turns his head to look back and upwards, irresistibly. A vague glimmer is wandering over the slope, brighter toward the edge of the plateau; that is all he can see of the vast conflagration, which is little enough compared with the glare of the nocturnal sea in the era of its fecundation. The firmament is especially astonishing, the *Aigue* having vanished, leaving only the redness—a kind of aurora borealis. The shower of bolides continues to fall.

"What's going on?" he wonders. "Why that enormous dissimilarity between the Tornadre and the Iazare?"

Eventually, he leans over Luce. She is still pale and motionless, but her breath is perceptible—the breath of sleep rather than unconsciousness. He calls out to her, raising his voice: "Luce! Luce!"

She shivers and moves her head gently. That is an infinite joy amid the gloom, and, with sobs of happiness, he embraces her, and continues calling out to her. He murmurs a few tender words.

Finally, the eyelids open and the young woman's gaze, full of dreams and darkness, falls upon Sévère.

"Ah!" he cries. "We're finally victorious. The Tornadre has not devoured you."

Standing up, with his arms folded, he conceives a desire—the promise of climbing up again, alone, toward the south-west, to follow the story of the cataclysm. Voices are raised on the slope however, and the sound of barking.

Understanding that it is the Corne's servants, Luce and Sévère wait for them, embracing one another, in a bliss so great that tears are streaming down their cheeks.

Note

Monsieur Sévère Lestang has, in fact, published the story of the Tornadre cataclysm (*chez* Germer-Ballière). For seven days the *Aigue* was visible over the plateau, and the conflagration with *neither heat nor consumption* persisted for those seven days—as attested, in addition to Monsieur Lestang and the inhabitants of the plateau, by a scientific commission that arrived on the final day of the phenomenon. There were some dead to mourn, but relatively few, the majority of individuals having fled after the beginning of the night of August 10.

As for the conclusions of the scientific investigation, it must be confessed that they were entirely negative; no plausible theory was offered. The one interesting fact, which might prove, at a later date, to lead to some discovery, is this:

the Tornadre plateau rests on a rocky mass of about 150 billion cubic meters, which is evidently of stellar origin; it is *a colossal bolide*, fallen near the Iaraze valley in prehistoric times.

Camille Debans: *The Story of an Earthquake*
(1892)

In the 1890s, a generation before Hugo Gernsback, Louis Figuier (1819-1894), editor of the French popular science magazine La Science Illustrée, *made a concerted effort to define and delimit the genre of* roman scientifique, *using that term to head a series of feuilletons that ran in his magazine from 1888 to 1905. One writer who became a regular contributor to Figuier's magazine was Camille Debans (1834-1910), who contributed seven stories in all, including "Histoire d'un tremblement de terre" (26 November 1892-24 December 1892; tr. as "The Story of an Earthquake").[35]*

"Histoire d'un tremblement de terre," like many popularizing endeavors by Camille Flammarion and S. Henry Berthoud, masquerades as an item of nonfiction presented in narrative form in the interests of dramatization, although it is a work of fiction whose careful use of real places and false dates are tactical exercises intended to create a sense of verisimilitude.

B.S.

On 18 November 1834, at 7.35 a.m., the ships at sea in the Pacific Ocean off the coast of Chile experienced a violent shock. Something like a terrible frisson ran through their hulls from one end to the other, causing their timbers to creak and their masts to groan; then, after five or six seconds of suspension, they resumed their progress, without anyone being able to account for the strange phenomenon. They subsequently learned that the shock had simply been the repercussion of the Talcahuano earthquake—a repercussion felt more than three hundred leagues away at sea.[36]

The mariners who put into Concepcion Bay a few days later no longer found the town and learned that the ships anchored in the harbor had almost all perished.

---

[35] Debans' novel *The Misfortunes of John Bull* (1884) is available from Black Coat Press (ISBN 978-1-61227-411-9).

[36] The earthquake whose devastation was still visible when *H. M. S. Beagle* called in at Concepcion Bay in March 1834 and was reported in Charles Darwin's journal to have destroyed Talcahuano (not for the first or the last time), must have taken place sometime before the date included in this story. Concepcion was itself devastated by a quake in February 1835, also reported in Darwin's journal. Talcahuano was most recently destroyed in the earthquake of February 2010, so the story has not lost its timeliness.

Concepcion Bay is one of the largest and most splendid havens on the Pacific coast of South America. It is five leagues across from north to south, and more than fifteen kilometers from east to west. Seen from anchorage, it appears immense. With the naked eye, in clear weather, one can scarcely make out the eastern and northern coasts, almost continually veiled by a light mist, which lends a mysterious charm to the horizon.

Talcahuano is a small town with white houses, distributed in a disorderly fashion over a peninsula in the south-east of the bay.

Behind Talcahuano, the foothills of the Cordilleras rise up immediately, covered by luxuriant vegetation and populated by innumerable herds of livestock. To the west, the principal hill of the town slopes down to fade away in a vast plain once occupied by the sea, extending between two mountains extending from the interior all the way to the town of Concepcion, which is the capital of the province.

Talcahuano no longer keeps count of earthquakes. Since its foundation—which was, parenthetically, due to French navigators—that small town has been destroyed at least fifteen times. Thus, its houses are constructed in anticipation of the frequent shocks to which it is subject. There are very few habitations of brick or stone, but in general, they are more or less spacious huts built in mud and supple wood. They have no foundations; the floorboards rest on enormous cylindrical logs, and the houses can, in consequence, move forwards and backwards without being damaged.

Experience has demonstrated that this plan is the most favorable in the event of volcanic eruptions, but from the point of view of road-building and the alignment of streets, that mode of construction offers inconveniences, the least of which is to annoy the Alcalde.

In fact, every inhabitant possesses a garden behind his house. When the requirements of cultivation cause him to feel the necessity of enlarging his garden, the proprietor contents himself with pushing his house, which slides over the logs and advances one, two or three meters toward the middle of the street. His garden therefore grows by as much on the side hidden from the public highway. This operation, repeated several time in accordance with need by each proprietor, ends up producing streets of microscopic width, whose irregular contours would make the most tortuous Flemish streets seem rectilinear by comparison.

When the encroachment reaches such proportions that the street is in danger of being replaced by a connecting wall, however, the Alcalde intervenes and lets it be known to the inhabitants, with a blast of his trumpet, that he is giving them twenty-four hours to readjust the alignment of their domiciles—and a pair of oxen harnessed to each house is sufficient to carry out the Alcalde's order.

Earthquakes are not rare events in Peru, and more especially in Chile. Valparaiso suffers fifteen earthquakes a year, but if these disquieting events are not the preliminary effects of volcanic eruptions in the Cordilleras, the inhabitants content themselves with coming out of their houses in order not to be crushed by collapsing ceilings.

In Copiapo, a small town in the north famous for its copper and silver mines, especially the Gallos family's silver mine, into the depths of which one goes down by means of a staircase carved in the silver mass, the earth is always quaking. The oscillations are not very obvious, but it is sufficient to lean on the wall of a hut to feel the perpetual trepidation of the ground immediately.

Thus, there are people in Chile who have been shaken by a hundred, a hundred and fifty, or even two hundred earthquakes.

For them, there are unequivocal signs by which one is able in advance to recognize the intensity of the terrible event: an increasingly heavy atmosphere, a sky veiled by hot vapors, nervous anxieties that extend in ascending progression from men to women, from women to animals, and from species to species thereafter, all the way to dogs, mules and horses, which are the most sensitive to the perturbations Thus, there are few examples of a mule or a horse continuing to walk during the five or six seconds preceding the subterranean noise and the trepidation of the earth.

Well, in spite of these premonitory symptoms, in spite of the habituation and in spite of everything, there is no Chilean who does not have an indescribable terror of earthquakes. Strangely enough, the older they get—which is to say, the more volcanic shocks they experience—the more fearful they become. I merely observe that; I shall not seek to explain it.

Now, toward the end of the month of October 1834, two volcanoes situated in the territory of Araucania, which were thought to have been extinct for half a century, vomited flame and a certain quantity of lava. On the other hand, it was learned that in San Carlos de Chiloé, in the archipelago of that name, three or four oscillations of a particular character had been felt.

People were, in consequence, expecting an imminent catastrophe. Every day they heard muffled detonations in the mountain, followed by long rumbles, as if thunder were growling. And the day after, they would hear from the vaqueros or the inhabitants of Concepcion that blocks of granite had been detached from the summits to tumble noisily into the precipices.

The old men who had escaped two or three destructions of their town felt gripped by fear and slept with one eye open, ready take up their families. Devoutly religious, like all Chileans, they implored the infinite mercy of God, and only found the appeasement for which they were avid in prayer.

The terror, which had been increasing since the beginning of the month, began to calm down after the twelfth of November. Alarming news became rarer, and it was thought that once again, they might get away with an alarm.

Talcahuano is an essentially joyful town. One could erect a temple to pleasure there. There is perhaps no country in the world, not forgetting Italy and Spain, where more effort is expended on follies, feasting, frantic dancing, guitar-music and egg punch. It seems that the poor Chileans and their amiable womenfolk are in haste to savor the fruits of life, and that tomorrow is, for them, the improbable date of an unhoped-for future.

Empedicles, I believe, reproached the inhabitants of Agrigentum for living life at a gallop, as if they were going to die the next day, and building their houses as if they were going to live forever. One might have made the same reproach to the Chileans of Talcahuano, except for the construction of the houses, for the dwellings and their inhabitants alike gave the appearance of awaiting the end of the world with a philosophy far more Christian that that of the vainglorious Sicilian rhetorician.

As soon as the inhabitants of Talcahuano were convinced that all danger had vanished, joy and feasting hastened to resume their empire over the light-hearted town.

A few *tertulias*—that being the name of the dances hosted in the region by people of certain importance—has taken place on the evening of the twelfth, and as no bad news came to subdue the town the following day, there was a big party at the home of one of the principal ship-suppliers. Naturally, almost all the captains and officers of the ships calling at Talcahuano were invited.

There was a considerable hotchpotch of nationalities—something akin to a miniature Tower of Babel—in the tradesman's drawing rooms, which did not prevent the young Chilean woman from being very amiable, and everyone was delighted.

The captains of the majority of the ships then got together to offer in their turn to throw an equally fine party for their hosts, and the date of that maritime *tertulia* was fixed for 17 November.

A magnificent and spacious American whaler, a three-master, was chosen with common accord by the mariners as the least oily and most elegant venue that could be presented to Talcahuanan high society. All the sailors worked in shifts to scrub and polish the deck that was to serve as a dance floor and the lower deck, where the gambling tables, boudoirs and sleeping quarters were set up. Flowers were brought aboard to surround and ornament the masts. The most delicate ear in the harbor was chosen and dispatched on reconnaissance to Concepcion, with instructions to bring back the best guitar-pluckers in the town. A piano was unearthed, hoisted aboard, and thoroughly retuned for the occasion.

Finally, when the preparations were concluded, it was all so beautiful that the mariners dared not stroll on their own decks.

The great day arrived. The launches and dinghies from all the ships, graciously decked with flags, gathered almost simultaneously on what was known as Talcahuano pier. The guests embarked successively, and were ferried to the *Ocean Queen*, where the party was soon in full swing.

Oh, it was a beautiful ball! A magnificent and picturesque *tertulia!* Among the mariners there were no dress suits, but long the frockcoats that mariners call "mainsails." Everyone had gloves, of course, but in their pockets or clutched in the left hand, to show that they were familiar with society conventions. On the

Chilean side, there was full European costume; for the ladies, that meant an overabundance of silk, feathers, velvet, ostrich-plumes and Chinese crepes.

They danced; they danced for a long time, and in every style: English jigs, boleros, tarantellas, waltzes, minuets, even quadrilles, not forgetting the Chilean *zamacueca* and the Peruvian *refalosa*.

At midnight, everyone went down to the lower deck for supper. A few sleepy children were put to bed in the officer's cabins, and the party resumed more hectically and more noisily than ever.

During that intermission, the sailors, who were wide-eyed with astonishment, having never seen such a hurly-burly before, performed all the dances they knew on the deck, with all the more enthusiasm because someone had broken open a barrel of rum in the *Ocean Queen*'s forecastle during the society supper.

The guests' supper was a true banquet. The men charged with serving at table had a great deal of difficulty satisfying the desires of senoritas who asked them to transport to some fortunate officer another the sparkling glasses in which they had dipped their red lips by way of a preliminary—a gracious custom of that liberal region.

In brief, by three o'clock in the morning, the stores being exhausted, and various groups experiencing the need to surrender their moist foreheads to the caresses of the open air, they left the table to return to the dances. On arriving on deck, however, they perceived that the sea had become choppy. The ship was pitching somewhat, although, strangely enough, there was no wind. It was, therefore, very difficult to dance. Anyone who had suggested bringing the party to an end at that point would, however, would have been very unpopular. What should they do, then? The young women's feet were twitching with impatience.

A local merchant offered to let the soirée continue on land at his house and drink his cellar dry. The motion was welcome with an enthusiastic acclamation. They embarked at the double, and twenty minutes later, the *Ocean Queen* had become the most silent of whaling-ships. The only people still aboard were drowsy sailors, two or three weary officers no longer seduced by the splendors of society, and three or four sleeping children, whose mothers, avid to dance, had not wanted to burden themselves with them, and had confided them to the guard of the first mate when he took over the four o'clock watch.

In almost all the towns of South America, especially those on the Pacific coast, night-watchmen still exist whose functions, in addition to nocturnal policing, consist of crying the time every thirty minutes. For Europeans that custom has something primitive about it, which brings a smile to the lips, but in a land where, in spite of the luxury and the fêtes, the majority of the indigenes sweat in poverty, that fashion of substituting Christians for clocks testifies to a certain eccentric solicitude for the needs of the inhabitants.

Thus, the watchmen in question, who are known as *serenos* and perform their duties on horseback, are continually shouting, simultaneously: *"Son last tres!"* or *"Cuatro! Son las quarto y media!"*—and they add *lluvia*, rain, or *sereno*, fine weather, according to the circumstances. Finally, when five o'clock sounds, hey announce it and the sing a prayer, which begins: *"Ave, Maria, purissima, castissima, inviolatissima, etc."*—a touching fashion of concluding their tiring work by actions of grace piously addressed to the mother of Our Savior. Then they go to bed, having been relieved of their service by the diurnal watchmen known as *vigilantes*.

That morning, well before the guests of the maritime *tertulia* had decided that they would go to finish their party on land, the *serenos* of Talcahuano had been exchanging anxious comments as they passed one another in the streets. The atmosphere was stifling in its heaviness, and the sea could be heard roaring in a lugubrious fashion in spite of the absence of a breeze.

On the mountain, five or six times, the dogs had uttered plaintive howls that put a chill in the bones. One of those landslides I mentioned had launched the echoes of its detonation into the precipices. In sum, for those experienced individuals, there was reason to fear an imminent catastrophe, and the best thing to do was prudently to seek shelter.

One old *sereno*, who heard five o'clock chime as he was going past the house where the ball had resumed at full tilt, uttered his call, muttered his prayer, and did not hesitate to add thereafter, to characterize the weather that was brewing, the terrible word *temblor*: earthquake.

The other *serenos* repeated it. Not one of the fanatical dancers heard that threat, but the other inhabitants leapt out of bed, as if the fatal word had been shouted over the town by the brazen breast of a giant taller than the mountain.

At six o'clock, all the inhabitants of Talcahuano were in the streets, in the squares, discussing what action they ought to take. A light tremor had already occurred. The old *sereno* had not been too quick off the mark.

The old people were interrogated; people ran home to gather up their most precious possessions; women and children were taken to places of safety.

The ball, however, was still in full swing. Too preoccupied with their own salvation, the fugitives had not thought to warn the dancers. One vigilante, however, who was passing by the house of the merchant where people were gorging themselves on pleasure with so much insouciance, knocked on a window, and when the window was opened, he uttered the frightful word: *"Temblor!"*

Pronounced by the policeman, it had the effect of the Biblical *Mene Mene Tekel Upharsin*. The guitars stopped dead, as if they had already been swallowed up; glasses fell from the hands of those who were completing their drunkenness, and who had sobered up on the spot. A livid pallor passed like a fog over all the faces that had been reddened by fatigue and sleeplessness an instant before. There was a redoubtable silence for a couple of minutes.

Then a voice cried: *"Fuera!"* Outside!

The *vigilante*, who had paused momentarily before that spectacle, tried to resume his course, but his horse refused to move, as if its four feet had been planted in the ground, and began to tremble in all its limbs. In the distance, already outside the town, the procession of Talcahuano's inhabitants was heading in haste toward the heights of Cap Estero, the culminating point of the peninsula separating Concepcion Bay from San Vicente Bay.

Scarcely had the word *fuera* been pronounced than the crowd of dancers poured out through the doors, windows and any other exists like a whirlwind. The Chileans, crazed by fear, no longer had any consciousness of their dignity, nor of the frailty of women and children. They crushed and trampled a fallen mass in order to get out more rapidly.

It must be said, in praise of the mariners, that not one of those rude whalers and not one of the other seafarers took a single step before the women and children were safe and sound.

But it was already too late. Scarcely twenty people made it out into the street before a frightful subterranean din was heard and the first shock was felt.

The house tottered; there were frightful cracks; the entire town was enveloped by dust—or smoke; who could tell?

Everyone fled as fast as possible.

Then, suddenly, the mountain began to roar violently; a second shock, which nothing could resist, was announced by a subterranean rumble of indescribable power.

Ordinarily, the oscillations of earthquakes are horizontal, passing from north to south or east to west. That day, at a few minutes to seven, the oscillations were produced vertically—which is to say, from bottom to top. It was as if a subterranean force wanted to lift up the terrestrial crust by battering it with repeated blows. As you can imagine, the houses, shaken in that terrible fashion, could not resist for long, and the entire town was reduced to a heap of rubble in a matter of seconds. Further abominable clouds of dust emerged from that mass, threatening to asphyxiate the fugitives and those trapped beneath the debris of the collapsed houses.

At every moment, the crowd gathered on Cap Estero saw terrified fugitives emerging from that dust and coming to join them, and fifteen minutes later, when a count was made, only a few people failed to respond to the roll-call.

By virtue of a kind of miracle, almost everyone had escaped. The houses were so lightly-built that their fall had only caused a few mishaps here and there, and there was still hope of finding a few bruised absentees, wounded but not dead.

In the bay, the sea was choppy without being menacing. All the ships at anchor were swaying gently, and among the unfortunates who had just witnessed the destruction of their homes, the young women in party dresses, the charming mothers whose sleeping children had remained aboard the *Ocean Queen*, rejoiced in the good fortune that had providentially kept their cherished infants away from the terrible danger; they wept with joy and delight for their miraculously preserved sons.

Half an hour had gone by since the last terrible shock that had flattened the town; a rather benign tidal wave had arrived to lick the nearest debris after crossing the pier, and then everything had returned to its habitual order.

On the horizon to the west, the breaking clouds allowed the sight of a broad sheet of azure. The clouds of dust that had risen skywards at the moment of the catastrophe were now falling back slowly, taking on bizarre forms, over the rubble lying in the place where Talcahuano had been an hour before.

The unfortunate refugees on Cap Estero gazed at all that with bleak and desperate expressions, but as the loss of their little houses was, after all, the only misfortune they had to deplore, given that the merchandise and objects of value had been recovered before the collapse, a few people better tempered than the rest of the population were beginning to shake off their torpor.

On the other hand, the mariners who had mingled with the crowd pronounced reassuring words; people encouraged one another.

In a region where such dangers are constantly suspended over one's head, there are no long hours to devote to despair. In brief, there was a *sursum corda*, and the five or six thousand unfortunates sketched a movement toward their crumbled town.

But what had just happened was merely a preface. The drama was to be terrible, bloody, irremediable, and the unspeakable terror that the witnesses to that drama experience was such that several among them were aged by years in a matter of minutes. Two or three young women saw their hair turn white in an hour.

Just as the desolate caravan moved off in order to go take possession of the locations that had been their home, their domain and their fortune, the dogs resumed howling furiously, and the sky was suddenly covered by dense vapors.

From the direction of the mountains a ripping sound resounded. What a noise that must have been! The ripping of rocks!

And the earth, shaken again in a disorderly fashion, began to tremble beneath the feet of the poor Chileans, who fell to their knees and struck their breasts, confessing their sins.

The padres mingled with that frightened crowd, pale-faced and with trembling hands, also on their knees, distribute their blessings and murmured absolutions, which were divined rather than heard, through their taut lips and clenched teeth.

Suddenly, a man, his eyes horribly widened by fear, stood up to his full height and, without being conscious of what he was doing, extended his arms in the direction of the mountains. All gazes followed the indication, and they saw something that few people in the world can boast of having seen. A broad peak situated to the right of the plain that has been mentioned, on the far side of which Concepcion stood, had just split in two, and that was the ripping that had been heard. A precipice had opened up, of a depth as-yet-incalculable. To the right and left, walls of granite; in the depths, perhaps a new valley.

The padres, men, women, mariners—everybody—thought that it was all over, and that in five minutes they would be swallowed up by that frightful furnace; and yet, that was not the most horrible thing.

An unusual sound was produced in the middle of the bay; then the noise became a racket, and commanded the attention of a few wretches who still had the strength to look and listen. In the space of ten minutes they witnessed the most grandiose, and simultaneously the most infernal, spectacle that could ever be imagined.

This would be unbelievable were there not still, at the time of writing, people who were eye-witnesses of what I am relating. A crevasse had opened up in the sea, in the middle of the bay. The force of dislocation that had just acted upon the mountain was now exercising its limitless power on the rocks of the sea-bed, and suddenly, with a vertiginous rapidity, the entire bay emptied, as if by magic.

The stupor that overwhelmed the poor refugees on Cap Estero I shall not attempt to describe; but from the middle of that astounded crowd, three or four shrill screams rose up.

What am I saying?

They were the howls of lionesses rather than screams. There was nothing human about them: they were eruptions of savage voices.

And immediately, women richly clad in silk and velvet, with their feet elegantly shod, were seen to leap toward the shore, extending their writhing arms desperately, and then fall to the ground, inanimate, so suddenly had their strength abandoned them, unless they were caught by their companions. Those women were the young mothers who had been rejoicing a little while before at the idea that they had left their children asleep aboard the *Ocean Queen*.

What a horrible spectacle they beheld now! The waters, in retreating, had dragged with them the majority of the ships at anchor in the harbor. Those that had been unable to resist the terrible current of a sea that seemed to be taking flight had been dragged into the sheer depths and torn apart before anyone could ascertain how many men they were dragging to their doom.

In the middle of the bay, a mighty whirlpool, as horrible as the Maëlstrom, had formed in the blink of an eye and pitilessly swallowed up everything that the retreating waters had drawn into its funnel.

Ships of large dimension were seen entering the gyratory radius of the whirlpool and, launched like arrows, making five or six rotations on the rim of the gulf, then going to break up on the sharp points of rocks at the bottom.

In the rigging or on the decks, a few men clinging to ropes waited for a miracle. From afar, one could divine that they were uttering roars or sobs of despair.

That mass of water, twenty leagues square on the surface, drained away almost entirely. The bay was empty. About ten ships, among them the *Ocean Queen*, solidly moored by four anchors, had resisted the catastrophe. Tipped over on the bed of sand or mud, they were lying partly broken, for the majority, in colliding with rocky spurs, had lost part of their rigging by virtue of the violence of the impact.

The masses of water were finishing their disappearance into the bed of the bay when frightened me were seen appearing on the surviving ships. Their sole desire, spurred by folly or fear, it was easily divined, was to take refuge on land.

But where? And how?

To traverse the mud, where the low-lying areas were still full of water, seemed impossible, and in any case, the nearest of those stricken vessels was at least twelve hundred meters from Cap Estero.

Some appeared to resign themselves to waiting, but simultaneously, from the poop-decks of two ships, one of them English and the other French, mariners were seen letting themselves slide down broken masts and ropes that were hanging over the side. They had decided to cross the dried-up sea, without thinking that, in case the Ocean reclaimed its rights, it might be better to await the final result of the earthquake.

Those madmen, therefore, ventured on to the bed of the bay, precipitately fleeing their wrecked ships, thus setting a deadly example that was almost immediately followed by fearful members of other crews. That happened just at the moment when several further shocks, much less violent, came to presage the last convulsions of the ground.

As is readily understandable, however, the mass of the water of the Pacific Ocean, driven back momentarily by the volcanic commotion, and suspended by some unknown power, was soon precipitated into that harbor, which seemed to have attempted to escape its empire.

Concepcion Bay is, as it were, closed to the west by an island, Quiriquina, to the right and left of which are two channels, through which ships enter the port. With a frightful din, two liquid mountains raced through each issue toward the dried-up bay. After having passed Quiriquina, those two mountains joined up and formed a foaming mass of such elevation that the refugees on Cap Estero, the crown of which is more than two hundred meters above sea level, thought they would be reached, knocked down and dragged away.

But where the drama took on gigantic proportions was in the place where the stricken ships were awaiting their fate; it was from the rocks that the mariners attempting to reach land saw that mighty wall advancing with vertiginous rapidity, beneath the weight of which they were about to be crushed. In that supreme moment, they experienced such terror that, in order to hurl one last cry of despair at the heavens, the force of their lungs was multiplied tenfold—for, in spite of the roar of the immense wave, a clamor was heard.

Some lay down silently. Others turned intrepidly toward the wave and waited for it, folding their arms; then it was all over.

When the first mate of the *Ocean Queen* had anticipated the assault of that unique tidal wave, his first thought had been to shut the children confided to his care in their cabins. After that he had set about doing everything humanly possible to save them, and himself with them. A consummate mariner, sailing in the region for nearly twenty years and familiar with the maritime accidents that are the ordinary consequence of earthquakes, he had assumed that the greatest danger had not passed, and that the offensive return of the waves would be the solemn moment of life or death.

In a few words, too colorful, too technical and above all too strong for us to think of reporting them here, he had demonstrated to the few men who had remained aboard with him after the party that to flee across the bed of the bay would be to run to certain death. The sea would return with incalculable violence; if there as a means of salvation—and one alone—it lay in the absolute abandonment of the ship to the caprice of the advancing liquid mountain. In consequence, the four chains that retained the anchors were let loose, and when the *Ocean Queen*—which, moreover, had not suffered overmuch—was completely disengaged from anything that could offer resistance to the rushing water, they waited. Some other ships imitated the maneuver. A few preferred to trust to the force of their anchors and chains and consolidated their moorings instead.

Moreover, when those brave seamen, in whom one would certainly have found the poet's triple bronze,[37] saw that frightful giant wall of water, white with foam and already laden with wrecks and corpses, racing across the bed of the bay, not one lost hope completely.

The mate retained his presence of mind; he ordered all his men below decks; all the hatches were hastily closed and everyone lay down, seeking a point of support so as not to be hurled against the walls of the hull. Who can ever know what a world of thought, what a poem of terror, despair and—who knows?—hope went through those men's heads during that solemn minute. Not one pronounced a word; only the cabin-boy was breathing loudly as he wrapped himself up in the captain's mattress, in accordance with the advice given to him by the boatswain. In one of the locked cabins a child was weeping and calling for his mother.

The noise suddenly redoubled, became horrible and made the ears bleed; a cold sweat streamed on the faces of all the men, and yet a single word was heard: "Ready!" It was the first mate again, whose composure had not deserted him.

What happened then? It seemed that the *Ocean Queen* was being crushed; a horrible cracking sound was heard; what remained of the masts was evidently torn away. The foot of the mizzen mast, which was supported on the bunkroom, splintered; a piece of wood struck the boatswain and killed him.

---

[37] The reference is to a phrase used by Horace; subsequent to this story's publication, it was borrowed by Robert Frost for the title of a poem that is nowadays more famous than the original reference.

There was a frightful buzz; there was an irresistible surge; the beautiful ship, which handled like a dream at sea, was rolled over and over twenty times; the unfortunate mariners, thrown between the ceiling and the floor every time, received bruises or injuries every time, sometimes fatal. However, an oath, a sigh or a cry announced from time to time that it was not all over yet.

Those who were still alive were unaware of what had become of them. On every side the seething of the sea could still be heard; fortunately, they could also sense that the *Ocean Queen*, although rolled by the waves like an enormous ball thrown at top speed, was no longer on the bottom. In addition, it had not run into any obstacle since the moment when a submarine wave, perfectly appreciable, had snatched it from the rocks on which it lay.

Those who could still make these reflections did not have long to wait. There was a horrible jolt; the ship split open; several gaps were distinctly perceived in the sleeping quarters, and all noise ceased.

Elsewhere, for the poor Chilean refugees on the heights of Cap Estero, the splendor and the horror of the spectacle had been indescribable. At the sight of the immense sea hurtling toward the wrecked ships and the imprudent sailors who had ventured on to the bed of the bay, a horrible frisson had gripped the terrified spectators of the sinister drama. To the clamor raised by the mariners who were about to be swallowed up, a more compact and sonorous clamor replied. Everyone had extended their arms toward the unfortunates and uttered a cry that was a farewell.

Almost at the same moment, however, the attention of the refugees shifted to the ships thus far spared from the fury of nature. To begin with, there were many mariners in the crowd on Cap Estero, including almost all the captains in the association to whom the previous day's *tertulia* was due. In the midst of them was a young blond man with a distinguished physiognomy; he was the captain of the Ocean Queen.

After having examined attentively the various measures and precautions taken aboard the menaced vessels to escape the terrible danger of being crushed, the young mariner seemed content with what had been done aboard his ship and advanced toward the group where the young mothers whose children were aboard were standing, mad with grief and fear. In a calm, voice he sought to reassure them, affirming that his first mate was the one man who might save a ship in such circumstances. He explained what the mate had done, and that it was probable that there would only be unimportant misfortunes to regret. The children being placed in bunks and retained by pivoting planks, it was necessary, in his opinion, to retain hope.

The poor mothers wanted nothing more than to believe him. One of them gazed at him in desperate gratitude, in which one could read thanks for his generosity, but also an absolute incredulity with regard to what he had said. He turned round to hide the sentiment painted on his face, for he had les faith than anyone in the possibility of snatching any prey whatsoever from the advancing Ocean.

The moving liquid mountain, which everyone was following with their eyes, horribly sick at heart, soon came within a few meters of the first ship. That was a moment of terror, during which no one breathed. The poor vessel disappeared, swallowed up. The immense collapse of the breakers fell successively upon each ship. The *Ocean Queen*'s turn came. The whaler was drowned by the waves.

Then, continuing its frightful progress toward the shore, the gigantic wave, which seemed to be growing as it advanced, threatened the coast and passed over it, as if it were now going to cover the land that had attempted to dispute its empire. Finally, it rose so high that the unfortunates on Cap Estero, seeing it rising toward them, forgot Talcahuano, the *Ocean Queen* and everything else for a moment, in order to carry out a rapid retreat.

But that was the sea's final effort; it came to break at their feet, and then began to retreat slowly. In the direction of Talcahuano the wave had passed rapidly and noisily over the debris of the town, smashing everything in its path that the range of the earthquake had spared. Its momentum had carried it over the slopes of the mountain well beyond the town, to such a height that the voyagers to whom the story is told nowadays would not believe it if irrefutable evidence did not remain to prove the veracity of the fact.

A cry of agony, a further clamor of despair, escaped every mouth and the sight of that irremediable catastrophe.

This time, Talcahuano was completely destroyed, and everything that the unfortunate town still contained was lost forever, including the lives of the poor people who had been unable to flee or who were trapped beneath the debris of their houses. A horrible death! A horrible ruination!

Suddenly, an exclamation of timid joy rang out in the midst of the general stupor. The captain of the *Ocean Queen* shouted: "Look! Look!" And with his finger he pointed at the side of the mountain, on which the sea had finally stopped, and which it was abandoning quite rapidly. The breach full of a ship was stuck in the ground, and the mariner's eye had recognized the *Ocean Queen*.

Yes, the sea's momentum had been so powerful that the vessel had been transported over the town and well beyond, halfway up the first of the foothills of the Cordilleras.

As I have said, no one would believe it if that extraordinary wreck were not still there as I write these lines and were not the objective of curious excursions by all the travelers who visit Talcahuano.

Without wondering if the sequence of misfortunes was at an end, the crowd rushed toward the *Ocean Queen*. It was necessary to find out what had become of the men they had seen a short while before. Feeling a little hope reborn in their hearts, the young mothers took the lead, so rapidly that even the captain had difficulty keeping up with them.

Finally, they arrived. As the captain was figuring out what the easiest way would be to climb up on to the deck, and how he could maintain himself there, it became evident that efforts were being made inside to open the hatch to the bunkroom.

There was an indescribable excitement. Agile as a cat, the captain bounded to the hatch, and forced it open with impatient violence.

A blood-stained man with his head half-broken then appeared and tumbled into the arms of the young mariner, who embraced him enthusiastically without being able to suppress the sobs of joy that were tearing his breast. The man was the first mate, cruelly wounded but alive. Providence had owed him that.

"The others?" the captain interrogated.

"Dead!" the poor man replied, losing consciousness.

Fortunately, he was mistaken; for emotion, joy and dread were taking on superhuman proportions when the crying of a child as heard. In two bounds the captain was inside the bunkroom, opened the cabin from which the cried were coming, and picked up a pink baby boy, who did not have a scratch.

He was passed from hand to hand to his mother, who fled with him like a wounded lioness, while the other young women darted glances of hatred at her. When the other cabins were searched, one more wounded infant was found, dying. Two others were dead. The mother of one of them, suddenly afflicted with madness, went straight toward the sea and let herself fall into it from the height of a rock.

"I can't see the cabin-boy!" said the captain.

Scared, his hair bristling and his eyes wide, a child of about twelve appeared in his turn, and, realizing that he was safe, was seized by a frightful nervous fit.

While all this was happening, the sea had retreated, only leaving behind, in the place where Talcahuano had existed that morning, a sandy beach on which a few wrecks could be seen, and one or two corpses.

When the victims of the disaster redirected their gazes toward the sea, they perceived a few ships that had resisted the powerful effort of the sea. Two or three of those that had entrusted to the solidity of their chains and anchors were still struggling against the final convulsions of the Ocean. Others, which had been believed lost since the commencement of the earthquake, were visible on the horizon, coming back to their moorings.

In sum, in spite of the magnitude of the disaster, more ships had been saved than one would have dared to hope.

The *Ocean Queen* stayed on the mountain as a memorial of the earthquake of 18 November. For some time, the poor of Talcahuano went to take it apart in order to provide wood for their fires and salvage the ironwork, which sold at a high price, but a decree by the Alcalde issued in 1844 specified punishments for anyone who touch the wrecked vessel again. A cross was set up on its poop, and the *Ocean Queen* was considered henceforth as a kind of historic monument.

For the benefit of people naturally disposed to incredulity, we shall content ourselves with recalling that, in an earthquake in Peru, several ships experienced the same fate as the *Ocean Queen*. A Peruvian naval corvette was hurled a long way inland and a considerable number of men perished, but the most extraordinary of all was an American steamship which was carried by the sea eight hundred meters beyond the beach.

Finally, a circumstance even more astonishing was produced in Calcutta during the cyclone that cost the English so dear in 1864. A magnificent ship of three thousand tones was seized by the wind—you read that correctly, by the wind—and thrown a hundred meters inland, where it was embedded up to the gunwales. That one is also still there; it has been converted into a hospital.

Furthermore, all the details that we have just offered the reader have been furnished by Don Pedro B***, a resident of Conception. Don Pedro is none other than the *Ocean Queen*'s cabin-boy, who refused to allow himself to be repatriated—for, after the fright he had had, he would not consent to set foot on a ship again for a long time.

Louis Gallet: *The Death of Paris*
(1892)

"La Mort de Paris" by the prolific writer Louis Gallet (1835-1898) first appeared in 1892 in La Nouvelle Revue, *and is here translated as "The Death of Paris." It is a slightly offbeat addition to the rich tradition of stories featuring the ruins of Paris, offering an account of how the city and its remaining inhabitants perish from suddenly-accelerated climate change—the advent of a new Ice Age—rather than poking fun at the mistaken conclusions of far-future archeologists. Its conscious affiliation to the tradition, however, adds an extra gloss to what might otherwise have been an ordinary disaster story, equipping it with a delicately ironic elegiac quality. The author was best known for his operatic libretti, and "Le Mort de Paris" has a kind of operatic sweep and flourish about it that suits its theme very well.*

B.S.

So, this is what the Seer said:

For twelve centuries Paris had been expanding at the foot of the metal tower that remains almost the sole vestige of the former city, which a very ancient tradition names the Eiffel Tower, without anyone knowing exactly where the name came from, the archeologists having failed completely to reach agreement on the matter. The city was immense, sheltering in its ten-story houses crowned with vast terraces a population of six million souls. Its prosperity was great, although it had no longer been the capital of the United States of Europe for a long time. It had, however, remained famous throughout the world for its worship of pleasure. All the peoples driven away from the North by the invasion of the ice had their representatives there, no longer forming any but a single nation.

Powerful Russia had flowed like a river into Asia; Germany only existed as a memory; all of noble Europe was asleep in polar silence.

The United States of Europe then had Marseille as a capital; those of Africa had Algiers.

Mediterranean and aerial communications already being very rapid in those days, the two cities in question exchanged their correspondence and newspapers several times every day, always full of stories about the admirable Paris that, although then situated at the northern extremity of Europe, dispossessed of its political suzerainty, was still the astonishment of the world. Science nevertheless expressed serious anxiety in its regard. The earth was subject to a cooling whose zone was describing increasingly large circles around the pole. But Paris, well-heated, abundantly provided with all industrial riches, laughed at the prophets of doom. The great city had always had enormous depths of skepticism.

And, in truth, the strength of Paris was marvelous then, able to inspire a boundless confidence in its duration, or at least in its means of salvation if, perchance, the existence of its inhabitants should one day be compromised. Gigantic airships with ten rows of propellers striped its sky with rapid flight; smaller ones, as elegant and gilded as royal galleys, crossed paths in daylight or, by night, fitted at the prow with multicolored beacon lights, constellated the sky like a dust of wandering stars.

In streets sixty meters wide, pedestrians circulated without fear between the tall houses. There were only a few electric carriages by then, airships being much more convenient and less dangerous than terrestrial vehicles. As for horses, they had been ameliorated to such an extent over the centuries that none remained, except for a few specimens absolutely pure in form but incapable of any service. Those masterpieces of plasticity were preciously conserved in zoological museums. Perhaps a few still exist today, but nobody knows where they are. The Museum of Algiers has one, but it is stuffed, exhibited alongside the last elephant, another species vanished in the wake of the pitiless hunting once carried out for the collection of ivory, which has been so advantageously replaced today by compressed paper products.

In numerous gymnasia the population incessantly maintained flexibility with the rudest exercises. The race had become very beautiful, no trace of senility appearing on faces, the incessantly functioning skin admitting no wrinkles, so it was difficult to distinguish an old man from a young one. As for women, it was as if they were uniformly fixed at the age of twenty, and it was not rare, even at close range, for a grandmother to be mistaken for her granddaughter, so much progress had the art of preservative ointments made.

All of that population, communally rich in amiable intelligence, was admirably healthy. For a long time there had been no more physicians; they had been replaced by chemists and simple physiologists. Having penetrated all the secrets of nature and catalogued all the microbes, those scientists had then rested, sagely content to watch humanity live and die.

There were no longer any public libraries or museums, literature and art having no reason to exist in a society that was attached above all to the materiality of things and had long since done away with sentimental speculations and esthetic theories. The language, moreover, had become very simple, although it was composed of all the ancient languages once spoke by the various races of the two worlds. From the exchange of vocables, syntax and formulae of abbreviation, a universal language had been born, in which the verb only played a minor role, giving ground to the precious noun and the adjective, the only ones indispensable, in sum, to the relations of practical life.

Thus, once-enormous newspapers had been reduced to the dimensions of a minuscule sheet. A few sentences gave the political news or recounted the most recent events; there had been no commentary for a long time, and all polemic had been suppressed. An item announced a fact, nothing more; the readers drew their own conclusions. The old argumentative journalists had been replaced by gymnasiarch-reporters whose renown was that of the aeronef moving with the greatest rapidity and flying most speedily to the theater of events.

A little music was still made in great halls: music in which research and the collision of enemy sonorities was pushed to the highest degree of refinement, and which produced, in the nervous system of its listeners, sensations of an extraordinary acuity.

In sum, the people were happy, and grateful to be so, which is rare. As long as no one spoke to them about God, death or amour, which engender pain, nor about the family, whose affections and proofs are subversive of all tranquility, they confessed themselves content; they went through life with a philosophical egotism that made them as beautiful and as joyful as their rich means permitted.

When it was too cold in Paris, when the snow became too frequent, the ordinary people found shelter in the winter gardens, immense palaces of glass in which spring was restored to them; the richest flew away in some pleasure airship to Algiers, or, if the temperature in Algiers seemed too low, all the way to Lake Chad, already bordered with magnificent habitations. That was a matter of a few hours. Many of those holidaying in Algiers returned to Paris once a week to take care of business.

Over the last few years the cold had increased markedly in the middle of each winter, and the snow had fallen with greater force. Snowstorms had been photographed in which the flakes seemed to touch one another and, so to speak, fuse together. But those snowfalls did not last long, and powerful apparatus loaded with special products melted them instantaneously and sent them in seething streams into the drains, all the way to the Seine, which transported them seawards.

One day, after an entire week of weather so spring-like that a few Japanese plum-trees had flowers in the gardens, which caused Parisians, eternally inclined to enthusiasm, to anticipate an exceptionally mild season, the sky was suddenly covered with exceedingly opaque clouds, so low that the summit of the metal tower disappeared, no longer allowing anything to be seen at night but the glow of its beacon, displayed like a bloodstain in the shifting darkness.

The public airships were obliged to modify their service, and, at times, to suspend it entirely, being unable to travel in the almost-constant darkness without danger of collision. Only a few private craft took the risk; for two hours there was a criss-crossing of vague streaks of colored light in the dirty sky, and the loud blaring of sirens sowing alarm in the air, as sinister as the cries of murdered monsters.

Many accidents occurred; two airships, each carrying a hundred passengers, crashed and fell, broken, on the hills of the Point-de-Jour, bristling with cupolas and iron steeples, from which bloody human rags were soon suspended in a sinister fashion.

A police edict then forbade all circulation, until the menacing clouds had dissipated. The temperature was mild. A slight breeze sometimes rose up, and then a whiteness would appear in the sky, and snow would begin to fall, slowly, in large flakes widely separated at first, but then thicker, so thick that within an hour there would be more than sixty centimeters in the streets. The snow-melting machines immediately went into action then and torrents of water flowed toward the river.

That lasted throughout the whole of one night, the snow falling incessantly and pitilessly, and the machines sweeping it away with mathematical regularity. In private meetings, in elegant clubs, the frightened faces of men and women could be seen at the windows, against the bright background of red wallpaper, gazing at the white shroud falling like an endless bolt of cloth, wondering whether it was going to last forever, and whether they would ever be able to go home. The sages were already asleep, ignorant of the event. A few enraged gamblers laughed, forgetting in the fever of baccarat the vague emotion, the fear of the inevitable unknown that had already gripped the souls round them.

In the morning, it became visible that what had been reckoned an event was about to become a disaster. The policemen responsible for manning the machines were exhausted by fatigue and only working tiredly. At about nine o'clock, when the pale daylight had difficulty piercing the gray backcloth of the sky, the dissolving salts required for the alimentation of the apparatus ran out.

While people ran around all the depots in the city, soon realizing that all the reserves had been exhausted by the exceptional requirements of the night, the snow continued to fall with a ferocious regularity, a scourge more terrible in its mild appearance than a devouring but extinguishable fire or invasive but fleeting floodwater, a pale mass rising in imperceptible layers to disquieting heights, eroding and devouring houses at the base, giving the eye the sensation of an entire city buried in a white immensity.

The electric streetlights, left illuminated since the previous evening, shone at ground level over the snow, sparkling with crystals, when dusk came again; the henceforth-invincible scourge had closed all doors. The sounds of the city were stifled beneath that thick, soft carpet.

A great torpor reigned, when, suddenly, toward midnight, a violent wind blowing from due north traversed space, shaking and breaking up the clouds, tearing them like masses of cotton wool, chasing them across the immense sky. And the moon appeared, cold and pure against the black firmament, where a few rare stars were quivering in the depths.

The thermometer descended well below zero and the snowy mass solidified into uneven ice. Then, clamors rose up from the city, the flames of torches flickered in the streets and the squares, and human masses escaped through windows that had become doors, fearful and dismal, traversed by the shrill cries of women, disrupted by sudden falls, forming terrible eddies in the obscure river of beings in flight.

Forgetting those that the snow slowly buried in obstructed houses, the people ran toward the only possible salvation. At the doors of garages, in the shops where airships, ready rigged, extended in the shadows, awaiting the moment to resume their flight in the open sky, groups collided, swearing at one another and fighting.

There was no longer any right, or law, neither servants nor masters. The supreme struggle for existence commenced.

In the radiant light of the second day the engines of the airships began to make their formidable respiration heard. On the white bed of snow, there were black and red stains, of mud and blood, were crowds had trampled and fought.

Finally, two airships rose up, to the cries of their triumphant passengers. The gigantic machines, of a solid but old model, only had canvas propellers, rendered rigid by the ice, when they tried to turn under the impulsion of their robust metallic armatures, cracks were heard in the canvas, here and there, and the progress of the airships became awkward and heavy. A false impulsion by one of the engineers caused their prows to collide. Both oscillated, drew back, and then resumed their convergent course. Then a collision more terrible than the preceding one occurred. One of the disemboweled ships fell like a great dead bird, and, breaking through the crust of ice, plunged profoundly into the snow, while the other, lurching like a doomed kite, came to plunge, skimming the surface, into the middle of the howling crowd.

No one ran to help the wounded. In any case, the sky overhead was darkening again, snow was threatening. The rigged airships, boarded in haste, were launched into the air. A few soon disappeared into the white depths; others fell, their propellers hanging limply, as if some invisible hunter had pierced them with his arrows. Nothing more: to the first layer of frozen snow a new layer was added by falling flakes.

Outside the suburbs, files extended like caravans of black ants. They could not advance beyond a kilometer; soon, they ran into inaccessible banks, and then, the cold afflicting them with immobility, they stayed where they were, frozen in their march. After a brief interval, everything became white again, and nothing revealed the place where the buried caravan had passed.

In the city—that city of six million beings—the human masses had melted, condensed into a single mass, huddled in the immense central square dominated by the metal tower. Already, the snow had reached halfway up the vast arches supporting the first stage. Weary and shivering, men, women and children gazed, waiting for help, incapable of action. Around them, in the immense circle of the horizon, only the summits of edifices any longer emerged. The city had already disappeared, leveled by the snow.

In the air there was no sound, not a single wing.

Finally, among those who were still capable of movement after three days of intense cold and invasive snow, a group formed that began to march toward the tower. There salvation might lie, if the snow continued to fall.

There were cried of "The tower! The tower!" And a counter-movement began among the people, many of whom had not thought at first about that refuge.

The elevators were no longer functioning, already seized by the icy snow. They hastened toward the stairs. There was a frightful struggle there. Before that narrow passage people grabbed one another by the throat or by the hair; in the heavy air, the sound of gunshots was scarcely perceptible, along with a brief flash; and black masses fell, their flesh splashed with blood. With teeth clenched, without a cry, they fought.

Finally, the file of the victorious, pale, their hands red, plunged into the narrow stairway. Shivering in the icy wind, not daring to grip the metal guardrails, which burned the palms if touched, they climbed the steps. And behind them, and around them, the virgin snow rose too, extending its immaculate cloak over Paris.

When they reached the beacon, night had fallen again: a night as pure as the one before, with a blue-tinted moon, sending darts with a thousand icy points at the earth. On high, in the stairway of the tower and on the platform of the beacon, there was a great and formidable silence. And the moonlight, stiff forms, with convulsed faces, leaned over, through the iron latticework, searching the dark horizon for something that was not there.

At daybreak, on the platform of the beacon, clinging to the bars, there were a few men, eyes terribly open—eyes of stone now—frozen forever, gazing in vain at the four points of the horizon from which something might come.

Paris was dead.

The snow soon changed into an immense glacier. The rains of spring came, which washed the mass and made it shine in the sunlight like a lake of glaucous crystal. And when, in that part of the vast polar desert, a few airships still risked themselves in the south, the explorers perceived quite distinctly, beneath the transparent ice, the enormous mass of the edifices, steeples, bell

Georges Bethuys: *Cataclysm*
(Georges-Frédéric Espitallier; 1896)

Not long after Louis Figuier began running feuilletons *as a regular feature of* La Science Illustrée, *the other leading magazine of the same sort,* La Science Française, *followed suit. Its editor, Émile Gautier (1853-1937) seemed to have a strong prejudice in favor of futuristic fiction and stories dealing with future wars, publishing, among other items, an exceedingly long serial by "Captain Danrit," the jingoistic doyen of French future war fiction.*[38]

Eventually, Gautier switched to a serial entitled Conte bleu *[a designation applied to all kinds of fanciful tales, from fairy tales to anecdotal tall tales], bearing the signature G. Bethuys. Something odd then happened. The third episode of that story—a sarcastic but earnest account of two military men visiting an industrialist who claims to have solved "the social problem," although his son, who has ambitions to be an alchemist, denies the claim vehemently— carried the usual "to be continued" at the end, but no continuation actually appeared; instead, the next issue of the magazine began a new story by the same author, "Cataclysme," here translated as "Cataclysm," without explanation.*

It is possible, given its content, that it was "Cataclysme"—a conte bleu if ever there was one—which had actually been intended to appear under the former title, but that the wrong manuscript had somehow ended up with the printer. Whatever the reason for the confusion, however, "Cataclysme," was the last piece of fiction published in La Science Française, *which stuck rigorously to non-fiction thereafter.*

A search for further information about G. Bethuys via the catalogue of the Bibliothèque Nationale and Google Books grants snippet access to an interview in the aeronautical periodical Technique, *which reveals that that name was one of the many pseudonyms employed by the interviewee,* Technique's *editor, George-Frédéric Espitallier. Espitallier, who had risen to the military rank of Lieutenant Colonel while in service, was a prolific writer on military technology from 1892 onwards, under his own and many other names. Whether he ever completed the ill-fated serial begun as* Conte bleu—*which was shaping up to be one of the most interesting stories in* Science Française—*I do not know, although he did publish a book entitled* L'Homme en nickel *in 1897.*[39]

B.S.

---

[38] For more about Captain Danrit, see *Undersea Odyssey*, published by Black Coat Press (ISBN 978-1-935558-81-1).

[39] Available from Black Coat Press as *The Nickel Man* (ISBN 978-1-61227-445-4).

That year, the elements seemed completely out of sorts. It's true that people say that every year, which appears to indicate that being out of sorts is the elements' natural state. Which was good luck for Max Eginhard, who, having nothing else to do, thanks to his considerable fortune, had devoted himself to meteorology. When the weather is fine, meteorology is a sinecure, while one throws oneself into it wholeheartedly when atmospheric disturbances are abundant.

The origins of Max Eginhard's considerable fortune were not lost in the night of time, and his intimate friends still remembered the epoch when his maternal grandfather had sold cloth for other reasons than to oblige his friends.

The said grandfather possessed an uncultivated plot of land on the heights of Chaillot; the idea had occurred to him to increase the size of that embryonic property. Who could tell? Wasn't there going to be building in the neighborhood?

"Great cities grow westwards."

He therefore bought land that cost him very little, but remained on his hands, with the result that when he married off his daughter, he gave it to her, in order to get rid of it once and for all.

The son-in-law, who was devoid of flair, found at first that this unproductive terrain was more cumbersome than a bad of loose change, but when the operations commenced that were to culminate in the transformation of the Monceau and Marbeuf districts, he finally perceived his father-in-law's clearsightedness; the fallow land was an investment for the father of a family. One morning, he woke up as rich as the late Croesus. With the fortune, he became bold, but without acquiring the flair that was definitely not part of his patrimony; he bought vast steppes east of Paris, not doubting that the great city, in letting out its belt, would rapidly transform them into residential housing.

Alas, he forgot that "great cities grow westwards." He died before having seen anything built on his land but a few ragpickers' shacks—tenants not accustomed to paying high rents. Nevertheless, thanks to the immovable properties he owned to the west, his heritage left no cause for complaint.

His heir had been brought up in the comfortable idleness befitting his fortune and had as little flair as his father, with the result that one day, having finished with the partying in which he had indulged more out of snobbery than temperament, he woke up one day to find himself a trifle empty. It was then that he discovered a vocation for meteorology.

It began with rather vague indications. Looking at the sky as he got up in the morning, he said: "Look, it's going to be a fine day," or: "The sky's cloudy; it's going to rain." These observations, judicious as they were, did not exceed, as you can see, the bounds of banality—but, the desire gripping him to know more about them, he stuck his nose into books, put a weathervane on his house and bought barometers of various kinds in order to check them against one another.

He did not fail to attend meetings the many organizations in which the most modest members could, if they had a mind to do it, contribute their little stone to the edifice of science, in the form of notes, contributions and lectures that did not have the solemn and intimidating manner of communications to the Académie des Sciences. And as he generously subsidized scientific enterprises, he very soon won the consideration that attaches to Maecenases.

He was not entirely satisfied, however, being ambitious for the kind of apostolate that consists of instructing one's contemporaries. Not daring to set his sights as high as a chair in the Collège de France, he affiliated himself to the Mutual Admiration Society, the Panphilotechnique, which offered to let him teach geology courses under its auspices.

That was not really his subject, but, all things considered, geology and meteorology are not without points in common; they even provide one another with mutual support. He only had to read up on the former science before teaching it. That is what he did.

Utterly ignorant of everything that it comprised, he possessed the unappreciable advantage, he said, of starting without preconceptions. Received ideas and acquired theories did not exist for him; he would be able to give the science a new impetus, by virtue of his new and profound observations.

His inaugural lesson was a colossal success. Addressing himself to Parisians, he thought that he ought to chose a "very Parisian" subject: the constitution of the Paris basin. The orator renewed that already-old theme by the unexpectedness of his exposition and gave it the piquant zest of a contemporary manner of speech.

"Messieurs," he said, in substance, "the Paris basin merits that name because it affects the form of one of those household utensils known as bowls. And if, not content to examine the inside of the bowl, we seek to take account of its underside, we observe that the Parisian ground is not just one bowl but a stack of bowls, of increasing dimensions the deeper one goes, because the containing vase has to be larger than the vase contained."

This reason seemed to convince the audience; one young lady, especially, sitting in the front row, did not hide her admiration for the eloquent professor, who continued:

"And that holds good to the enormous thickness—yes, truly enormous—of six hundred meters, where the stack rests on a bed of sand—Gault sand—disposed there for the express purpose of collecting the water filtered by that vast basin, while underneath, a clay mold, forming an impermeable bed, like any respectable clay, retains that water, under pressure, that the artesian wells bring back, in part, to the light of day.

"If, departing from the center of this improbable pile of vessels—I mean Paris—we now follow a radius outwards, it's natural, is it not, that we successively encounter the different layers, each one terminated by a border from which one falls on to the following plate. That change of terrain is clearly marked, especially as one walks eastwards, because, in distant epochs, waters have eroded all the soft or sandy parts partly masking the more ancient formations, as they still cover them in the plains of Beauce and Normandy—with the result that, in advancing toward the Vosges, one encounters a series of crests one after another, some of which form veritable cliffs; and these crests seem to have been placed there so expressly to serve as barriers against floods of invaders that the towns and villages that mark them out almost all bear the names of battles.

"First there is the superb arc of a circle passing through Montereau, Nogent, Sézanne, Epernay and Laon, which limits the tertiary bowl—which is to say, the soil of the Île-de-France itself, well-named, for, as Monsieur de Lapparent[40] says: 'the tertiary massif, eaten away along its border, seems like an island, emerging in abrupt cliffs from the bosom of a vast chalky plain. From time to time, a profound fissure interrupts the cliff and a river flows through it as if through a gully. Thus does the Seine at Moret, the Marne at Epernay, the Vesle and the Aisne outside Reims, the Oise at Chauny, the Brèche at Clermont, the Thévain on the outskirts Beauvais, anticipating the moment when, united in a single flow, the waters of all these rivers quit the tertiary mass between Meulan and Mantes by another defile, the latter less visible because of the rapid rise of the limestone in Normandy.'

"Beneath that tertiary bowl, there is the enormous and thick chalky plateau of Champagne, limited by the arc of Troyes, Brienne, Vitry, Saint-Menehould and Valmy. Then the less accentuated crest of the Argonne, departing from which we encounter the greensand of the Barois, before reaching the Jurassic strata of the arc that goes from Chatillon-sur-Seine to Chaumont, Toul and Verdun. Is that all? No, for beyond that is the concentric line from Langres to Montmédy and Mexières, which forms yet another line of defense—the first."

Here the orator thought it appropriate to include a little patriotic couplet pronounced with a tremolo befitting morsels redolent with pathos.

"Oh, Messieurs, as I speak, the diplomats are trying to calm the hot heads of dispute raised once again by the hereditary enemy. Is it not to be feared that the great voice of the canon might suddenly interrupt the conference and overturn protocol? This very day we find ourselves under arms, on the frontier, and, in order to defend the territory of our dear fatherland foot by foot, we shall be able to take advantage of obstacles that Nature herself has been able to design on our soil!"

A murmur of enthusiasm ran through the audience, and an old white-haired gentleman got to his feet to utter an energetic: "Vive la France!" while waving his hat.

---

[40] Albert Lapparent (1839-1908) helped draw up the geological map of France, which Eginhard is interpreting in a slightly flippant fashion, as well as writing numerous books on the subject.

It was under the emotion of that vibrant peroration that Monsieur Eginhard bowed to his audience and gathered his papers together.

A few moments later, he went out into the street and headed for home. But at the moment when, getting down from the carriage, he was about to go through the door, two people hurried forward. They were, on the one hand, the young lady who had shown so much enthusiasm at the beginning of the lecture, and, on the other, the old patriot who had so vigorously applauded its conclusion.

"Just one word, Monsieur!" cried the lady.

"I need to talk to you!" shouted the gentleman.

Eginhard was perplexed.

"Madame...Monsieur...the street is doubtless not the most propitious place for conversation, and, if you would like to come up to my study..."

"Monsieur," the old patriot insinuated, as they climbed the stairs, "What I have to say to you will brook no delay, and if Mademoiselle will be kind enough to permit..."

"But no, Monsieur, my confidence is certainly as urgent as yours..."

"Madame...Monsieur, please," the professor interjected. "Gallantry dictates my duty, and since you have only one word to say, Madame, be good enough to come in, while Monsieur will wait for a moment in the drawing-room."

Scarcely had the study door closed than the young woman said, excitedly: "Your lecture was sublime. It has inspired me with such enthusiasm that I have come to ask you: will you marry me?"

It must be admitted that, thus taken by surprise, Monsieur Eginhard could not find a reply before the lady had taken up the thread of her discourse. "Oh, I know! That goes against what is conventionally called propriety in your country. Personally, I'm an American—an American of Spanish origin; I have the blood of Pizarro in my veins, and I'm volcanic, as one says in your country. I'm rich; I love science and travel. A scientist like you needs a wife who understands him and who can also liberate him from the anxieties and material cares that waste his energy; I will be that wife..."

Eginhard was quite nonplused by this unexpected passion, so brutally introduced into his life. He was not immune to flattery, however, and, on raising his eyes, perceived that his interlocutrice was pretty. But still! To have to reply immediately, without having had time to reflect...

"Well," said the other, in a conclusive fashion. "That's settled. I'll go and announce it to my family—and now, you can admit the old gentleman."

She was already opening the door. "Oh! I forgot to tell you my name. Carmencita Calcinata y Constancia. Here's my card."

Eginhard darted a glance at it while she made her exit like a gust of wind.

"Why," he said. "She's one of my tenants in the Marboeuf district."

He did not have time to take the course of his reflections any further, however, for the little old man irrupted into the room. He introduced himself: "Victor de Sourdillon, senior clerk in the Ministry of Foreign Affairs, retired. My occupation has given me a nose for European complications, and after one retires, the instincts of the profession subsist. Well, Monsieur, I've come to tell you, because you appear to me to be the enlightened patriot of whom I've dreamed, that we are dancing on a volcano."

"It's certain, Monsieur..." Eginhard interrupted himself, searching for the name."

"De Sourdillon," the other finished, naming himself again.

"It's certain Monsieur de Sourdillon, that the Parisian basin, without exactly being a volcano, is in a state of perpetual agitation—which is a bad omen for the solidity of our monuments. We are sinking, Monsieur, and Fourier—not the Phalansterian but Fourier the mathematician, less well-known to the general public because he was more sensible—has calculated how many millions of years..."

"Oh, never mind such distant catastrophes. War is at our gates! Have you read yesterday's newspapers? The latest uprising in Armenia has lit the fuse. Germany is taking advantage of it to contest our most sacred rights, and England is ready once again to eat the chestnuts that we have pulled out of the fire. The political barometer is exceedingly low."

"The barometer! That reminds me that I omitted to look at mine today."

While he went over to the instruments, Monsieur de Sourdillon continued: "Well, Monsieur, that situation cannot last. I thought that, in a democratic State, it was the responsibility of every citizen to help, within the measure of his means, to solve the great problems seething on the green carpet of democracy."

"The barometer's going down," said the other, who was doubtless listening distractedly."

"With a few friends, I've founded the Foreign Club,[41] in which we examine questions of foreign politics, with the objective of giving the minister the benefit of our enlightenment: that's first-rate private initiative, and very valuable, for, not having the prejudices of career diplomats, for the most part, we're able to bring new and often unexpected solutions to weighty questions. That is the eminently useful work in which I'm inviting you to collaborate. A man of your competence has a place marked out for him among us..."

Eginhard was following his own train of thought. "The barometer's truly afflicted with St. Vitus' Dance. Look at that crazy curve! What perturbations! I wouldn't be astonished if there were serious changes in the sunspots."

"You ask me: why have you given a foreign name to an association so truly French? To which I reply that, 'club' being an English word, it's entirely natural to attach an epithet of the same provenance to it. Then again, do we, the French, have a short and clear word to express the same idea? Evidently not, and in consequence..."

---

[41] "Foreign Club" is rendered in English in the original.

"The seismographs are also indicating abnormal vibrations of our terrestrial crust..."

"Ah, the seismographs! Oh well—but isn't it strange that the repercussions make themselves felt in the chronic agitation of our colliding nations?"

"That's an eminently philosophical point of view, which does you credit, Monsieur."

"We understand one another marvelously, and I shall hasten to inform my committee that you're accepting the presidency of the Foreign Club."

"But Monsieur..."

"Don't protest; it's settled—and as it's necessary not to restrict ourselves to vain words, I shall publish a pamphlet tomorrow concerning the defense of our frontier, basing my argument on your admirable theories regarding the forms of the terrain. Oh, the tertiary cliff—what a role, what a great role I shall reserve for it, in accordance with the enormous role it has played in history!"

At that moment, through the open window, they heard the cry of a news-vendor, running and shouting at the top of his voice: "Get *La Patrie*! Latest news! Germans at the frontier! Grave complications in the East! Mass conscription! Get *La Patrie*!"

"Eh? What is he shouting?" said Monsieur de Sourdillon, choked by emotion. "You'll soon see whether my fears were chimerical! I'll go call a meeting of the Club immediately. You'll come—tomorrow, eight o'clock in the morning. Don't miss it!"

He seized his hat and gloves and hurtled away, leaving Monsieur Eginhard bewildered, his head leaning out of the window, while other hawkers were running from all directions, barking their disturbing news—and the passers-by, suddenly gathering, were snatching the papers from their hands.

What a lot of events in so few minutes in the life of the pseudo-intellectual! An engagement on the hoof; affiliation to a Club of amateur diplomats; and war, the threat of war, about to trouble the quietude of his placid egotism!

He tried to go back to work and, sitting down at his desk, took up the notes he had prepared for his second lecture. He read aloud, striving to acquire an oratorical tone.

"Nature loves variety; she has taken care to compose the bowls stacked in our Parisian basin of different materials; and, the better to limit that ancient cradle of our fatherland, she has caused to surge from her loins three enormous supports, made of granite and eruptive rocks: three solid boundaries emerging from the primitive crust, constituting a sort of gigantic basket, into which are fitted the sedimentary layers, whose edges are lifted by the irresistible upward surge.

"Everything rests on the solidity of those supports. If the whim took them, under and energetic interior pressure, to draw closer together, the stack of dishes would be shattered, and towns and villages would fall pell-mell into the cracks, along with their inhabitants.

"Fortunately, such a catastrophe is improbable; I will say more..."

Eginhard interrupted himself to look at his seismograph, which was definitely going crazy.

"Either I'm much mistaken," he said, "or we're going to have an earthquake..."

And, as the barometer no longer appeared to him to be on its best behavior, he added: "...and a cyclone," while the newsvendors were shouting outside, advertising the political storm.

A gust of wind seemed to confirm his prognostications. He got up to close the window, just as his *valet de chambre* came in and presented him with a letter on a tray. It was written on scented paper, in an elongated green-tinted envelope sealed with aventurine.

Eginhard opened it and read these lines, written in a delicate hand, and unsteady orthography:

Mi amigo,

I will not abandon you to the perils of an invasion, siege, famine and bombardment. I shall elope with you, and we will depart for the Argentine Republic, where my flocks graze, tomorrow morning, by the eight o'clock train.

Carmencita.

An elopement and a meeting of the Foreign Club at the same time was too much, and in the absence of the gift of ubiquity...

Desperate to resolve this difficulty appropriately, Eginhard went to bed with a headache.

On getting into bed it seemed to him that the ground gave way beneath him, which he attributed to the nervous state he was in—but he could not mistake for an illusion the whistling of the wind, which was raging, furiously shaking the shutters.

Nevertheless, he got to sleep in the end.

How long was he asleep? He would have been incapable of answering that question when, feeling himself abruptly shaken, prodded and poked, he woke up in the midst of a frightful racket.

Opening his eyes with difficulty, in the dark, it seemed at first to be impossible to take account of what was happening around him.

He was lying on the carpet, his limbs bruised and aching, in the midst of a chaotic mess of colliding furniture and the noise of breaking glass and porcelain.

From the lower floors of the house—doubtless from the entrails of the earth—rose strange rumblings and dull cracking sounds, to which other cracking sounds, more sinister still, replied in the walls, shaking on their foundations...

And the floor was oscillating like the deck of a ship...

The sudden horror of that anguished awakening squeezed the unfortunate professor's throat and paralyzed his screams.

He groped around him, crawling through the debris until he finally bumped into the door.

He stood up, tried to open it, and succeeded in spite of the resistance of the frame, put out of square by the shocks.

Throughout the house, from top to bottom, there were already lugubrious interjections, overlapping calls for help, slamming doors and cries of fright. Then, by the light of candles lit by feel, white shadows moved—people in night-shirts running in panic.

People called for help, and people helped themselves, but, not dead but wounded, they all found themselves standing up and more-or-less intact. The walls had not collapsed, and they thought themselves fortunate to have got away with the fear and the material damage that the nascent daylight permitted them to estimate.

Two further shocks made themselves felt, but the people were battle-hardened, and they were over quickly. Nevertheless, the tenants, fearing that the house might collapse on their heads, felt an urgent need to get out.

Eginhard had gone back into his room and, searching for his scattered clothes, dressed in haste, but he did not want to leave without having consulted his cherished instruments, in order to demand the secret of the abrupt cataclysm. The recording devices were lying around all over the place. He gathered them together. As was only to be expected, the seismographs displayed an enormous smear where the pen had marked crazy oscillations.

As he sought to replace on the table the objects that had been thrown on the floor, the meteorologist noticed his compass, and was suddenly struck by a strange and inexplicable fact. The needle had deviated by an entire quadrant!

There was no doubt about it; he was perfectly familiar with the orientation of the walls of the house, whose windows opened due east and west; the compass was now pointing at one of them. Was it necessary to suppose that the building had suddenly been rotated by ninety degrees? Or had terrestrial magnetism suddenly undergone in implausible metamorphosis?

Eginhard remembered in a timely fashion that in many circumstances, earthquakes have provoked rotatory movements. It seemed that the house really had fallen victim to an effect of that sort. It was a miracle that it had resisted such an effort, which inertia usually transforms into a torsion dislocating the entire edifice.

It was urgently necessary to get out of the tottering building. Instinctively, the professor put his compass in his pocket and went down to the street as quickly as possible. He was not unsurprised to observe that the walls, in spite of a few cracks that rendered the anticipated torsion manifest, had nevertheless remained almost vertical on their foundations; it was, therefore, the foundations themselves that had rotated—and as the house had conserved its position relative to the other houses in the street, the whole street must have been subject to the same movement. Eginhard verified that by taking out his compass and orientating it. His bewilderment knew no bounds, however, when he observed that the angle of deviation was even greater than it had been a short while before. The movement was continuing! Paris was slowly rotating!

A thought suddenly occurred to the scientist...the thought of a landlord. His properties that had been east of Paris the day before were moving northwards. Oh, if the movement could only continue, what value they would acquire!

"Great cities grow westwards!"

He did not have time to take the reflections that were already consoling him for the public misfortune any further. In the street, where people were running around lamenting their fate, coming from opposite directions, Carmencita and Monsieur de Sourdillon appeared, hurtling toward Eginhard.

"*Querido!*" cried one.

"Dear Master!" exclaimed the other.

And the latter murmured, bad-temperedly, on perceiving the Argentinian: "Oh—that madwoman again!"

"Come quickly," Carmencita continued, breathlessly. "Let's run to the station. I won't stay a moment longer in this Babylon, crushed by divine wrath."

"Our friends are already assembled at the Club," said the other. "I've come to collect you."

"Ah!" Eginhard replied. "In the great peril that threatens France, while the enemy hordes are already at our gates, my place is at the frontier. I'm hastening there! I'm must fly!"

He did, indeed, fly,[42] dragged away by the robust and volcanic foreigner. But Sourdillon would not surrender his prey and lengthened the stride of his short legs to catch up with the couple.

"You're right—to the frontier! I'll bring the entire Club to the frontier with us!"

Eginhard would dearly have like to climb into a fiacre and obtain a little relief from so much emotion, but the earthquake had cracked all the causeways and overturned the wooden sidewalks, and no carriage was risking traveling in all that chaos. It was therefore necessary to make his decision and go on foot— but they could not agree to a direction. Sourdillon wanted to go to the Gare de l'Est and Carmencita the Gare de l'Ouest.

It was Eginhard, again, who cut to the heart of the question by saying: "What good will that do, since Paris has rotated? The eastbound railway will no longer take us to Le Havre, and the westbound one will surely take us to Bordeaux. All roads lead to Rome...but I'm still not absolutely convinced of that, for if we're on a rotating platform, there must be, at the edge of that inopportune

---

[42] A common, untranslatable pun: *voler* means both to fly and to steal, so Eginhard is not literally flying here, but only being stolen by the passionate Carmencita.

circle, a disjunction of roads, railways, and even rivers—with the result that it would require a hazard that I would qualify as providential if the rotation should stop at the exact moment when the line to Chalon happened to be passing that to Amiens, or for the waters of the Oise to flow into the bed of the Seine. I would be curious, all the same, to know whether the rupture has taken place at the rim of the tertiary bowl, as it would be logical to suppose..."

"In that case," said Carmencita, "in order to satisfy the old gentleman, let's go to the Gare de Lyon; that will be the best way of going northwards; we'll finish up reaching the sea and a steamer that will take us to my homeland. I don't say that there are no earthquakes there, but one never sees cities spinning like tops."

The old gentleman was only semi-satisfied to be thus designated, but he contented himself with this transactional proposition. "Very well," he said. "I'll go fetch the Club members."

Gallantly, Eginhard offered his arm to the Argentinian woman, who set off, swaying on her hips like a launch agitated by the swell and watching her slender feet, only wanting to set them down judiciously in the midst of the confused rubble that had once been the flat surface of a pavement.

At that moment, some bill-posters passed by at a run, their ladders on their shoulders, leaving behind them, displayed on the walls, placards in which the municipal council reassured the public against any panic.

This was their approximate tenor:

Citizens

At the very moment when the enemy is invading our frontiers, and English fleets are menacing our African possessions, and even our Mediterranean coast, a frightful cataclysm has just struck your city.

The authorities owe you the truth; they will hide nothing from you. The terrain that once constituted the Île-de-France, under subterranean forces that it is not possible for us at present to check, and for which the Prefecture of Police will take sole responsibility, has become unstuck and is rotating on its axis. What was north is now south. That, without doubt, will be no bad thing, for, after all, it is only just that everyone should enjoy in turn the advantages and inconvenience of location and orientation. Where the question becomes complicated, however, is the manner in which the edge of this islet accords with the neighboring regions that have remained in place, immobile.

It was inevitable that his readjustment would take place as best it could, and that it would be much like what happens when a clumsy domestic sticks the limbs of a carelessly broken statue back together. The fracture will have dragged Melun away, leaving Fontainebleau immobile in its sands and its forest, breaking the Seine between the two towns; the Marne has been severed between Château-Thierry and Epernay, the Aisne near Craonne, the Oise below the Fère and the rest in accordance.

The railway lines stop, broken at that improbable cut-off point, along with the telegraph lines. Employees are reconnecting the wires in all directions as quickly as possible and at random, but the Paris offices are confounded by the Chinese puzzle posed by the inevitable entanglement resulting from such a reconnection; the distribution tables are now a mosaic devoid of significance.

In sum, Paris is without communications. We resemble shipwreck-victims on a vessel derived of a rudder, and, to complete the analogy, we shall probably run out of water. During the rotation, in fact, our aqueducts have broken, and if they still carry a liquid having all the appearances of water, it is because they have collected it from the lakes in which rivers abruptly cut off from their mouths are accumulating. How can such water be assessed? It is no longer that beverage, as pure as it was hygienic, that we have disputed for so long with the river-dwellers of the Avre and the Loing! Today, they are keeping their water, and we Parisians, after so many sacrifices agreed by your Municipal Councils—drawn on the public purse, of course—we are reduced to drinking an unnamable liquid. The Board of Hygiene, urgently consulted, has unanimously decided that it would be better not to drink it, thus absorbing unknown microbes to which we have not had the leisure to become accustomed in the manner of Mithridates, as happens every summer for the waters of the Seine, surreptitiously introduced into our conduits.

Such is the situation, dear fellow citizens.

But that is not all.

We have received, just now, an alarming phonogram from the observatory, and are delivering it to your appreciation: 'The latitude of Paris is gradually but sensibly increasing.'

"That's horrible! It's terrible!" Eginhard exclaimed, having read it aloud. "And unless the Earth has chosen a new axis of rotation, which science refuses to admit, I don't see what it implies."

He had not finished expressing this remark when more bill-posters stuck up a new poster beside the first. This one was signed by a well-known promoter of the Paris Seaport[43] and was thus conceived:

---

[43] The person the author has in mind is almost certainly J. Émile Labadie, who published *Étude sur Paris-port-de-mer* in 1886 and engaged in a long battle with the government regarding the practicality of his plan to render the Seine navigable by oceangoing merchant ships all the way to Paris. He was not alone, however; Prosper Germain's *Paris-port-de-mer* (1912) listed 24 such proposals made since the 18th century. Nor has the idea ever died, a similar proposal was submitted to the President of the Republic as recently as 2009 by Antoine Grumbach.

VICTORY

That which the authorities have refused to our legitimate claims, nature has given us gratis: PARIS SEAPORT is a reality, without it costing our shareholders a single sou! All that it required was a simple cataclysm.

While Paris was being shaken by the worrying earthquake that terrified us all last night, the Massif Central of France was subjected to an even more frightful convulsion and was raised up by several hundred meters. The news reached us by means of the optical telegraph that has just been established, in a matter of hours, between the two lips of the fracture that appeared so strangely at the edge of the tertiary basin of Paris.

Lifted up with the central plateau, however, were the sedimentary layers that were spread out at its feet, which now form an immense inclined plane, extending all the way to La Manche. Over the soft clays and marls interposed between these various layers, Paris is gently sliding, along with its suburbs, and in a few hours it will be on the shore of the sea, doubtless destroying the mortal enemies of the great project of PARIS SEAPORT, Rouen and Le Havre, unless those conceited cities have already sunk beneath the waves in the same seesaw motion that elevated the Auvergnat plateau!

Only one thing remains for us to desire: that our vessel will stop in time and not, by virtue of its acquired velocity, fall into the sea—for it is much heavier than water and would doubtless sink, in spite of the motto of the city of Paris: fluctuat nec mergitur.[44]

It is Melun that is serving as our prow—Melun, which a fortunate evolution of the basin has carried northwards. The PARIS SEAPORT Company invites all its supporters to go to Melun, in order to be the first to salute the sea. A special train has been organized for ten o'clock in the morning at the Gare de Lyon.

HURRAH!

"Quickly, to the Gare de Lyon!" cried Eginhard, gripped by enthusiasm.

He spotted some porters who had thought of improvising *filanzanes*, in order to transport their fellow citizens like simple Hovas,[45] on the backs of men, through the obstacles of the disrupted streets. Soon, he and his companion were on their way to the Gare de Lyon at the steady trot of these businessmen of a new breed.

---

[44] "Battered by the waves, but unsinking." The city's emblem is a ship, presumably reflecting the fact that the shape of its original site, the Île de la Cité, is somewhat reminiscent of a ship floating on the Seine.

[45] Hovas are natives of Madagascar, where *filanzanes*—light chairs suspended by ropes between two long poles supported on the shoulders of four bearers—were once used as a standard means of transport.

One might have thought, in fact, that all Paris had arranged to meet there; the station platforms were crowded with people who were taking the army trains, and Eginhard fell into the arms of Monsieur de Soudillon, who was surrounded by the kindly members of the Foreign Club. They were all shouting as loudly as they could, while waving little tricolor flags: "To the front! To the front!"

An ovation was given to the already-celebrated professor of geology, who nevertheless demurred when asked to make a speech.

"This is not the time for words, my friends," he said, "but for actions. At the frontier, we shall find the words that set hearts on fire!"

A formidable pressure transported his entire audience on to the first train to depart; the locomotive whistled, and the train was soon rolling northwards at top speed.

Eginhard was sitting between Carmencita and Sourdillon, who were both intent on serving as deacons to the high priest of science, and both talking at the same time about different things. Pulled in opposite directions by these demanding acolytes, the professor did not know which one to listen to, and clasped his head, which seemed to be about to explode, with feverish hands.

Dominating the tumult of the carriage, Sourdillon was sketching a plan of diplomatic diversion, in which the members of the Foreign Club would be sent forth as sharpshooters to negotiate with the enemy. In the meantime the leader of the band would go to appeal for help to the Pope and the Negus, hoping that the slowness of protocol would permit them to bring the Church's cannons and the Libya lions to bear before the end of hostilities.

While these words were hammering Eginhard's right ear, however, the latter was lending his left ear to less transcendent suggestions.

"In my homeland," murmured the Argentinian woman, we sing this:
"Olé!
"The storm bursts in the bosom of the earth,
"The hurricane roars in my heart,
"The volcano vomits lava, and my heart breaks, vomiting its blood!
"Who betrays us dies; and we die afterwards!"
Damn it! thought the scientist. *That's enough to dispel any thought of treason.*

"Our mothers carry daggers in their stockings, and we hide revolvers in our belts, *mio caro*, to reckon with the unfaithful. Oh, let's flee, let's flee to the pampas of my native land!"

The conversation on this theme seemed rather embarrassing for Eginhard, who was doubtless unfamiliar with the practice of replacing the mandolin with a revolver.

Fortunately, they were approaching the terminus; the locomotive slowed down, its brakes screeching, and soon stopped, steaming, beside the platform of Melun station.

"All change!" cried the employees—which was perfectly natural, since the broken track stopped there, to the despair of the troops who were occupying the station, the town and its surroundings. Their mobilization orders had specified that they ought to embark at six o'clock in the morning for Belfort. It was midday; the line no longer existed, and instead of going south-east, the ground itself was taking them northwards. A colonel tackled the stationmaster, complaining that the Network Commission ought to have been able to anticipate the eventuality.

"And in the meantime, the enemy is free to establish themselves on our territory, take out fortifications and advance on Paris. What's going to happen, when they arrive on the Epernay-Craonne-La Fère line, and no longer recognize the valleys through which all invasions take place? They're going to say that our maps are worse than ever! And not to be there to land a blow!"

The promoter of Paris Seaport provided a fortunate diversion by intervening. "Oh, Messieurs, be glad that you're not on the eastern front; isn't it at least as honorable to maintain a garrison in an entrenched camp that's on the move? Spare a thought for the perplexity of the enemy, whose objective has slipped away and vanished! Their cleverly ripened plan has gone down the river; their preparations were in vain; everything has to be started again, and, confronted by the strangeness of the phenomenon, their strategic science remains indecisive: a momentary hesitation! But that's salvation! Our armies, of which you are only on part, gentlemen, will easily form up in a province on the flank of their line of operations and…but what's that? A pigeon coming down!"

They ran to the bird, under the wing of which appeared a light tube contain dispatches, and while they looked everywhere for an authority to whom the grave responsibility of reading them could be left, everyone began to discuss the thorny question raised by the arrival of the carrier-pigeon.

Certainly, the bird possessed an admirable instinct, and, crossing mountains and oceans, was able to return to its dovecot, without anyone having sufficiently explained, in my opinion, by what mysterious cerebral mechanism it bring that incomprehensible sense of direction into play—but how could it recognize it if, as in the present case, the entire country containing its shelter had started to displace itself on the round ball? Even the cleverest had to admit that they did not know; it was a miracle that the pigeon, evidently bound for Paris, had landed on the Île-de-France in distress.

At the same time, someone wondered exactly where that crazily drifting ship was. A former naval officer proposed to take a bearing, as if on board. It was necessary to run around all the optician's shops in the town to find a sextant and the mercury to form and artificial horizon to substitute for the marine horizon.

Finally equipped, the former frigate captain stood with his legs apart, as if to resist the swaying of a deck, consulted his chronometer, raised the sextant toward the sun, and...

A frightful clamor stopped him in mid-gesture.

"The sea! The sea!" cried a thousand voices.

Binoculars were immediately aimed. A few kilometers away, a cloud of dust rose up, denouncing the rapid progress of that singular sled, and when the wind dispersed the cloud, the waves were shining in the distance.

At a vertiginous speed, they advanced toward the roaring gulf. Everything was going to fall into it. Only one hope remained, which was that the moving stratum was thicker than the water was deep.

To begin with, on reaching the cliffs that had one sheltered so many charming seaside resorts, which had already disappeared beneath the waters, the enormous calcareous mass cracked as it fell.

There was an immense scream of terror, while a frightful shock knocked people down on top of one another, and buildings collapsed with an indescribable din.

Then, equilibrium was gradually restored, and, the surface of the land not sinking any lower than the level of the water, the gigantic islet continued to slide over the bed of La Manche.

Extreme situations temper the character of individuals. All the emotions that the passengers on that singular raft had experienced in a few hours had hardened them, and, from the moment that they had withstood the initial impact, it seemed that they no longer had any reason to be afraid.

However, as they got nearer to the deepest water, the water-level reached the surface of the ground, invading the lower areas first and forcing the inhabitants—I mean the passengers—to take refuge on higher ground. Soon, though, they had passed the thalweg and as they climbed up the opposite slope, the land gradually emerged again.

Hope was reborn, and Sourdillon tried to profit from it to harangue the club members, while the prefect, to whom the carrier-pigeon had been taken, appeared waving a piece of paper over his head. It was the dispatch.

"Rejoice, Messieurs. Our eastern frontier is no longer under threat. The elevation of our central plateau had as its counterpart the collapse of the Rhineland, which is under water. It's a barrier sufficient against any invasion, for the moment. We no longer have anything to do but march upon the conquest of England."

At the same moment, a new impact shook the ground; the raft had run aground on the English shore, crushing Portsmouth, Brighton and Newhaven and stopping when it ran into the South Downs.

England was no longer a island!

Sourdillon wanted to run ahead, in order to be the first to set foot on British soil, as the Norman conqueror had once done. He took Eginhard by the arm to drag him away, but the latter took out his watch.

"What time," he asked, "is the train to Liverpool, and what day is the liner to America?"

It was Carmencita who replied, and with what an incendiary gaze! "We'll be able to say," she added, "that to go and get married, we haven't taken a banal vehicle."

"Oh, we'll come back," he assured her, "for I haven't forgotten that I own land in Paris that is now west of the city, and 'great cities grow westwards'— it'll be worth a fortune before long. But I don't want to occupy myself any longer with geology, or meteorology—they're too complicated."

Raoul Bigot: *The Iron That Died*
(1918)

"Le Fer qui meurt" by Raoul Bigot (1874-1928), here translated as "The Iron that Died," was originally published in the 15 December 1918 issue of the popular magazine Lectures Pour Tous, *only a month after the armistice that brought the Great War to a close. It had obviously been written while the war was still raging, and clearly belongs to the glut of propagandistic speculative fiction that began production in 1917, evidently with the active encouragement of George Clemenceau. On publication, therefore, it became something of a curious anomaly: an accidental "alternative history." It was by no means the only story of the period to meet that fate, to which all speculative fictions dealing with contemporary events are exceedingly vulnerable, but it is one of the most extravagant. It is also notable for introducing a motif that had the distinction of being taken up subsequently by writers in all three of the nations that developed a robust tradition of speculative fiction, in France by S. S. Held in* La Mort du fer *(1931), in the U.S.A. by David H. Keller in* The Metal Doom *(1932,) and in England by "Wayland Smith" (Victor Bayley) in* The Machine Stops *(1936), thus permitting an intriguing comparison of cultural attitudes.*

Raoul Bigot went on to publish a two longer works of speculative fiction in Lectures Pour Tous, *one of them in collaboration with E. M. Laumann. "Le Fer qui meurt" was rapidly followed by "Nounlegos" (1919,) a novella that offers an unusually detailed account of a literal kind of "mind-reading," applying the hypothetical technology to the melodramatic unraveling of an audacious and exceptionally well-planned crime.[46]*

B.S.

For forty-eight hours Lieutenant Jacques had not had a moment's rest. Since the beginning of the attack violently launched by the enemy, his battery, installed not far from the front line, had come under particularly heavy fire from the opposing artillery; he was the sole surviving officer, with a personnel reduced by almost half. The orders were imperative; it was necessary, whatever the cost, to continue the barrage under the hail of the 20s and the 150s.

With his habitual detached expression, the lieutenant was going from gun to gun, inspecting his men and giving advice whenever an incident threatened to stop the fire. Nothing seemed to move him, and his imperturbable calm tem-

---

[46] Included in *On the Brink of the World's End*, Black Coat Press (ISBN 978-1-61227-474-4).

pered the courage of his soldiers better than more or less nervous speeches. From time to time he went into his hole in order to take cognizance of the news that he was able to receive thanks to the improvised wireless receiver he had installed there.

Good news was transmitted by him directly to his men, and he took to each gun, personally, the new instructions for firing when orders instructed him to change target.

But his physical resistance was at an end this evening; he perceived that in reading a communication saying:

Enemy attack definitively failed. On target one, a burst every quarter hour. Measures taken to resupply you 23 hours and evacuate your wounded. Your fire very efficacious.

Then he made one last round, spreading the consoling information, gave a few orders, and headed for his mattress, felling exhausted.

Lieutenant Jacques had not been born to be a soldier. Rather delicate in health, repelled by any violent exercise, he only felt alive in the research laboratory that he had entered as soon as his scientific education was complete. He deemed himself fortunate to have been able to penetrate right away into one of the all-too-rare great French industrial enterprises that had understood the technical, economic and moral importance of those research laboratories, so well-developed in certain countries industrially younger than France.

He had found his way, and had rapidly rendered appreciated services. At the outbreak of the war, as a complement officer, he had rejoined his regiment. Patriotic and scrupulous, he did his duty without ostentation; the cerebral labor that it demanded was mere child's play to him; he was able to carry out his functions while leaving his mind to work in much higher spheres. Naturally, his scientific preoccupations were orientated toward means of war, and he had astonished his comrades many a time by describing to them, a year before they made their appearance, new machines that seemed to him to be necessary. He gladly repeated that the means of making war were, in sum, very restricted. The present adversaries only used engines of limited local operation, which, in order to produce their effect, had to be employed in considerable numbers.

In order to beat Germany rapidly, it was necessary to be able to do to it, over the thousands of kilometers of the front, at the rear, among its innumerable armies and even on its own territory, by means of a general catastrophe comparable to a major epidemic of the plague or cholera, what the Bocho-Maximalist[47] virus had done to the old Greater Russia or what a torpedo did to a defenseless steamer. But those points of comparison did not furnish any datum to solve the problem. The creation of a general epidemic in Germany was impossible; it was,

---

[47] "Maximalist" is an approximate translation of "Bolshevik," "Bocho" is an improvised derivative of Boche, signifying the German origin of Marxist-Leninist theory.

in any case, repugnant to the French character, all the more so as Germany had already attempted to employ it.

As for interior decomposition originating from politics, it was necessary not to think of it; the entire history of Germany was there to prove that the German people were made to obey; it could not be other than an arm; it needed its government to think for it.

It was also utopian to think of blowing up the enemy country like a poor ship!

And Lieutenant Jacques sank into profound reflections in search of a method that might disarm the abhorred enemy at a stroke.

Gradually, sudden and strange gleams were produced in his mind, unexpected connections between experiments he had carried out on the contexture and fragility of metals and curious anomalous electrical phenomena that he had promised to look into in future.

He forced his mind to follow those two questions in parallel, and an idea of genius slowly crystallized in his mind.

During the frightful attack that had been repelled, thanks in large measure to the conduct of his battery, it seemed to him that the idea took on a definitive form.

And lying down on his bed of straw, he said to himself: *I've found it!* Then he thought he had the strength to reflect—but physical fatigue got the better of him. He murmured: "That's it: I'll write to the President of the Council."[48] Then, worn out, he fell into a profound sleep.

Lieutenant Jacques of the 3rd battery, 10th artillery regiment,
to Monsieur the President of the Council of Ministers.

I have the honor of informing you that I have discovered a previously-unknown means of war, capable in a matter of hours of provoking an unprecedented catastrophe over enemy territory, placing our enemies at our mercy. The method requires:

A new material, rather important but not extraordinary;

An ensemble of measures easy to take and to apply simultaneously to all fronts and to neutral frontiers, but the strict execution of which is a vital condition to protect the Allies against a catastrophe identical to the one that must be provoked in the central empires;

Absolute discretion, because, if the enemy were informed of the project, it could not only diminish the magnitude of the result but suppress it completely by a very simple means;

A narrow coordination with the general strategy that would certainly modify the plans presently decided.

---

[48] The President of the Council, or Prime Minister, of France in 1918 was Georges Clemenceau.

For all these reasons, recourse to the usual channels with be absolutely impractical; the number and nature of the questions raised would require the examination of my proposal by a large number of committees and bureaux, which would find it absolutely impossible to reach accord before, by one of the devious means that are unknown to us, but which we sense, the enemy would be informed of the idea and undertake the simple measure to which I have made allusion.

I will add that add that all these preparations for execution should not give, either to our agents or the enemy, if it should become aware of them, any indication of the goal pursued.

Only one man in France can examine the ensemble of these questions and decide on them; that man is you, Monsieur President.

Public opinion has brought your energy to power; I am presenting it with the opportunity to make use of it for the greater good of the country.

Lieutenant Jacques.

The military office of the President of the Council, to which that letter was sent, did not attach much importance to it; nevertheless, information was sought regarding the officer so scantly respectful of hierarchical channels.

That information was such that the skepticism of the President's entourage was shaken, and in order to avoid any blunder, the letter was presented to the President of the Council. The latter ordered that a senior officer be immediately sent to Lieutenant Jacques to demand the principle of his project and a few details that would permit a judgment as to whether the proposal merited study.

The officer returned swiftly.

The lieutenant had simply replied that, on his honor, he guaranteed the veracity of what he had put forward, but that, for the reasons indicated in the letter, he would only explain his project to the President of the Council in person.

From his short mission, the impression that Jacques had made on him, the conversations he had had with his military superiors and with the director of the Company that had employed him before the war, the officer reported the conviction that the proposal could not be summarily dismissed. The Premier telephoned G.H.Q. to send Lieutenant Jacques to see him.

The first interview between the great clear-sighted and unshakably determined politician and the calm and resolute young scientist was a rapid clash of swords.

"Monsieur, you have sent me this letter; you have refused explanations to the superior officer I sent to you. I want to believe that you are not playing a practical joke and that you've reflected that causing the man who concentrates the energy and will of France in his hands to waste his time is almost a crime. Explain your project to me rapidly."

"Monsieur President, the time has not yet come. I would explain to you what you would not believe. First, it is necessary for me to prove to you that the fundamental idea is sound, and I ought to commence with an experiment."

He took a small container out of his jacket pocket the size of a pocket electric torch.

"With this," he continued, "by borrowing for a few seconds an electric current just sufficient to illuminate an ordinary light bulb, I could destroy the world.

"You're shaking your head, Monsieur President, wondering if I'm not mad. Come with me to a place where I can carry out my experiment without doing any damage, and you'll see, you'll believe, and afterwards, you'll hear and comprehend my project."

The President asked for a telephone connection.

"Colonel, do you have an old building in your arsenal that's a hindrance to you and you'd like to see disappear? Good...I'll come to see you tomorrow then."

As he was about to hang up the receiver, Lieutenant Jacques made a gesture.

"Pardon me, Monsieur President, but a few preliminary precautions are indispensable; will you permit me to indicate them before you?"

In response to an affirmative sign, Jacques took he telephone and gave a few instructions.

When the communication was terminated, the President said: "So, Monsieur, we'll leave from here at ten-thirty tomorrow."

The next day, at ten-thirty precisely, the President of the Council and Lieutenant Jacques climbed into an automobile, which took them to an arsenal situated in a large Parisian suburb. Jacques made sure that the prescribed instructions had been carried out. Satisfied with his examination, he returned to the President, who was talking to the colonel in command.

"I'm ready, Monsieur President. Colonel, you know the conditions. Come back in an hour; you'll be able to observe that the building won't inconvenience you any longer."

At a sign of assent from the great master, the colonel went away. An hour later, when he came back, nothing remained of the large hangar but a layer of dust.

The President, in an attitude of profound reflection, was staring at the accumulation at his feet. Lieutenant Jacques was placidly making notes. The arrival of the director of the arsenal recalled them to reality.

The President showed the Colonel what remained of the large edifice, with an expression that said: *How was it done? I don't know.* Then he addressed himself to Jacques.

"What you've just done is prodigious, but I can't conceive its application to the war. I don't understand."

"Now I can explain to you, Monsieur President."

A few days later, the lieutenant was summoned to the Presidency.

"Monsieur Jacques; as you will have anticipated, my decision is made; we're going to attempt your extraordinary operation. The triumph of civilization and humanity justifies it. But I ought not to be the only one informed. In order to bear all its fruits, your action needs to be intimately linked with that of our armies, and it isn't me who commands them."

"I've thought of that. As you've finally succeeded in convincing all the Allies to name a single generalissimo,[49] it's him that it's necessary to inform. We three alone informed, without saying a word to anyone whatsoever, will ensure triumph. I've brought a plan of organization and execution such that all those who will be involved will have no suspicion of the work that they are preparing."

"That's my opinion too. I've summoned the commander-in-chief."

As he said that, the President opened the door to a small room adjacent to his office. With the door securely closed, the three individuals remained in conference for half a day.

The allied offensive that had been expected did not happen, all the armies receiving strict orders to stay on the defensive and maintain pressure on the enemy by means of an uninterrupted harassment of the front and rear lines. Considerable concentrations of automobile trucks carrying various materiel were, however, organized not far from the lines, as well as large quantities of munitions and provisions of every sort.

The President of the Council had enormous difficulty, politically, defending himself against reproaches for inaction; he repeated incessantly that: "We're waiting for the right moment," citing the authority of the decisions of the generalissimo, who, appointed by all the Allies, was shielded from the ill humor of parliamentarians.

In the meantime, Jacques worked. To the Swiss frontier and three points on the western front he brought electric power lines from the nearest large generating stations. He had bizarre electrical machines constructed, which bore no resemblance to those known prior to that day; those machines were set up in armored bunkers instructed at the extremities of new lines.

Crews of sappers carried out various maneuvers at the front.

After a few months of intensive labor, Jacques, in the course of a meeting with his two highly-placed collaborators, declared to them: "I'm ready. It's certain that all the precautions have been taken on the Franco-Anglo-Belgian-American, Italian and Greek fronts. On our front, we have succeeded at three points, taking advantage of watercourses, in establishing the necessary connections. If the order is sent to close the Swiss frontier, in the agreed fashion, both

---

[49] Ferdinand Foch was appointed commander-in-chief of the Allied armies in the Spring of 1918.

on the French side and the Italian side, the cataclysm can by unleashed within forty-eight hours.

"Half an hour after that release, the observers at the front, the barrage balloons and the airplanes, having been alerted to the phenomena to look for, will inform us as to whether or not that first action has been successful. It is, in fact, necessary to anticipate that the mechanisms established with great difficulty at the front might have suffered deterioration; if the result is negative we shall then be obliged to launch the catastrophe through Switzerland. In that case, you know the measures taken to limit the damage, and those permitting our neighbors to remedy the general upheaval that they will suffer.

"If, on the contrary, as it is necessary to hope, the result is good, our emissaries will act in the agreed fashion to oblige Switzerland to take the measures that will safeguard that country; in addition, reliable men will depart for selected points where, even independently of the Federal Government, they can proceed with simple operations that will protect the country from all contagion. That is the system that will be employed in Holland and Demark. France will have made the maximum efforts to ensure that those who have not intervened in the struggle do not have to suffer the rude blow that her adversaries are going to receive.

"Among the enemy, it will be devastating. They will not be able to carry out any defensive move; their famous methodical organization does not permit the rapid comprehension of new things and the consequent making of the necessary decisions. The unexpected is for them a terrible obstacle that stops them, obliging a laborious cerebral effort, which necessities consultations in order to accommodate the abnormal in a familiar frame. They will not yet have grasped the situation as whole when our endeavor will be complete.

"Squadrons of reconnaissance aircraft will keep us up to date with the progress of the disaster. Then, General, it will be up to you to conclude the task."

Lieutenant Jacques had never made such a long speech; in spite of all his calmness, the frightful grandeur of what was about to occur at a gesture from him had overexcited him a little.

For a few seconds silence reigned between the three men on whom the destiny of the world depended.

The meditation terminated, they settled with a common accord the ultimate details of the execution of the gigantic project. At the moment of separation, they thought that they would not see one another again until "afterwards"—which is to say, after the great victory—brought them together and, moved, they embraced fraternally.

A few days after that meeting, the allied front was abuzz with rumors. It appeared that something gave was happening among the Boches. Fires could be seen in large agglomerations; munitions depots were exploding. The aviators reported that they had observed and absolute cessation of movement on the railways.

Messages providing more detailed information signaled that a large number of destructions were visible behind all the enemy lines. The messages multiplied, making the entire world aware of the extraordinary cataclysm that was invading enemy territory. The ruination and conflagrations reached Berlin, Vienna and all the way to Constantinople.

A sentiment of surprise, rapidly turning to amazement, and then changing into rage and utter despair, takes possession of Germany and its allies.

On the other side of the front, the first news is welcomed with calm, people being somewhat suspicious of everything that seems supernaturally favorable, but events hurry on; the terrible epidemic that is ravaging the central empires is recorded step by step; a wild joy takes possession of everyone; people run out into the streets and embrace one another, weeping with joy. The tombs of those "Died for France and the Allies" are covered with flowers, and loud voices declare to the dear departed; "You are avenged!"

Then the great awaited new bursts like a clap of thunder: the entire front moves; the French, the English, the Americans, the Italians, the Serbs and the Greeks plunge forward, reducing to nothing the rare resistances of a completely demoralized enemy.

What, then, has happened?

Three days after the last meeting of those who were about to save the civilized world, General von Schünburg arrived, out of breath, at Nuremburg railway station just in time to take the westbound train.

After having expelled the occupants of a carriage that suited him and rebuked the employees who did not exhibit sufficient urgency with regard to a man of his importance—he was in command of an army corps—he installed himself. Then, with an anxious expression, he took two telegrams out of his pocket and reread them attentively. What could they signify? One of the two telegrams came from the commandant of his army at the front, the other from the Minister of War, giving him the order to return to his post immediately "in view of extraordinary circumstances." He had, therefore, been obliged to interrupt his leave, although he had only arrived in Nuremburg the day before.

Tyrannical with his subordinates, he showed, like all Prussian officers, an absolute discipline with regard to his superiors. Thus, he did not protest against the order that deprived him of the distractions he had promised himself, but preoccupied himself with the reason that had provoked it. What could the extraordinary circumstances in question be?

The train stopped at a small station through which it should have passed at speed. Leaning out of the window, von Schünburg could see an agitated man making broad gestures speaking to the locomotive's driver. He was about to send for news when the train moved off again at a much reduced speed, which it maintained.

The general, his conscience tranquil, made himself comfortable in a corner, and fell asleep shortly thereafter.

A sudden shock wakes him up. The train has stopped abruptly. This time, the general gets down; if the driver has not been warned that he has the honor of conducting the commandant of an army corps, he will go to inform him in energetic terms.

Around the machine there is a circle formed by railway employees and a few passengers. The locomotive has derailed; the accident has been caused the rupture of the rails, which have split over a length of several meters.

Thanks to its low speed, the machine had not traveled far; it has traced a furrow in the gravel and has stopped against a rail of the adjacent track—which, someone remarks, has been split by the impact over a distance of several meters. The machine is obstructing both tracks; circulation will certainly be interrupted for several hours.

The train manager informs the passengers that there is a station only three kilometers further on, and that the simplest thing is to head for it on foot; from there they can telegraph for a train to be formed and come to pick up the passengers stranded by the breakdown.

Von Schünburg sees wan faces peering at him, which might, in emitting the complaints of people who cannot swallow their anger, offend the dignity of the high rank he represents. He therefore contains himself and, responding to the salute addressed to him a moment before by a young officer of pretentious appearance striking the regimental pose, authorizes the latter to accompany him in attaining the advertised station.

At the station there is an extraordinary hubbub; all the station personnel are afflicted by panic. There is good reason; no train has passed through for an hour; the last one to arrive derailed while stopping, the rails having twisted and broken beneath the locomotive at the moment the engineer applied the brake. It is necessary to believe that the shock was rude and had broken the wheels, for they had given way shortly afterwards and the machine is now maintained on the ground by a part of its mechanism and its axles.

The general went directly to the station-master; authorizing himself by his rank, and even exhibiting his two telegrams. He ordered imperatively that a train be formed immediately. The station-master raised his arms to the heavens in a gesture of despair; all the dispatches he had received were incomprehensible; they talked of derailed rains and catastrophes, but nothing precise could be obtained therefrom except that railways circulation appeared to have stopped completely. Furthermore, telegraphic communication had been progressively cut off, without it being possible to determine the cause. At that very moment, information had just arrived that extraordinary phenomena were occurring at the large freight terminal created to serve the munitions factory with which the little town had been honored in 1915: the rails were disappearing and wagons were collapsing.

Exasperated by that verbiage, which he attributed to a fit of madness provoked in a feeble mind by the announcement of a vulgar railway accident, von Schünburg sent the officer accompanying him to request on his behalf the elements necessary to form a train and headed for the buffet.

For nearly an hour, von Schünburg ate and drank copiously, isolated in a small separate room.

As he lit a cigar he thought about the officer, who had not come back, but his well-garnished stomach inclined him temporarily to indulgence toward the subaltern who seemed to be taking a long time to carry out his orders. Suddenly, a man brought him a note scribbled by his companion, which told him that what the station-master had said was unfortunately correct; he had not been able to find and rolling-stock in s for state to travel. On the indication that he might perhaps find something at the munitions factory, he had gone there.

After having taken cognizance of that message, the general noticed that the man who had brought it seemed to be on the brink of fainting.

"What's happening, then?"

"Frightful things."

"Let's go, then!"

Getting up, with difficulty, von Schünburg decided to make a tour in order to restore order.

At that moment, a cry of "Fire!" resounded. At the door of the buffet, the general stopped, dazedly. A short distance away the deformed locomotive had collapsed completely, and the coals, still incandescent, had set fire to the mass of fuel in the tender, of which nothing remained but vestiges.

The wagons had crumbled; only the planks and drapes seemed intact; the gas reservoir of one was letting out gas through its walls, and a gust of wind had caused the cloud of gas to make contact with the sparks of the fire; in an instant, flames engulfed the train. In a matter of moments, the entire station would be on fire!

The general followed the crowd that was fleeing through the only available exit, toward the freight terminal.

There, he was obliged to admit that the rumors reaching him were accurate. Where the rails had been, nothing could now be seen but streaks of dark dust; nothing remained of wagons but plants and partitions; it was as if the framework had been volatilized.

He stopped in front of a train loaded with munitions and contemplated the large shells that were heaped up pell-mell. He struck one of them with the tip of his cane and stopped, stupefied.

Come on! He was dreaming. It wasn't possible!

He repeated the experiment; his cane had pierced the shell; under the slight impact, the magnificent steel of the German factories had shattered, laying bare the redoubtable explosive.

Mechanically, he did it again, and every time, his stick disaggregated one of the shells of which he was so proud.

As if under the influence of a hallucination, he struck with harder blows, hoping finally to hear the metallic sound usually rendered by those large jewels of death, which only Germany had been able to prepare in advance—but he encountered nothing but soft sounds, which the friable envelopes made as they crumbled, laying bare their hideous yellow souls.

Then, griped by vertigo, he fled. But he did not get far.

A few hundred meters away, and immense whirlwind of flames burst forth. He only just had time to think: *The munitions factory!* before he was swept away and crushed by the torrent of gas, materials and debris of all kinds projected in all directions by the explosion of a considerable mass of munitions and thousands of tons of explosives.

Lieutenant Jacques' method was triumphant.

It really was an idea of genius that he had had, of provoking, by means of a new phenomenon of the electric order, what he called a "molecular disease of iron." Under the impact of that special wave, iron and steel took on an intimate vibratory movement—for nothing was revealed at the outset—that provoked an extreme fragility in the metal. Under the effect of the stresses to which it was subjected, the metal broke; the disintegration continued by virtue of the annihilation of molecular attraction, and the iron was reduced to dust. And the most extraordinary thing was that the malady was eminently contagious; the vibration was transmitted with a speed so reduced that it was difficult to explain scientifically, but it was transmitted from one piece to another, even when there was only an insignificant contact between them.

What had happened at the station where General von Schünburg had had such a tragic end to his dinner was only one small scene in the terrible drama that shook Germany and extended to Austria, Bulgaria and Turkey. The disease progressed, following the facile route of the railway, and multiplied, without any break in continuity, at the inexorable velocity of fifty kilometers an hour, sowing terror everywhere.

The first effects were those already known: the rails broke and disintegrated, leading to frightful derailments; the locomotives and the metal parts of the wagons soon followed, and by means of the fires in the engines, the gas in the wagons and electrical short-circuits, the trains fell prey to flames. In the big stations, above all, the accumulation of materials subject to that extraordinary decomposition led almost immediately to devastating conflagrations.

Metal bridges attained by the epidemic collapsed noisily.

At army railways depots, the accumulation of munitions and cannons offered a magnificent field for the extension of the molecular disease, whose ravages spread, reducing the results of the efforts of Boche industry to nothing.

Near the front, the stations of the various engineering and artillery stores are naturally afflicted; in the munitions depots, the casings of shells disintegrate before the fearful eyes of the personnel, who flee madly in all directions, often with reason, for the fires produced there, as everywhere, lead in places to mighty explosions; the latter spread from one accumulation to another. Projectiles and cartridges of every caliber, grenades, rockets, canisters of incendiary liquids and gas cylinders form gigantic firework displays, of which only those who are able to contemplate the most massive destructions accomplished in the course of the war can have any idea.

The contagion continues; a simple momentary contact between an item attained by the mysterious disease and a healthy piece contaminates the latter, which becomes susceptible in its turn of transmitting the plague. Many bizarre incidents result therefrom.

Projectiles unloaded from a cart at the moment when the fatal wave reaches them carry the germ inexorably into the munitions depots of batteries where they are stored; if those projectiles are immediately employed, it is to the cannons that they communicate the decomposition still latent within them; in that case, it is a rare gun that resists the first shot; at the second, the breech, under the pressure of the gases, explodes with a bang.

In the interior, the railway stations are not the only places attained; industrial communications are a facile route of penetration which the molecular disease comes implant itself in the enemy's factories. By way of wagons, and the conveyor belts that load and unload them, the vibratory shock imperceptible invests the frameworks of the vast proud halls; as time goes by, they collapse noisily, contaminating the machine-tools and the components under construction, reducing the martial and economical equipment so laboriously constructed to nothing.

But that is not all; many tramway rails are connected to those of the railways. By way of them, the funeral frisson reaches the hearts of cities.

Tramway rails, in order to reduce the effects of electrolysis provoked by the currents, are linked to the great cast iron conduits that distribute water and gas; those electrical links, in copper cables prior to the war, have been replaced by pieces of soft iron, because Germany needs to make use of its entire stocks of copper in munitions; those cables are, therefore, further vehicles that tranquilly absorb the electrical wave broadcast from the French front; and those routes offer a magnificent means of fulfilling the mission for which it has been created.

It reaches the electricity stations and water distribution stations and destroys them. It reaches the gas factories, and its destructive power is amply displayed; the apparatus of the manufacture and purification of the gas, and the gasometers, disintegrate under its action. The gas and incandescent hearths are liberated; their encounter produces cataclysms; gigantic flames rise up to enormous heights, as if to underline the amplitude of the punishment for the terrified populations.

The devastating scourge follows its inflexible law; the major conduits that have brought it to the places where gas is produced have not caused it to disdain the secondary iron conduits that aliment certain districts; it arrives to prove its power by provoking conflagrations that the disappearance of the water mains does not allow to be combated.

The fluvial routes do not remain immune; bridges and locks are infected, and break; cisterns empty; their contents produce floods.

Any yet more: the ravages are not only exercised on land, the ports are subject to it as well. Maritime railway stations docks and warehouses are gripped and disappear in the torment. Naval shipyards are not sheltered from the blows of the invisible enemy, which shows no mercy to any of the atoms of iron that it encounters in its path. The gigantic or modest hulls of cruisers under repair and submarines under construction disappear rapidly from the places where they are being prepared for further depredations.

The ships in dock receive the unforgiving flux via the apparatus for loading coal and the embarkation gangways; in a matter of hours they are on the sea-bed. Several large battleships, confronted by the inexplicable disease, decide to leave, but many of them carry away the fatal germ that a fortuitous contact has transmitted to them. At sea, their hulls dissolve and they plunge abruptly beneath the waves.

The initial shock provoked at three points of the enemy railway network by the intermediary connections established with great difficulty had succeeded in reaching the adversary in all its vital and sensitive spots, thanks to the prodigious continuity of the metal components that cover all the civilized or supposedly civilized nations with a slender but tangled network that binds together all toil and production.

Germany, Austria-Hungary, Bulgaria and Turkey were reduced to helplessness. The destruction extended, alas, to the territories occupied by the ferocious aggressors, but that was the ransom of the triumph.

As for neutrals, to the great satisfaction of the three protagonists of the momentous affair, they had not suffered. The molecular disease had been transmitted from the front; the anticipated protective measures had been taken in time; the railway lines linking them to the central empires had been cut.

The task of Lieutenant Jacques was accomplished; he had refused in advance all the flattering proposals made to him. He would return to his cherished laboratory; he had a great problem to solve—to the molecular disease of iron that his genius had created, he needed to find a remedy. That would be his work during the peace, the glorious and just peace that the beaten enemy was now demanding on its knees, and which would be signed the next day.

"Lieutenant! Lieutenant! The colonel has arrived to congratulate the battery!"

It is only at the third announcement of that news, shouted by his orderly, that Lieutenant Jacques, after twelve hours of deep sleep, wakes up.

Henri Falk: *The Age of Lead*
(1919)

Little biographical information regarding Henri Falque (1881-1937), who signed almost all his published writings Henri Falk, is recoverable from contemporary sources, save for the dates of his birth and death, and what little can be inferred from the record of his publications.

"L'Age de Plomb" (here translated as "The Age of Lead") is likely to have been written during or just after the Great War, although the book is undated and bibliographical notations merely offer the guess that it was published circa 1922. Its plot appears to be an absurdist transfiguration of life under bombardment. It features an epidemic of alopecia induced by solar radiation that spreads from the tropics to infect the entire world and begins to develop more serious side effects, which requires the protection of homes by lead armor and necessitates the carrying of lead umbrellas by those venturing outside, if not by entire lead-lined costumes—a circumstance that inevitably precipitates international and international conflicts to secure supplies of the newly precious metal. The scourge proves temporary, but the arbitrary ending looks suspiciously akin to a convenience not far removed from waking up after a dream.

B.S.

I. An Inconceivable Epidemic

It is irrefutable that the Gabon enjoys an elevated temperature, and it is no less certain that the days pass placidly there, exempt from the ridiculous trepidation of European life. Libreville, the colony's capital, is a delightful seaport, with its picturesque aloe- and mangrove-wood huts, surrounded by gardens overflowing with abundant vegetation or dominated by cacti, lentisks, houseleeks and bocabungas. There are also sturdier edifices, built for the use of white men, but in the indigenous style; the bank is a beautiful building in pink brick, ornamented with genista bark, and the Lieutenant-Governor's palace a pretty tricolor house in peperino stone, aloe-wood branches and carob hearts.

Pasturelands extend around the city, which nourish numerous livestock—notably herds of buffalo whose steaks, braised with Congo onions, provide feasts for travelers. Eucalyptus and coconut woods punctuate the grasslands, where cockatoos, garden warblers and marmosets frolic.[50] Rattlesnakes and shrews swarm in the long grass.

The native villagers are gentle and cheerful by nature, shiny black in color; they are no more cannibals that the permanent secretary of the Académie Française. Everything in this blissful place seems, therefore, to respire the sweetness of life; and everything there was, indeed, respiring when, at 5:45 p.m. on March 21, 19**, a strange combination of circumstances contrived to disturb the legitimate quietude of M. Parmesif, the colony's Lieutenant-Governor.

Under the veranda with blue-paned bay windows, judiciously opening on to the cool shade of the garden, the Lieutenant-Governor and his faithful secretary, the elegant Monsieur Saumaître, both clad in white linen suits, were slowly drinking exquisite iced lemonade through straws. Between suctions, they were smoking odorous cigars, and whether they were sucking or puffing to the sway of their rocking-chairs, the mute and blissful gentlemen were not thinking about anything at all.

Their thought-free silence was suddenly torn apart by cries, sobs and an eruption of howls from Mademoiselle Lotte Parmesif, aged seven. The little girl was holding a bizarre package: a sort of ball of flaccid flesh, which she threw on to the table bearing the lemonade. The ball unwound; paws and a head emerged, and a frightful, unidentifiable little creature began bounding around the room. Meanwhile, Lotte curled up, weeping in her father's arms, and moaned: "Adolphe! Something's wrong with Adolphe, Papa!"

The Lieutenant-Governor then recognized the bounding animal as young Adolphe, the child's pet capuchin monkey. "Catch him! Catch him, Saumaître!"

The elegant secretary bounded in pursuit of the minuscule quadrumane, and collected it from the wardrobe, using a monocle as bait. "Why, what's wrong with the monkey?" he asked in his turn, while the trembling animal rolled its frightened eyes.

"Something that's causing him to lose his hair," declared Parmesif—and he pulled out a few tufts that were still clinging to Adolphe's thigh, as easily as one removes the leaves from an overcooked artichoke. The capuchin monkey offered no resistance, nor did it cry; it did not seem to feel any pain; it limited itself to shivering, while stupidly clacking its jaws. Lotte began to cry again.

"Come on, calm down," her father said. "If Adolphe's ill, we'll look after him."

As he dried the child's tears, Madame Parmesif came in like a gust of wind. She was a handsome plump lady, with thick blonde hair and a little make-

---

[50] Falk's natural history is blithely askew; several of the species of the species he mentions in this chapter are not native to Central Africa. The most obvious sore thumbs are marmosets (*ouistitis* in French) and the capuchin monkey (*sapajou* in French), which are only found in South America, but his entire approach is cavalier.

up on her eyebrows and a face, dressed in a jonquil kimono. She was followed by a mournful dog. She seemed very excited. "Gustave!" she said, violently. "Take a look at Top!"

Monsieur Parmesif observed that his wife's spaniel was losing its hair as copiously as his daughter's capuchin monkey.

"Yes," Madame Parmesif went on, "Top and Adolphe! Can you explain it?"

"Some kind of contagious alopecia," he suggested.

He had scarcely made this remark when an even strange phenomenon renewed his amazement. A bird had just fallen through an open window in the glazed ceiling; its wings could no longer sustain it, because it was very nearly de-feathered. Almost at the same time, Sokota, the Congolese servant, came on to the veranda; she was crying, and carrying a cage containing what was surely the most ridiculous parrot in the world.

Kiko had ceased to be the splendid multicolored macaw of the front steps; nothing more remained to him but a row of colored feathers on his head and rump—with the result that, with his round eyes, his brick-red skin, the row of feathers on his head and his guttural squawks, he resembled a grotesque and tiny caricature of a naked Indian on the warpath.

Young Lotte howled even more loudly.

"Come on, Sokota!" said Monsieur Parmesif, impatiently. "Take the child away—we have to talk."

"The post, Monsieur le Lieutenant-Gouverneur."

"Thanks, Saumaître... why... well... that's odd! And this letter too... and this.... read this, Saumaître..."

The handsome Madame Parmesif and the impeccable Saumaître seized the papers that the Lieutenant-Governor's feverish hand was holding out to them, and it was their turn to utter an arpeggio of exclamations.

This resulted from the correspondence from Libreville and its surroundings, which revealed that all the animals on the land and in the air were losing their fur and feathers, at variable speeds but to a similar degree—that of total deprivation. For no apparent reason, the cattle, sheep, horses, dogs, cats, pigs and rabbits on the farms, all the poultry in the chicken-runs, the animals living in luxury in the houses and the wild animals in the woods, were being visibly transformed into supernudities—if one might put it thus—as wretched as they were baroque.

With his thumb on his forehead, Parmesif reflected. Violently, he cried: "Good God! What's all this about? A veritable conspiracy of beasts. Here, where we're so tranquil! We must mount an investigation, demand reports, and produce them. What do you think of this business, Saumaître?

The perfect secretary replied, deferentially: "It seems to require attention."

"Come in!" shouted Parmesif.

A black manservant came in, with several telegrams in his hand. The Lieutenant-Governor opened them anxiously. He read aloud:

"From Najalé: *Maritime Commissioner to Lieutenant-Governor. Conspicuous rain of bird feathers on coast. Please telephone instructions.*

"From the Administration at Nyanga: *Administrative livestock herds victim general alopecia. Please send official veterinarian urgently.*

"From Mayouniba: *Rubber plantations in danger. General shriveling of district vegetation. Awaiting orders.*

"From Lastourville: *Epidemic in park. Ostriches deplumed. Telegraph advice.*

"And from the plantations of Franceville: *Banana-trees suffering. Coconut-palms dying. Send help urgently.*"

The pale Madame Parmesif said: "The coconut-palms? The banana-trees? Oh!"

"Yes," said her husband, whose face was crimson. "The plants are joining in now. Damn it, Saumaître, what does it all mean?"

"I don't know, sir."

Behind the door, however, loud voices were raised. Two black men were arguing bitterly.

"No see Massa Tenant-gov'nor!" declare the butler.

"Me haf talk him urgent!" protested another voice, which Parmesif recognized as that of one of his old farmers."

A white-haired native came in, with his peaked straw hat in his hands. He was dressed up, wearing a blue jacket, khaki trousers, and a red cretonne cravat; yellow gloves compensated for the grey nudity of his feet. There was a shiny watch-chain in his waistcoat, but no watch. Without any preamble, he began: "Mass gov'nor, you cattle is losing dey skin."

"Their skin? Jibber-jabber! Their hair, you mean?"

"No, no. Dey hair already gone. Now dey skin is fallin... like dis." And the old man demonstrated by detaching a long strip of epidermis from his arm.

"Oh! What! Saumaître, telephone Monsieur Réminiscent—tell him to come and see me immediately."

"Very well."

While his secretary strode stiffly to the telephone, Parmesif set his elbows on the balcony of the veranda. He could see his daughter and her companion immobile in the garden, contemplating the ground as if petrified. Their attitude alarmed him, but his alarm increased while he mechanically directed a circular glance outside.

He called his wife. "Come and look at this, dear!"

Madame Parmesif hurried to his side.

"Look at the trees," he continued. "Look! Our beautiful magnolia: don't the leaves seem to you to have dried up, as if they'd been burned?"

"Yes," she said, in a choked voice. "Neither its leaves, not those of the other trees, have their natural tint any longer. One might think that they were dying, that they were shriveling up fatally. Oh, my dear, extraordinary things are happening around us. And what's the matter with Lotte and Sokota?"

She called to her daughter. The child raised her head and threw herself upon the bosom of the old black woman, tearfully. She was clutching a handful of dry grass. Very anxiously, Madame Parmesif said: "Come here right away!"

They hurried over, and little Lotte, her face flooded with tears, held out a bunch of yellowed flowers to her mother.

"Look what's become of them, Mama!"

Indeed, the flowers, which had been alive, colorful and odorous a day earlier—even an hour earlier—were no longer anything but specters of their former selves, devoid of brightness or perfume.

"Is like dat ever'where, de flow," said Sokota. "Is all sick, gwin to die."

"Gustave, Gustave—I'm frightened!"

Parmesif gestured to his wife to shut up, for their daughter was looking at them in terror. He promised the child a large coconut, and she left, consoled. Left alone with Madame Parmesif, he said: "Do you want to drive the child out of her mind?"

"I'm terrified myself," she replied.

In an agitated voice, he went on: "Calm down. All these fantastic phenomena must have a causal explanation. Anyway, here's the vet."

II. Réminiscent's Diagnosis

The official veterinarian, Monsieur Réminiscent, arrived at a trot, sweating and out of breath. He was the Lieutenant-Governor's neighbor, and while bending down to kiss Madame Parmesif's sadly-extended hand, he explained that he had escaped between two consultations. He was a short stout man with a black goatee and a ruddy and acne-ridden complexion, obviously a drinker. A fan woven from little wrinkles spread out from each of his little eyes; he rolled his rs as if he were pulverizing bricks.

"Excuse me," he said, "for only staying a moment. My office has been invaded. Apart from my assistant, my wife and my three daughters, I have my niece, Aunt Anaïs and the son of the fruiterer who works in my office pounding pomades and mixing distempers…"

"Well, in a word, Monsieur Réminiscent, can you explain to us…are we dealing with an epidemic?"

"Not exactly—an epizootic disease."

"All right. Do you know that it extends much further than you think? I have reports, letters and telegrams here; it's affecting almost the whole colony."

"No!"

"It's therefore necessary to take immediate measures—but in order to take them, we need to know the cause…"

"I've found it."

"Oh, do tell us!" begged Madame Parmesif.

"Well, here it is: the skin of the infected animals is falling off in strips and sheets; it's a progressive desquamation, in consequence of a sort of molting."

"What?"

"Well, we're in serpent territory. Large and small, they're abundant in the country, and even in the city. No longer ago than yesterday, I found a grass snake asleep on my doormat. Now, we're in the season when snakes shed their skin; that molting has become contagious, that's all."

A silence veiled by amazement greeted this revelation. The audience reflected. Monsieur Saumaître, with a great deal of courteous reverence, objected: "It would be the first time…"

"Perhaps—but in matters of science, it's necessary not to despair of anything. This epizootic disease leads me to infer that molting, in snakes, is microbial in origin—and the molt microbe has just turned noxious. Some animals must have consumed shreds of snakeskin left in corners. They've molted in their turn. Others have eaten their skin—or even absorbed contaminated pellicles without eating them, via the dust in the air or in some other way.

"You're not unaware that, for example, scarlet fever is contagious in humans during the season of desquamation. The molt is evidently an analogous sort of fever, for it's accompanied in animals, to begin with, by an elevation of temperature and a congestion of the pharynx. It only remains to identify the molt microbe, for which I have already reserved a name: *Bacillus reminiscens*. Now, this infinitely small organism has revealed itself to be all the more virulent in taking effect for the first time. That's the cause of the lightning spread of the epizootic condition. I've made up lotions and unguents: makeshift therapies. What we need is a serum, then a prophylactic vaccine. We shall find them. It's an important matter." And he clicked his heels joyfully.

"But what about the birds?" said Madame Parmesif.

"Birds scavenge, pecking the ground. Besides, don't forget that some birds also molt."

"They lose their feathers, not their skin!"

"A difference of degree, a question of more or less. Here's something that will convince you. I've made use of the experimental method, highly recommended in science. I took two canaries; to one, I gave snakeskin, via the beak; to the other, nothing. The experimental canary lost its feathers and its skin twice as fast as the control canary. It's peremptory. Have you any sick animals here?"

"First of all, there's poor Top here," sighed Madame Parmesif. "Look, he's almost hairless…"

"Indeed. It's not pretty. And his skin is starting to come away too. Perfect. Same treatment as the comrades: applications of my lotion, *reminiscine.* For the larger animals, Monsieur le Gouverneur, use a brush to wash them with *reminiscol*, my liniment. You can obtain these products from me."

"No internal remedy?"

"A little later, a few good purges, Monsieur le Gouverneur. Would you excuse me, Madame? I have to attend to my fellow citizens."

"Just a moment. What about the plants? How do you explain their withering?"

"That's not within my competence—you'll have to ask a botanist. Personally, I think it might be due to the depredations of an insect analogous to *Phylloxera*, which I'm not qualified to discover. On which note…"

He bade farewell.

"Shall we have the pleasure of seeing you this evening?" asked Madame Parmesif.

"I shall try to escape briefly, my dear Madame. No one has been talking about anything but your reception for a week. I shall try to put in an appearance."

"Alas," she said, plaintively, "I fear that these events do not bode well."

"So far as I'm concerned, I don't deplore them," the veterinarian replied. "Be tranquil, dear Madame. Your *soirée* will be brilliant."

The general opinion, after his departure, was that Monsieur Réminiscent was becoming unbearable, but that one had to smile at him, since he had suddenly become the arbiter of destiny in Libreville and its surrounds.

III. The Governor's Soirée

As night fell, however, even more serious news pushed public concern with the mysterious malady of plants and animals into the background, for the epidemic had taken a further leap: it had begun to attack human beings—colored people, fortunately. A number of natives had suddenly begun to lose their skin, and there was a discordant concert of groans throughout the city. In response to entreaties, the sorcerers were selling strong liquor and organizing sacred dances, for whose favorable effects the participants waited in vain. That evening, therefore, when the elite of Librevillean society met at the Lieutenant-Governor's house, the only subject of conversation was the dread of seeing the malady afflict white people and suddenly experiencing, at ten o'clock or thereabouts, the terror of knowing that the white race had been contaminated in its turn.

In fact, while the guests savored iced syrups in the delightfully starry night, listening to the tenor Caruso in phonographic form, the police captain—who was twirling his moustache while flirting with the postmaster's wife—had a feeling that the moustache in question had come away in his hand. It had—and that distinguished officer was not the only victim of such a sinister accident. In the course of that memorable soirée, the epidermis of every guest began to denude itself, to varying degrees but appreciable in every case.

119

Monsieur Pitourin-Mocquard, the president of the Court, who was talking about literature with Madame Parmesif, suddenly found that a tuft of his beautiful beard had become detached from his chin, and was scattered over his waistcoat and trousers. As for Madame Parmesif, while trying to extract a hairpin from the edifice of her coiffure, she also pulled away, without the slightest difficulty, a handful of her golden hair. Some people lost their eyelashes, others an eyebrow or two, others their bodily hair—and everyone realized that it hardly mattered where the malady first exhibited itself in any individual case; experiment proved that the enigmatic alopecia was rapidly becoming total.

It seemed certain that the loss of hair would be succeeded by a period of desquamation. This lamentable prospect distressed the most highly-placed hearts. Only Monsieur Parmesif, habitually clean-shaven and already bald, conserved his self-composure, as befit a leader of men. He calmly interrogated, not the veterinarian—who had abruptly become a dull nonentity—but Dr. Columat, the city's leading physician.

Amid a group of listeners hanging on to his every word, the latter replied: "I don't understand it at all. This story of contagion from the molting of snakes is, of course, utterly grotesque. I'm inclined to think that we're the victims of a virulent dermatosis, probably of parasitic origin. Is it a kind of leprosy? Is it a blood-infection? Is it the effect of a trypanosome? Is it...?"

He was interrupted by one of his listeners, a retired ship's captain and a distinguished naturalist. "Excuse me, Doctor, but one fact ought to be noted whose omission might corrupt any hypothesis. Concurrently with ours, a contagious infection is corroding plants, producing parallel effects. The light of these electric lamps is sufficient to show us the ravages produced: the leaves on the trees are curling up, as if burnt; those fleshy plants, hitherto so plump, are flattened, as if emptied out; these flowers, blooming vividly yesterday, are now faded and sickly, and will be dead tomorrow. Why?"

This interruption only served to increase the general anxiety. Everyone now sensed that a single unknown and deadly influence was extending over both kingdoms of nature throughout the Gabon.

"And what do you conclude, Monsieur?" the physician asked the naturalist.

"I conclude, Doctor, that this is not a matter of parasitic manifestation—and the hypothesis I offer far surpasses yours in amplitude. I suspect that the air of the Gabon is presently subject to a chemical modification—that the atmosphere in which we are all plunged contains some unknown new gas which, without destroying life itself, is harmful to living tissues. In my opinion, we should not even be talking about contagion. If a storm bursts and we are all wet, does that mean that rain is contagious? Oh, my God...!"

While speaking, the naturalist had been rubbing his cheeks rather vigorously, and that gesture had just ripped away one of his fine side-whiskers.

"Hair today," he said, sadly, "tomorrow the epidermis, the dermis the day after. It could be that within a week, this corrosive gas will make us all, beasts and humans alike, into pitiful flayed creatures."

A woman fainted. The reception ended with lugubrious farewells.

Once he was alone with his secretary, the Governor declared: "We must telegraph the Ministry."

The composition of an explicit dispatch kept them up all night.

IV. The Peeled Equator

The next day the citizens abroad in Libreville only recognized one another with the greatest difficulty. To avoid the scarcely attractive appearance of partial depilation, men had shaved off their beards and moustaches. It was as if an army of actors had taken possession of the city, to the exclusion of all other inhabitants. Alone in the midst of public distress, the wigmakers were walking on air. They could not meet demand, and became insolent—which, for the favored individuals, save for a few honorable exceptions, constituted the greatest satisfaction in the world.

At 10 a.m., Monsieur Parmesif was still asleep, worn out by fatigue. All night long, he had been subjected to the lamentations of his wife, who was already half-bald; young Lotte, in her turn, was losing her golden curls, her parents' silken pride and joy. When the Governor had negligently opened his eyes, however, and run them—distractedly at first, then with fascination—over a telegram from the Minister, he leapt out of bed, got dressed and raced to the office, where Monsieur Saumaître was waiting for him, as hairless and shiny as an egg.

"Read this!" cried Parmesif.

And Monsieur Saumaître read:

Same phenomena observed in Congo, English East Africa, Singapore, Borneo, Brazil. Colombia. International investigation begun. Cause of epidemic still unknown. Keep population calm. Will telegraph instructions as soon as possible.

The two men looked at one another in amazement.

"In that case," Parmesif exclaimed, spinning a little terrestrial globe, "it's the entire equator that's peeling!"

After reflection, Monsieur Saumaître replied: "The entire equator is, indeed, peeling."

They sank into meditation. They visualized the Earth, effectively girdled around its zero degree of latitude by peoples of the most disparate sorts, but equally terrified by the common peril. At the same time, they estimated that, if the doctor's hypothesis was false, the naturalist's was insufficient, for it seemed impossible to them that the terrestrial atmosphere should be contaminated

121

uniquely around the perimeter corresponding to the globe's greatest circumference. Why there? Why not elsewhere?

Other distressing news reached them; vessels that had been sailing for several days in the vicinity of the equator were reaching port with their crew and passengers losing their skins; it seemed that their maritime voyage had accentuated the effects of the mysterious malady. In some voyagers, the skin was crumbling into dust, in others it was coming away in shreds. Their despair appeared to be attenuated when they learned that the same disease was ravaging land-dwellers—and it really was a matter of ravaging now, for the epidemic, whose initial effects had seemed more ridiculous than dangerous, soon took on a manifest character of gravity.

Some people fell victim to intense nervous afflictions; many field workers were subject to a weakening of their sight, and to lesions in the eye that were sometimes manifest as cataracts. In many cases, the spleen seemed to be affected; it diminished in volume and became spongy. Phenomena of rapid consumption were observed in children. Many of them displayed profound lesions in the skin comparable to burns, painless but destructive of the tissues.

As for the vegetation, it was reminiscent of an autumn in Tibet after a hot summer: the reddened foliage of the trees hung down miserably, or was strewn funereally over the ground. It seemed that the universal malady was enveloping the peeling equator like a devouring sash, some vast cousin of the shirt of Nessus—and an intolerable anguish consumed all the inhabitants of the globe's torrid region.

V. The Scourge Spreads

For the Equator, the initial seat of the epidemic, already only constituted a minor part of the contaminated regions. The scourge was not only gaining in vigor but also in extent, and its stain was spreading implacably toward the temperate zones of both hemispheres.

A month after its appearance, the "universal leprosy" encircled the entire ring extended between the Tropic of Cancer and the Tropic of Capricorn—and it was no longer mere lieutenant-governors and colonial officials who were agitatedly reporting by telegram to the metropolitan authorities; now it was the Metropolises themselves, the great civilized States of the planet's temperate zones, that were exchanging urgent messages.

The army of scientists was mobilized. This time, it was up to them, and them alone, to save human existence, if that were possible. That army, however, was not composed entirely of generals, and the collision of hypotheses only generated discussion, and no light. The enigma, it is true, was becoming more complicated, for the scourge was now exercising its influence excessively on inanimate objects. Thus, it had become impossible in the affected regions to take photographs; all plates and films, freshly taken out of their boxes, were found to be clouded in advance of their exposure to daylight. It was also impossible to make wireless telegraphy apparatus work—during the day, at least, for communication was reestablished at night. Why?

It was these particular perturbations, even more inexplicable than the others in the minds of the multitude, that drew the researches of the scientists in a new direction. By this time, Mexico, the United States, Morocco, Algeria, Arabia, Egypt, Persia, Hindustan and Tonkin—which is to say, all the countries in the Northern Hemisphere within the 30th degree of latitude—and the corresponding regions in the Southern Hemisphere, were prey to the scourge, whose violence was increasing every day.

In the equatorial regions deaths were multiplying, and the appearance of men and animals at the moment of death was as follows: epidermis completely hairless; skin ulcerated in the regions of the body most hidden from the Sun; intense conjunctivitis; blepharitis and cataracts. The cutaneous wounds did not manifest any tendency to heal.

Thus, on the one hand there was a progressive and continuous burning of organic tissues; on the other, a cessation by night of certain magnetic perturbations. The conclusion drawn from this assembly of facts by several scientific conferences was that the initial cause of the scourge must be attributed to the source of all heat and all light: the Sun.

It became, in fact, increasingly probable that some specific solar activity had entered into play—but what? The telescopes of all the observatories in the world were aimed at the star. Nothing abnormal was observed. It seemed to the astronomers of Paris and Uppsala that the sunspots, generally dark red in color, were turning blood-red—but they had not changed in their form, their number or their extent. Besides, their influence on the seasons, and particularly on the terrestrial temperature, was still debatable. The Academies, in public sessions, whose conclusions were distributed in official communiqués, declared that sunspots could not be causing any disease of the skin or of the cuticles of plants.

Meanwhile, the scourge continued its methodical and ineluctable progress.

VI. Monsieur Galfo

Now, it seemed to have been determined by destiny that Monsieur Parmesif, a tiny particle of humanity, would play an important role in this adventure of universal interest, either individually or in terms of his family. Abandoning the affairs to the colony to the hands of Monsieur Saumaître for a few weeks, on the Minister's authority, he followed the example of all the people in the affected regions who were able to move. He took his wife and daughter north, specifically to Neuilly-sur-Seine, the town of his birth, where he owned a small house.

France was still unaffected, but the minds of her people—like all others at similar latitudes—were singularly overexcited. Parmesif, who announced his imminent return to the Gabon among the circle of his acquaintances, was unanimously admired. The Minister promised him the Croix d'Officier de la Légion d'Honneur and as Saumaître was, after all, entirely competent, Parmesif decided to wait for a decrease in the epidemic before going back to Libreville. He followed the newspaper reports of the daily progress of the scourge with a sort of avid horror.

One afternoon, he was scanning the "latest" edition of the *Bonsoir* when he read:

One of our eminent young scientists, M. Stéphane Galfo, has today delivered a report on the scourge to the Académie des Sciences. The document remains secret, but a highly qualified authority has been able to assure us that it reveals the cause—and, in consequence, the remedy—of the "universal leprosy". The world will learn important things tomorrow.

The other evening newspapers carried near-identical articles.

"Galfo!" he said to his wife. "Isn't that...?"

"Yes!" she exclaimed. "Stéphane Galfo is one of my cousins—Uncle Victor's son. We were once very close..."

"Where does he live?"

"Wait a minute..."

Madame Parmesif went into her bedroom. She came back with a little address-book and found her husband with his hat already on his head. "If he hasn't moved," she said, "his address is 17A, Rue Herschel."

Parmesif bounded into the Avenue de Neuilly, and then into an automobile.

Galfo had not moved. Having rung three times on the threshold of the fourth-floor apartment occupied by his cousin by marriage, however, Parmesif received the response, from a burly and arrogant maid, that Monsieur Galfo was not seeing anyone. "You're not the first to come today, and you certainly won't be the last!"

Indeed, a gentleman who had just climbed the stairs stopped on the landing and asked for Monsieur Galfo.

The maid replied to both visitors: "No one. Monsieur is seeing absolutely no one; he's given orders."

"I beg your pardon," said Parmesif. "Here's my card. I'm his cousin, temporarily in Paris. I've come from the Gabon for urgent consultation. His cousin, be sure to tell him..."

The maid took Parmesif's card, with an expression of disgust and closed the door again. "I don't think," the latter said to the other visitor "that you have any chance of getting in."

"Yes I do, Monsieur—I'm the representative of an important scientific journal."

"Nothing to do with us," Parmesif declared. "Ah! Now we'll see!"

The door had opened again. Come in, you," the maid said to him.

"Madame, I…" said the representative.

"No, not you!" And she slammed the door violently.

"It's unfortunate," Parmesif pronounced, "that one can't be left alone in one's own home. Where is my dear cousin?"

The chambermaid introduced him into a small scantily furnished drawing-room. "Wait," she said, and went out.

Parmesif sat down in an old green plush armchair. Shortly afterwards, he saw a thin, pale fellow of about thirty come in. The newcomer had a long beard and a soft smile; the gaze of blue eyes seemed very refined and benevolent.

Parmesif threw himself into the young man's arms. "Galfo! My dear cousin!" He recounted, very rapidly, the story of his arrival in Paris with his family, and went on: "I'll get straight to the point. Later, I hope, you will fill me in about your life and work. I know that you're a scientist…"

"Since yesterday evening," said Galfo, smiling.

"Right! I'm no better informed than I am. My wife, your cousin, is desperate—bald, my dear friend, absolutely bald—and my daughter is also very ill. Is it really true that you have made a discovery?"

"Yes—yesterday. My report has been in the hands of the Dean of the Faculty of Sciences for a few hours. It will be made public tomorrow."

"Then tell me, quickly—what is the cause of the scourge?"

"My dear cousin," Galfo replied, calmly, "I cannot, in deference to the Dean, who has accepted my report, reveal any of my observations."

"Even to me—to me your cousin…?"

"My cousin is only one man. Besides, the peril will not have increased greatly in one more day. Nevertheless, informally, I recommend that you…"

VII. J. S. Barcklett

He interrupted himself. A noise of loud voices was resonating in the antechamber. The maid was shouting: "Nothing doing, I tell you! He's not seeing anyone."

A sonorous foreign accent replied: "But I want to see him. I have to!"

The maid began to shouted even louder, but abruptly fell silent. A moment later, she presented herself, rather shamefacedly. "This gentleman," she said "insisted so strongly…he's come from America."

"Whether from America or Asnières, I don't want to see anyone," he said, with gentle firmness.

Meanwhile, Parmesif had glanced at the card and read:

J. S. BARCKLETT
Philadelphia
U.S.A.

Galfo continued: "Some machine salesman—Americans are great producers."

Parmesif, who was thinking hard, cried: "I have it! Barcklett of Philadelphia! Either I'm much mistaken, or he's a multimillionaire."

"Definitely!" said the chambermaid—after which she bit her lip.

"I've seen his photograph," Parmesif continued. "I'll recognize him. Let him in, my boy—you've nothing to lose."

"All right," said Galfo.

When the maid had gone out, Parmesif added: "If Barcklett's put himself out, old chap, it's because it's an important business matter. He's a big financier, one of the richest owners in the Klondike…"

At that moment, a broad-shouldered individual with a round head, a ruddy face and a carefully shaped moustache dressed in a suit the color of tobacco made a rapid entrance.

"That's him!" Parmesif murmured to Galfo.

The American had not come in alone, though: he was followed by a young woman, whose beauty, complexion and slimness were ideal. She was clad in a white muslin dress, slightly off-the-shoulder, which displayed the nape of her gracious neck. Her cheerful smile, revealing dazzling teeth, lit up the little room.

The foreigner, his palm open, hesitated between the two men. "Monsieur Galfo?" In response to a movement from the scientist, he went on: "Delighted. J. S. Barcklett of Philadelphia here, and his daughter Winnie."

She smiled, archangelically. "Bonjour, Monsieur," she said, extended a slender and vigorous hand to the blushing Galfo.

"Introduce me," whispered Parmesif.

"Oh, sorry! My cousin, Gustave Parmesif, Lieutenant-Governor of the Gabon."

Parmesif bowed formally. Barcklett shook his hand, and continued, in incorrect but comprehensible French: "If you will permit, let's sit down. I'll explain why I'm here. My daughter and I have come for a short stay in Paris. Winnie is very interested in your literature, and I introduced myself this morning to the secretariat of the Faculty, in order to enroll her in Professor Poule's course on your Baudelaire…"

"Oh, I'm so fond of Baudelaire!" sighed the young woman, raising eyes like green lakes toward the ceiling.

"Then we took a walk through the Sorbonne, admiring the paintings and colored frescos. We passed in that manner from the Faculty of Letters to that of Sciences. There, on a staircase, I saw two lavishly decorated gentlemen talking animatedly. While examining a bas-relief, I lent an ear. One, who had long grey hair and a hooked chin…"

"The Dean," said Galfo.

"…was saying to the other, who had two noses—or rather, one nose with a double bump…"

"I know who you mean. Then…"

"…he said to him: 'This Galfo's report will produce a thunderbolt.' Yes, he said thunderbolt. And the other added: 'What a rush there'll be tomorrow…' They drew away. I didn't hear any more—but I remembered the name: Galfo. At the secretariat of the Faulty, I learned that you had a laboratory…"

"Of radiophysics, to be exact."

"But neither at the secretariat nor at your laboratory, which was locked, could I obtain your private address."

"Orders have been given to that effect."

"Well, I got your address all the same, like everything else I want—and here I am. Since there'll be a rush, there must be a product. You give me the name of the product right away, and this evening, I'll send out all the possible instructions. Tomorrow, I'll be the owner of large quantities, and tomorrow, at the same time. You'll get your hands on a check at the America Eagle, the amount of which I'm waiting for you to name."

While speaking, he fetched a checkbook and a pen out of his pocket.

Galfo remained nonplussed. Parmesif assumed an advantageous pose.

"What sum, Monsieur?" Barcklett repeated, his pen raised.

"Monsieur," Galfo replied, blushing again, "I'm not a businessman but a man of science. I can't sell you the name or the formula of a remedy, the knowledge of which will necessarily be entailed by that of the cause of the scourge. There will be nothing—absolutely nothing—secret, and in consequence, I do not consider that I have the right to sell you anything."

As he said this, Galfo received a jab in his side from Parmesif's elbow.

Winnie took up the thread: "Monsieur Galfo, what you say is very nice, and very French, but you must do as I ask. You're going to give my Papa the name of the remedy immediately, and I will write something on the check myself, which Papa will sign. There you are!" She matched words with action, held out the checkbook to her father, and placed the check on the table.

"No," Galfo protested, "that's not necessary." And, revealing what he would doubtless have kept quiet if Barcklett had come alone, he declared: "The remedy is lead."

"Lead?"

"Yes, Monsieur. I'll explain…"

"Don't bother. I don't have a minute to lose before giving my instructions. I'll buy all the lead available immediately. Winnie?"

"Papa?"

"Are you coming, child? You need to buy an entire library for Professor Poule's course."

"No, Papa. I've changed my mind. Poetry no longer interests me. I want to study radiophysics—with Monsieur Galfo, if he's agreeable…"

"If I'm agreeable! Oh, Mademoiselle!"

"When will you show me your laboratory? Tomorrow?"

"Of course, Mademoiselle—tomorrow."

Galfo stared for a long time at the door through which Winnie Barcklett had disappeared from view.

Meanwhile, Parmesif examined the check. "$5000," he said. "That's nice—which doesn't alter my opinion that you've been swindled. You should have obtained a contract of partnership with a share of the profits. Now, will you explain to me?"

"Tomorrow…" Murmured Galfo, as if transported by a dream.

And Parmesif could not dissipate his cousin's dreaminess.

VIII. A Sensational Report

In any case, his curiosity was satisfied—along with that of the entire world—the following morning. The newspapers had never appeared with such gigantic headlines:

UNIVERSAL ALOPECIA VANQUISHED.
ITS CONQUEROR STÉPHANE GALFO.

VICTORY OF FRENCH SCIENCE:
YOUNG SCIENTIST DEFEATS THE SCOURGE

MIND TRIUMPHS OVER MATTER
THANKS TO STÉPHANE GALFO'S DISCOVERY

There followed various paeans in praise of the master, in the Pindaric mode. Most of the papers also took it upon themselves to explain the discovery either by summarizing or by paraphrasing his report, in consequence offering murky enlightenment. Some more wisely limited themselves to reproducing the text. It was conceived as follows:

Monsieur le Doyen,

About a month ago, I was able to observe certain inexplicable perturbations in the functioning of the exceedingly sensitive apparatus comprising the radiophysics laboratory that you were kind enough to allocate to me.

At intervals that were initially widely spaced, but then became closer, they were abruptly deprived of their electric charges, with no apparent cause.

I became greatly troubled when, in the course of spectrographic research, I noticed the appearance of new lines in the solar spectrum—lines quite distinct from those studied by Frauenhofer and so completely mapped by Angström.

128

That fact put me on the track. Having charged an electroscope, I directed a ray of sunlight upon it I saw the gold leaf fall back almost immediately to the zero point of the scale. My conclusion was, therefore, that solar radioactivity had suddenly increased, in such a proportion that the effects would be manifest both rapidly and violently.

But why had the scourge begun to produce its effects at the Equator, which then extended toward the Poles? Evidently, because the Sun's ray fall vertically at the Equator, the increase in radioactivity was manifested more quickly there; as distances from the Equator increase, the rays fall more obliquely, by virtue of the well-known "cosine law," and are therefore less powerful. That is why the phenomenon, which, in reality commenced everywhere at the same time, appeared to spread from the Equator to the Poles. As for its effects, they are those, immensely amplified, of a source of "gamma rays."

It is known that among physical agents, these rays are in the first rank as regards their harmfulness; not content with acting at the surface, like heat, light and ultra-violet radiation, they act internally, by virtue of their property of traversing the various tissues of an organism to a greater or lesser depth. They have a pernicious effect on all living cells, especially the cells of certain particular organs, which are the genital organs, nerve-ganglions, white corpuscles and the skin. In brief, even at low doses, they provoke a premature senescence of all living cells—and, if the dose is sufficient, their definitive death.

Now, all the observed phenomena are evidently identical with those determined by gamma radiation. Not being a doctor of medicine, I will not enter into detail regarding the syndromes whose pathology I have only sketched out.

How can the peril be averted? The gravity of past, present and future accidents necessitates the creation, with the briefest possible delay, of all the known means of protection against solar radioactivity.

In the present state of our knowledge, there is one product, and one alone, that is completely opaque to gamma radiation: lead, whether isolated or in combination, in glass or crystal, canvas or rubber. In this regard, radiologists have shown us the way: they possess sufficiently complete protective apparatus. The defense of the hands, as is well-known, is achieved by means of leaded rubber gloves, that of the eyes by leaded glass spectacles, that of the body by aprons made out of leaded cloth. In our case, however, the dangerous radiations do not emerge from a source that can be channeled; they surround the interested parties in all directions, and there will have to be a considerable practical adaptation of existence to these new conditions—if, at least, as seems probable, humankind desires to continue to exist.

This is not the place to imagine the protective devices that will doubtless see the light of day in countless varieties. My purpose was merely to specify the origin of the scourge, thus to indicate the remedy.

It will be as well to utilize the devices in question as quickly as possible, for there can be no further doubt, at present, that the gamma rays have already begun their silent ravages upon the organisms of this country. I estimate that, if no precautions are taken, we shall have the first serious incidents to deplore within the next fortnight.

IX. The Run on Lead

Equity demands that it be noted that other radiologists had carried out analogous experiments at the same time as Monsieur Galfo, leading to identical conclusions, but they had formulated them less rapidly. The young scientist's priority being established, therefore, the new rays emitted by the Sun were named "Galfo rays." That was incontestably a source of illustration for the scientific hero, but no profit derived from it for him, nor to those to whom the scourge had, thus far, delivered honest benefits. Within a few hours, all the physicians, including the most specialized lost their entire clientele; pharmacists lamented beside their immense neglected stocks of lotions, depuratives and philodermic unguents. If Galfo's observations had not been irrefutable, several trades unions would have launched furious lawsuits against him. No one, however, undertook any such economic action, for they were prey to more pressing worries; it was, in effect, a matter of everyone procuring, without delay, the quantity of lead necessary to protect his life.

On the day when the panacea was revealed, the scourge had reached the 44th degree of latitude—which represented, for France, a line drawn almost directly between Morcenx and Puget-Théniers. In consequence, Toulouse was peeling, as were Mont-de-Marsan, Albi, Avignon and Nîmes. The run on lead therefore began, with lightning rapidity. "Run on lead" is not sufficiently precise; on the part of the masses, there was a race for available lead susceptible of furnishing the desired protection; and on the part of businessmen there was a run on the metal itself. In the space of a few hours, therefore, the run on lead reached vertiginous heights—heights all the more fantastic because the mineral deposits happened to be on the property of a few individuals and societies, which regulated the extraction of the primary material at their convenience. Thanks to the advantage he had over his peers, Barcklett was the largest owner of the precious metal, the Lead King.

In France, mines of cerussite and galena, the carbonates and sulphates from which lead is extracted, are situated in Brittany and Auvergne. In the short time available, Barcklett had only been able to purchase four—but he possessed one of them in America, where lead ores are rare. Above all, however, he was assured of the definite sale of the entire disposable production of his factories. In league with a few rich financiers, he soon achieved dominion over the run.

Before the crisis, the average price of lead had been about forty centimes a kilogram; within 48 hours it passed three francs. Undoubtedly, the trust-owners would have been able to let it go higher still, but they rightly feared the intervention of governmental powers in a matter of general concern.

For their part, the factory-owners formed cartels; in very little time, certain wholesalers built up enormous fortunes. All the installations that could be adapted to the metallurgy of lead were dedicated to that work, and a few days sufficed to modify the economics of human life completely.

X. The Age of Lead

It was individual initiative that first came into play. Every individual exerted his ingenuity to obtain effective protection for himself. All the sheets of lead that producers and merchants possessed were bought up, and the buyers remained huddled in their houses or sitting under sheets of lead all day long. These fortunate individuals were, inevitably, a tiny minority.

On the advice of the Académie of Sciences, urgently convened, the Government put up posters advising citizens to spend the day, as far as possible, in their cellars, the Sun's radioactivity being attenuated by walls and thwarted by layers of earth. It was, however, necessary to be lodged in buildings equipped with sufficiently deep cellars; this was not the case for the poorer classes and the mobile population. This is why deplorable excesses occurred; makeshift crews of diggers were not content to excavate subterranean shelters; they laid bare water and gas pipelines in order to take possession of the pipes, producing floods and explosions. Troops had to use force to limit the damage.

Fortunately, this convulsive period of incoherent individual efforts did not last long. Analogous scenes, more or less violent, having unfolded in all countries, the course of everyday transactions almost came to a standstill, and it was absolutely necessary to plan and then construct the necessary means of safe circulation from one state or region to another, as well as coming and going within the bounds of an individual city.

In the first place, a large number of locomotives and carriages were armored with thick sheets of lead, and the companies did their best to reduce traffic by day and increase nocturnal traffic. The crowding of the rails resulted in a series of nocturnal bottlenecks and accidents. The first consequence of the measures taken was, therefore, a transport crisis. Little by little, as they say, things piled up.

Maritime traffic was also slowed down considerably—even more so than terrestrial traffic, at least in the early days. As it was not possible for ships only to cross the oceans by night, it was necessary to bring all transoceanic vessels successively into dry dock, in order to cover their decks in layers of lead sufficient to protect the passengers. For some vessels this work changed the height of the flotation line and, in consequence, their stability, so it was necessary to modify their construction. Submarines were used for short journeys and for coastal trade, but they did not win the favor of the public. The attraction of protection by lead was such that, when one ship foundered, the story went around that a rich upstart who had had a suit made out of lead fabric, flatly refused to take it

131

off; he buckled his lifejacket over the top of it and, when he came into contact with the waves, inevitably sank like a stone.

Such were the first incidents of international circulation. They were reiterated for some time, but the cities adapted rapidly. Four days after the great revelation, lead fabric hats, coats and cloaks were already to be found in the stores, as well as lead gloves and footwear. That was, however, only a stopgap measure, firstly because the hastily fabricated garments and accessories were only of use to people of medium build, and secondly because, even in themselves, they represented such a weight that walking, or any movement at all, became extremely difficult. The hats weight about three kilos, as much as a veritable helmet, and the seven-kilo boots nailed feet to the sidewalk. The attire of a deep-sea diver, in the capacity of an "antiradioactive suit" became what a smock and trousers had formerly been to a workman, aerial everyday wear. Such costumes were, however, the privilege of the rich; the poor found themselves deprived. The result of that was the pillaging of boutiques, which was violently repressed.

The Government, very agitated, resolved to take general measures—but it did not know exactly what to do. Fortunately, its task was alleviated thanks to a Senor Lopez, a Spanish umbrella-merchant. The said Lopez had an idea, simple in principle, but which was deemed a stroke of genius and enjoyed spectacular success: the idea of a leaden parasol, which he named the "pararad."

This portable shelter ensured a relative protection—but the pararad was found to be somewhat impractical, for, constructed in haste on a massive scale, it could not be closed; it was, in sum, a heavy and voluminous mushroom, under which it was, strictly speaking, possible to walk along the street but which occasioned serious annoyance indoors. As it was larger than a single-batten doorway, it greatly complicated the business of passing from one room to another, and the spectacle of several members of the same family coming and going through their apartment under pararads, complaining and cursing when they met, was painfully comical. Besides, one entire category of human beings, even in the highest ranks of society, could not be equipped with them: children.

In fact, the manufacturers had not yet had the time to produce small pararads; the large ones were too heavy, and dragged down their terrified slender carriers when they fell. Babies also remained unprotected, for it was most uncomfortable to support a nursling and a pararad at the same time. To humanity's shame, some women abandoned the former in favor of the latter. A makeshift provision was devised: children under six were drawn along in small carriages covered by lead awnings, and they were maintained indoors beneath little lead-leaf roofs, and forbidden to move. This prohibition, which prevented them from engaging in their customary play, brought about an unprecedented epidemic of infantile melancholy.

An entire mass of living beings was still endangered, however: animals. They were interesting to the extent that they were useful to humans; it was therefore necessary to protect beasts of burden, farmyard animals and livestock.

The Chamber experienced stormy sessions. They began, of course, by covering the Bourbon Palace, the Senate, the Elysée Palace, the Banque de France and all administrative buildings with impenetrable leaden carapaces, the lives of administrative personnel being, in their eyes, the most precious of all. It was, however, also necessary to think about safeguarding that of the nation, especially in the persons of its soldiers and its children, for representatives without a nation no longer represent anything but themselves—which is to say, not very much, relatively speaking.

All the available lead was, therefore, requisitioned by the State, and the trusts had to surrender it. It was realized a little later that it would have been expedient to tax them before effecting the requisition, and long debates began in national assemblies in relation to that tax, without reaching any conclusion.

Meanwhile, the authorities did not remain inactive; taking inspiration from the pararad model, they ordered the construction of huge shelters equipped with leaden cupolas, underneath which markets could be held. They lead-lined hospitals, subsidized theaters and schools—but the protection of houses remained the responsibility of individuals. A multitude of lawsuits was launched between tenants and landlords, each party imputing to the other the duty of protecting rented accommodation and paying for that protection. In addition, some buildings collapsed, because they were unable to support the supplementary weight of the lead that had been abruptly inflicted upon them.

A question of equal gravity was that of lighting. To garnish windows with lead was to suppress light. The leaded glass from which radiologists' eyeshields were constructed was certainly available, but in very small quantity and at an extremely high price. Human beings enclosed in dark places during the day therefore illuminated their environments for several weeks with artificial light, which resulted in an excessive rise in the price of means of lighting. In this interval, an Italian chemist, Doctor Finoli, discovered the formula of a glass opaque to radioactivity but translucent; it was a silicate of lead, thorium and tin obtained by the fusion of specific fractions of pure sand, red lead, thorianite and stannic dioxide. The glass in question only permitted a blurred vision, but it permitted the revival of sunlit indoor existence. At the same time, the factories began to produce vast numbers of thin lead sheets cut to size, which served to paper the walls of continually-inhabited rooms, and the government introduced a wise measure; in order prevent monopolizers from covering more rooms in lead wallpaper than they needed to live, they instituted a ration-card giving each person the right to 4.9 square meters of protection, with a premium for numerous families—which was very popular. The system functioned well, save for a certain amount of black marketeering.

At the end of the day, however, social life mostly takes place outside private dwellings, so the clothing industry, under the pressure of necessity, made astonishing progress. Fabrics were woven rapidly in all colors—but all those colors, mixed with lead, retained dark shades, giving entire costumes a metallic aspect of the strangest effect.

Good tailors produced bespoke clothing not deprived of a massive elegance. For men, the initial fashion was for long raglan overcoats, bowler hats with broad curved brims that marked the face and neck from the Sun, lead gauntlets to hide the wrists and canvas shoes, for it had not been possible to combine lead and leather. For women, there were ample cloaks and hats of every shape profoundly enclosing the head—and it was rather amusing to see light ornaments, such as feathers, tulle and lace surmounting such heavy headgear.

It is also necessary to relate that headaches became endemic, especially among people obliged to circulate in confined spaces and travel underground, as on subway trains. In truth, nothing was more irritating than feeling crushed by the heat and the weight of clothing that was entirely unnecessary during the subterranean journey—but where and how could cloakrooms be installed? By virtue of that fact, underground railways lost a large fraction of a clientele that they had, on the contrary, expected to increase, since subterranean journeys offered full security. Reality often takes responsibility for giving the lie to the most logical inductions in such a manner.

If journeys in the open air regained favor, however, sedentary work in the same conditions was abandoned, as far as possible, for it was more agreeable to work underground, in the costumes of the past, than above ground in the new armor. That is why the jobs of sewer-workers miners and tunnelers became highly sought-after by the working classes; among commercial employees there was a marked preference for working in basements. These preferences resulted in considerable perturbations of wage-scales, in consequence of abrupt and frequent strikes. As it was necessary, though, in the final analysis, to seek work where it was to be found, the conditions of proletarian existence were not greatly modified.

On the other hand, that of the leisured class was completely transformed. Its members almost never went out any more by day; social life became primarily nocturnal. Elegant beauties could not reconcile themselves to putting on such heavy apparel. They remained seated or lying down until nightfall beneath magnificent lead awnings provided by their admirers; in cases of urgency they climbed into armored automobiles and were driven to the shops or pleasure spots by chauffeurs liveried in lead. The fashion was established of going to dinner in the cellars of fashionable restaurants; there, amid wine-racks full of bottles sparkling in the illumination, between varnished tuns and hogsheads, on carpets of fine sand, refined guests sat down before the most delicate foodstuffs, not without having selected for themselves, directly from the racks—that was the fad of the moment—the wines that they would drink.

In the streets, the general appearance of passers-by, which had at first been that of pachyderms, gradually became, thanks to the ingenuity of tailors and couturiers, that of gigantic insects: cloaks of every sort, very ample and darkly metallic in color, resembled the wing-cases of enormous beetles, especially among women, who further emphasized the resemblance with hats whose feathers were similar to antennae and thin legs similar to the feet of scarabs.

Automobile omnibuses were reminiscent of the military vehicles that had been named "tanks". Horses, whether in harness or mounted, were caparisoned in "plumbite," a thick leaden cloth that was solid and not very costly. Dogs—cherished pets, at least, were walked entirely covered in little leaden cloaks with four sleeves, which protected their bodies and limbs but had the inconvenience of inhibiting their capers. All in all, the general aspect of the streets, as much by virtue of the dark envelopes of living beings as by the leaden cladding of houses, became sad and grey.

Certain buildings, however, remained deprived of all protection longer than the rest: military barracks. Administrative formalities, projections, estimates and all sorts of conditions routinely slowed down the placement of protective sheathing. At the same time, a committee was studying the alternative project of a leaden uniform, which was followed by several others. The scientists were thus able to study at their leisure the subsequent effects of "radiopathy" on the soldiers: extreme irritability, intense anemia, loss of strength, disturbances of vision, loss of hair—including eyelashes, eyebrows and beards—and acute erythema, often accompanied by lesions in all the parts of the body exposed to solar radiation.

To ward off these disastrous consequences, all permissions compatible with concerns of national defense were granted. Military personnel were thus able to take shelter among civilians. One arm of the military gave the authorities particular anxiety: the cavalry. How could their mounts be maintained in a serviceable state? Mounted regiments were urgently reassembled in wine-growing regions, and the horses sent down into the immense cellars of the great producers. In the final count, the administration paid up for a million leaden helmets and cloaks, of a model that recommended itself by its heavy warrior-like grace.

The Ministry of Agriculture found itself facing problems at least as worrying. In the majority of communes, the insouciant peasants were not taking any protective measures. It required the balding and death of numerous animals to force their owners to utilize the lead sheets deposited in the town halls by the care of the prefects. Another question remained to be resolved; it was not only a matter of conserving the animals, but also their feed. Now, the herbage was perishing; the meadows once green and lush, were turning brown and developing immense bare patches, and the naked red earth presented the appearance of wounds in the scorched earth.

The destruction of vegetation constituted the worst disaster of all, for without plants, there would be no more animals, and without animals, no more humans. The idea that seemed the most practical was to build frameworks over large areas that could be roofed with leaded glass, and gather the livestock in these "sheltered pastures". Under the leaded glass the meadows survived; everywhere else, they stopped growing, and then began to die. As for the trees, there was no remedy. Thus, with the summer barely begun, an autumnal landscape was already in the process of dying—or, rather a landscape that was rugged, bleak and burned in appearance, as in the approaches to large deserts. It seemed that a leprosy issued from the abyss was slowly eating away the terrestrial flesh, all the way down to the stones that were its bones.

In the savage countries, the decimated populations embarked on merciless slaughter, everyone attributing the scourge to the malice of his neighbors. The policed nations were less inclined to accept it as destiny, and gradually contrived, by the solidarity of research and effort, to thwart its cruelty—but existence had become ponderous and grey. Humankind had been happy during the Age of Gold, active during the Age of Silver, bellicose during the Age of Iron. Now it became neurasthenic—and that was the Age of Lead.

XI. A Radiological Idyll

It would, however, be an exaggeration to claim that the whole world was unhappy. To begin with, those enriched by the scourge—the "leprosy profiteers," as some newspapers called them—almost all led an ecstatic life of feasts, balls and orgies. Then there were the philosophers, for whom the calamity formed a precious subject of meditation; the believers, to whom it appeared as an ordeal imposed by Heaven and necessary to salvation; and the men of science of every category, who "laid"[51]—according to the technical expression—communications of every sort. There were also those in love, for love, "invincible in combat," triumphs over all enemy forces.

Among the latter, amid the general distress, Winnie and Monsieur Galfo flourished. It will perhaps be remembered that the ravishing American had been overtaken by a sudden and immoderate taste for research in radiophysics. Entirely devoted to his speculations on the Bourse, Barcklett had left her completely at liberty, according to the transatlantic fashion. Winnie, therefore, frequented the young man's laboratory assiduously. Utterly disgusted with literature, she had enrolled at the Faculty of Sciences as an honorary auditor, purchased an intimidating stack of radiological treatises, and remained for long hours in her "scientific home," according to her own exquisite expression. There, she examined the apparatus, admired everything, and understood nothing.

Galfo found her adorable. Furthermore, alone with him, the young woman was scarcely at risk, either from the viewpoint of honor or that of health. Galfo was too honest a fellow to take the slightest liberty with regard to a woman,

---

[51] This metaphor does not translate; the French *pondre* (from the Latin *pono*, to lay) is used literally to mean "to lay an egg" but is also used metaphorically to mean "to write [creatively]," when the writing process in question is imagined to be awkward.

even a pretty one, without express encouragement; that eventuality being realized, Galfo was capable of protecting his laboratory and apartment fully. Barcklett had furnished him with an imperious superfluity of lead—it was the least he owed him. Thus, an idyll was secured between teacher and pupil, among various instruments, the names of which she asked with an apprehensive and curious smile.

"Oh, dear master, dear friend, will you tell me what that pretty little copper apparatus is, which resembles a photographic apparatus?"

"A spectroscope, Winnie."

"What is it for?"

"For examining the solar spectrum."

"Oh! I'm afraid!"[52]

"Don't worry. 'Spectrum' means a colored image of all the shades of the rainbow or a soap-bubble."

"I can look at it then?"

"Of course. Put your eye to that objective. The vertical stem is directed at the Sun. Can you see the lines of the spectrum?"

"Oh! How pretty it is! The ribbon of Iris! What about the Galfo rays—can I see them?"

"Certainly. Look to the left, at those dazzling red radiations, as if the shade were intended to evoke the profound burns that they cause..."

"Oh! Frightful! Show me something else..."

"This is a spectrograph. It's not sufficient to see the lines of the spectrum; it's necessary to conserve the trace. My spectrograph measures them and, by virtue of the adaptation of photographic apparatus, fixes the in black and in color. Look at this collection of prints..."

"Oh! Marvelous! Oh, dear Stéphane, how I love radiophysics! Show me more. There—what's that?"

With their fingers, and sometimes their arms, enlaced, they strolled tenderly over the rubber-lined floor of the laboratory...

"That, Winnie, is a radiosclerometer, which measures the penetration of radioactive rays; their penetrative force is appraised automatically by reading the graduated scale in front of which that little needle is moving. And this is Wilson's electrometer..."

"Our president?"

"No, but a man just as great. The electrometer is designed to register radiation; a gold leaf gets further away from or closer to this polished copper disk."

"Oh! Splendid! And all this works?"

"In normal conditions, marvelously. Presently, all my apparatus becomes worthless as soon as solar light reaches it, so it's all protected."

---

[52] This joke doesn't translate either; Winnie has misunderstood "*spectre solaire*" [solar spectrum] as "solar spectre."

"And this?"

"That's FitzHerald's polaristroboscope[53]... and here's the Coolidge bulb, the empress of bulbs, which permits the production of a quantity of X-rays unknown until today. American genius, you observe, has given rise to astonishing progress in radiophysics."

"Oh, how polite you are to tell me that, dear Stéphane!"

"Dear Winnie!"

A kiss united their lips—and if the tension and attraction of their souls could have been measured in units of electrical force, it would doubtless have sent the needle of the Thomson electrodynamometer crazy. They therefore made a mutual promise to unite themselves in the bonds of matrimony, and Winnie immediately started planning the furnishing of a leaden nest where their protected happiness might curl up amorously.

A shadow fell upon the scene, though; when Winnie revealed her intentions to Barcklett, the latter reacted as he would have done to a traveling salesman of sewing-machines.

"You can't marry that unprepossessing scientist, whose exact worth is my $5000—assuming that he still has them."

"He's worth every penny that he's earned for you, Papa."

"You're talking sentiment, child, and I'm talking business. It's not the same language."

"My language is that of the heart, Papa. Stéphane doesn't even have your $5000 any longer, for he spent them on sweets and cream cakes for me. He's a gallant man."

"A mighty imbecile. He'll never get rich. Making a deal without assuring himself of a percentage of my profits was a costly omission. The daughter of the Lead King can't marry the Prince of Fools."

"She will marry him."

---

[53] I have been content to contract Falk's "Fitz Herald" rather than substituting the likelier FitzGerald, because I cannot find any evidence that the Irish physicist George FitzGerald (1851-1901) invented anything that might be called a "polaristroboscope." The latter word does, however, produce one hit on Google, from a document presented to the Académie des Sciences, so Falk was not the first to coin it and might well have appropriated it from elsewhere. "Radiosclerometer" is also not unknown, although Falk presumably improvised that one for the purposes of Galfo's imagined research. With regard to subsequently mentioned apparatus, the new light bulb developed for General Electrics by William Coolidge was distinguished by its use of a "ductile tungsten" filament and did not produce abundant X-rays. William Thomson (later Lord Kelvin) did patent an electrodynamometer, although the invention is generally credited to Werner von Siemens, and Galfo would surely have had a more recent model.

"Don't count on it. I've got a magnificent match for you: the son of the Iced Fruit King..."

"He can drown himself in one of his vats!" cried Winnie. "I don't want your ices—I want my Galfo!"

He being stubborn and she obstinate, agreement was problematic.

"If that's the way it is," he concluded, "we're going back to Philadelphia on the next steamer."

XII. A Business Dinner

Sitting in the drawing-room of a sumptuous hotel, Winnie was smoking a cigarette dreamily. Barcklett was reading the evening papers. It was only 2 p.m., but as the wireless telegraph did not work by day, the major evening dailies had brought forward their printing times.

"There's a very interesting article in the Times," he told his daughter, "entitled *What of the Planets?* The reporter writes: *Astronomical observations reveal that solar radioactivity is not only affecting the Earth. Thus, Mars has changed color; it was red and has become green. The vegetation covering its surface, which formerly had a carmine-poppy tint, has doubtless been subject to Galfo radiation, for it has faded and withered, changing to the most lamentable greenness.* You ought to read it, having become a 'scientist'..." And he uttered a little snigger, which was apparently unwelcome, for his daughter turned her back on him, blowing out cigarette smoke forcefully.

"Ah! Ah!" Barcklett went on. "The run on the 'Winnie' is still going on. Your name had brought the mine good luck. I'll order further prospecting."

Without replying, the young woman looked out of the window, at a lower-class wedding procession: the traditional landaus were rolling slowing along, their thin horses fatigued by their leaden caparisons; as the weather was magnificent, the hoods were open, and seen room above, the entire wedding-party—groom, bride, relatives and guests—resembled a series of big bells set in pairs on the benches. The bride was only identifiable by the veil of classic muslin covering her lead hat; the couple's black-gloved hands were joined...

The young American sighed, and turned to her father. "Are you still brutally inflexible?"

"It's marvelous," he replied. "I no longer know how much money I have. The government's promising taxation. It will promise it until the end of the world—that's perfect. What?"

A gilt-edged hotel bellboy brought a folded piece of paper on a sliver tray.

"For you, Winnie," said Barcklett. "A telegram."

She opened it and read:

Beloved darling! I have just made an immense discovery. Can you come to the laboratory? My cousin Parmesif, who is with me, swears that our happiness is guaranteed. Come quickly, I beg you.

She rang, and the bellboy reappeared.

"My car."

The bellboy bowed and disappeared.

"Are you going out, Winnie?"

"Yes."

"We're dining at eight, don't forget—we're going to the Opéra. I'm going to the Club now."

He rang. The bellboy reappeared.

"My car."

The bellboy bowed and disappeared.

Twenty minutes later, Winnie was listening, with great delight, to Galfo's revelations.

She threw her arms around his neck. "I had a presentiment of something good, darling! You must dine with us...Monsieur Parmesif too. And the three of us will—how can I put it?—*have Papa where we want him.*"

"The situation is delicate in one respect," Parmesif opined. "Your father won't promise anything without reasoned explanations—and once the explanations have been given, will he still promise?"

Winnie replied, haughtily: "Papa has many faults, but he has the greatest quality of all: he's honest."

"That is also," Parmesif replied, gallantly, "the greatest of skills."

"For now," said Winnie, "I shall telephone my father to tell him that I'm bringing two guests."

Around a brightly-lit, flower-laden table, three guests in suits and the charming Winnie were consuming a choice meal. The tender flesh of admirable pullets swelled out, superabundantly stuffed with truffles.

Winnie launched the attack with vigor and simplicity. "Papa!"

"My child?"

"What do you say to this news: Monsieur Galfo is capable of making you sudden millions, or impoverishing you so sternly that we would be almost ruined?"

Galfo blushed. Parmesif smiled graciously. Barcklett, with his fists set solidly on the table, scarcely frowned, and replied: "That's certainly news. Well, if it can be proven, I'll offer Monsieur Galfo..."

"Your daughter, Papa?"

"No."

"Then he'll keep quiet, and you'll be ruined. You'll keep quiet, my love!"

"Yes," Galfo replied, coughing with emotion.

"May I be permitted, Monsieur," Parmesif put in, "to point out that my cousin Galfo is from an excellent family, that, in spite of his youth, he is famous, and that his science will one day..."

Winnie interrupted him. "Monsieur Parmesif, it's necessary not to discuss sentiment with Papa. Instead, dictate the terms of an agreement..."

"Very well," Parmesif went on, without seeming disconcerted—for the interruption had been planned in advance—"I propose to Monsieur your father the following formula: 'If Monsieur Galfo makes me a profit of so many dollars, I promise to give him my daughter.'" Addressing himself to Barcklett, he added: "That profit should be matched, I think, by a similar sum paid to my cousin."

"What profit?" asked Barcklett. "I want a million dollars, minimum."

Winnie shrugged her shoulders. "Make the contract out for two million, Papa—you see that we have nothing to fear. I add that if you refuse, dear Galfo will say nothing to you, but will talk to others—and the others will have you where they want you. There you are."

"All right," said Barcklett. "Two million. I'm listening. Talk."

"Very well, Monsieur," Galfo declared, in a voice whose assurance he tried to maintain. "Sell all your lead immediately. Tomorrow, its value will go down; the day after, it will go down even further, and within a week, it will be worthless."

"Why?"

"Because your stocks will become unnecessary, because the cruel Sun will become our benevolent Sun again, returning progressively to its normal activity."

"How? Explain!"

"This is how it is. After having observed an increasing perturbation of my measuring apparatus, and having tracked that effect to its maximum, I observed a few days ago that instead of continuing its ascent, the curve had rapidly turned downwards. It tended to become parallel to the time axis on the diagrams on which I inscribe the phenomenon on an hourly basis. Finally, this very morning, my measurements showed that the decrease of penetrating radiation is quite clear; the curve is declining slowly toward the abscissa."

Galfo fell silent. The American looked at him. After a moment's reflection, he replied: "I don't understand any of that—but it's not your explanation that's important: it's the fact."

He scribbled figures in his notebook, then shook Galfo's hand, saying: "Take my daughter. I'm off to the telephone."

XIII. Epilogue

The nightmare that had weighed upon the world gradually vanished. A month after Galfo's prediction, the Sun had lost all radioactivity and lead almost all its value. That sad metal took a long time to resume its normal course. Nevertheless, the effects of the scourge persisted among the afflicted organisms. A large number of human beings, until they died, no longer knew any but a diminished, painful life complicated by such accidents as dyspepsia or failing eyesight. A deficiency of white blood corpuscles became the rule among all those who had not protected themselves sufficiently; they were recognizable by their waxy pallor.

In sum, it is incontestable that an entire generation was sacrificed, to varying degrees—but what is a generation in the sequence of centuries? A wrinkle that is born, propagates and dies on the infinite and moving sea of time.

Of all the heroes of the faithful preceding narrative, only Monsieur Saumaître, the Lieutenant-Governor's elegant secretary, who had been ordered to remain at his post, was profoundly affected; the Galfo rays produced certain devastating consequences in him. Completely sterilized, the honest man decided not to marry the woman he loved, and languished and died shortly thereafter in the accursed Gabon, which he had never left. The sad end of that worthy official was, however, compensated by his superior's good fortune; Monsieur Parmesif received in France the high distinction that he might never have obtained far from the metropolis and nearer to the Sun; named Officier de la Légion d'Honneur, he was also promoted to the office of Governor of a lovely colony. To complete his happiness, his wife's hair grew again, sufficiently for her to wear a bob.

Galfo went to live in the United States, commissioned by the American government to set up the largest radiophysics laboratory in the world. Winnie became Madame Galfo. Barcklett, a manifest billionaire, now adores his son-in-law.

The moribund plants gradually recovered their vigor and beauty. All the creatures of nature rejoiced in concert, finally liberated from their burdensome terror—except for the fish, which the scourge had not attained, and which remained, in consequence, strangers to the universal delight.

The Age of Lead was over, well and truly finished. It was then that the military administration finally started distributing a million lead uniforms and helmets...

Maurice Leblanc: *The Tremendous Event*
(1920)

Le Formidable Événement [*The Tremendous Event*] *was first serialized in* Je Sais Tout *in 1920, then collected in book form by publisher Pierre Lafitte that same year.*

It was Lafitte who steered Maurice Leblanc (1864-1941) towards writing detective novels à la Conan Doyle's. After reading a few samples, Leblanc brought Laffite his first Arsène Lupin story for Je Sais Tout, *a magazine, which Lafitte had launched in 1904. Lafitte, a smart publisher, immediately saw the potential in the character and the rest is, as they say, history.*

Leblanc began his literary career as a journalist, contributing to Gil Blas, Le Figaro, Comœdia *and* Le Journal. *He had also written a few novels influenced by Guy de Maupassant and Gustave Flaubert. He was grateful to Lafitte for having helped him find his way, and dedicated his first collection of Lupin stories to him, writing "You put me on a road where I did not believe that I should ever venture."*

Lafitte had christened the imprint in which he published Leblanc's—and later, Gaston Leroux'—books "Extraordinary Adventures." The Tremendous Event *is, indeed, an "extraordinary adventure" in all the meanings of the term because it belongs to both the detective story and the* roman scientifique. *Leblanc was still clearly influenced by World War I, Thus, in the last chapter he shows Germany, without shame, offering an alliance to France to invade Great Britain. "Delenda Britannia!" Leblanc ends the novel with the signing of a pact between England and France in which they declare eternal friendship and found the basis of a United States of Europe. This conclusion appears to be somewhat optimistic in light of Brexit, when France and Germany now sit side by side!*

The Tremendous Event *begins as a sentimental novel, then turns into science fiction before settling into being almost a western. Indeed, Leblanc introduced "Cowboys and Indians" in this new "no man's land," whose presence he cleverly explains, in order to pen a story in the vein of Fenimore Cooper. All the subtleties of civilization, all social and moral conventions, vanish in favor of a return to primordial instincts, abuse of force, theft, plunder, and murders.*

J.-M.L.

AUTHOR'S NOTE

The tremendous event of the 4th. of June, whose consequences affected the relations of the two great Western nations even more profoundly than did the war, has called forth, during the last fifty years, a constant efflorescence of books, memoirs and scientific studies of truthful reports and fabulous narratives. Eye-witnesses have related their impressions; journalists have collected their articles into volumes; scientists have published the results of their researches; novelists have imagined unknown tragedies; and poets have lifted up their voices. There is no detail of that tragic day but has been brought to light; and this is true likewise of the days which went before and of those which came after and of all the reactions, moral or social, economic or political, by which it made itself felt, throughout the twentieth century, in the destinies of the world.

There was nothing lacking but Simon Dubosc's own story. And it was strange that we should have known only by reports, usually fantastic, the part played by the man who, first by chance and then by his indomitable courage and later still by his clear-sighted enthusiasm, was thrust into the very heart of the adventure.

To-day, when the nations are gathered about the statue over-looking the arena in which the hero fought, does it not seem permissible to add to the legend the embellishment of a reality which will not misrepresent it? And, if it is found that this reality trenches too closely upon the man's private life, need we object?

It was in Simon Dubosc that the western spirit first became conscious of itself and it is the whole man that belongs to history.

M.L.

Part One: William the Conqueror

I. The Suit

"Oh, but this is terrible!" cried Simon Dubosc. "Edward, just listen!"

And the young Frenchman, drawing his friend away from the tables arranged in little groups on the terraces of the clubhouse, showed him, in the late edition of the *Argus*, which a motorcyclist had just brought to the New Golf Club, this telegram, printed in heavy type:

Boulogne, 20 May. The master and crew of a fishing-vessel which has returned to harbor declare that this morning, at a spot mid-way between the French and English coasts, they saw a large steamer lifted up by a gigantic waterspout. After standing on end with her whole length out of the water, she pitched forward and disappeared in the space of a few seconds.

Such violent eddies followed and the sea, until then quite calm, was affected by such abnormal convulsions that the fishermen had to row their hardest to avoid being dragged into the whirlpool. The naval authorities are sending a couple of tugs to the site of the disaster.

"Well, Rolleston, what do you think of it?"

"Terrible indeed!" replied the Englishman. "Two days ago, the *Ville de Dunkerque*. Today another ship, and in the same place. There's a coincidence about it..."

"That's precisely what a second telegram says," exclaimed Simon, continuing to read:

The steamer sunk between Folkstone and Boulogne is the transatlantic liner Brabant, of the Rotterdam-America Co., carrying twelve hundred passengers and a crew of eight hundred. No survivors have been picked up. The bodies of the drowned are beginning to rise to the surface.

There is no doubt that this terrifying calamity, like the loss of the Ville de Dunkerque *two days ago, was caused by one of those mysterious phenomena which have been disturbing the Straits of Dover during the past week and in which a number of vessels were nearly lost, before the sinking of the* Brabant *and the* Ville de Dunkerque.

The two young men were silent. Leaning on the balustrade which runs along the terrace of the clubhouse, they gazed beyond the cliffs at the vast circle of the sea. It was peaceful and kindly innocent of anger or treachery; its near surface was crossed by fine streaks of green or yellow, while, farther out, it was flawless and blue as the sky and, farther still, beneath the motionless cloud, grey as a great sheet of slate.

But, above Brighton, the sun, already dipping towards the downs, shone through the clouds; and a luminous trail of gold-dust appeared upon the sea.

"*La perfide!*" murmured Simon Dubosc. He understood English perfectly, but always spoke French with his friend. "The perfidious brute: how beautiful she is, how attractive! Would you ever have thought her capable of these malevolent whims, which are so destructive and murderous? Are you crossing to-night, Rolleston?"

"Yes, Newhaven to Dieppe."

"You'll be quite safe," said Simon. "The sea has had her two wrecks; she's sated. But why are you in such a hurry to go?"

"I have to interview a crew at Dieppe to-morrow morning; I am putting my yacht in commission. Then, in the afternoon, to Paris, I expect; and, in a week's time, a cruise to Norway. And you, Simon?"

Simon Dubosc did not reply. He had turned toward the clubhouse, whose windows, in their borders of Virginia creeper and honeysuckle, were blazing with the sun. The players had left the links and were taking tea beneath great many-colored sunshades planted on the lawn. The *Argus* was passing from hand to hand and arousing excited comments. Some of the tables were occupied by young men and women, others by their elders and others by old gentlemen who were recuperating their strength by devouring platefuls of cake and toast.

To the left, beyond the geranium-beds, the gentle undulations of the links began, covered with turf that was like green velvet; and right at the end, a long way off, rose the tall figure of a last player, escorted by his two caddies.

"Lord Bakefield's daughter and her three friends can't take their eyes off you," said Rolleston.

Simon smiled:

"Miss Bakefield is looking at me because she knows I love her; and her three friends because they know I love Miss Bakefield. A man in love is always something to look at; a pleasant sight for the one who is loved and an irritating sight for those who are not."

This was spoken without a trace of vanity. For that matter, no man could have possessed more natural charm or displayed a more alluring simplicity. The expression of his face, his blue eyes, his smile and something personal, an emanation compounded of strength and suppleness and healthy gaiety, of confidence in himself and in life, all contributed to give this peculiarly favored young man a power of attraction to whose spell the onlooker readily surrendered.

Devoted to outdoor games and exercises, he had grown to manhood with those young postwar Frenchmen who made a strong point of physical culture and a rational mode of life. His movements and his attitudes alike revealed that harmony which is developed by a logical training and is still further refined, in those who comply with the rules of a very active intellectual existence, by the study of art and a feeling for beauty in all of its forms.

For him, indeed, as for many others, liberation from the lecture-room had not meant the beginning of a new life. If, by reason of a superfluity of energy, he was impelled to give much of his time to games and to attempts at establishing records which took him to all the running-grounds and athletic battlefields of Europe and America, he never allowed his body to take precedence of his mind. Every day, come what might, he set apart the two or three hours of solitude, of reading and meditation, which the intellect requires for its nourishment, continuing to learn with the enthusiasm of a student who is prolonging the life of the school and university until events compel him to make a choice among the paths which he has opened up for himself.

His father, to whom he was bound by ties of the liveliest affection, was puzzled:

"After all, Simon, what are you aiming at? What's your object?"

"I am training."

"For what?"

"I don't know. But an hour strikes for each of us when we must be fully prepared, well equipped, with our ideas in good order and our muscles absolutely fit. I shall be ready."

And so he reached his thirtieth year. It was at the beginning of that year, at Nice, through Edward Rolleston, that he made Miss Bakefield's acquaintance.

"I am sure to see your father at Dieppe," said Rolleston. "He will be surprised that you haven't returned with me, as we arranged last month. What shall I say to him?"

"Say that I'm stopping here a little longer... or no, don't say anything... I'll write to him... to-morrow perhaps... or the day after..."

He took Rolleston's arm:

"Tell me, old chap," he said, "tell me. If I were to ask Lord Bakefield for his daughter's hand, what do you think would happen?"

Rolleston appeared to be nonplussed. He hesitated and then replied:

"Miss Bakefield's father is a peer, and perhaps you don't know that her mother, the wonderful Lady Constance, who died some six years ago, was the granddaughter of a son of George III. Therefore she had an eighth part of blood royal running in her veins."

Edward Rolleston pronounced these words with such unction that Simon, the irreverent Frenchman, could not help laughing:

"The deuce! An eighth! So that Miss Bakefield can still boast a sixteenth part and her children will enjoy a thirty-second! My chances are diminishing! In the matter of blood royal, the most that I can lay claim to is a great-grandfather, a pork-butcher by trade, who voted for the death of Louis XVI! That doesn't amount to much!"

He gave his friend a gentle push:

"Do me a service. Miss Bakefield is alone for the moment. Keep her friends engaged so that I can speak to her for a minute or two: I shan't be longer."

Edward Rolleston, a friend of Simon's who shared his athletic tastes, was a tall young man, too pale, too thin and so long in the back that he had acquired a stoop. Simon knew that he had many faults, including a love of whisky and the habit of haunting private bars and living by his wits. But he was a devoted friend, in whom Simon was conscious of a genuine and loyal affection.

The two men went forward together. Miss Bakefield came to meet Simon, while Rolleston accosted her three friends.

Miss Bakefield wore an absolutely simple wash frock, without any of the trimmings that were then the fashion. Her bare throat, her arms, which showed through the muslin of her sleeves, her face and even her forehead under her hat were of that warm tint which the skin of some fair-haired women acquires in the sun and the open air. Her eyes were almost black, flecked with glittering specks of gold. Her hair, which shone with metallic glints, was dressed low on the neck in a heavy coil. But these were trivial details which you noted only at leisure, when you had in some degree recovered from the glorious spectacle of her beauty in all its completeness.

Simon had not so recovered. He always paled a little when he met Miss Bakefield's eyes, however tenderly they rested on him.

"Isabel," he said, "are you determined?"

"Quite as much as yesterday," she said, smiling; "and I shall be still more so to-morrow, when the moment comes for action."

"Still... We have known each other hardly four months."

"Meaning thereby?..."

"Meaning that, now that we are about to perform an irreparable action, I invite you to use your judgment..."

"Rather than listen to my love? Since I first loved you, Simon, I have not been able to discover the least disagreement between my judgment and my love. That's why I am going with you to-morrow morning."

"Isabel!"

"Would you rather that I left to-morrow night with my father? On a voyage lasting three or four years? That is what he proposes, what he insists upon. It's for you to choose."

While they exchanged these serious words, their faces displayed no trace of the emotion which thrilled the very depths of their beings. It was as though, in being together, they experienced that sense of happiness which gives strength and tranquility. And, as the girl, like Simon, was tall and bore herself magnificently, they received a vague impression that they were one of those privileged couples whom destiny selects for a life more strenuous, nobler and more passionate than the ordinary.

"Very well," said Simon. "But let me at least appeal to your father. He doesn't know..."

"There is nothing he doesn't know, Simon. And it is precisely because our love displeases him and displeases my stepmother even more that he wants to get me away from you."

"I insist on this, Isabel."

"Speak to him, then, Simon, and, if he refuses, don't try to see me to-day. To-morrow, a little before twelve o'clock, I shall be at Newhaven. Wait for me by the gangway of the steamer."

He had something more to say:

"Have you seen the *Argus*?"

"Yes."

"You're not frightened of the crossing?"

She smiled. He bowed over her hand and kissed it and said no more.

Lord Bakefield, a peer of the United Kingdom, had been married first to the aforesaid great-grand-daughter of George III. and secondly to the Duchess of Falconbridge. He was the owner, in his own right or his wife's, of country-houses, estates and town properties which enabled him to travel from Brighton to Folkstone almost without leaving his own domains. He was the distant player who had lingered on the links; and his figure, now less remote, was appearing and disappearing according to the lay of the ground. Simon decided to profit by the occasion and to go to meet him.

He set out resolutely. In spite of the young girl's warning and though he had learnt, from her and from Edward Rolleston, something of Lord Bakefield's true character and of his prejudices, he was influenced by the memory of the cordial welcome which Isabel's father had invariably accorded him hitherto.

This time again the grip of his hand was full of geniality. Lord Bakefield's face—a round face, too fat for his thin and lanky body, too florid and a little commonplace, though not lacking in intelligence—lit up with satisfaction.

"Well, young man, I suppose you have come to say good-bye? You have heard that we are leaving?"

"I have, Lord Bakefield; and that is why I should like a few words with you."

"Quite, quite! You have my attention."

He bent over the tee, building up, with his two hands, a little mound of sand on whose summit he placed his ball; then, drawing himself up, he accepted the brassy which one of his caddies held out to him and took his stand, perfectly poised, with his left foot a little advanced and his knees very slightly bent. Two or three trial swings, to assure himself of the precise direction; a second's reflection and calculation; and suddenly the club swung upwards, descended and struck the ball.

The ball flew through the air and suddenly veered to the left; then, curving to the right after passing a clump of trees which formed an obstacle to be avoided, it fell on the putting-green at a few yards' distance from the hole.

"Well done!" cried Simon. "A very pretty shot!"

"Not so bad, not so bad," said Lord Bakefield, resuming his round.

Simon did not allow himself to be disconcerted by this curious method of beginning an interview and broached his subject, without further preamble:

"Lord Bakefield, you know who my father is, a Dieppe ship-owner, with the largest merchant-fleet in France. So I need say no more on that side."

"Capital fellow, M. Dubosc," said Lord Bakefield, approvingly. "I had the pleasure of shaking hands with him at Dieppe last month. Capital fellow."

Simon continued, delightedly:

"Let us consider my own case. I'm an only son. I have an independent fortune from my poor mother. When I was twenty, I crossed the Sahara in an aeroplane without touching ground. At twenty-one, I made the record for the running mile. At twenty-two, I won two events at the Olympic Games: fencing and swimming. At twenty-five, I was the world's champion all-round athlete. And mixed up with all this was the Morocco campaign: four times mentioned in dispatches, promoted lieutenant in the reserve, awarded the military medal and the medal for saving life. That's all. Oh no, I was forgetting: a Masters in letters, laureate of the Academy for my essays on the Grecian ideal of beauty. There you are. I am twenty-nine years of age."

Lord Bakefield looked at him with the tail of his eye and murmured:

"Not bad, young man, not bad."

"As for the future," Simon continued, without waiting, "that won't take long. I don't like making plans. However, I have the offer of a seat in the Chamber of Deputies at the coming elections, in August. Of course, politics don't much interest me. But after all... if I must... And then I'm young: I shall always manage to get a place in the sun. Only, there's one thing... at least, from your point of view, Lord Bakefield. My name is Simon Dubosc. Dubosc in one word, without the particle... without the least semblance of a title... And that, of course..."

He expressed himself without embarrassment, in a good-humored, playful tone. Lord Bakefield, the picture of amiability, was quite unperturbed. Simon broke into a laugh:

"I quite grasp the situation; and I would much rather give you a more elaborate pedigree, with a coat-of-arms, motto and title-deeds complete. Unfortunately, that's impossible. However, if it comes to that, we can trace back our ancestry to the fourteenth century. Yes, Lord Bakefield, in 1392, Mathieu Dubosc, a yeoman in the manor of Blancmesnil, near Dieppe, was sentenced to fifty strokes of the rod for theft. And the Duboscs went on valiantly tilling the soil, from father to son. The farm still exists, the farm *du Bosc*, that is *du Bosquet*, of the clump of trees..."

"Yes, yes, I know," interrupted Lord Bakefield.

"Oh, you know," repeated the younger man, somewhat taken back.

He intuitively felt, by the old nobleman's attitude and the very tone of the interruption, the full importance of the words which he was about to hear.

And Lord Bakefield continued:

"Yes, I happen to know... When I was at Dieppe last month, I made a few inquiries about my family, which sprang from Normandy. Bakefield as you may perhaps not be aware, is the English corruption of Bacqueville. There was a Bacqueville among the companions of William the Conqueror. You know the picturesque little market-town of that name in the middle of the Pays de Caux? Well, there is a fourteenth-century deed in the records at Bacqueville, a deed signed in London, by which the Count of Bacqueville, Baron of Auppegard and Gourel, grants to his vassal, the Lord of Blancmesnil, the right of administering justice on the farm du Bosc... the same farm du Bosc on which poor Mathieu received his thrashing. An amusing coincidence, very amusing indeed: what do you think, young man?"

This time, Simon was pierced to the quick. It was impossible to imagine a more impertinent answer couched in more frank and courteous terms. Quite baldly, under the pretense of telling a genealogical anecdote, Lord Bakefield made it clear that in his eyes young Dubosc was of scarcely greater importance than was the fourteenth-century yeoman in the eyes of the mighty English Baron Bakefield and feudal lord of Blancmesnil. The titles and exploits of Simon Dubosc, world's champion, victor in the Olympic Games, laureate of the French Academy and all-round athlete, did not weigh an ounce in the scale by which a British peer, conscious of his superiority, judges the merits of those who aspire to his daughter's hand. Now the merits of Simon Dubosc were of the kind which are amply rewarded with the favor of an assumed politeness and a cordial handshake.

All this was so evident and the old nobleman's mind, with its pride, its prejudice and its stiff-necked obstinacy, stood so plainly revealed that Simon, who was unwilling to suffer the humiliation of a refusal, replied in a rather impertinent and bantering tone:

"Needless to say, Lord Bakefield, I make no pretension to becoming your son-in-law just like that, all in a moment and without having done something to deserve so immense a privilege. My request refers first of all to the conditions which Simon Dubosc, the yeoman's descendant, would have to fulfil to obtain the hand of a Bakefield. I presume that, as the Bakefields have an ancestor who came over with William the Conqueror, Simon Dubosc, to rehabilitate himself in their eyes, would have to conquer something—such as a kingdom—or, following the Bastard's example, to make a triumphant descent upon England? Is that the way of it?"

"More or less, young man," replied the old peer, slightly disconcerted by this attack.

"Perhaps too," continued Simon, "he ought to perform a few superhuman actions, a few feats of prowess of world-wide importance, affecting the happiness of mankind? William the Conqueror first, Hercules or Don Quixote next?... Then, perhaps, one might come to terms?"

"One might, young man."

"And that would be all?"

"Not quite!"

And Lord Bakefield, who had recovered his self-possession, continued, in a genial fashion:

"I cannot undertake that Isabel would remain free for very long. You would have to succeed within a given space of time. Do you consider, M. Dubosc, that I shall be too exacting if I fix this period at two months?"

"You are much too generous, Lord Bakefield," cried Simon. "Three weeks will be ample. Think of it: three weeks to prove myself the equal of William the Conqueror and the rival of Don Quixote! It is longer than I need! I thank you from the bottom of my heart! For the present, Lord Bakefield, good-bye!"

And, turning on his heels, fairly well-satisfied with an interview which, after all, released him from any obligation to the old nobleman, Simon Dubosc returned to the clubhouse. Isabel's name had hardly been mentioned.

"Well," asked Rolleston, "have you put forward your suit?"

"More or less."

"And what was the reply?"

"Couldn't be better, Edward, couldn't be better! It is not at all impossible that the decent man whom you see over there, knocking a little ball into a little hole, may become the father-in-law of Simon Dubosc. A mere nothing would do the trick: some tremendous stupendous event which would change the face of the earth. That's all."

"Events of that sort are rare, Simon," said Rolleston.

"Then, my dear Rolleston, things must happen as Isabel and I have decided."

"And that is?"

Simon did not reply. He had caught sight of Isabel, who was leaving the clubhouse.

On seeing him, she stopped short. She stood some twenty paces away, grave and smiling. And in the glance which they exchanged there was all the tenderness, devotion, happiness and certainty that two young people, can promise each other on the threshold of life.

II. The Crossing

The next day, at Newhaven, Simon Dubosc learnt that, at about six o'clock on the previous evening, a fishing-smack with a crew of eight hands had foundered in sight of Seaford. The cyclone had been seen from the shore.

"Well, captain," asked Simon, who happened to know the first officer of the boat which was about to cross that day, having met him in Dieppe, "well captain, what do you make of it? More wrecks! Don't you think things are beginning to get alarming?"

"It looks like it, worse luck!" replied the captain. "Fifteen passengers have refused to come on board. They're frightened. Yet, after all, one has to take chances..."

"Chances which keep on recurring, captain, and over the whole of the Channel just now..."

"M. Dubosc, if you take the whole of the Channel, you will probably find several hundred craft afloat at one time. Each of them runs a risk, but you'll admit the risk is small."

"Was the crossing good last night?" asked Simon, thinking of his friend Rolleston.

"Very good, both ways, and so will ours be. The *Queen Mary* is a fast boat; she does the sixty-four miles in just under two hours. We shall leave and we shall arrive; you may be sure of that, M. Dubosc."

The captain's confidence, while reassuring Simon, did not completely allay the fears which would not even have entered his mind in ordinary times. He selected two cabins separated by a stateroom. Then, as he still had twenty-five minutes to wait, he repaired to the harbor station.

There he found people greatly excited. At the booking-office, at the refreshment-bar and in the waiting-room where the latest telegrams were written on a black-board, travelers with anxious faces were hurrying to and fro. Groups collected about persons who were better-informed than the rest and who were talking very loudly and gesticulating. A number of passengers were demanding repayment of the price of their tickets.

"Why, there's Old Sandstone!" said Simon to himself, as he recognized one of his former professors at a table in the refreshment-room.

And, instead of avoiding him, as he commonly did when the worthy man appeared at the corner of some street in Dieppe, he went up to him and took a seat beside him:

"Well, my dear professor, how goes it?"

"What, is that you, Dubosc?"

Beneath a silk hat of an antiquated shape and rusty with age was a round, fat face like a village priest's, a face with enormous cheeks which overlapped a collar of doubtful cleanliness. Something like a bit of black braid did duty as a necktie. The waistcoat and frockcoat were adorned with stains; and the overcoat, of a faded green, had three of its four buttons missing and acknowledged an age even more venerable than that of the hat.

Old Sandstone—he was never known except by this nickname—had taught natural science at Dieppe College for the last twenty-five years. A geologist first and foremost and a geologist of real merit, he owed his by-name to his investigations of the sedimentary formations of the Norman coast, investigations which he had extended even to the bottom of the sea and which, though he was nearly sixty years of age, he was still continuing with unabated enthusiasm. Only last year, in the month of September, Simon had seen him, a big, heavy man, bloated with fat and crippled with rheumatism, struggling into a diver's dress and making, within sight of Saint-Valéry-en-Caux, his forty-eighth descent. The Channel from Le Havre to Dunkirk and from Portsmouth to Dover, no longer had any secrets for him.

"Are you going back to Dieppe presently, professor?"

"On the contrary, I have just come from Dieppe. I crossed last night, as soon as I heard of the wreck of the English fishing-smack, you know, between Seaford and Cuckmere Haven. I have already begun to make inquiries this morning, of some people who were visiting the Roman camp and saw the thing happen."

"Well?" said Simon, eagerly.

"Well, they saw, at a mile from the coast, a whirl of waves and foam revolving at a dizzy speed round a hollow center. Then suddenly a column of water gushed straight up, mixed with sand and stones, and fell back on all sides, like a rain of rockets. It was magnificent!"

"And the fishing-smack?"

"The fishing-smack?" echoed Old Sandstone, who seemed not to understand, to take no interest in this trivial detail. "Oh, yes, the fishing-smack, of course! Well, she disappeared, that's all!"

The young man was silent, but the next moment continued:

"Now my dear professor, tell me frankly, do you think there's any danger in crossing?"

"Oh, that's absurd! It's as though you were to ask me whether one ought to shut oneself in one's room when there is a thunder-storm. Of course the lightning strikes the earth now and again. But there's plenty of margin all round... Besides, aren't you a good swimmer? Well, at the least sign of danger, dive into the sea without delay: don't stop to think; just dive!"

"And what is your opinion, professor? How do you explain all these phenomena?"

"How? Oh, very simply! I will remind you, to begin with, that in 1912 the Somme experienced a few shocks which amounted to actual earthquakes. Point number one. Secondly, these shocks coincided with local disturbances in the Channel, which passed almost unnoticed; but they attracted my attention and were the starting point of all my recent investigations. Among others, one of these disturbances in which I am inclined to see the premonitory signs of the present water spouts, occurred off Saint-Valéry. And that was why you caught me one day, I remember, going down in a diving-suit just at that spot. Now, from all this, it follows..."

"What follows?"

Old Sandstone interrupted himself, seized the young man's hand and suddenly changed the course of the conversation:

"Now tell me, Dubosc," he said, "have you read my pamphlet on the cliffs of the Channel? You haven't, have you? Well, if you had, you would know that one of the chapters, entitled, 'What will occur in the Channel in the year 2000,' is now being fulfilled. D'you understand? I predicted the whole thing! Not these minor incidents of wrecks and water spouts, of course, but what they seem to announce. Yes, Dubosc; whether it be in the year 2000, or the year 3000, or next week, I have foretold in all its details the unheard-of, astounding, yet very natural thing which will happen sooner or later."

He had now grown animated. Drops of sweat beaded his cheeks and forehead; and, taking from an inner pocket of his frockcoat a long narrow wallet, with a lock to it and so much worn and so often repaired that its appearance harmonized perfectly with his green over-coat and his rusty hat:

"You want to know the truth?" he exclaimed. "It's here. All my observations and all my hypotheses are contained in this wallet."

And he was inserting the key in the lock when loud voices were raised on the platform. The tables in the refreshment-room were at once deserted. Without paying further heed to Old Sandstone, Simon followed the crowd which was rushing into the waiting-room.

Two telegrams had come from France. One, after reporting the wreck of a coasting-vessel, the *Bonne Vierge*, which plied weekly between Calais, Le Havre and Cherbourg, announced that the Channel Tunnel had fallen in, fortunately without the loss of a single life. The other, which the crowd read as it was being written, stated that "the keeper of the Ailly lighthouse, near Dieppe, had at break of day seen five columns of water and sand shooting up almost simultaneously, two miles from the coast, and stirring up the sea between Veules and Pourville."

These telegrams elicited cries of dismay. The destruction of the Channel Tunnel, ten years of effort wasted, millions of pounds swallowed up: this was evidently a calamity! But how much more dreadful was the sinister wording of the second telegram! Veules! Pourville! Dieppe! That was the coast which they would have to make for! The steamboat, in two hours' time, would be entering the very region affected by the cataclysm! On sailing, Seaford and Hastings; on nearing port, Veules, Pourville and Dieppe!

There was a rush for the booking-office. The stationmaster's and inspectors' offices were besieged. Two hundred people rushed on board the vessel to recover their trunks and bags; and a crowd of distraught travelers, staggering under the weight of their luggage, took the uptrain by assault, as though the sea walls and the quays and rampart of the cliffs were unable to protect them from the hideous catastrophe.

Simon shuddered. He could not but be impressed by the fears displayed by these people. And then what was the meaning of this mysterious sequence of phenomena, which seemed incapable of any natural explanation? What invisible tempest was making the waves boil up from the depths of a motionless sea? Why did these sudden cyclones all occur within so small a radius, affecting only a limited region?

All around him the tumult increased, amid repeated painful scenes. One of these he found particularly distressing; for the people concerned were French and he was better able to understand what they were saying. There was a family, consisting of the father and mother, both still young, and their six children, the smallest of whom, only a few months old, was sleeping in its mother's arms. And the mother was imploring her husband in a sort of despair:

"Don't let us go, please don't let us go! We're not obliged to!"

"But we are, my dear: you saw my partner's letter. And really there's no occasion for all this distress!"

"Please, darling!... I have a presentiment... You know I'm always right..."

"Would you rather I crossed alone?"

"Oh no! Not that!"

Simon heard no more. But he was never to forget that cry of a loving wife, nor the grief-stricken expression of the mother who, at that moment, was embracing her six children with a glance.

He made his escape. The clock pointed to half-past eleven; and Miss Bakefield ought to be on her way. But, when he reached the quay, he saw a motorcar turning the corner of a street; and at the window of the car was Isabel's golden head. In a moment all his gloomy thoughts were banished. He had not expected the girl for another twenty minutes; and, though he was not afraid of suffering, he had made up his mind that those last twenty minutes would be a period of distress and anxiety. Would she keep her promise? Might she not meet with some unforeseen obstacle?... And here was Isabel arriving!

Yesterday he had determined, as a measure of precaution, not to speak to her until they had taken their places on the boat. However, as soon as Simon saw her step out of the car, he ran to meet her. She was wrapped in a grey cloak and carried a rug rolled in a strap. A sailor followed with her travelling-bag.

"Excuse me, Isabel," said Simon, "but something so serious has happened that I am bound to consult you. The telegrams, in fact, mention a whole series of catastrophes which have occurred precisely in the part which we shall have to cross."

Isabel did not seem much put out:

"You're saying this, Simon, in a very calm tone which does not match your words at all."

"It's because I'm so happy!" he murmured.

Their eyes met in a long and penetrating glance. Then she continued:

"What would you do, Simon, if you were alone?"

And, when he hesitated what to answer:

"You would go," she said. "And so should I..."

She stepped onto the gangway.

Half an hour later, the *Queen Mary* left Newhaven harbor. At that instant, Simon, who was always so completely his own master and who, even in the most feverish moments of enthusiasm, claimed the power of controlling his emotions, felt his legs trembling beneath him, while his eyes grew moist with tears. The test of happiness was too much for him.

Simon had never been in love before. Love was an event which he awaited at his leisure; and he did not think it essential to prepare for its coming by seeking it in adventures which might well exhaust his ardor:

"Love," he used to say, "should blend with life, should form a part of life and not be added to it. Love is not an aim in itself: it is a principle of action and the noblest in the world."

From the first day when he saw her, Isabel's beauty had dazzled him; and he needed very little time to discover that, until the last moment of his life, no other woman would ever mean anything to him. The same irresistible and deliberate impulse drove Isabel towards Simon. Brought up in the south of France, speaking French as her native tongue, she did not feel and did not evoke in Simon the sense of embarrassment that almost invariably arises from a difference of nationality. That which united them was infinitely stronger than that which divided them.

It was a curious thing, but during these past four months, while love was blossoming within them like a plant whose flowers were constantly renewed and constantly increasing in beauty, they had had none of those long conversations in which lovers eagerly question each other and in which each seeks to find entrance into the unknown territory of the other's soul. They spoke little and rarely of themselves, as though they had delegated to gentle daily life the task of raising the veils of the mystery one by one.

Simon knew only that Isabel was not happy. After losing at the age of fifteen a mother whom she adored, she failed to find in her father the love and the caresses that might have consoled her. Moreover, Lord Bakefield almost immediately fell under the dominion of the Duchess of Falconbridge, a vain, tyrannical woman, who rarely stirred from her villa at Cannes or her country seat near Battle, but whose malign influence exerted itself equally close at hand and far away, in speech and by letter, on her husband and on her stepdaughter, whom she persecuted with her morbid jealousy.

Naturally enough, Isabel and Simon exchanged a mutual promise. And, naturally enough, on coming into collision with Lord Bakefield's implacable will and his wife's hatred, they arrived at the only possible solution, that of running away. This was proposed without heroic phrases and adopted without any painful struggle or reluctance. Each formed a decision in perfect liberty. To themselves their action appeared extremely simple. Loyally determined to prolong their engagement until the moment when all obstacles would be smoothed away, they faced the future like travelers turning to a radiant and hospitable country.

In the open Channel a choppy sea was beginning to rise before a steady light breeze. In the west the clouds were mustering in battle array, but they were distant enough to promise a calm passage in glorious sunshine. Indifferent to the assault of the waves, the vessel sped straight for her port, as though no power existed which could have turned her aside from her strict course.

Isabel and Simon were seated on one of the benches on the after deck. The girl had taken off her cloak and hat and offered to the wind her arms and shoulders, protected only by a cambric blouse. Nothing more beautiful could be imagined than the play of the sunlight on the gold of her hair. Though grave and dreamy, she was radiant with youth and happiness. Simon gazed at her in an ecstasy of admiration:

"You don't regret anything, Isabel?" he whispered.

"No!"

"You're not frightened?"

"Why should I be, with you? There is nothing to threaten us."

Simon pointed to the sea:

"That will, perhaps."

"No!"

He told her of his conversation with Lord Bakefield on the previous day and of the three conditions upon which they had agreed. She was amused, and asked him:

"May I too lay down a condition?"

"What condition, Isabel?"

"Fidelity," she replied, gravely. "Absolute fidelity. No lapses! I could never forgive anything of that sort."

He kissed her hand and said:

"There is no love without fidelity. I love you."

There were few people around them, for the panic had affected mainly the first-class passengers. But, apart from the two lovers, all those who had persisted in crossing betrayed by some sign their secret uneasiness or their alarm. On the right were two old, very old clergymen, accompanied by a third, a good deal younger. These three remained unmoved, worthy brothers of the heroes who sang hymns on the sinking *Titanic*. Nevertheless, their hands were folded as though in prayer. On the left was the French couple whose conversation Dubosc had overheard. The young father and mother, leaning closely on each other, searched the horizon with fevered eyes. Four boys, the four older children, all strong and robust, their cheeks ruddy with health, were coming and going, in search of information which they immediately brought back with them. A little girl sat crying at her parents' feet, without saying a word. The mother was nursing the sixth child, which from time to time turned to Isabel and smiled at her.

Meanwhile, the breeze was growing colder. Simon leant toward his companion:

"You're not feeling chilly, Isabel?" he said.

"No, I'm used to it..."

"Still, though you left your bag below you brought your rug on deck, very wisely. Why don't you undo it?"

The rug was still rolled up in its straps; and Isabel had even passed one of the straps around an iron rod, which fastened the bench to the deck, and buckled it.

"My bag contains nothing of value," she said.

"Nor the rug, I presume?"

"Yes, it does."

"Really? What?"

"A miniature to which my poor mother was very much attached, because it is a portrait of her grandmother painted for George III."

"It has just a sentimental value, therefore?"

"Oh dear no! My mother had it set in all her finest pearls, which gives it an inestimable value to-day. Thinking of the future, she left me, in this way, a fortune of my own."

Simon laughed:

"And that's the safe!"

"Yes, that's the safe!" she said, joining in his laughter. "The miniature is pinned to the middle of the rug, between the straps where no one would think of looking for it. You're laughing, but I am superstitious where that miniature is concerned. It's a sort of talisman..."

For some time they spoke no further. The coast had disappeared from sight. The swell was increasing and the _Queen Mary_ was rolling a little.

At this moment they were passing a beautiful white yacht.

"That's the Comte de Bauge's *Castor*," cried one of the four boys. "She's on her way to Dieppe."

Two ladies and two gentlemen were lunching under an awning, Isabel bowed her head so as to hide her face.

This thoughtless movement displeased her; for, a moment later, she said (and all the words which they exchanged during these few minutes were to remain engraved on their memories):

"Simon, you really believe, don't you, that I was entitled to leave home?"

"Why," he exclaimed, in surprise, "don't we love each other?"

"Yes, we love each other," she murmured. "And then there's the life which I was leading with a woman whose one delight was to insult my mother..."

She said no more. Simon had laid his hand on hers and nothing could reassure her more effectually than the fondness of that pressure.

The four boys, who had disappeared again, came running back:

"You can see the company's mail-boat that left Dieppe at the same time that we left Newhaven. She's called the *Pays de Caux*. We shall pass her in a quarter of an hour. So you see, mama, there's no danger."

"Yes, but it's afterwards, when we get closer to Dieppe."

"Why?" objected her husband. "The other boat hasn't signaled anything extraordinary. The danger is altering its position, moving farther away..."

The mother made no reply. Her face retained the same piteous expression. The little girl at her knee was still silently crying.

The captain passed Simon and saluted.

And a few more minutes elapsed.

Simon was whispering words of love which Isabel did not catch very distinctly. The little girl's constant tears were causing her some distress.

Shortly after, a gust of wind made the waves leap higher. Here and there streaks of white, seething foam appeared. There was nothing remarkable in this, as the wind was gaining in force and lashing the crests of the waves. But why did these foaming billows appear only in one part and that precisely the part which they were about to cross?

The father and mother had risen to their feet. Other passengers were leaning over the rails. The captain was seen running up the poop-steps.

And it came suddenly, in a moment.

Before Isabel and Simon, sitting self-absorbed, had the least idea of what was happening, a frightful clamor, made up of a thousand shrieks, rose from all parts of the boat, from port and starboard, from stem to stern, even from below; from every side, as though the minds of all had been obsessed by the possibility of disaster, as though all eyes, from the moment of departure, had been watching for the slightest premonitory sign.

A monstrous sight. Three hundred yards ahead, as though in the center of a target at which the bows of the vessel were aimed, a hideous fountain had burst from the surface of the sea, bombarding the sky with masses of rock, blocks of lava and flying masses of spray, which fell back into a circle of foaming breakers and yawning whirlpools. And a wind of hurricane force gyrated above this chaos, bellowing like a bull.

Suddenly silence fell upon the paralyzed crowd, the deathly silence that precedes an inevitable catastrophe. Then, yonder, a rattle of thunder that rent the air. Then the voice of the captain at his post, roaring out his orders, trying to shout down the monster's myriad voices.

For a moment there seemed some hope of salvation. The vessel put forth so great an effort that she appeared to be gliding along a tangent away from the infernal circle into which she was on the point of being drawn. But it was a vain hope! The circle seemed to be increasing in size. Its outer waves were approaching. A mass of rock crushed one of the funnels.

And again there were shrieks, followed by a panic and an insane rush for the life-boats; already some of the passengers were fighting for places...

Simon did not hesitate. Isabel was a good swimmer. They must make the attempt.

"Come!" he said. The girl, standing beside him, had flung her arms about him. "We can't stay here! Come!"

And, when she struggled, instinctively resisting the course which he had proposed, he took a firmer hold of her.

She entreated him:

"Oh, it's horrible... all these children... the little girl crying!... Couldn't we save them?"

"Come!" he repeated, in a masterful tone.

She still resisted him. Then he took her head in his two hands and kissed her on the lips:

"Come, my darling, come!"

The girl fainted. He lifted her in his arms and threw one leg over the rail:

"Don't be afraid!" he said. "I will answer for your life!"

"I am not afraid," she said. "I am not afraid with you..."

They leapt into the water.

III. Good-Bye, Simon

Twenty minutes later, they were picked up by the *Castor*, the yacht which by this time had passed the *Queen Mary*. As for the *Pays de Caux*, the steamer sailing from Dieppe, subsequent inquiries proved that the passengers and the crew had compelled the captain to flee from the scene of the disaster. The sight of the huge water spout, the spectacle of the ship lifting her stern out of the waves, rearing up bodily and falling back as though into the mouth of a funnel, the upheaval of the sea, which seemed to have given way beneath the assault of maniacal forces and which, within the circumference of the frenzied circle, revolved upon itself in a sort of madness: all this was so terrifying that women fainted and men threatened the captain with their levelled revolvers.

The *Castor* also had begun by fleeing the spot. But the Comte de Bauge, detecting through his field-glasses the handkerchief which Simon was waving, persuaded his sailors, despite the desperate opposition of his friends, to put about, while avoiding contact with the dangerous zone.

For that matter, the sea was subsiding. The eruption had lasted less than a minute; and it was as though the monster was now resting, sated, content with its meal, like a beast of prey after its kill. The squall had passed. The whirlpool broke up into warring currents which opposed and annulled one another. There were no more breakers, no more foam. Beneath the great undulating shroud which the little waves, tossing in harmless frolic, spread above the sunken vessel, the tragedy of five hundred death-struggles was consummated.

Under these conditions, the rescue was an easy task. Isabel and Simon, who could have held out for hours longer, were taken to the two cabins and supplied with a change of clothing. Isabel had not even lost consciousness. The yacht sailed away immediately. Those on board were eager to escape from the accursed circle. The sudden subsidence of the sea seemed as dangerous as its fury.

Nothing occurred before they reached the French coast. The oppressive, menacing lull continued. Simon Dubosc, directly he had changed his clothes, joined the count and his party. A little embarrassed in respect of Miss Bakefield, he spoke of her as a friend whom he had met by chance on the *Queen Mary* and by whose side he had found himself at the moment of the catastrophe.

For the rest, he was not questioned. The company on board the yacht were still profoundly uneasy; the thought of what might happen obsessed them. Further events were preparing. All had the impression that an invisible enemy was prowling stealthily around them.

Twice Simon went below to Isabel's cabin. The door was closed and there was no sound from within. But Simon knew that Isabel, though she had recovered from her fatigue and was already forgetting the dangers which had threatened them, nevertheless could not shake off the horror of what she had seen. He himself was still terribly depressed, haunted by the vision so frightful that it seemed the extravagant image of a nightmare rather than the memory of an actual thing. Was it true that they had one and all lost their lives: the three clergymen with their austere faces, the four happy, cheerful boys, their father and mother, the little girl who had cried, the child that had smiled at Isabel, the captain and every single individual of all those who had covered the *Queen Mary*'s decks?

About four o'clock, the clouds, unrolling in blacker and denser masses, had conquered the heavens. Already the watchers felt the first breath of the great squalls whose precipitous onset was at hand, whose battalions, let loose across the Atlantic, were about to rush into the narrow straits of the Channel and mingle their devastating efforts with the mysterious forces rising from the depths of the sea. The horizon was blotted out as the clouds released their contents.

But the yacht was nearing Dieppe. The Count and Simon Dubosc, each gazing through a pair of binoculars, cried out as with one voice, struck at the same moment by the most unexpected sight. Looking at the row of buildings, which line the long sea front like a tall rampart of brick and stone, they could plainly see that the roof and upper story of the two largest hotels, the Imperial and the Astoria, situated in the middle, had collapsed. And the next instant they caught sight of other houses which were tottering, leaning forward, fissured and half-demolished.

Suddenly a flame shot up from one of these houses. In a few minutes there was a violent outbreak of fire; and on every side, from one end of the sea front to the other, a panic-stricken crowd, whose shouts they could hear, came pouring down the streets and running to the beach.

"There is no doubt about it," spluttered the Count. "There has been an earthquake, a very violent shock, which must have synchronized with the sort of waterspout in which the *Queen Mary* disappeared."

When nearer, they saw that the sea must have risen, sweeping over the sea wall, for long streaks of mud marked the lawns, while the beach to right and left was covered with stranded shipping.

And they saw too that the end of the jetty and the lighthouse had disappeared, that the breakwater had been carried away and that boats were drifting about the harbor.

The wireless telegram announcing the wreck of the *Queen Mary* had redoubled the panic. No one dared fly from the peril on land by taking to the open sea. The relatives of the passengers stood massed together, in witless and hopeless waiting, on the landing stage and what remained of the jetty.

In the midst of all this turmoil, the yacht's arrival passed almost unperceived. Each was living for himself, without curiosity, heedless of all but his own danger and that of his kinsfolk. A few distraught journalists were darting about feverishly for news; and the port-authorities subjected Simon and the Count to a hasty and perfunctory enquiry. Simon evaded their questions as far as possible. Once free, he escorted Isabel to the nearest hotel, saw her comfortably settled and asked her for permission to go in search of information. He was uneasy, for he believed his father to be in Dieppe.

The Duboscs' house stood at the first turning on the great slope which climbs to the top of the cliffs on the left, itself hidden behind a clump of trees and covered with flowers and creepers, it had a series of terraced gardens which overlooked the town and the sea. Simon was at once reassured on learning that his father was in Paris and would not be home until next day. He was also told that they had felt only a slight shake on this side of Dieppe.

He therefore went back to Isabel's hotel. She was still in her room, however, needing rest, and sent down word that she would rather be alone until the evening. Somewhat astonished by this reply, the full meaning of which he was not to understand till later, he went on to his friend Rolleston's place, failed to find him in, returned to his own house, dined and went for a stroll through the streets of the town.

The damage was not so widespread as he had supposed. What is usually described as the first Dieppe earthquake, to distinguish it from the great upheaval of which it was the forerunner, consisted at most of two preliminary oscillations, which were followed forty seconds later by a violent shock accompanied by a tremendous noise and a series of detonations. As for the tidal wave, improperly called an *eager*, which rushed up the sea front, it had but a very moderate height and a quite restricted force. But the people whom Simon met and those with whom he talked remembered those few seconds with a terror which the hours did not appear to diminish. Some were still running with no idea of where they were going, while others—and these were the greater number—remained in a state of absolute stupefaction, making no reply when questioned or answering only with incoherent sentences.

It was of course different in a town like this from elsewhere. In these long-settled regions, where the soil had assumed its irrevocable configuration hundreds and hundreds of years ago and where volcanic manifestations were not even contemplated as possible, any phenomenon of the kind was peculiarly alarming, illogical, abnormal, and in violent contradiction with the laws of nature and with those conditions of security which each of us has the right to regard as unchanging and as definitely fixed by destiny.

And Simon, who since the previous day had been wandering to and fro in this atmosphere of distraction, Simon, who remembered Old Sandstone's unfinished predictions and who had seen the gigantic waterspout in which the _Queen Mary_ was swallowed up, Simon asked himself:

"What is happening? What is going to happen? In what unforeseen fashion and by what formidable enemy will the coming attack be delivered?"

Though he had meant to leave Dieppe on that night or the following morning, he felt that his departure would be tantamount to a desertion just when his father was returning and when so many symptoms announced the imminence of a final catastrophe.

"Isabel will advise me," he said to himself. "We will decide together what we have to do."

Meantime night had fallen. He returned to the hotel at nine o'clock and asked that Isabel should be told. He was amazed, almost stunned by the news that Miss Bakefield had gone. She had come down from her room an hour earlier, had handed in at the office a letter addressed to Simon Dubosc and had suddenly left the hotel.

Disconcerted, Simon asked for explanations. There seemed to be none to give, except that one of the waiters said that the young lady had joined a sailor who seemed to be waiting for her in the street and that they had gone off together.

Taking the letter, Simon moved away with the intention of going to a café or entering the hotel, but he had not the courage to wait and it was by the light of a street lamp that he opened the envelope and read:

"I am writing to you with absolute confidence, feeling happy in the certainty that everything I say will be understood and that you will feel neither bitterness nor resentment, nor, after the first painful shock, any real distress.

"Simon, we have made a mistake. It is right that our love, the great and sincere love which we bear each other, should dominate all our thoughts and form the object of our whole lives, but it is not right that this love should be our only rule of conduct and our only obligation. In leaving England we did what is only permissible to those whose fate has persistently thwarted all their dreams and destroyed all their sources of joy. It was an act of liberation and revolt, which people have a right to perform when there is no other alternative than death. But is this the case with us, Simon? What have we done to deserve happiness? What ordeals have we suffered? What efforts have we made? What tears have we shed?

"I have done a great deal of thinking, Simon. I have been thinking of all those poor people who are dead and gone and whose memory will always make me shudder. I have thought of you and myself and my mother. Her too I saw die. You remember: we were speaking of her and of the pearls which she gave me when dying. They are lost; and that distresses me so terribly!

"Simon, I don't want to consider this and still less all the horrors of this awful day as warnings intended for us two. But I do want them to help us to look at life in a different way, to help us put up a prouder and pluckier fight against the obstacles in our path. The fact that you and I are alive while so many others are dead forbids us to suffer in ourselves any sort of weakness, untruth or shuffling, anything that cannot face the broad light of day.

"Win me, Simon. For my part, I shall deserve you by confidence and steadfastness. If we are worthy of each other, we shall succeed and we shall not need to blush for a happiness for which we should now have to pay—as I have felt many times to-day—too high a price of humiliation and shame.

"You will not try to find me, will you, Simon?

"Your promised wife,

"Isabel."

For a few moments Simon stood dumbfounded. As Isabel had foreseen, the first shock was infinitely painful. His mind was full of conflicting ideas which eluded his grasp. He did not attempt to understand nor did he ask himself whether he approved of Isabel's action. He suffered as he had never known that it was possible to suffer.

And suddenly, in the disorder of his mind, among the incoherent suppositions which occurred to him, there flashed a horrible thought. It was obvious that Isabel, determined to submit to her father before the scandal of her flight was noised abroad, had conceived the intention of returning to Lord Bakefield. But how would she put her plan into execution? And Simon remembered that Isabel had left the hotel in the most singular fashion, abruptly, on foot and accompanied by a sailor carrying her bag. Now the landing-stage of the Newhaven steamers was close to the hotel; and the night-boat would cast off her moorings in an hour or two.

"Can she be thinking of crossing?" he muttered, shuddering as he remembered the upheavals of the sea and the wreck of the *Queen Mary*.

He rushed towards the quay. Despite Isabel's expressed wish, he intended to see her; and, if she resisted his love, he would at least implore her to abandon the risk of an immediate crossing.

Directly he reached the quay, he perceived the funnels of the Newhaven steamer behind the harbor railway-station. Isabel, without a doubt, was there, in one of the cabins. There were a good many people about the station and a great deal of piled-up luggage. Simon made for the gangway, but was stopped by an official on duty:

"I have no ticket," said Simon. "I am looking for a lady who has gone on board and who is crossing to-night."

"There are no passengers on board," said the official.

"Really? How's that?"

"The boat is not crossing. There have been orders from Paris. All navigation is suspended."

"Ah!" said Simon Dubosc, with a start of relief. "Navigation is suspended!"

"Yes; that is to say, as far as the line's concerned."

"What do you mean, the line?"

"Why, the company only troubles about its own boats. If others care to put to sea, that is their look-out; we can't prevent them."

"But," said Simon, beginning to feel uneasy, "I suppose none has ventured to sail just lately?"

"Yes, there was one, about an hour ago."

"Oh? Did you see her?"

"Yes, she was a yacht, belonging to an Englishman."

"Edward Rolleston, perhaps?" cried Simon, more or less at a venture.

"Yes, I believe it was, Rolleston. Yes, yes, that's it: an Englishmen who had just put his yacht in commission."

Simon suddenly realized the truth. Rolleston, who was staying at Dieppe, happened to hear of Isabel's arrival, called at her hotel and, at her request, gave orders to sail. Of course, he was the only man capable of risking the adventure and of bribing his crew with a lavish distribution of bank notes.

The young Englishman's behavior gave proof of such courage and devotion that Simon at once recovered his normal composure. Against Rolleston he felt neither anger nor resentment. He mastered his fears and determined to have confidence.

The clouds were gliding over the town, so low that their black shapes could be distinguished in the darkness of the night. He crossed the front and leant upon the balustrade which borders the Boulevard Maritime. Thence he could see the white foam of the heavy breakers on the distant sands and hear their vicious assault upon the rocks. Nevertheless, the expected storm was not yet unleashed. More terrible in its continual, nerve-racking menace, it seemed to be waiting for reinforcements and to be delaying its onslaught only to render it more impetuous.

"Isabel will have time to reach the other side," said Simon.

He was now quite calm, full of faith in the present and the future. In absolute agreement with Isabel, he approved of her departure; it caused him no suffering.

"Come," he thought, "it is time to act."

He now recognized the purpose in view of which he had been preparing for years and years: it was to win a woman who was dearer to him than anything on earth and whose conquest would force him to claim that place in the world which his merits deserved.

He had done with hoarding. His duty was to spend, ay, to squander, like a prodigal scattering gold by the handful, without fear of ever exhausting his treasure.

"The time has come," he repeated. "If I am good for anything, I must prove it. If I was right to wait and husband my resources, I must prove it."

He began to walk along the boulevard, his head erect, his chest expanded, striking the ground with a ringing step.

The wind was rising to a gale. Furious showers swept the air. These were trifles to a Simon Dubosc, whose body, clad at all times of the year in light materials, took no heed of the rough weather and, even at the end of a day marked by so many trials, did not betray the slightest symptom of fatigue.

In truth, he felt inaccessible to ordinary weaknesses. His muscles were capable of unlimited endurance. His arms, his legs, his chest, his whole body, patiently exercised, were able to sustain the most violent and persistent efforts. Through his eyes, ears and nostrils he participated acutely in every vibration of the outer world. He was without a flaw. His nerves were perfectly steady. His will responded to every demand. He had the faculty of making up his mind at the first warning. His senses were always on the alert, but were controlled by his reason. He had keen intelligence and a clear, logical mind. _He was ready.

He was ready. Like an athlete at the top of his form, he owed it to himself to enter the lists and accomplish some feat of prowess. Now, by a wonderful coincidence, it seemed that events promised him a field of action in which this feat of prowess might be performed in the most brilliant fashion. How? That he did not know. When? That he could not say. But he felt a profound intuition that new paths were about to open up before him.

For an hour he walked to and fro, fired by enthusiasm, quivering with hope. Suddenly a squall leapt at the sea front, as though torn from the crest of the waves; and the rain fell in disorderly masses, hurtling downwards in all directions.

The storm had broken and Isabel was still at sea.

He shrugged his shoulders, refusing to admit a return of anxiety. If they had both escaped from the wreck of the *Queen Mary*, it was not in order that one of them should now pay for that unexpected boon. No, come what might, Isabel would reach the other side. Fate was protecting them both.

Through the torrents of rain pouring across the parade and by the flooded streets, Simon returned to the Villa Dubosc. An indomitable energy bore him up. And he thought with pride of his beautiful bride, who, disdainful like himself of the day's accumulated ordeals and untiring as he, had gone forth bravely into the terrors of the night.

IV. The Great Upheaval

The next five days were of those whose memory oppresses a nation for countless generations. What with hurricanes, cyclones, floods, swollen rivers and tidal waves, the coasts of the Channel and in particular the parts about Fécamp, Dieppe and Le Tréport suffered the most infuriate assaults conceivable.

Although a scientist would not admit the least relation between this series of storms and the tremendous event of the 4th of June, that is to say, of the last of these five days, what a strange coincidence it was! How could the masses ever since help thinking that these several phenomena all formed part of one connected whole?

In Dieppe, the undoubted center of the first seismic disturbances, in Dieppe and the outlying districts hell was let loose. It was as though this particular spot of the earth's surface was the meeting-place of all the powers that attack and devastate and undermine and slay. In the whirlpools, or the water spouts, or the eddies of overflowing rivers, under the crash of uprooted trees, crumbling cliffs, falling scaffoldings and walls, tottering belfries and factory-chimneys and of all the objects carried by the wind, the deaths increased steadily. Twenty families were thrown into mourning on the first day, forty on the second. As for the number of victims destroyed by the great convulsion which accompanied the tremendous event, it was doubtful whether this was ever accurately estimated.

As happens in such periods of constant danger, when the individual thinks only of himself and those akin to him, Simon knew hardly anything of the disaster save through the manifestations that reached him directly. After receiving a wireless telegram from Isabel which assured him of her safety, he spread the newspapers only to make certain that his flight with her was not suspected. With the rest—details of the foundering of the *Queen Mary*, articles in which his presence of mind, his courage and Isabel's pluck were extolled, or in which the writer endeavored to explain the convulsions in the Channel—with all this he had hardly time to concern himself.

He remained with his father. He told him the secret of his love, told him the story of the recent incidents, told him of his plans. Together they wandered through the town or out into the country, both of them drenched and blinded by the showers, staggering under the squalls and bowing their heads beneath the bombardment of slates and tiles. The trees and telegraph-poles along the road were mown down like corn. Trusses of straw, stacks of fodder, faggots of wood, palings, coils of wire were whirled through the air like autumn leaves. Nature seemed to have declared a merciless war upon herself for the sheer pleasure of spoiling and destroying.

And the sea was still trundling its gigantic waves, which broke with deafening roar. All navigation between France and England was suspended. Wireless messages signaled the danger to the great liners coming from America or Germany; and none of them dared enter the hell that was the Channel.

On the fourth day, the last but one, Tuesday the 3rd of June, there was a slight lull.

The final assault was marshalling its forces. M. Dubosc worn out with fatigue, did not get up that afternoon. Simon also threw himself on his bed, fully dressed, and slept until evening. But at nine o'clock a shock awakened them.

Simon thought that the window, which suddenly burst open, had given away under the pressure of the wind. A second shock, more plainly defined, brought down the door of his room; and he felt himself spinning on his own axis, with the walls circling round him.

He ran downstairs and found his father in the garden with the servants, one and all bewildered and uttering incoherent phrases. After a long pause, during which some tried to escape while others were on their knees, there was a violent downpour of rain, mingled with hail, which drove them indoors.

At ten o'clock they sat down to supper. M. Dubosc did not speak a word. The servants were livid and trembling. Simon retained in the depths of his horrified mind an uncanny impression of a shuddering world.

At ten minutes to eleven there was another vibration, of no great violence, but prolonged, with beats that followed one another very closely, like a peal of bells. The porcelain plates fell from the walls; the clock stopped.

All the inmates of the house went out of doors again and crowded into a little thatched summer house lashed by slanting rain.

Half-an-hour later, the tremors recommenced and from this time onwards, were so to speak, incessant. They were faint and remote at first, but soon grew more and more perceptible, like the shivers of fever which rise from the depths of our flesh and shake us from head to foot.

This ended by becoming a torture. Two of the maids were sobbing. M. Dubosc had flung an arm about Simon's neck and was stammering terrified and meaningless words. Simon himself could no longer endure this execrable sensation of earthquake, this vertigo of the human being losing his foothold. He felt that he was living in a disjointed world and that his mind was registering absurd and grotesque impressions.

From the town arose an uninterrupted clamor. The road was crowded with people fleeing to the heights. A church-bell filled the air with the doleful sound of the tocsin, while the clocks were striking the twelve hours of midnight.

"Let us go away! Let us go away!" cried M. Dubosc.

Simon protested:

"Come, father, there's no need for that! What have we to fear?"

But one and all were seized with panic. Everybody acted at random, making unconscious movements, like a crazy piece of machinery working backwards. The servants went indoors again, looking about them stupidly, as do those who go over a house which they are leaving for the last time. Simon, as in a dream, saw one of them cramming a canvas bag with the gilt candlesticks and silver boxes of which he had charge, while another wrapped himself in a table-cloth and a third filled his pockets with bread and biscuits. He himself, turning by instinct to a small cloakroom on the ground floor, put on a leather jacket and changed his shoes for a pair of heavy shooting-boots. He heard his father saying:

"Here, take my pocketbook. There's money in it, bundles of notes: you'd better have it..."

Suddenly the electric light went out; and at the same time they heard, in the distance, a strange thunder-clap, curiously different from the usual sound of thunder. It was repeated, with a less strident din, accompanied by a subterranean rattling; and then, growing noisier again, it burst a second time in a series of frightful detonations, louder than the roar of artillery.

Then there was a frantic rush for the road. But the fugitives had not left the garden when the frightful catastrophe, announced by so many manifestations, occurred. The earth leapt beneath their feet and instantly fell away and leapt again like an animal in convulsions.

Simon and his father were thrown against each other and then violently torn apart and hurled to the ground. All around them was the stupendous uproar of a tottering world in which everything was collapsing into an incredible chaos. The darkness seemed to have grown denser than ever. And then, suddenly, there was a less distant sound, a sound which touched them, so to speak, a sort of cracking noise. And shrieks rose into the air from the very bowels of the earth.

"Stop!" cried Simon, catching hold of his father, whom he had succeeded in rejoining. "Stop!"

He felt before him, at a distance of a few inches, the utter horror of a gap-ing abyss; and it was from the bottom of the abyss that the shrieks and howls of their companions rose.

And there were three more shocks...

Simon realized a moment later that his father, clutching his arm, was drag-ging him away with fierce energy. Both were clambering up the road at a run, groping their way like blind men through the obstacles with which the earth-quake had covered it.

M. Dubosc had a goal in view, the Caude-Côte cliff, a bare plateau where they would be in absolute safety. But, on taking a crossroad, they struck against a band of maddened creatures who told them that the cliff had fallen, carrying numerous victims with it. All that these people could think of now was to run to the seashore. With them, M. Dubosc and his son stumbled down the paths which led to the valley of Pourville, whose beach lies in a cove some two miles from Dieppe. The front was obstructed by a crowd of villagers, while others were tak-ing shelter from the rain behind the bathing-huts overturned by the wind. Others again, as the tide was very low, had gone down the sloping shingle and crossed the sands and ventured out to the rocks, as though the danger had ended there and there only. By the uncertain light of a moon which strove to pierce the curtain of the clouds, they could be seen wandering to and fro like ghosts.

"Come, Simon!" said M. Dubosc. "Let's go over there..."

But Simon held him back:

"We are all right here, father. Besides, it seems to be calming down. Take a rest."

"Yes, yes, if you like," replied M. Dubosc, who was in a greatly dejected mood. "And then we will go back to Dieppe. I want to make sure that my boats have not been knocked about too much."

A squall burst, laden with rain.

"Don't move," said Simon. "There's a bathing-hut a few yards off. I'll just go and see..."

He hurried away. But there were already three men lying under the hut, which they had lashed to one of the buttresses of the parade. Others came up and tried to share the shelter. Blows were exchanged. Simon intervened. But the earth shook once more; and they could hear the crash of cliffs falling to right and left.

"Where are you, father?" cried Simon, running back to the spot where he had left M. Dubosc.

Finding no one there, he shouted. But the roar of the gale smothered his voice and he did not know in what direction to seek. Had his father been overcome by fresh fears and gone closer to the sea? Or had he, in his anxiety for his boats, returned to Dieppe as he had hinted?

At a venture—but is it right to apply this term to the unconscious decisions which impel us to follow our destined path?—Simon began to run along the sand and shingle. Then, through the maze of slippery rocks, hampered by the snares spread by the wrack and seaweed, stumbling into pools of water in which the towering breakers from the open sea had died away in swirling eddies or in lapping waves, he joined the ghostly figures which he had seen from a distance.

He went from one to another and, failing to see his father, was thinking of returning to the parade, when a small incident occurred to make him change his mind. The full moon appeared in the sky. She was covered again immediately, then reappeared; and several times over, between the ragged clouds, her magnificent radiance flooded the sky. At this juncture, Simon, who had veered towards the right of the beach, discovered that the fallen cliffs had buried the shore under the most stupendous chaos imaginable. The white masses were piled one atop the other like so many mountains of chalk. And it looked to Simon as if one of these masses, carried by its own weight, had rolled right into the sea, whence it now rose some three hundred yards away.

On reflection, he could not believe this possible, the distance being far too great; but then what was that enormous shape outstretched yonder like a crouching animal? A hundred times, in his childhood, he had paddled his canoe or come fishing in this part; and he knew for certain that nothing rose above the waters here.

What was it? A sand bank? But its outlines seemed too uneven and its grey color was that of the rocks, naked rocks, without any covering of wrack or other seaweed.

He went forward, actuated in part by an eager curiosity, but still more by some mysterious and all-powerful force, the spirit of adventure. The adventure appealed to him: he must go up to this new ground whose origin he could not help attributing to the recent earthquake.

And he went up to it. Beyond the first belt of sand, beyond the belt of small rocks where he stood, was the final bed of sand over which the waves rolled eternally. But from place to place there rose still more rocks, so that he was able, by a persistent effort, to reach what appeared to be a sort of promontory.

The ground underfoot was hard, consisting of sedimentary deposits, as Old Sandstone would have said. And Simon realized that, as a result of the violent shocks and of some physical phenomenon whose action he did not understand, the bed of the sea had been forced upwards until it overtopped the waves by a height which varied in different places, but which certainly exceeded the level of the highest spring tides.

The promontory was of no great width, for by the intermittent light of the moon Simon could see the foam of the breakers leaping on either side of this new reef. It was irregular in form, thirty or forty yards wide in one part and a hundred or even two hundred in another; and it ran on like a continuous embankment, following more or less closely the old line of the cliffs.

Simon did not hesitate. He set out. The hilly, uneven surface, at first interspersed with pools of water and bristling with rocks which the stubborn labors of the sea had pushed thus far, became gradually flatter; and Simon was able to walk at a fair pace, though hampered by a multitude of objects, often half-buried in the ground, which the waves, not affecting the bottom of the sea, had been unable to sweep away: meat-tins, old buckets, scrap-iron, shapeless utensils of all kinds covered with sea-weed and encrusted with little shells.

A few minutes later, he perceived Dieppe lying on his right, a scene of desolation which he divined rather than saw. The light of conflagrations not wholly extinguished reddened the sky; and the town looked to him like an unhappy city in which a horde of barbarians had sat encamped for weeks on end. The earth had merely shuddered and an even more stupendous disaster had ensued.

At this moment, a fine tracery of grey clouds spread above the great black banks which were driving before the gale; and the moon disappeared. Simon felt irresolute. Since all the lighthouses were demolished, how would he find his way if the darkness increased? He thought of his father, who was perhaps anxious, but he thought also—and more ardently—of his distant bride whom he had to win; and, as the idea of this conquest was blended in his mind—he could not have said why—with visions of dangers accepted and with extraordinary happenings, he felt vaguely that he would be right in going on. To go on meant travelling towards something formidable and unknown. The soil which had risen from the depths might sink again. The waves might reconquer the lost ground and cut off all retreat. An unfathomable gulf might yawn beneath his footsteps. To go on was madness.

And he went on.

V. Virgin Soil

It was hardly later than one o'clock in the morning. The storm was less furious and the squalls had ceased, so that Simon suddenly began to walk as quickly as the trifling obstacles over which he stumbled and the dim light of the sky would permit. For that matter, if he branched off too far in either direction, the nearer sound of the waves would serve as a warning.

In this way he passed Dieppe and followed a direction which, while it varied by reason of curves and sudden turns, nevertheless, in his opinion, ran parallel with the Norman coast. During the whole of this first stage of his journey, he was only half-aware of what he was doing and had no thought but of making headway, feeling certain that his explorations would be interrupted from one minute to the next. It did not seem to him that he was penetrating into unlimited regions, but rather that he was really persistently pushing towards a goal which was close at hand, but which receded so soon as he approached it and which was no other than the extreme point of this miraculous peninsula.

"There," he said to himself. "There it is. I've got there. The new ground goes as far as that..."

But the new ground continued to stretch into the darkness; and a little later he repeated:

"It's over there. The line of breakers is closing up. I can see it."

But the line opened out, leaving a passage by which Simon pursued his way.

Two o'clock... Half-past two... Sometimes the water was up to his knees, sometimes his feet sank into a bed of thicker sand. These were the low-lying parts, the valleys of the peninsula; and there might perhaps be some, thought Simon where these beds would be deep enough to bar his passage. He went on all the more briskly. Ascents rose in front of him, leading him to mounds forty or fifty feet in height, whose farther slopes he descended rapidly. And, lost in the immensity of the sea, imprisoned by it, absorbed by it, he had the illusion that he was running over its surface, along the back of great frozen, motionless waves.

He halted. Before him a speck of light had crossed the darkness, a long, a very long way off. Four times he saw the flame reappear at regular intervals. Fifteen seconds later came a fresh series of flashes, followed by a similar interval of darkness.

"A lighthouse!" murmured Simon. "A lighthouse which the disaster has spared!"

Just here the embankment ran in the direction of the lighthouse; and Simon calculated that it would thus end at Tréport, or perhaps farther north, if the lighthouse marked the estuary of the Somme, which was highly probable. In that case he would have to walk four or five hours longer, at the same swift pace.

But he lost the intermittent gleams as suddenly as he had caught sight of them. He looked and failed to find them and felt overwhelmed, as though, after the death of these little twinkling flames, he could no longer hope ever to escape from the heavy darkness which was stifling him or to discover the tremendous secret in pursuit of which he had darted. What was he doing? Where was he? What did it all mean? What was the use of making such efforts?

"Forward!" he cried. "At the double! and we don't do any more thinking. I shall understand presently, when I get there. Until then, it's a matter of going on and on, like a beast of burden."

He spoke aloud, to shake off his drowsiness. And, as a protest against a weakness of which he was ashamed, he set off at a run.

It was a quarter past three. In the keener air of the morning he was conscious of a sense of well-being. Moreover, he noticed that the obscurity around him was becoming lighter and was gradually lifting like a mist.

The first glimmer of dawn appeared. The day broke quickly and at last the new land was visible to Simon's eyes, grey, as he had supposed, and yellower in places, with streaks of sand and hollows filled with water in which all sorts of fish were seen struggling or dying, with a whole galaxy of little islands and irregular shoals, beaches of fine, close-packed gravel, tracts of seaweed and gentle undulations, like those of a rich plain.

And in the midst of it all there was ever a multitude of objects whose real shape could no longer be distinguished, remnants enlarged and swollen by the addition of everything that could be encrusted or fastened on them, or else eaten away, worn out, corroded, or disintegrated by everything that helps to dissolve or to destroy.

They were flotsam and jetsam of all kinds. Past counting, glistening with slime, of all types and of all materials, of an age to be reckoned in months or years, it might be in centuries, they bore witness to the unbroken procession of thousands and thousands of wrecks. And, as many as were these remnants of wood and iron, so many were the human lives engulfed in companies of tens and hundreds. Youth, health, wealth, hope: each wreck represented the destruction of all their dreams, of all their realities; and each also recalled the distress of the living, the mourning of mothers and wives.

And the field of death stretched away indefinitely, an immense, tragic cemetery, such as the earth had never known, with endless lines of graves, tombstones and funeral monuments. To the right and left there was nothing, nothing but a dense fog rising from the water, hiding the horizon as completely as the veils of night and making it impossible for Simon to see more than a hundred yards in front of him. But from this fog new land-formations continued to emerge; and this seemed to him to fall so strictly within the domain of the fabulous and the incredible that he easily imagined them to be rising from the depths on his approach and assuming form and substance to offer him a passage.

A little after four o'clock there was a return of the gale, an offensive of ugly clouds emitting volleys of rain and hail. The wind made a gap in the clouds, which it drove north and south, and then, on Simon's right, parallel with a belt of rosy light which divided the waves from the black sky, the coast line became visible.

It was a vaguely defined line which might have been taken for a fine streak of motionless clouds; but he knew its general appearance so well that he did not hesitate for a moment. It was the cliffs of the Seine-Inférieure and the Somme, between Le Tréport and Cayeux.

He rested for a few minutes; then, to lighten his outfit, he pulled off his boots, which were too heavy, and his leather jacket, which was making him too hot. Then taking his father's wallet out of the jacket, he found in one of the pockets two biscuits and a stick of chocolate which he himself had put there, so to speak, unwittingly.

After making a meal of these, he set out again briskly, not with the cautious gait of an explorer who does not know where he is going and who measures his efforts, but at the pace of an athlete who has fixed his timetable and keeps to it in spite of obstacles and difficulties. A strange light-heartedness uplifted him. He was glad to expend so much of the force which he had been storing for all these years and to expend it on a task of which he knew nothing, but of which he felt the exceptional greatness. His elbows were well tucked in and his head thrown back. His bare feet marked the sand with a faint trail. The wind bathed his face and played in and out of his hair. What joy!

He kept up his pace for nearly four hours. Why should he hold himself in? He was always expecting the new formation to change its direction and, bending suddenly to the right, to join the coast of the Somme. And he went forward in all confidence.

At certain points, progress became arduous. The sea had got up; and here and there the waves, rushing over those places where the sand, though clear of the water, was unprotected by a barrier of rocks, formed in the narrower portions actual rivers, flowing from one side to the other, which Simon had to wade, almost knee-deep in water. Moreover, he had taken so little food that he began to be racked with hunger. He had to slow down. And another hour went by.

The great squalls had blown over. The returning sea fogs seemed to have deadened the wind and were now closing in on him again. Once more Simon was walking through moving clouds which concealed his path from him. Less sure of himself, attacked by a sudden sense of loneliness and distress, he soon experienced a lassitude to which he was unwilling to surrender.

This was a mistake. He recognized the fact: nevertheless, he struggled on as though in fulfillment of the most imperious duty. With an obstinate ring in his voice, he gave himself his orders:

"Forward: Ten minutes more!... You must!... And, once more, ten minutes!"

On either side lay things which, in any other circumstances, would have held his attention. An iron chest, three old guns, small-arms, cannonballs, a submarine. Enormous fish lay stranded on the sand. Sometimes a white seagull circled through space.

And so he came to a great wreck whose state of preservation betrayed a recent disaster. It was an overturned steamer, with her keel deeply buried in a sandy hollow, while her black stern stood erect, displaying a broad pink stripe on which Simon read:

"The *Bonne Vierge*, Calais."

And he remembered. The *Bonne Vierge* was one of the two boats whose loss had been announced in the telegrams posted up at Newhaven. Employed in the coasting-trade between the north and west of France, she had sunk at a spot which lay in a direct line between Calais and Le Havre; and Simon saw in this a positive proof that he was still following the French coast, passing those sea-marks whose names he now recalled: the Ridin de Dieppe, the Bassure de Baas, the Vergoyer and so on.

It was ten o'clock in the morning. From the average pace which he had maintained, allowing for deviation and for hilly ground, Simon calculated that he had covered a distance of nearly forty miles as the crow flies and that he ought to find himself approximately on a level with Le Touquet.

"What am I risking if I push on?" he asked himself. "At most I should have to do another forty miles to pass through the Straits of Dover and come out into the North Sea... in which case my position would be none too cheerful. But it will be devilish odd if, between this and that, I don't touch land somewhere. The only trouble is, whether it's forty miles on or forty miles back, those things can't be done on an empty stomach."

Fortunately, for he was feeling symptoms of a fatigue to which he was unaccustomed, the problem solved itself without his assistance. After going around the wreck, he managed to crawl under the poop and there discovered a heap of packing-cases which evidently formed part of the cargo. All were more or less split or broken or gaping at the corners. But one of them, whose lid Simon had no difficulty in prying open, contained tins of syrup, bottles of wine and stacks of canned foods: meat, fish, vegetables and fruits.

"Splendid!" he said, laughing. "Luncheon is served, sir. On top of that, a little rest; and the sooner I'm off the better!"

He made an excellent lunch; and a long siesta, under the vessel, among the packing-cases, restored his strength completely. When he woke and saw that his watch was already pointing to noon, he felt uneasy at the waste of time and suddenly reflected that others must have taken the same path and would now be able to catch him up and outstrip him. And he did not intend this to happen. Accordingly, feeling as fit as at the moment of starting, provided with the indispensable provisions and determined to follow up the adventure to the very end, without a companion to share his glory or to rob him of it, he set off again at a very brisk, unflagging pace.

"I shall get there," he thought, "I mean to get there. All this is an unprecedented phenomenon, the creation of a tract of land which will utterly change the conditions of life in this part of the world. I mean to be there first and to see... to see what? I don't know, *but I mean to do it.*"

What rapture to tread a soil on which no one has ever set foot! Men travel in search of this rapture to the utmost ends of the earth, to remote countries, no matter where; and very often the secret is hardly worth discovering. As for Simon, he was having his wonderful adventure in the heart of the oldest regions of old Europe. The Channel! The French coast! To be treading virgin soil here, of all places, where mankind had lived for three or four thousand years! To behold sights that no other eye had ever looked upon! To come after the Gauls, the Romans, the Franks, the Anglo-Saxons and to be the first to pass! To be the first to pass this way, ahead of the millions and millions of men who would follow in his track, on the new path which he would have inaugurated!

One o'clock... Half-past one... More ridges of sand, more wrecks. Always that curtain of clouds. And always Simon's lingering impression of a goal which eluded him. The tide, still low, was leaving a greater number of islands uncovered. The waves were breaking far out to sea and rolling across wide sand banks as though the new land had widened considerably.

About two o'clock in the afternoon, he came upon higher undulations followed by a series of sandy flats in which his feet sank to a greater depth than usual. Absorbed by the dreary spectacle of a ship's mast protruding from the sand, with its tattered and colored flag flopping in the wind, he pressed on all unsuspecting. In a few minutes, the sand was up to his knees, then half-way up his thighs. He laughed, still unheeding.

In the end, however, unable to advance, he tried to return: his efforts were useless. He attempted to lift his legs by treading, as though climbing a flight of stairs, but he could not. He brought his hands into play, laying them flat on the sands: they too went under.

Then he broke into a flood of perspiration. He suddenly understood the hideous truth: he was caught in a quicksand.

It was soon over. He did not sink with the slowness that lends a little hope to the agony of despair. Simon fell, so to speak, into a void. His hips, his waist, his chest disappeared. His outstretched arms checked his descent for a moment.

He stiffened his body, he struggled. In vain. The sand rose like water to his shoulders, to his neck.

He began to shout. But in the immensity of these solitudes, to whom was his appeal addressed? Nothing could save him from the most horrible of deaths. Then it was that he shut his eyes and with clenched lips sealed his mouth, which was already full of the taste of the sand, and, in a fit of terror, he gave himself up for lost.

VI. Triumph

Afterwards, he never quite understood the chance to which he owed his life. The most that he could remember was that one of his feet touched something solid which served him as a support and that something else enabled him to advance, now a step, now two or three, to lift himself little by little out of his living tomb and to leave it alive. What had happened? Had he come upon a loose plank of the buried vessel whose flag he saw before him? He did not know. But what he never forgot was the horror of that minute, which was followed by such a collapse of all his will and strength that he remained for a long time lying on a piece of wreckage, unable to move a limb and shuddering all over with fever and mental anguish.

He set off again mechanically, under the irresistible influence of confused feelings which bade him go forward and reconnoiter. But he had lost his former energy. His eyes remain obstinately fixed upon the ground. For no appreciable reason, he judged certain spots to be dangerous and avoided them by making a circuit, or even leapt back as though at the sight of an abyss. Simon Dubosc was afraid.

Moreover, after reading on a piece of wood from a wreck the name of Le Havre, that is to say, the port which lay behind him, he asked himself anxiously whether the new land had not changed its direction; whether, by doubling upon itself, it was not leading him into the widest part of the Channel.

The thought of no longer knowing where he was or where he was going increased his lassitude twofold. He felt overwhelmed, discouraged, terribly alone. He had no hope of rescue, either by sea, on which no boat would dare put out, or from the air, which the sea-fog had made impossible for aeroplanes. What would happen then?

Nevertheless he walked on; and the hours went by; and the belt of land unrolled vaguely before his eyes the same monotonous spectacle, the same melancholy sand-hills, the same dreary landscapes on which no sun had ever shone.

"I shall get there," he repeated, stubbornly. "I mean to get there; I must and shall."

Four o'clock. He often looked at his watch, as though expecting a miraculous intervention at some precise moment, he did not know when. Worn out by excessive and ill-directed efforts, exhausted by the fear of a hideous death, he was gradually yielding beneath the weight of a fatigue which tortured his body and unhinged his brain. He was afraid. He dreaded the trap laid for him by the sands. He dreaded the threatening night, the storm and, above all, hunger, for all his provisions had been lost in the abyss of the quicksand.

The agony which he suffered! A score of times he was on the point of stretching himself on the ground and abandoning the struggle. But the thought of Isabel sustained him; and he walked on and on.

And then, suddenly, an astonishing sight held him motionless. Was it possible? He hesitated to believe it, so incredible did the reality seem to him. But how could he doubt the evidence of his eyes?

He stooped forward. Yes, it was really that: there were footprints! The ground was marked with footprints, the prints of two bare feet, very plainly defined and apparently quite recent.

And immediately his stupefaction made way for a great joy, aroused by the sudden and clear conception of a most undeniable fact: the new land was indeed connected, as he had supposed, with some point on the northern coast of France; and from this point, which could not be very remote, in view of the distance which he himself had covered, one of his fellow-creatures had come thus far.

Delighted to feel that there was human life near at hand, he recollected the incident where Robinson Crusoe discovers the imprint of a naked foot on the sand of his desert island:

"It's Man Friday's footprint!" he said, laughing. "There is a Friday, too, in this land of mine! Let's see if we can find him!"

At the point where he had crossed the trail, it branched off to the left and approached the sea. Simon was feeling surprised at not meeting or catching sight of anyone, when he discovered that the author of the footprints, after going round a shapeless wreck, had turned and was therefore walking in the same direction as himself.

After twenty minutes, the trail, intersected by a gully which ran across it, escaped him for a time. He found it again and followed it, skirting the base of a chain of rather high sand-hills, which ended suddenly in a sort of craggy cliff.

On rounding this cliff Simon started back. On the ground, flat on its face, with the arms at right angles to the body, lay the corpse of a man, curiously dressed in a very short, yellow leather waistcoat and a pair of trousers, likewise leather, the ends of which were bell-shaped and slit in the Mexican fashion. In the middle of his back was the hilt of a dagger which had been driven between the shoulder-blades.

What astonished Simon when he had turned the body over was that the face was brick-red, with prominent cheek bones and long, black hair: it was the undoubted face of a Indian. Blood trickled from the mouth, which was distorted by a hideous grin. The eyes were wide open and showed only their whites. The contracted fingers had gripped the sand like claws. The body was still warm.

"It can't be an hour since he was killed," said Simon, whose hand was trembling. And he added, "What the deuce brought the fellow here? By what unheard-of chance have I come upon a Indian in this desert?"

The dead man's pockets contained no papers to give Simon any information. But, near the body, within the actual space in which the struggle had taken place, another trail of footsteps came to an end, a double trail, made by the patterned rubber soles of a man who had come and gone. And, ten yards away, Simon picked up a gold hundred-franc piece, with the head of Napoleon I and the date 1807.

He followed this double trail, which led him to the edge of the sea. Here a boat had been put aground. It was now easy to reconstruct the tragedy. Two men who had landed on this newly-created shore had set out to explore it, each taking his own direction. One of them, an Indian, had found, in the hulk of some wreck, a certain quantity of gold coins, perhaps locked up in a strongbox. The other, to obtain the treasure for himself, had murdered his companion, and reembarked.

Thus, on this virgin soil, Simon was confronted—it was the first sign of life—with a crime, with an act of treachery, with armed cupidity committing murder, with the human animal. A man finds gold. One of his fellows attacks and kills him.

Simon pushed onwards without further delay, feeling certain that these two men, doubtless bolder than the rest, were only the forerunners of others coming from the mainland. He was eager to see these others, to question them upon the point whence they had started, the distance which they had covered and many further particulars which as yet remained unexplained.

The thought of this meeting filled him with such happiness that he resisted his longing for rest. Yet what a torture was this almost uninterrupted effort! He had walked for sixteen hours since leaving Dieppe. It was eighteen hours since the moment when the great upheaval had driven him from his home. In ordinary times the effort would not have been beyond his strength. But under what lamentable conditions had he accomplished it!

He walked on and on. Rest? And what if the others, coming behind him from Dieppe, should succeed in catching him up?

The scene was always the same. Wrecks marked his path, like so many tombstones. The mist still hung above the endless graveyard.

After walking an hour, he was brought to a stop. The sea barred his way.

The sea facing him! His disappointment was not unmixed with anger. Was this then the limit of his journey and were all these convulsions of nature to end merely in the creation of a peninsula cut off in this meaningless fashion?

But, on scanning from the sloping shore the waves tossing their foam to where he stood, he perceived at some distance a darker mass, which gradually emerged from the mist; and he felt sure that this was a continuation of the newly-created land, beyond a depression covered by the sea:

"I must get across," said Simon.

He removed his clothes, made them into a bundle, tied it round his neck and entered the water. For him the crossing of this strait, in which, besides, he was for some time able to touch bottom, was mere child's play. He landed, dried himself and resumed his clothes.

A very gentle ascent led him, after some five hundred yards, to a reef, overtopped by actual hills of sand, but of sand so firm that he did not hesitate to set foot on it. He therefore climbed till he reached the highest crest of these hills.

And it was here, at this spot—where a granite column was raised subsequently, with an inscription in letters of gold: two names and a date—it was here, on the 4th of June, at ten minutes past six in the evening, above a vast amphitheater girt about with sand-hills like the benches of a circus, it was here that Simon Dubosc at last saw, climbing to meet him, a man.

He did not move at first, so strong was his emotion. The man came on slowly, sauntering, as it were, examining his surroundings and picking his way. When at last he raised his head, he gave a start of surprise at seeing Simon and then waved his cap. Then Simon rushed towards him, with outstretched arms and an immense longing to press him to his breast.

At a distance the stranger seemed a young man. He was dressed like a fisherman, in a brown canvas smock and trousers. His feet were bare; he was tall and broad-shouldered. Simon shouted to him:

"I've come from Dieppe. You, what town do you come from? Did you take long to get here? Are you alone?"

He could see that the fisherman was smiling and that his tanned, clean-shaven face wore a frank and happy expression.

They met and clasped hands; and Simon repeated:

"I started from Dieppe at one in the morning. And you? What port do you come from?"

The man began to laugh and replied in words which Simon could not understand. He did not understand them, though he well enough recognized the language in which they were uttered. It was English, but a dialect spoken by the lower orders. He concluded that this was an English fisherman employed at Calais or Dunkirk.

He spoke to him again, dwelling on his syllables and pointing to the horizon:

"Calais? Dunkirk?"

The other repeated these two names as well as he could, as though trying to grasp their meaning. At last his face lit up and he shook his head.

Then, turning round and pointing in the direction from which he had come, he twice said:

"Hastings... Hastings..."

Simon started. But the amazing truth did not appear to him at once, though he was conscious of its approach and was absolutely dumbfounded. Of course, the fisherman was referring to Hastings as his birthplace or his usual home. But where had he come from at this moment?

Simon made a suggestion:

"Boulogne? Wimereux?"

"No, no!" replied the stranger. "Hastings... England..."

And his arm pointed persistently to the same quarter of the horizon, while he as persistently repeated:

"England... England..."

"What? What's that you're saying?" cried Simon. And he seized the man violently by the shoulders. "What's that you're saying? That's England behind you? You've come from England? No, no! You can't mean that. It's not true!"

The sailor struck the ground with his foot:

"*England!*" he repeated, thus denoting that the ground which he had stamped upon led to the English mainland.

Simon was flabbergasted. He took out his watch and moved his forefinger several times round the dial.

"What time did you start? How many hours have you been walking?"

"Three," replied the Englishman, opening his fingers.

"Three hours!" muttered Simon. "We are three hours from the English coast!"

This time the whole stupendous truth forced itself upon him. At the same moment he realized what had caused his mistake. As the French coast ran due north, from the estuary of the Somme, it was inevitable that, in pursuing a direction parallel to the French coast, he should end by reaching the English coast at Folkstone or Dover, or, if his path inclined slightly toward the west, at Hastings.

Now he had not taken this into account. Having had proof on three occasions that France was on his right and not behind him, he had walked with his mind dominated by the certainty that France was close at hand and that her coast might loom out of the fog at any moment.

And it was the English coast! And the man who had loomed into sight was a man of England!

What a miracle! How his every nerve throbbed as he held this man in his arms and gazed into his friendly face! He was exalted by the intuition of the extraordinary things which the tremendous event of the last few hours implied, in the present and the future; and his meeting with this man of England was the very symbol of that event.

And the fisherman, too, felt the incomparable grandeur of the moment which had brought them together. His quiet smile was full of solemnity. He nodded his head in silence. And the two men, face to face, looking into each other's eyes, gazed at each other with the peculiar affection of those who have never been parted, who have striven side by side and who receive together the reward of their actions performed in common.

The Englishman wrote his name on a piece of paper: William Brown. And Simon, yielding to one of his natural outbursts of enthusiasm, said:

"William Brown, we do not speak the same language; you do not understand me and I understand you only imperfectly; and still we are bound together more closely than two loving brothers could be. Our embrace has a significance which we cannot yet imagine. You and I represent the two greatest and noblest countries in the world; and they are mingled together in our two persons."

He was weeping. The Englishman still smiled, but his eyes were moist with tears. Excitement, excessive fatigue, the violence of the emotions which he had experienced that day, produced in Simon a sort of intoxication in which he found an unsuspected source of energy.

"Come," he said to the fisherman catching hold of his arm. "Come, show me the way."

He would not even allow William Brown to help him in difficult places, so determined was he to accomplish this glorious and magnificent undertaking by his unaided efforts.

This last stage of his journey lasted three hours.

Almost at the start they passed three Englishmen, to whom Brown addressed a few words and who, while continuing on their road, uttered exclamations of surprise. Then came two more, who stopped for a moment while Brown explained the situation. These two turned back with Simon and the fisherman; and all four, on coming closer to the sea, were attracted by a voice appealing for help.

Simon ran forward and was the first to reach a woman lying on the sand. The waves were drenching her with their spray. She was bound by cords which fettered her legs, held her arms motionless against her body, pressed the wet silk of her blouse against her breast and bruised the bare flesh of her shoulders. Her black hair, cut rather short and fastened in front by a little gold chain, framed a dazzling face, with lips like the petals of a red flower and a warm, brown skin, burnt by the sun. The face, to an artist like Simon, was of a brilliant beauty and recalled to his mind certain feminine types which he had encountered in Spain or South America. Quickly he cut her bonds; and then, as his companions were approaching before he had time to question her, he slipped off his jacket and covered her beautiful shoulders with it.

She gave him a grateful glance, as though this delicate act was the most precious compliment which he could pay her:

"Thank you, thank you!" she murmured. "You are French, are you not?"

But groups of people came hurrying along, followed by a more numerous company. Brown told the story of Simon's adventure; and Simon found himself separated from the young woman without learning more about her. People crowded about him, asking him questions. At every moment fresh crowds mingled with the procession which bore him along in its midst.

All these people seemed to Simon unusually excited and strange in their behavior. He soon learnt that the earthquake had devastated the English coast. Hastings, having been, like Dieppe, a center of seismic shocks, was partly destroyed.

About eight o'clock they came to the edge of a deep depression quite two-thirds of a mile in width. Filled with water until the middle of the afternoon, this depression, by a stroke of luck for Simon, had delayed the progress of those who were flying from Hastings and who had ventured upon the new land.

A few minutes later, the fog being now less dense, Simon was able to distinguish the endless row of houses and hotels which lines the sea fronts of Hastings and St. Leonards. By this time, his escort consisted of three or four hundred people; and many others, doubtless driven from their houses, were wandering in all directions with dazed expressions on their faces.

The throng about him became so thick that soon he was able to see nothing in the heavy gloom of the twilight but their crowded heads and shoulders. He replied as best he could to the thousand questions which were put to him; and his replies, repeated from mouth to mouth, aroused cries of astonishment and admiration.

Gradually, lights appeared in the Hastings windows. Simon, exhausted but indomitable, was walking briskly, sustained by a nervous energy which seemed to be renewed as and when he expended it. And suddenly he burst out laughing to think—and certainly no thought could have been more stimulating or better calculated to give a last fillip to his failing strength—to think that he, Simon Dubosc, a man of the good old Norman stock, was setting foot in England at the very spot where William the Conqueror, Duke of Normandy, had landed in the eleventh century! Hastings! King Harold and his mistress, Edith of the swan's neck! The great adventure of yore was being reenacted! For the second time the virgin isle was conquered... and conquered by a Norman!

"I believe destiny is favoring me, my Lord Bakefield," he said to himself.

The new land joined the mainland between Hastings and St. Leonards. It was intersected by valleys and fissures, bristling with rocks and fragments of the cliffs, in the midst of which lay, in an indescribable jumble, the wreckage of demolished piers, fallen lighthouses, stranded and shattered ships. But Simon saw nothing of all this. His eyes were too weary to distinguish things save through a mist.

They reached the shore. What happened next? He was vaguely conscious that someone was leading him, through streets with broken pavements and between heaps of ruins, to the hall of a casino, a strange, dilapidated building, with tottering walls and a gaping roof, but nevertheless radiant with electric light.

The municipal authorities had assembled here to receive him. Champagne was drunk. Hymns of rejoicing were sung with religious fervor. A stirring spectacle and, at the same time, a striking proof of the national self-control, this celebration improvised in the midst of a town in ruins. But every one present had the impression that something of a very great importance had occurred, something so great that it outweighed the horror of the catastrophe and the consequent mourning: France and England were united!

France and England were united; and the first man who had walked from the one country to the other by the path which had risen from the very depths of the ancient Channel that used to divide them was there, in their midst. What could they do but honor him? He represented in his magnificent effort the vitality and the inexhaustible ardor of France. He was the hero and the herald of the most mysterious future.

A tremendous burst of cheering rose to the platform on which he stood. The crowd thronged about him, the men shook him by the hand, the ladies kissed him. They pressed him to make a speech which all could hear and understand. And Simon, leaning over these people, whose enthusiasm blended with his own exaltation, stammered a few words in praise of the two nations.

The frenzy was so violent and unbridled that Simon was jostled, carried off his feet, swept into the crowd and lost among the very people who were looking for him. His only thought was to go into the first hotel that offered and throw himself down on a bed. A hand seized his; and a voice said:

"Come with me; I will show you the way."

He recognized the young woman whom he had released from her bonds. Her face likewise was transfigured with emotion.

"You have done a splendid thing," she said. "I don't believe any other man could have done it... You are above all other men..."

An eddy in the crowd tore them apart, although the stranger's hand clutched his. He fell to the floor among the overturned chairs, picked himself up again and was feeling at the end of his tether as he neared one of the exits, when suddenly he stood to attention. Strength returned to his limbs. Lord Bakefield and Isabel were standing before him.

Eagerly Isabel held out her hand:

"We were there, Simon. We saw you. I'm proud of you, Simon."

He was astonished and confused.

"Isabel! Is it really you?"

She smiled, happy to see him so much moved in her presence.

"It really is; and it's quite natural, since we live at Battle, a mile away. The catastrophe has spared the house but we came to Hastings to help the sufferers and in that way heard of your arrival... of your triumph, Simon."

Lord Bakefield did not budge. He pretended to be looking in another direction. Simon addressed him.

"May I take it, Lord Bakefield, that you will regard this day's work as a first step towards the goal for which I am making?"

The old nobleman, stiff with pride and resentment, vouchsafed no reply.

"Of course," Simon continued, "I haven't conquered England. But all the same there seem to be a series of circumstances in my favor which permit me at least to ask you whether you consider that the first of your conditions has been fulfilled."

This time Lord Bakefield seemed to be making up his mind. But, just as he was going to reply—and his features expressed no great amount of good will—Isabel intervened:

"Don't ask my father any questions, Simon... He appreciates the wonderful thing that you have done at its true value. But you and I have offended him too seriously for him to be able to forgive you just yet. We must let time wipe out the unpleasant memory."

"Time!" echoed Simon, with a laugh. "Time! The trouble is that I have only twelve days left in which to triumph over all the labors put upon me. After conquering England, I have still to win the laurels of Hercules... or of Don Quixote."

"Well," she said, "in the meantime hurry off and go to bed. That's the best thing you can do for the moment."

And she drew Lord Bakefield away with her.

VII. Lynx-Eye

"What do you say to this, my boy? Did I prophesy it all, or did I not? Read my pamphlet on the Channel in the Year 2000, and you'll see. And then remember all I told you the other morning, at Newhaven station. Well, there you are: the two countries are joined together as they were once before, in the Eocene epoch."

Awakened with a start by Old Sandstone, Simon, with eyes still heavy with slumber, gazed vacantly at the hotel bedroom in which he had been sleeping, at his old professor, walking to and fro, and at another person, who was sitting in the dark and who seemed to be an acquaintance of Old Sandstone's.

"Ah!" yawned Simon. "But what's the time?"

"Seven o'clock in the evening, my son."

"What? Seven o'clock? Have I been sleeping since last night's meeting at the Casino?"

"Rather! I was strolling about this morning, when I heard of your adventure. 'Simon Dubosc! I know him.' said I. I ran like mad. I rapped on the door. I came in. Nothing would wake you. I went away, came back again and so on, until I decided to sit down by your bedside and wait."

Simon leapt out of bed. New clothes and clean linen had been laid out in the bathroom; and he saw, hanging on the wall, his jacket, the same with which he had covered the bare shoulders of the young woman whom he had released.

"Who brought that?" he asked.

"That? What?" asked Old Sandstone.

Simon turned to him.

"Tell me, professor, did anyone come to this room while you were here?"

"Yes, lots of people. They came in as they liked: admirers, idle sight-seers..."

"Did a woman come in?"

"Upon my word, I didn't notice... Why?"

"Why?" replied Simon, explaining. "Because last night, while I was asleep, I several times had the impression that a woman came up to me and bent over me..."

Old Sandstone shrugged his shoulders:

"You've been dreaming, my boy. When one's badly overtired, one's likely to have those nightmares..."

"But it wasn't in the very least a nightmare!" said Simon, laughing.

"It's stuff and nonsense, in any case!" cried Old Sandstone. "What does it matter? There's only one thing that matters: this sudden joining up of the two coasts... It's fairly tremendous, what? What do you think of it? It's more than a bridge thrown from shore to shore. It's more than a tunnel. It's a flesh-and-blood tie, a permanent junction, an isthmus, what? The Sussex Isthmus, the Isthmus of Normandy, they've already christened it."

Simon jested:

"Oh, an isthmus!... A mere causeway, at most!"

"You're driveling!" cried Old Sandstone. "Don't you know what happened last night? Why, of course not, the fellow knows nothing! He was asleep! Then you didn't realize that there was another earthquake? Quite a slight one, but still... an earthquake? No? You didn't wake up? In that case, my boy, listen to the incredible truth, which surpasses what anyone could have foreseen. It's no longer a question of the strip of earth which you crossed from Dieppe to Hastings. That was the first attempt, just a little trial phenomenon. But since then... oh, since then, my boy... you're listening, aren't you? Well, there, from Fécamp to Cape Gris-nez in France and from the west of Brighton to Folkstone in England: all that part, my boy, is now one solid mass. Yes, it forms a permanent junction, seventy to ninety miles wide, a bit of exposed ground equivalent at least to two large French departments or two fair-sized English counties. Nature hasn't done badly... for a few hours' work! What say you?"

Simon listened in amazement:

"Is it possible? Are you sure? But then it will be the cause of unspeakable losses. Think: all the coast-towns ruined... and trade... navigation..."

And Simon, thinking of his father and the vessels locked up in Dieppe harbor, repeated:

"Are you quite sure?"

"Why, of course I am!" said Old Sandstone, to whom all these considerations were utterly devoid of interest. "Of course, I'm sure! A hundred telegrams, from all sides, vouch for the fact. What's more, read the evening papers. Oh, I give you my word, it's a blessed revolution!... The earthquake? The victims? We hardly mention them!... Your Franco-English raid? An old story! No, there's only one thing that matters to-day, on this side of the Channel: England is no long-er an Island; she forms part of the European continent; she is riveted on to France!"

"This," said Simon, "is one of the greatest facts in history!"

"It's _the_ greatest, my son. Since the world has been a world and since men have been gathered into nations, there has been no physical phenomenon of greater importance than this. And to think that I predicted the whole thing, the causes and the effects, the causes which I am the only one to know!"

"And what are they?" asked Simon. "How is it that I was able to pass? How is it..."

Old Sandstone checked him with a gesture which reminded Simon of the way in which his former lecturer used to begin his explanations at college; and the old codger, taking a pen and a sheet of paper, proceeded:

"Do you know what a fault is? Of course not! Or a horst? Ditto! Oh, a ge-ology lesson at Dieppe college was so many hours wasted! Well, lend me your ears, young Dubosc! I will be brief and to the point. The terrestrial rind—that is, the crust which surrounds the internal fireball, of solidified elements and erup-tive or sedimentary rocks—consists throughout of layers superposed like the pages of a book. Imagine forces of some kind, acting laterally, to compress those layers. There will be corrugations, sometimes actual fractures, the two sides of which, sliding one against the other, will be either raised or depressed. Faults is the name which we give to the fractures that penetrate the terrestrial shell and separate two masses of rock, one of which slides over the plane of fracture. The fault, therefore, reveals an edge, a lower lip produced by the subsidence of the soil, and an upper lip produced by an elevation. Now it happens that suddenly, after thousands and thousands of years, this upper lip, under the action of irre-sistible tangential forces, will rise, shoot upwards, and form considerable out-throws, to which we give the name of horsts. This is what has just taken place... There exists in France, marked on the geological charts, a fault known as the Rouen fault, which is an important dislocation of the Paris basin. Parallel to the corrugations of the soil, which have wrinkled the cretaceous and tertiary depos-its in this region from north-east to north-west, it runs from Versailles to seven-ty-five miles beyond Rouen. At Maromme, we lose it. But I, Simon, have found it again in the quarries above Longueville and also not far from Dieppe. And lastly I have found it... where do you think? In England, at Eastbourne, between Hastings and Newhaven! Same composition, same disposition. There was no question of a mistake. It ran from France to England! It ran under the Channel... Ah, how I have studied it, my fault, Old Sandstone's fault, as I used to call it! How I have sounded it, deciphered its meanings, questioned it, analyzed it! And then, suddenly in 1912, some seismic shocks affected the table lands of the Seine-Inférieure and the Somme and acted in an abnormal manner as I was able to prove—on the tides! Shocks in Normandy! In the Somme! Right out at sea! Do you grasp the strangeness of such a phenomenon and how, on the other hand, it acquired a significant value from the very fact that it took place along a fault? Might we not suppose that there were stresses along this fault, that captive forces were seeking to escape through the earth's crust and attacking the points of least resistance, which happened to lie precisely along the lines of the faults?... You may call it an improbable theory. Perhaps so; but at any rate it seemed worth verifying. And I did verify it. I made diving-experiments within sight of the French coast. At my fourth descent, in the Ridin de Dieppe, where the depth is only thirty feet, I discovered traces of an eruption in the two blocks of a fault all of whose elements tallied with those of the Anglo-Norman fault... That was all I wanted to know. There was nothing more to do but wait... a century or two... or else a few hours... Meanwhile it was patent to me that sooner or later the fragile obstacle opposed to the internal energies would break down and the great upheaval would come to pass. It has come to pass."

Simon listened with growing interest. Old Sandstone illustrated his lecture with diagrams drawn with broad strokes of the pen and smeared with blots which his sleeve or fingers generously spread all over the paper. Drops of sweat also played their part, falling from his forehead, for Old Sandstone was always given to perspiring copiously.

He repeated:

"It has come to pass, with a whole train of precursory or concomitant phenomena: submarine eruptions, whirlpools, boats and ships hurled into the air and drawn under by the most terrible suction; and then seismic tremors, more or less marked, cyclones, waterspouts and the devil's own mischief; and then a cataclysm of an earthquake. And immediately afterwards, indeed at the same moment, the shooting up of one lip of the fault, projecting from one coast to the other, over a width of seventy or eighty miles. And then, on the top of it, you, Simon Dubosc, crossing the Channel at a stride. And this perhaps was not the least remarkable fact, my boy, in the whole story."

Simon was silent for some time. Then he said:

"So far, so good. You have explained the emergence of the narrow belt of earth which I walked along and whose width I measured with my eyes, I might say, incessantly. But how do you explain the emergence of this immense region which now fills the Straits of Dover and part of the Channel?"

"Perhaps the Anglo-Norman fault had ramifications in the affected areas?"

"I repeat, I saw only a narrow belt of land."

"That is to say, you saw and crossed only the highest crests of the upheaved region, crests forming a ridge. But this region was thrown up altogether; and you must have noticed that the waves, instead of subsiding, were rolling over miles of beach."

"That is so. Nevertheless the sea was there and is there no longer."

"It is there no longer because it has receded. Phenomena of this extent produce reactions beyond their immediate field of activity and give rise to other phenomena, which in turn react upon the first. And, if this dislocation of the bottom of the Channel has raised one part, it may very well, in some other subma-rine part, have provoked subsidences and ruptures by which the sea has escaped through the crust. Observe that a reduction of level of six to nine feet was enough to turn those miles of barely covered beach into permanent dry land."

"A supposition, my dear professor."

"Nothing of the sort!" cried Old Sandstone, striking the table with his fists. "Nothing of the sort! I have positive evidence of this also; and I shall publish all my proofs at a suitable moment, which will not be long delayed."

He drew from his pocket the famous locked wallet, whose grease-stained leather had caught Simon's eye at Newhaven, and declared:

"The truth will emerge from this, my lad, from this wallet in which my notes have been accumulating, four hundred and fifteen notes which must needs serve for reference. For, now that the phenomenon has come to pass and all its mysterious causes have been wiped out by the upheaval, people will never know anything except what I have observed by personal experiments. They will put forward theories, draw inferences, form conclusions. *But they will not see.* Now I... have *seen.*"

Simon, who was only half listening, interrupted:

"In the meantime, my dear professor, I am hungry. Will you have some dinner?"

"No, thanks. I must catch the train to Dover and cross to-night. It seems the Calais-Dover boats are running again; and I have no time to lose if I'm to pub-lish an article and take up a definite position." He glanced at his watch. "Phew! It's jolly late!... If only I don't lose my train!... See you soon, my boy!"

He departed.

The other person sitting in the dark had not stirred during this conversation and, to Simon's great astonishment, did not stir either after Old Sandstone had taken his leave. Simon, at switching on the light, was amazed to find himself face to face with an individual resembling in every respect the man whose body he had seen near the wreck on the previous evening. There was the same brick-red face, the same prominent cheekbones, the same long hair, the same buff leather clothing. This man, however, was very much younger, with a noble bear-ing and a handsome face.

"A true Indian chief," thought Simon, "and it seems to me that I have seen him before... Yes, I have certainly seen him somewhere. But where? And when?"

The stranger was silent. Simon asked him:

"What can I do for you, please?"

The other had risen to his feet. He went to the little table on which Simon had emptied his pockets, took up the coin with the head of Napoleon I which Simon had found the day before and, speaking excellent French, but in a voice whose guttural tone harmonized with his appearance, said:

"You picked up this coin yesterday, on your way here, near a dead body, did you not?"

His guess was so correct and so unexpected that Simon could but confirm it:

"I did... near a man who had just been stabbed to death."

"Perhaps you were able to trace the murderer's footprints?"

"Yes."

"They were prints of bathing-shoes or tennis-shoes, with patterned rubber soles?"

"Yes, yes!" said Simon, more and more puzzled. "But how do you know that?"

"Well, sir," continued the man whom Simon silently called the Indian, without replying to the question, "Well, sir, yesterday one of my friends, Badiarinos by name, and his niece Dolores, wishing to explore the new land after the convulsions of the morning, discovered, in the harbor, amid the ruins, a narrow channel which communicated with the sea and was still free at that moment. A man who was getting into a boat offered to take my friend and his niece along with him. After rowing for some time, they saw several large wrecks and landed. Badiarinos left his niece in the boat and went off in one direction, while their companion took another. An hour later, the latter returned alone, carrying an old broken cashbox with gold escaping from it. Seeing blood on one of his sleeves, Dolores became alarmed and tried to get out of the boat. He flung himself upon her and, in spite of her desperate resistance, succeeded in tying her up. He took the oars again and turned back along the new coast line. On the way, he decided to get rid of her and threw her overboard. She had the good luck to fall on a sandbank which became uncovered a few minutes later and which was soon joined to the mainland. For all that, she would have been dead if you had not released her."

"Yes," murmured Simon, "a Spaniard, isn't she? Very beautiful... I saw her again at the casino."

"We spent the whole evening," continued the Indian, in the same impassive tones, "hunting for the murderer, at the meeting in the casino, in the bars of the hotels, in the public-houses, everywhere. This morning we began again... and I came here, wishing also to bring you the coat which you had lent to my friend's niece."

"It was you, then?"

"Now, on entering the corridor upon which your room opens, I heard someone groaning and I saw, a little way ahead of me—the corridor is very dark—I saw a man dragging himself along the floor, wounded, half-dead. A servant and I carried him into one of the rooms which are being used for infirmary purposes; and I could see that he had been stabbed between the shoulders... as my friend was! Was I on the track of the murderer? It was difficult to make enquiries in this great hotel, crammed with the mixed crowd of people who have

191

come here for shelter. At last I discovered that, a little before nine o'clock, a lady's maid, coming from outside, with a letter in her hand, had asked the porter for M. Simon Dubosc. The porter replied, 'Second floor, room 44.'"

"But I haven't had that letter!" Simon remarked.

"The porter, luckily for you, mistook the number. You're in room 43."

"And what became of it? Who sent it?"

"Here is a piece of the envelope which I picked up," replied the Indian. "You can still make out a seal with Lord Bakefield's arms. So I went to Battle House."

"And you saw... ?"

"Lord Bakefield, his wife and his daughter had left for London this morning, by motor. But I saw the maid, the one who had been to the hotel with a letter for you from her mistress. As she was going upstairs, she was overtaken by a gentleman who said, 'M. Simon Dubosc is asleep and said I was to let no one in. I'll give him the letter.' The maid therefore handed him the letter and accepted a tip of a louis. Here's the louis. It's one with the head of Napoleon I and the date 1807 and is therefore precisely similar to the coin which you picked up near my friend's body."

"And then?" asked Simon, anxiously. "Then this man... ?"

"The man, having read the letter, went and knocked at room 44, which is the next room to yours. Your neighbor opened the door and was seized by the throat, while the murderer, with his free arm, drove a dagger into his neck, above the shoulders."

"Do you mean to say that he was stabbed instead of me?..."

"Yes, instead of you. But he is not dead. They will pull him through."

Simon was stunned.

"It's dreadful!" he muttered. "Again, that particular way of striking!..."

After a short pause, he asked:

"Do you know nothing of the contents of the letter?"

"From some words exchanged by Lord Bakefield and his daughter the maid gathered that they were discussing the wreck of the *Queen Mary*, the steamer on which Miss Bakefield had been shipwrecked the other day and which must be lying high and dry by now. Miss Bakefield appears to have lost a miniature."

"Yes," said Simon, thoughtfully, "yes, I dare say. But it is most distressing that this letter was not placed in my own hands. The maid ought never to have given it up."

"Why should she have been suspicious?"

"What! Of the first person she met?"

"But she knew him."

"She knew this man?"

"Certainly. She had often seen him at Lord Bakefield's; he is a frequent visitor to the house."

"Then she was able to give you his name?"

"She told me his name."

"Well?"

"His name's Rolleston."

Simon gave a start.

"Rolleston!" he exclaimed. "But that's impossible!... Rolleston! What madness!... What's the fellow like? Give me a description of him."

"The man whom the maid and I saw is very tall, which enables him to bend over his victims and stab them from above between the shoulders. He is thin... stoops a little... and he's very pale..."

"Stop!" ordered Simon, impressed by this description, which was that of Edward. "Stop!... The man is a friend of mine and I'll answer for him as I would for myself. Rolleston a murderer! What nonsense!"

And Simon broke into a nervous laugh, while the Indian, still impassive, resumed:

"Among other matters, the maid told me of a public house, frequented by rather doubtful people, where Rolleston, a great whiskey drinker, was a familiar customer. This information was found to be correct. The barman, whom I tipped lavishly, told me that Rolleston had just been there, at about twelve o'clock, that he had enlisted half-a-dozen rascals who were game for anything and that the object of the expedition was the wreck of the *Queen Mary*. I was now fully informed. The whole complicated business was beginning to have a meaning; and I at once made the necessary preparations, though I made a point of coming back here constantly, so that I might be present when you awoke and tell you the news. Moreover, I took care that your friend, Mr. Sandstone, should watch over you; and I locked your pocketbook, which was lying there for anybody to help himself from, in this drawer. I took ten thousand francs out of it to finance our common business."

Simon was past being astonished by the doings of this strange individual. He could have taken all the notes with which the pocketbook was crammed; he had taken only ten. He was at least an honest man.

"Our business?" said Simon. "What do you mean by that?"

"It will not take long to explain, M. Dubosc," replied the Indian, speaking as a man who knows beforehand that he has won his cause. "It's this. Miss Bakefield lost, in the wreck of the *Queen Mary*, a miniature of the greatest value; and her letter was asking you to go and look for it. The letter was intercepted by Rolleston, who was thus informed of the existence of this precious object and at the same time, no doubt, became acquainted with Miss Bakefield's feelings towards you. If we admit that Rolleston, as the maid declares, is in love with Miss Bakefield, this in itself explains his pleasant intention of stabbing you. At any rate, after recruiting half-a-dozen blackguards of the worst kind, he set out for the wreck of the *Queen Mary*. Are you going to leave the road clear for him, M. Dubosc?"

Simon did not at once reply. He was thinking. How could he fail to be struck by the logic of the facts that had come to his notice? Nor could he forget Rolleston's habits, his way of living, his love of whisky and his general extravagance. Nevertheless, he once more asserted;

"Rolleston is incapable of such a thing."

"All right," said the Indian. "But certain men have set out to seize the *Queen Mary*. Are you going to leave the road clear for them? I'm not. I have the death of my friend Badiarinos to avenge. You have Miss Bakefield's letter to bear in mind. We will make a start then. Everything is arranged. Four of my comrades have been notified. I have bought arms, horses and enough provisions to last us. I repeat, everything is ready. What are you going to do?"

Simon threw off his dressing-gown and snatched at his clothes:

"I shall come with you."

"Oh, well," said the Indian smiling, "if you imagine that we can venture on the new land in the middle of the night! What about the water courses? And the quicksands? And all the rest of it? To say nothing of the devil's own fog! No, no, we shall start to-morrow morning, at four o'clock. In the meantime, eat, M. Dubosc, and sleep."

Simon protested:

"Sleep! Why, I've done nothing else since yesterday!"

"That's not enough. You have undergone the most terrible exertions; and this will be a trying expedition, very trying and very dangerous. You can take Lynx-Eye's word for it."

"Lynx-Eye?"

"Antonio or Lynx-Eye: those are my names," explained the Indian. "Then to-morrow morning, M. Dubosc!"

Simon obeyed like a child. Since they had been living for the past few days in such a topsy-turvy world, could he do better than follow the advice of a man whom he had never seen, who was a Indian and who was called Lynx-Eye?

When he had had his meal, he glanced through an evening paper. There was an abundance of news, serious and contradictory. It was stated that Southampton and Le Havre were blocked. It was said that the British fleet was immobilized at Portsmouth. The rivers, choked at their mouths, were overflowing their banks. Everywhere all was disorder and confusion; communications were broken, harbors were filled with sand, ships were lying on their sides, trade was interrupted; everywhere devastation reigned and famine and despair; the local authorities were impotent and the governments distraught.

It was late when Simon at last fell into a troubled sleep.

It seemed to him that after an hour or two someone opened the door of his room; and he remembered that he had not bolted it. Light footsteps crossed the carpet. Then he had the impression that someone bent over him and that this someone was a woman. A cool breath caressed his face and in the darkness he divined a shadow moving quickly away.

He tried to switch on the light, but there was no current.

The shadow left the room. Was it the young woman whom he had released, who had come? But why should she have come?

VIII. On the War-Path

At four o'clock in the morning, the streets were almost empty. A few fruit and vegetable carts were making their way between the demolished houses and the shattered pavements. But from a neighboring avenue there emerged a little cavalcade in which Simon immediately recognized, at the head of the party, astride a monstrous big horse, Old Sandstone, wearing his rusty top-hat, with the skirts of his black frockcoat overflowing either side of a saddle with bulging saddlebags.

Next came Antonio, a.k.a. Lynx-Eye, likewise mounted; then a third horseman, perched like the others behind heavy saddlebags; and lastly three persons on foot, one of whom held the bridle of a fourth horse. The three pedestrians had brick-red faces and long hair and were dressed in the same style as Lynx-Eye, in soft leggings with leather fringes, velveteen breeches, flannel girdles, wide-brimmed felt hats, with gaudy ribbons: in short, a heterogeneous, picturesque band, with many-colored accoutrements, in which the adornments dear to circus cow-boys were displayed side by side with those of one of Fenimore Cooper's Indians, or one of Gustave Aimard's scouts.[54] They carried rifles slung across their shoulders and revolvers and daggers in their belts.

"What the deuce!" exclaimed Simon. "Why, this is a martial progress! Are we going among savages?"

"We are going into a country," replied Antonio, gravely, "Where there are no inhabitants, no inns, no victuals, but where there are already visitors as dangerous as beasts of prey, which is why we have to carry two days' provisions and two days' supply of oats and compressed fodder for our mounts. This, then, is our escort. These are the brothers Mazzani, the elder and the younger. This is Forsetta. Here is Mr. Sandstone. Here, on horseback, is one of my personal friends. And here, lastly, for you, is Orlando III, out of Chiquita."

And, at a sign from the Indian, a noble animal was led forward, lean, sinewy and nervous, standing very high on its long legs.

Simon mounted, much amused:

"And you, my dear professor?" he said to Old Sandstone: "Are you one of the party?"

"I lost my train," said the old fellow, "and on returning to the hotel I met Lynx-Eye, who recruited me. I represent science and am entrusted with the geo-

---

[54] Gustave Aimard (1818-1883) was the author of numerous books about Latin America and the American frontier.

logical, geographical, cerographical, stratigraphical, paleontological and other observations. I shall have plenty to do."

"Forward, then!" commanded Simon. And, taking the lead with Antonio, he at once said, "Now tell me about your companions. And you, Lynx-Eye, where do *you* hail from? After all, if there are still a few specimens of Indians left, they're not out for a good time on the highways of Europe. Confess that you are, all of you, made up and disguised."

"They are no more made up than I am," said Antonio. "We come from the other side. For my part, I am the grandson of one of the last remaining Indian chiefs, Long Carbine who ran away with the little daughter of a Canadian trapper. My mother was a Mexican. You see that, though there's a mixture, our origins are beyond dispute."

"But afterwards, Lynx-Eye? What has happened afterwards? I'm not aware that the British government provides for the descendants of the Sioux or Mohicans?"

"There are other concerns besides the British government," said the Indian.

"What do you mean?"

"I mean there are concerns which are interested in keeping us going."

"Really? What are they?"

"The motion picture firms."

Simon struck his hand against his forehead:

"What an idiot I am! Why didn't I think of that? Then you are..."

"Simply film actors from the Far West, the Prairies and the Mexican frontier."

"That's it! That's it!" cried Simon. "I have seen you on the screen, haven't I? And I've seen... hold on. I remember now, I've seen the fair Dolores also, haven't I? But what are you doing in Europe?"

"An English company sent for me and I engaged a few friends over there, who, like myself, are the very mixed descendants of American Indians, Mexicans and Spaniards. Now, M. Dubosc, one of these friends of mine—the best, for I can't say much for the others, and I advise you, if the occasion should arise, to be very careful with Forsetta and the Mazzani brothers—the best, M. Dubosc, was murdered the day before yesterday by Rolleston. I loved Badiarinos as a son loves his father. I have sworn to avenge him. There you have it."

"Lynx-Eye, grandson of Long Carbine," said Simon, "we will avenge your friend, but Rolleston is not guilty of his murder..."

For a man like Simon, to whom practical navigation, in the air or on the sea, had given a keen sense of direction and who, moreover, kept on consulting his compass, it was child's play to reach a spot whose latitude and longitude he was able to determine more or less exactly. He galloped due south, after making the calculation that, if nothing forced them to turn aside, they would have to cover a distance of about thirty miles.

Almost immediately, the little troop, leaving on their left the line of ridges which Simon had followed a few days before, struck off across a series of rather lower sand-hills, which nevertheless were high enough to overlook immense beds of yellow mud, covered with a network of small, winding streams. This was the slime deposited by the rivers of the coast and carried out to sea by the tides and currents.

"Grand alluvial soil," said Old Sandstone. "The water will form channels for itself. The sandy parts will be absorbed."

"In five years," said Simon, "we shall see herds of cattle grazing on the very bed of the sea; and five years later there will be railway-lines across it and palatial hotels standing in the middle."

"Perhaps; but, for the moment the situation is not promising," observed the old professor. "Look here, look at this newspaper, published yesterday evening. In both France and England the disorder is complete. Social and economic life has been suddenly paralyzed. No more public services. Letters and telegrams may or may not be delivered. Nothing definite is known; and people are saying the most extraordinary things. The cases of insanity and suicide, it seems, are numberless. And the crimes! Isolated crimes, crimes committed by gangs of criminals, riots, shops and churches pillaged wholesale. It's an absolute chaos; we are back in the dark ages."

The stratum of mud, formerly swept by the ground-wash, was not very thick; and they were able, time after time, to venture upon it without the least danger. For that matter, it was already indented with footprints, which also marked the still moist sand of the hills. They passed the hulk of a steamboat round which some people had established a sort of camp. Some were poking about the hull. Others were entering by the battered funnel, or demolishing the woodwork with hammers, or breaking open cases of more or less intact provisions. Women of the people, women in rags and tatters, wearing the look of hunted animals, sat on pieces of timber, waiting. Children ran about, playing; and already, marking a first attempt at communal life, a peddler was moving through the crowd with a keg of beer on his back, while two girls, installed behind a tottering bar, were selling tea and whisky.

Farther on, they saw a second camp and, in all directions, men prowling about, solitary individuals, who, like themselves, were reconnoitering.

"Capital!" cried Simon. "The prairie lies stretched before us, with all its mysteries and all its lurking dangers. Here we are on the war-path; and the man who leads us is an Indian chief."

After they had trotted for two hours at a brisk pace, the prairie was represented by undulating plains, in which sand and mud alternated in equal proportions and in which hesitating streams of no great depth were seeking a favorable bed. Over it hung a low, thick, stationary fog, apparently as solid as a ceiling.

"What a miracle, my dear Old Sandstone!" cried Simon, while they were following a long ribbon of fine gravel which stretched before them, like a sunken path winding through the greensward of a park. "What a miracle, an adventure of this sort! A horrible adventure, certainly; a disaster causing superhuman suffering, death and mourning; but extraordinary adventure, the finest that a man of my age could dream of. It's all so prodigious!"

"Prodigious, indeed!" said Old Sandstone, who, faithful to his mission, was pursuing his scientific investigations. "Prodigious! Thus, the presence of this gravel in this place constitutes one of the unprecedented events of which you are speaking. And then look at that bank of great golden fish lying over there, with their upturned bellies..."

"Yes, yes, professor," replied Simon. "It's impossible that such an upheaval should not usher in a new age! If I look at the future as people sometimes look at a landscape, with my eyes half-closed, I can see... heavens, what don't I see!... What don't I imagine! What a tragedy of folly, passion, hatred, love, violence, and noble efforts! We are entering upon one of those periods in which men are full to overflowing of energy, in which the will goes to the head like a generous wine!"

The young man's enthusiasm ended by annoying Old Sandstone, who moved away from his expansive companion, grumbling:

"Simon, the memory of Fenimore Cooper is making you lose your head. You're getting too talkative, my son."

Simon was not losing his head, but he was possessed by a burning fever and, after the hours which he had experienced two days before, was quivering with impatience to return, so to speak, to the world of abnormal actions.

In point of fact, Isabel's image was before him in all his thoughts and in all his dreams. He paid hardly any attention to the precise aim of his expedition or to the campaign which they were undertaking to recover a certain object. The precious miniature was hidden in the rug where he was sure to find it. Rolleston? His gang of ruffians? Men stabbed in the back? A pack of inventions and nightmares! The only reality was Isabel. The only aim before him was to distinguish himself as a knight fighting for the love of his lady.

Meanwhile there were no longer any camps around wrecks, nor parties of people searching for valuables, but only individual prowlers and very few of these, as though most of the people were afraid to go too far from the coast. The surface was becoming more broken, consisting, no doubt, as Old Sandstone explained, of former sand banks which the seismic disturbances had shaken down and mixed with the underlying sedimentary strata. They had to go out of their way to avoid not shattered rocks indeed, nor compact cliffs, but raised tracts of ground that had not yet assumed those definite forms in which we perceive the action of time, of time which separates, classifies and discriminates, which organizes chaos and gives it a durable aspect.

They crossed a sheet of perfectly clear water, contained within a circle of low hills. The bottom was carpeted with little white pebbles. Then they descended, between two very high banks of mud, a narrow gully through which the water trickled in slender cascades. As they emerged from this gully, the Indian's horse shied. A man was kneeling on the ground, groaning and writhing in pain, his face covered with blood. Another man lay near him, his white face turned to the sky.

Antonio and Simon at once sprang from their horses. When the wounded man raised his head, Simon cried:

"Why, I know him... it's Williams, Lord Bakefield's secretary. And I know the other too: it's Charles, the valet. They have been attacked. What is it, Williams? You know me, Simon Dubosc."

The man could hardly speak. He spluttered:

"Bakefield... Lord Bakefield..."

"Come, Williams, tell me what happened?"

"Yesterday... yesterday..." replied the secretary.

"Yes, yesterday you were attacked. By whom?"

"Rolleston..."

Simon started:

"Rolleston! Did he kill Charles?"

"Yes... I... I was wounded... I have been calling out all night. And, just now, another man..."

Antonio put a question:

"You were attacked again, were you not, by some thief who wanted to rob you... And, when he heard us coming, he too stabbed you and took to his heels? Then he is not far away?"

"There... there," stammered Williams, trying to stretch out his arm.

The Indian pointed to footsteps which led to the left, up the slope of the hills:

"There's the trail," he said.

"I'll follow it up," said Simon, leaping into the saddle.

The Indian protested:

"What's the use?"

"Use? The scoundrel must be punished!"

Simon went off at a gallop, followed by one of the Indian's companions, the one who rode the fourth horse and whose name he did not know. Almost immediately, at five hundred yards ahead, on the ridge of the hills, a man rose from the cover of some blocks of stone and made away at the top of his speed.

Two minutes later, Simon reached these blocks and exclaimed:

"I see him! He's going around the lake which we crossed. Let's make straight for him."

He descended the farther slope and forced his horse into the water, which, at this point, covered a layer of mud so deep that the two riders had some difficulty in getting clear of it. When they reached the opposite shore, the fugitive, seeing that there were only two of them, turned round, threw up his rifle and covered them:

"Halt," he commanded, "or I fire!"

Simon was going too fast and could not pull up.

At the moment when the shot rang, he was at most twenty yards from the murderer. But another rider had leapt between them and was holding his horse, reared on its hind legs, like a rampart in front of Simon. The animal was hit in the belly and fell.

"Thanks, old chap, you've saved my life!" cried Simon, abandoning the pursuit and dismounting to help the other, who was in an awkward position, jammed under his horse and in danger of being kicked by the dying brute.

Nevertheless, when Simon endeavored to extricate him, the fallen rider did nothing to assist his efforts; and, after releasing him with some difficulty, he perceived that the man had fainted.

"That's odd!" thought Simon. "Those fellows don't usually faint over a fall from a horse!"

He knelt down beside the other and, seeing that his breathing was embarrassed, undid the first few buttons of his shirt and uncovered the upper part of his chest. He was stupefied and for the first time looked at his companion, who hitherto, in the shadow of his broad-brimmed hat, had seemed to him like the other Indians of the escort. The hat had fallen off. Quickly, Simon lifted an orange silk kerchief bound round the head and neck of the supposed Indian, whose hair escaped from it in thick black curls.

"The girl!" he muttered. "Dolores!"

Once more he had before his eyes the vision of radiant beauty to which his mind had recurred several times during the past two days, though no emotion mingled with his admiration. He was so far from any thought of concealing this admiration that the young woman, on recovering consciousness, surprised it in his gaze. She smiled:

"I'm all right now!" she said. "I was only stunned."

"You're not in pain?"

"No. I am used to accidents. I've often had to fall from my horse for the films... This one's dead, isn't he? Poor creature!"

"You've saved my life," said Simon.

"We're quits," she replied.

Her expression was grave and harmonized with her slightly austere features. Hers was one of those beautiful faces which are peculiarly disconcerting by reason of the contrasts which they present, being at once passionate and chaste, noble and sensuous, pensive and enticing.

Simon asked her, point blank:

"Was it you who came to my room yesterday, first in broad daylight and afterwards at night?"

She blushed, but admitted:

"Yes, it was I."

And, at a movement of Simon's, she added:

"I felt uneasy. People were being killed, in town and in the hotel. I had to watch over you, who had saved my life."

"I thank you," he said once more.

"Don't thank me. I have been doing things in spite of myself... these last two days. You seem to me so different from other men!... But I ought not to speak to you like this. Don't be vexed with me!"

Simon held out his hand to her, when suddenly she assumed a listening attitude and then, after a moment's attention, straightened her clothes, hid her hair beneath her kerchief and put on her hat.

"It's Antonio," she said, in a different tone. "He must have heard the firing. Don't let him know that you recognized me, will you?"

"Why?" asked Simon, in surprise.

She replied, in some embarrassment:

"It's better... Antonio is very masterful. He forbade me to come. It was only when he was naming the three Indians of the escort that he recognized me; I had taken the fourth Indian's horse... So, you see..."

She did not complete her sentence. A horseman had made his appearance on the ridge. When he came up to them, Dolores had unfastened her saddlebags and was strapping them to the saddle of Simon's horse. Antonio asked no questions. There was no exchange of explanations. With a glance he reconstructed the scene, examined the dead animal and, addressing the young woman by her name, perhaps to show that he was not taken in, said:

"Have my horse, Dolores."

Was it the mere familiarity of a comrade, or that of a man who wishes, in the presence of another man, to assert his rights or his pretentions to a woman? His tone was not imperious, but Simon surprised the glance that flashed anger on the one side and defiance on the other. However, he paid little attention, being much less anxious to discover the private motives which actuated Dolores and Antonio than to elucidate the problem arising from his meeting with Lord Bakefield's secretary.

"Did Williams say anything?" he asked Antonio, who was beside him.

"No, he died without speaking."

"Oh! He's dead!... And you discovered nothing?"

"Nothing."

"Then what do you think? Were Williams and Charles sent to the *Queen Mary* by Lord Bakefield and his daughter and were they to find me and help me in my search? Or did they go on their own account?"

They soon joined the three pedestrians of the escort, to whom Old Sandstone, with a cluster of shells in his hand, was giving a geological lesson. The three pedestrians were asleep.

"I'm going ahead," said Antonio to Simon. "Our horses need a rest. In an hour's time, set out along the track of the white pebbles which I shall drop as I go. You can ride at a trot. My three comrades are good runners."

He had already gone some paces, when he returned and, drawing Simon aside, looked him straight in the eyes and said:

"Be on your guard with Dolores, M. Dubosc. She is one of these women of whom it is wise to beware. I have seen many a man lose his head over her."

Simon smiled and could not refrain from saying:

"Perhaps Lynx-Eye is one of them?"

The Indian repeated:

"Be on your guard, M. Dubosc!"

And with these words he went his way. They seemed to sum up all that he thought of Dolores.

Simon ate, stretched himself out on the ground and smoked some cigarettes. Sitting on the sand, Dolores unpicked a few seams of the wide trousers which she was wearing and arranged them in such a fashion that they might have been taken for a skirt.

An hour later, as Simon was making ready to start, his attention was attracted by a sound of voices. At some little distance, Dolores and one of the three Indians were standing face to face and disputing in a language which Simon did not understand, while the brothers Mazzani were watching them and grinning.

Dolores' arms were folded across her breast; she stood motionless and scornful. The man, on the contrary, was gesticulating, with a snarling face and glittering eyes. Suddenly he took both Dolores' arms and, drawing her close to him, sought her lips.

Simon leapt to his feet. But there was no need of intervention; the Indian had at once recoiled, pricked at the throat by a dagger which Dolores held before her, the handle pressed against her bosom, the point threatening her adversary.

The incident was not followed by any sort of explanation. The Indian made off, grumbling. Old Sandstone, who had seen nothing, tackled Simon on the subject of his geological fault; and Simon merely said to himself, as Dolores tightened her saddle-girth:

"What the deuce are all these people up to?"

He did not waste time in seeking for an answer to the question.

The little band did not overtake Antonio until three hours later, when he was stooping over the ground, examining some footprints.

"There you are," he said to Simon, straightening his back. "I have made out thirteen distinct tracks, left by people who certainly were not travelling together. In addition to these thirteen highwaymen—for a man has to be a pretty tough lot to risk the journey—there are two parties ahead of us: first, a party of four horsemen and then, walking behind them—how many hours later I couldn't say—a party of seven on foot, forming Rolleston's gang. Look, here's the print of the patterned rubber soles."

"Yes, yes," said Simon, recognizing the footprint which he had seen two days before. "And what do you conclude?"

"I conclude that Rolleston, as we knew, is in it and that all these gentry, separate prowlers and parties, are making for the *Queen Mary*, the last large Channel boat sunk and the nearest to this part of the coast. Think, what a scoop for marauders!"

"Let's push on!" cried the young man, who was now uneasy at the thought that he might fail in the mission which Isabel had allotted to him.

One by one, five other tracks coming from the north—from Eastbourne, the Indian thought—joined the first. In the end they made such an intricate tangle that Antonio had to give up counting them. However, the footprints of the rubber soles and those of the four horses continued to appear in places.

They marched on for some time. The landscape showed little variety, revealing sandy plains and hills, stretches of mud, rivers and pools, of water left by the sea and filled with fish which had taken refuge there. It was all monotonous, without beauty or majesty, but strange, as anything that has never been seen before or anything that is shapeless must needs be strange.

"We are getting near," said Simon.

"Yes," said the Indian, "the tracks are coming in from all directions; and here even are marauders returning northwards, laden with their swag."

It was now four in the afternoon. Not a rift was visible in the ceiling of motionless clouds. Rain fell in great, heavy drops. For the first time they heard the overhead roar of an aeroplane flying above the insuperable obstacle... They followed a depression in the ground, succeeded by hills. And suddenly a bulky object rose before them. It was the *Queen Mary*. She was bent in two, almost like a broken toy. And nothing was more lamentable, nothing gave a more dismal impression of ruin and destruction than those two lifeless halves of a once so powerful thing.

There was no one near the wreck.

Simon experienced an extreme emotion on standing before what was left of the big boat which he had seen wrecked so terribly. He could not approach it without that sort of pious horror which one would feel on entering a mighty tomb haunted by the shades of those whom we once knew. He thought of the three clergymen and the French family and the captain; and he shuddered at remembering the moment when, with all the strength of his will and all the imperious power of his love, he had dragged Isabel towards the abyss.

A halt was called. Simon left his horse with the Indians and went forward, accompanied by Antonio. He ran down the steep slope which the stern of the vessel had hollowed in the sand, gripped with both hands a rope which hung beside the rudder and in a few seconds, with the assistance of his feet and knees, reached the stern rail.

Although the deck had listed violently to starboard and a sticky mud was oozing through the planking, he ran to the spot where Isabel and he had sat. The bench had been torn away, but the iron supports were still standing and the rug which she had slung to one of them was there, shrunk, heavy with the water dripping from it and packed, as before the shipwreck, in its straps, which were untouched.

Simon thrust his hand between the wet folds of the rug, as he had seen Isabel do. Not feeling anything, he tried to unfasten the straps, but the leather had swollen and the ends were jammed in the buckles. Then he took his knife, cut the straps and unrolled the rug. The miniature in its pearl setting was gone.

In its place, fixed with a safety-pin, was a sheet of paper.

He unfolded it. On it were these hastily written words, which Isabel evidently intended for him:

"I was hoping to see you. Haven't you received my letter? We have spent the night here—In an absolute hell on earth! and we are just leaving. I am uneasy. I feel that someone is prowling around us. Why are not you here?"

"Oh!" Simon stammered, "it's incredible!"

He showed the note to Antonio, who had joined him, and at once added:

"Miss Bakefield!... She spent the night here... with her father... and they have gone! But where? How are we to save them from so many lurking dangers?"

The Indian read the letter and said, slowly:

"They have not gone back north. I should have seen their tracks."

"Then...?"

"Then... I don't know."

"But this is awful! See, Antonio, think of all that is threatening them... of Rolleston pursuing them! Think of this wild country, swarming with highwaymen and footpads!... It's horrible, horrible!"

Part Two: No Man's Land

I. Inside the Wreck

The expedition so gaily launched, in which Simon saw merely a picturesque adventure, such as one reads of in novels, had suddenly become the most formidable tragedy. It was no longer a matter of cinema Indians and circus cowboys, nor of droll discoveries in fabled lands, but of real dangers, of ruthless brigands operating in regions where no organized force could thwart their enterprises. What could Isabel and her father do, beset by criminals of the worst type?

"Good God!" exclaimed Simon. "How could Lord Bakefield be so rash as to risk this journey? Look here, Antonio, the lady's-maid told you that Lord Bakefield had gone to London by train, with his wife and daughter..."

"A misunderstanding," declared the Indian. "He must have seen the duchess to the station and arranged the expedition with Miss Bakefield."

"Then they're alone, those two?"

"No, they have two manservants with them. It's the four riders whose tracks we picked up."

"What imprudence!"

"Imprudence, yes. Miss Bakefield told you of it in the intercepted letter, counting on you to take the necessary measures to protect her. Moreover, Lord Bakefield had given orders to his secretary, Williams, and his valet, Charles, to join them. That is why those two poor fellows were put out of action on the road by Rolleston and his six accomplices."

"Those are the men I'm afraid of," said Simon, hoarsely. "Have Lord Bakefield and his daughter escaped them? Did the departure of which Miss Bakefield speaks take place before their arrival? How can we find out? Where are we to look for them?"

"Here," said Antonio.

"On this deserted wreck?"

"There's a whole crowd inside the wreck," the Indian affirmed. "Here, we'll begin by questioning the boy who is watching us over there."

Leaning against the stump of a broken mast, stood a lean, pasty-faced guttersnipe, with his hands in his pockets, smoking a huge cigar. Simon went up to him, muttering:

"Very like one of Lord Bakefield's favorite Havanas... Where did you sneak that cigar?" he asked.

"I ain't sneaked nuffin, sure as my name's Jim. It was giv' me."

"Who gave it you?"

"My old man."

"Where is he, your old man?"

"Listen..."

They listened. A noise echoed beneath their feet in the bowels of the wreck. It sounded like the regular blows of a hammer.

"That's my old man, smashin' 'er up," said the urchin, grinning.

"Tell me," said Simon, "have you seen an elderly gentleman and a young lady who came here on horseback?"

"Dunno," said the boy, carelessly. "Ask my old man."

Simon drew Antonio to where a companion-ladder led from the deck to the first-class cabins, as a still legible inscription informed them. They were going down the ladder when Simon, leading the way, struck his foot against something and nearly fell. By the light of a pocket-torch he saw the dead body of a woman. Though the face, which was swollen and bloated and half eaten away, was unrecognizable, certain signs, such as the color and material of clothes, enabled Simon to identify the French lady whom he had seen with her husband and children. On stooping, he saw that the left hand had been severed at the wrist and that two fingers were lacking on the right hand.

"Poor woman!" he faltered. "Unable to remove her rings and bracelets, the blackguards mutilated her!" And he added. "To think that Isabel was here, that night, in this hell!"

The corridor which they entered as they followed the sound of hammering led them astern. At a sudden turning a man appeared, holding in his hand a lump of iron with which he was striking furiously at the partition-wall of a cabin. Through the ground-glass panes in the ceiling filtered a pale white light which fell full upon the most loathsome face imaginable, a scoundrelly, pallid, cruel face, with a pair of bloodshot eyes and an absolutely bald skull dripping with sweat.

"Keep your distance, mates! Everybody do the best he can in his own! There's plenty of stuff to go round!"

"The old man ain't much of a talker," said the urchin's shrill voice.

The boy had accompanied them and stood, with a bantering air, puffing great whiffs of smoke. The Indian handed him a fifty-franc note:

"Jim, you have something to tell us. Out with it."

"That's all right," said the boy. "I'm beginnin' to twig this business. Come along 'ere!"

Guided by the boy, Antonio and Simon passed along other corridors where they found the same fury of destruction. Everywhere fierce-looking ruffians were forcing locks, tearing, splitting, smashing, looting. Everywhere they were seen creeping into dark corners, crawling on their hands and knees, sniffing out booty and seeking, in default of gold or silver, bits of leather or scrap-metal that might prove marketable.

They were beasts of prey, carrion brutes, like those which prowl about a battlefield. Mutilated and stripped corpses bore witness to their ferocity. There were no rings left upon the bodies, no bracelets, watches, or pocketbooks; no pins in the men's ties; no brooches at the women's throats.

From time to time, here and there, in this workyard of death and hideous theft, the sound of a quarrel arose; two bodies rolling on the ground; shouts, yells of pain, ending in the death-rattle. Two plunderers came to grips; and in a moment one of them was a murderer.

Jim halted in front of a roomy cabin, the lower part of whose sloping floor was under water; but on the upper part were several cane deck chairs which were almost dry.

"That's where they spent the night," he said.

"Who?" asked Simon.

"The three what come on horseback. I was the first on the wreck with my old man. I saw 'em come."

"But there were four of them."

"There was one what lay down outside to guard the horses. The other three went to get something out of the rug where you didn't find nuffin; and they 'ad their grub and slept in 'ere. This mornin', after they left, my old man come to go through the cabin and found the old gent's cigar-case here.

"So they went away again?"

The boy was silent.

"Answer my question, can't you, boy? They left on horseback, didn't they, before the others got here? And they're out of danger?"

The boy held out his hand:

"Two notes," he demanded.

Simon was on the point of flying at him. But he restrained himself, gave the boy the notes and pulled out his revolver:

"Now then!"

The boy shrugged his shoulders:

"It's the notes is making me talk, not that thing! Well, it's like this: when the old gent wanted to start this mornin', he couldn't find the old chap what was guarding the four horses near the stern of the vessel, what you got up by."

"But the horses?"

"Gone!"

"You mean, stolen?"

"Arf a mo! The old gent, his daughter and the other gent went off to look for him, following the track of the 'osses alongside the wreck. That took them to the other part of the *Queen Mary*, just to the place where the starboard lifeboat was stove in. And then—I was on deck, like I was just now, and I see the whole business as if it was the movies—there was five or six devils got up from behind the lifeboat and rushed at 'em; and a great tall bloke a-leadin' of 'em with a re-volver in each fist. I wouldn't say everythink passed off quiet, not on neither side. The old gent, 'e defended himself. There was some shootin'; and I see two of 'em fall in the scrimmage."

"And then? And then?" Simon rapped out, breathlessly.

"I don't know nuffin about then. A change of pickshers, like at the movies. The old man wanted me for somefink; he took me by the scruff o' the neck and I lost the end o' the film like."

It was now Simon's turn to seize the young hooligan by the scruff of the neck. He dragged him up the companion-ladder and, having reached a part of the deck where the whole wreck was visible, he said:

"It was over there, the lifeboat?"

"Yuss, over there."

Simon rushed to the stern of the vessel, slid down the rope and, followed by the Indian and the boy, ran alongside the steamer to the lifeboat which had been torn from the *Queen Mary*'s deck and cast on the sands some twenty yards from the wreck. It was here that the attack had taken place. Traces of it remained. The body of one of those whom the boy had described as "devils" was half-hidden in a hollow.

But a cry of pain rose from behind the boat. Simon and the Indian ran round it and saw a man cowering there, with his forehead bound up in a blood-stained handkerchief.

"Rolleston!" cried Simon, stopping short in bewilderment. "Edward Rolleston!"

Rolleston! The man whom all accused! The man who had planned the whole affair and recruited the Hastings blackguards in order to make a dash for the wreck and steal the miniature! Rolleston, the murderer of Dolores' uncle, the murderer of William and Charles! Rolleston, Isabel's persecutor!

Nevertheless Simon hesitated, profoundly troubled by the sight of his friend. Fearing an outburst of anger on the Indian's part, he seized him by the arm:

"Wait a moment, Antonio! First, are you really certain?"

For some seconds, neither stirred. Simon was thinking that Rolleston's presence on the battlefield was the most convincing proof of his guilt. But Antonio declared:

"This is not the man I met in the corridor of the hotel."

"Ah!" cried Simon. "I was sure of it! In spite of all appearances, I could not admit..."

And he rushed up to his friend, saying:

"Wounded, Ted? It's not serious, is it, old man?"

The Englishman murmured:

"Is that you, Simon? I didn't recognize you. My eyes are all misty."

"You're not in pain?"

"I should think I was in pain! The bullet must have struck against the skull and then glanced off; and here I've been since this morning, half dead. But I shall get over it."

Simon questioned him anxiously:

"Isabel? What has become of her?"

"I don't know... I don't know," the Englishman said, with an effort. "No... no... I don't know..."

"But where do you come from? How do you come to be here?"

"I was with Lord Bakefield and Isabel."

"Ah!" said Simon. "Then you were of their party?"

"Yes. We spent the night on the *Queen Mary*... and this morning we were set upon here, by the gang. We were retreating, when I dropped. Lord Bakefield and Isabel fell back on the *Queen Mary*, where it would have been easier for them to defend themselves. Rolleston and his men were not firing at them, however."

"Rolleston?" echoed Simon.

"A cousin of mine... Wilfred Rolleston, a damned brute, capable of anything... a scoundrel... a crook... oh, a madman! A real madman... a dipsomaniac..."

"And he's like you in appearance, isn't he?" asked Simon, understanding the mistake that had been made.

"I suppose so."

"And it was to steal the miniature and the pearls that he attacked you?"

"That... and something else that he's even more keen on."

"What?"

"He's in love with Isabel. He asked her to marry him at a time when he hadn't fallen so low. Then Bakefield kicked him out."

"Oh, it would be too awful," stammered Simon, "if that man had succeeded in kidnapping Isabel!"

He stood up. Rolleston, exhausted, said:

"Save her, Simon."

"But you, Ted? We can't leave you..."

"She comes first. He has sworn to have his revenge; he has sworn that Isabel shall be his wife."

"But what are we to do? Where are we to look for her?" cried Simon, in despair.

At that moment Jim came up, all out of breath. He was followed by a man whom Simon at once recognized as a groom in Lord Bakefield's service.

"The bloke!" cried Jim. "The one what looked after the horses... I found him among the rocks... d'you see? Over there? They'd tied him up and the horses were tied up in a sort of cave like..."

Simon lost no time:

"Miss Bakefield?"

"Carried off," replied the man. "Carried off... and his lordship as well."

"Ah!" cried Simon, overwhelmed.

The man continued:

"Rolleston is their leader, Wilfred Rolleston. He came up to me this morning at sunrise, as I was seeing to the horses, and asked me if Lord Bakefield was still there. Then, without waiting for an answer, he knocked me flat, with the help of his men, and had me carried here, where they laid an ambush for his lordship. They didn't mind what they said before me; and I learnt that Mr. Williams, the secretary, and Charles, my fellow-servant, who were to have joined us and increased the escort, had been attacked by them and, most likely, killed. I learnt too that Rolleston's idea was to keep Miss Bakefield as a hostage and to send his lordship to his Paris banker's to get the ransom. Later on, they left me alone. Then I heard two shots and, a little after, they returned with his lordship and Miss Bakefield. Both of them had their hands and feet tied."

"At what time did all this happen?" asked Simon, quivering with impatience.

"Nine o'clock, sir, or thereabouts."

"Then they have a day's start of us?"

"Oh, no! There were provisions in the saddlebags. They sat eating and drinking and then went to sleep. It was at least two o'clock in the afternoon when they strapped his lordship and Miss Bakefield to a couple of horses and started."

"In what direction?"

"That way," said the manservant, pointing.

"Antonio," cried Simon, "we must catch them before night! The ruffian's escort is on foot. Three hours' gallop will be enough..."

"Our horses are badly done up," objected the Indian.

"They've got to get there, if it kills them."

Simon Dubosc gave the servant his instructions:

"Get Mr. Rolleston under shelter in the wreck, look after him and don't leave him for a second. Jim, can I count on you?"

"Yes."

"And on your father?"

"All depends."

"Fifty pounds for him if the wounded man is in Brighton, safe and sound, in two days' time."

"Make it a hundred," said Jim. "Not a penny less."

"Very well, a hundred."

At six o'clock in the evening, Simon and Antonio returned to the Indians' camp. They quickly bridled and saddled their horses, while Old Sandstone, who was strolling around, ran up to them shouting:

"My fault, Simon! I swear we are over my fault, the fault in the Paris basin, which I traced to Maromme and near the Ridin de Dieppe... the one whose fracture caused the whole upheaval. Get on your horse, so that I may give you my proofs. There's a regular Eocene and Pliocene mixture over there which is really typical... Heavens, man, listen to me, can't you?"

Simon stepped up to him and, with drawn features, shouted:

"This is no time to listen to your nonsense!"

"What do you mean?" stammered the old fellow, utterly bewildered.

"Mean? Why, shut up!"

And the young man leapt into the saddle:

"Are you coming, Antonio?"

"Yes. My mates will follow our trail. I shall leave a mark from spot to spot; and I hope we shall all be united again to-morrow."

As they were starting, Dolores, on horseback, brought up her mount alongside theirs.

"No!" said Antonio. "You come on with the others. The professor can't walk all the time."

She made no reply.

"I insist on your keeping with the others," repeated the half-breed, more severely.

But she set her horse at a trot and caught up with Simon.

For more than an hour they followed a direction which Simon took to be south by south-east, that is to say, the direction of France. The half-breed thought the same:

"The main thing," he said, "is to get near the coast, as our beasts have only enough food to last them till to-morrow evening. The water question also might become troublesome."

"I don't care what happens to-morrow," Simon rejoined.

They made much slower progress than they had hoped to do. Their mounts were poor, spiritless stuff. Moreover, they had to stop at intervals to decipher the tracks which crossed one another in the wet sand or to pick them up on rocky ground. Simon became incensed at each of these halts.

All around them the scene was like that which they had observed early in the afternoon; the land rose and fell in scarcely perceptible undulations; it was a dismal, monotonous world, with its graveyards of ships and skeleton steamers. Prowling figures crossed it in all directions. Antonio shouted questions to them as he passed. One of them said that he had met two horsemen and four pedestrians leading a couple of horses on which were bound a man and a woman whose fair hair swept the ground.

"How long ago was this?" asked Simon, in a hoarse voice.

"Forty minutes, or fifty at the most."

He dug his heels into his horse's flanks and set off at a gallop, stooping over the animal's neck in order not to lose the scoundrel's track. Antonio found it difficult to follow him, while Dolores erect in her saddle, with a serious face and eyes fixed on the distant horizon, kept up with him without an effort.

Meanwhile the light was failing, and the riders felt as though the darkness were about to swoop down on them from the heavy clouds in which it was gathering.

"We shall get there... we must," repeated Simon. "I feel certain we shall see them in ten minutes..."

He told Dolores in a few words what he had heard of Isabel's abduction. The thought that she was in pain caused unendurable torture. His overwrought mind pictured her a captive among savages torturing her for their amusement, while her blood-bedabbled head was gashed by the stones along the track. He followed in imagination all the stages of her last agony; and he had such a keen impression of speed contending with death, he searched the horizon with so eager a gaze, that he scarcely heeded a strident call from the half-breed, a hundred yards in the rear.

Dolores turned and calmly observed:

"Antonio's horse has fallen."

"Antonio can follow us," said Simon.

For a few moments, they had been riding through a rather more uneven tract of land, covered with a sort of downs with precipitous sides, like cliffs. A fairly steep incline led to a long valley, filled with water, on the brink of which the bandits' trail was plainly visible. They entered the water, making for a place on the opposite edge which seemed to them, at a distance, to be trampled in the same way.

The water, which barely reached the horses' hocks, flowed in a gentle current from left to right. But, when they had covered a third of the distance, Dolores struck Simon's horse with her long reins:

"Hurry!" she commanded. "Look... on the left..."

On the left the whole width of the valley was blocked by a lofty wave which was gathering at either end into a long, foaming breaker. It was merely a natural phenomenon; as a result of the great upheaval, the waters were seeking their level and invading the lower tracts. Moreover, the flow was so gradual that there was no reason to fear its effects. The horses, however, seemed to be gradually sinking. Dragged by the current, they were forced to sheer off to the right; and at the same time the opposite bank was moving away from them, changing its aspect, shifting back as the new stream rose. And, when they had reached it, they were still obliged, in order to escape the water, which pursued them incessantly, to quicken their pace and trot along the narrow lane enclosed between two little cliffs of dried mud, in which thousands upon thousands of shells were encrusted like the cubes of a mosaic.

Only after half an hour's riding were they able to clamber to a table-land where they were out of reach. It was as well, for their horses refused to go any farther.

The darkness was increasing. How were they to recover the tracks of Isabel and her kidnappers? And how could their own tracks, buried beneath this enormous sheet of water, be recovered by Antonio and his men?

"We are separated from the others," said Simon, "and I don't see how our party can be got together again."

"Not before to-morrow, at all events," said Dolores.

"Not before..."

And so these two were alone in the night, in the depths of this mysterious land.

Simon strode to and fro on the plateau, like a man who does not know on what course to decide and who knows, moreover, that there is no course on which he can decide. But Dolores unsaddled the horses, unbuckled the saddle-bags and said:

"Our food will hold out, but we have nothing to drink. The spare water-bottles were strapped to Antonio's saddle."

And she added, after spreading out the two horse-rugs:

"We will sleep here, Simon."

II. Along the Cable

He fell asleep beside her, after a long spell of waking during which his un-easiness was gradually assuaged by the soft and regular rhythm which marked the young girl's breathing.

When he woke, fairly late in the morning, Dolores was stooping and bathing her beautiful arms and her face in the stream that flowed down the hillside. She moved slowly; and all her attitude, as she dried her arms and put back her hair, knotting it low on her neck, were full of a grave harmony.

As Simon stood up, she filled a glass and brought it to him:

"Drink that," she said. "Contrary to what I thought, it's fresh water. I heard our horses drinking it in the night."

"That's easily explained," said Simon. "During the first few days, the rivers of the old coasts filtered in more or less anywhere, until forced, by their increasing flow, to wear themselves a new course. Judging by the direction which this one seems to follow and by its size, it should be a French river, doubtless the Somme, which will join the sea henceforth between Le Havre and Southampton. Unless..."

He was not certain of his argument. In reality, under the implacable veil of the clouds, which were still motionless and hanging very low, and without his compass, which he had heedlessly handed to Antonio, he did not know how to take his bearings. He had followed in Isabel's track last evening; and he hesitated to venture in either direction now that this track was lost and that there was no clue to justify his seeking her in one direction rather than in another.

A discovery of Dolores put an end to his hesitation. In exploring the immediate surroundings, the girl had noticed a submarine cable which crossed the river.

"Capital!" he said. "The cable evidently comes from England, like ourselves. If we follow it, we shall be going towards France. We shall be sure of going the same way as our enemies and we shall very likely pick up some information on the road."

"France is a long way off," Dolores remarked, "and our horses perhaps won't last for more than another half day."

"That's their lookout," cried Simon. "We shall finish the journey on foot. The great thing is to reach the French coast. Let us make a start."

At two hundred yards' distance, in a depression of the soil, the cable rose from the river and ran straight to a sand bank, after which it appeared once more, like one of those roads which show in sections on uneven plains.

"It will lead you to Dieppe," said a wandering Frenchman, whom Simon had stopped. "I've just come from there. You've only to follow it."

They followed it in silence. A mute companion, speaking none save indispensable words, Dolores seemed to be always self-absorbed, or to heed only the horses and the details of the expedition. As for Simon, he gave no thought to her. It was a curious fact that he had not yet felt, even casually, that there was something strange and disturbing in the adventure that brought him, a young man, and her, a young woman, together. She remained the unknown; yet this mystery had no particular attraction for him, nor did Antonio's enigmatic words recur to his memory. Though he was perfectly well aware that she was very beautiful, though it gave him pleasure to look at her from time to time and though he often felt her eyes resting on him, she was never the subject of his thoughts and did not for a moment enter into the unbroken reflections aroused by his love for Isabel Bakefield and the dangers which she was incurring.

These dangers he now judged to be less terrible than he had supposed. Since Rolleston's plan consisted in sending Lord Bakefield to a Paris banker to obtain money, it might be assumed that Isabel, held as a hostage, would be treated with a certain consideration, at least until Rolleston, after receiving a ransom, made further demands. But, when this happened, would not he, Simon, be there?

They were now entering a region of a wholly different character, where there was no longer either sand or mud, but a floor of grey rock streaked with thin sheets of hard, sharp-edged stone, which refused to take the imprint of a trail and which even the iron of the horses' shoes failed to mark. Their only chance of information was from the prowlers whom they might encounter.

These were becoming more and more numerous. Two full days had elapsed since the emergence of the new land. It was now the third day; and from all parts, from every point of the sea-side counties or departments, came hastening all who did not fear the risk of the undertaking: vagabonds, tramps, poachers, reckless spirits, daredevils of all kinds. The ruined towns poured forth their contingent of poverty-stricken, starving outcasts and escaped prisoners. Armed with rifles and swords, with clubs or scythes, all these brigands wore an air that was both defiant and threatening. They watched one another warily, each of them gauging at a glance his neighbor's strength, ready to spring upon him or ready to act in self-defense.

Simon's questions hardly evoked as much as a grumbling reply:

"A woman tied up? A party? Horses? Not come my way."

And they went on. But, two hours later, Simon was greatly surprised to see the motley dress of three men walking some distance ahead, their shoulders laden with bundles which each of them carried slung on the end of a stick. Weren't those Antonio's Indians?

"Yes," murmured Dolores. "It's Forsetta and the Mazzani brothers." But, when Simon proposed to go after them, "No!" she said, without concealing her repugnance. "They're a bad lot. There's nothing to be gained by joining them."

But he was not listening; and, as soon as they were within hearing, he shouted:

"Is Antonio anywhere about?"

The three men set down their bundles, while Simon and Dolores dismounted and Forsetta, who had a revolver in his hand, thrust it into his pocket. He was a great giant of a fellow.

"Ah, so it's you, Dolores?" he said, after saluting Simon. "Faith, no, Antonio's nowhere hereabouts. We've not seen him."

He smiled with a wry mouth and treacherous eyes.

"That means," retorted Simon, pointing to their burdens, "that you and Mazzani thought it simpler to go hunting in this direction?"

"May be," he said, with a leer.

"But the old professor? Antonio left him in your charge."

"We lost sight of him soon after the *Queen Mary*. He was looking for shells. So Mazzani and I came on."

Simon was losing patience. Dolores interrupted him:

"Forsetta," she said gravely. "Antonio was your chief. We four were fellow workers; and he asked if you would come with him and me to avenge my uncle's death. You had no right to desert Antonio."

The Indians looked at one another and laughed. It was obvious that notions of right and wrong, promises, obligations, duties of friendship, established rules, decent behavior, all these had suddenly become things which they had ceased to understand. In the stupendous chaos of events, in the heart of this virgin soil, nothing mattered but the satisfaction of the appetites. It was a new situation, which they were unable to analyze, though they hastened to profit by its results without so much as discussing them.

The brothers Mazzani lifted their bundles to their shoulders. Forsetta went up to Dolores and stared at her for a moment without speaking, with eyes that glittered between his half-closed lids. His face betrayed at the same time hesitation and a brutal desire, which he made no attempt to conceal, to seize the girl as his prey.

But he restrained himself and, picking up his bag, moved off with his companions.

Simon had watched the scene in silence. His eyes met Dolores'. She blushed slightly and said, in a low voice:

"Forsetta used to know how to keep his distance... The air of the prairie, as you say, has acted on him as it has on the others."

Around them, a bed of dried wrack and other seaweeds, beneath which the cable disappeared for a length of several miles, formed a series of hills and valleys. Dolores decided that they would halt there and led the horses a little way off, so that they should not disturb Simon's rest.

As it happened, Simon, having lain down on the ground and fallen asleep, was attacked, knocked helpless, gagged and bound before he was able to offer the least resistance to his assailants. These were the three Indians, who had returned at a run.

Forsetta took possession of Simon's pocketbook and watch, tested the firmness of his bonds and then, flat on his stomach, with one of the Mazzanis on either side, crawled under the wrack and seaweed towards the spot where the girl was tending the horses.

Simon repeatedly saw their supple bodies wriggling like reptiles. Dolores, who was busied over the saddlebags, had her back to them. No feeling of uneasiness warned her of her danger. In vain Simon strove against his bonds and uttered shouts which were stifled by his gag. No power could prevent the Indians from attaining their aim.

The younger Mazzani was the swifter of the two. He suddenly sprung upon Dolores and threw her down, while his brother leapt upon one of the horses and Forsetta, holding another by the bridle, gave his orders in a hoarse tone of triumph:

"Lift her. Take away her rifle... Good! Bring her here... We'll tie her on."

Dolores was placed across the saddle. But, just as Forsetta was uncoiling a rope which he carried round his waist, she raised herself upon the horse's neck, towering over young Mazzani and, raising her arm, struck him full in the chest with her dagger. The Indian fell like a stone against Forsetta; and, when the latter had released himself and made as though to continue the struggle on his own account, Dolores was already before him, threatening him point-blank with her rifle, which she had recovered:

"Clear out," she said. "You too, Mazzani, clear out."

Mazzani obeyed and flew off at a gallop. Forsetta, his features convulsed with rage, withdrew with deliberate steps, leading the second horse. Dolores called to him:

"Leave that horse, Forsetta! This moment... or I fire!"

He dropped the bridle and then, twenty paces farther on, suddenly turned his back and fled as fast as he could run.

Simon was impressed not so much by the incident itself—a mere episode in the great tragedy—as by the extraordinary coolness which the girl had displayed. When she came to release him, her hands were cold as ice and her lips quivering:

"He's dead," she faltered. "The young Mazzani is dead..."

"You had to defend yourself," said Simon.

"Yes... yes... but to take a man's life... how horrible! I struck instinctively... as though I were acting for the films: you see, we rehearsed this scene a hundred times and more, the four of us, the Mazzanis, Forsetta and I, in the same way, with the words and gestures in the same order... Even to the stab! It was young Mazzani himself who taught me that; and he often used to say: 'Bravo, Dolores! If ever you play the kidnapping-scene in real life, I'm sorry for your adversary!'"

"Let's hurry," said Simon. "Mazzani may try to avenge his brother's death; and a man like Forsetta doesn't easily give up..."

They continued on their way and once more came upon the cable. Simon went on foot, abreast of Dolores. By turning his head a little, he could see her sad face, with its crown of black hair. She had lost her broad-brimmed hat, as well as her bolero, which was strapped to the saddle of the horse stolen by Mazzani. A silk shirt revealed the modelling of her breasts. Her rifle was slung across her shoulders.

Once more the region of streaked stone extended to the horizon, dotted with wrecks as before and crossed by the wandering shapes of looters. Clouds hung overhead. From time to time there was the humming of an aeroplane.

At noon Simon calculated that they had still twelve or fifteen miles to cover and that therefore they might be able to reach Dieppe before night. Dolores, who had dismounted and, like him, was walking, declared:

"We, yes, we shall get there. But not the horse. He will drop before that."

"No matter!" said Simon. "The great thing is for us to get there."

The rocky ground was now interspersed with tracts of sand where footprints were once more visible; and among other trails were those of two horses coming in their direction along the line of the cable.

"Yet we passed no one on horseback," said Simon. "What do you make of it?"

She did not reply; but a little later, as they reached the top of a slope, she showed him a broad river mingling with the horizon and barring their progress. When they were nearer, they saw that it was flowing from their right to their left; and, when they were nearer still, it reminded them of the stream which they had left that morning. The color, the banks, the windings were the same. Simon, disconcerted, examined the country around to discover something that was different; but the landscape was identical, as a whole and in every detail.

"What does this mean?" muttered Simon. "There must be an inexplicable mirage... for, after all, it is impossible to admit that we can have made a mistake."

But proofs of the blunder committed were becoming more numerous. The track of the two horses having led them away from the cable, they went down to the riverbank and there, on a flat space bearing the traces of an encampment, they were compelled to recognize the spot where they had passed the previous night!

Thus, in a disastrous fit of distraction due to the attack by the Indians and the death of the younger Mazzani, both of them, in their excitement, had lost their bearings, and, trusting to the only indication which they had discovered, had gone back to the submarine cable. Then, when they resumed their journey, there had been nothing, no landmark of any kind, to reveal the fact that they were following the cable in the reverse direction, that they were retracing the path already travelled and that they were returning, after an exhausting and fruitless effort, to the spot which they had left some hours ago!

Simon yielded to a momentary fit of despondency. That which was only a vexatious delay assumed in his eyes the importance of an irreparable event. The upheaval of the 4th of June had caused this corner of the world to relapse into absolute barbarism; and to struggle against the obstacles which it presented called for qualities which he did not possess. While the marauders and outcasts felt at home from the beginning in this new state of things, he, Simon Dubosc, was vainly seeking for the solution of the problems propounded by the exceptional circumstances. Where was he to go? What was he to do? Against whom was he to defend himself? How was he to rescue Isabel?

As completely lost in the new land as he would have been in the immensity of the sea, he ascended the course of the river, following, with a distraught gaze, the trace of the two trails marking the sand, which was wet in places. He recognized the prints left by Dolores' sandals.

"It's no use going in that direction," she said. "I explored all the surrounding country this morning."

He went on, however, against the girl's wishes and with no other object than that of acting and moving. And, so doing, in some fifteen minutes' time he came upon a spot where the bank was trampled and muddy, like the banks of a river at a ford.

He stopped suddenly. Horses had passed that way. The mark of their shoes was plainly visible.

"Oh!" he cried, in bewilderment. "Here is Rolleston's trail!... This is the distinct pattern of his rubber soles! Can I believe my eyes?"

Almost immediately his quest assumed a more definite form. Fifty yards higher were the traces, still plainly marked, of a camp; and Simon declared:

"Of course!... Of course!... It was here that they landed last night! Like us, they must have fled before the sudden rise of the water; and like us, they camped on the further side of a hill. Oh," he continued, despairingly, "we were less than a mile from them! We could have surprised them in their sleep! Isn't it frightful to think that nothing told us of it... and that such an opportunity..."

He squatted on his heels and, bending over the ground, examined it for some minutes. Then he rose, his eyes met those of Dolores and he said, in a low voice:

"There is one extraordinary thing... How do you explain it?"

The girl's tanned face turned crimson; and he saw that she guessed what he was about to say:

"You came here this morning, Dolores, while I was asleep. Several times your footsteps cover those of our enemies, which proves that you came after they were gone. Why didn't you tell me?"

She was silent, with her eyes still fixed upon Simon's and her grave face animated by an expression of mingled defiance and fear. Suddenly Simon seized her hand:

"But then... but then you knew the truth! Ever since this morning, you have known that they went along the riverbank... Look... over there... you can see their tracks leading eastward... And you never told me! Worse than that... Why, yes... it was you who called my attention to the cable... It was you who set me going in a southerly direction... towards France... And it is through you that we have lost nearly a whole day!"

Standing close up to her, with his eyes plumbing hers, holding her fingers in his, he resumed:

"Why did you do that? It was an unspeakable piece of treachery... Tell me, why? You know that I love Miss Bakefield, that she is in the most terrible danger and that to her one day lost may mean dishonor... and death... Then why did you do it?"

He said no more. He felt that, in spite of her appearance, which was impassive as usual, the girl was overcome with emotion and that he was dominating her with all the power of his manhood. Dolores' knees were giving way beneath her. There was nothing in her now but submissiveness and gentleness; and, since, in their exceptional position, no reserve could restrain her confession or check her impulsiveness, she whispered:

"Forgive me... I wasn't thinking... or rather I thought of no one but you... you and myself... Yes, from the first moment of our meeting, the other day, I was swept off my feet by a feeling stronger than anything in this world... I don't know why... It was your way of doing things... your delicacy, when you threw your coat over my shoulders... I'm not used to being treated like that... You seemed to me different from the others... That night, at the Casino, your triumph intoxicated me... And since then my whole life has been centered on you... I have never felt like this before... Men... men are brutal to me... violent... terrible... They run after me like brutes... I loathe them... You... you... you're different... With you I feel a slave... I want to please you... Your every movement delights me... With you I am happier than I've ever been in my life..."

She stood drooping before him, with lowered head. Simon was bewildered at the expression of this spontaneous love, which to him was so completely unforeseen, which was at once so humble and so passionate. It wounded him in his love for Isabel, as though he had committed an offence in listening to the girl's avowal. Yet she spoke so gently; and it was so strange to see this proud and beautiful creature bowing before him with such reverence that he could not but experience a certain emotion.

"I love another woman," he repeated, to set up definitely the obstacle of this love, "and nothing can come between us."

"Yes," she said. "Nevertheless I hoped... I don't know what... I had no object in view... I only wanted us to be alone together, just the two of us, as long as possible. It's over now. I swear it... We shall find Miss Bakefield... Let me take you to her: I think I shall be better able than you..."

Was she sincere? How could he reconcile this offer of devotion with the passion to which she had confessed?

"What proof have you?" asked Simon.

"What proof of my loyalty? The absolute acknowledgement of the wrong which I have done and which I wish to repair. This morning, when I came here alone, I looked all over the ground to see if there was anything that might give us a clue and I ended by discovering on the edge of this rock a scrap of paper with some writing on it..."

"Have you it?" cried Simon, sharply. "Has she written? Miss Bakefield, I mean?"

"Yes."

"It's for me, of course?" continued Simon, with increasing excitement.

"It's not addressed. But of course it was written for you just as yesterday's message was. Here it is..."

She held out a piece of paper, moist and crumpled, on which he read the following words, hastily scribbled in Isabel's hand:

"No longer making for Dieppe. They have heard a rumor of a fountain of gold... a real, gushing spring, it seems. We are going in that direction. No immediate cause for anxiety."

And Dolores added:

"They left before daybreak, going up the river. If this river is really the Somme, we must suppose that they have crossed it somewhere, which will have delayed them. So we shall find them, Simon."

III. Side by Side

The jaded horse was incapable of further service. They had to abandon it, after emptying the saddlebags and removing the rug, which Dolores wrapped about her like a soldier's cloak.

They set out again. Henceforth the girl directed the pursuit. Simon, reassured by Isabel's letter, allowed Dolores to lead the way and twenty times over had occasion to remark her perspicacity and the accuracy of her judgment or intuition.

Then, less anxious, feeling that she understood, he became more talkative and abandoned himself, as on the previous day, to the burst of enthusiasm which the miracle of this new world awakened in him. The still unsettled coast line, the irresolute river, the changing hues of the water, the ever-varying forms of the heights and valleys, the contours of the landscape, hardly more definite as yet than those of an infant's face: all of this, for an hour or two, was to him a source of wonder and exaltation.

"Look, look!" he cried. "It is as though the landscape were amazed at showing itself in the light of day! Crushed until now beneath the weight of the waters, buried in darkness, it seems embarrassed by the light. Each detail has to learn how to hold itself, to win a place for itself, to adapt itself to new conditions of existence, to obey other laws, to shape itself in accordance with other purposes, in short, to live its life as a thing of earth. It will grow acquainted with the wind, the rain, the frost; with winter and spring; with the sun, the beautiful, glorious sun, which will fertilize it and draw from it all the appearance, color, service, pleasure and beauty which it is capable of yielding. A world is being created before our eyes."

Dolores listened with a charmed expression that spoke of the delight which she felt when Simon spoke for her benefit. And he, all unawares, meanwhile became kindlier and more attentive. The companion with whom chance had associated him was assuming more and more the semblance of a woman. Sometimes he reflected upon the love which she had revealed to him and asked himself whether, in professing her readiness to devote herself, she was not seeking above all to remain by his side and to profit by the circumstances which brought them together. But he was so sure of his own strength and so well protected by Isabel that he took little pains to fathom the secrets of this mysterious soul.

Three times they witnessed murderous conflicts among the swarm of vagabonds who were checked by the barrier of the river. Two men and a woman fell, but Simon made no attempt to defend them or to punish the criminals:

"It is the law of the strongest," he said. "No police! No judges! No executioners! No guillotine! So why trouble ourselves? All social and moral acquisitions, all the subtleties of civilization, all these melt away in a moment. What remains? The primordial instincts, which are to abuse your strength, to take what isn't yours and, in a moment of anger or greed, to kill your fellows. What does it matter? We are back in the troglodyte age! Let each man look to himself!"

The sound of singing reached them from somewhere ahead, as though the river had transmitted its loud echo. They listened: it was a French rustic ditty, sung in a drawling voice to a tuneful air. The sound drew nearer. From the curtain of mist a large open boat came into view, laden with men, women and children, with baskets and articles of furniture, and impelled by the powerful effort of six oars. The men were emigrant sailors, in quest of new shores on which to rebuild their homes.

"France?" cried Simon, when they passed.

"Cayeux-sur-Mer," replied one of the singers.

"Then this river is the Somme?"

"It's the Somme."

"But it's flowing north!"

"Yes, but there's a sharp bend a few miles from here."

"You must have passed a party of men carrying off an old man and a girl bound to two horses."

"Haven't seen anything of that sort," declared the man.

He resumed his singing. Women's voices joined in the chorus; and the boat moved on.

"Rolleston must have branched off towards France," Simon concluded.

"He can't have done that," objected Dolores, "since his present objective is the fountain of gold which someone mentioned to him."

"In that case what has become of them?"

The reply to this question was vouchsafed after an hour's difficult walking over a ground composed of millions upon millions of those broken seashells which the patient centuries use in kneading and shaping of the tallest cliffs. It all crackled under their feet and sometimes they sank into it above their ankles. Some tracts, hundreds of yards wide, were covered with a layer of dead fish on which they were compelled to trudge and which formed a mass of decomposing flesh with an intolerable stench to it.

But a slope of hard, firm ground led them to a more rugged promontory overhanging the river. Here a dozen men, grey before their time, clothed in rags and repulsively filthy, with evil faces and brutal gestures, were cutting up the carcass of a horse and grilling the pieces over a scanty fire fed with sodden planks. They seemed to be a gang of tramps who had joined forces for looting on a larger scale. They had a sheepdog with them. One of them stated that he had that morning seen a party of armed men crossing the Somme, making use of a big wreck which lay stranded in the middle of the river and which they had reached by a frail, hastily constructed bridge.

"Look," he said, "there she is, at the far end of the cliff. They slid the girl down first and then the old, trussed-up chap."

"But," asked Simon, "the horses didn't get across that way, did they?"

"The horses? They were done for. So they let them go. Two of my mates took three of them and have gone back to France with them... If they get there, it'll be a bit of luck for them. The fourth, he's on the spit: we're going to have our dinner off him... After all, one must eat!"

"And those people, where were they going?" asked Simon.

"Going to pick up gold. They were talking of a fountain flowing with gold pieces... real gold coins. We're going too, we are. What we're wanting is arms: arms that are some use."

The tramps had risen to their feet; and, obeying an unconcerted and spontaneous movement, they gathered round Simon and Dolores. The man who had been speaking laid his hand upon Simon's rifle:

"This sort of thing, you know. A gun like that must come in handy just now... especially to defend a pocketbook which is probably a fat one... It's true," he added, in a threatening tone, "that my mates and I have got our sticks and knives, for when it comes to talking."

"A revolver's better," said Simon, drawing his from his pocket.

The circle of tramps opened out.

"Stay where you are, will you?" he bade them. "The first of you who moves a step, I shoot him down!"

Walking backwards, while keeping the men covered with his revolver, he drew Dolores to the end of the promontory. The tramps had not budged a foot.

"Come," whispered Simon. "We have nothing to fear from them."

The boat, completely capsized, squat and clumsy as the shell of a tortoise, barred the second half of the river. In foundering she had spilt on the sloping shore a deck cargo of timber, now sodden, but still sound enough to enable Rolleston's gang to build a footbridge twelve yards long across the arm of the river.

Dolores and Simon crossed it briskly. It was easy after that to go along the nearly flat bottom of the keel and to slide down the chain of the anchor. But, just as Dolores reached the ground, a violent concussion shook the chain, of which she had not yet let go, and a shot rang out from the other bank.

"Ah!" she said. "I was lucky: the bullet has struck one of the links."

Simon had faced round. Opposite them, the tramps were venturing on the footbridge one by one.

"But who can have fired?" he demanded. "Those beggars haven't a rifle."

Dolores gave him a sudden push, so that he was protected by the bulk of the wreck:

"Who fired?" she repeated. "Forsetta or Mazzani."

"Have you seen them?"

"Yes, at the back of the promontory. You can understand, a very few words would enable them to make a deal with the tramps and persuade them to attack us."

They both ran round to the other side of the stern. From there they could see the whole of the footbridge and were under cover from the snipers. Simon raised his rifle to his shoulder.

"Fire!" cried Dolores, seeing him hesitate.

The shot rang out. The foremost of the vagabonds fell. He roared with pain, holding his leg. The others hurried back, dragging him with them, and the promontory was cleared of men. But, though the tramps could not risk going on the footbridge, it was no less dangerous for Dolores and Simon to leave the protected area formed by the wreck. Directly they became visible, they were exposed to Forsetta's or Mazzani's fire.

"We must wait till dark," Dolores decided.

For hours, rifle in hand, they watched the promontory, on which a head and shoulders or gesticulating arms appeared at frequent intervals and from which on several occasions also the threat of a levelled rifle forced them to hide themselves. Then, as soon as the darkness was dense enough, they set off again, convinced that Rolleston's trail would continue to ascend the Somme.

They travelled quickly, never doubting that the two Indians and the vagabonds would pursue them. Indeed, they heard their voices across the water and saw fleeting glimmers of light on the same bank as themselves.

"They know," said Dolores, "that Rolleston went in this direction and that we, who are looking for him, are bound to keep to it."

After two hours' progress, during which they groped their way, guided from time to time by the vague shimmering of the river, they reached a sort of isolated chaos into which Simon wearily cast the light of his electric torch. It consisted of enormous blocks of hewn stone, sunk in some lighter, marble, as far as he could see, and partly awash.

"I think we might stop here," said Simon, "at all events till daybreak."

"Yes," Dolores said, "at daybreak you go on again."

He was surprised by this reply:

"But you too, I suppose, Dolores?"

"Of course; but wouldn't it be better for us to separate? Soon Rolleston's trail will leave the river and Forsetta is sure to catch you up, unless I draw him off on another trail."

Simon did not quite understand the girl's plan:

"Then what will you do, Dolores?" he asked.

"I shall go my own way and I shall certainly draw them after me, since it's I they want."

"But in that case you'll fall into the hands of Forsetta and Mazzani, who means to avenge his brother's death..."

"I shall give them the slip."

"And all the brutes swarming in these parts: will you give them the slip too?"

"We're not discussing my affairs, but yours: you have to catch Rolleston. I am hampering your efforts. So let us separate."

"Not at all!" protested Simon. "We have no right to separate; and you may be sure that I shan't leave you."

Dolores' offer aroused Simon's curiosity. What was the girl's motive? Why did she propose to sacrifice herself? In the silence and the darkness, he thought of her for a long while and of their extraordinary adventure. Starting in pursuit of the woman whom he loved, here he was bound by events to another woman, who was herself pursued; and of this other woman, whose safety depended on his and whose fate was closely linked with his own, he knew nothing but the grace of her figure and the beauty of her face. He had saved her life and he scarcely knew her name. He was protecting her and defending her; and her whole soul remained concealed from him.

He felt that she was creeping closer to him. Then he heard these words, which she uttered in a low and hesitating voice:

"It's to save me from Forsetta, isn't it, that you refuse my offer?"

"Of course," he said. "He's terribly dangerous."

She replied, in a still lower voice and in the tone of one making a confession:

"You must not let the threat of a Forsetta influence your conduct... What happens to me is of no great account... Without knowing much about my life, you can imagine the sort of girl I was: a little cigarette-seller hanging about the streets of Mexico; later, a dancer in the saloons at Los Angeles..."

"Hush!" said Simon, placing his hand over her mouth. "There must be no confidences between you and me."

She insisted:

"Still you know that Miss Bakefield is running the same danger as myself. By remaining with me, you sacrifice her."

"Hush!" he repeated, angrily. "I am doing my duty in not leaving you; and Miss Bakefield herself would never forgive me if I did otherwise!"

The girl irritated him. He suspected that she regarded herself as having triumphed over Isabel and that she had been trying to confirm her victory by proving to Simon that he ought to have left her.

"No, no," he said to himself, "it's not for her sake that I'm staying with her. I'm staying because it's my duty. A man does not leave a woman under such conditions. But is she capable of understanding that?"

They had to leave their refuge in the middle of the night, for it was stealthily invaded by the river, and to lie down higher up the beach.

No further incident disturbed their sleep. But in the morning, when the darkness was not yet wholly dispersed, they were awakened by quick, hollow barks. A dog came leaping towards them at such a speed that Simon had no time to do more than pull out his revolver.

"Don't fire!" cried Dolores, knife in hand.

It was too late. The brute turned a somersault, made a few convulsive moments and lay motionless. Dolores stooped over it and said, positively:

"I recognize him, he's the tramps' dog. They are on our track. The dog had run ahead of them."

"But our track's impossible to follow. There's hardly any light."

"Forsetta and Mazzani have their torches, just as you have. Besides, the firing would have told them."

"Then let's be off as quickly as possible," Simon proposed.

"They will catch us up... at least, unless you abandon your search of Rolleston."

Simon seized his rifle:

"That's true. So the only thing is to wait for them here and kill them one by one."

"That's so," she said. "Unfortunately..."

"Well?"

"Yesterday, after firing at the tramps, you did not reload your rifle."

"No, but my cartridge-belt is on the sand, at the place where I slept."

"So is mine; and both are covered by the rising water. Therefore there are only the six cartridges of your Browning left."

IV. The Battle

All things considered, their best chance of safety would have been to plunge into the river and escape by the left bank. But this plan, which would have cut them off from Rolleston and which Simon did not wish to adopt except in the last extremity, must have been foreseen by Forsetta, for, as soon as light was clear enough, they saw two tramps going up the Somme on the opposite bank. Under these conditions, how were they to land?

Shortly afterwards, they saw that their retreat was discovered and that the enemy was profiting by their hesitation. On the same bank as themselves, some five hundred yards down-stream, appeared the barrel of a rifle. Up-stream an identical menace confronted them.

"Forsetta and Mazzani," declared Dolores. "We are cut off right and left."

"But there's nobody in front of us."

"Yes, the rest of the tramps."

"I don't see them."

"They are there, believe me, in hiding and well sheltered."

"Let's rush at them and get by!"

"To do that, we should have to cover a bare patch under the crossfire of Mazzani and Forsetta. They are good shots. They won't miss us."

"Then what?"

"Well, let's defend ourselves here."

It was good advice. The cargo of marble blocks, piled higgledy-piggledy like a child's building-bricks, formed a thorough citadel. Dolores and Simon climbed it and at the top selected a fort, protected on all sides, from which they could see the slightest movements of their enemies.

"They're coming," Dolores declared, after an attentive scrutiny.

The river had deposited along the banks trunks of trees and enormous roots, drifting it was impossible to say whence, which Forsetta and Mazzani were using to cover their approach. Moreover, at each rush forward they protected themselves with broad planks which they carried with them. And Dolores called Simon's attention to the fact that more things were moving across the bare plain; more shields improvised of all sorts of stray materials: coils of rope, broken parts of boats, fragments of pontoons and pieces of boilerplate. All these things were creeping imperceptibly, with the sure, heavy pace of tortoises making for the same goal, along the radius that led to the center. And the center was the fortress. The tramps were investing it under the orders of Mazzani and Forsetta. From time to time a limb or a head appeared in sight.

"Ah!" said Simon, in a voice filled with rage. "If only I had a few bullets, wouldn't I stop this inroad of wood lice!"

Dolores had made a display of the two useless rifles, in the hope that the threatening aspect would intimidate the enemy. But the confidence of the attackers increased with the inactivity of the besieged. It was even possible that the two Indians had scented the ruse, for they scarcely attempted to conceal themselves.

To show his skill, one of them—Forsetta, Dolores declared—shot down a seagull skimming along the river. Mazzani accepted the challenge. An aeroplane, humming in their direction and flying lower than most, seemed suddenly to drop from the clouds and silently glided across the river, over the blocks of marble. When it came level, Mazzani threw up his rifle, slowly took aim and fired. The pilot was hit, bore downwards, heeled over on either side alternately, until he seemed about to capsize, and passed on, disappearing in a zig-zag flight like that of a wounded bird.

And suddenly, Simon having shown his head, two bullets fired by the two Indians ricocheted from the nearest stone surface, detaching a few splinters.

"Oh, please don't be so imprudent!" Dolores implored.

A drop of blood trickled down his forehead. She staunched it gently with her handkerchief and murmured:

"You see, Simon, those men will get the better of us. And you still refuse to leave me? You risk your life, though nothing can affect the issue?"

He pushed her away from him:

"My life is not at stake... Nor yours either... This handful of wretches will never get at us."

He was mistaken. Some of the vagabonds were within eighty yards of them. They could hear them talking together; and the men's hard faces, covered with grey stubble, shot up from behind their bucklers like the head of a Jack-in-the-box.

Forsetta was shouting his orders:

"Forward!... There's no danger!... They've no ammunition!... Forward, I tell you! The Frenchman's pockets are stuffed with notes!"

The seven tramps ran forward as one man. Simon levelled his revolver briskly and fired. They stopped. No one was hit. Forsetta was triumphant:

"They're done for!... Nothing but short-range Browning bullets!... At them!"

He himself, protecting his body with a piece of sheet-iron, ran up at full speed. Mazzani and the tramps formed up in a circle at thirty or forty yards.

"Ready!" bellowed Forsetta. "Out with your knives!"

Dolores remarked to Simon that they must not remain in their observation-post, since most of their enemies would be able to reach the foot of the fortress unseen and slip between the marble blocks. They slid through a gap which formed a chimney from the top to the ground.

"There they are! There they are!" said Dolores. "Fire now!... Look, here's a chink!"

Through this chink Simon saw two big ruffians walking ahead of the rest. Two shots rang out. The two big ruffians fell. The party halted for the second time, hesitating what to do.

Dolores and Simon profited by this delay to take refuge at the extreme edge of the river. Three single blocks of marble formed a sort of sentry-box, with an empty space in front of it.

"Charge!" shouted Forsetta, joining the men. "They're trapped! Mazzani and I have got them covered. If the Frenchman stirs, we'll shoot him down!"

To meet the charge, Simon and Dolores were obliged to stand up and half-expose themselves. Terrified by the Indian's threat, Dolores threw herself before Simon, making a rampart of her body.

"Halt!" ordered Forsetta, restraining his men's onrush. "And you, Dolores, you leave your Frenchman! Come! He shall have his life if you leave him. He can go: it's you I'm after!"

Simon seized the girl with his left arm and drew her back by main force:

"Not a movement!" he said. "I forbid you to leave me! I'll answer for your safety. As long as I live those brutes shan't get you."

And, with the girl pressed against the hollow of his shoulder, he stretched out his right arm.

"Well done, M. Dubosc!" jeered Forsetta. "Seems that we're sweet on the fair Dolores and that we're sticking to her! Those Frenchmen are all alike! Chivalrous fellows!"

With a wave of the hand he gathered up the tramps for the final attack:

"Now then, mates! One more effort and all the notes are yours! Mazzani and I bag the pretty lady. Is that right, Mazzani?"

All together they came rushing on. All together, at an order from Forsetta, they hurled, like so many projectiles, the pieces of wood and iron with which they had protected themselves. Dolores was not hit, but Simon, struck on the arm, dropped his Browning at the very moment when he had fired at Mazzani and brought him down. One of the tramps leapt upon the pistol, which had rolled away, while Forsetta struggled with Dolores, avoiding the girl's dagger and imprisoning her in his arms.

"Oh, Simon! I'm done for!" she screamed, trying to hang on to him.

But Simon had the five tramps to deal with. Unarmed, with nothing but his hands and feet to fight with, he was shot at three times by the man who had picked up his pistol and was clumsily firing off the last few cartridges. He staggered for a moment under the weight of the other brutes and was thrown to the ground. Two of them seized his legs. Two others tried to strangle him, while the fifth still kept him covered with his empty pistol.

"Simon, save me!... Save me!" cried Dolores, whom Forsetta was carrying off, wrapped in a blanket and bound with a rope.

He made a desperate effort, escaping his assailants for a few seconds, and, before they had time to come to close quarters again, acting on a sudden impulse he threw his pocketbook to them, shouting:

"Hands off, you blackguards! Share that between you! Thirty thousand!"

The bundles of notes fell out of the leather wallet and were scattered over the ground. The tramps did not hesitate, but plumped down on their hands and knees, leaving the field to Simon.

Fifty yards away, Forsetta was running along the river, with his prey slung over his shoulder. Farther on, the two tramps posted on the other bank were punting themselves across on a raft which they had found. If Forsetta came up with them, it meant his safety.

"He won't get there," Simon said to himself, measuring the distance with his eye.

With a quick movement, he snatched the knife of one of his aggressors and set off at a run.

Forsetta, who believed him to be still struggling with the vagabonds, did not hurry. He had, so to speak, rolled Dolores round his neck, holding her legs, head and arms in front of him and crushing them to his chest with his rifle and his brawny arms. He shouted to the two men on the raft, to stimulate their ardor:

"Here's the girl! She's my share... You shall have all her jewels!"

The men warned him:

"Look out!"

He turned, saw Simon at twenty paces' distance and tried to throw Dolores to the ground with a heave of the shoulder, like an irksome burden. The girl fell, but she had so contrived matters, under cover of the suffocating blanket, that at the moment of falling she had a good grip on the barrel of the Indian's rifle; and in her fall she dragged him down with her.

The few seconds which Forsetta needed to recover his weapon were his undoing. Simon leapt upon him before he could take aim. He stumbled once more, received a dagger-thrust in the hip and went down on his knees, begging for mercy.

Simon released Dolores' bonds; then, addressing the two tramps who, terror-stricken when on the point of touching ground, were now trying to push off again:

"See to his wound," he ordered. "And there's the other Indian over there: he's probably alive. Look after him too, you shall have your lives."

The tramps were scattering so rapidly in the distance, with Simon's banknotes, that he gave up all idea of pursuing them.

Thus he remained master of the battle-field. Dead, wounded, or in fight, his adversaries were defeated. The extraordinary adventure was continuing as it were in a savage country and against the most unexpected background.

He was profoundly conscious of the incredible moments through which he was passing, on the bed of the Channel, between France and England, in a region which was truly a land of death, crime, cunning and violence. And he had triumphed!

He could not refrain from smiling and, leaning with both hands on Forsetta's rifle, he said to Dolores:

"The prairie! It's Fenimore Cooper's prairie! The Far West! It's all here: the attack by Sioux, the improvised blockhouse, the abduction, the fight, with the chief of the Pale-Faces coming out victorious!..."

She stood facing him, very erect. Her thin silk blouse had been torn in the struggle and hung in strips around her bosom. Simon added, in a tone of less assurance:

"And here's the fair Indian."

Was it emotion, or excessive fatigue after her protracted efforts? Dolores staggered and seemed on the verge of fainting. He supported her, holding her in his arms:

"You're surely not wounded?" he said.

"No... A passing giddiness... I have been badly frightened... And I had no business to be frightened, since you were there and you had promised to save me. Oh, Simon, how grateful I am to you!"

"I have done what anyone would have done in my place, Dolores. Don't thank me."

He tried to free himself, but she held him and, after a moment's silence, said:

"She whom the chief calls the fair Indian had a name by which she was known in her own country. Shall I tell you what it was?"

"What was it, Dolores?"

In a low voice, without taking her eyes from his, she replied:

"The Chief's Reward!"

He had felt, in his inner consciousness, that this magnificent creature deserved some such name, that she was truly the prey which men seek to ravish, the captive to be saved at any cost, and that she did indeed offer, with her red lips and her brown shoulders, the most wonderful of rewards.

She had flung her arms about his neck; he was conscious of their caress; and for a moment they stood like that, motionless, uncertain of what was coming. But Isabel's image flashed across his mind and he remembered the oath which she had required of him:

"Not a moment's weakness, Simon. I should never forgive that."

He pulled himself together and said:

"Get some rest, Dolores. We have still a long way to go."

She also recovered herself and went down to the river, where she bathed her face in the cool water. Then, getting to work immediately, she collected all the provisions and ammunition that she could find on the wounded men.

"There!" she said, when everything was ready for their departure. "Mazzani and Forsetta won't die, but we have nothing more to fear from them. We will leave them in the charge of the two tramps. The four of them will be able to defend themselves."

They exchanged no more words. They went up the river for another hour and reached the wide bend of which the people from Cayeux had told them. At the very beginning of this bend, which brought the waters of the Somme direct from France, they picked up Rolleston's trail on a tract of muddy sand. The trail led straight on, leaving the course of the river and running north.

"The fountains of gold lie in this direction evidently," Simon inferred. "Rolleston must be at least a day's journey ahead of us."

"Yes," said Dolores, "but his party is a large one, they have no horses left and their two prisoners are delaying their progress."

They met several wanderers, all of whom had heard the strange rumour which had spread from one end of the prairie to the other and all of whom were hunting for the fountain of gold. No one could give the least information.

But a sort of old crone came hobbling along, leaning on a stick and carrying a carpetbag with the head of a little dog sticking out of it.

The dog was barking like mad. The old crone was humming a tune, in a faint, high-pitched voice.

Dolores questioned her. She replied, in short, sing-song sentences, which seemed a continuation of her ditty, that she had been walking for three days, never stopping... that she had worn out her shoes... and that when she was tired... she got her dog to carry her:

"Yes, my dog carries me," she repeated. "Don't you, Dick?"

"She's mad," Simon muttered.

The old woman nodded in assent and addressed them in a confidential tone:

"Yes, I'm mad... I used not to be, but it's the gold... the rain of gold that has made me mad... It shoots into the air like a fountain... and the gold coins and the bright pebbles... fall in a shower... So you hold out your hat or your bag and the gold comes pouring into it... My bag is full... Would you like to see?"

She laughed quietly and, beckoning to Simon and Dolores, took her dog by the scruff of the neck, dropped him on the ground and half-opened her bag. Then, again in her sing-song voice:

"You are honest folk, aren't you?... I wouldn't show it to anyone else... But you won't hurt me."

Dolores and Simon eagerly bent over the bag. With her bony fingers the old woman first lifted a heap of rags kept there for Dick's benefit; she then removed a few shiny red and yellow pebbles. Beneath these lay quite a little hoard of gold coins, of which she seized a generous handful, making them clink in the hollow of her hand. They were old coins of all sizes and bearing all sorts of heads.

Simon exclaimed excitedly:

"She comes from there!... She has been there!"

And shaking the mad woman by the shoulders, he asked:

"Where is it? How many hours have you been walking? Have you seen a party of men leading two prisoners, an old man and a girl?"

But the madwoman picked up her dog and closed her bag. She refused to hear. At the most, as she moved away, she said, or rather sang to the air of a ballad which the dog accompanied with his barking:

"Men on horseback... They were galloping... It was yesterday... A girl with fair hair..."

Simon shrugged his shoulders:

"She's wandering. Rolleston has no horses..."

"True," said Dolores, "but, all the same, Miss Bakefield's hair is fair."

They were much astonished, a little way on, to find that Rolleston's trail branched off into another trail which came from France and which had been left by the trampling of many horses—a dozen, Dolores estimated—whose marks were less recent than the bandits' footprints. These were evidently the men on horseback whom the madwoman had seen.

Dolores and Simon had only to follow the beaten track displayed before their eyes on the carpet of moist sand. The region of shells had come to an end. The plain was strewn with great, absolutely round rocks, formed by pebbles agglomerated in marl, huge balls polished by all the submarine currents and deep-sea tides. In the end they were packed so close together that they constituted an insuperable obstacle, which the horsemen and then Rolleston had wheeled round.

When Simon and Dolores had passed it, they came to a wide depression of the ground, the bottom of which was reached by circular terraces. Down here were a few more of the round rocks. Amid these rocks lay a number of corpses. They counted five.

They were the bodies of young men, smartly dressed and wearing boots and spurs. Four had been killed by bullets, the fifth by a stab in the back between the shoulders.

Simon and Dolores looked at each other and then each continued in independent search.

On the sand lay bridles and girth, two nosebags full of oats, half-emptied meat-tins, unrolled blankets and a spirit-stove.

The victims' pockets had been ransacked. Nevertheless, Simon found in a waistcoat a sheet of paper bearing a list of ten names—Paul Cormier, Armand Darnaud, etc.—headed by this note:

"Forêt d'Eu Hunt."

Dolores explored the immediate surroundings. The clues which she thus obtained and the facts discovered by Simon enabled them to reconstruct the tragedy exactly. The horsemen, all members of a Norman hunt, camping on this spot two nights before, had been surprised in the morning by Rolleston's gang and the greater number massacred.

With such men as Rolleston and his followers, the attack had inevitably ended in a thorough loot, but its main object had been the theft of the horses. When these had been taken after a fight, the robbers had made off at a gallop.

"There are only five bodies," said Dolores, "and there are ten names on the list. Where are the other five riders?"

"Scattered," said Simon, "wounded, dying, anything. I daresay we should find them by searching about? But how can we? Have we the right to delay, when the safety of Miss Bakefield and her father is at stake? Think, Dolores: Rolleston has more than thirty hours' start on us and he and his men are mounted on excellent horses, while we... And then where are we to catch them?"

He clenched his fists with rage:

"Oh, if I only knew where this fountain of gold was! How far from it are we? A day's march? Two days'? It's horrible to know nothing, to go forward at random, in this accursed country!"

V. The Chief's Reward

During the next two hours they saw, in the distance, three more corpses. Frequent shots were fired, but whence they did not know. Single prowlers were becoming rare; they encountered rather groups consisting of men of all classes and nationalities, who had joined for purposes of defense. But quarrels broke out within these groups, the moment there was the least booty in dispute, or even the faintest hope of booty. No discipline was accepted save that imposed by force.

When one of these wandering bands seemed to be approaching them, Simon carried his rifle ostentatiously as though on the point of taking aim. He entered into conversation only at a distance and with a forbidding and repellent air.

Dolores watched him uneasily, avoiding speech with him. Once she had to tell him that he was taking the wrong direction and to prove his mistake to him. But this involved an explanation to which he listened with impatience and which he cut short by grumbling:

"And then? What does it matter if we keep to the right or to the left? We know nothing. There is nothing to prove that Rolleston has taken Miss Bakefield with him on his expedition. He may have imprisoned her somewhere, until he is free to return for her... so that, in following him, I risk the chance of going farther away from her..."

Nevertheless, the need of action drew him on, however uncertain the goal to be achieved. He could never have found heart to apply himself to investigations or to check the impulse which urged him onward.

Dolores marched indefatigably by his side, sometimes even in front. She had taken off her shoes and stockings. He watched her bare feet making their light imprint in the sand. Her hips swayed as she walked, as with American girls. She was all grace, strength and suppleness. Less distracted, paying more attention to external things, she probed the horizon with her keen gaze. It was while doing so that she cried, pointing with outstretched hand:

"Look over there, the aeroplane!"

It was right at the top of a long, long upward slope of the whole plain, at a spot where the mist and the ground were blended until they could not say for certain whether the aeroplane was flying through the mist or running along the soil. It looked like one of those sailing-ships which seem suspended on the confines of the ocean. It was only gradually that the reality became apparent: the machine was motionless, resting on the ground.

"There is no doubt," said Simon, "considering the direction, that this is the aeroplane that crossed the river. Damaged by Mazzani's bullet, it flew as far as this, where it managed to land as best it could."

Now the figure of the pilot could be distinguished; and he too—a strange phenomenon—was motionless, sitting in his place, his head almost invisible behind his rounded shoulders. One of the wheels was half-destroyed. However, the aeroplane did not appear to have suffered very greatly. But what was this man doing, that he never moved?

They shouted. He did not reply, nor did he turn round; and, when they reached him, they saw that his breast was leaning against the steering-wheel, while his arms hung down on either side. Drops of blood were trickling from under the seat.

Simon climbed on board and almost immediately declared:

"He's dead. Mazzani's bullet caught him sideways behind the head... A slight wound, of which he was not conscious for some time, to judge by the quantity of blood which he lost, probably without knowing... Then he succeeded in touching earth. And then... then I don't know... a more violent hemorrhage, a clot on the brain..."

Dolores joined Simon. Together they lifted the body. No footpads had passed that way, for they found the dead man's papers, watch and pocket-book untouched.

His papers, on examination, were of no special interest. But the route-map fixed to the steering-wheel representing the Channel and the old coast lines, was marked with a dot in red pencil and the words:

"Rain of gold."

"He was going there too," Simon murmured. "They already know of it in France. And here's the exact place... twenty-five miles from where we are... between Boulogne and Hastings... not far from the Banc de Bassurelle..."

And, quivering with hope, he added:

"If I can get the thing to fly, I'll be there myself in half an hour... And I shall rescue Isabel..."

Simon set to work with a zest which nothing could discourage. The aeroplane's injuries were not serious: a wheel was buckled, the steering rod bent, the feed pipe twisted. The sole difficulty arose from the fact that Simon found only inadequate tools in the toolbox and no spare parts whatever. But this did not deter him; he contrived some provisional splices and other repairs, not troubling about their strength provided that the machine could fly for the time required:

"After all," he said to Dolores, who was doing what she could to help him, "after all, it is only a question of forty minutes' flight, no more. If I can manage to take off, I'm sure to hold out. Bless my soul, I've done more difficult things than that!"

His joy once more bubbled over in vivacious talk. He sang, laughed, jeered at Rolleston and pictured the ruffian's face at seeing this implacable archangel descending from the skies. All the same, rapidly though he worked, he realized by six o'clock in the evening that he could scarcely finish before night and that, under these conditions, it would be better to put off the start until next morning. He therefore completed his repairs and carefully tested the machine, while Dolores moved away to prepare their camp. When twilight fell, his task was finished. Happy and smiling, he followed the path on his right which he had seen the girl take.

The plain fell away suddenly beyond the ridge on which the aeroplane had stranded; and a deeper gully, between two sand-hills, led Simon to a lower, basin-shaped plain, in the hollow of which shone a sheet of water so limpid that he could see the bed of black rock at the bottom.

This was the first landscape in which Simon perceived a certain charm, a touch of terrestrial and almost human poetry; and at the far end of the lake there stood the most incredible thing that could be imagined in this region which only a few days earlier had been buried under the sea: a structure which seemed to have been raised by human hands and which was supported by columns apparently covered with fine carving!

Dolores stepped out of it. Tall and shapely, with slow, sedate movements, she walked into the water, among some stones standing upright in the lake, filled a glass and, bending backwards, drank a few sips. Nearby, a trace of steam, rising from a pannikin on a spirit-stove, hovered in the air.

Seeing Simon, she smiled and said:

"Everything's ready. Here's tea, white bread and butter."

"Do you mean it?" he said, laughing. "So there were inhabitants at the bottom of the sea, people who grew wheat?"

"No, but there was some food in that poor airman's box."

"Very well; but this house, this prehistoric palace?"

It was a very primitive palace, a wall of great stones touching one another and surmounted by a great slab like those which top the Druid dolmans. The whole thing was crude and massive, covered with carvings which, when examined closely, were merely thousands of holes bored by mollusks.

"Lithophilic mollusks, Old Sandstone would call them. By Jove, how excited he would be to see these remains of a dwelling which dates thousands and thousands of centuries back and which perhaps has others buried in the sand near it... a whole village, I dare say! And isn't this positive proof that this land was inhabited before it was invaded by the sea? Doesn't it upset all our accepted ideas, since it throws back the appearance of men to a period which we are not prepared to admit? Oh, you Old Sandstone, if you were only here! What theories you could evolve!"

Simon evolved no theories. But, though the scientific explanation of the phenomenon meant little to him, how acutely he felt its strangeness and how deeply stirring this moment seemed to him! Before him, before Dolores, rose another age and in circumstances that made them resemble two creatures of that age, the same desolate, barbarous surroundings, the same dangers, the same pitfalls.

And the same peace. From the threshold of their refuge stretched a placid landscape made of sand, mist and water. The faint sound of a little stream that fed the lake barely disturbed the infinite silence.

He looked at his companion. No one could be better adapted to the surrounding scene. She had its primitive charm, its wild, rather savage character and all its mysterious poetry.

The night stretched its veil across the lake and the hills.

"Let us go in," she said, when they had eaten and drunk.

"Let us go in," he said.

She went before, then, turned to give him her hand and led him into the chamber formed by the circle of stone slabs. Simon's lamp was there, hanging from a projection in the wall. The floor was covered with fine sand. Two blankets lay spread.

Simon hesitated. Dolores held him by a firmer pressure of the hand and he remained, despite himself, in a moment of weakness. Besides, she suddenly switched off the lamp and he might have thought himself alone, for he heard nothing more than the infinitely gentle lapping of the lake against the stones upon the beach.

It was then and really not until then that he perceived the snare which events had laid for him by drawing him closer to Dolores during the past three days. He had defended her, as any man would have done, but her beauty had not for a moment affected his decision, or stimulated his courage. Had she been old or ugly, she would have found the same protection at his hands.

At the present moment—he realized it suddenly—he was thinking of Dolores not as a companion of his adventures and his dangers but as the most beautiful and attractive of creatures. He reflected that she, perturbed like himself, was not sleeping either, and that her eyes were seeking him through the darkness. At her slightest movement, the delicate perfume with which she scented her hair, mingled with the warm emanations that floated on the breeze.

She whispered:

"Simon... Simon..."

He did not reply. His heart was oppressed. Several times she repeated his name; then, no doubt believing him asleep, she rose and her naked feet lightly touched the sand. She went out.

What was she going to do? A minute elapsed. There was a sound as of rustling clothes. Then he heard her footsteps on the beach, followed almost immediately by the splash of water and the sound of drops falling in a shower. Dolores was bathing in the darkness.

Simon was next hardly able to detect what was scarcely more perceptible than the swan's gliding over the surface of the pond. The silence and peace of the water remained unbroken. Dolores must have swum towards the center of the lake. When she returned, he once more heard the pattering of drops and the rustle of clothes while she dressed.

He rose suddenly, with the intention of going out before she entered. But she was quicker than he anticipated and they met on the threshold. He drew back, while she asked him:

"Were you going, Simon?"

"Yes," he said, seeking a pretext. "I am anxious about the aeroplane... some thief..."

"Yes... yes," she said, hesitatingly. "But I should like first... to thank you..."

Their voices betrayed the same embarrassment and the same profound agitation. The darkness hid them from each other's eyes; yet how plainly Simon saw the young woman before him!

"I've behaved as I should to you," he declared.

"Not as other men have done... and it is that which touched me... I was struck by it from the beginning..."

Perhaps she felt by intuition that any too submissive words would offend him, for she did not continue her confession. Only, after a moment's pause, she murmured:

"This is our last night alone... Afterwards we shall be parted by the whole of life... by everything... Then... hold me tight to you for a little... for a second..."

Simon did not move. She was asking for a display of affection of which he dreaded the danger all the more because he longed so eagerly to yield to it and because his will was weakening beneath the onslaught of evil thoughts. Why should he resist? What would have been a sin and a crime against love at ordinary times was so no longer at this period of upheaval, when the play of natural forces and of chance gave rise for a time to abnormal conditions of life. To kiss Dolores' lips at such a moment: was it worse than plucking a flower that offers itself to the hand?

They were united by the favoring darkness. They were alone in the world; they were both young; they were free. Dolores' hands were outstretched in despair. Should he not give her his own and obey this delicious dizziness which was overcoming him?

"Simon," she said, in a voice of supplication. "Simon... I ask so little of you!... Don't refuse me... It's not possible that you should refuse me, is it? When you risked your life for mine, it was because you had a... a feeling... a something... I am not mistaken, am I?"

Simon was silent. He would not speak to her of Isabel, would not bring Isabel's name into the duel which they were fighting.

Dolores continued her entreaties:

"Simon, I have never loved anyone but you... The others... the others don't count... You, the look in your eyes gave me happiness from the first moment... It was like the sun shining into my life... And I should be so happy if there were a... a memory between us. You would forget it... It would count for nothing with you... But for me... it would mean life changed... beautified... I should have the strength to be another woman... Please, please, give me your hand... Take me in your arms..."

Simon did not move. Something more powerful than the impulse of the temptation restrained him: his plighted word to Isabel and his love for her. Isabel's image blended with Dolores's image; and, in his faltering mind, in his darkened conscience, the conflict continued...

Dolores waited. She had fallen to her knees and was whispering indistinct words in a language which he did not understand, words of plaintive passion of whose distress he was fully sensible, and which mounted to his ears like a prayer and an appeal.

In the end she fell weeping at his feet. Then he passed by, without touching her.

The cold night air caressed his features. He walked away at a rapid pace, pronouncing Isabel's name with the fervor of a believer reciting the words of a litany. He turned towards the plateau. When almost there, he lay down against the slope of the hill and, for a long time before falling asleep, he continued to think of Dolores as of someone whose memory was already growing dim. The girl was becoming once more a stranger. He would never know why she had loved him so spontaneously and so ardently; why a nature in which instinct must needs play so imperious a part had found room for such noble feelings, humility and delicacy and devotion.

In the earliest moments of the dawn he gave the aeroplane a final examination. After a few tests which gave him good hopes of success, he went back to the dwelling by the lake. But Dolores was gone. For an hour he searched for her and called to her in vain. She had disappeared without even leaving a footprint in the sand.

On rising above the clouds into the immensity of a clear sky all flooded with sunlight, Simon uttered a cry of joy. The mysterious Dolores meant nothing to him now, no more than all the dangers braved with her or all those which might still lie in wait for him. He had surmounted every obstacle, escaped every snare. He had been victorious in every contest; and perhaps his greatest victory was that of resisting Dolores' enchantment.

It was ended. Isabel had triumphed. Nothing stood between her and him. He held the steering-wheel well under control. The motor was working to perfection. The map and the compass were before his eyes. At the point indicated, at the exact spot, neither too much to the right nor too much to the left, neither overshooting nor falling short of the mark, he would descend within a radius of a hundred yards.

The flight certainly took less than the forty minutes which he had allowed for. In thirty at most he covered the distance, without seeing anything but the moving sea of clouds rolling beneath him in white billows. All he could do now was to fling himself upon it. After stopping his engine, he drew closer and closer, describing great circles. Cries or rather shouts and roars rose from the ground, as though multitudes were gathered together. Then he entered the rolling mist, through which he continued to wheel like a bird of prey.

He never doubted Rolleston's presence, nor the imminence of the fight which would ensue between them, nor its favorable outcome, followed by Isabel's release. But he dreaded the landing, the critical rock on which he might split.

The sight of the ground showing clear of the mist reassured him. A wide and, as it seemed to him, almost flat space lay spread like an arena, in which he saw nothing but four disks of sand which must represent so many mounds and which could be easily avoided. The crowd kept outside this arena, save for a few people who were running in all directions and gesticulating.

At closer quarters, the soil appeared less smooth, consisting of endless sand-colored pebbles, heaped in places to a certain height. He therefore gave all his attention to avoiding collision with these obstacles and succeeded in landing without the slightest shock and in stopping quite quietly.

Groups of people came running about the aeroplane. Simon thought that they wished to help him to alight. His illusion did not last long. A few seconds later, the aeroplane was taken by assault by some twenty men; and Simon felt the barrels of two revolvers pushed against his face and was bound from head to foot, wrapped in a blanket, gagged and deprived of all power of movement, before he could even attempt the least resistance.

"Into the hold, with the rest of them!" commanded a hoarse voice. "And, if he gives trouble, blow out his brains!"

There was no need for this drastic measure. The manner in which Simon was bound reduced him to absolute helplessness. Resigning himself to the inevitable, he counted that the men carrying him took a hundred and thirty steps and that their course brought him nearer to the roaring crowd.

"When you've quite done bawling!" grinned one of the men. "And then make yourselves scarce, see? The machine-gun's getting to work."

They climbed a staircase. Simon was dragged up by the cords that bound him. A violent hand ransacked his pockets and relieved him of his arms and his papers. He felt himself again lifted; and then he dropped into a void.

It was no great fall and was softened by the dense layer of captives already swarming at the bottom of the hold, who began to swear behind their gags.

Using his knees and elbows, Simon made room for himself as best he could on the floor. It must have been about nine o'clock in the morning. From that moment, time no longer counted for him, for he thought of nothing but how to defend the place which he had won against any who might seek to take it from him, whether former occupants or newcomers. Voices muffled by gags uttered furious snarls, or groaned, breathless and exhausted. It was really hell. There were dying men and dead bodies, the death-rattle of Frenchmen mingling with Englishmen, blood, sticky rags and a loathsome stench of carrion.

During the course of the afternoon, or it might have been in the evening, a tremendous noise broke out, like the sound of a great sheaf of rockets, and forthwith the numberless crowd roared at the top of its voice, with the frenzied fury of an insurgent mob. Then, suddenly, through it all, came orders shouted in a strident voice, more powerful than the tumult. Then a profound silence. And then a crack of sharp, hurried explosions, followed by the frightful rattle of a machine-gun.

This lasted for at least two or three minutes. The uproar had recommenced; and it continued until Simon could no longer hear the fizzing of the fireworks and the din of the shooting. They seemed still to be fighting. They were dispatching the wounded amid curses and shrieks of pain; and a batch of dying men was flung into the hold.

The evening and the night wore through. Simon, who had not touched food since his meal with Dolores beside the lake, was also suffering cruelly from the lack of air, the weight of the dead and the living on his chest, the gag which bruised his jaw and the blanket which wrapped his head like a blind, air-tight hood. Were they going to leave him to die of starvation and asphyxia, in this huddle of sticky, decomposing flesh, above which floated the inarticulate plaint of death?

His bandaged eyes received a feeling as though the day were breaking. His torpid neighbors were swarming like slimy reptiles in a tub. Then, from above, a voice growled:

"No easy job to find him!... Queer notions the chief has! As well try and pick a worm out of the mud!"

"Take my boat-hook," said another voice. "You can use it to turn the stiffs over like a scavenger sorting a heap of muck... Lower down than that, old man! Since yesterday morning, the bloke must be at the bottom..."

And the first voice cried:

"That's him! There, look, to the left! That's him! I know my rope around his waist... Patience a moment, while I hook him!"

Simon felt something digging into him that must have been the spike of the boat hook catching in his bonds. He was hooked, dragged along and hoisted from corpse to corpse to the top of the hold. The men unfastened his legs and told him to stand up:

"Now then, you! Up with you, my hearty!"

His eyes still bandaged, he was seized by the arms and led out of the wreck. They crossed the arena, whose pebbles he felt under foot, and mounted another flight of steps, leading to the deck of another wreck. There the men halted.

From here, when his hood and gag were removed, Simon could see that the arena in which he had landed was surrounded by a wall made of barricades added according to the means at hand: ships' boats, packing-cases and bales, rocks, banks of sand. The hulk of a torpedo-boat was continued by some cast-iron piping. A stack of drainpipes was followed by a submarine.

All along this enclosure, sentinels armed with rifles mounted guard. Beyond it, kept at a distance of more than a hundred yards by the menace of the rifles and of a machine-gun levelled a little way to the rear, the swarm of marauders was eddying and bawling. Inside, there was an expanse of yellow pebbles, sulphur-colored, like those which the madwoman had carried in her bag. Were the gold coins mixed with those pebbles and had a certain number of resolute, well-armed robbers clubbed together to exploit this precious field? Here and there rose mounds resembling the truncated cones of small extinct volcanoes.

Meantime, Simon's warders made him face about, in order to bind him to the stump of a broken mast, near a group of prisoners whom other warders were holding, like so many animals, by halters and chains.

On this side was the general staff of the gang, sitting for the moment as a court-martial.

In the center of a circle was a platform of moderate height, edged by ten or a dozen corpses and dying men, some of the latter struggling in hideous convulsions. On the platform a man who was drinking sat or rather sprawled in a great throne-like chair. Near him was a stool with bottles of champagne and a knife dripping with blood. Beside him was a group of men with revolvers in their hands. The man in the chair wore a black uniform relieved with decorations and stuck all over with diamonds and precious stones. Emerald necklaces hung round his neck. A diadem of gold and gems encircled his forehead.

When he had finished drinking, his face appeared. Simon started. From certain details which recalled the features of his friend Edward Rolleston, he realized that this man was no other than Wilfred Rolleston. Moreover, among the jewels and necklaces, was a miniature set in pearls, the miniature and the pearls of Isabel Bakefield.

VI. Hell on Earth

A rascally face was Wilfred Rolleston's, but above all a drunkard's face, in which the noble features of his cousin Edward were debased by the habit of debauch. His eyes, which were small and sunk in their sockets, shone with an extraordinary glitter. A continual grin, which revealed red gums set with enormous, pointed teeth, gave his jaw the look of a gorilla's.

He burst out laughing:

"M. Simon Dubosc? M. Simon Dubosc will pardon me. Before I deal with him, I have a few poor fellows to dispatch to a better world. I shall attend to you in three minutes, M. Simon Dubosc."

And, turning to his henchman:

"First gentleman."

They pushed forward a poor devil quaking with fear.

"How much gold has this one stolen?" he asked.

One of the warders replied:

"Two sovereigns, my lord, fallen outside the barricades."

"Kill him."

A revolver-shot; and the poor wretch fell dead.

Three more executions followed, performed in as summary a fashion; and at each the executioners and their assistants were seized with a fit of hilarity which found expression in cheers and the cutting of many capers.

But when the fourth sufferer's turn came—he had stolen nothing, but was under suspicion of stealing—the executioner's revolver missed fire. Then Rolleston leapt from his throne, uncoiled his great height, towered above his victim's head and buried his knife between his shoulder-blades.

It was a moment of delirious delight. The guard of honor yelped and roared, dancing a frantic jig upon the platform. Rolleston resumed his throne.

After this, an axe cleft the air twice in succession and two heads leapt into the air.

All these monsters gave the impression of the court of some nigger monarch in the heart of Africa. Liberated from all that restrains its impulses and controls its actions, left to itself, with no fear of the police, mankind, represented by this gang of cut-throats, was relapsing into its primitive animal state. Instinct reigned supreme, in all its fierce absurdity. Rolleston, the drink-sodden chieftain of a tribe of savages, was killing for killing's sake, because killing is a pleasure not to be indulged in everyday life and because the sight of blood intoxicated him more effectually than champagne.

"It's the Frenchman's turn"; cried the despot, bursting into laughter. "It's M. Dubosc's turn! And I will deal with him myself!"

He stepped down from his throne again, holding a red knife in his hand, and planted himself before Simon:

"Ah, M. Dubosc," he said, in a husky voice, "you escaped me the first time, in a hotel at Hastings! Yes, it appears I stabbed the wrong man. That was a bit of luck for you! But then, my dear sir, why the deuce, instead of making yourself scarce, do you come running after me... and after Miss Bakefield?"

At Isabel's name, he suddenly blazed into fury:

"Miss Bakefield! My fiancée! Don't you know that I love her! Miss Bakefield! Why, I've sworn by all the devils in hell that I would bury my knife in the back of my rival, if ever one dared to come forward. And you're the rival, are you, M. Dubosc? But, my poor fool, you shouldn't have let yourself get caught!"

His eyes lit up with a cruel joy. He slowly raised his arm, while gazing into Simon's eyes for the first appearance of mortal anguish. But the moment had not yet come, for he suddenly stayed the movement of his arm and sputtered:

"I have an idea!... An idea... not half a bad one!... No, not half! Look here... M. Dubosc must attend the little ceremony! He will be glad to know that the lot of his dear Isabel is assured. Patience, M. Dubosc!"

He exchanged a few words with his guards, who gave signs of their hearty approval and were at once rewarded with glasses of champagne. Then the preparations began. Three guards marched away, while the other satellites seated the dead bodies in a circle, so as to form a gallery of spectators round a small table which was placed upon the platform.

Simon was one of the gallery. He was again gagged.

All these incidents occurred like the scenes of an incoherent play, stage-managed and performed by madmen. It had no more sense than the fantastic visions of a nightmare; and Simon felt hardly more alarmed at knowing that his life was threatened than he would have felt joy at seeing himself saved. He was living in an unreal world of shifting figures.

The guard of honor fell in and presented arms. Rolleston took off his diadem, as a man might take off his hat in sign of respect, and spread his diamond-studded tunic on the deck, as people might spread flowers beneath the feet of an advancing queen. The three attendants who had been ordered away returned.

Behind them came a woman escorted by two coarse, red-faced viragoes.

Simon shuddered with despair; he had recognized Isabel, but so much changed, so pale! She swayed as she walked, as though her limbs refused to support her and as though her poor distressful eyes could not see plainly. Yet she refused the aid of her companions. A male prisoner followed her, held on a leash like the others. He was an old, white-haired parson.

Rolleston hurried to meet her whom he called his fiancée, offering her his hand and leading her to a chair. He resumed his tunic and took his place beside her. The clergyman remained standing behind the table, under the threat of a revolver.

The ceremony, of which the details must have been arranged beforehand, was short. The parson stammered the customary words. Rolleston declared that he took Isabel Bakefield to be his wife. Isabel, when the question was put, bowed her head in assent, Rolleston slipped a wedding-ring upon her finger; then he unfastened from his uniform the miniature set in pearls and pinned it to the girl's bodice:

"My wedding-present, darling," he said, cynically.

And he kissed her hand. She seemed overcome with dizziness and collapsed for a moment, but recovered herself immediately.

"Till this evening, darling," said Rolleston, "when your loving husband will visit you and claim his rights. Till this evening, darling."

He made a sign to the two viragoes to lead their prisoner away.

A few bottles of champagne were opened, the clergyman received a dagger-thrust as his fee and Rolleston, waving his glass and staggering on his legs, shouted:

"Here's the health of my wife! What do you say to that, M. Dubosc? She'll be a lucky girl, eh? To-night makes her King Rolleston's bride! You may die easy, M. Dubosc."

He drew near, knife in hand, when suddenly there broke out, from the arena, a succession of crackling noises, followed by a great uproar. The fireworks were beginning again, as on the night before.

In a moment the scene was changed. Rolleston appeared to sober down at once. Leaning over the side of the wreck, he issued his commands in a voice of thunder:

"To the barricades! Every man to his post!... Independent fire! No quarter!"

The deck resounded with the feet of his adherents, who rushed to the ladders. Some, the favored members of the guard of honor, remained with Rolleston. The remaining captives were tied together and more cords were added to the bonds that bound Simon to the foot of the mast.

However, he was able to turn his head and to see the whole extent of the arena. It was empty. But from one of the four craters which rose in the center a vast sheaf of water, steam, sand and pebbles spurted and fell back upon the ground. In the midst of these pebbles rolled coins of the same color, gold coins.

It was an inconceivable spectacle, reminding Simon of the Iceland geyser. The phenomenon was obviously capable of explanation by perfectly natural causes; but some miraculous chance must have heaped together at the exact spot where this volcanic eruption occurred the treasures of several galleons sunk in times gone by. And these treasures, now dropping like rain on the surface of the earth, must have slipped gradually to the bottom of the huge funnel in which the new forces, concentrated and released by the great upheaval, were boiling over now.

Simon had an impression that the air was growing warmer and that the temperature of this column of water must be fairly high, which fact, even more than fear of the pebbles, explained why no one dared venture into the central zone.

Moreover, Rolleston's troops had taken up their position on the line of the barricades, where the firing had been, furious from the first. The mob of marauders, massed at a hundred yards beyond, had at once given way, though here and there a band of lunatics would break loose from the crowd and rush across the slope. They toppled over, ruthlessly shot down; but others came on, bellowing, maddened by those golden coins which fell like a miraculous rain and some of which rolled to their feet.

These men in their turn spun on their heels and dropped. It was a murderous game, an absolute massacre. The more favored, those who escaped the bullets, were taken prisoners on the line of the barricades and set aside for execution.

And suddenly all grew quiet again. Like a fountain when the water is turned off, the precious sheaf wavered, grew smaller and smaller and disappeared from sight. The troops remaining at the barricades completed the rout of the assailants, while the satellites who made up the guard of honor gathered the gold in rush baskets collected at the fore of the wreck on which Rolleston was performing his antics. The harvest did not take long. The baskets were brought up briskly and the sharing began, a revolting and grotesque spectacle. Eyes burned with greed, hands trembled. The sight, the touch, the sound of the gold drove all these men mad. No famishing beasts of prey, disputing a bleeding quarry, could display greater ferocity and spite. Each man hid his booty in his pockets or in a handkerchief knotted at the corners. Rolleston put his into a canvas bag which he held clasped in his arms:

"Kill the prisoners, the new ones as well as the others!" he shouted, relapsing into drunkenness. "Have them executed! After that, we'll string them all up, so that they can be seen from everywhere and nobody will dare attack us. Kill them comrades! And M. Dubosc to begin with! Who'll attend to M. Dubosc? I haven't the energy myself."

The comrades rushed forward. One of them, more agile than the rest, seized Simon by the throat, jammed his head against the broken mast and, pressing the barrel of his revolver against his temple, fired four times.

"Well done!" cried Rolleston! "Well done!"

"Well done!" cried the others, stamping with rage around the executioner.

The man had covered Simon's head with a strip of cloth already spotted with blood, which he knotted round the mast, so that its ends, brought level with the forehead and turned upwards, looked like a donkey's ear, which provoked an explosion of merriment.

Simon did not feel the least surprise on discovering that he was still alive, that he had not even been wounded by those four shots fired point-blank. This was the way of the incredible nightmare, a succession of illogical acts and disconnected events which he could neither foresee nor understand. In the very article of death, he was saved by circumstances as absurd as those which had led him to death's threshold. An unloaded weapon, an impulse of pity in his executioners: no explanation gave a satisfactory reply.

In any case, he did not make a movement which might attract attention and he remained like a corpse within the bonds which held him fixed in a perpendicular position and behind the veil which hid his face, the face of a living man.

The hideous tribunal resumed its functions and hurried over its verdicts, while washing them down with copious libations. As each victim was condemned, a glass of spirits was served, the tossing off of which was meant to synchronize with a death-struggle. Foul jests, blasphemies, laughter, songs, all mingled in an abominable din which was dominated by Rolleston's piercing voice:

"Now have them hanged. Tell them to string up the corpses! Fire away, comrades! I want to see them dancing at the end of their ropes when I come back from my wife. The queen awaits me! Here's her health, comrades!"

They touched glasses noisily, singing until they had escorted him to the ladder; then they returned and immediately set to work upon the loathsome business which Rolleston had judged necessary to terrorize the distant crowd of marauders. Their jeers and exclamations enabled Simon to follow the sickening incidents of their labors. The dead were hanged, with head or feet downwards alternately, from everything that projected from the ship's deck or its surroundings; and flagstaffs were stuck between their arms, with a blood-soaked rag floating from each.

Simon's turn was approaching. A few dead bodies at most divided him from the executioners, whose hoarse breathing he could hear. This time nothing could save him. Whether he was hanged or stabbed the moment they saw that he was still alive, the issue was inevitable.

He would have made no attempt to escape, if the thought of Isabel and Rolleston's threats had not exasperated him. He reflected that at that moment Rolleston, the drunkard and maniac, was with the girl who for years had been the object of his desire. What could she do against him? Captive and bound, she was a prey vanquished beforehand.

Simon growled with rage. He contracted his muscles in the impossible hope of bursting his bonds. The period of waiting suddenly became intolerable; and he preferred to draw upon himself the anger of all those brutes and to risk a fight which might at least give him a chance of safety. And would not his safety mean Isabel's release?

Something unexpected, the sensation of a touch that was not brutal but, on the contrary, furtive and cautious, gently persuaded him to silence. A hand behind his back was untying his hands and removing the ropes which held him bound against the mast, while an almost inaudible voice whispered in his ear:

"Not a movement!... Not a word!..."

The cloth around his head was slowly withdrawn. The voice continued:

"Behave as if you were one of the gang... No one is thinking about you... Do as they do... And, above all, no hesitation!"

Simon obeyed without turning round. Two executioners, not far away, were picking up a corpse. Sustained by the thought that nothing must disgust him if he meant to rescue Isabel, he joined them and helped them to carry their burden and hang it from one of the iron davits.

But the effort exhausted him: he was tortured by hunger and thirst. He turned giddy and was seeking for a support when some one gently seized his arm and drew him toward Rolleston's platform.

It was a sailor, with bare feet and dressed in a blue serge pea-jacket and trousers; he carried a rifle across his back and wore a bandage which hid part of his face.

Simon whispered:

"Antonio!"

"Drink!" said the Indian, taking one of the bottles of champagne; "and look here... here's a tin of biscuits. You'll need all your strength..."

After the shocks of the frightful nightmare in which he had been living for thirty-six hours, Simon was hardly capable of surprise. That Antonio should have succeeded in slipping among the gang of criminals accorded, after all, with the logic of events, since the Indian's object was just to be revenged on Rolleston.

"Did you fire at me with a blank cartridge?" asked Simon, "and saved my life?"

"Yes," replied the Indian. "I got here yesterday, when Rolleston was already beginning to drive back the mob of three or four thousand ruffians crowding round the fountains. As he was recruiting all who possessed firearms and as I had a rifle, I was enlisted. Since then, I've been prowling right and left, in the trenches which they've dug, in the wrecks, more or less everywhere. I happened to be near his platform when they brought him the papers found on the airman; and I learnt, as he did, that the airman was no other than yourself. Then I watched my opportunity and offered myself as an executioner when it came to a matter of killing you. But I didn't dare warn you in his presence."

"He's with Miss Bakefield, isn't he?" asked Simon anxiously.

"Yes."

"Were you able to communicate with her?"

"No, but I know where she is."

"Let's hurry," said Simon.

Antonio held him back:

"One word. What has become of Dolores?"

He looked Simon straight in the eyes.

"Dolores left me," Simon replied.

"Why?" asked Antonio, in a harsh voice. "Yes, why? A woman alone, in this country: it's certain death! And you deserted her?"

Simon did not lower his eyes. He replied:

"I did my duty by Dolores... more than my duty. It was she who left me."

Antonio reflected. Then he said:

"Very good. I understand."

They moved away, unobserved by the rabble of henchmen and executioners. The boat—a Channel packet whose name Simon read on a faded pennant: the *Ville de Dunkerque*; and he remembered that the *Ville de Dunkerque* had been sunk at the beginning of the upheaval—the boat had not suffered much damage and her hull was barely heeling over to starboard. The deck was empty between the funnels and the poop. They were passing the hatch of a companion way when Antonio said:

"That's Rolleston's lair."

"If so, let's go down," said Simon, who was quivering with impatience.

"Not yet; there are five or six accomplices in the gangway, besides the two women guarding Lord Bakefield and his daughter. Come on."

A little farther, they stopped in front of a large tarpaulin, still soaked with water, which covered one of those frames on which the passengers' bags and trunks are stacked. He lifted the tarpaulin and slipped under it, beckoning to Simon to lie down beside him.

"Look," he said.

The frame contained a skylight protected by stout bars, through which they saw down into the long gangway skirting the cabins immediately below the deck. In this gangway a man was seated with two women beside him. When Simon's eyes had become accustomed to the semidarkness which showed objects somewhat vaguely, he distinguished the man's features and recognized Lord Bakefield, bound to a chair and guarded by the two viragoes whom Rolleston had placed in charge of Isabel. One of these women held in her heavy hand, which pressed on Lord Bakefield's throat, the two ends of a cord passed round his neck. It was clear that a sudden twist of this hand would be enough to strangle the unfortunate nobleman in the space of a few seconds.

VII. The Fight for the Gold

"Silence!" whispered Antonio, who divined Simon's feeling of revolt.

"Why?" asked Simon. "They can't hear."

"They can. Most of the panes are missing."

Simon continued, in the same low tone:

"But where's Miss Bakefield?"

"This morning I saw her, from here, on that other chair, bound like her father."

"And now?"

"I don't know. But I suppose Rolleston has taken her into his cabin."

"Where's that?"

"He's occupying three or four, those over there."

"Oh," gasped Simon, "it's horrible! And there's no other way out?"

"None."

"Still, we can't..."

"The least sound would be Miss Bakefield's undoing," Antonio declared.

"But why?"

"I am sure of it... All this is thought out... That threat of death to her father; it's blackmail. Besides..."

One of the women moved to a cabin door, listened and returned, sniggering:

"The chit's defending herself. The chief will have to employ strong measures. You're resolved to go through with it, are you?"

"Of course!" said the other, nodding in the direction of her hand. "Twenty quid extra for each of us: it's worth it! On the word of command, pop! And there you are!"

The old man's face remained impassive. His eyes were closed; he appeared to be asleep. Simon was distracted:

"Did you hear? Isabel and Rolleston: she's struggling with him..."

"Miss Bakefield will hold out. The sentence of death has not been issued," said Antonio.

One of the men keeping watch at the entrance to the gangway now came along on his rounds, walking slowly and listening. Antonio recognized him:

"He's one of the original accomplices. Rolleston had all his Hastings stalwarts with him."

The man shook his head:

"Rolleston is wrong. A leader doesn't concern himself like that with trifles."

"He's in love with the girl."

"A funny way of being in love!... He has been persecuting her now for four days."

"Why does she refuse him? To begin with, she's his wife. She said yes just now."

"She said yes because, ever since this morning, some one has been squeezing dear papa's throat."

"Well, she'll say yes presently so that it shan't be squeezed a little tighter."

The man bent down:

"How's the old chap doing?"

"Impossible to say!" growled the woman, who held the cord. "He told his daughter not to give in, said that he'd rather die. Since then, you'd think he's sleeping. It's two days since he had anything to eat."

"All this sort of thing," retorted the sentry, moving off, "isn't business. Rolleston ought to be on deck. Suppose something happened, suppose we were to be attacked, suppose the enclosure was invaded!"

"In that case, I've got orders to finish the old man off."

"That wouldn't make us come out on top."

A short time elapsed. The two women talked in very low tones. At moments Simon seemed to hear raised voices from the cabin:

"Listen," he said. "That's Rolleston, isn't it?"

"Yes," said the Indian.

"We must do something, we must do something," said Simon.

The door of the cabin was flung open violently. Rolleston appeared. He shouted angrily to the women:

"Are you ready? Count three minutes. In three minutes strangle him," and, turning round, "You understand, Isabel? Three minutes. Make up your mind, my girl."

He slammed the door behind him.

Quick as thought, Simon had seized Antonio's rifle, but, hampered by the bars, he was unable to take aim before the villain had closed the door.

"You will spoil everything!" said Antonio, crawling from under the tarpaulin and wresting the rifle from him.

Simon, in turn, stood up, with distorted features:

"Three minutes! Oh, poor girl, poor girl!"

Antonio tried to restrain him:

"Let's think of something. There must be a porthole in the cabin."

"Too late. She will have killed herself by then. We must act at once."

He reflected for a moment, then suddenly began to run along the deck and, reaching the hatch of the companion way, jumped to the bottom. The gangway began with a wider landing where the sentry sat playing cards and drinking.

They rose. One of them commanded:

"Halt! No passage here!"

"All hands on deck! Every man to his post," shouted Simon, repeating Rolleston's words. "At the double! And no quarter! The gold! The rain of gold has started again!"

The men leapt to their feet and made off up the companion. Simon darted down the gangway, ran into one of the two women, whom his shouts had attracted, and flung the same words at her:

"The gold! The rain of gold! Where's the chief?"

"In his cabin," she replied. "Tell him!"

And she made off in her turn.

The other woman, who held the cord, hesitated. Simon felled her with a blow on the point of the chin. Then, without troubling about Lord Bakefield, he rushed to the cabin. At that moment, Rolleston opened the door, shouting:

"What's up? The gold?"

Simon laid hold of the door to prevent his closing it and saw Isabel, at the back of the cabin, alive.

"Who are you?" asked the villain, uneasily.

"Simon Dubosc."

There was a pause, a respite before the struggle which Simon believed inevitable. But Rolleston fell back, with haggard eyes:

"M. Dubosc?... M. Dubosc?... The one who was killed just now?"

"The same," said a voice in the gangway. "And it was I who killed him, I, Antonio, the friend of Badiarinos whom you murdered."

"Ah!" groaned Rolleston, collapsing. "I'm done for!"

He was paralyzed by his drunkenness, by his state of stupor and even more obviously by his natural cowardice. Without offering the least resistance, he allowed himself to be knocked down and disarmed by Antonio, while Simon and Isabel rushed into each other's arms.

"My father?" murmured the girl.

"He's alive. Don't be afraid."

Together they went to release him. The old lord was at the end of his forces. It was all that he could do to kiss his daughter and press Simon's hand. Isabel too was on the verge of swooning; shaken with a nervous tremor, she fell into Simon's arms, faltering:

"Oh, Simon, you were just in time. I should have killed myself!... Oh, what degradation!... How shall I ever forget?"

Great as was her distress, she had nevertheless the strength to check Antonio's hand when he raised it to stab Rolleston:

"No, please don't... Simon, you agree, don't you? We haven't the right..."

Antonio protested:

"You're wrong, Miss. A monster like that has to be got rid of."

"Please!"

"As you will. But I shall get him again. We have an account to settle, he and I. M. Dubosc, lend me a hand to tie him up!"

The Indian lost no time. Knowing the ruse which Simon had employed to remove the guards, he expected them to return at any moment, no doubt escorted by their comrades. He therefore shoved Rolleston to the other end of the corridor and bundled him into a dark cupboard.

"Like that," he said, "his accomplices won't find their chief and will look for him outside."

He also bound and locked up the big woman, who was beginning to recover from her torpor. Then, despite the exhausted condition of Lord Bakefield and his daughter, he led them to the companion.

Simon had to carry Isabel. When he reached the deck of the *Ville de Dunkerque*, he was astounded to hear the rattling sounds and to see the great sheaf of pebbles and water spurting towards the sky. By a lucky coincidence, the phenomenon had occurred just as he announced it and caused an excitement by which he had time to profit. Isabel and Lord Bakefield were laid under the tarpaulin, that part of the wreck being deserted. Then Antonio and Simon went to the companion in quest of news. A band of ruffians came pouring down it, shouting:

"The chief! Where's Rolleston?"

Several of them questioned Antonio, who pretended to be equally at a loss:

"Rolleston? I've been hunting for him everywhere. I expect he's at the barricades."

The ruffians streamed back again, scampering up on deck. At the foot of the platform they held a conference, after which some ran towards the enclosing fence, while others, following Rolleston's example, shouted:

"Every man to his post! No quarter! Shoot, can't you, down there?"

"What's happening?" whispered Simon.

"They're wavering," said Antonio, "and giving way. Look beyond the enclosure. The crowd is attacking at several points."

"But they're firing on it."

"Yes, but in disorder, at random. Rolleston's absence is already making itself felt. He was a leader, he was. You should have seen him organize his two or three hundred recruits in a few hours and place each man where he was best suited! He didn't only rule by terror."

The eruption did not last long and Simon had an impression that the rain of gold was less abundant. But it exercised no less attraction upon those whose work it was to collect it and upon others who, no longer encouraged by their leader's voice, were abandoning the barricades.

"Look," said Antonio. "The attacks are becoming fiercer. The enemy feels that the besieged are losing hold."

The slope was invaded from every side; and small bodies of men pushed forward, more numerous and bolder as the firing became less intense. The machine-gun, whether abandoned or destroyed, was no longer in action. The chief's accomplices, who had stood in front of the platform, finding themselves unable to enforce their authority and restore discipline, leapt into the arena and ran to the trenches. They were the most resolute of the defenders. The assailants hesitated.

So, for two hours, fortunes of the fight swayed to and fro. When night fell, the battle was still undecided.

252

Simon and Antonio, seeing the wreck deserted, collected the necessary arms and provisions. They intended to prepare for flight at midnight, if circumstances permitted. Antonio went off to reconnoiter, while Simon watched over the repose of his two patients.

Lord Bakefield, although fit to travel, was still badly pulled down and slept, though his sleep was disturbed by nightmares. But Simon's presence restored to Isabel all her energy, all her vitality. Sitting side by side, holding each other's hands, they told the story of those tragic days; and Isabel spoke of all that she had suffered, of Rolleston's cruelty, of his coarse attentions to her, of the constant threat of death which he held over Lord Bakefield if she refused to yield, of the nightly orgies in camp, the bloodshed, the tortures, the cries of the dying and the laughter of Rolleston's companions...

She shuddered at certain recollections, nestling against Simon as though she feared to find herself once more alone. All around them was the flash of firearms and the rattle of shots which seemed to be coming nearer. A din at once confused and terrific, made up of a hundred separate combats, death-struggles and victories, hovered above the dark plain, over which, however, a pale light appeared to be spreading.

Antonio returned in an hour's time and declared that flight was impossible:

"Half the trenches," he said, "are in the hands of the assailants, who have even penetrated into the enclosure. And they won't let any one pass, any more than the besieged will."

"Why?"

"They're afraid of gold being taken away. It seems that there's a sort of discipline among them and that they're obeying leaders whose object is to capture from the besieged the enormous booty which they have accumulated. And, as the assailants are ten or even twenty to one, we must expect a wholesale massacre!"

The night was full of tumult. Simon observed that the dense layer of clouds was breaking up in places and that gleams of light were falling from the starry sky. They could see figures darting across the arena. Two men first, then a number of others boarded the *Ville de Dunkerque* and went down the nearest companion way.

"Rolleston's accomplices returning," murmured Antonio.

"What for? Are they looking for Rolleston?"

"No, they think he's dead. But there are the bags, the bags filled with coin, and they are all going to fill their pockets."

"The gold is there, then?"

"In the cabins. Rolleston's share on one side; his accomplices on the other."

Below deck quarrels were beginning, followed almost immediately by a general affray, which was punctuated by yells and moans. One by one the victors emerged from the companion way. But shadows crept down it all night long; and the newcomers were heard searching and destroying.

"They'll find Rolleston in the end," said Simon.

"I don't care if they do," said Antonio, with a grin which Simon was to remember thereafter.

The Indian was getting together their arms and ammunition. A little before daybreak, he awoke Lord Bakefield and his daughter and gave them rifles and revolvers. The final assault would not be long delayed; and he calculated that the *Ville de Dunkerque* would be the immediate objective of the assailants and that it would be better not to linger there.

The little party therefore set out when the first pale gleams of dawn showed in the sky. They had not set foot on the sand of the arena before the signal for the attack was given by a powerful voice which sounded from the bulk of the submarine; and it so happened that, at the very moment when the final offensive was launched, when the besieged, better armed than the attackers, were taking measures of defense which were also better organized, the roar of the eruption rent the air with its thousand explosions.

Then and there, the enemy's onslaught became more furious, and the besieged began to retreat, as Simon and Antonio perceived from the disorderly rush of men falling back like trapped animals, seeking cover behind which to defend themselves or hide.

In the middle of the arena, the scorching rain and the showers of falling pebbles created a circular empty space; nevertheless, some of the more desperate assailants were bold enough to venture into it and Simon had a fleeting vision in which he seemed to see—but was it possible?—Old Sandstone running this way and that under a strange umbrella made of a round sheet of metal with the edge turned down.

The mob of invaders was growing denser. They collided with groups of men and women, brandishing sticks, old swords, scythes, hill-hooks and axes, who fell upon the fugitives. Simon and Antonio were twice obliged to take part in the fighting.

"The position is serious," said Simon, taking Isabel aside. "We must risk all for all and try to find a way through. Kiss me, Isabel, as you did on the day of the shipwreck."

She gave him her lips, saying:

"I have absolute faith in you, Simon."

After many efforts and two brushes with some ruffians who tried to stop them, they reached the line of the barricades and crossed it without hindrance. But in the open space outside they met fresh waves of marauders breaking furiously against the defenses, including parties of men who seemed to be running away, rather than pursuing a quarry. It was as though they themselves were threatened by some great danger. Fierce and murderous for all that, they plundered the dead and wildly attacked the living.

"Look out!" cried Simon.

It was a band of thirty or forty street-boys and hooligans, among whom he recognized two of the tramps who had pursued him. At sight of Simon, they egged on the gang under their command. By some ill chance Antonio slipped and fell. Lord Bakefield was knocked down. Simon and Isabel, caught in an eddy, felt that they were being stifled by a mass of bodies whirling about them. Simon, however, succeeded in seizing hold of her and levelling his revolver. He fired three times in succession. Isabel did likewise. Two men dropped. There was a moment's hesitation; then a new onslaught separated the lovers.

"Simon, Simon!" cried the terrified girl.

One of the tramps roared:

"The girl! Carry her off! She'll fetch her weight in gold!"

Simon tried to reach her. Twenty hands opposed his desperate efforts; and, while defending himself, he saw Isabel pushed towards the barricades by the two tramps. She stumbled and fell. They were trying to raise her when suddenly two shots rang out and both fell headlong.

"Simon! Antonio!" cried a voice.

Through the fray Simon saw Dolores, sitting erect on a horse all covered with foam. Her rifle was levelled and she was firing. Three of the nearest aggressors were struck. Simon contrived to break away, run to Isabel and join Dolores, to whom Antonio at the same time was bringing Lord Bakefield.

Thus the four were together again, but each was followed by the rabble of persistent marauders, and these were reinforced by dozens of others, who loomed out of the fog and doubtless imagined that the stake in such a battle, in which the number of their opponents was so small, must be the capture of some treasure.

"There are more than a hundred of them," said Antonio. "We are done for."

"Saved!" cried Dolores, who now ceased firing.

"Why?"

"Yes, we must hold out... one minute..."

Dolores' reply was drowned in the uproar. Their assailants came along with a rush. With their backs against the horse, the little party faced in all directions, firing, wounding, killing. With his left hand Simon discharged his revolver, while with his right hand, which gripped his rifle by the barrel, whirling it to terrible effect, he held the enemy at a distance.

But how could they resist the torrent, continually renewed, that rushed upon them. They were submerged. Old Lord Bakefield was struck senseless with a stick; and one of Antonio's arms was paralyzed by a blow from a stone. Any further resistance was out of the question. The hideous moment had come when people fall, when their flesh is trampled underfoot and torn asunder by the enemy's claws.

"Isabel!" murmured Simon, crushing her passionately in his arms.

They dropped to their knees together. The beasts of prey fell upon them, covering them with darkness.

A bugle sounded some distance away, scattering its lively notes upon the air. Another call rang out in reply. It was a French bugle sounding the charge.

A great silence, heavy with fear, petrified the hordes of pillagers. Simon, who was losing consciousness, felt that the weight above him was lightened. Some of the beasts of prey were taking flight.

He half-raised himself, while supporting Isabel, and the first thing that struck him was Antonio's attitude. The Indian, with drawn face, was gazing at Dolores. Slowly and steadily he took a few steps towards her, like a cat creeping up to its prey, and suddenly, before Simon could intervene, he leapt on the crupper behind her, passed his arms under hers and dug his heels into the horse, which broke into a gallop along the barricades, towards the north.

From the opposite direction, through the mist, appeared the sky-blue uniforms of France.

VIII. The High Commissioner for the New Territories

"My fault!... Now aren't you convinced, as I am, that this is a ramification of my fault, ending in a _cul-de-sac_? So that all the eruptive forces immobilized in the direction of this blind alley have found a favorable position... so that all these forces... you grasp the idea, don't you?"

Simon grasped it all the less inasmuch as Old Sandstone was becoming more and more entangled in his theory, while he, Simon, was wholly absorbed in Isabel and had ears for hardly anything but what she was telling him.

They were all three a little way outside the barricades, among the groups of tents around which the soldiers, in overalls, and fatigue-caps, were moving to and fro and preparing their meals. Isabel's face was already more peaceful and her eyes less uneasy. Simon gazed at her with infinite tenderness. In the course of the morning the fog had at last dispersed. For the first time since the day when they had travelled together on the deck of the _Queen Mary_, the sun shone in a cloudless sky; and one might almost have thought that nothing had occurred between that day and this to divide them. All evil memories faded away. Isabel's torn dress, her pallor and her bruised wrists were the reminder merely of an adventure already remote, since the glorious future was opening out before them.

Inside the barricades, a few soldiers scurried round the arena, stacking the dead bodies, while others, farther back, stationed on the wreck of the _Ville de Dunkerque_, removed the sinister shapes hanging from their gibbets. Near the submarine, in an enclosed space guarded by many sentries, some dozens of prisoners were herded and were joined at every moment by fresh batches of captives.

"Of course," resumed Old Sandstone, "there are many other obscure points; but I shall not leave this until I have studied all the causes of the phenomenon."

"And I," said Simon, laughing, "should very much like to know how you managed to get here."

This was a question which possessed little interest for Old Sandstone, who replied, vaguely:

"How do I know! I followed a crowd of good people..."

"Good looters and murderers!"

"Oh, do you think so? Yes, it may be... it seemed to me, sometimes... But I was so absorbed! So many observations to make! Besides, I was not alone... at least, on the last day."

"Really? Who was with you?"

"Dolores. We made the whole of the last stage together; and it was she who brought me here. She left me when we came in sight of the barricades. For that matter, it was impossible to enter this enclosure and examine the phenomena more closely. Directly I went forward, pom-pom went the machine-gun! At last, suddenly, the crowd burst the dike. But what puzzles me now is that these eruptions seem already to be decreasing in violence, so that we can foresee the end of them very shortly. True, on the other hand..."

But Simon was not listening. He had caught sight, in the arena, of the captain commanding the detachment, with whom he had not been able to exchange more than a few words that morning, as the officer had at once gone in pursuit of the fugitives. Simon led Isabel to the tent, set aside for her, in which Lord Bakefield was resting, and joined the captain, who cried:

"We are straightening things out, M. Dubosc. I've sent a few squads north; and all these bands of cut-throats will fall into my hands or into those of the English troops, who, I'm told, have arrived. But what savages! And how glad I am that I came in time!"

Simon thanked him in the name of Lord Bakefield and his daughter.

"It's not I whom you should thank," he replied, "but that strange woman, whom I know only by the name of Dolores, and who brought me here."

The captain related how he had been operating since three o'clock in the outposts of Boulogne, where he was garrisoned, when he received from the newly appointed military governor an order instructing him to move towards Hastings, to take possession of the country as far as mid-way between the two coasts and to put down all excesses ruthlessly.

"Well, this morning," he said, "when we were patrolling two or three miles from there, I saw the woman ride up at a gallop. She told me in a few words what was happening inside these barricades, which she had not been able to pass, but behind which Simon Dubosc was in danger. Having succeeded in catching a horse, she had come to beg me to go to your assistance. You can imagine how quickly I marched in the direction she gave me, as soon as I heard the name of Simon Dubosc. And you will understand also why, when I saw that she in her turn was in danger, I rushed in pursuit of the man who was carrying her off."

"What then, captain?"

"Well, she returned, quite quietly, all alone on her horse. She had thrown the Indian, whom my men picked up in the neighborhood, rather the worse for his fall. He says he knows you."

Simon briefly related the part which Antonio had played in the tragedy.

"Good!" cried the officer. "The mystery is clearing up!"

"What mystery, captain?"

"Oh, something quite in keeping with all the horrors that have been committed!"

He drew Simon to the wreck and down, the companion-ladder.

The wide gangway was littered with empty bags and baskets. All the gold had disappeared. The doors of the cabins occupied by Rolleston had been demolished. But, outside the last of these cabins and a little before the cupboard into which Antonio had locked Rolleston on the previous evening, Simon, by the light of an electric torch switched on by the officer, saw a man's body hanging from the ceiling. The knees had been bent back and fastened to keep the feet from touching the floor.

"There's the wretched Rolleston," said the captain. "Obviously he has got no more than his deserts. But, all the same... Look closely..."

He threw the rays of the lamp over the upper part of the victim's body. The face, covered with black clotted blood, was unrecognizable. The drooping head displayed the most hideous wound: the skull was stripped of its skin and hair.

"It was Antonio who did that," said Simon, remembering the Indian's smile when he, Simon, had expressed the fear that the ruffians might succeed in finding and releasing their chief. "After the fashion of his ancestors, he has scalped the man whom he wished to punish. I tell you, we're living in the midst of savagery."

A few minutes later, on leaving the wreck, they saw Antonio who was talking to Dolores near the spot where the submarine strengthened the former line of defense. Dolores was holding her horse by the bridle. The Indian was making gestures and seemed to be greatly excited.

"She's going away," said the officer. "I've signed a safe-conduct for her."

Simon crossed the arena and went up to her:

"You're going, Dolores?"

"Yes."

"Where?"

"Where my horse chooses to take me... and as far as he can carry me."

"Won't you wait a few minutes?"

"No."

"I should have liked to thank you... So would Miss Bakefield..."

"Miss Bakefield has my best wishes!"

She mounted. Antonio snatched at the bridle, as though determined to detain her, and began to speak to her in a choking voice and in a language which Simon did not understand.

She did not move. Her beautiful, austere face did not change. She waited, with her eyes on the horizon, until the Indian, discouraged, released the bridle. Then she rode away. Not once had her eyes met Simon's.

She rode away, mysterious and secretive to the last. Simon's refusal, his conduct during the night which they had passed in the prehistoric dwelling must have humiliated her profoundly; and the best proof was this departure without farewell. But, on the other hand, what miracles of dogged heroism she must have wrought to cross this sinister region by herself and to save not only the man who had spurned her but the woman whom that man loved above all things in this world!

A hand rested on Simon's shoulder:

"You, Isabel!" he said.

"Yes... I was over there, a little farther on... I saw Dolores go."

The girl seemed to hesitate. At length, she murmured, watching him attentively:

"You didn't tell me she was so strikingly beautiful, Simon."

He felt slightly embarrassed. Looking her straight in the eyes, he replied:

"I had no occasion to tell you, Isabel."

At five o'clock that afternoon, the French and British troops being now in touch, it was decided that Lord Bakefield and his daughter should make part of an English convoy which was returning to Hastings and which had a motor-ambulance at its disposal. Simon took leave of them, after asking Lord Bakefield's permission to call on him at an early date.

Simon considered that his mission was not yet completed in these days of confusion. Indeed, before the afternoon was over, an aeroplane alighted in sight of the camp and the captain was asked to send immediately reinforcements, as a conflict appeared inevitable between the French and a British detachment, both of which had planted their colors on a ridge overlooking the whole country. Simon did not hesitate for a moment. He took his place between the two airmen.

It is needless to describe in all its details the part which he played in this incident, which might have had deplorable results: the way in which he threw himself between the adversaries, his entreaties, his threats and, at last, the order to withdraw which he gave to the French with such authority and such persuasive force. All this is history; and it is enough to recall the words uttered two days later by the British prime minister in the House of Commons:

"I have to thank M. Simon Dubosc. But for him, there would have been a stain upon our country's honor; French blood would have been shed by English hands. M. Simon Dubosc, the wonderful man who crossed what was once the Channel at one stride, understood that it would be necessary, at least for a few hours, to exercise a little patience towards a great nation which for so many centuries has been accustomed to feel that it was protected by the seas and which suddenly found itself disarmed, defenseless, deprived of its natural ramparts. Let us not forget that Germany, that very morning, with her customary effrontery, offered France an alliance and proposed the immediate invasion of Great Britain by the whole of the united forces of the two countries. _Britannia delenda est!_ Mr. Speaker, it was Simon Dubosc who gave the reply, by achieving the miracle of a French retreat! All honor to Simon Dubosc!"

France at once recognized Simon's action by appointing the young man high commissioner for the new French territories. For four days longer he was ubiquitous, flying over the province which he had conquered, restoring order, enforcing harmony, discipline and security. Pursued and captured, all the bands of pillagers and spoilers were duly brought to trial. Aeroplanes sailed the heavens. Provision-lorries ran in all directions, assuring travelers the means of transport. Chaos was becoming organized.

At last one day, Simon called at Lord Bakefield's country house near Battle. Here too tranquility had returned. The servants had resumed their duties. Only a few cracks in the walls, a few gaps in the lawns reminded them of the hours of terror.

Lord Bakefield, who appeared to be in excellent health, received Simon in the library and gave him the same cordial welcome as on the Brighton golflinks:

"Well, young man, where do we stand now?"

"On the twentieth day after my request for your daughter's hand," said Simon, smiling, "and as you gave me twenty days in which to perform a certain number of exploits, I come to ask you, on the appointed date, whether I have, in your opinion, fulfilled the conditions settled between us."

Lord Bakefield offered him a cigar and handed him a light.

He made no further reply. Simon's exploits and his rescue of Lord Bakefield when at the point of death, these obviously were interesting things, deserving the reward of a good cigar, with Isabel's hand perhaps thrown into the bargain. But it was asking too much to expect thanks as well and praise and endless effusions. Lord Bakefield remained Lord Bakefield and Simon Dubosc a nobody.

"Well, see you later, young man... Oh, by the way! I have had the marriage annulled which that reptile Rolleston forced upon Isabel... The marriage wasn't valid of course; but I've done what was necessary just as though it had been. Isabel will tell you all about it. You'll find her in the park."

She was not in the park. She had heard that Simon had called and was waiting for him on the terrace.

He told her of his interview with Lord Bakefield.

"Yes," she said, "my father accepts the position. He considers that you have satisfied the ordeal."

"And you, Isabel?"

She smiled:

"I have no right to be more difficult than my father. But remember that there were not only his conditions: there was one added by myself."

"Which condition was that, Isabel?"

"Have you forgotten?... On the deck of the *Queen Mary*?"

"Then, Isabel, you doubt me?"

She took both his hands and said:

"Simon, it sometimes makes me rather sad to think that in this great adventure it was not I but another who was your companion in danger, the one whom you defended and who protected you."

He shook his head:

"No, Isabel, I never had but one companion, you, Isabel, and you alone. You were my only aim and my only thought, my one hope and my one desire."

After a moment's reflection, she said:

"I talked of her a good deal with Antonio, on the way home. Do you know, Simon, that girl is not only very beautiful, but capable of the noblest, loftiest feelings? I know nothing of her past; according to Antonio, it had its unsettled moments. But since then... since then... in spite of her present mode of life, in spite of all the admiration which she attracts, she leads an existence apart. You alone have really stirred her feelings. For you, from what I can see for myself and from what Antonio told me—and he, after all, is only a rejected and embittered lover—for you Dolores would have laid down her life and that from the first day. Did you know that, Simon?"

He was silent.

"You are right," she said. "You can't answer. However, there is one point, Simon, on which I ask you to tell me the absolute truth. I can look you straight in the face, can I not? There is not in the depths of your being a single memory that comes between us?... Not a weakness?... Not a disloyal thought?"

He pressed her to him and, with his lips on hers, said:

"There's you, Isabel, and you alone: you in the past and you in the future."

"I believe you, Simon," she declared.

The wedding took place a month later; and they went to live in the wreck of the *Ville de Dunkerque*, the official residence of the French high commissioner of the new territories.

It was here that the draft agreement was signed, in accordance with Simon Dubosc's proposal and his preliminary investigations, for the great canal which was to bisect the Isthmus of Normandy, allotting to each country, right and left, an almost equal portion of land.

Here too was signed the solemn covenant by which Great Britain and France declared eternal friendship and laid the foundations of the United States of Europe.

And it was here that four children were born to Isabel and Simon.

In after years, Simon often went on horseback or by aeroplane, accompanied by his wife, to visit his friend Edward Rolleston. When he had recovered from his wounds, Rolleston set to work and became the manager of a large fishing-industry on the new English coast, in which he employed Antonio. Rolleston married. The Indian lived alone for a long time, waiting for her who never came and of whom no one ever spoke. But one day he received a letter and went away. Some months later, he wrote from Mexico announcing his marriage to Dolores.

But Isabel and Simon's favorite walk led them to Old Sandstone's house. He lived in a little bungalow, close to the prehistoric dwelling by the lake, where he pursued his research into the new land. The showers of gold, now exhausted, no longer interested him; moreover, the problem had been solved. But what an indecipherable riddle was this building, standing on a site of the Eocene period!

"There were apes in those days," Old Sandstone declared. "There's no doubt of that. But men! And men capable of building, of ornamenting their dwellings of carving stone! No, I confess this is a phenomenon which unsettles all one's ideas. What do you make of it, Simon?"

Simon made no reply. A boat was rocking on the lake. He took his place in it with Isabel and rowed with a care-free mind; nor did Dolores' image ever rise from this limpid water, in which she had bathed on a certain voluptuous evening. Simon was the husband of one alone and this was the woman whom he had won.

René Pujol: *The Black Sun*
(1921)

"Le Soleil noir", translated as "The Black Sun," was originally published in Lectures Pour Tous *as a three-part serial in March-May 1921.*

René Pujol (1878-1942) was a journalist who branched out after the Great War into the production of popular fiction and theatrical sketches, also writing librettos for comic opera, sometimes using the pseudonym René Pons. He went on to work prolifically as a screenwriter and director in the cinema during the 1930s. He ventured into the realms of speculative fiction several times, notably with La Planète invisible *(1931) and* La Chasse aux chimères *(1932) (translated as* The Chimerical Quest, *Black Coat Press, ISBN* 978-1-61227-488-1).

Le Soleil noir *is very much darker in tone and more coldly cynical than his other works—evidently a result of being written in the immediate aftermath of the Great War. It is not the most extreme of the cynical studies of catastrophe published in the aftermath of the war, but it is one of the most stylishly laconic. It makes an interesting companion with J. H. Rosny's classic* La Force mysté-rieuse *(1913). Although the plots and fundamental attitudes of the two stories are similar, and their development equally conscientious, Pujol's clearly bears the traces and scars of the real catastrophe that had occurred in the interim. It was an unusually sophisticated work for the rather downmarket* Lectures Pour Tous *to publish, and might have been accepted, or even commissioned, with* La Force mystérieuse *in mind, as the editors tried to reposition the periodical at the higher market level of* Je Sais Tout, *but whether that is the case or not, they never published anything else nearly as corrosively downbeat in the magazine thereafter, and might have instructed the author to bring it to its rather abrupt conclusion.*

Partly because it is too short to make a book, Le Soleil noir *went unreprinted until 1984, so it is not as well-known as some of the other works of a similar tripe published in the same period, such as Henri Allorge's* Le Grand cataclysme *(1922) and Ernest Pérochon's* Les Hommes frénétiques *(1925), but it does not suffer by comparison with them, and is one of the finest examples of cataclysmic fiction, perhaps the deftest of all in the delicacy of its touch and the subtlest in terms of its depiction of psychological reactions to unexpected and uncomprehended disaster.*

B.S.

I.

Jane was pretty. Nevertheless, the sentiment she inspired was not so much admiration as a keen interest, so intelligent was she divined to be, incapable of vulgar thoughts and miscalculations. She had magnificent eyes whose exact color was unknown; their irises were tinted with blue and green, and speckled with flecks of gold that augmented their brightness.

That day, I was contemplating her in silence. I was taking pleasure in detailing her delicate features while she leaned over her embroidery. Sometimes, she bit her lip lightly, and then pushed back a rebellious curl that was tickling her ear. I smiled tenderly at my fiancée. My happiness was complete.

Jane had been in my house since the previous day, with her father and mother, Monsieur Jérôme Sterneballe and Madame Amélie Sterneballe. Christmas falling on a Friday, the businessman was having "a long weekend." They had closed their shop for three days—for my future father-in-law kept an optician's boutique in the Rue Sainte-Catherine in Bordeaux, and they had come to spend their vacation under my roof.

I was in charge of the school at Roque de Thau, near Blaye. I loved that region, between the placid waters of the Gironde and the vineyards that produced a justly reputed wine. The commune being small, I did not have many pupils, and my work was not difficult. Fond of my métier, I was passionate about shaping the young souls confided to me.

"Where's Papa?" Jane asked.

"He's finishing painting the wine-store door."

If I dare express myself thus, painting was Monsieur Sterneballe's Ingres violin. The honorable optician spent his leisure time covering with multicolored layers anything that seemed to him to be worthy of his brush. Every time he came to see me he brought his pots of paint. It was sufficient to count them to know how many days he intended to devote to me. Thanks to him, as much as to the old woman who served as my housekeeper, a "Carabosse" of whom I had only ever known the nickname, La Barboque, my house was a jewel of neatness.

It is no bad thing to have laborious distractions. For my part, I profited from my hours of liberty to cultivate a piece of land situated behind the school, and no one went past my enclosure without complimenting me on my vegetables or my fruit trees.

"One day," said Jane, "Papa will paint himself—you'll see!"

I started to laugh at the idea that the long, thin figure of Monsieur Sterneballe might be ornamented by tattoos. The worthy man was approaching sixty. Commercial cares had marked his physiognomy with two deep wrinkles that, departing from the base of his nose, gave the illusion that his cheeks were crumpled like crepe. As for his forehead, it was striped from one temple to the other by three rigorously parallel furrows whose extremities were lost in hair that was still thick.

"You're teasing," I told my fiancée. "You'll be cruel to me if I become too old."

"Oh, I'll be very peevish," she replied, laughing.

"Then you'll have changed a great deal."

"We continued to chat merrily, while maintaining the beautiful fire that was blazing between two cast iron andirons.

The bells were ringing for the end of vespers and, a few minutes later, we heard children chattering in the road.

The previous evening, we had gone to midnight mass. It had been bitterly cold, with a sharp north wind that drew tears. When we returned we had huddled around the table to have supper.

"Would you like a game of chess?" I proposed.

"Good idea. A game, and a return match."

I had just set up the chessboard when someone knocked. It was Léonce Mistouflet, one of the Baron de Lansac's tenant farmers.

"A thousand apologies and beg pardon," he said, shaking my hand. "I'm disturbing you, Monsieur Dantenot."

"Not at all, Monsieur Mistouflet."

"Yes, I'm disturbing you. You're being polite, but it doesn't alter the fact..."

"No matter...what can I do for you?"

The fellow was not embarrassed. Before felling some oaks to sell the wood, he wanted to consult the official land register in order to determine the limits of his forest. He had come on the afternoon of Christmas day in order not to lose an hour of the working day.

"I know that everything is shut," he said, "but you're so obliging, Monsieur Dantenot..."

"A secretary of the Mairie ought not to spare his trouble," I replied. "Come with me; it won't take long."

I picked up my cap and we left. The weather was splendid. It was as warm as spring. I made that remark to my companion.

"Don't talk to me about it," he said. "That old devil of a sun is lashing out today. One would think it were May."

And he lamented the irregularity of the seasons, affirming that nature had been more reasonable once. One had hot weather in summer, cold in winter and rain in autumn, as regular as a musical score.

I listened to him with a distracted ear, for I was in a hurry to get back to Jane. I unrolled the plan, on which I pointed out to the farmer the part that interested him. He ran his rugged index-finger over it slowly, the fingernail as hard and yellow as horn.

"Yes, that's it, yes...I see...it's there. So, Féraud comes as far as here? That's curious... Anyway, thank you, Monsieur Dantenot."

"No trouble, Monsieur Mistouflet."

"I won't hurry going back to the farm. It's not right to be sweating in December."

I went back with him as far as the house. The village was almost deserted. Père Fouessart, who was suspected of being a centenarian, was smoking his pipe in his doorway. We exchanged a few cordial remarks.

"I put myself in the sun to soothe my rheumatism," he said, "but it was so hot that I came back into the shade."

"With these satanic seasons," Mistouflet said to him, "one no longer knows which foot to dance on."

"Oh," the old man replied, philosophically, "it's been a long time since I danced on either foot."

"Joker!" said the farmer. Addressing me with gravity, he added: "I'll be frank, Monsieur Dantenot. All these upsets that are ruining us come from the telegraph. These electricities, these waves, as the newspaper says, are troubling the sky. They claim that it's progress. Progress? I bow my head—but what good will progress do when nothing germinates any longer?"

I kept quiet. He seized me be the shoulder in a familiar fashion.

"You who are studious, Monsieur Dantenot, you ought to write articles about that. Too many cannon shots were fired during the war, and now we're being poisoned by airplanes. And the clouds? No one even thinks about them, the clouds! If I were something in the government, I'd have all the inventors shot."

"*Au revoir*, Monsieur Mistouflet."

"Bonsoir, Monsieur Dantenot...and thank you for showing me the register."

Jane was waiting for me with impatience. We started playing, pushing the pawns after mature reflection, because we were both serious players.

The contest had been seriously engaged when Madame Sterneballe came into the dining room. The good woman was scarlet.

"Oh, my children," she said, letting herself fall into a chair. "I can't digest my lunch. I have the vapors, and they're choking me..." She rolled her anxious eyes and fanned herself nervously with her handkerchief.

Jane hastened to run in search of melissa cordial. I made a circuit of the room several times, making vague remarks, which is the usual fashion in which men make themselves useful.

Madame Sterneballe was suffocating. Her plump, short hands were trembling.

"I was in the drawing room," she said, "reading the feuilleton. I suddenly felt my temples becoming moist...and a ball forming in my stomach..."

Jane handed her a glass, which she emptied in brief draughts, while continuing to talk.

"In order not to alarm anyone I went to sit down outside...but it didn't pass... I'm streaming from head to toe. Oh, my God...! What's wrong with me? A congestion?"

"Don't be alarmed, Madame," I said to her. "Everyone's complaining about the heat today."

Jane looked at me with a mocking expression. She thought that I simply wanted to reassure her mother, and doubtless judged that I lacked imagination. Madame Sterneballe was of the same opinion, for she shrugged her shoulders and repeated: "Heat in December? You're not thinking, Roger!"

Monsieur Sterneballe appeared in his turn. He was even redder than his wife.

"Well!" he said. "What does this comedy signify? I can no longer stand the heat!"

"You too!" stammered Madame Sterneballe. "Then I'm not ill?"

"It's the sun that's ill. It thinks it's April!"

I went out immediately. As soon as I had crossed the threshold I was astonished to feel the caress of a veritable summer breeze. I went to consult the thermometer. It marked twenty-eight degrees. I took out my watch. It was half past three.

"What do you think of it, Roger?"

It was Monsieur Sterneballe, who had rejoined me. I spread my arms and let them drop to indicate my ignorance. We advanced into the middle of the courtyard in order to examine the sky.

An elongated cloud, pink and gray, was floating at the zenith, and the sun was resplendent in the occident, where it would soon disappear. Nothing in particular attracted our attention. It was a superb day, and nothing more.

The almanac told us that the sun would set at three fifty-six. When it had sunk beneath the horizon, the temperature gradually dropped. The twilight was, however, exceptionally beautiful.

After dinner, we perceived that the fire had gone out. It was definitely not cold, and it wasn't relit.

We did not accord an extraordinary importance to what had happened during the day. We talked about the whims of nature, Indian summers—in brief, we exchanged banalities, the same ones people must have been emitting on the same subject in all the houses in the village. We did not stay up very long, because we had gone to bed late the day before.

I dozed off into a dreamless sleep. A kind of oppression woke me up. I propped myself up on my elbow and, having taken a deep breath without experiencing the slightest pain, acquired the certainty that my discomfort came from having too many bedclothes. I therefore cast off the eiderdown and went back to sleep—but not for long, for the same sensation forced me to open my eyes again. Irritated, I leapt out of bed, opened the widow and leaned on the sill. I stayed there for some time, breathing I the slightly cooler air delightedly.

Myriads of stars were resplendent in the firmament. The moon was silvering the roofs of houses. Dogs were responding to it, as if to invite one another mutually to redouble their vigilance. The sound of the flow of the Gironde reached me, as faint as the rustle of the willows in the Avenue du Port. Everything gave an impression of tranquility and absolute security. I went back to bed without reclosing the window. I thought it original to sleep in the open air, so to speak, at the end of December.

II.

I got up at daybreak. It was already after seven. No one was moving yet in the house. I went down to the garden in order to dig over a patch of ground that I wanted to sow. I had only been working for five minutes when I was sweating as if it were the middle of summer. I took off my jacket and the pullover I wore outside, rolled up my shirt sleeves, and continued plying the spade vigorously.

Fradinotte, my neighbor, went past driving a cart full of dung. He called to me over the garden wall.

"Hey, Monsieur Dantenot, is the soil good?"

"Not bad, not bad..."

"In any case, it's not last night's frost that has hardened it. If this goes on, the vine shoots are going to sprout, and the first cold snap will cut them down."

"Damn! That would be annoying."

"It's what we call a false spring. Let's hope everything will sort itself out. It's not warm weather we need, but a thick carpet of snow, to destroy those accursed insects! Hup, Bourrin! Hup!"

And his donkey pulled away while I went back to work.

"What an admirable man!" said Jane, suddenly, who had just arrived. "Come in quickly. You deserve the nice buttered toast I've made for you."

I readjusted my pince-nez in order to see my fiancée better. Every time I saw her she seemed to me to be more exquisite.

Hazard alone had allowed me to make her acquaintance. Monsieur Sterneballe was not my optician, but having noticed a pince-nez in his window whose frame seemed to me to be solid, I had gone in to buy it. An enchantress served me: that was Jane. She had admitted to me since that I had been ridiculous. I no longer knew what I was saying, and made a mistake in the number of diopters. Those who have been in love will comprehend the disturbance in question, which infallibly reveals the sincerity of the heart.

I went back the following Thursday. I bought another pince-nez, and that second conversation with Jane only reinforced my sentiment.

I have never been very bold. Every week, regularly, I went back to Sterneballe's with the formal intention of declaring my love, but as soon as I went into the shop, my courage vanished, anguish gripped my throat, and I went away having bought another pair of spectacles.

During the Easter vacation, I went to change my lenses five days in succession. On the last day, Monsieur Sterneballe emerged from his back room.

"Jane," he said, "your mother's asking for you. I'll take care of Monsieur."

When the young woman had disappeared, he looked me full in the face, with a gravity that was not devoid of sympathy.

"Monsieur," he said to me, "You're ruining yourself on lorgnons. You're a great breaker of lenses and a famous executioner of frames. You'd be better off addressing yourself to a wholesaler."

Nonplussed, I attempted a weak smile while darting a glance at the door, mentally making my preparations for flight.

"I wouldn't be sorry to know who you are," continued Monsieur Sterneballe, deliberately cutting off the route of my retreat.

As I was incapable of articulating a single word, I handed him my card.

"Aha!" he said. "You're a schoolteacher? I have a young cousin in the educational corps...Philippe Escarpit."

"He was in my class!" I exclaimed, in a stentorian voice.

Thank you, Philippe Escarpit. I never told you so, but you rendered me a sterling service. I spoke about you emotionally, I felt an extraordinary affection for your person. You abruptly became my best friend, my brother. I enquired after your health, your aspirations. I learned with immense pleasure that you were about to get married. Ah, family life! The wife sowing beside the lamp...the children playing on the carpet...the grandparents generously dispensing the advice of experience...

I was so enthusiastic and eloquent that I nearly reduced the good Madame Sterneballe, who had come to join her husband, to tears.

Regretfully, I finally took my leave. Monsieur Sterneballe accompanied me to the threshold of his shop. There, he said to me: "*Au revoir*, Monsieur Dantenot. I'll expect you tomorrow, since you're on vacation. And henceforth, don't feel obliged to buy spectacles in order to chat to my daughter."

In losing his best client, he was gaining a son-in-law...

"This is for you, Monsieur Greedyguts."

I bit into the enormous slice of buttered toast, which I washed down with a cup of milky coffee. Madame Sterneballe gave me honorable competition, for she had a good appetite.

At about nine o'clock I was scanning the newspapers that the postman had just delivered, when I was summoned. Monsieur Sterneballe was standing in front of the thermometer, shaking his head pensively.

"Twenty-eight degrees!" he said. "It's climbing visibly."

"That's odd," I said. "We had the same temperature yesterday evening."

"We're passing that, my dear!"

Gradually, the level of the red liquid rose in the tube of the thermometer. The ascent was slow but regular. In a quarter of an hour the level reached twenty-nine degrees, in half an hour, thirty.

"Fantastic! Fantastic!" murmured my future father-in-law. "Your instrument isn't out of order?"

"I don't think so. Let's go and consult the one at the Mairie."

"*Cristi!* What a heatwave!" sighed Monsieur Sterneballe.

The thermometer at the Mairie was fixed in the upper corner of the panel containing official notices and parliamentary speeches deemed worthy of display, which no one bothered to read. The said panel, facing south-east, was, in consequence, in full sunlight.

"Twenty-nine degrees and three tenths!" exclaimed Monsieur Sterneballe.

The Maire, Monsieur Nattechoux, was signing a few documents. He came out on hearing voices, to inform us that his amazement equaled ours. He uttered a few unnecessary observations on meteorology, and then took the *Petite Gironde* out of his pocket. The great Bordelais daily contained an article thus conceived:

We had the benefit on Friday of an ideal evening. The day had been rather sullen until, at about three o'clock, the solar rays increased in strength. Our fellow citizens, who were very numerous in the streets of the city center, where they were admiring the sumptuous window-displays in the large stores, observed that the temperature changed rapidly and agreeably. Even after the disappearance of the sun, a warm breeze was blowing, and the majority of strollers took off their overcoats and mantles with satisfaction.

Interrogated on the phenomenon, one of our most eminent astronomers at the observatory in Floirac attributed it to an abnormal atmospheric current. According to him, a veritable wave of sirocco, born in the confines of the Sahara, has crossed the Mediterranean and made its influence felt over the major part of Europe. That explanation would seem plausible if the same temperature—twenty-eight degrees—had not been registered at the same time in Madrid, Paris and London.

As on the previous evening, we examined the sun. It had an unsustainable glare, and the purity of the sky was absolute.

The intensity of the radiation was no longer augmenting with the same intensity. At eleven o'clock, the thermometer had scarcely passed thirty degrees. I ceased keeping watch on it after that, because we had a marriage to celebrate.

The nuptial cortege did not take long to appear. Behind a violin scratched by an idle fiddler, the spouses and the guests were bathed in sweat. They hastened to arrive in order to take shelter from the burning rays. The women especially, wrapped up in their winter clothes, overloaded with woolens and furs, were in torment. The bride's godfather was walking bare-headed, and had confided his top hat to his god-daughter.

The ceremony commenced with the reading of the contract. While I pronounced that standard phrases that I knew by heart, I observed the assembly, whose members seemed weight down by fatigue.

"Monsieur Robert-Émile Dufraison, do you consent to take for your legitimate wife...?"

My gaze was obstinately attached to the bride's godfather. The old man was experiencing an undeniable disturbance. He was opening and closing his mouth like a fish out of water, and his eyelids were rounding out immeasurably.

"Mademoiselle Ernestine-Gabrielle Tardivaud, do you consent to take for...?"

The godfather was as red as a poppy. Suddenly, he collapsed, delivering a rude blow of the fist to his neighbor's nose. There was a frightful tumult, an indescribable disorder. The women were all talking at once; a few children were crying; the men were interrogating one another. I had never seen such chaos.

"Air...! Air...!" I said, in a comminatory tone.

People drew apart slightly, and I laid the invalid out on the floor. He was completely inert, but his pulse was beating fairly clearly. At hazard, I was about to carry our respiratory movements, when Doctor Caffier came across the Place de la République. He leapt down from his cabriolet, fitted the safety-chain to the wheel, cleaved through the crowd authoritatively, and crouched down next to the old man.

"It's sunstroke," he said. "Roll back his sleeve—we're going to bleed him right away."

I obeyed, while he selected a lancet from his medical bag.

"Sunstroke!" people repeated. "Sunstroke in December! Oh la la! Sunstroke!"

The vein traced a little blue line on the white skin. With a swift gesture, Monsieur Caffier plunged his lancet into it. I saw half the blade disappear into the flesh and went pale, without letting go of the poor man's arm.

A drop of blood pearled at the edge of the little wound. That was all. The wound remained open, but no other drop appeared.

"Hmm! Hmm!" said the doctor without concealing his apprehension.

He made a second cut with the lancet, deeper and a little higher up. This time, I did not perceive a single drop of blood. He leaned over the sick man, stuck his ear to the chest directly over the heat, then got up and said, in a low voice: "He's dead."

The silence was absolute; everyone heard the words. Ernestine-Gabrielle Tardivaud fainted, uttering a terrible cry. The men took off their hats with a unanimous gesture. An old woman—I learned subsequently that it was the dead man's wife—screeched, in an extraordinarily shrill voice: "It's not true...it's not true..."

It was true, however. The man had died. The sun had just claimed its first victim.

Tears flowed and lamentations rose up. I was in haste to rejoin my future father-in-law, on whom that tragic scene had made a deep impression, but I was obliged to assist Monsieur Nattechoux to draw up, under the dictation of Doctor Caffier, a kind of witness-statement, to the bottom of which he added his signature, and to wait until the cadaver was taken away—with the result that it was one o'clock when we set off back to the school, and Jane and her mother were beginning to get anxious about our tardiness.

In the afternoon, the heat became torrid. The ardor of the sun was such that we dared not budge from the apartment. The thermometer, which I had taken into the kitchen—which is to say, into the shade—rose to thirty-five degrees. We closed the shutters and lowered the blinds, and Monsieur and Madame Sterneballe had a fine siesta.

Jane and I were not thinking about sleeping. Very close to one another, looking into one another's eyes, tenderly holding hands, we were making marvelous plans and building castles in Spain.

III.

Jane, Monsieur Sterneballe and I left early the next morning, at sunrise, to go fishing for shrimp.

The harbor of Roque de Thau is very narrow. Upriver of the landing-stage where the paddle-steamers operating as ferries between Bordeaux and Pauillac put in, a canal had been dug into which the barges and lighters come; when those small boats are loaded with barrels they take advantage of the tide to go slowly up the river.

Beyond the landing-stage, marshy meadows constitute the shore of the Gironde. Reeds grow in the mud and rattle their long leaves in the slightest breeze. On the seaward side, the Île Verte and the Île-sans-Pain bar the horizon with an emerald line. Further away, in front of the old citadel of Blaye, Fort Paté crouches in the middle of the muddy water, and in clear weather the other side of the estuary can be vaguely made out.

All three of us coiffed in vast straw hats, for the day promised to be as hot as the preceding one, we went to cast our rudimentary nets. I had fabricated those instruments myself, by fixing canvas sacks to barrel-hoops. A cod's head and some sheep-bones served us as bait.

The fishing promised to be excellent. In twenty minutes we had caught nearly half a kilo of shrimp, which were competing with one another to leap out of the basket in which we had imprisoned them. Monsieur Sterneballe was proud of having caught an American perch that measured about five centimeters from head to tail. He was already glimpsing a monster fry-up.

In the meantime, the wind got up. At first it was an imperceptible breeze blowing from the west, but its strength increased with great rapidity. The river became wrinkled, and then veritable waves unfurled toward us. My hat blew away, and I had to run after it at top speed to catch up with it.

A furious squall bent the reeds; such a whistling filled our ears that we almost had to shout to make ourselves heard.

"There's going to be a storm!" howled Monsieur Sterneballe.

The sky, however, remained absolutely pure.

We packed our baggage. An instinctive fear drove us toward my home. It was not rain that we feared, since there was not a single cloud in the sky, but we needed to feel a roof over our heads. We succeeded quite easily in getting out of the meadow where we had installed ourselves in order to fish, but once we were on the road, the wind was lashing us sideways, and we only advanced at the cost of great effort.

Jane clung to my arm, laughing nervously. Monsieur Sterneballe talked continuously, and I heard intermittently the words: "...tornado...tempest...worse than the equinox..." I made no reply, occupied as I was in protecting my fiancée.

We were emerging from the Avenue du Port when a frightful gust assailed us. I had the presence of mind to lie down on the ground, and I dragged Jane down with me as I fell. I felt a sharp pain in my knee, but did not pay overmuch attention to it.

Monsieur Sterneballe was literally lifted from the ground. I saw him oscillate, trying to regain his equilibrium, take two or three enormous strides, and, as if launched by a catapult, was hurled head-first into the wall of a fisherman's hut build on the roadside.

Leaving my fiancée lying in the dust, I crawled toward my future father-in-law. He was squatting on his haunches, seemingly stunned, with an enormous bump on his forehead. I asked him if he was hurt, but he was content to protest that he did not understand it at all.

Reassured on his account, I turned toward Jane. She had succeeded in dragging herself along on her knees, and was soon beside us. We went around the hut in order to get to the eastern side.

When we were in shelter, we were shaken by an uncontrollable hilarity. Nothing about our adventure seemed tragic. The sun was still resplendent.

The cyclone reached its peak. We only truly had the impression of danger when we saw a poplar snapped clean through near its base.

Then a willow was uprooted and transported fifty meters like a wisp of straw. A runaway horse went passed at a gallop, an empty trap rattling along at its heels. In the blink of an eye it reached the barrier of the railway crossing. It slipped on a rail and collapsed. After kicking all four feet it succeeded in getting up, and continued its hectic course toward Bribazac and Villeneuve.

A loud crack terrified us. Monsieur Sterneballe jumped to the right, and I drew Jane desperately to the left. At the same moment, the hut collapsed, noisily. Its wooden roof flew away and came down in a nearby field.

"We can't stay here!" shouted Monsieur Sterneballe.

Putting our arms around one another in order to oppose the greatest resistance to the impetuous wind, which was suffocating us, we headed toward the school, stumbling at every step. We had the good fortune to reach the goal without any further accident.

Madame Sterneballe's expression brightened at the sight of us. A pad of cotton wool soaked in phenol was applied to Monsieur Sterneballe's bump, and his head was wrapped in an immaculate turban.

Something warm and sticky was trickling down my leg. It was blood. When I lay down on the road I must have knelt on the shard of bottle-glass or a trenchant flint, because I had a deep cut underneath the knee-cap. It needed a serious bandage.

Jane, luckier than us, had not suffered any injury. She had lost most of her hairpins, and magnificent blonde tresses were flowing over her shoulders. Oh, that sumptuous mantle! I could not weary of admiring it.

In the haste of our flight we had abandoned our nets, and, as one can imagine, our straw hats had abandoned us, but the famous basket of shrimp was still there. We decided to boil them for lunch.

The fury of the atmosphere did not abate. The old house moaned, the wind growled and blew under the door, like a malevolent beast. The windows were shaken, as if someone were trying to open them, and we heard the shutters on the first floor slapping the façade furiously.

I went upstairs to fix them to their hooks, and did not succeed without difficulty. The gusts were as hot as the breath of a forge. Dust was swirling furiously, drawing in its rotation pieces of paper, bits of straw and hay, and detritus of every sort. And above the demented atmosphere, the blinding sun continued to describe its immutable parabola.

In the company of Monsieur Sterneballe, I absorbed the formidable aerial turmoil for a long time. The wind was not blowing in a regular fashion. The principal current was from west to east, from the ocean to the land, but bizarre whirlwinds were forming here and there, the force of which was vertical, from top to bottom. In my courtyard, for example, a tin-plate trough, from which my chickens and guinea-fowl came to rink in ordinary times, rose ten meters into the air, fell back almost in the same place, and immediately repeated the same ascent.

After the midday meal, La Barboque left us to go to vespers. We saw her drawing away prudently, moving along the walls—which was not a superfluous precaution, for the roadway was strewn with tiles and slates dislodged from roofs.

When we had drunk the coffee, I read aloud from the *Petite Gironde*. Naturally, the meteorological bulletin was on the first page, and contained more precise information than the one the previous day. Nevertheless, the commentary was sparse. The specialists were limiting themselves to recording the facts, and reserving their judgment.

The heatwave had descended on all five continents of the world. The rise in temperature was proportionately less in the tropical zone. On the other hand, the northern regions had passed without transition from the harshest winter to the most clement summer. Christiania, Viborg, Archangel and Omsk had never known such days. The thaw of the Siberian rivers had begun, and ships were signaling by wireless small icebergs off the coast of Iceland. A telegram from the Klondike said that the torrents of the gold country were threatening to inundate the majority of the claims. There was no information from Patagonia or the Antarctic region.

One American astronomer, bolder than his colleagues, attempted to give an explanation of the phenomenon. He spoke of an "excitation of solar incandescence due to causes of a mysterious nature" and left it at that. Another, a Dane, signaled the appearance of a monstrous sunspot, ten times larger than that of 2 February 1905, but confessed that the spot in question, observed on the equator of the star, had only been visible for a few minutes on 25 December. Already, an Englishman had categorically denied the claim, and, supporting his assertion on the anterior observations, demonstrated that although sunspots were modified with a disconcerting rapidity, they also disappeared just as suddenly. He affirmed that the gaseous eruptions that had taken place in that epoch had not been much more powerful than those once studied by Julius Mayer and Helmholtz, and that the protuberances were not abnormal. He then recalled that, every eleven years, the sun is the theater of crises that, although taking place two hundred million kilometers from Earth, are not without effect on our more modest globe.

Agreement was only unanimous on one point: all the scientists predicted the imminent return of the cold.

"We don't know much more than we did before," said Monsieur Sterneballe, when I finished reading. "I don't know whether or not the cold will be back soon, but what's certain is that the heat is increasing."

He was not mistaken. We were crimson and we were stifling. It seemed to us that we were in an oven, breathing fiery air.

I had the idea of watering the parquet copiously. The evaporation, very rapid, procured us some relief. We continued to throw water on it, in spite of the lamentations of Madame Sterneballe, who swore to the great gods that we were going to make the floorboards rotten.

That Sunday promised to be a mortally long day. The growling of the hurricane prevented us from thinking clearly, and a strange melancholy began to take possession of us. Jane attempted to sing in order to dissipate the sadness, but Madame Sterneballe asked her to stop, and all four of us remained dismal and preoccupied, waiting.

I received a visit from Monsieur Nattechoux, who was alarmed by the prolonged tempest. Considering me as a serious and sensible man, he had come to ask me what he ought to do.

"Do what?" sad Monsieur Sterneballe. "You don't, I suppose, have the pretention of being able to vanquish the elements?"

The Maire of Roque de Thau scratched his head in perplexity. "Obviously not...but within the limit of our forces...it's necessary to make some sort of plan..." Changing the subject, he said: "The wind has pulled my vines out of the ground."

That news appeared to consternate Madame Sterneballe, who usually had scant interest in agriculture. Monsieur Nattechoux addressed himself to her.

"It's ruination, Madame! The poles have been torn up and the stocks completely dislodged." With an energetic gesture, the countryman concluded: "My duty as the principal municipal magistrate is to comfort my administratees."

"Well said!" said Monsieur Sterneballe,

Sensing approval, Monsieur Nattechoux no longer hesitated: "Will you come with me, Dantenot?" he asked.

"We'll go," said Monsieur Sterneballe, spontaneously.

The ladies protested; they did not want to let us go out. I affirmed that we were taking absolutely no risk; the Maire insisted on the imperious character of his duty, my future father-in-law made a moving speech about the role of educated men, and Jane and her mother gave in.

It was not a banal departure. Under the leaden sun, buffeted by an infernal wind, we walked slowly, lending one another our arms like three drunkards, the Maire raising his thin face proudly; Monsieur Sterneballe affecting a solemn expression and me limping on my left leg.

The extent of the disaster terrified us. The closer we got to the river, the more the effects of the tempest were aggravated.

Trees that were still standing were very scarce. Save for the lowest fields, the vines were no more than tangles of branches. The embankment of the railway had protected a small area of the plain, but what subsisted was insignificant. The catastrophe was complete and irreparable.

Monsieur Nattechoux gazed fixedly at the earth. The man was suffering. Better than us, he understood what the destruction of the vineyards signified. It would require several years of labor before anyone could pick a single grape...

The postman came to meet us, tottering like us. He shouted in Monsieur Nattechoux's face: "It's not working anymore!"

"What?" shouted the Maire.

"The telegraph!"

And, with his head tucked in his shoulders, he headed for the railway station.

Mademoiselle Tournemire, the post office receiver, was smiling and relaxed. While chatting, she polished her fingernails with sustained application.

"It's not working anymore?" asked Monsieur Nattechoux, repeating what the postman had said.

"No, completely dead," said Mademoiselle Tournemire, lightly. "See for yourself. I'm going to call..."

Very elegantly, she activated the Morse key.

"Nothing," she said. "Silence. But it's not surprising. This stiff breeze has knocked down the telegraph poles."

"Ah! The stiff breeze...," sniggered Monsieur Sterneballe.

Mademoiselle Tournemire pouted delightfully. "Some squabble, isn't it? Do you have a headache, Monsieur?"

"Yes," said Monsieur Sterneballe, outraged by such insouciance.

"As soon as communications are restored," Monsieur Nattechoux instructed, "send the postman to inform me."

"Yes, Monsieur le Maire. But the workmen are so slow that we'll probably be cut off until the end of the week."

When we had set out again, Monsieur Sterneballe's indignation burst forth. "That silly girl is insupportable," he said. "The sky could fall and she'd go on polishing her nails."

"She's young," said the Maire sententiously. "She doesn't reflect on the consequences. You, Monsieur Sternecanne, you reflect."

"Sterneballe," my father-in-law corrected, immediately. "Indeed, I'm reflecting...do you know whether the train from Bordeaux has arrived?"

"It isn't time."

It did not arrive that evening, however, because of the rupture of a viaduct in the vicinity of Bordeaux.

IV.

Almost the entire population of the village was on the waterfront, fixed in the grim and silent resignation that is quickly acquired in grief.

The Gironde had the appearance of an angry sea. Meter-high waves were crashing upon the bank with such force that the ground shook and a watery spray rose up above the foam.

The pontoon of the landing-stage no longer existed; the swell had broken its moorings. The gangway was still there, oscillating in mid-air like the arm of a gigantic crane. It certainly would not be there for long, for its worm-eaten tie-beams were giving way and splintering.

In the canal, it was worse. Two lighters, the *Étoile 124* and the *Guillaume-de-Rosa* were colliding repeatedly; at each impact the hulls resonated lugubriously. A dozen men, clinging to the end of a cable, were hauling obstinately, with the efforts of the damned, but the river paid no heed to those pygmies.

We watched the destruction of the two boats, our hearts sinking. The *Étoile 124* was lifted up in such a way that her prow came crashing down on the deck of the *Guillaume-de-Rosa*. A wave then caused her to fall back heavily, and the water followed into her black belly, where a hole was gaping. That produced a frightful gurgling, and the *Étoile 124* sank to the level of her rail. She did not sink completely—the canal was not deep enough for her to be able to disappear. The *Guillaume-de-Rosa* was then broken herself, falling like a battering-ram upon the wreck of the other boat.

A clamor rose up from all mouths, for the barrels forming the cargo rolled off one by one, cracking and tinting the canal with bloody reflections. One man was struggling like a madman in the hands of several others. It was the owner of the *Guillaume-de-Rosa*, who wanted to kill himself. His comrades held on to him, but they had the appearance of executioners ferociously prolonging the torture of a victim.

The crowd flooded back in disorder toward the landing-stage. We followed, almost dragged along involuntarily, and were obliged to brace ourselves in order not to be pushed too close to the edge.

Less than a hundred meters away, a boat was struggling against the wind and the current. It was probably from the Île Verte, and was trying to land. For people were steering her—or rather maintaining her, for they were visibly incapable of maneuvering.

Curiosity maintained us motionless. Monsieur Nattechoux's fingernails dug into my arm, and Monsieur Sterneballe was moving his lips actively, like a priest reciting his breviary.

An old fisherman was gesticulating in a disorderly fashion. He was so far forward that the water was up to his knees. Making his hands into a loudhailer in front of his mouth he shouted words that no one could hear.

The men on the boat were harassed. They replaced one another at the oars, but their skiff was waltzing in such a way that one might have thought that they were rowing in the air. One of the two was repeatedly catching crabs. The inevitable occurred. The boat seesawed slowly and turned turtle with an almost mechanical precision.

Everyone fell silent. The old fisherman came back to firm ground, his fists in his pockets, like a man whose work was concluded.

The four unfortunates splashed, disappeared and reappeared, like novice swimmers in a fish pond. They were so close that we could make out two black dots—their eyes—in the white oval of their face. We knew that they were going to die.

"Let's go...let's go...," stammered Monsieur Sterneballe.

We set off without letting go of one another, Monsieur Nattechoux, Monsieur Sterneballe and I, like three friends at the exit from a play. The intensity of the tempest was diminishing. It was after four o'clock; the sun was no longer shining. It was a great relief no longer to feel its rays. My skin was dry and hot, as in the aftermath of a bout of fever.

Monsieur Nattechoux did not communicate his impressions to us. He was not sad; only one word could translate his state of mind: he was stupefied. In his distress, he blew his nose on a tricolor cloth; it was his mayoral sash, which he had been carrying in his pocket.

He left us at our door.

"Bonsoir, Monsieur Corneballe," he said.

"Sterne...Sterneballe," said the optician, with a hint of irritation. "Buck up, Monsieur le Maire. Days that follow one another don't resemble one another."

"Fortunately," said Monsieur Nattechoux.

"He's a good fellow," said Monsieur Sterneballe, when we were alone, "but he hasn't invented the coffee-grinder. Did you notice that he always gets my name wrong?"

Jane and her mother were embroidering peacefully in the dining room. Madame Sterneballe scrupulously described her real and imaginary illnesses, and finally ceded the floor to her husband. The worthy man, as talkative as her, started to recount in detail everything that we had seen. When he finished his story, night was almost complete.

I wanted to call La Barboque to light the lamp, but Jane stopped me,

"Let me do it," she said. "Your housekeeper isn't in her normal state."

"What's wrong with her, then?"

"Hmm!" said Madame Sterneballe. "I believe she's been hitting the wine bottle too hard."

"La Barboque? That's not her habit."

"Listen to her singing..."

In the kitchen, La Barboque was mistreating the crockery, and howling a refrain: *La fille alla-t'au bois/Larirette, larifla!*"

"I can't tolerate that," I said, indignantly, while Jane suppressed an impulse to laugh.

Standing in front of her oven, La Barboque was striking a saucepan conscientiously with a metal spoon. She did not even hear me come in.

"Well!" I said.

She turned round. She had daubed her face with soot, and in that black mask, her eyes sparkled like carbuncles.

"Monsieur," she said, "I know all that. If I'm cooking a bar of soap, it's because the catechism is important. But no dandy is going to lead me by the nose!"

She came to me, claws forward. I seized her by the wrists in order to defend myself, but she allowed herself to be mastered meekly. She was as cold as marble."

"Bang!" she said. "You can't stop rabbits from jumping on the rubber."

La Barboque was not drunk. The sun had driven her mad.

I am not very impressionable; even so, anguish penetrated my heart. I scarcely had the strength to take the poor wretch to her nephew's house, and I took refuge in my bedroom without having anything to eat.

The wind had dropped completely. The constellations strewed the sky with twinkling fireflies. The blue darkness of the night invited dreams.

But what was the significance of the heat that was gripping me, irritating my lungs and forcing me to forget the winter?

Silence was the master of nature. Mystery was floating therein. Exhausted by the emotions and exertions of the day, however, I did not have the courage to try to investigate it.

I went to sleep thinking about Jane, our imminent union, and the happiness that awaited us...

I didn't know...

I didn't know...

V.

The pain of my wound woke me up. It was still dark, but an indecisive glimmer brightened the orient and gradually caused the stars to fade. The angelus rang, with little irregular and feeble chimes that encouraged the supposition that the bell-ringer was still half-asleep.

Under my window, a cock crowed. I saw him singing, his chest thrust out, his feet apart; then he listened, until a response reached him, and seemed satisfied. Around him, the hens were actively pecking the ground, and seemed to be exchanging reflections on their finds.

Not a cloud in the sky; the air was absolutely limpid. It was another day of beautiful weather that was announced, a day of heatwave.

The aurora was as red as the reflection of a titanic furnace. The last stars went out, and the sun appeared above Fradinotte's house. All the colors changed, becoming vivid. The occident remained tinted ultramarine by the fleeing shadow. The blinding disk remained tangential to the ridge of the roof for a few seconds, and then rose into the sky.

There was movement on the ground floor. I went downstairs to drink milky coffee. By tacit accord, we avoided mentioning La Barboque. Madame Sterneballe, wrapped in a white apron, had already wrung the neck of a chicken that she was planning to fry on the stove with potatoes and onions.

Monsieur Sterneballe was anxious. It was the first time in thirty years that he had not been in his shop at the habitual hour.

"There are no trains, of course," he told me confidentially. "There are no boats, I'll give you that...but I can't resign myself, even so...I'm annoyed...it's impossible for me to think about anything else. I can hear the neighbors gossiping—people in commerce are so malevolent. They'll believe that I'm rich enough to take vacations like a State employee. Not to mention that Monday is the best day of the week for us. All the people in the area will go to Bordeaux to get what they need. What will my clients think when they find my iron shutter lowered? I like you, Roger, but truly I regret having come to Roque de Thau..."

I listened to him with patience and deference. It's better to let people of a certain age talk. If one interrupts them, it annoys them and makes them angry.

"You're making too much bad blood," Madame Sterneballe told him. "Me, I'd be consoled if it weren't as hot."

In this story, the question of heat is sempiternal. The word recurs constantly at the end of my sentences, but I can't do otherwise. The temperature was rising incessantly; we were living in a steam-bath. It was in vain that we sought to procure ourselves even a semblance of freshness. We had given up watering the parquet, because the evaporation eventually saturated the atmosphere with humidity.

Monsieur Sterneballe wanted to open the windows; Madame Sterneballe preferred to keep them closed, and I agreed with her. It was a little less stifling inside than outside.

The absence of trains naturally deprived us of mail. I was put out by that, because I looked forward to my morning paper impatiently. I needed news, gossip. I understood that a cataclysm of an unprecedented kind as menacing the solar world, but the worst that I supposed as far from the truth.

As I found out later, the hurricane on 26 December had not simply devastated France. The entire atmosphere was in revolt. In the valley of the Rhône, framed by the Cévennes and the foothills of the Alps, nothing had resisted. The tempest had overturned the express trains, undermined tall buildings, scythed down the trees. Entire villages were no longer anything but ruins. All the coastal areas had been swept by tidal wave. The dyke at Cherbourg had been demolished; the ships at anchor in the port of Saint-Nazaire had been smashed against the quays.

The Eiffel Tower had held firm, as well as the pylons of the big wireless telegraphy station at Croix d'Hins; by contrast, the antenna of the German station at Nauen, which had told so many lies during the war, no longer existed. It was, therefore, via France that the old and new continents were still in communication.

The American telegrams were frightening in their laconism. The region surrounding the Great Lakes was no more than a desert. In New York, the skyscrapers had been decapitated, and the tons of materials that had fallen around them had struck countless victims. Several quarters of San Francisco no longer existed. In the Rocky Mountains, landslides had caused serious damage in several cities.

South America, Australia, Africa and Asia were mute, and their silence was more terrible than the most terrible news.

The British Admiralty did not publish any list of maritime losses, nor did the Veritas bureau. The telegraphists of the semaphores however, were not unaware of the number of shipwrecks. For twelve hours, uninterruptedly, they had received the tragic signal: S.O.S... S.O.S... S.O.S... It was by launching those three letters into space, thousands of miles around them, that ships in perdition requested help. One could not hear those desperate appeals, converging from all the points of the ocean, without experiencing an atrocious sentiment of impotence and terror.

A large number of boats escaped destruction, but they were not the transatlantic liners, the leviathans; they were the nutshells, the cod-fishers, the broad and flat coasters. They danced, ripping their rigging, but did not sink. The fashion in which the others agonized will forever remain a secret.

The dispatches of the last hour—the qualification was all too exact—announced cataclysms of every sort. Formidable torrents poured down from the Alps, the melting of the snows occurring suddenly. The dykes gave way in Holland and the Belgian lowlands, where immense plains were submerged. Everywhere, a number of mortal congestions caused by the heat were recorded. In the beginning, the sun only killed with a kind of discretion. It was the skirmish before the hecatomb.

Such was the beginning of the reign of Fear.

Monsieur Sterneballe was the most clear-sighted of the four of us, because he had nothing to do other than observe. Madame Sterneballe was occupied with the housework, and Jane and I with our future. We were choosing furniture in catalogues, discussing the styles!

My future father-in-law interrupted our tête-à-tête. He took me into the courtyard.

"Roger," he said, "I'm frightened."

I wanted to reply with a joke, but his face was so distressed that I kept quiet.

"Frigh-ten-ed!" he repeated, stressing the syllables. "The strength of the sun is increasing by the minute..."

"The increase can't be indefinite."

"How do you know?"

"It's never been seen!"

"What has happened in the last three days has never been seen either. We're in December! In December, it ought not to be, it *can't* be, so hot!"

"At the Equator, however..."

"We're not at the Equator! And even at the Equator, we'd have reason to tremble."

"Because the sun is in effervescence," I said, lightly.

"Precisely, Roger. The sun is our master, it can roast us as a cooking-fire roasts a vulgar chicken."

"Bah! It's been tranquilly playing its role for millions of years..."

"You can't deny that some phenomenon has exaggerated its ardor! Your cabbages, the cabbages of which you were so proud, are no more than yellow balls, fuming and rotting. The fields? Not a blade of green grass! I'm wondering, anxiously, whether our organism can resist for much longer."

He leaned over to repeat, in a low voice: "I'm wondering..."

I revolted. "What! You think that we...?"

To my unfinished sentence he replied by nodding his head affirmatively. And I felt incapable of protesting, for his conviction impressed me.

A glance around the courtyard reassured me. The weather was fine. Cocks and hens were pecking the ground here and there, plumping themselves up with pleasure. The sky was almost white, by virtue of the brightness of the light.

"You're a pessimist," I told him.

"I am since this morning. I've put the thermometer outside again. Do you know what it did, the thermometer? It burst. Now, it's graduated up to fifty degrees...it seems to me that that's a figure that justified my pessimism."

Raising his two clenched fists over his head, he said: "What's going on up there? What's happening...?"

We took some prudent measures to give us the illusion of security. Our apartment was a greenhouse, for the heat came in through the windows but didn't go out, so we nailed thick canvas over all the embrasures. The result of that padding was a relatively cool demi-obscurity.

Jane amused herself somewhat poking fun at her father. He didn't care. He made an inventory of all the receptacles, from the buckets and pitchers to the most modest pots, and we filled them the pump. That small task was extremely difficult, because the iron of the handle burned our fingers.

When we had finished, we seemed to be emerging from a steam-bath.

"Now," said Monsieur Sterneballe, "we're ready; we have no more to do than wait."

But several distractions were reserved for us. Blisters that soon formed on our skin made us itch intolerably. Madame Sterneballe supported that torture poorly—which, fortunately did not last long. The blisters disappeared, leaving a large number of little scarlet circles on our bodies.

Then came the flies. They arrived in swarms, slipping through the cracks in the doorways and windows and coming down the chimney. With great sweeps of dusters we made relentless and joyful war on them. They were gradually vanquished, and hundreds of shriveled strewed the floor.

Lunch was sad; my artificial cheerfulness did not fool anyone.

We started a game of lotto thereafter, but it lacked enthusiasm. Madame Sterneballe went to sleep over her cards. She woke up suddenly with a start.

"Fifteen! I've got it!" And after an attentive examination: "I beg your pardon. I haven't got it."

A visit from the curé, Abbé Escatafal, revived us.

"Can you guess what I've come to tell you?" he said, sitting down.

"Frost!" I said, gaily.

"Alas, no," he replied. "Monsieur Nattechoux is dead."

The Maire of Roque de Thau had left for his property at Gauriac. He had been found lying face down on the road, in a pool of blood."

"Congestion...hemorrhage...," said Monsieur Sterneballe. "He was already having trouble yesterday...he was mangling proper nouns..."

"There's panic in the village," the Abbé continued.

"Do you think that it will get even hotter?" Jane asked.

"I don't know, Mademoiselle. As the Scriptures say, the designs of the Almighty are impenetrable."

"You're being tragic," I said. "All this will sort itself out. It's sufficient to have a little logic to..."

"There's logic intervening!" riposted the curé. "It has nothing to do with this affair! Extraordinary events are manifest, a prodigious upheaval is occurring, and you talk about logic! That's pride, Monsieur Dantenot. Human logic is probably not universal logic. The laws of your physicists and your astronomers are based on hypotheses that I defy you to verify. We want to know everything, to explain everything, to regulate everything, but we don't know the most elementary things...you're protesting? Tell me, then, what flame is...! You remain silent, naturally. That won't prevent you, in a little while, if it gets hotter, from affirming that it's because of this, and if it gets cooler, that it's because of that... I've studied, like you, and I'm not so categorical. Logic? Today is not its reign. In the meantime, I'm going to go around the houses to comfort the inhabitants..."

"The wisest thing would be to return to the presbytery," said Monsieur Sterneballe.

"No, Monsieur," said Abbé Escatafal, "I have a role to fulfill. In the thirty years that I've been exercising my ministry it has never been difficult. I'd be unworthy of the soutane if I showed reluctance at the first danger."

We never saw him again. He must have perished like Monsieur Nattechoux.

VI.

The temperature increased incessantly. My apartment resembled the coal-bunker of a steamship.

Madame Sterneballe was suffering more than the rest of us. I calculated that if the increase of the heat continued, our organism could not resist until sunset. Strangely lucid, I foresaw that our last moments would be frightful. Even so, I risked a joke.

"It's the ruination of the coal-merchants."

I was talking to the deaf. Jane and her mother, overwhelmed and exhausted, seemed to be asleep. Monsieur Sterneballe never left the window. Through a gap in the curtain, he watched the shadow of the house advance further and further toward the road. But the sun wasn't disappearing rapidly enough.

To fight against an enemy, even if defeat is inevitable, is a consolation, and even a distraction, but there is nothing more depressing than passive resistance to a torture. I bit my fists because I was unable to offer Jane any relief.

Monsieur Sterneballe did not manifest any madness. Suddenly, we saw him steep several napkins in a pitcher.

"Compresses!" cried Madame Sterneballe.

We applied them to our burning foreheads, and savored a moment of indescribable wellbeing. Confidence returned.

At about three o'clock, Madame Sterneballe had a brief fainting fit. A drop of ether reanimated her, but I understood that she was at the end of her resources. In any case, we were all the color of brick, and it was evident that our collapse was only a matter of minutes.

Alone in my house, I had not made a gesture. My sensations were bizarre. When one comes home from hunting, in snowy weather, one installs oneself voluptuously beside the fire. One gets too hot, one almost burns. It is sufficient to step back to be more at ease, and yet one says there, heels on the andirons, torpid and somnolent. I was in exactly that state.

"Oh, how will I feel!" said Jane, in a plaintive voice.

Monsieur Sterneballe contemplated her sadly. I got up and I drank a draught from a large glass of water.

I was ready to fight, but against whom? Against what?

I learned later that the disorganization of Europe commenced that afternoon. All public services had been functioning until then, all the factories were working. It had not occurred to any government, or any employer, to stop the social machine because the weather was hot. Every man was therefore left to his own initiative, and resistance was more or less prolonged in accordance with his environment or his personal energy. Curiously enough, the ministries did not shut down any more than usual. On the other hand, trains stopped in the middle of the countryside, no matter where. But no traveler survived to tell the story of what had happened...

A noise of hooves attracted my attention. I perceived one of my best pupils, little Florimond Lestaque, who was galloping while weeping. The poor child had doubtless just witnessed a horrible scene and was fleeing at random.

I wanted to call out to him, but I did not have time. Before arriving at my door he fell as if he had received a sledgehammer blow on the back of his neck.

"What's that?" asked Jane.

Swiftly, I replied: "Nothing...nothing at all..."

Monsieur Sterneballe came toward me. He looked at the little cadaver, lying under the terrible sun.

"Our turn will come," he breathed in my ear.

"No," I said, clenching my fists.

He thought I had a means of delaying the final outcome. His face cleared. He pointed to the two women.

"Them first," he said.

But seeing my eyes fill with tears, he turned his back on me.

"Imbecile!" he murmured.

He had never been rude in my regard.

The howl of a wounded dog, a prolonged and heart-rending plaint, suddenly broke the luminous and sinister silence. The beast went past, flat out, suffering without understanding why. It was a large and sleek sheepdog, with a long tongue hanging down. It swerved, and without paying any heed to a thread of barbed wire that tire its flank, it succeeded in slipping through the ventilation-shaft of a cellar. Its muffled moans became more lugubrious, and it fell silent. It seemed to me that the ventilation shaft was the maw of a monster that had swallowed it in order to abridge its suffering.

Delirium afflicted me, to my great satisfaction, for it attenuated my physical sensibility. Multicolored lights danced before my eyes. The state in which I found myself is difficult to describe; it was compounded out of an indifference in the face of death and a clairvoyance that left me under no illusion as to my fate.

The head of the dog reappeared in the ventilation shaft. It immediately went back into the shadow. Then a sense of reality returned to me. The cellar made me think of other cellars more spacious and more tenebrous. I started capering like a madman.

"The quarries! The quarries!"

I shouted those words, clamored them, sang them.

"The quarries! The quarries! The quarries!"

Without lifting a finger, Madame Sterneballe said: "It's like La Barboque!"

"Make no mistake!" I replied. "I have all my common sense. Let's take refuge in the quarries of Le Mugron!"

Like an echo, Monsieur Sterneballe repeated: "In the quarries of Le Mugron."

Le Mugron is a hill, a calcareous cliff that roses to the south of Roque de Thau and extends as far as Rigalet. People extract building stone from it, with the result that a large number of runnels have been excavated in it. It was of those tunnels, those profound quarries, that I had just thought. How cool they must be!

"Let's go! Let's go!" said Monsieur Sterneballe.

But I had recovered all my reason.

"We won't reach Le Mugron like this," I said. "If we don't take precautions, the sun will kill us."

"That's true," said Monsieur Sterneballe. "Roger, you've saved us! We're going to shelter under umbrellas."

"That won't be sufficient," I said. "Let me think, let's not rush..."

The obeyed me with a child-like docility. Under our hats we rolled up damp sheets. But it was important to protect our bodies as well as our heads. I found nothing better than pouring a bucket of water over Monsieur Sterneballe's shoulders. His wife did not consent to an analogous treatment without jibbing.

"At my age!" she said. "I'll catch a cold!"

While she was arguing, Jane doused her copiously. She screeched like an osprey, and finally resigned herself. We soon had every appearance of survivors of a shipwreck. Our garments stuck to our bodies, and we spread a veritable rain at every movement.

"Let's go," I said.

I went out first. I had not taken ten steps when I doubted the success of my plan. The ground burned our feet. A thick mist was disengaged from our cloths. We advanced in a flameless conflagration. We had less than a kilometer to travel to each the entrance to the first tunnel. I don't know how much or how little time it took to cover that distance. The soles of my shoes were like hot irons. Monsieur Sterneballe was moaning.

We finally got there. Our clothes, completely dry, were irritating the skin. We dived into the black hole of the quarry.

The gallery descended at a gentle slope. We plunged on into the darkness. The further we went, the cooler the atmosphere became. We breathed in life greedily, dilating our lungs. The nightmare was over.

We embraced one another with intoxication, unable to see one another. At the end of the tunnel, the orifice was like a little blue dot.

VII.

If the first hour was exquisite, it was necessary for us to admit thereafter that our change of domicile had been effected too lightly. In the precipitation of our departure, we had not brought any food. We also lacked matches, and Monsieur Sterneballe only had a tinder lighter that could not give us any assistance. Sitting side by side on a long stone, we dared not move any further away from the exit, for the quarries of Le Mugron comprise several levels. We might have fallen and broken our necks.

The entrance to the tunnel became gradually darker, for night had to be descending over the earth. We were not too hot, but we were hungry and thirsty. Anguish was strangling us. I had difficulty chasing away the thought that we were buried alive. An insipid odor of mildew assailed us, similar to that which expands when gravediggers lift up the stone of a tomb. Then too, we were anxious because we did not know what was happening outside.

We wanted to talk, conversation being, in that darkness, the most reassuring manifestation of life, but we could not find anything to say. Jane, who was pressing against me, was trembling like a leaf. From time to time, Madame Sterneballe uttered deep sighs.

"We were wrong not to have eaten a more substantial lunch," said my future father-in-law. "I feel a ferocious appetite."

"Me too," said Madame Sterneballe. "I could eat no matter what."

I replied to them, dully: "I'll go look for some food."

I immediately repented of having pronounced that sentence. I waited for protestations, but only Jane replied: "Mightn't it be dangerous to go out?"

Monsieur Sterneballe reassured her, too affirmatively for my liking: "It's not as hot at night."

I was annoyed with him. He ought to have forbidden me to sacrifice myself. I felt safe on my stone, beside the woman I loved. Our suffering was still benign. Why not endure it for one more day?

"Bring something to drink," said Madame Sterneballe.

That order scandalized me. But my fury gave way to dejection when Jane added: "Hurry up, Roger. The sooner you go, the sooner you'll be back..."

I kissed her rapidly in the darkness. My kiss was lost in her hair.

"Adieu," I said, in a tremulous voice.

A hand palpated my side—that of my future father-in-law, seeking mine in order to shake it effusively.

"Would you like me to come with you?" he asked.

Madame Sterneballe immediately protested: "Don't leave us alone in this gulf?"

"All right, all right, I'll stay," said the optician, without insisting. "Let me tell our young friend what it's necessary to do."

I no longer had the initiative for the dangerous operation. I was about to risk my carcass benevolently—why had I been so talkative?—and Monsieur Sterneballe, abusing the authority of age, wanted to direct me from his place, as strategists behind the lines direct armies.

"Take my big square basket. Do you have tinned food?"

"No," I riposted, outraged by such a perfect indifference to the risks I was about to run.

"Pity. Get the ham, then..."

"And the rest of the chicken," said Madame Sterneballe.

"There's half a cheese in the larder," Jane recalled.

"Perfect," said Monsieur Sterneballe. "Don't forget the bread. We French don't know how to eat without bread. Hurry, Roger—a prolonged absence would make us anxious."

I had a desire to weep. Those people, who comprised my entire family, were only thinking about their stomachs! They were sacrificing me lightly in order to be able to satisfy their hunger.

I could not stay at the expense of my self-respect. I left.

The adieux were conventional. I kissed Jane a second time, at the invitation of her mother. That was the last favor accorded to the condemned man.

My knee was hurting badly. I limped up the slope that led up to the orifice. The heat increased at every step.

So much the better! I thought, at the peak of my indignation. I'm going to collapse immediately. That will teach them!

It would have taught them absolutely nothing. In any case, I didn't collapse. Breathless, slightly suffocated, I understood that I could resist. I paused on the threshold of the tunnel. My silhouette must have been cut out in the opening, against the sky, perceptible to Monsieur Sterneballe.

I waited for a cry, an appeal, in order to retrace my steps. I did not hear any. So I launched forth, vomiting imprecations.

The stars had never been so numerous or so scintillating. Their tiny lights danced in space. Bolides traced long phosphorescent streaks.

Crickets were singing.

I was scarcely sensible to the beauty of nature; nevertheless, it reassured me. I gradually got used to the heat, which must have been about forty degrees.

I went as rapidly as my myopia permitted. Before reaching the first house I made out a large heap in the middle of the road. It was a cow, already bloated, its legs stiff. A little further on there was another body, that of a man. My hair prickled. That macabre encounter took away all my valor. If I continued, it is because vanity is more powerful than cowardice.

The village was dark, peaceful and welcoming. I introduced myself to my home with an artificial assurance. If I had not found the matches in their usual place I would have fled.

Everything was in order, and yet I was groping. It took me five minutes to discover Monsieur Sterneballe's square basket. With a perfect docility I stuffed into it my ham, half a loaf of bread, two or three pieces of chicken and the cheese, all pell-mell. I added three bottles of wine, the end of a sausage and a few apples that were sitting on a shelf.

The clock chimed eight. The first stroke froze me to the spot. Then it appeared marvelous and comforting that the clock had tranquilly continued its work, as if the duration of time mattered more than events. I went back up with a kind of piety, and it was to the clock that I addressed my adieu as I left.

It was, in any case, a false exit, because, in spite of Monsieur Sterneballe's recommendation, I had forgotten the candles. I took two packets, and headed for the quarry

As I approached the dead man lying in the road I experienced a veritable terror again. I turned my head away and passed by rapidly on the verge. The dry grass crackled underfoot. That reminded me about the excessive heat. In reality, my mission had not been very difficult, but in remembering the details, I convinced myself that I ha jut accomplished an extraordinary exploit. I was in haste to arrive in order to recount my odyssey.

As I set foot on the rounded platform in front of the quarry I experienced a joy as great as that of a pursued badger reaching its sett. I lit a candle and went into the tunnel. It was about two meters high and as many wide. The walls were yellowed, perfectly dry, and the ground was constituted by a thick layer of stone dust, known locally as "perruche." I was very satisfied. In a loud voice I asked: "Where are you?"

My phrase echoed in the distance. Someone replied: "Yoo-hoo!"

The most eloquent sentence could not have charmed me more; I had recognized Jane's voice.

"I'm intact," I went on, thinking that it might interest them.

"Have you got something to eat?" demanded Monsieur Sterneballe.

"Yes, glutton," I said, but as I pronounced the latter word with a measure of discretion, my future father-in-law did not hear it.

All three of them were still sitting on the stone. The light of the candle cast great moving shadows over their features. They laughed, and that made me think of the dead man lying on the road.

"There's the blessed basket!" said Monsieur Sterneballe.

He set about taking inventory of the provisions. I poured a few stops of stearine on to the ground and the candle remained upright.

"It all went well?" said the optician. "I had to reassure the ladies..."

So, during my absence, he had transformed my perilous adventure into a pleasant stroll! It was with the laudable intention of "reassuring the ladies," but it vexed me profoundly.

"I'll wager that you haven't brought a knife!" said Madame Sterneballe.

I made a movement of annoyance.

"How are we going to cut the ham without a knife?"

"I'm a birdbrain," I said. "Would you like me to make another trip?"

"Of course not! We'll do without, that's all."

The bread was broken into four hunks of approximately equal size. The division of the chicken was less equitable. My share consisted of a part of the carcass, which I gnawed philosophically, while Madame Sterneballe tore apart an entire wing.

"No notable incidents?" asked Monsieur Sterneballe, his mouth full.

My good humor returned at that question. Without urgency, in a casual manner, I began my story.

I am still amazed by the embellishments that I took pleasure in adding to it. To hear me, I had only progressed with extreme difficulty, sustained by the imperious desire to discover alimentary supplies. I had found three dead cows, a semi-carbonized man and an agonizing dog. I made much of the dog.

"What a spectacle! The unfortunate quadruped was whining..."

But Monsieur Sterneballe was battling with the ham.

"It's resisting! It's resisting!" he said.

In fact, the ham, thickest and compact, was formally refusing to be divided. Madame Sterneballe recommenced her jeremiads on the subject of the knife. I then discovered a folding pen-knife in my waistcoat pocket, whose timid offensive against the tough meat permitted me to finish my story.

The golden halo of our candle rendered the darkness around us more impenetrable. The light isolated us in the middle of the gallery as in a closed room. We chatted insouciantly, for a fault—or a virtue—of human beings is to forget their troubles when they are no longer experiencing them.

If we avoided making plans for the future, it was because we estimated that our situation was temporary. We did not think we would be inhabiting those catacombs, which had to be singularly favorable to rheumatism, for long.

"Do you think that the human race will perish?" Monsieur Sterneballe asked me, in a light tone." And without waiting for my response, he added: "The disorder must be serious in the cities. People must be killing one another recklessly, because the troublemakers are always on the lookout for an opportunity to turn society upside down."

"I think, on the contrary, that the sun will have put everyone in accord, even the Bolsheviks and the bourgeois."

Later, I was to learn what had happened. The tunnels of the Paris Metro and the London "Tube" were filled with a tumultuous crowd. Deaths by asphyxiation and crushing were multiplied. In certain places the crush was such that the cadavers remained upright between the living, advancing and recoiling with them in accordance with the eddies, with a lugubrious impassivity. The sewers had been much sought after, and the victims there had been numerous.

Existing social inequalities had rapidly disappeared, to give way to others. The privilege of strength had been imposed. Powerful muscles and automatic weapons conferred an undeniable superiority on their possessors. It was not rare to see a scholarly professor or an influential politician behaving respectfully before a dock worker he would have scorned a few days before.

Monsieur Sterneballe lamented the possible pillage of his shop in Bordeaux. While he waxed lyrical in his lamentations, Madame Sterneballe started snoring without discretion, which was a fashion of sounding the curfew. We decided to look for a sufficiently comfortable place to spend the night. I therefore picked up the candle, and we moved away, carrying the ham.

The gallery turned abruptly to the right and divided into two tunnels. I followed the wider one, which plunged into the depths of the hill. A few beams and stays reminded me of the possibility of collapses. The sound of our footsteps was amplified in the sepulchral silence. We were overwhelmed by all the shadow; we said nothing.

Suddenly, all four of us came to a halt, like a squadron in response to its leader's command. We had just heard something: a bizarre cry, strident and quavering, deformed by the echoes, and also by our fear.

We waited for another cry, but a heavy silence had fallen again. I was incapable of taking a step, either forwards or backwards, and my companions were no more sure of themselves than me. What mysterious being was troubling our retreat?

Three hammer-blows struck on a plank resounded violently. We looked at one another fearfully, ready to panic. But the cry resounded again under the vault, and we realized this time that it was the whinny of a horse.

Twenty meters further on, a door sealed the tunnel. As it was maintained by a simple peg, I opened it.

A fairly sizeable chamber had been hollowed out in the friable stone. The chamber served as a stable, a feed-store and a depository for tools. Quarrymen's picks, shovels and saws were stacked up in one corner, near a heap of straw and several bales of hay, which embalmed it.

The horse, a dappled pony, was attached to a bar of its empty manger. It extended its quivering nostrils toward us, and delivered several kicks to the partition of its stall. It had eaten all of its litter that it had been able to reach, and it was hunger that was causing it to whinny. It had probably not had any care for two or three days.

Jane caressed it amicably. It placed its large head on my fiancée's shoulder.

"It's blind," she said.

The animal's eyes were only two milky globes. Its infirmity rendered it more sympathetic. I gave it a copious ration of hay, which it started to chew incontinently with its long yellow teeth.

"We'll call it Coco," said Jane.

A copper plate was nailed to the snaffle. I read: *Fourtané Auguste, owner*. But we were never to make the acquaintance of Fourtané Auguste.

Ever practical, Monsieur Sterneballe scattered the straw. Ten minutes later, we were sleeping in the obscurity of a dreamless slumber. That was truly our best night, in the course of that period of frightful and exhausting emotions.

VIII.

It was at dusk that I emerged from our subterranean refuge for the second time. Monsieur Sterneballe had come with me as far as the orifice. He was sprightly until the moment when the heat became unbearable for him. Then he wished me *bon voyage* and quickly went back into the tunnel like a snail into its shell.

When the fire follet of his candle had vanished, I felt my heart sink. I sat down on the threshold to accustom my organism to the ambient temperature.

My horizon was rather limited. To my right bristled a wood whose trees were completely denuded of leaves. To my left, some distance away, the river was flowing toward the ocean. In front of me, the roofs of a hamlet were outlined against the sky. The landscape was familiar, and yet it seemed to me to be different. I soon understood why.

Nature had lost its habitual coloration. Everything had become ruddy black, like a heath after one of those fires that, passing at the speed of a galloping horse, only burns the grass and brushwood, the leaves and twigs, leaving the pines upstanding like specters.

The road extended its ribbon. I walked with a long stride in order to arrive before dark. The Shepherd's Star was shining in the sky; the Great Bear designed its trapezium.

The dead cow and the cadaver of the man made les impression on me than the previous day, but as I penetrated into the village I shivered. Everything evoked flight, precipitate abandonment. The doors were ajar, the houses dark. The walls gave off an ardent heat, like the walls of an oven.

At home, I stripped the sheets from my bed. I was afraid of dying, of dying alone. I nevertheless remembered Madame Sterneballe's reproaches, and I collected knives and forks. There was no hurry, but I was as nervous as a traveler at risk of missing his train.

I knocked on the grocer's door; a yapping replied. I knocked again in order to hear the dog again. It replied to me, and I went in. It ran forward madly, bumping its muzzle against my wounded knee and drawing a cry of pain from me.

"Madame Ferry, are you there?"

She was there, but silent: the silence of eternity. I only saw her when I had a candle in my hand. She was collapsed on her counter, her arms extended, as if to defend her cash register.

What I did then was purely mechanical. I transformed myself into a burglar. I emptied the shelves of the shop, taking possession of sugar, tins of sardines, a small tub of herring, a lump of lard, two boxes of biscuits and six liters of wine, and I wrapped that precious merchandise up in my bed-sheets.

I hoisted the heavy bale on to my shoulder like a peddler's pack.

I set forth on the way back, but stopped several times to catch my breath. Suddenly, the dog crossed the road a few paces in front of me, and I understood that it was accompanying me. That witness to my burglary embarrassed me. I threw stones at it, but in vain. It attached itself to my heels, prudently maintaining itself out of reach. My poor eyesight prevented me from following all its movements, but it sometimes whimpered, as if to say to me: *Let me be your slave...I shall love you...no one but me is alive on this earth of desolation...let's join forces...*

Near the quarry it barked with a full voice and someone whistled to it. Monsieur Sterneballe was waiting for me at the orifice of the gallery. A human shadow appeared.

"I'm heavily laden," I said, cheerfully, "but I won't be obliged to return to the village tomorrow. The ladies aren't too impatient?"

To my great surprise, a nasal voice replied to me: "I don't know, Monsieur, to what ladies you're referring. What village do you mean?"

"Who are you?" I replied.

"If our interrogations overlap," the unknown man remarked, "We'll talk for a long time without learning anything. First, I want to know where I am. Oh, you have light—so much the better!"

I had just lit my candle in order to identify the individual. The unknown was a short man about fifty years old, his face lost in a bushy beard, with prominent blue eyes. He had little hair, as I observed when he politely took off his hat. His thin body was adrift in an ample frock coat that had emerged from the hands of a good tailor but was presently dirty and torn.

He submitted meekly to my suspicious examination.

"You asked me who I am?" he said. "That's a legitimate curiosity. I won't offer you my card, because it's not a time for ceremony, and in any case, I've mislaid my wallet. I'm Onésime Cynécarmieux, astronomer at the Observatory at Floirac. Do you know the Observatory at Floirac? Three domes surrounded by beautiful trees, resembling three white mushrooms in a lawn. What poetry, Monsieur! But perhaps I'm keeping you?"

That loquaciousness stunned me slightly.

"What do you want with me?" I said, still on my guard.

"Nothing, Monsieur. I'm a man in need of everything who dare not ask for anything. Do you understand that? I believe that I'm emerging from a bout of hot fever. I have vague memories...I was watching the sun, Monsieur...and *crack!* a rift in my intelligence. It's not pleasant. I remember a prolonged journey...extremely prolonged...to the point that I have bloody feet...literally bloody...and here I am, dazed, but in full possession of my mental faculties. Where am I?"

"Roque de Thau."

"In what part of the Gironde is that place situated?"

"Near Blaye."

"No," said Monsieur Cynécarmieux, firmly.

"What do you mean, no?"

"You won't make me believe that I've come all the way to Blaye on foot. It's risible, Monsieur. I walk like a woodlouse. To Roque de Thau, me! If it weren't the end of the world, I'd make a communication to the Académie des Sciences."

"What make you suppose that it's the end of the world?"

He put the tip of his index finger under his right eyelid. "My eye."

"Your eye?"

"My astronomer's eye, stuck to the objective of a telescope. I know what I know.

"Very well, Monsieur," I said, "but you've left me in the heat for a long time, when it's infinitely cooler in the quarries. Ask me for the information that's useful to you, and make use of it!"

Monsieur Cynécarmieux clicked his tongue. "The heat is making you irritable," he said. "That's normal. I have no more information to ask of you. I know where I am—that's already a great deal. In a few hours when I die, I'll think that it's in Roque de Thau."

"Make arrangements not to die," I advised him.

"A delicate arrangement, Monsieur…actually, I don't know your name…a delicate and superfluous arrangement. I repeat to you that it's the end of the world."

"That's possible," I said, "but I'm stubborn in living."

"You're not wrong, Monsieur…but I, although as stubborn as you, am obliged to die. I'm frightfully ill and I have no shelter. Phoebus has miraculously taken pity on me, but tomorrow morning, he will expedite me *ad patres*, in Roque de Thau."

"This quarry is as much yours as mine."

"Thank you," he said. "I feared being indiscreet. But I'll make you a confession devoid of artifice: I'm dying of hunger."

"Ah!" I said, vaguely.

"I even have a weakness in that regard; if not, I would have had the pleasure of making your acquaintance. You're scowling, Monsieur I-don't-know-your name. Don't worry—I won't deplete your provisions. You're free to leave me in the claws of famine."

"I'm not as devoid of compassion as you might suppose," I said, sulkily.

"Be careful—I might take you at your word."

The strange fellow had the effrontery to joke!

"I'm not a parasite," he went on. "Tappers give me the creeps. However, I'm ready to be a parasite, a glutton and perhaps a drunkard. Messer Gaster is a tyrant whose orders one doesn't dispute for long. In consequence, no surprise: if you offer me something to eat, I'll accept."

"I offer you something to eat," I said.

"I ought to refuse," he replied. "I'm ready to die, and I'll draw away from it only to catch it up later. It's puerile, Monsieur…what is your name?"

"Dantenot."

"You're really going to give me something to eat?"

"Yes."

"Then don't let me languish any longer."

"Follow me inside…there are people waiting for me."

"You're not alone? Your comrades might not be as magnanimous as you."

"Come on—this heat is crippling us. I'm with my fiancée, her father and her mother."

"I'm ashamed to be introduced to them in this state."

He was trotting behind me like a rat.

"Bloody feet!" he said. "But I'll forget those miseries, since I'm going to satisfy myself before bidding farewell to the world."

"I forbid you to talk in that fashion to the people you're going to see," I said, dryly. "Madame Sterneballe is already sufficiently alarmed…"

"I shall observe the formalities, Monsieur Dantenot. You're energetic? So am I, damn it! It will be amusing to struggle against destiny..."

Monsieur Cynécarmieux plunged into the quarries, blowing hard, in the manner of a seal.

"The first breath of fresh air I've had!" he said, "It's good, it's comforting. I'll take it in liters, cubic meters. You're my good genie, Monsieur Dantenot. It's building stone that's extracted here, isn't it? I'm no geologist, but I know a little about it, all the same. Oh, the geologists! Not a morsel will remain of their Jurassic, Hercynian, etcetera, rocks. All that will be igneous rock...simply igneous. Are you taking me far, Monsieur Dantenot? Apologies, but I have bloody feet."

The candle lighting the Sterneballes' refuge appeared as a yellow dot in the darkness.

"That's it?" asked Monsieur Cynécarmieux. "Oh, I'll be able to eat...eat..."

His nasal voice had tender inflections. He sniffed noisily.

"I'm weeping...veritably, I'm weeping...it's hunger that's making me weep. It's a physiological emotion..."

Monsieur and Madame Sterneballe were wondering anxiously what the arrival of that phonographic voice signified. Instinctively, they had placed themselves in front of their daughter, as if to protect her against a possible danger. I saw my mother-in-law sketch a furtive sign of the cross.

"It's Roger!" cried Jane, the first to recognize me.

My presence reassured everyone. I explained briefly how I had encountered Onésime Cynécarmieux.

"Monsieur is an astronomer?" asked Monsieur Sterneballe.

"At the Observatory of Floirac...three white domes...mushrooms in a clump of grass..."

"The comparison is striking," said Monsieur Sterneballe. "I'm in a somewhat similar line..."

"Aha! A professor of sciences?"

"I'm an optician—Rue Sainte-Catherine."

"Delighted," said Monsieur Cynécarmieux. "Aiee! Permit me to sit down. I have bloody feet...I've come from Bordeaux by road..."

"That's a record!"

"A Marathonian record...I'd make a communication to the Académie des Science is it weren't the end...but no, no! I promised your son-in-law. Evohé! We're going to eat!"

I unwrapped my riches, as the conquerors of old unwrapped their booty on returning from a victorious expedition, in the midst of the most exuberant enthusiasm. The blind horse stamped its hooves in order to join in.

Monsieur Cynécarmieux abridged the inventory; he had already nibbled through a few biscuits, but that only served to exasperate his hunger. He demanded a full dinner.

The meal was substantial, but without a satisfactory complement, because we had to eat without bread.

"Reason is ordering me to stop," said Monsieur Cynécarmieux. "I'd gladly swallow that ham, but indigestion would be bound to follow. Now, I don't want to suffer during the few hours that...that...separate us from further events."

Monsieur Sterneballe was listening attentively.

"Why is it so hot outside?" he demanded.

Monsieur Cynécarmieux became agitated. "What? You don't know the causes? May I speak, Monsieur Dantenot? It's so interesting!"

He was begging me, with his ten fingers in his beard. I sensed that what he was about to say would deliver a rude blow to Jane's tranquility and her mother's, but I was so eager to be better informed myself that I acquiesced.

We were grouped round the candle, our eyes fixed on the hirsute little man. His nasal voice rose up.

"Where should I begin? You're not unaware of the movements of the heavenly bodies?"

"Gravitation...gyration...," said Monsieur Sterneballe, with a knowing expression.

"Nothing is motionless in the celestial desert...the stars, the planets, the satellites of every dimension, bolides, comets...everything is in motion at vertiginous speeds. The parabolas overlap, the curves intersect, the ellipses are intertwined...there are thousands, hundreds of thousands of movements in the ether."

"All of that must be admirably regulated!" Monsieur Sterneballe ecstasized.

"No need! Millions of leagues separate the stars. It takes them hundreds of centuries to get significantly closer to one another. The small ones gravitate round the medium-sized ones, the medium-sized around the large, and the large around incandescent monsters. Why that intersidereal restlessness? Gyration and gravitation, as you said just now, Monsieur...yes, that's it, that appears to be it...until an individual cleverer than Newton has built a more ingenious theory and is lucky enough to find practical confirmations in nature. One can find all that one wants in nature, and even what one doesn't want, with patience and a little luck..."

He reflected momentarily on what he had just said.

"I could have written that," he said, "but my future has been so rudely broken..."

He was going astray, and I brought him back to his subject. "Tell us about the heat, Monsieur Cynécarmieux."

"I'm coming to that...but it exasperates me when people batter my ears with the same old stuff: perfect order, perfect movements, perfect trajectories...everything perfect, what! Except for what's happening to us... Order in the world? Then why is there radium in the sun, and uranium too, and oxygen here, nitrogen there, iron on the Earth, aluminum on some other planet? Disorder, muddle, strife!"

"You're troubling me," said Monsieur Sterneballe.

The little astronomer tugged at his beard as if to uproot it.

"I'm an anarchist of science, Monsieur! I claim that everything in the astral world is adrift! In a few million years, the pole star might indicate south. As for the moon, we'll long since have shed it along the way; it will be beautiful around some other sphere that we've grazed in passing."

"We won't be here to see that," said Monsieur Sterneballe.

"We won't be here to see the last quarter of the present moon..."

"Monsieur!" I said, angrily.

"Pardon me, Monsieur Dantenot...apologies..."

He continued, with a stunning volubility: "We Terrans, we depend on the sun. It makes the rain and the fair weather here. It hasn't always been tender in our regard. It made the Deluge, emptied the Aquitanian gulf... For a long time, though, it's been tender...a moderate and constant temperature. Perhaps its personal cuisine has sometimes not quite succeeded...chemical cataclysms have resulted on the subject of which the scientists trade insults, but they're no more than trivia. The gravest matter is the deviation of the entire system toward the constellation Lyra. It's in the course of that deviation that our sun has run into a dead star..."

"A dead star?"

"A black sun, if you prefer. Stars are born and die, only they live for millions of centuries. It appears that that's nothing by comparison with eternity. Then, when the stars are dead, they no longer shine, one can no longer distinguish them in the infinite obscurity. They circulate discreetly, and, in truth, without concern for accidents. On the twenty-fifth of December our shiny sun encountered a black sun. Telescopy should have spread the rumor, but we didn't hear anything. One of my colleagues simply saw a patch that was promptly erased...nothing broke, but the temperature has increased, for every impact engenders heat..."

Monsieur Cynécarmieux stood up in order to gesticulate more freely.

"It's the bankruptcy of physics and thermodynamics. There are laws concerning the velocity of the transmission of heat; they're false! Everything is false! Everything is false!"

We didn't know what to say. My mind was exceedingly troubled. More fortunate than us, Madame Sterneballe scarcely understood, for she had fallen asleep.

"The temperature's rising!" said Monsieur Cynécarmieux. "It will go one rising. It will rise until no one exists to observe that it's still rising! The solar clouds are eight thousand degrees. There are perhaps twenty or twenty-five thousands of them, or more. Must I insist of the consequences? You can foresee them as well as me, so there's no point in dissimulating them. We're all going to

298

die together, on Venus, on Earth, on Mars. Civilization will be destroyed, along with human beings, but the elite will have the sole consolation of thinking that the planets will be rejuvenated, that the heat will invigorate them, that this catastrophe will double the duration of the existence of our group, which is nevertheless one of the paltriest in creation. Heatstrokes first, then conflagrations, then boiling, then evaporation…we'll witness the conflagrations…perhaps the boiling…but surely not the rest…"

"Will it take long?" asked Monsieur Sterneballe.

"Ask the physicists! They'll search their logarithmic tables, and by hurrying a little, perhaps they'll have time to publish new erroneous calculations… But the wisest course is not to worry about anything. Eat when one is hungry, drink when one is thirsty, and sleep while awaiting the final insensibility…"

Heads in our hands, we listened to him. When he shut up, the silence overwhelmed us.

IX.

Monsieur Cynécarmieux woke up agitated. He stretched himself, clucking like a mother hen. As soon as I heard him I lit the candle. At that moment, the blind horse demanded its pittance imperiously. It sniffed the hay, but only took a few wisps between its thick lips.

"It's thirsty," said Monsieur Cynécarmieux.

But what could I give it to drink? Of liquid, in fact, we only possessed three bottles of wine. The question of thirst would soon arise for us, as for the horse.

After our breakfast, we took stock of our provisions. Jane and I set about dividing the food into rations, while my father-in-law and Monsieur Cynécarmieux fraternized, lying in the hay. My fiancée was amused by the situation, but I felt invaded by pessimism. By eking out our provisions strictly, we had enough food for a week. But what would become of the world in seven days?

We organized ourselves, in order to avoid the afflictions of our implacable enemy, the heat. Gradually, it was infiltrating the quarry. The invasion was slow, but the number of calories was increasing sensibly by the hour. A hundred meters from the entrance it was no longer easy to breathe. It was important, however, in order to preserve our cool air, to seal the tunnel hermetically, as far as possible from the cul-de-sac we occupied.

After having removed the door of the redoubt where the horse was enclosed, we fixed it at the junction that the tunnel formed with the central gallery. It fitted perfectly. In order to render our artificial wall airtight, it was sufficient to fill the gaps and interstices with rags obtained by ripping up a sheet. Monsieur Cynécarmieux calculated that we were then assured of a reserve of about five hundred cubic meters of cool air.

That installation took up most of the day. Jane and her mother helped us in the measure of their strength. The astronomer had filled a role that was not without analogy to that of a circus ringmaster. He had not worked much and had talked non-stop. His nasal verbiage irritated me, but silence would have irritated us more.

When the door swung on its hinges, I experienced a proud satisfaction. We were now in a retrenchment where the defense would be dogged.

"Shall we dine?" said Monsieur Cynécarmieux. "To favor the digestion, we can then go to the threshold, in order to see what has become of nature. The birds will no longer be singing…they've stuck out their tongues…cooee…"

"You'll cut off our appetite," said Monsieur Sterneballe, half serious and half in jest.

"So much the better—the food will last longer."

Everyone wanted to economize on the food. In spite of those good intentions, the others agreed that the ration was insufficient. I flatly refused to increase it, and no one dared insist. It was thus that, without perceiving it myself, I became the chief of our little colony.

The candles were consumed with alarming rapidity. A time would come when we would be plunged irredeemably into darkness. It was hence necessary to restrict our light, mediocre as it was, and remain for hours in bleak obscurity. Jane's hands gripped mine nervously; my dear fiancée was placing all her hope and all her confidence in me. But what could I do to save us?

At about six o'clock, Monsieur Cynécarmieux and I set forth. Monsieur Sterneballe was not sorry to be the immovable guardian of his wife and daughter. He abandoned the glory of conquests to us, without jealousy. To give himself a little exercise, he came with us as far as the door of our subterrain. He tugged on my sleeve and whispered: "We only have one bottle of wine left."

"I know," I replied, in the same tone.

"Good," he said. "I was just discharging my responsibility."

The astronomer was the most curious among us. He had the vocation of an explorer.

"The left-hand corridor leads to the exit," he said. Not worth the trouble of going to overheat our blood. Suppose we follow the right-hand tunnel?"

I told him that my intention was to go to the village. He dissuaded me.

"The temperature has risen, Monsieur Dantenot. You'd fall on the road, and no one would come to our aid."

I let him know the situation: "We don't have any more to drink."

"Damn!" he said, perplexed. "Thirst is even more redoubtable than hunger. But there's always water underground! I'm certain that in excavating some gallery, the workers have broken into some seam. We'll find it!"

"And if we don't find it?"

"We'll find it!" he repeated, forcefully. There's water in all mines. While digging, one always finds pockets of it. What desolated the owner of this quarry will be our good fortune. Limpid fresh water will flow down our esophagus. We'll look for the spring tomorrow morning; that will extract us from our lugubrious idleness."

The tunnel we were exploring was rigorously horizontal. It permitted access to another gallery much wider than the one we knew. Monsieur Cynécarmieux stumbled upon the track of a narrow-gauge railway.

"This is the high road of our city," he said. "This gallery is parallel to the first, therefore, and a little to the left. Let's turn right again."

"We're risking getting lost, Monsieur Cynécarmieux," I said, hesitantly, intimidated by the dark mystery that surrounded us.

"Well," he said, "there is a lack of street signs. We can always baptize the galleries..."

We were intelligent men, serous functionaries; in spite of that, we started arguing like children. The first gallery obviously ought to have been called the Roger Gallery, but I ceded my rights to Madame Sterneballe, and in consequence, we called it the Amélie Gallery. The communicating tunnel was named the Onésime Passage, and the astronomer was prouder of that than if he's discovered a star telescopically. The central avenue, with the narrow-gauge railway, being the most beautiful, became the Jane Gallery.

A philosopher has said that man is a strange animal. We were in a frightful situation, the old world was in its death-throes above our heads, life was disappearing from the surface of the globe, and we were taking pleasure in ridiculously baptizing he excavations of our mole-maze.

Monsieur Cynécarmieux had found a little fossil incrusted in the stone. Everything was a matter of dissertation for him. He was so occupied in spouting banalities from the scholarly manual about ammonites and belemnites that I invited him to shut up twice, in vain. I put a hand over his mouth and blew out my candle.

He did not protest, because he quickly understood why I had submitted him to that rather cavalier treatment.

We were not alone in the Jane Gallery. In the direction of the exit, someone was walking with a light. A few seconds sufficed for me acquire the certainty that he was heading toward us.

"Let's move back," said Monsieur Cynécarmieux. "He hasn't seen us. He's a human being like us, but we don't need to make his acquaintance. If we make his acquaintance, we won't have the cruelty to abandon him to his misery. Now, we're vagabonds ourselves..."

I had not followed the same reasoning when I had und him, Cynécarmieux, suffering from hunger at the entrance to the quarry. However, I might have followed his advice if I had not heard the indefinable sound of scraping, of friction, that the intruder was making. I wanted to know the cause of that noise.

Lurking in the Onésime passage like bandits in ambush, we waited.

The light was that of a lantern whose ring the man was holding in his hand. He was pushing a barrel, a demi-hogshead.

It was my neighbor Fradinotte!

I was gripped by emotion. The old vine-grower, under the menace of an atrocious death, was saving himself, along with the wine of his vineyard. Nothing had been able to persuade him to abandon his full barrel. He might not have been able to bring his savings, but he had not been able to separate himself from his wine, a magical panacea.

Monsieur Cynécarmieux, who could not abide thirty seconds of immobility, caused a pebble to rattle. Ceasing to roll his barrel, Fradinotte raised his lantern at arm's length and scrutinized the shadows.

"Who goes there?" he shouted.

"Friends," the astronomer replied. "We're brothers before eternity..."

The vintner judged the muscular value of Cynécarmieux at a glance. "Be off," he said. "I don't know you."

"Me neither," said the scientist, tenaciously, "but we'll gladly enter into relations. Show yourself, Monsieur Dantenot, for the worthy fellow has no confidence in me."

At the sight of me, Fradinotte's cunning visage relaxed. We shook hands.

"Bonsoir, Monsieur Dantenot," he said, as if we were in the square of Roque de Thau. "You're alive?"

"My God, yes...and you too, Fradinotte?

"Not without difficulty. Since Christmas, it's been necessary to box clever for that. It's a memorable epoch."

He had a live chicken in his pocket. The terrified fowl stuck out its neck and contemplated us with its round eyes. Fradinotte sat down on his barrel.

"I don't know what's become of my wife," he said, without apparent emotion. "She wanted to go out and didn't come back. It's the story of all the victims. I went to ground in my cellar. I slept. On the second day I thought about the quarry. I didn't think I'd find you here..."

Monsieur Cynécarmieux tapped the barrel with his curved index finger. "Is it full?" he asked.

"Of the 1912," said Fradinotte. "It's the one I like best."

"Are you going to let us taste it?"

Fradinotte avoided the question. With a thrust of his thumb he indicated the route he had just traveled. "Don't go that way," he said. "There are some there squabbling."

"Who?"

"People from Berson and strangers. That's why I'm leaving those parts. The people from Berson claim that the quarry belongs to them. The strangers, who arrived in an automobile, want to stay. Every man for himself, you understand..."

"They're fighting?" said Monsieur Cynécarmieux.

"They're making their preparations for it. Don't get mixed up in it, Monsieur Dantenot. We'll doubtless see one another again. Bonsoir."

He left us in the shadows without asking us whether we had light. He shoved his barrel carefully, the chicken still sticking its head out of his pocket."

"Old miser!" said Monsieur Cynécarmieux.

But the sharp sound of a gunshot made us forget Fradinotte. A battle had started at the other end of the gallery.

The wisest thing would have been not to go any closer, but the demon of curiosity was needling us. Without consulting one another, we made our way up the slope. I must admit that Monsieur Cynécarmieux did not dispute the position of patrol leader.

We covered at least two hundred meters. Heat and bitter smoke caught us in the throat. There was a bend in the galley, and we didn't go round the corner. A violent, blinding light filled the subterrain. The strangers had aimed the headlight of their auto at the people from Berson. Five black silhouettes were gesticulating in the dazzling light.

Incontestably, the attackers had the advantage. They could see without being seen, because they remained behind the reflector. In both camps, people had revolvers, and were not neglecting to fire them.

The bullets ricocheted as far as us. If even half of them had struck home, the besiegers and the besieged would have been exterminated. But it is difficult to aim with Brownings, and the majority of the shots were too high.

Suddenly, darkness filled the quarry again. A bullet had smashed the searchlight. Then we heard furious cries and more gunshots.

The vanquished disbanded; they passed in front of us in the darkness. There were three or four. One of them brushed me.

Then the victors went past, three in number. They were shining an electric pocket torch intermittently, and talking breathlessly.

"Are you wounded, Pierre?"

"I've broken my radius. It doesn't hurt too much."

"The brutes! If we unearth them, we'll exterminate them without mercy."

"They fled like rabbits."

"All the same, it's good to breathe this cool air."

"My arm's swelling up. It's necessary to stop the bleeding."

"I've got a handkerchief; we'll make a bandage."

They were ten paces away from us. The electric torch illuminated them imperfectly. In the little cone of light, I saw a bloody arm, bare to the elbow, and the energetic face of a man in his prime. Then the light went out with an abrupt click, and the three men plunged on, with a vague hubbub of voices.

"We've had a narrow escape," said Monsieur Cynécarmieux. "If they'd discovered us they'd have killed us without giving us time to protest. The fabulist was right, Monsieur Dantenot: to live happily, live hidden..."

I was in a hurry to get back to our encampment, because I was fearful now for the security of Jane and her parents. We groped our way along Onésime Passage. We pricked up our ears frequently, but the silence of the quarry was now undisturbed.

Once we were back we consolidated our door by means of three beams whose extremities we succeeded in wedging in the stone.

Monsieur Sterneballe, his wife and his daughter were asleep. My future father-in-law interrogated us in a thick voice. I contented myself with telling him that all was well.

It took me a long time to go to sleep. Alongside me, Monsieur Cynécarmieux turned over and over on his bed of straw.

"Can't you sleep?" I asked him, discreetly.

"No," he replied, his voice hoarse. "I'm thirsty."

I was thirsty too. And the blind horse was thirsty. And we would all be thirsty soon, without being able to suffer it with as much resignation as the blind horse.

I had nightmares. It seemed to me that I was eating mouthfuls of salt, while Monsieur Cynécarmieux, having made a gash in his wrist, was drinking his own blood avidly, and that Monsieur Sterneballe was drinking a cup of molten lead...

X.

Monsieur Cynécarmieux was sucking pebbles. A monotonous rattle was escaping from the throat of the blind horse. The shadow was heavy.

We had been thirsty for hours and hours. We could no longer eat. We were waiting for a miracle or the deliverance of death. We preferred to remain in the dark because our faces made us fearful.

Days had passed. I had been suffering for longer than the others because I had given my last drop of wine to my fiancée. Jane was not complaining, but her mother was whining for two. As for Monsieur Sterneballe, he sometimes said: "What can we do?"

In vain, I tried to forget our fate; I had only one thought, one desire: to drink.

To drink... To empty in a single draught a glass of crystalline water. To make the impetuous jet of a siphon spurt into a glass of vermouth. To drink... To pour old wine, Fradinotte's wine, the color of brick, as smooth as oil, into a glass in the form of a tulip. To drink... Glasses, bottles, babbling brooks...

I was becoming slightly delirious.

In the company of Monsieur Cynécarmieux I had explored the quarry from top to bottom within a radius of a kilometer. The galleries ramified infinitely, going upwards and downwards, and intersecting, but the walls were immutably dry; no trickle of water filtered through the white dust.

We had not encountered either Fradinotte or he strangers. There was nothing astonishing about that; the quarry extended a long way in the direction of Rigalet; it pierced the chain of hills like an immense anthill.

I had candles and matches in my pocket. I took four boxes and rolled them up in a strip of sheet, and I left. They heard me, but no one asked where I was going.

I only lit my candle when I reached the Jane Gallery. There was a heavy, overwhelming heat there. I was weak but resolute. I wanted to drink or die.

I went into a tortuous tunnel, so low that I was obliged to walk bent double. Rockfalls had occurred, and black soil had slid through the crevices in the saltpetrous stone. I picked up a handful of that earth. It was dry. No water; still no water!

The tunnel was long. It ended in another tunnel that descended at a forty-five degree angle, so I let myself slide down it, and I reached a high and broad excavation with an arched ceiling like the cupola of an oven.

I slipped through a fissure and found myself in a new gallery. It appeared to me that there was an odor of damp there. The soil was, in fact, damp, but so very little! That gave me a new burst of energy, however. But the galleries succeeded one another, changing direction every ten meters, with the result that it was difficult to get my bearings. My last candle was diminishing. When I perceived that, there were only a few centimeters left. It was impossible that it would last long enough to permit me to get back to our redoubt.

Darkness was certain death, but I wasn't afraid; I was suffering too much. I changed course as frequently as possible, rendering the maze inextricable. I no longer knew whether I was looking for a spring or a tomb.

That prolonged, desperate course exhausted my feeble strength. My candle fell to the ground and went out; the bottles slipped out of my hand and I heard the sound of breaking glass. I sank down, utterly resigned, and I lost consciousness...

It's probable that my faint was brief. On coming round, I reassembled my ideas painfully. I had the tranquil conviction that I was doomed. Only one thing rendered me desperate: expiring far away from my fiancée. I was no longer anything but a little child, humble before the definitive mystery.

Suddenly, it seemed to me that I felt something cool in my back, between the shoulder blades. The sensation was agreeable. The coolness increased, descending, bathing me delightfully...

I felt the wall. It was damp.

"Water!"

I recovered my strength with a surge. Feverishly, I searched for my matches. The light of the sizzling sulfur caused the stone to sparkle. The water was trickling drop by drop along the wall.

My candle had fallen a few paces away. I lit it, trembling, and placed it on a flat stone.

Water—I had water! It was filtering imperceptibly, not forming a stream or a pool, and was lost between the stones, but it was water,

I stuck my lips to the wall, and sucked in a mouthful of mud. I had water, but I could not drink.

To recover my calmness, I strode back and forth clasping my temples as if to extract an idea from my head. Then I planted myself in front of the semblance of a spring, hypnotized by that possibility of salvation.

An inspiration struck me. With my fingernails I hollowed out a little excavation in the rock that the damp had rendered spongy. Then, with a handful of earth, I fashioned a kind of beak. At the end of that beak a drop formed, then another, and another, and a fourth...

One bottle had broken but I still had three. I placed one of them under the falling drops. With incredible patience I waited, counting the drops savoring them with my gaze.

When there was a little water in the bottom of the bottle, I drank it. I recommenced twice, ten times, insatiably, and it was only after I had half-extinguished the furnace of my stomach that I thought about those who were dying elsewhere.

I would have experienced a veritable remorse had I drunk any more. I replaced the bottle; I extinguished the candle. I no longer had either the right or the desire to die.

How long did it take me to fill the three bottles? I don't know. When I had finished, I thought about going back. I no longer had any more than half an hour of candlelight. I expelled the doubt and apprehension from my mind, and I set out. At the end of the tunnel I made a cross on the wall to mark the place, and wondered whether I ought to turn left or right. I opted for left. I ran like a madman, calling out so loudly that my voice became hoarse, pivoting in all directions—and I suddenly found myself back at the spring, at which I had arrived from the other end of the corridor.

Then I collapsed and wept silently.

The candle flickered, flared up and went out. The darkness imprisoned me. Nevertheless, I set forth again. I still had thirty matches. I struck one at the intersection.

I soon had only three left.

I advanced with rage, but not so rapidly as to break my precious bottles. My wounded knee as still making me suffer; my leg was heavy and numb. I felt the walls with my free hand, and I walked, and walked, and walked...

Finally, my foot hit something hard that rendered a slight metallic sound. I bent down. I had tumbled over the rails of the central gallery.

Never had Providence been thanked with so much fervor.

Ten minutes later, I was in our cavern. The horse was snoring lugubriously in the darkness.

"Jane!" I called.

A feeble sigh was exhaled. An anguish gripped my heart. I struck a light. Madame Sterneballe was sitting down, supporting Jane's inert lead on her lap. Monsieur Sterneballe and Monsieur Cynécarmieux were lying face to face on the straw.

"I have water!" I cried, triumphantly.

That phrase suddenly rendered them life. I gave one bottle to Jane, another to her mother, the third to the men.

"After you," stammered Monsieur Cynécarmieux.

"No, Monsieur," said Monsieur Sterneballe. "You're the guest."

They drank religiously, with a kind of unction, and their features relaxed, the hallucination disappearing from their pupils. I begged them to be moderate, to slake their thirst prudently; they listened to me, regretfully.

Jane thought about the horse, which had not yet drunk anything. I agreed to return to the spring with the astronomer. We gathered our bottles, which we arranged in a large plasterer's bucket. On hearing the handle clink against the iron, the horse whinnied dully.

"You'll be able to drink soon," said Madame Sterneballe, amicably. "Be patient. These messieurs are going to the fount."

Monsieur Cynécarmieux, who had recovered his usual loquacity, told me how, during my absence, he had gone as far as the orifice of the quarry.

"I dragged myself to the top of the Amélie Gallery. What a steam-bath! I wanted to commit suicide, but I didn't have the strength. I crawled on to the ground, far enough from the hole. I was cooking, frying…it was dark outside, but the shadow was splashed with red reflections..."

"The trees were burning," said Monsieur Sterneballe.

"They had to burn, planted like torches in the middle of the roasted countryside. Solid and liquid matter were heated more than the air, which is easily traversed and only conserves a fraction of the heat. The water must have disengaged floods of vapor; it has been raining, or will rain boiling water! And yet, if anything can save the Earth, it's water. Perhaps the sun will grow weary before having emptied the oceans. Since we've been imprisoned, the temperature hasn't increased too rapidly, because of the intense evaporation. We're the impotent witnesses to a monstrous struggle between the elements."

His laughter resembled the grating pulley of a well.

"Are we leaving for the marvelous spring, Monsieur Dantenot?"

"Whenever you wish, Monsieur Cynécarmieux."

Suddenly I recoiled. The specter of Fradinotte was standing on the threshold of the cavern. He really was a specter, lived, fleshless, the skin plastered on the skeleton, the eyes flamboyant and terrible.

"Give me something to eat," said the specter, in a hoarse voice.

No one budged. Monsieur Sterneballe was sitting on the dismantled crate that enclosed our meager reserves.

"Give me something to eat," Fradinotte repeated.

Monsieur Cynécarmieux went to place himself in front of him.

"You're the man with the barrel?" he said. "We can't do anything for you. I can see that you're in a pitiful state, but we won't soften. We don't have a crumb to give you."

"You have food. Give me something to eat!"

The astronomer wagged his index finger in a sign of refusal. "Your insistence is misplaced," he said. "Monsieur Dantenot is as poor as you. He is good enough to tolerate me, and I'm only an intruder. I am, therefore, willing to be cut in two for him, and I intend him to know it."

"Give me something to eat!" said Fradinotte again.

"No," the astronomer replied, with implacable firmness.

"We might, perhaps...," I began.

"Oh, no, no!" said Monsieur Sterneballe and Monsieur Cynécarmieux, severely.

Fradinotte fell to his knees, his arms extended toward me. "Monsieur Dantenot, something to eat! Just a mouthful."

"Gives us something to drink!" replied Monsieur Cynécarmieux, suddenly.

The old vintner made a gesture of revolt. "Never!" And he added, dolorously. "The barrel is smashed, smashed..."

"You're lying," Monsieur Cynécarmieux said to him. "Give, give...you want to eat; we want to drink..."

"Give us wine and we'll give you herring..."

"Since I swear to you that the barrel is smashed..."

I no longer had any pity. The avarice of the wretch scandalized me. Madame Sterneballe proffered, harshly: "Two bottles of wine for one herring..."

"You're torturers" clamored Fradinotte. "God will avenge me, for you'll die sooner than me! You'll die of thirst! And I'll eat—I'll eat you! Ah, you refuse to give me something to eat! Torturers!"

"Go away!" intimated Monsieur Cynécarmieux."

"Not before spitting in your face!"

"Give us wine, or get out."

"Here! Here's wine for you!"

Monsieur Cynécamieux received a punch that instantly tumefied his right eye. He riposted as best he could, but he did not have the strength. Fradinotte, mad with rage, knocked him down, crushed him with his knees and took hold of his throat.

Stunned, we saw Monsieur Cynécarmieux agitating frenziedly, clawing at Fradinotte's face with his fingernails, but the latter squeezed with an incredible force.

Madame Sterneballe and her daughter screamed. Monsieur Sterneballe was still protecting the crate. I stepped forward swiftly in order to liberate Monsieur Cynécarmieux. As I leaned forward, the vintner butted me with his head and the blood sprang from my nose. Then I seized a bottle by the neck and I struck, once.

Fradinotte let go and gripped his head in both hands. He opened his mouth to shout an insult, and then fled at top speed.

XI.

Hunger, to begin with, is not very dolorous. It is irritating, but tolerable. It causes a sensation of emptiness in the body, with a few dizzy spells. Then there are torsions of the entrails, stabling pains, a finally an indescribable suffering, like a cruel bite that never ends.

Ten times, perhaps, I tried to go out. I ran into the heat as if it were a wall. Then, flanked by Monsieur Cynécarmieux, I traveled the quarry in every direction. We found several springs, but not the slightest nourishment. I strove to find subterranean mushrooms, because I knew they existed, but we never succeeded in finding a tunnel where they grew.

Our sleep had become very irregular, for our organisms were no longer obedient to the alternation of day and night. Monsieur Sterneballe and Monsieur Cynécarmieux distracted one another with interminable conversation.

For myself, I was no longer capable of taking an interest in anything. My strength gradually disappeared. My love for Jane, without having diminished, was no longer manifest in any but a vague fashion. For her part, my fiancée never addressed herself to me except to ask me for something. She only questioned me or commanded me.

Madame Sterneballe kept her gestures to a strict minimum. Her existence had become vegetative. She did not recriminate, did not speak, did not act. Her gaze fixed, she dreamed.

The blind horse still had a provision of hay and ate when it was hungry. Suddenly, the idea occurred to me of killing it and nourishing ourselves on its flesh. I ruminated the project for some time before communicating it to Monsieur Cynécarmieux. He qualified it as genius, and Monsieur Sterneballe accepted its realization with a blissful smile.

However, we could not bring ourselves to kill the animal. Our thinness became frightful. We went regularly to fetch water and experienced a sensible relief in swallowing the liquid. Monsieur Cynécarmieux almost always accompanied me. The little man had an extraordinary energy. Like all braggarts, he was always talking about acing, and acted when it was possible. It was him who shook us up, who obliged us to take a little exercise, and who conserved within us, not the appetite for but the possibility of living.

Once, when we were coming back to our refuge laden with full bottles, we heard a voice. It repeated two almost-identical syllables, which we did not understand at first.

It was the cry of great distress; "Maman! Maman! Maman!"

We had suffered so much that we were inaccessible to pity. The man who is suffering no longer has any generosity, but he is curious. We hoped to see a being more unfortunate than us.

There was a man lying in the shadow. His eyes were so unaccustomed to any light that the flame of our candle forced him to turn his head way. He stopped crying out and waited.

Monsieur Cynécarmieux inspected him cautiously. The man was inoffensive. He gave him a drink. The unknown man emptied the bottle. He drank so avidly that the water spilled from the corners of his lips and over his beard.

"It's good," said the man, "but it's very late."

He looked at us. His eyebrows frowned and his eyes rolled.

"Thieves!" he said. "You've taken my package!"

He threw himself triumphantly on something lying by the wall.

"Aha! I've got it back. Ha ha ha!"

Terrified, we recoiled. The man was pressing to his breast a severed arm, an arm with livid flesh, the biceps of which had been lacerated, torn apart, as if gnawed...

"Human flesh!" said Monsieur Cynécarmieux.

With a cheerful expression, the man said: "I shall never again eat anything else..."

Indeed he did not, for he expired a minute later. We drew away silently from his cadaver and the half-devoured arm.

"We'll arrive at that!" said the astronomer, suddenly.

"Rather die!" I retorted, indignantly.

"One says that...and then...and then...do you believe, Dantenot, that we'll arrive at that?"

"Better to die immediately!"

"We have to kill the horse!" he said, authoritatively.

And when we went into the cavern, he said to Monsieur Sterneballe: "We have to kill the horse."

My future father-in-law stood up.

"Where are you going?" asked Monsieur Cynécarmieux.

"I'm going away with the ladies."

"We need you. Three won't be too many."

"I've never been able to kill a chicken," said the optician, piteously.

Monsieur Cynécarmieux lost his temper. "So you want to live? Do you want to enable your wife and daughter to live? Let's kill the horse. Mesdames, go out."

He had departed from his habitual politeness. The ladies went out, and the three of us remained.

"This is what we're going to do," said Monsieur Cynécarmieux, lowering his voice, as if the horse might have been able to understand. "We're going to tie its feet so that it can't kick."

"Yes," I acquiesced.

He pointed to a huge quarryman's sledgehammer.

"Then, we're going to hit it with that."

"Yes," I said, again.

"Who's going to hit it and bleed it?"

"Dantenot, of course."

"Pardon!" I exclaimed. "Why me, rather than you?"

He pulled a face, expressing weariness and scorn.

"This is ridiculous," he said. "Let's draw straws."

He picked up three pieces of straw and offered them to us. Monsieur Sterneballe drew first; suspiciously, I chose after him.

"You have the shortest one," said Monsieur Cynécarmieux.

I didn't protest.

The blind horse meekly allowed its hind feet to be tied, with pieces of string that we cut laboriously. It made a few difficulties when we tried to tie the front feet. Monsieur Cynécarmieux calmed it down.

"La...la...hold firm, Monsieur Sterneballe! La...la..."

But the horse remained upright. The astronomer braced himself, and pushed hard. The animal fell on to its flank.

"Over to you," said Monsieur Cynécarmieux to me. "Strike behind the ear. I'll hold the head."

I picked up the hammer. To grant myself a few seconds respite, I rolled up my sleeves to the elbow.

"Behind the ear," insisted Monsieur Cynécarmieux.

I struck weakly. It caused me a bizarre impression. The horse shuddered.

"Harder!" cried the astronomer.

I struck again, but weakly again.

"He said harder!" vociferated Monsieur Sterneballe.

But those memories are too atrocious...

The days continued to succeed one another. I believe that in order to cook the meat we built a fire in the feed-trough.

We argued. We wept. We recited prayers. Monsieur Cynécarmieux was hardly ever with us. He was afraid of being killed. However, no desire to murder him ever took hold of me. I had too many phantoms in my nightmares.

I don't remember anything more.

Everything was lost in darkness. Death was no longer a terrifying leap into the unknown, but a rational terminus...

"Come!"

The resumption of my human existence commenced with that word, uttered by Monsieur Cynécarmieux.

"Come!"

I was obliged to walk, to crawl. I don't know; I never will know...

"Come!"

Night. But cold night. A January night, with a serene moon in the middle of a pure sky, strewn with stars. The earth I trod was bare, but the atmosphere seemed normal.

It is necessary to have lived through that hour to comprehend...

The rest no longer belongs to a storyteller. Philosophers, statisticians and economists have, in any case, said enough. They have described the formation of the new society, composed of survivors issued from the mines and caverns where they had taken refuge. They have explained that enough engineers survived to have the tyranny of science recognized, enough advocates to constitute a truly political parliament, enough energetic men to take possession of the wealth of deserted Asia and Africa.

Change oscillates; the problem of Constantinople remains entire; the next election will determine the scrutiny of lists, with proportional representation of minorities.

The passions are the same in the embryonic new humankind. Humans are still human. I like them anyway, because they don't prevent me from being happy with Jane and the son that was born to us.

The appeased autumn sun is gilding my wife's forehead. She is rocking the sleeping infant. She has forgotten—I have forgotten myself—all our suffering. God is good, since he had permitted us to emerge unscathed and better from the terrible ordeal.

In the poultry-yard, Monsieur Sterneballe is repainting the henhouse. In the main courtyard, my mother-in-law and Monsieur Cynécarmieux are playing backgammon. We are all united in an indefectible manner, as if to affirm the verity of the Arab proverb:

Fear assembles individuals and inspires a mutual love in them.

Colonel Royet: *On the Brink of the World's End*
(1928)

The final item in the anthology, is a short novel, "À deux doigts de la fin du monde" bylined by "Colonel Royet"—who also wrote as Max Colroy, although that was probably not, as some sources suggest, his real name—here translated as "On the Brink of the World's End." It was first published in 1928 by Ferenczi as a "roman inédit" [previously unpublished novel], although it appears to have been designed for publication as a feuilleton, *and might well have been written some years before its publication.*

The "Colonel Royet" signature initially appeared in tandem with that of Paul d'Ivoi on feuilletons *produced prior to the Great War, which he presumably helped the more experienced author to keep going during problematic periods, and then reappeared during the war on jingoistic propaganda pieces before continuing to feature thereafter on various garish thrillers as well as a twenty-part future war epic,* La Guerre est déclarée *[War is Declared] issued by Tallandier in 1931. Little seems to be known about the person behind the name, which might or might not have been borrowed from Colonel Hippolyte Royet of the National Guard, who played a significant role in the suppression of the Lyon insurgency of 1834.*

"À deux doigts de la fin du monde" belongs to the pulpish phase of the evolution of the roman scientifique, *but it warrants particular attention within that arena by virtue of the manner in which it stretches its melodrama to an unusual extreme, and also because of the feverishly colorful fashion in which it deploys the popular notion of the "mad scientist" as a threat to the relative stability of the world. The scientific background of the story is extremely dubious—a frequent feature of popular thrillers of the period—but the nettle is grasped in with an unusually firm hand that adds to the story's vivacity.*

B.S.

Introduction

For long hours, I have mediated before these pages, hesitantly, with a heavy heart, my head vertiginous, as if on the edge of an abyss...

Ought I to make public these memories of one of the most anguished and tragic periods through which humankind has passed, without being aware of it?

Was it permissible for me to evoke the terrible threat that the future might reserve for us?

Oh, what perplexity was mine before the ultimate decision!

However, I have decided. The terrible secret is choking me. For more than twenty years I have kept it, having sworn to do so to Monsieur Luissant, the venerated President of the Republic. Today, my oath is no longer binding, because the illustrious Statesman summoned me to his deathbed in order to release me from it—me, the last survivor of *those who knew*. More than that, the great and good citizen engaged me to publish my notes and memories.

"Now that panic is no longer to be feared," he pronounced, in a voice already faint, "it's necessary for people to know how close they came to Oblivion. Perhaps the frightful vision of the accident that nearly destroyed life on our globe will render them better."

In delivering the lines to the printer, it is, therefore, a terrible will of which I am the executor.

It is also a confession, for which I glimpse the appeasement of a dolorous remorse. Although entirely virtuous, a responsibility weighs cruelly upon my life. Too sensitive and too pusillanimous, I lacked decision. I allowed a frightful peril to grow before me, without denouncing it. My determination stood up just in time to prevent the definitive catastrophe, but too late to obliterate the effect of frightful misfortunes already consummated.

Perhaps people will consent to absolve me on imagining the heights of alarm and terror that I was obliged to scale. But above my imperishable dolor, crushing my weak personality, *the Fact* will be imposed, colossal in itself, disconcerting in its causes.

The Fact!

The World nearly perished.

The cause?

An unforeseen cosmic phenomenon? A cataclysm of the physical order? An unleashing of natural forces?

No.

Terrestrial life was threatened by a single man, simultaneously a genius and a madman.

And the reason for that monstrous aberration?

An amorous despair!

I. Roger Livry

The fifth of August 192*.

That date hammers my skull, an ineradicable obsession that marks the point of departure of the fantastic adventure in which I was involved.

That morning, I was very happy. In agreement with my principal, I had organized the syllabus of my course in philosophy for the next scholarly year. With a light heart, I had just saluted the gold-lettered frontispiece of Louis le Grand. For two months, I was departing on vacation, bidding farewell to my Lycée, and to noisy and agitated Paris. I was finally going to take refuge in a "retreat" that I had chosen some time before: a hemicycle of high mountains in the Savoy, with the blue line of an Alpine lake in a valley.

My suitcases buckled, and my ticket in my pocket, I call in at Fontenay-sous-Bois to bid farewell to Roger Livry, perhaps to make one last attempt to drag him along with me. But will he break with his need for isolation? Will he consent to abandon his laboratory, interrupt his research as an alchemist of genius?

I ring the bell at the gate of his villa. Little Tourte, Livry's "laboratory assistant," comes to answer it.

"Is Roger here?"

"Yes, M'sieur, in the laboratory—but we're leaving soon on a journey."

"On a journey!"

Why has Roger not told me about that project? Slightly anxious, I hasten my steps, heading straight toward the glazed roof of the laboratory, which is shining through the girdle of trees, in the filtered sunlight.

I knock discreetly and go in, as is my habit, without waiting to be invited.

As soon as he perceives me on the threshold, Roger looks at me suspiciously. He interrupts his work momentarily, which consists of arranging bottles of blue glass in the padded compartments of a black case with copper corners—a case similar to those used by commercial travelers.

Others are arranged around him, waiting to be loaded.

"Secret keeper! You didn't tell me you were leaving!"

Under that amicable reproach, which I try to clothe in a jovial tone, I cannot entirely hide my perplexity.

For a moment, Roger hesitates to reply, but then snaps: "Well, yes, I'm going to the Camp de Châlons."[55]

"The Camp de Châlons? You want to see Suippes again, then, the chalk trenches, the frightful mud where we suffered and fought?"

Roger does not reply. He checks the stopper of one of the blue bottles. Abruptly, a suspicion grips me. The Camp de Châlons! But that is where Capitaine Berjac is garrisoned—the husband of Mademoiselle Thiérard-Leroy!

Does Roger intend to inflict the futile torture on himself of proximity to the woman who, in his mind, ought to be his wife?

Perhaps—because, his eyes vague, he seems to have forgotten my presence by his side; a bitter crease purses his lip; he has plunged once again into the dolorous dream that that hunts him.

---

[55] The Camp de Châlons, or Camp de Mourmelon, was a huge tract of land transformed into a military base in 1857, which became the showcase of Napoléon III's Imperial Army, employed for vast parades. In the early twentieth century it also became an important center for experiments in aviation. During the Great War it had close links with the nearby Camp de Suippes, close to the Front, also used as a training ground and to store stocks of chemical weapons.

In my turn, once again, I evoke, angrily, the absurd and unrealizable amorous dream that has poisoned the life, to calm and so rational, of Roger Livry.

How could one imagine that that man of science, concentrated in study, rendered even more antisocial, almost misanthropic, by the years of the war, could have been struck by a thunderbolt? And yet, that was what had happened seven months before.

One day in January, an untimely hazard took Livry to the home of Monsieur Thiérard-Leroy, the director of the Observatory.

Irony! His visit had only one objective, to solicit some statistical information of a meteorological nature, but it needed no more than a brief appearance of the astronomer's daughter in her father's study to cast a profound and durable disturbance into my unfortunate friend's soul.

I saw Roger arrive at my home like a madman the next day, begging me to go incontinently to Monsieur Thiérard-Leroy's house. Without further ado, on behalf of my comrade, I was to ask him for the hand of his daughter!

And, without any objection, I submitted to that irrational and precipitate demand, because I could not refuse Roger anything.

We had been united by the bonds of a fraternal amity since our first days at school; having entered the École Normale at the same time, we had lived side by side ever since. By virtue of delicacy, simplicity and modesty, Roger had been able to level our very different situations, and render a narrow intimacy possible between the multimillionaire that he was and a poorly-recompensed debutant schoolteacher like me.

In addition, in spite of its singularity, my embassy to Monsieur Thiérard-Leroy inspired high hopes in me. In spite of his rough exterior of a gangling and inelegant, almost hirsute man of study, Roger was, in sum, very presentable. After a session with the hairdresser and a lesson to teach him to tie his cravat, he would be able, like anyone else, to pay court to and please a young woman. Then again, in matters more serious than physique and costume, he offered what is conventionally known as a brilliant catch.

An orphan, Livry had inherited a colossal fortune from his uncle, a wealthy ironmaster, estimated at a hundred and twenty millions at least; and what was certainly better, in the eyes of a man of science like Monsieur Thiérard-Leroy, my friend had always made the noblest uses of his enormous income. A sworn enemy of luxury and snobbery, scornful of the idle life of pleasure that seemed open to him, Roger had been passionate about the study of chemistry since his adolescence. Exceptionally endowed with mathematical skills, he had initially gone into the Normale-Sciences, and had then resigned on graduating, desiring to devote himself more freely to scientific experiments and the experiments he carried out relentlessly.

Finally, during the hostilities, his conduct had been admirable. He had involved himself in the gas war, pursuing research at the front, under shell fire, into the toxic substances employed by our pitiless enemies, inventing replies as he went along to their odious malevolence.

Five palms of his military cross and a red ribbon testified to his heroism.

Thus, I was beginning to count on the success of my comrade's project, perhaps a trifle eccentric and unreflective, when, as soon as I spoke, Monsieur Thiérard-Leroy placed a brutal impossibility before me; his daughter was engaged to be married to a childhood friend, Monsieur Berjac, an artillery officer; the marriage was arranged for the end of April.

What could I say to Roger's dolor when he learned about the abrupt termination of his first idyll?

It was so violent, so unmeasured, that I envisaged with anguish a morbid depression in that powerful brain, overtaxed by study and the terrible years lived since 1914.

Alas, since that fatal day, my friend's singular attitude had reinforced my fears. There was a series of furious crises, during which Roger uttered extraordinary threats, punctuated with phases of listlessness that were even more worrying.

Then, a kind of rage for work reassured me a little. Did not the laboratory where his perpetual effort was extended offer the best distraction from his troubles?

So, at that moment, my anxiety was perfectly legitimate, on seeing him abruptly quitting his elected refuge in order to go toward an indeterminate goal.

The Camp de Châlons! What projects might be lurking inside his head?

I wanted to reassure myself.

"You've chosen a singular place for a vacation," I said, taking advantage of a moment when he had interrupted his meditation in order to resume the organization of his strange luggage.

Roger raised his head. "A vacation? You're joking, out there, I'll be better able to carry out the decisive experiments."

"Right! The war's over—and you've done enough in that accused region."

Roger clenched his fists.

"No, the war isn't over! Humans haven't ceased to be the shame of terrestrial life."

"You're very hard on your fellows."

The chemist laughed sardonically.

"Look at Jobert! Another serpent I've warmed in my bosom..."

Evidently, the example of Jobert seemed well chosen to support the rancor that Roger had against the human species—and my friend continued to evoke the disquieting physiognomy of his former assistant.

"I associated him with my work; I confided a part of my secrets to him—not all, fortunately. The rogue thanked me afterwards by stealing two centigrams of radium from me—which is nothing—and three hundred grams of Omega acid, which is more serious." Roger brandished one of the blue bottles that he was

317

in the process of packing carefully into his case, and added: "Look! A phial like this one..." An excitement illuminated his gaze. "With this, I could turn the world upside down!"

Poor Roger. I judged it pointless to object to his startling affirmation.

"Fortunately, you're loyal to me, my boy," the chemist said, in a more placid tone, giving an amicable tap on the shoulder to young Tourte, who had just come in, his arms laden with packages.

"And me?" I said, in a tone of mild reproach. "You don't count me for anything?"

At that appeal, Roger relaxed. "Paul, my brother, take pity on my poor nerves, raked by suffering. Don't abandon me. You can—you ought to—help me in my great task. Look, come with me!"

He takes hold of my hands and pressed them feverishly.

A brief hesitation, an egotistical impulse, quickly strangled, and I renounce the snowy summits of the great Alps in order to go with Roger to the dismal plains of barren Champagne.

I don't have the right to leave him to struggle alone in the morbid crisis that he's going through.

I can see very well what he intends to do at the Camp de Châlons; if necessary, I can oppose his possible eccentricities.

Then again, perhaps he doesn't know about the presence of the Berjac household in that region.

"Go back to Paris quickly," Roger concluded. "In two hours, I'll pick you up with your suitcases."

Without resistance, I consented.

Little Tourte escorted me back to the gate. Opening the batten of the door, the boy stood aside; then, tugging my sleeve, he pointed in the direction of the Bois de Vincennes.

"Jobert! Again!"

I saw an emaciated and bilious face disappear; it was, indeed Livry's former laboratory assistant.

"Every time anyone goes out, he's there, watching."

While walking to the station, I tried to divine the reason for the surveillance exercised over the villa by that maniac. The idea occurred to me to alert the police—but what was the point, since, in a matter of hours, Roger would have left Fontenay. If Jobert manifested himself again when we returned, we would think again.

Why, oh why, alas, did I not yield to that first impulse by provoking the arrest of the radium thief that same day?

How many subsequent catastrophes would have been avoided!

II. Étienne Tourte, Apprentice Pastry-Cook

In the golden haze of the setting sun, the first military barracks raised on the edge of the Camp de Châlons emerged on the horizon.

Now we are penetrating the long street of the singular village that is Mourmelon-le-Grand: poor dwellings that the furies of the war have brought back to their origins as shacks weatherproofed with the aid of biscuit-tins, coiffed with tin-plate roofs, the debris of food-cans.

In the church square, the auto stops in front of a hotel that has remained almost intact.

The choice of our rooms is quickly made, because questions of comfort have never had great weight in Roger's preoccupations.

He is far more interested in the transport of the two cases secured to the roof of the limousine. There are a thousand recommendations to avoid collisions. He does not take his eyes off them until they are installed in his room.

They worry me, those cases with copper corners, which suggest the most fantastic reflections to the idlers assembled in front of the automobile.

"A photographer," suggests one.

"No, they're glider pilots," whispers another, with a knowing look— because, after a suspension, piloting gliders has become the order of the day again and the Camp de Châlons has become the terrain of choice for the pioneers of the new aviation; every new arrival is willingly seen as a seeker of wings.[56]

"That's the very thing," mutters Roger, who has overheard the comment in passing. "We'll be glider pilots. An excellent pretext for not exposing our flank to curiosity-seekers. Anyway, as soon as possible I want to be at home. Let's look for a house for sale."

I start in surprise. Now Roger is thinking of becoming a property-owner in this desolate place.

It's necessary to convince myself of that, when my friend drags me to see the village notary the next day. Roger asks for a furnished house, with the provision that it must be isolated and surrounded by large grounds.

Mention is made to him of a former brasserie situated outside the locality on the road to Suippes—but the buildings have been slightly damaged by the bombardments.

Roger wants to visit it immediately.

I still remember the painful impression that gripped me when the clerk serving as our guide opened the door of an enclosure surrounded by high but

---

[56] Gliding clubs proliferated after the Great War, when an intense interest developed in extending distance and altitude records. Activity was particularly marked in Germany because of the prohibition of training for powered flight there, and there was a competitive reaction in northern France.

breached walls. In the middle stood a large building, half in ruins. The roof stripped of some of its tiles, the shutters worm-eaten and dislocated, a lantern sustained with great difficult by its rusty iron fittings: such was the unappetizing spectacle that one discovers on the threshold of the "property."

The interior of the building does not cede anything to the exterior appearance in dilapidation and dirtiness. Our entry has the effect of scaring away a band of rats, the sole masters of the dismal abode. In the rooms, there are broken windows, partly collapsed ceilings and fractured floor-tiles.

"A few minor repairs will be made, on the entitlement of war damage," said the clerk, to clear his conscience.

"I like the place as it is," says Roger. "I'll buy it."

Two days later, it's done. Roofers have replaced a few tiles; glazers have replaced a few broken panes. The worst of the dust has been swept away by vigorous thrusts of a broom. A local merchant has provided "furniture." Not without audacity, he names thus some primitive camping material undoubtedly collected from the nearby trenches.

For his part, young Tourte occupied himself buying a stove and household utensils from a bazaar. With the best will in the world, the laboratory assistant offered to resume his original métier as scullion.

It was, in fact, by virtue of a singular misunderstanding that the boy found himself in Livry's service in the quality of apprentice chemist.

A few days after Jobert's abrupt departure, my friend had decided to look for another laboratory assistant. One Sunday, without realizing that he would find all the shops closed, he dragged me to the Rue des Ecoles, to his supplier of chemical products, from whom he was going to seek the necessary indications.

"In any case," Roger repeated to me, in a tone of mystery and mistrust, I want two hands, hands from which I demand neither science nor intelligence, which will handle my retorts without wanting to know what they contain."

We ran into closed shutters, of course.

Resentfully, the chemist stamped his foot on the asphalt; then he stated walking, mechanically following the sidewalk of a street going down toward the Boulevard Saint-Germain.

Suddenly, he stopped dead, his cane pointing to the front of a shop that more the sign: *Laboratory*.

He pronounced the word in a loud voice; I read it in my turn. Unlike the other shop fronts, that one allowed its frosted glass windows to appear. On the door, a handle seemed to invite entry.

"Let's see," said Roger, who did not renounce his obsessions easily.

He crossed the road and opened the door of the shop.

We both had a moment of amazement; then our gazes met and we smiled. Before us appeared the preparation-room of a pastry-cook or a confectioner. Shiny pans were handing on the wall; on the shelves were molds of every form, bottles of candy, and to flatter or nostrils, the characteristic odor of chocolate mingled with vanilla and caramel.

In the room, with his elbows on the table, an adolescent was reading. He was little more than a child, clad in the classic costume of pastry-makers, a white hat and smock.

Ah, the hazard of destiny. Who could have suspected then that my life, those of our fellows, and the fate of the world, were going to depend on a heroic gesture on the pats of that apprentice pastry-cook?

At the sight of us the child got up and then advanced toward the threshold. He removed his hat politely.

"What can I do for you, M'sieur?"

"Nothing, my friend," said Roger, smiling. "We've made a mistake. Excuse us."

"No offense taken!"

"So, why did Messieurs the confectioners take it into their heads to baptize their back-kitchen a laboratory?"

At the slightly scornful expression "back-kitchen," the gamin raised his head, not without pride. "Well, M'sieur, we do chemistry here. We distill sugar, we manipulate perfumes and essences."

The statement took on weight primarily because of our interlocutor's attitude—that of a young cockerel rearing up—and by the moderated guttural accent of the Parisian slum-dweller. It amused us enormously.

"You're laughing, Messieurs," the contrite pastry-cook went on. "You're mocking me. Well, for sure, it's not chemistry as I'd like to learn it, true chemistry with bases, acids, metalloids, so-called organic substances…chemistry as this book explains it." With a resentful gesture he indicated the book left open on the kitchen table. Then, ceding to the insouciant and cheerful philosophy that seems to be integral to the Parisian poor, he added: "Anyway, what do I care? I know it's not for me, the fine things one learns in lycées, and all the tricks I see through the windows of the Sorbonne when I pass by with my basket on my head. One isn't a prince!"

Livry seemed prodigiously interested.

"Would you like to learn chemistry, then—real chemistry?" he asked, in a soft voice.

"Oh, M'sieur…"

The apprentice pastry-cook put his hands together, as if in adoration of a distant and fugitive dream.

"Do you want to come with me?" said Roger. "You can help in my laboratory."

"A laboratory like the one in the Sorbonne, with retorts and test-tubes and electric machines and microscopes?"

"Yes," said Roger, smiling. "A laboratory even better equipped than the one at the Sorbonne."

The gamin looked my friend straight in the eyes. "No! You're poking fun at a poor kid!"

"I'm perfectly serious."

I judged it appropriate to intervene. "But it will be necessary to consult your family, won't it, young man?"

A shadow of sadness veiled the boy's gaze. "My family! Well, Monsieur, unless I call the macadam Papa and the railings of the market in the Place Maubert Mama, I can't name them for you, my family."

"You're a foundling?" I said, compassionately.

"Yes, since it's the custom to call children like that 'lost'."

He was decidedly interesting, that gamin, with his intelligent expression and his street urchin repartee.

"By the way, what's your name?"

"Étienne Tourte, M'sieur...Étienne after the statue of the man in the square where they picked me up—you know, Étienne Dolet, who was put to death, back in the day, to teach him to live.[57] Tourte because that's the name, or the nickname, of the worthy woman who picked me up: Mère Tourte, well-known in the neighborhood—she sold fries at the Maubert market."

"Good! The good lady serves as your adoptive mother?"

"She served, M'sieur, but not anymore. She died last year—died of grief because her eldest, Gustave, died in the war. A strapping fellow Gustave—he was a roofer; he taught me to run over the roofs. Those were good times—you could breathe the air, not like here in the ovens. The Boches killed him; that changed my life, and to console myself, I took up science."

With the back of his sleeve, he wiped away a tear that was running down his cheek. Poor kid!

"What about your employer?"

"My boss? He's one who won't keep me back. I work in his house during the week."

Two days later, Étienne Tourte arrived in Fontenay. With an indescribable joy, he traded the white hat and smock of a pastry-maker for the grey smock of a laboratory assistant.

Today, without false shame, he declared himself ready to resume his place among the saucepans.

Roger was delighted with that solution. "That way we won't waste our time eating out, and we'll have no need to introduce strangers here. We'll be able to work in peace." Then, encouraging Tourte with an amicable tap: "Agreed, my lad; make us truffle sauces and champagne-style kidneys if it amuses you..."

---

[57] Étienne Dolet (1509-1546) was a French scholar and printer burned in the Place Maubert, along with his books, on the orders of the theological faculty of the Sorbonne, on a trumped-up charge of atheism.

"And desserts, of course!"

"Thumbs up for the desserts. In a few days, you'll be able to serve us *bombes glacées*, I can sure you of that."

The last words vibrated like a threat. The allusion to bombs plunged me into an anguish compounded from amazement and fear. What chemical work did he intend to do in this similar place?"

That same evening, Roger permitted me to glimpse the stupefying path into which his delirious brain was urging him.

III. Nightmarish Discourse

It was a heavy and sultry evening, with rumbles of thunder in the distance.

After dinner, well cooked, in truth, by little Tourte, Roger sent the boy away. When we were alone, with an abrupt gesture, he threw away a half-consumed cigarette and came toward me. A willful movement of his head seemed to drive away a final hesitation.

"Paul," he said, in a very calm voice, "you're a courageous man, and also a philosopher, so, you ought not to fear death?"

At that unexpected interpellation, I had a surge of anxiety, but since my friend was offering me the opportunity for a lesson in morality, I quickly recovered my aplomb in order to launch the reply: "Certainly, I don't fear death; like many others, I risked it for four years, at the front—but on the other hand, I don't fear life." Making my thought more specific, I went on: "Life is a duty that makes all the obligations of humanity concrete, and that duty sometimes requires more resolution and sacrifice. Because of that, all life ought to be sacred to us—our own as well as other people's..."

A fugitive irony traversed my interlocutor's physiognomy, but he hastened to approve: "I think exactly as you do. Suicide, like individual murder, is a cowardly and stupid act." He became strangely animated. "There's something better to do: radically suppress the cause of human miseries by suppressing the world, by stifling at a stroke the existences that trouble and poison the Earth's surface."

"Damn! You're lapsing into integral nihilism, my friend. Fortunately, you're not yet in a position to load the bomb that will blow this poor terraqueous ball to smithereens."

"How do you know? Have you ever thought about the end of the world?"

Roger looked me straight in the eyes. That fiery gaze reignited all my anxieties. To avoid a more serious excitation, I was obliged to follow him in his lucubrations.

"The end of the world?" I said. "Certainly, I've read all the scientific anticipations, all the fantastic presumptions, all the legends related to the question. Periodically, besides, amateur astronomers a hundred-sou astrologers take the trouble to announce the abrupt termination of our celestial voyage. This very day, if you search hard enough, you'll find, somewhere in the sky, the comet that's due to pulverize us. Since the year 1000 of sinister memory, prophets of that stripe have never shut up shop, but as the Earth isn't doing too badly..."

"Let's leave the jokes there, please, and remain in the domain of pure science. The Earth won't die from the impact of a comet; celestial mechanics are too well-regulated for that. The Earth will perish from cold."

"Yes," I risked, to temper the violence of Roger's words. "I estimate, like you, that when the Sun is extinguished..."

"The Sun!" My friend shrugged his shoulders in order to emphasize the scorn he accorded o my hypothesis. "The Sun! But my poor Paul, although it's true that in the first ages of the Earth, the Sun stored enormous quantities of heat inside our globe, at the present moment, it only contributes in trivial proportions to the maintenance of normal temperature. Look, it's as if you tried to heat the Place de la Concorde with a lighted candle. Oh, don't smile; it's not a laughing matter. Merely allow me to help you grasp the true—the only—reason that guarantees the terrestrial crust against the mortal cold of space."

"I'm listening like a docile pupil, happy to be instructed."

"Well, it's the 320 kilometers of atmosphere that constitute a gaseous mattress around us, impermeable to the cold outside. And do you know the indispensable agent of that impermeability?"

"Tell me."

"Water vapor." And, in a tone of complaint: "What! You didn't know, then, that water vapor regulates all terrestrial life? Suppress the water vapor, and you suppress life, because you permit the cold of space to penetrate all the way to the solid surface. Now, the cold of space reaches 270 degrees below zero..."

"Brrr! You're giving me cold chills in my back."

Without paying any heed to the interruption, Roger continued: "But to extinguish life on Earth completely, there's no need to envisage that extreme temperature. A great scientist, Charles Martins, has demonstrated that a decline of only six degrees in the mean temperature of France would bring the Alpine glaciers all the way to Paris.[58]

"I've calculated myself that a decline of forty-three degrees in the normal temperature of the globe would lead to the solidification of the oceans and transform the continents into vast deserts of ice."

"Fortunately, they're entirely theoretical calculations."

"No, it's been observed; it's a fact of our geological history. Millions of years ago, when the overheated surface was covered with gigantic flora, when fantastic animals, the bones of which we've discovered, pullulated on land and

---

[58] The author adds a note at this point bearing the single word "Authentic." The reference is to Charles Frédéric Martins (1806-1889), a botanist and meteorologist who carried out extensive comparative studies of glaciers and concluded that the mean temperature during "ice ages" was only a few degrees lower than the present mean.

under water, when an intense life was established everywhere, the ice abruptly surged forth, stifling all creatures, animals and plants, and doubtless also the humans of those times—for there's no proof that, amid that exasperation of vital forces, human, civilizations and empires didn't exist in those distant ages.

"The result of it was an anesthesia of seeds, a destruction of species, a kind of end of the world, so abrupt and unexpected that science hasn't yet been able to offer a plausible explanation of the mystery." In a lower voice, Roger added: "Today, I believe that I've solved it, the mystery..."

He uttered a sigh, marking a pause. Then, with an ever-increasing tone of hatred, he went on: "After centuries, millennia of death, the resurrection came! There were other lives, other plants, other beasts and other humans. Was that life any better than the one swallowed up by the shroud of ice? It doesn't appear so, at least if I can judge by the odious spectacle of our present world."

Livry stood up; he strode back and forth, making broad gestures, and continued to emit his anathemas: "Today, what do we see, in spite of the apparent and illusory progress of civilization? Everywhere, the onslaught of base instincts and evil passions. Everywhere, lies, hypocrisy and fraud. Yesterday's atrocious war is only one incidence of that universal degradation. Half of humankind seems to me to be hell-bent on despoiling, torturing and destroying the other half. And if we look at the material signs, don't we find symptoms of decadence and decrepitude in all races and all classes? What is more abominable than the world of today?"

Roger stopped in front of me, his arms folded. His face was crimson with anger, his gaze fiery. He burst forth: "Paul, believe me, it's time, high time, to plunge the world that is coming apart and suffering—oh yes, suffering!—back into oblivion."

Poor Roger. At that moment, he was causing me a frightful pain, and a profound pity. Beneath the crazy words of an unhappy man, I sensed the distress of a grief-stricken soul, an exceedingly sharp dolor. I was, however, convinced of the impracticality of his hallucinatory threats; I was far more fearful of other, more direct, acts of violence against the Berjac household.

"I understand. You're meditating a book, a scientific work serving as the frame for a philosophical idea: a dream of the end of the world by cold, such as has happened in prehistory, such as occurred millions of years ago..."

Strident, demonic laugher cut off the thread of my speech.

In a harsh, metallic, arrogant voice-a voice whose tone made me shiver, Roger roared: "No, you don't understand! It's not a matter of a dream, but a reality; not contemplative philosophy, but imminent facts."

He made a violent effort to get a grip on himself.

"Excuse my nerves, Paul—but I want to finish where I should have begun. In this very place, I possess the substance that renders me master of lowering, as I wish, the temperature of the globe."

The chemist took me into the next room, where he had put the cases brought from Fontenay. He pointed to them with an emphatic gesture.

"This is the means by which we'll conduct the world to its final end!"

I don't flinch. He has just opened one of the cases. It contains the phials of blue glass that I've already seen, contained in their felt sheaths. The chemist takes one out, removes the stopper, and pours a few drops into a saucer.

Without emotion, I gaze at the syrupy blue-tinted liquid that my comrade caresses—I can't think of a better word—and trickles between his fingers.

Obligingly, he explains:

"In the first box is my provision of the Omega acid. In the other, lined with platinum sheets, my radium is at the center of an asbestos mattress—for radium is a terribly inconvenient metal; it eats through everything, including glass."

Now he brandishes the ebonite case inclosing the strange substance discovered by the admirable Curie household.

"It's a big as a penholder! One wouldn't suspect that the contents are worth twelve millions!"

"Twelve millions!" I repeat, stunned.

"Yes, ten grams of radium...I have as much in my laboratory at Fontenay...and that's just a beginning. I've made a contract with the largest manufacturers of chemical products for them to procure me, within a year, the forty grams I'll need."

What point is there in protesting loudly? In his dementia, the poor fellow is multiplying, at the demand of his crazy imagination, the few particles of radium that he possesses.

He replaces the tube of radium and closes the two boxes carefully.

"Tomorrow, I'm expecting to receive at the railway station the glass tanks destined to contain the Omega acid, as well as the meteorological instruments that will enable me to observe the results. In four days, everything will be ready. While awaiting the definitive action, this first experiment will give an idea of the means at my disposal..."

It was heart-rending.

But once again, his grating laughter bursts forth in the silence.

"If the astronomer Thiérard-Leroy were able to suspect it, I think he'd have judged it futile to marry his daughter Hélène last April twenty-fourth to Capitaine Berjac of the three-oh-sixth artillery, eh!"

Those words make me shiver. Roger knows the names, he remembers the date. He's dominated by the obsession of that accursed marriage.

Doubtless spurred on by that reminiscence, the madman cedes to the cruel emprise of his distress. He becomes delirious.

"Oh, the blind lovers, they can't see Death. It's descending from on high, all white, as white as a bride... It's snow...it's ice... I'm summoning it, I'm attracting it, I'm guiding it...it extends its white shroud over them, over us, over the entire earth..."

"Roger, I beg you..."

The exhortations to calm remain stuck in my throat. I'm alone with the poor madman, in that remote house where the storm is rumbling, where the wind is howling, where the ground, beneath the harsh glare of lightning-flashes, seems to be carpeted with frost.

Truly, in that moment of alarming nightmare, I think I see around me the dead earth invoked by the demented vision, the crust of crystallized snows of the glacial epoch.

And Roger, his arms raised toward the havens, continues to vociferate:

"Tremble, beings and things...

"Dust will return to dust...

"I am the Man of the Apocalypse!"

IV. A Seeker of Wings

After that fearful evening, I knew the terrors of a night of fever and insomnia.

The next morning, Roger seemed to me to be fresh and well-disposed. In accordance with orders given the previous day, the auto, which had been put in the garage at the hotel, came to pick us up to take us to the station. In no time at all, we were there.

Numerous packages had arrived, addressed to the chemist. Roger arranged with the dispatch office for them to be transported and then we climbed back into the automobile.

Roger is driving; I am sitting beside him. A beautiful day is in prospect, tempered by an easterly wind.

That regular wind encourages trials in unpowered flight, for on the horizon, in the direction of the Ferme de Bouy,[59] two great white birds are furrowing the sky, alternately appearing and disappearing behind clumps of fir-trees,

On the road, we catch up with a strange machine being towed by a tractor.

"Well, well!" says Roger. "That's a new idea! Oscillating wings..."

In fact, by virtue of the speed of travel, the wings of the alerion[60] in tow, stretched over a supple armature, are beating the air regularly like those of an enormous bird.

---

[59] The Ferme de Bouy, in the heart of the Camp de Châlons, was the training center for the Fourth Army during the Great War.

[60] An *alérion* [alerion] is a heraldic eagle; it was adopted by the designer Louis Peyret for the Peyret Alérion single-seat glider, which won the first British Glider Competition in 1922, piloted by Alexis Maneyrol; the two were fêted when they returned home. The term became briefly commonplace in application to gliders in general, and even to other small aircraft.

But the auto of the seekers of wings turns right on to a side road, clearing the road ahead.

Roger was about to activate the accelerator.

"What if we go and watch?" I proposed

He shrugged slightly. "Poor inventor! If he knew, he wouldn't risk breaking his bones in a crude machine."

"If he knew what?"

My question must have seemed naïve, because Roger became irritated. "That we'll soon be dead, of course!" Then, after a gesture, he conceded: "But if it's agreeable to you to go see at close range the attempts those larvae are making to crawl above ground, let's go!"

He turned the steering-wheel. Following the alerion, our vehicle reached the crest overlooking the plain, from which the machines were being launched.

We were soon on the fringe formed by the curiosity-seekers who were limiting the improvised aerodrome.

Two flying-machines were already in the air. Attention was, however, concentrated on the flying machine that had just arrived. In the circle of watchers, the name of the inventor was whispered: Guy Mayrol.

He proceeds with his preparations for take-off. The aides extend the "sandow" that is to project the alerion.[61] Guy Mayrol takes his place in the pilot's seat and utters a brief cry. That is the signal. The elastic cables relax; like an arrow, the alerion departs into space.

Almost immediately, alas, the apparatus stalls, descends in a spiral, and crashes on the hillside.

The crowd runs forward. Roger and I follow.

Fortunately, the fall has been gentle. The pilot stands up, unharmed.

In spite of his chagrined declarations of a short while before, my friend examines the flying machine lying on the grass with interest. Mayrol, a very young man with a sympathetic face, contemplates the injured machine with an expression of dolor and discouragement.

In the meantime, Livry has taken his notebook out of his pocket, and traces a sketch, while casting a glance over the various parts of the apparatus, measuring the inclination of the wings with the gaze, and then jots down equations.

I prefer to see him like that.

Suddenly, he approaches Guy Mayrol, and in a very soft voice, which I have not heard for a long time, he murmurs in his ear: "Will you permit me to give you some advice, Monsieur...?"

---

[61] A "sandow" was originally an elastic device used for exercising the arms, named after and marketed by the pioneering body-builder Eugen Sandow. The term was borrowed for application to catapults employed for launching gliders in France during the 1920s, but its fashionability was brief.

Mayrol looks at the unknown man with astonishment, but lets him speak without impatience. God knows how much advice he had heard!

However, the aviator follows the explanation, nods his head, and finally stuffs the piece of paper that Roger has just torn out of his notebook into his pocket.

After that incident, my friend rejoins me. We climb back into the automobile. Roger redirects the vehicle toward Mourmelon-le-Grand.

"You see, you're interested nevertheless in the future of unpowered flight," I say, to break the silence.

He makes a gesture of protest.

"Oh, don't exaggerate! I found myself in a position to procure that seeker some satisfaction. His wings are too narrow, the center of gravity of the apparatus is set too low. And yet, he understood the problem. If he listens to me, tomorrow he'll fly like a bird." Then, in an ironic tone: "Isn't it customary to grant small favors to those condemned to die?"

I keep quiet. What point is there is persisting?

In any case, we've arrived at our rickety château.

As soon as the threshold is crossed, Tourte, in a white apron, contrasting with the face, reddened by the fire of the oven, hands Roger a letter.

He opens it, scans it, and flies into a fury again.

"What is it?" I ask.

"Here, read it."

It's a letter from Philippe, the old domestic who serves as a concierge at the villa in Fontenay. Two banal pages to say that everything is in order, as at Monsieur's departure; one page of salutations. Then, at the bottom, a postscript that makes me jump.

I ought to tell Monsieur that Monsieur Jobert presented himself at four o'clock yesterday, asking to speak to Monsieur. I told him that Monsieur was absent.

The return to the scene of that individual caused me an indefinable malaise. But what could be the objective of that tireless pursuit?

"Perhaps Jobert wanted to solicit a re-entry into grace in your regard?"

My supposition provoked a shake of the head on the chemist's part—but the arrival of the station cart deflected attention to another object.

He supervised the unloading of various parcels. Until dusk, we were occupied in unpacking the crates sent from Paris.

First there were thick crystal tanks that Roger had placed in the middle of the empty space behind the house.

"This will be what I'll call our cold trap," he declared. "With four nuclei of that sort, I can bring the world to its end."

I let him talk, and helped him to install other apparatus of current usage in meteorological observatories.

Afterwards, it was necessary to distribute a whole series of maximum and minimum thermometers. One was set at ground level, another lodged in a shell-hole ten meters deep, which we were obliged to dry out first. It was hard work dredging the white mud of the calcareous soil. My pupils at Louis-le-Grand would have laughed if they could have seen their philosophy professor in his shirt sleeves, like a well-digger.

"Now I need a thermometer on the roof, as high as possible," Roger murmured.

"I'll climb up," said Tourte, sketching a joyful caper.

Poor boy! Your destiny, to which ours was linked in an extraordinary fashion, obliged you to be an accomplished gymnast and daredevil!

The work took us until nightfall.

Surprised by the darkness, Roget consented to put off filling the tanks with the Omega acid, and the entrance on stage of the radium, until the next day.

For my part, I was exhausted. So, after a summary dinner, I wasn't sorry to go up to my bedroom and find my poor camp-bed.

V. Drama, Heroism and Folly

Roger's imperative voice extracted me from slumber.

"Quickly, get up!" my friend shouted. "It's four o'clock. The wind's favorable. If you want to, come and see Mayrol fly."

I got dressed in haste.

We arrived at the terrain just as the young pilot had finished his preparations for take-off.

At the sight of the apparatus, Roger's face brightened. "He's followed my advice!" he said. "His center of gravity seems appropriate, the wings are now aligned with the axis of horizontal stability. Ha ha! We might see some interesting things!"

I couldn't see any of the improvements mentioned, which might have existed only in Roger's hallucinated eyes, but I approved of what he said regardless.

To my great surprise, though, as soon as he saw us, the young man ran toward us. His extended hands sought those of the chemist.

"Oh, Monsieur, my dear Monsieur, how I thank you. Without great confidence, I confess—forgive me, but I've already had so many disappointments—I adapted my supportive surface to the mathematical points fixed by your drawing. I twisted my ailerons according to our sketch. Well, at dawn I made a trial; it seemed to me that my apparatus was a hundred kilos lighter, that it was supported in the air with an unusual force."

"It doesn't astonish me," said Roger, with amazing self-assurance.

Mayrol contemplated him, with a passionate admiration painted in his gaze. "But who are you, then, to have given me, without even knowing me, an idea from which I might obtain glory and money? For I sense that this time, I shall get there!"

"Me! My young friend, if you knew who I am, you'd doubtless lavish me with more execration than gratitude. I'm the Man of the Apocalypse."

For a moment, Mayrol was silent, disconcerted by those strange words. Without lingering any longer in astonishment, however, he installed himself on the seat of his apparatus, and made a gesture bidding the gawkers to stand aside.

The alerion was launched. To everyone's amazement, it rose twenty meters in an admirable fashion. Then the great white bird began to describe circles with a perfect regularity.

The spectators, whose number was increasing by the minute, were astonished and ecstatic.

The pilot seemed sure of himself. No oscillation indicted any disequilibrium. Occasional abrupt downward plunges were halted by a graceful upward curve toward the sky.

"One would think it were a seagull flying over the waves!"

That reflection by an officer rendered the appearance of that extraordinary flight exactly.

And I repeated the thought that Livry had a considerable part in the success that seemed increasingly certain.

It was marvelous—and how troubling!

Troubling?

Even more so than I imagined at the time.

Who would have been capable of foreseeing that Livry had just created, with his own hands, the supreme antidote, by which the Earth might escape the evil of death?

Time went by.

Large placards displayed on the ground in succession indicated to the pilot the results acquired.

One hour thirty. One hour fifty...

The alerion continued to rise and descend with a remarkable facility. One gradually got so used to seeing it soaring in the sky that at length, the spectacle became natural, banal, almost tedious.

Roger became impatient.

"Damn it! We're wasting our time. I'm sure the man will keep flying until his strength runs out. Let's go..."

He turned round, took a step forward, and then stopped, nailed to the ground.

His face had gone white; his hands were agitated by a convulsive tremor.

I shivered in anguish. Was Roger about to have a fit, there, in public?

Mechanically, my eyes searched the people surrounding us.

Many officers, sportsmen, chauffeurs, a few peasants—and, six paces behind, a group composed of two amazons and two cavaliers: a colonel and a captain of artillery.

Of the two women, the first as red-haired, her hair tight at the temples, her body roughly-hewn, with a mannish appearance. At first glance one divined a horsewoman, sacrificing all coquetry to the practice of her habitual sport. At any rate, I scarcely accorded a glance to the plain and graceless individual in question, who seemed to be there to serve as a counterfoil to the prettiness of her neighbor.

By a striking contrast, the other amazon gave the impression of a being all finesse and charm. A slim figure, as supple as a liana; an ideal face illuminated by large dark blue eyes, slightly sad; tufts of fleecy blonde hair escaping the edges of a straw boater. That ravishing creature almost inspired a sentiment of tender pity with her lily-like fragility.

It was toward her that Roger's mad gaze was directed. Abruptly, I understood.

The unfortunate hazard that, to all indications, it was necessary to expect at any moment, had occurred. It had brought before us Madame Berjac, the daughter of the astronomer Thiérard-Leroy.

Alas, I sensed then the extent to which the sudden and insane passion of my friend was justified.

That adorable woman was one of those predestined to charm and seduce at first glance. Others, like me at that moment, would have been able to admire, to love, such an exquisite work of art, a fragile item of Dresden china perceived in a display-case in a museum. It would have required a truly great assurance of one's heart and one's reason to remain insensible before such ideal grace.

An incident as rapid as lightning suspended my reflections. How can I describe the sudden succession of anguishes and fears with which those few seconds were filled?

Amid the acclamations of the increasingly dense crowd, the alerion was approaching the ground, ready to touch down at its point of departure as lightly as a bird. Mayrol had beaten the record for altitude and distance.

At the same moment, however, dominating all the other sounds, a loud cry of distress resounded.

I turned round, and horror gripped me before the imminence of a frightful drama.

Frightened by the large shadow of the apparatus sweeping over the ground and by the precipitate cheers of the spectators, Madame Berjac's horse has leapt sideways. Then, with a single movement, the beast has reared up on its hind legs. For an inappreciable time it remains in that unstable equilibrium, of which circus exercises only give a faint idea. It is a complete straightening, which horsemen have baptized with the significant expression "the candle." It constitutes the most redoubtable defense that a horse can oppose, because the weight of the rider and the instinctive action exercised on the reins combine to tip the mount backwards. Then the rider is crushed! A vice clasps the victim between the ground and the mass of the beast seeking a point of support in order to get up again. With the disposition of ladies' saddles the danger is even more horrible, for the amazon remains the prisoner of the forks sustaining her, and those forks intervene to produce frightful and mortal wounds.

Such is the perilous situation of the frail young woman. One senses, one sees, that she is doomed!

Cries rise up, horrified screams, in which impotence and dolor are mingled.

Pricking his horse with a furious thrust of the spur, Capitaine Berjac launches himself toward his companion, but, frightened in its turn, the animal swerves.

Among the pedestrians, people make as if to run forward.

Before all the rest, a man beside me has bounded forward.

With an incredible leap, of which only a professional acrobat would seem to me to be capable, he leaps at the horse's head, grabs the reins and clings on to them.

There is a violent shock, and under the effort of that counterweight, Madame Berjac's mount falls back to the ground. Other people have thrown themselves upon the beast, gripping it everywhere, immobilizing it. In the midst of the crowd I distinguish the savior who has fallen under the hooves of the horse, and then Capitaine Berjac, who carries his inanimate wife away in his arms.

All that, I repeat, has taken place so rapidly that the different phases of the scene have raced ahead of my impressions, my intentions and my movements.

Like my neighbors, I disposed myself to run, to bring help, but I did not have time to put one foot in front of the other before it was all over.

Only then did I recognize Roger as the man who had just been disengaged from between the horse's hooves. All at once, he is dusted down, asked if he is injured and congratulated for his coolness.

In my turn I approached my friend, and without a word, I squeezed his hands in mine.

"Let's go, quickly!" he murmured in my ear, in a halting voice. "I can't take any more!"

Poor Roger. At that moment, I was able to fathom the depth of his incurable wound,

He let in the clutch, and the auto sped away in fourth gear through the stony ruts of a scarcely-traced path, fleeing toward Mourmelon. The machine truly seemed to embrace its master's rancor.

There was a series of terrible jolts, shocks to break the springs. For a moment I feared that Roger, vanquished by sickness of living, might precipitate himself voluntarily toward a mortal catastrophe.

An abrupt application of the brake nearly sent me hurtling over the hood.

"Hold tight, there," muttered the driver, in the irritated tone that was the surest indication of his interior turmoil.

We had just stopped less than a meter from an immense haycart blocking the Rue de Mourmelon, into which we had plunged. With imperative blasts of the horn, Roger forced it to let him pass.

Before I had recovered from my emotion, the auto had traversed the village and stopped in front of the gate of our sullen dwelling.

Roger went up to his room and shut himself in. I judged that it was best to respect that grim isolation.

In any case, Roger reappeared against at lunch time.

Sitting facing me, he dispatched his meal without saying a word, and then, having swallowed the last mouthful, he said: "To work! I want the experiment to be in full swing by the end of the week, so that we're feeling the first effects of the cold.

With a sardonic smile, he added: "The lovers of equitation can enjoy the time they have left. Before autumn, I promise them a Siberian temperature. At least the amazons will remain by the fireside."

I abstained from any reflection.

VI. Jobert's Letter

The next day, from dawn onwards, the chemist applied himself to delicate and slow manipulations. As meticulously as if he were carrying out a real experiment, he distributed the Omega acid. In successive layers, the syrupy liquid was spread out in the glass tanks. With scrupulous attention, Roger supervised the crystallization of the liquid, in such a fashion, he claimed, as to render the mass perfectly homogeneous.

My role was limited to following the chemist's work as a mere spectator. Roger had insisted on distributing the radium personally in the gelatinous mass formed by the aid.

With the aid of a long hollow platinum needle, he introduced traces of the precious substance particle by particle, in such a way as to impregnate the crystalline block. Eventually, the monotonous gesture seemed to make my skin crawl.

The ringing of the bell by the postman bringing the morning mail offered me a pretext to escape momentarily. I ran to the gate.

There was a letter addressed to me. I opened the envelope. A piece of lined paper escaped from it—vulgar letter paper of the liked that is usually offered in cafés to customers who ask for "something to write on."

At the first glance I deciphered Jobert's signature, a jerky, jagged scrawl with downstrokes interrupted by jumps.

In that scrawled page a graphologist would have discovered indications of envy, rage, pride and also a clearly emphasized cerebral derangement.

In fact, it was a veritable ultimatum that, via my intermediary, Jobert was addressing to Livry.

Judge for yourselves:

Monsieur Paul Lefort

Your friend Livry can hide at the Camp de Châlons, but I have penetrated the goal of the secret experiment he is preparing. I can foresee its incalculable consequences: to transform into arable land the chalky steppes of dusty Champagne, to change deserts into pastureland and heaths into forests. Now, having contributed to his works since their outset, it is only just that I participate in the glory of the grandiose results. Knowing that you are the only person possessing any influence over Livry, I am using your intermediary to make him understand his duty and to express my formal desires.

Either Livry will summon me and associate me with his work, not as an assistant but as a collaborator treated on a footing of absolute equality, or he will make me a gift in full property of the quantity of radium necessary to continue my research on the modification of calcareous matter on my own—a quantity that I fix at twenty grams.

My science is worth as much as his, and I cannot admit that his insolent wealth gives him the power to humiliate my poverty and arrest the impetus of my genius. In the scientific domain, as in any other, property is theft. Thus, equal shares, if he does not want to exhaust my patience and my resignation.

With best wishes, sincerely,

Jobert

The author of that statement was truly endowed with a strong dose of unconsciousness or effrontery. I judged that it was better to bring my friend up to date with the situation. I would see what he said.

More pensive than irritated, the chemist listened to a brief account of his ex-assistant's actions and movements since the day he had left the laboratory at Fontenay. He frowned on taking cognizance of the letter, and then nodded his head, as if those incoherent lines seemed perfectly normal to him.

In sum, the audacious pretentions of the rogue did not make him unduly indignant. He contented himself with pinching his lips, and they looked me in the face.

"Your Jobert possesses what we call scientific intuition, you know. I wouldn't have thought him that strong."

I couldn't help smiling at that unexpected appreciation. "Let's see—if I've understood correctly, Jobert intends to regenerate infertile soil, and become a benefactor of humankind. Now, it seems to me that you're marching toward an exactly opposite goal; instead of creating, you intend to destroy."

"That's true—but Jobert has nevertheless glimpsed one of the applications of my method, and that's not bad. Even so, it would be unfortunate if he took the theory too far, and especially the practice, for then..."

Roger left the sentence dangling.

"Then?" I prompted.

"Nothing. There's no need to develop my hypothesis, firstly because Jobert doesn't possess a sufficient quantity of radium, and secondly because you wouldn't understand a word of my explanations."

As the play of my features must have testified some resentment at that appreciation, however, my savant friend deigned to talk.

"Don't get annoyed! My research rests on theories so new, so troubling and so extraordinary that they almost escape our sense and reason. To make a palpable and so to speak, mechanical proof of them demands the help of higher mathematics, the integral calculus, because there alone can the notion of infinity be distinctly clarified. I'll spare you that demonstration, but in order that you can grasp it, I'll attempt a vulgarization by enunciating the as-yet-vague results in which the future laws of chemistry and physics are based.

"Inorganic ferments exist, which play in matter the role that microbes play in living beings. In consequence, large-scale effects—or, if you prefer, powerful reactions—can be produced by very small quantities of substance, possessed of an appropriate power of dissociation..."

Taking me by the arm, Roger led me to the tank in which the mixture of radium and Omega acid was crystallizing.

"Look! You have before your eyes a striking example of what I'm saying. What is nowadays known as radioactivity is, more simply, the dematerialization of matter." With a hint of pride, he went on: "The other evening, I reminded you that water vapor in suspension in the atmosphere opposes the intrusion of the cold of space, just as the panes of a window protect a room from the effects of the exterior temperature. Well, I'm breaking a pane of the atmospheric greenhouse in which we live like fragile plants. I'm shattering the glass of the sky—and this is my stone!"

He took a droplet of the blue- and violet-tinted liquid, and made the gesture of throwing it violently into the air. Then he went on:

"My Omega acid completely dissociates the water vapor with which it comes into contact, by fixing the oxygen and liberating the hydrogen—which, by reason of its weak density, rises up to the upper limit of the atmosphere and is probably lost there. But a remarkable fact gives my discovery its full range: after the adjunction of radium, the dissociation produced at ground level simply by exposing the liquid to the exterior air is transmitted from one particle to another. Every molecule of water vapor attacked decomposes its neighbors, and so on, with a speed proportional to the extent of the radiant surface. If you like, compare that action, of which radium is the principal agent,[62] to that of a trail of powder. Remember too that the extraordinarily intense phenomenon discovered by me, will be exercised equally from sea level all the way to the highest atmospheric layers.

"As an immediate consequence, no more evaporation of water! And evaporation, which constitutes the great thermic regulator of the globe, is as necessary to the life of the planet as respiration is to us. Conclude!"

But it was the madman who, in a tone without reply, provided the hallucinatory conclusion himself:

"Given the surfaces of radiant acid that I shall employ, six months will suffice to lower the temperature of the globe to a hundred and fifty degrees below zero. I estimate that no living organism will be able to resist such a climate.

"On the other hand, the surprise will be too abrupt for any organization to be made against such cold. All the heat and protection furnished by present habitations or vestments would become illusory. In any case, what would one eat? No more animals to butcher, no more running water. All movement impossible!

"From that moment on, after a brief struggle, life will disappear without there being any need to wait for the next year, when the temperature will drop a further hundred degrees, or the next century, when the advance of the ice will complete the covering of the entire globe."

In truth, it was horrific, that tale in the fashion of Edgar Poe, which Livry developed with an indisputable appearance of scientific precision.

Roger triumphed over my emotion. He had undoubtedly found the means to test my shaken suspicion.

"Have you grasped now the colossal phenomenon of the dematerialization of matter—a phenomenon characterized by an extraordinary liberation of energy? Here, I'm employing that energy to destroy the water vapor in the atmosphere, and indirectly, to produce cold. Jobert is thinking of using it in another way, to destroy chalk...but let's leave that; the energy can manifest itself in thousands of forms. You know at least some of them..."

As I opened my eyes wide in astonishment, Roger smiled ironically. "Of course! You must have heard mention of heat, electricity and light!"

"I understand," I murmured.

I could not help being gripped by the grandeur of those magisterial views; I completely forgot that the speech-maker was mad!

But I was troubled even more when Roger declared, in his modest tone: "After all, I only have the chance of putting these theories into practice, of giving them the consecration of experiment—and what an experiment! But I don't have the merit of having invented them; they were proposed by Gustave Le Bon.

---

[62] Author's note: "An experiment by Marie Curie has demonstrated that radium decomposes liquid water, ice or water vapor with an extraordinary intensity." Marie Curie made this point explicitly in her Nobel Prize lecture in 1911.

And let me just remind you of a sentence written by that great physicist in his book on *The Evolution of Matter*: 'The scientist who finds a means of liberating economically the forces that matter contains will instantaneously change the face of the world.'"[63]

And Roger sniggered.

"My insolent fortune, as Jobert puts it, has permitted me to pay the price—but I have found it!"

I lived a fearful moment then; a horrible conviction imposed itself on my mind: sound in body and mind, Roger was telling the truth! Had I not unknowingly witnessed the beginning of the titanic and mortal experiment of which the world was about to die?

No! It was too absurd.

If I had abandoned myself to it, I would rapidly have acquired the tremulous mentality of a man of the year one thousand, terrorized by legends and predictions.

Alas, my perplexities were, as yet, only at their beginning.

The next day I was woken up by Livry's triumphant shouting.

"Hey Paul! Come down quickly! Come and look: the temperature has already dropped three degrees since yesterday at the same time."

In fact, on setting foot in the courtyard, I felt a chilly wind strike me in the face.

He was exultant, and at eight o'clock he declared, with a proud joy: "Six degrees below normal. That's not bad for a start."

In truth, the weather seemed to be complicit with his mania. By the end of the day, we had the impression of a veritable cold snap. In the course of the night, I found myself obliged to add a traveling rug to my light bedcovers; I was freezing.

In the two days that followed, the cold got worse. A bitter north wind blew outside. That was abnormal for the middle of August, but in sum, the seasons to which we have become accustomed in recent years have similar whims.

On the morning of the third day, Roger could not retain his joy on observing that the short grass was covered by white frost.

In the course of the afternoon, however, an unexpected blow put a brake on that enthusiasm. Roger was cheerfully getting ready to go for an excursion by automobile—in order to take temperature readings in the surrounding area, he said—when a telegraphist came to the door. He held out a dispatch. Roger broke the gummed seal with an expression of ill humor. "Why won't they leave me in peace?" he grumbled.

---

[63] Gustave Le Bon's far-sighted account of *L'Évolution de la matière* was published in 1905.

As soon as he had read the telegram, however, his physiognomy revealed a violent emotion.

"The wretch!" he murmured. "He's gone stark raving mad, then!"

As my gaze sought an explanation, he passed me the blue paper.

In my turn, I was choked by indignation and dolor after having read the frightful lines:

Public prosecutor, Seine, to Roger Livry, chemist, Mourmelon.

Property Fontenay burgled last night by unknown malefactor. Custodian murdered. Please return urgently.

"Jobert!"

The name escaped my lips, containing a formal accusation in itself.

"Yes, the rogue has put his threats into action. He's stolen my radium!"

"What are you going to do, then?"

"Return to Paris. It's necessary. I want to be sure about Philippe's fate. Poor fellow!"

His real affliction gave way to a burst of egotistical ill-humor. "To be disturbed like this at the most interesting point of my experiment!"

"You can interrupt it, to resume it later."

"No! Here, everything will remain in place. The phenomenon will proceed without us, for years if necessary. No one will suspect it, and the house can look after itself. All the same, it's vexing!"

Half an hour later, after having locked up the rickety château as best we could, we were speeding along the road to Paris.

VII. The Cold

The sad voyage is accomplished without a word being exchanged.

At six o'clock we arrive outside the gate of the villa in Fontenay. The house is full of agents of the Sûreté. The examining magistrate is completing his investigation in the laboratory.

All the luxury of the property is contained in that large low building behind the villa, in the middle of a veritable park that extends between the railway line and the Bois de Vincennes. There, Roger has realized a marvelous installation, equipped with the most advanced and most costly apparatus. To science he has been unable to refuse anything, not even an electric furnace that burns three thousand francs' worth of current an hour every time it is switched on.

We head in that direction, but as we approach the door, amazement nails me to the ground. The frame of carved stone—of millstone—in which the solid grille and the thick battens of the door were enclosed, has completely disappeared. The battens and the metal hinges are lying on the ground, leaving an opening excavated in the supporting brickwork; one might think it a construction at its outset.

"Walk!" whispers Roger, in a low voice. "And above all, stop looking astonished!" And as my bewilderment is not dissipated swiftly enough for his liking, he adds, impatiently: "Better than anyone else, I ought to understand how Jobert got in there. A simple dissociation of the calcareous stone sustaining the door, with the aid of the Omega acid. Have you forgotten my explanations already?"

Shivering, I followed my comrade.

Reciprocal introductions with the magistrate are followed by the latter's explanations.

"The door of your laboratory was being repaired, which facilitated the malefactor's intrusion" says the magistrate, without hesitating over what seems to him to be an evident observation.

Roger nods his head. At the same time, a glance instructs me to keep quiet. The magistrate continues is reconstruction of the crime.

In the middle of the night, the murderer climbs the wall of the property. Then he introduces himself into the laboratory through the open breach, goes straight to the strong-box; removes a steel panel with the aid of an explosive—a chlorated powder, according to the experts.

In spite of the care taken by the burglar to cover the front of the strongbox with blankets, the noise of the explosion is heard by old Philippe, the villa's guardian. He comes running, but on the threshold of the laboratory he falls, pierced with two thrusts of a dagger. The poor man is dying at the Hôpital Saint-Antoine. Nevertheless, thanks to the light of a lantern, he thinks he has recognized his attacker; he has designated Jobert, the former laboratory assistant of the master of the house.

"Everything indicates, in any case, that the crime has been committed by someone very familiar with the habits of your house," concludes the examining magistrate. "Had you, then, large sums of money in that strongbox?"

"Not a centime of cash, but ten grams of radium, representing a value of more than two millions."

The judge started. I stifled a cry of amazement. Had Roger really spent such a sum buying radium?"

Without excitement, however, the chemist proceeded with a rapid inventory.

"He has also stolen a demijohn containing twenty-five liters of Omega acid," he murmured in my ear. "And that's more serious..."

The last observations having been made, the examining magistrate retired, declaring that Jobert would be placed in the ranks of the most dangerous criminals; all the police forces would be launched on his heels.

"Will they succeed in arresting him?"

I formulated that question a few moments after the magistrate's departure, solely to break the somber silence in which Roger seemed to want to confine himself.

"I hope not!" he fulminated.

As I manifested a legitimate surprise in my expression, he explained: "I have no desire to see the Law doing chemistry on my back!"

"What do you mean?"

"That Jobert possesses a specimen of my acid, that he's divined too much of my work. I'd prefer that he doesn't talk, so, I want him to escape the searches."

"But he's a murderer! He merits a punishment!"

Roger shrugged his shoulders. "Like all of us, he's condemned to death. The Law can do no better."

I did not feel any desire to prolong that conversation, both idle and painful. I understood the urgent necessity of reaction.

To begin with, I wanted to liberate my mind from the doubt into which, reluctantly, Roger's extravagant claims had plunged me, on the subject of his purchases of radium.

That same evening, while my friend was at the Hôpital Saint-Antoine with his wounded servant, I went to the principal merchants of chemical products in the Latin quarter.

Livry had made large purchases from all of them.

From the very start, the merchants allowed me to discover that my friend's affirmations were still below the truth. Three months before, had he not concluded, in good and due form, an unusual contract for the supply of fifty grams of radium? At the current price of one million two hundred thousand francs per gram, he had thus engaged himself, with regard to the various producers of France and abroad, for a sum of about sixty million—a full half of his fortune.

On returning to the villa, I found Roger occupied with tidying up his laboratory. Without waiting any further, I could not master the impulse that drove me to try to talk some sense into him.

"Wretch!" I exclaimed. "Do you want to ruin yourself, then?"

He shrugged his shoulders.

"In a few months, we'll no longer be here. Do I still have to repeat that to you? So, tomorrow I'll go to my notary to tell him to sell my immovable property. Then, if necessary, I'll mortgage the villa at Fontenay..."

I let him talk. What was the point of countering such arguments? I would only try to see his notary, secretly, in order to prevent that irremediable eccentricity, which would put the unfortunate on the streets.

But would those officious precautions of a devoted friend be sufficient, against the obsessions of a willful individual like Roger?

No: at the rate things were going, very soon, circumstances would give me a duty to have resource to a dolorous extremity.

On the day when I found that it was impossible for me to defend Roger against himself, I would become culpable by keeping the secret of his folly; then, only one solution would appear possible: the internment of the poor fellow.

For some time already, would it not have been better to give the scientist the care required by his sick brain?

But our thoughts and our resolutions are truly submissive to strange oppositions!

From the moment that I began to encourage myself increasingly to take a decisive step, Roger seemed to be determined to adopt an absolutely normal attitude. And with regard to whom? With regard to the very people who might be called upon to judge his mental condition!

In the course of the Jobert affair he was summoned to numerous interviews with the examining magistrate, the head of the Sûreté, and the police commissioner of Vincennes. Was there an effort on his part to appear natural in order to remove any inclination on the part of the law to occupy themselves with his affairs? At any rate, I had never seen my friend Roger so amiable, such a brilliant conversationalist, so far from lunacy. The magistrates marveled at his logic and his intelligence. Behind his back, they addressed themselves to me to consecrate Livry as a superior man, a powerfully organized mind, a scholar of the first order.

He made the same impression on Dr. Revard, the celebrated surgeon and most prominent member of the Académie de Médecine. Roger had made his acquaintance at the bedside of poor Père Philippe, who was still battling between life and death. Quite naturally, the two men had allowed their conversations to stray on to scientific terrain. One day, to summarize his enthusiastic judgment on the subject of my friend, Revard, who was not reputed to be lavish with praise, whispered in my ear:

"Remember my diagnosis—your friend will be Galileo, Edison or Pasteur!"

After that, could one see me going to request the detention of Livry in an asylum? It would be me who was at risk of being treated as a madman and seeing myself locked up right away.

And yet, I retained the certainty that my friend was not cured. On the contrary, his strange ideas were becoming more profoundly rooted. Every morning, Roger came into my room brandishing the newspapers.

"I believe that's that, eh? Yesterday, fifteen degrees below normal. Winter temperatures at the beginning of autumn. The vines frozen in Champagne. Poor devils of vine-growers! If I could tell them how vain their lamentations are...

"And the meteorologists! Oh, it's necessary to hear them! They're serving us the cold wave, the perturbation of the regime of the winds, or even the sunspots! All the old majors are being worked to death. They're also accusing the Moon, of course. She has a broad back, the gentle Phoebe!

"Anyway, observe for yourself the unexpected activity with which the Omega acid is eating the water vapor. Since my cold machine has been functioning at Mourmelon, not a drop of rain—a sky purged of any trace of humidity."

In fact, a singular coincidence encouraged the extravagant fantasy of the destroyer of the world.

In the months since we had quit Mourmelon, the weather had cooled in a very abnormal fashion for the time of year. There was a veritable cold snap: a bitter north wind was blowing, as in December. Everywhere, that the popular sentiment could be grasped, on autobuses, at the restaurant, at street-corners, the plaints burst forth. On the doorsteps, housewives were affirming that the seasons had "turned round."

Finally, there was one symptom that could not help but impress me forcefully: well before the usual date of their departure, the swallows were flying south.

I have always judged the instinct of animals to be superior to the anticipations of humans. Were we really threatened by an exceedingly precocious winter of exceptional rigor?

That fortuitous accord between Roger's hallucinatory predictions and the reality of facts ended up troubling me in a singular fashion. In vain I waited for a change in the weather, one of those abrupt releases of a soft warm humidity that normally succeed dry and cool periods—but the days passed without modifying the state of the atmosphere, the meteorological bulletins recorded increasingly sullen temperatures, to the great joy of the chemist and my increasing nervousness

It was then that, the following week, an event occurred that was to furnish a new aliment to my anguish.

VIII. The Sower of Cataclysm

I have omitted to say that, to Livry's secret satisfaction, all efforts to pick up the trail of Jobert had remained vain.

At one moment, it had been suspected that the murder had taken refuge in his mother's house near Algiers. The window of a farmer, the woman lived at Bouffarik. But a search carried out in the poor old lady's home had demonstrated that Jobert was not there. That he had gone there after the crime was possible, even probable if one put weight on certain indications. Perhaps Jobert had yielded to the desire to embrace his old mother before leaving the country, and the old woman's denials did not determine anything with regard to that particular point; a mother does not betray her son! At any rate, everything indicated that the criminal had reached Algiers and had succeeded in embarking for an unknown destination.

Such was the state of the information on which the police were relying when there were earthquakes in the vicinity of Douera and Bouffarik, which plunged the region into consternation and terror.

The newspapers of the epoch have described in detail the frightful panic of the first moment, the villages in ruins, the dead and the living buried under the rubble, and also the noble rivalry of the rescuers coming from all directions.

While deploring that public misfortune I would doubtless only have taken a distant interest in those events if Roger had not given them a truly singular interpretation.

"You haven't guessed what had happened?" he asked me, after having read the news relating to the cataclysm attentively.

As I did not grasp the significance of the question I remained silent.

"Well," Roger cut in, "I'm convinced that Jobert has certainly taken refuge in Bouffarik with his mother. There, consciously or unconsciously, he has provoked the catastrophe."

"The catastrophe?"

"Of course—the earthquake.

I was accustomed to my poor friend's mystifying speech, but that was truly beyond measure. Following the strategy that I had imposed on myself in such circumstances, I did not pick up the strange affirmation.

Nevertheless, Roger followed his train of thought.

"The suspicion occurred to me immediately. A study of the geological map has confirmed it fully. In the region tested by the cataclysm the ground is constituted by siliceous strata alternating with calcareous layers. Suppress or dilute the layers of marble, chalk or marl and everything collapses, dislocated. You've realized the conditions that engender earthquakes."

Mockingly, he unleashed a few darts at me: "No, however little versed you are in studies of chemistry, you must remember the fundamental experiment: chalk dissolved by acid... What am I saying? I blush to have to remind you of the Latin classics, in which you were taught that Hannibal, in order to cross the Alps, dissolved the rocks with vinegar![64]

"Well, I repeat to you, my Omega acid, amalgamated with radium, also enjoys the property of attacking limestone, but in proportions..."

This time, I pricked up my ears; a new horizon had been abruptly revealed to my troubled eyes: a horizon of which Livry took charge of fixing the lines.

"Of course," he said, in a jovial tone, "I'm preaching to a convert! You've even been able to observe that Jobert has been able to volatilize calcareous stone instantaneously, in the form of the millstone doorposts of my laboratory. His recent theft permits him to do things on a larger scale, and undoubtedly, the terrible consequences of his manipulations have escaped him, for they will have en-

---

[64] This myth originated in the work of the Roman historian Livy; Polybius makes no mention of the preposterous alleged feat.

countered the mirage after which Jobert is running inconsiderately—the so-called regeneration of the soil."

Roger laughed. "A fine regeneration of the soil!"

For myself, I shivered.

For a moment, Roger remained thoughtful; then, in a more serious tone, he said: "Which doesn't alter the fact that the individual is now becoming very dangerous. I too would be able to ravage the earth, sow ruin, death and destruction here and there, but that would be local destruction, an absurd crime with no tomorrow.

"The end of the world, yes—that's a grandiose idea, as logical and ordered as a mathematical verity. It's an almost divine endeavor, in comparison with which a partial hecatomb appears to me to be abominable."

Full of his subject, Roger paced back and forth in the room, illuminated like a prophet. It was the first time that he had frightened me—really frightened, beyond any nervous sensation or imaginative shock. For the first time, my conviction was shaken.

Why? Because I had seriously envisaged the possible role that he attributed to Jobert. I had seen with my own eyes the solvent effects produced by the Omega acid. It was not unreasonable to calculate effects of the same sort multiplied to an extreme. At an infinitesimal dose, the radium had already determined extraordinarily energetic phenomena. What power could be attributed to the ten grams in Jobert's possession, to the eighty grams that Livry intended to employ one day? How could the limit be measured of the formidable reactions that might follow, since no laboratory had ever experimented with such quantities?

Thus, I almost admitted the thing that would have seemed insane a few months earlier: a man was able to provoke a cataclysm, an earthquake.

In that case...why deny another man the power to bring about an even greater upheaval, by imagining the destructive effect of the acid multiplied a hundredfold, multiplied almost infinitely?

Except that a doubt came to my rescue, to defend me against the definitive invasion of that frightful idea.

At its base, that reasoning depended on an entirely gratuitous hypothesis on Roger's part: the presence of the murder in Bouffarik on the day of the seismic shock, and the proven correlation between the phenomenon and manipulations of the Omega acid by his former assistant.

That doubt, to which my tottering reason clung, was to be cut away a week later.

There are dates that are landmarks in life. Thus, I will never forget that eighth of October 19**. It was my first lecture since the resumption of classes. In fact, I had been able to make Roger, who wanted to keep me with him, understand that it was necessary for me to resume my position at Louis-le-Grand, at least until the appointment of a substitute: a rule of decency that he could not make me violate, while awaiting the solicitation of a leave of absence that would permit me to devote myself to him.

Deep down, I experienced a secret joy at that resumption of contact with the academic world; for a few hours a week I would live in a saner and less troubling atmosphere than the one in which I had been plunged for two months.

Not that I begrudged the unfortunate Roger the worries, the difficulties and the tribulations. More than ever, I was prepared to sacrifice everything—my repose, my wellbeing, my career—in the attempt to free him from his terrible obsessions. There are duties of friendship that cannot be set aside.

By the very reason of my intentions, however, it seemed good to me to steep myself once again in my natural milieu. In teaching philosophy to others, it seemed to me that I ought to be the first to profit from my instruction.

Thus, I had devoted by initial lesson to Descartes, that great destroyer of preconceived ideas, that declared enemy of the imagination. Under the cover of admirable philosophy doubled with scholarly genius, I vituperated against the illusion of our senses, the tyranny of illusions, the false steps of reasoning.

In truth, I was speaking for myself.

With the fire of enthusiasm that sincerity gives, I uplifted my audience, I obtained a veritable success.

I left the class with my temples still throbbing, exhausted by physical effort but with a joyful heart, and a serene soul.

It appeared to me that I had reconquered my tranquility and my aplomb.

Joyful and resolute, I was leaving the lycée when someone tapped me on the shoulder.

"I've arrived in time to collect you," pronounced Roger's voice.

"You? Nothing serious, I hope?"

I had, in fact, left Roger in his laboratory, where he was ardently manufacturing further quantities of his acid, and I knew that the chemist was not easily distracted from his work.

He reassured me with a gesture. "Oh, simply a summons I received this morning from the head of the Sûreté."

"Ah! The Jobert affair again?"

"You've guessed correctly. According to the succinct note I've been sent, the blackguard has been found."

"You see!" I exclaimed, carried away. "Jobert had nothing to do with the earthquake, then, and everything you supposed the other day..."

With a gesture of his hand, Roger invited me to formulate my judgment with more reserve. "Gently—we'll see what they have to say to us at the Sûreté first. Thinking that the matter might interest you, I made a detour to pick you up."

He drew me toward his automobile.

Privately, I was counting in advance on a denouement that would complete the annihilation of the troubling suppositions of the preceding days. Already, I was muttering to myself inaudibly: "That will teach you not to get carried away in your hypotheses!"

We arrived at the Prefecture of Police. We were immediately received by Monsieur Régnaud, one of the deputy heads of the Sûreté.

"Well, Monsieur Livry," the functionary said, "you were right in opposing those who wanted to see Jobert as a thief attracted by the enormous intrinsic value of the radium. He has furnished us himself with proof that he's a simple madman...a dangerous madman, to be sure."

"He's been arrested?" asked the chemist, impatiently.

"No, but he undoubtedly will be, in a matter of days. He's taken the trouble to notify us of his presence in Messina."

"How?"

"An imprudence. He's written to his aged mother in Bouffarik. The letter was intercepted. The missive is sufficient for us to be convinced of his mental state, and also..." The deputy head of the Sûreté grumbled, in a lower voice: "And also the pitiful fashion in which the surveillance of the widow Jobert was exercised. Oh, the provincial police! In brief, by his own confession, our fugitive really did remain hidden in his hometown until the day after the catastrophe. In the midst of the panic, without being recognized, he even helped with the rescue of his mother, buried under the rubble of her house. He made himself scarce as soon as he saw the old woman recover her senses. He went to Bougie, embarked on an Italian fishing-smack and reached Sicily. All of that, narrated in his letter, is instructive, but in sum, quite banal. Where the banality ceases is when he explains the cataclysm. In my profession, I've often had occasion to examine cases of delusions of grandeur, but rarely like this one."

And Monsieur Régnaud, his hands on his hips, slowly shook his head as he said what he judged to be an enormity: "Can you imagine that Jobert accuses himself of having provoked the earthquake by means of his imprudent experiments? He asks his old mother, who almost fell victim to it, for forgiveness!"

Roger said nothing; he merely looked at me with an indefinable expression.

As for me, I had become livid.

"After that," the functionary concluded, "the wretch seems to require alienists rather than the court of assizes. In the meantime, we've taken steps to alert the Italian police and request his extradition. In a few days, I hope, we'll have him in Paris."

As if in a fog, I saw my companion get up and take his leave of the deputy chief.

I stiffened myself in order to imitate him and stood up.

In the broad administrative corridor, cold and bare, I was prey to a veritable vertigo. I had to lean on Livry's arm in order not to fall.

"Why, what's the matter?" said my friend, solicitously. "Are you feeling...faint?"

What was the matter!

For the first time since the beginning of the affair, the wall of incredulity that had protected me against definitive terror had been split; through that fissure, the last resistance attempted by my reason in revolt was about to drain away.

The veil of doubt had decidedly torn, allowing *the fact* to appear.

Mad, Roger undoubtedly was, in everything connected with his amour for Monsieur Thiérard-Leroy's daughter, but as soon as he was lodged in his scientific domain, madness gave way to an admirable clarity of sight—as witness the prodigious result of the advice given, off the cuff, to Guy Mayrol.

Amid the disorder of my thoughts in distress, that was the first proof that presented itself. A few days before, departing from the cliff of Boulogne, the aviator had made child's play of traversing the Channel and landing in a suburb of London. Then, only the day before, the newspapers had been full of his new exploit: Mayrol had launched himself from the summit of the Ballon d'Alsace, and after reaching an altitude of more than fifteen hundred meters, and flying over the valleys of the Saône and the Rhône, a blast of the mistral had carried him beyond Avignon.

In the course of the interviews to which he was obliged to submit, the hero of the day reported that a great part of his success was due to a mysterious unknown man, who had appeared and disappeared like the good genie of a tale, leaving behind him only a phantom name: the Man of the Apocalypse. And the press continued to discuss, to comment on and enliven Mayrol's confidence, surrounded henceforth with the Hoffmannesque attraction of the fantastic.

But I knew the truth: the Man of the Apocalypse was Livry.

Then, to complete the foundations of my judgment, came those striking coincidences—more than coincidences, *realizations*—corresponding to events announced by the chemist: the increasing marked lowering of the temperature; the duly-explained sorceries that were narrowly attached to Jobert's actions.

After that, how was it possible to persist in a blind negation?

Now, Roger, the friend of my childhood, the companion of my joys and troubles, appeared to me as the superhuman genius of annihilation and Death!

The simple role that I had attributed to myself was finished. It was no longer a matter of watching over a madman with prudent and compassionate attention. I had to enter into a struggle with a Force whose immeasurable power I already suspected.

No matter! The situation was revealed in such a way that I was condemned to march over my heart, to strangle my nerves, to stifle my self-esteem. Everything was effaced before a new instinct, which I discovered in my inner depths in those minutes of fearful suggestion: the instinct of survival—but an instinct enlarged beyond the interests of my own individuality.

Does Nature act, unknown to us, at opportune moments, to defend her creation and her creatures?

When a poor head allows itself to be invaded by such thoughts, there is nothing astonishing, is there, in seeing the body that supports it collapse?

The keen air outside whipped my blood. I straightened up again. I breathed out dely.

"There—that's better!" said Roger, as he installed me in his automobile.

"Yes. It was so hot in the offices of the Sûreté..."

Roger smiled in a Machiavellian fashion. "They've turned up the heating—and but that's only the beginning!" And in a tone of triumphant satisfaction: "In the plain of Châlons, for two days, it's been cold enough to split stones."

IX. The Release

"Are you asleep, Paul?"

It was the morning of the fifteenth of October when Roger came into my bedroom on tiptoe to murmur those words in my ear. His voice was grave; it was not accentuated by the amicable familiarity with which he came to wake me up when he needed me before the time I normally got up.

"I'm not asleep," I said. "What's wrong?"

Before replying, Roger turned the commutator placed at the head of my bed. The electric bulb lit up.

Then I was able to look at my friend. He was very pale; his tremulous hands were holding an unfolded newspaper.

In a muted tone that revealed a profound emotion, he pronounced: "You know, my projects might be modified completely..." He waved his arm in a veritably solemn gesture. "The world might live!"

To that colossal affirmation, I opposed a banal interrogation: "Why?"

"Because Capitaine Berjac is dead!"

Dazed, I was voiceless.

Roger held out *Le Matin* to me, which was delivered to the villa every day at six o'clock. With his finger, he indicated an article headlined: *Icy Autumn*.

First there was a sequence of dispatches coming from the eastern region, all signaling the disastrous precocity of winter cold. At Epernay, the thermometer had reached seventeen degrees below zero. At Sillery, the docks of the Vesle canal had been icebound for two days. Then a subheading made me shiver: *First victim: an officer drowned while skating*.

My heart constricted, I read the item:

Reims, 14 October, 9 p.m.
A serious accident has just plunged our region into consternation...

I read on without reading, my eyes only retaining the conclusion:

Capitaine Berjac leaves a young wife, the daughter of Monsieur Thiérard-Leroy, director of the Observatoire de Paris.

We salute with respect the grief that has struck that honorable family, as well as the officers of the 306ᵗʰ artillery.

I remained petrified. And as I kept silent, Roger's timid, almost ashamed voice murmured nearby: "Now she's free."

"Oh, Roger!"

I could not repress that exclamation, vibrant with indignation. What! My friend had arrived at that barbaric unconsciousness! Was not the poor officer, in sum, the indirect victim of the chemist's enterprises? He had died of the cold that the other had created.

At that moment, Roger horrified me.

To efface that painful impression, it was necessary for me to remount the current of our long friendship. It was necessary, above all, for me to tell myself that my judgment was iniquitous and absurd. One does not incriminate a madman. One disarms him.

Instead of playing the professor of morality with regard to Roger, it is necessary for me to take advantage of the lamentable event in order to render myself master of that powerful—and yet so feeble—mind. Rather than exasperate it further with vain remonstrations, I ought to encourage the fantasy that might deliver it to me.

Madame Berjac is free, so the world might be saved! Roger says so himself; he has shown me the terrain on which I must maneuver.

It was necessary to encourage his hopes but it was necessary above all to rein them in. My first efforts, therefore, were aimed at preventing him from making any inconsiderate move.

Straight away, I set aside the lugubrious shadow of Capitaine Berjac; I kept it for myself. And, in order to explain the critical tone of me exclamation, I did not recoil from a lamentable recantation.

"You're frightening me, Roger. You seem to me to be about to compromise, by an unreflective impatience, the happiness to which you might aspire one day."

"The happiness!" he murmured. The magic of that single word had cast a gleam over his sorrowful physiognomy. "Oh, tell me what I ought to do!"

"Wait! Let time, the great surgeon of the soul's wounds, do its work. That way, you'll show the tact of a man of heart, and that will be the supreme skill."

He listened to me with an extreme attention. Then, in a calm and resolute tone, he said: "I trust you; I'll follow your fraternal advice. But tell me again that I can hope!"

"You have the right to do so."

Oh, how dearly it cost me to formulate that affirmation, which hid a lie.

And in order to take immediate advantage of the scientist's good dispositions, I pointed at the frost that was covering the panes of the bedroom window.

"You can divine where it's necessary to begin?"

He passed his hand over his eyes, and, as if struck by a sudden revelation: "That's true! At Mourmelon, the Omega acid is continuing to operate. We'll go out there today; it will only take me a quarter of an hour to suspend the effect."

"Suspend? Why not destroy it permanently?"

After a hesitation marked by a contraction of his features, he said, in a dull voice: "I want to reserve the future."

At that moment it would have been maladroit to press harder. I attempted nevertheless to obtain an indication that might be of extreme importance later.

"You have a means, then, of stopping the effects of your cold?"

"Yes, a very simple means that renders the acid inert, just as gunpowder loses its properties of deflagration when it's moistened, and recovers them again when it's dried out."

"Will you explain it to me?"

Roger considered me with an expression in which I clearly discerned suspicion. Then, grimly, he said: "No."

But a first, enormous result had been acquired.

At ten o'clock in the morning we—Roger, Étienne and I—set off on the road to the Camp de Châlons.

Within two hours, the limousine drew up outside the abandoned house.

Since our abrupt recall to Paris, Étienne had returned there alone once a week, to remove the graphic recordings from the various meteorological instruments left at fixed points.

Nothing in the dismal dwelling had changed.

The sparse grass of the courtyard had disappeared under a layer of frost. The cold was biting; the sky had the dark blue tint of the great winter cold.

How could anyone suspect the colossal work of destruction that was being contrived there, in that square courtyard? How could one suspect those glaucous tanks, mimicking the appearance of bowls innocently set to collect rainwater?

One last time, Roger consulted the thermometers; then he came back to me. A melancholy smile wandered over his lips, and there was a hint of regret in his tone.

"As a scientist, I regret the action I'm about to take. I'm stopping an experiment at the moment when it's yielding prodigious results, more conclusive than those indicated to me by the calculations."

He shook his head, considering the receptacles.

"Now, let me cure this poor earth, which seemed so well lost. Give me ten minutes. Go and wait for me in the car."

I made no objection to the maniac's desire. I went away.

Faithful to his promise, the chemist reappeared a quarter of an hour later. As I interrogated him with my gaze he said: "It's done. In a matter of days, you'll be able to see."

After having relocked the door, my friend took his place in the automobile. He settled into the back seat. His eyes vague, his features relaxed, he smiled at his dream.

Poor fellow, I divined the vision that had just succeeded furious nightmares. That languor did not abandon him even when the auto came to a rather abrupt halt a few minutes after our departure. Roger continued to dream, while I leaned out of the window curiously.

We were near Mourmelon railway station and our vehicle had run into the tail end of a funeral cortege: officers and armed artillerymen surrounded the hearse, while other wore crowns with tricolor ribbons. I guessed the rest.

It was poor Capitaine Berjac that they were accompanying on his final voyage.

My heart constricted, I drew my head back in very rapidly, as if were guiltily ashamed to show myself.

Shivering, I looked at Roger.

He was still smiling at the angels.

X. The False Quietude

In the days that followed our journey to Mourmelon, Roger behaved with an admirable sagacity.

A radical transformation seemed to have taken place in him. No more of those monologues full of muffled and terrifying threats, no more of those fits of fury followed by phases of depression. He worked reasonably, applying himself to being and living, like everyone else.

Was it the force of his renascent passion that gave him such an empire over himself? Was it the abrupt change in the atmospheric conditions that was having a good influence on his temperament?

For, extraordinarily—and for me, conclusively, the dry cold had given way to a misty humidity. Everywhere, the thaw was announced: mild, rainy weather—"rotten weather," to employ the expressive term of the common people—set in. Then the sun began to shine, bringing with its radiance an Indian summer that contrasted in an exquisite fashion with the frosts of the previous days.

That remarkable relaxation, in accordance with the anticipations of the chemist, appeared to be the direct consequence of the visit to the house at the camp.

For me, it was a supplementary proof, and how suggestive!

So, in an undeniable fashion, Roger seemed to be on the road to recovery.

I congratulated myself and I trembled at the same time, because the divine amorous deception to which my friend was lending himself, and of which I had become the fearful accomplice, might well be doomed to end lamentably.

And when the moment of disillusionment came...

In the near future, I glimpsed the brutal end of the idyll on which Roger was building the future city of his happiness. Of what would he not be capable on observing for a second time the bankruptcy of his adorable and naïve confidence?

Fortunately, Roger opened up to me at the same time the hope of stopping future threats—and is such a prosaic fashion!

"Paul," he said to me, abruptly, "I want you to do something for me."

"Isn't that what I'm here for?"

"Oh, don't engage yourself so lightly. I know in advance that you have no liking for the task I want to confide to you. You're not a businessman."

Before knowing what he was getting at, I smiled, nodding my head.

"Bah!" Roger went on. "Out of friendship for me, you'll do it. You're to substitute for me in all matters concerned with the administration of my fortune. You're to deal with my suppliers, to do what's necessary to make the payments...because I have obligations to them. In any case, you'll only have to follow the indications of Sencier, my notary; I have every confidence in him. As for you, I don't need to tell you that I give you *carte blanche*. You'll act as I would."

And, putting his poor fiery head in his hands, he confessed: "I need to pull myself together, you see—a time of repose. For some time, I've been caressing a mad desire to lock the door of my laboratory; I no longer want to think about anything but my amour. So I'm asking you to be my steward, Can I count on you?"

"Can you doubt it for a moment, my friend?"

As I spoke those words I had a slight shudder, for already, the depths of my mind were pierced by the vague sensation that Roger had delivered himself to me.

He pushed me into the automobile himself, and gave the order to Julien to take me to his notary.

My head seething, I arrived at the offices of Maître Sencier, in the Faubourg Saint-Honoré. I received the most amiable welcome, which immediately put me at my ease.

My designation as substitute brought an unanticipated solution.

"I'll draw up a power of attorney for you," said the notary. "Then, furnished with the most extensive powers in all things, you can substitute yourself for the unfortunate scientist. In all conscience, we have the right to save his fortune. The purchases of radium...well, they'll fall of their own accord; we're due to pay on delivery of the merchandise; we won't pay, and the radium won't be delivered."

353

Thus spoke Maître Sencier.

That same evening, Roger signed a duly drawn-up power of attorney. Henceforth, I had free disposal of his wealth; I had him, bound hand and foot. He would no longer have a particle of radium, except for the few grams he already possessed.

This time, an immense relief invaded me entirely. Whatever might happen subsequently, Roger was no longer in a position to pursue his dream of ending the world.

And, sure of the future—oh, what an imbecile presumption as mine!—I let myself lapse into the pitiful, paltry and surely ignoble, but very human, observation that the world would not be saved, as I had believed momentarily, by the adorable tenderness of Amour, but thanks to the implacable and vile force of Money!

Roger kept his promise. He deserted his laboratory.

And that epoch marked, for him, more than a repose; it brought about a radical modification of all his anterior habits.

It was thus that Roger spent his days running around the tailors, shirt-makers and boot-makers most renowned in elegant society. One morning, he arrived with his beard trimmed and pointed, his hair parted from forehead to nape by a savant stripe. Another time, I surprised him abandoning himself to the care of a manicurist.

A manicurist in Roger's house! That small fact alone said a great deal to anyone who knew that antisocial seeker.

Then he turned his application toward various methods of physical culture. His dressing-room was garnished with the most complicated items of apparatus: exercisers, adjustable dumb-bells, electric masseurs. Within two weeks, my friend was unrecognizable. Instead of the tall, gangling, more-or-less hirsute fellow, almost neglectful in his attire, I had before me a veritable gentleman in a well-cut, dark-colored suit in perfect taste.

It had certainly required an extraordinary effort of will on Roger's part suddenly to become a man of the world in the accepted sense of the term.

That transformation accompanied a new and entirely unexpected way of life.

Roger dragged me to fashionable cabarets, passed in review the season's new plays, even strayed into dance halls.

Poor Roger! That new twist to his ideas ought to have delighted me, but it caused me an unbearable malaise. Without any great effort, I guessed why he was so determined to strip away his old self. Oh, he didn't confide in me—what tact, what scrupulousness he put into never mentioning his amour!

However, a few days before the end of the year, his almost grim reserve gave way to an impulsive desire, prompted by an unexpected occurrence.

Since dinner, Roger had seemed to me to be nervous, very distant from the conversation. Once or twice, he began to say something, and then stopped. Then, as we were going to our rooms, he abruptly retained me by the arm.

"Listen to me, Paul. I'm haunted by a project. In advance, I beg you not to turn me away from it. You've been able to observe with what discretion I've conducted myself with regard to Hélène Thiérard-Leroy." He had returned her maiden name to his beloved! "During her mourning, I've never sought to see her, to place myself in her path. And yet, I haven't been able to constrain myself to remaining without news of the person to whom I've dedicated me life. I'm made use of Étienne to keep me informed, in order to maintain a link with her, however tenuous."

I made a gesture.

"Oh, don't worry, it's not a matter of any indiscreet investigation, any un-timely step. The child has limited himself observing from a distance. By means of servants' gossip, he's kept up to date with her health and a thousand petty de-tails of her life: trivia for others, very precious things for me.

"Thus, I've learned about a voyage planed by Monsieur Thiérard-Leroy. With the aim of making her forget more surely the great emotions that have as-sailed her, the worthy man is taking his daughter to Biskra until the end of win-ter. He's using the pretext of a slight illness to take her to that marvelous oasis. It's a good opportunity!"

That blind optimism disturbed me. The name of Biskra, associated with illness, evoked before my vision the extreme winter station to which those con-sumptives who can no longer even support the Mediterranean climate are sent as a last resort. And the slender, transparent silhouette of poor little Madame Berjac traversed my memory...

I carefully refrained from communicating such somber apprehensions to my friend.

"So, I thought that we could also go to Biskra…oh, remaining in the shad-ows, I swear to you. I'm sure of myself. I won't risk my happiness by making an untimely move. But to be close to her, to breathe the same air, to love her with-out her suspecting it—what harm do you see in that?"

"None," I murmured. Oh, I didn't reveal my sentiment. What would have been the point? I could see that Roger was only consulting me for form's sake. Nothing in the world could have modified his resolution.

He seemed delighted by my acquiescence.

"We have no more to do than pack our trunks," he concluded. "Thiérard-Leroy is leaving on Saturday. I'll give him a start of one steamer; we'll take the next one. You can see that I'm being reasonable. Is that all right?"

The question was settled.

The next day, Roger was occupied with the preparations for the departure. I had to accompany him to the suppliers and complete a wardrobe for myself as becoming as his own.

355

"You understand," he had said to me. "You need two white flannel suits, and a dinner-jacket—that's indispensable for dinner at the hotel."

"Thumbs up for the dinner jacket."

Fundamentally, I was beginning to lend myself to his childishness.

After having seen everything in black, Roger now perceived everything rose-tinted—but through what a prism of illusions! How was it all going to end?

A new whim of Roger's reawakened my alarm momentarily. Among the numerous items of luggage, I distinguished the two famous cases that had served to transmit the Omega acid and the radium salts to the Camp de Châlons.

"What!" I exclaimed. "You're taking that dangerous paraphernalia to Biskra!"

He looked at me, smiling. "La la! You're not going to get excited about a few decigrams of radium and the bottle of acid that I have to hand? Out there, on the burning threshold of the desert, I can doubtless determine certain details that will be useful later."

"You intend to work, then?"

"No. Is it necessary to repeat to you that I've too many things in my head and I my heart to abandon myself to any serious work. I don't call work the two or three meteorological observations that I'll have the leisure to make in excellent conditions."

Truly, without ill grace, I no longer had the right to suspect my friend's intentions. Wasn't the presence of the young window the best guarantee henceforth against a possible reawakening of the chemist's frightful designs?

A few remarks exchanged with Étienne enabled me to glimpse how precarious that guarantee was.

It was the day of the departure of Monsieur Thiérard-Leroy and his daughter. Roger had insisted on dispatching his young factotum as a scout. Under the pretext of preparing for our installation in Biskra, Tourte was going to accompany the voyagers, in the shadows.

Needless to say, the most important part of his mission consisted of sending dispatches bearing news at the principal stages of the journey.

Faithful to his discretion, Roger did not want to appear. He charged me with embarking the boy at the Gare de Lyon.

While the car was going through Paris, I was struck by the child's sad expression.

"You're not looking forward to making a magnificent voyage?" I asked.

He shook his head. "No, Monsieur Paul. And now I can tell you why..."

He recounted the story of his petty intrigue, which I knew already by virtue of Roger's confidence.

"I'm afraid," he added, "because I think that Madame Berjac is very ill. A bad influenza."

Ah! My presentiments!

Four days later, Livry and I departed in our turn. Roger had the appearance and the manner of a happy man. The telegrams sent by Tourte said that the Thiérard-Leroys had arrived safely after an excellent crossing.

With a fine confidence, Roger, the implacable and terrible scientist, the Man of the Apocalypse, set forth on the road to happiness.

Personally, I had a heart bruised by an indefinable sadness. I was still assailed by the most somber presentiments.

Those presentiments crystallized in Marseilles, in the most frightful and unexpected form.

While traversing the great city to go to the boarding jetty of the transatlantic liners, we had the impression of a city in turmoil. The crowd was agitated by the frisson of anguish characteristic of great misfortunes. On the streets people were snatching the newspapers. In the tumult of overlapping cries, over the racket of the autobus rolling over the cobblestones, we could not discern the words being howled by the newsvendors.

"What's happened, then?" Roger asked, when we arrived at the port.

"What! Monsieur doesn't know?" said the loquacious southerner to whom my friend had addressed himself. "Alas, the news arrives more rapidly in Marseilles than in Paris, especially when it comes from Messina."

"Messina!" I exclaimed, seized by an emotion and a reminiscence.

"Terrible, Monsieur, terrible! Worse than in Japan... There's been an earthquake. There's no more left of Messina than a handful..."

A hasty reading of the first dispatches convinced us of the extent of the terrible disaster. And among the confusion of news transcribed as telegrams arrived and precipitate special editions were published, Roger indicated to me with a thrust of his fingernail a small item found in the *Petit Provençal*:

A bizarre prophecy

A few days before the catastrophe, the Crown Prosecutor received a strange letter sent by a certain Jobert, a French subject. Wanted for a crime committed in Paris, the individual had been arrested by the Sicilian police, and had then succeeded in escaping from the municipal prison.

In his letter to the magistrate, this Jobert, who is believed to be an anarchist madman, complained of various denials of justice committed in his regard, demanded the immediate restitution of papers and notes seized from him, and the cessation of the pursuits instituted.

If these conditions were not accepted and fulfilled, he threatened to destroy Messina from top to bottom before the end of the week.

"He's kept his word!" pronounced the chemist, with a troubling gravity.

"What! You judge the wretch capable of having unleashed such a catastrophe!" I exclaimed, fearfully.

"He had the means to do it, given the subsoil of the north-eastern tip of Sicily, disrupted by a series of anterior catastrophes: volcanic eruptions, earthquakes…a chaos of rocks in unstable equilibrium. I only hope that this time, Jobert has exhausted his supply of acid, or that he's perished." Then, in a tine of determination: "No matter! I'll clarify the matter. I want to know whether the man is dead or alive!"

Seeing me distressed, shivering with horror, he made an effort to chase away an importunate thought, perhaps of remorse. In a casual, almost scolding tone, he added: "What do you expect, my friend? It's a great misfortune, but any progress is costly. As soon as I'm a billionaire, I'll help to reconstruct Messina. But in the midst of all this, let's not miss our boat!"

XI. The Death's-Head

We are in Biskra.

About the first part of our journey, I shall say nothing. It only left me with vague and painful impressions. The terrible events in Messina had plunged me into a dire state of mind. Pitiless sea sickness accentuated those evil dispositions by keeping me bed-ridden in my cabin from the emergence from Marseilles to the landing in Philippeville.

Then there was a frightful day of jolts on the railway across a sullen landscape beneath a soot-black sky. That gray weather, which lent the high Algerian plateaux the aspect of the black plains of Artois, minus the towns, was worth the magic of a marvelous contrast when the train crossed the threshold of El Kantara.

Through the breach pierced in the somber rocks the golden vision of the sun-bathed desert appeared to our dazzled eyes, revealing palm trees and the gardens of the celestial paradise.

An hour later, our enchantment came to an end. Biskra offered itself to us, in its whiteness and its verdure.

Étienne was waiting for us at the station.

Roger's first words were to enquire about the Thiérard-Leroys. With a joyful animation, the child hastened to satisfy his master's anxious curiosity. The astronomer and his daughter were installed at the *Villa el Blod*—the White Villa—rented for the season; the young woman did not appear to have suffered from the fatigues of the journey. She spent long hours in her garden; she went out in her carriage.

"She's better, much better!" little Étienne whispered in my ear.

Good! The reassuring news was only designed to soothe Roger's confidence, about which I had begun to be slightly anxious. Things were arranging themselves in a better fashion than I had dared to anticipate. For the moment, therefore, there was nothing to do but abandon myself to the fortunate influence that emanated from the marvelous land, to take advantage in mid-December of the delightful temperature of a fine month of June in France.

We allowed Étienne to guide us to the Imperial Hotel.

It was an immense caravanserai responding to the uniform model that luxury hotels offer to well-off travelers everywhere.

With his habitual intelligence, our little courier had been able to choose a most agreeable apartment for us. Our bedrooms overlooked the palm trees of the oasis, with an extended view over the immensity of the desert. Another room destined to serve as a drawing room and study overlooked a gallery with arcades, beyond which was a Moorish courtyard paved with mosaics, ornamented with spurting fountains and orange-trees in tubs. It formed a delightful décor.

It is nearly seven o'clock. We dress for dinner; we are both inaugurating our dinner-jackets. I cannot help smiling on seeing us decked out as snobs when the immense mirror on one of the monumental lands reflects our image.

We penetrate into the vast dining-room: white tablecloths, flowers and green plants everywhere; crystal scintillating under the caress of the light. Waiters with felted footsteps circulate silently, like black phantoms, crossing one another's paths, avoiding one another, hastening in a perpetual farandole. In a corner, "lautars," or imitations thereof, their rounded torsos stuffed into embroidered jackets are picking out more-or-less Rumanian rhapsodies.

The diners are various: a few young women in bright pretty dresses, a few angular old women; the men are unobtrusive, dissolved in the same uniform blackness. How much I prefer the frame and public of our Parisian restaurants to that conventional luxury, those sad, extinct people with faces like those in a wax museum.

But what's the point in quibbling? All in all, the milieu isn't unpleasant. Everything invites me to live and let live, to chase away preoccupations and bad memories. I have only to take my inspiration from Roger, who seems to be enjoying his new existence with the amused astonishment and happy insouciance of a child.

Already he has chosen a table near a glazed bay window.

"That's Monsieur Barnett's table," remarks a maître-d'hôtel, in a tone that says a great deal about the importance he accords to that individual. Then, with an obsequious smile: "Here...the next table is free; the Messieurs will be very comfortable here."

We sit down. Soon, the Barnett in question, our neighbor, arrives. His advent suspends conversations and the sound of forks. There is good reason; never has such a strange spectacle been offered to my eyes.

Barnett certainly "makes an entrance," as the phrase is understood in the circus.

First, him: a skeleton in a black suit. Impossible to trace a more exact portrait of his ensemble. Oh, that frightful head with the bald cranium and the glabrous face, the ivory-tinted skin stuck to the bones; those frightfully hollow orbits, in which glaucous eye glimmer, immobile and expressionless; and those bloodless lips, drawn back to expose a double row of excessively white teeth. Then, to complete the hideous effect, a thin nose with hints of violet, which, seen from a certain angle, designs a hole in the wan face.

A death's-head!

Slightly behind that macabre individual comes a little man with an olive complexion and a face like a ferret, certainly a half-breed. Finally, closing the march, a negro of colossal stature with a horrible bestial visage, covered in scars.

The negro is wearing a somber livery overladen with silver ornaments, the outfit of a undertaker in full regalia. And, a contrast between the hideous and the pretty, his huge black paws are respectfully holding a rose-wood tray surmounted by a perch, on which are set two ravishing hummingbirds, two living jewels.

Open-mouthed, we watched that incoherent stage-setting. The continuation of the performance was to reserve further astonishments.

Barnett sat down in front of the only place-setting. Opposite him, the negro placed the perch, and then remained frozen a pace behind it, in the attitude of a vast, well-trained valet.

The half-breed took up a position to the right of the birds; from a leather case he took out a kind of little metal trough, perhaps silver-plated. He placed that bird-table accessory in front of the little creatures, and the hummingbirds set about pecking the minuscule seeds contained in the trough. Sometime, the attentive half-breed helped them by lifting a delicate ivory spatula to their beaks. With an imperturbable gravity, Barnet took his meal in parallel with that of the birds, while addressing gracious and encouraging words to them.

After a long moment of stupor, Roger and I ended up smiling at one another with our eyes. Then hypotheses flowed between us in whispers:

"A conjurer."

"A necromancer."

"A lion-tamer who's going to give a performance at the hotel,"

"A hypnotist."

We were mistaken. Barnett was none of those. After dinner, Étienne, who had been invited by Livry to take coffee in the hall in our company, revealed the quality of the extraordinary individual.

Barnett was simply a rich American, and an utter eccentric. After having been a master of the strange and redoubtable sect of the Ku Klux Klan, he belonged, it appeared, to one of the "suicide clubs" that exist in the United States. At dates fixed by solemn engagements the members of those associations have to pass over to the afterlife by the most expedient means.

Oh, Franklin, Grant and Washington, what would you have said if someone had told you that some of your descendants would sink into such morbid extravagances?

Barnett still had a year to go before the supreme date. He was employing that period of grace traveling in the company of the only two beings for which he experienced a human sentiment, his birds.

He possessed about two hundred birds belonging to the rarest and most magnificent species in the New World. That winged population occupied three-quarters of the ten-room apartment retained for the season at the Imperial Hotel. With the aid of trellis, the rooms had been transformed into aviaries. Three people were attached to that little society: an avian veterinarian—the half-breed we had seen during diner—and two negroes. Every day, at the whim of his fantasy, Barnett "invited" some of his pretty boarders to dinner. That evening, it had been the turn of the hummingbirds.

"What a crackpot!" I exclaimed, shrugging my shoulders

"Bah!" said Roger, with a serene indulgence. "Everyone's free. At least that one's not harming anyone."

And by a natural association of ideas, he returned to the other madman, the criminal and terrible madman. "Oh, I was thinking about Jobert. I think I've found a surer means than police searches of laying a hand on him." He took a piece of paper out of his pocket. "Look, read this advertisement that I intend to place in the most widespread newspapers. Tell me what you think."

I scanned the paper, on which was inscribed:

Monsieur Jobert may address himself in all confidence to Roger Livry. In the interests of science, Monsieur Livry will forget the past and invite his ex-assistant to reach an understanding with him.

"You're making a pact with that murderer, then?" I exclaimed.

Roger smiled. "There you go with your fine words. Above all, I want to be practical, and render Jobert harmless, by taking away his teeth.

"How?"

"By making him a proposition: either I'll buy the acid and the radium he stole at a price fixed by him, if he has any left, or I'll offer to let him work with me."

"With you? Père Philippe's murderer!"

"First of all, Philippe is out of danger; when he comes out of hospital in a few days' time I'll ensure him an income."

"But Jobert's a dangerous madman!"

"In that case, isn't it preferable to have him close at hand? You see, I intend to settle that matter before Mademoiselle Thiérard-Leroy becomes my wife. My responsibility is engaged, after all!"

Apart from that alarming confidence in the conclusion of his matrimonial projects, Roger seemed to the reasoning accurately; on analysis, his idea was perfectly defensible.

"Place your ad, then," I ended up saying. "We'll see whether Jobert reveals himself."

Glad to have convinced me, Roger took me out of the hotel,

"This magnificent might invites a stroll," he said. "Étienne can show us where the White Villa is." And, rapidly, to take away a suspicion that was already pricking me: "Oh, understand me clearly. If I want to know where she's living, it's to be sheltered from any involuntary indiscretion." In a lower voice, he pronounced, religiously: "For the moment, it's sufficient for me to breathe the air she breathes, the air charged with delightful scents."

Roger, the cold calculator, turned to lyricism: I couldn't help admiring the touching sincerity of the passion that guided him, and also the perfect delicacy with which it constrained his conduct.

So, that evening, we only saw from a distance the clump of palms and orange trees behind which the White Villa was sheltered. Roger resisted the desire, innocent I sum, to approach the wall. It was like a sacred terrain on to which he, being profane, could not stray without offending the divine creature who had captured his soul.

After a mute contemplation, during which his poor heart must have been singing a love song, my comrade took me back to the hotel.

In the hall, we encountered the macabre appearance of Barnett again.

The American is lying back in a rocking chair. In front of him there is a table laden with partly-emptied bottles. The ugly fellow isn't on a diet of orange-blossom water. He has fled the rigors of "dry" America, and is pouring himself draughts of whisky, which he mixes with champagne.

As we pass by, he makes an effort to salute us, and even to smile. Oh, that death's-head rictus! It's enough to give one nightmares.

Roger bows courteously; in the phase through which he is passing, he can draw upon immense indulgence for people and things. Personally, I only lift my fingers to the brim of my hat. I find him repulsive, that alcoholic with his counterfeit eccentricity. Our idlers ought to react once and for all against the blissful admiration of these Anglo-Saxon so-called eccentricities. On tracing them back to their source, one invariably finds a cerebral breakdown caused by the abuse of strong liquors.

And our friends from England and America enabled us to know, in the course of the Great War, real men veritably worthy of our admiration.

At any rate. I'd like to see that skeletal individual a hundred leagues from Biskra. Is that a presentiment? Barnett doesn't only cause me a disagreeable impression, he scares me!

XII. The Idyll Begins

What had to happen, has happened!

A fortnight ago, Roger entered into relations with the Thiérard-Leroys, and I needed that entire fortnight to determine the exact impression that the unexpected *coup-de-théâtre* made on me.

Unexpected? On reflection, I might, on the country, have calculated the probability of an encounter in a social circle as narrow as Biskra's as a virtual certainty.

It occurred, inevitably, at an intersection of two narrow streets in Old Biskra.

We had gone as far as that agglomeration of clay houses and walls of dry mud enclosing garden of palm trees a few kilometers from Biskra, to which tourists go in search of a sensation exactly similar, so the colonials say, to a village in the Sudan.

We were following one of the alleyways, where the high cob walls are prolonged by the branches of palm trees overhanging the enclosures. Thus are formed shady, profound and silent corridors full of mystery.

Suddenly, in a patch of light that was plastered on the ground by virtue of an intersection, a few paces away from us, I saw the astronomer Thiérard-Leroy and his daughter appear.

We had to back up against the wall to allow the young woman to pass, leaning on her father's arm. I experienced a horrible embarrassment. As for Roger, he was as pale as a corpse.

By virtue of an instinctive propriety, we saluted. With a mechanical gesture, the old man returned our salute; his eyes were vague and dolorous, doubtless fixed on distant preoccupations.

Madame Berjac looked directly at us, with a tranquil and gracious assurance. On discovering Roger, however, she experienced a shock. A pink tint appeared in her cheeks. She leaned more forcefully on her father's arm. Then, after having passed by, white and frail, she turned to look back.

And I saw that she was speaking animatedly to the old man.

Roger continued to lean back on the earthen wall, doubtless in order not to fall. Taking him gently by the arm, I led him away.

"My God, how I love her!" he murmured, in a breath. "How beautiful she is!"

Yes, more than beautiful, touching. She appeared to me as Dante's imagination invoked the shade of Beatrice walking amid the flowers of eternal gardens.

I drew my comrade outside the checkerboard of shadows, into the dazzling light of the sun.

We were getting ready to walk slowly in the direction of Biskra, when a slightly quavering voice behind us made itself heard.

"Pardon me, Messieurs..."

We turned round, and found ourselves face to face with Monsieur Thiérard-Leroy.

"You will excuse, Monsieur, a step that is doubtless inconsequent, when you know that it is dictated by an invalid who is very dear to me, my daughter."

"Cover yourself, Monsieur," said my friend, with profound deference, perceiving that the old man had remained bare-headed. "The sun..."

"The sun scarcely shines for me," replied the astronomer, with a sad smile.. He replaced his broad-brimmed panama. "I was saying that my daughter, Madame Berjac, doubtless under the suggestion of an invalid's illusion, thought she recognized in you a person who had saved her life last summer at the Camp de Châlons. She will continue to be eaten away by anxiety so long as she does not know for sure that her memories are playing her false." And in a more tremulous vice, the father added: "Now, Monsieur, my child's state of health does not permit any preoccupation. That is why you see me before you."

While Monsieur Thiérard-Leroy was pronouncing these words, I was watching Roger, anxiously.

He was biting his lip until it bled. Then he appeared to make an immense effort to regain full possession of himself. He succeeded.

"Monsieur," he said, in a tone of perfect modesty, "Madame your daughter is not mistaken. It was indeed me who, at the Camp de Châlons, last August, made an impulsive gesture, perfectly natural, with the aim of avoiding a serious accident."

The astronomer seized Livry's hands.

"You...you...! The unknown man about who she has spoken to me so often...! Monsieur, will you tell me your name?"

"Roger Livry."

The old man passed his hand over his forehead, searching for a memory; but the light was immediately extinguished. The name of Livry did not recall anything...

I preferred it that way!

He introduced himself in his turn. Then, in an imploring tine, he said: "Monsieur Livry, may I ask you for a favor?"

"Please do."

"I believe...I am sure...that my daughter would like to thank you herself. Excuse me, but I'm trying to do everything possible to help her get better. She has passed through such rude ordeals...that slight satisfaction... She's there, nearby, in our carriage..."

"Your desires and those of Madame your daughter are orders for me. In my turn, I would be very glad to salute her. But Madame Berjac should not exaggerate the gratitude she believes she owes me. At Châlons, I arrived before the others. All my good fortune was there!"

I marveled at my friend's good grace, the tact and the urbanity. At a deliberate pace, he followed Monsieur Thiérard-Leroy. Fifty meters away, behind a cactus hedge, the carriage was waiting.

How can I describe the expression of profound joy that illuminated the pale and charming visage of Madame Berjac when her "savior" was brought to her. In that joy, there was doubtless a little contentment at having divined as accurately, at having rediscovered "the unknown man" floating in her memory like an enigma, sometimes sweet and sometimes irritating. Perhaps there was something more!

The poor child was entering that terrible phase of tuberculosis in which life wants to blossom regardless, hastily, because it senses the threat at short range.

The word "frightful" came to mind. Alas, it was written in her waxen features, engraved in the overly blue veins of her diaphanous hands.

To confirm the lugubrious presages that I had formed since the departure from Paris, there was not even any need for the throaty cough that she tried to stifle in her lace handkerchief.

She was better, it had been said. A very relative better, which ordinarily accompanies the reaction consequent on a change of climate.

At the first glance, I acquired the cruel certainty that, barring a miracle, she was doomed.

As for Roger, during that first introduction, he remained the gallant man, full of reserve and attentiveness, that he had become.

How did he succeed in strangling the devouring passion that was setting him ablaze? Undoubtedly by developing an extraordinary will-power.

How, on the other hand, was he not struck by the mortal pallor spread over the face of the poor creature? Perhaps he had elevated his love into spheres so radiant that his dazzled eyes could no longer discern anything.

But I, who could see, was struck by a tragic horror when Roger said to me, pointing his finger at the cloud of dust raised by the carriage carrying Madame Berjac away: "Oh, my friend, I am so happy!"

I mentioned a miracle.

Is the miracle about to be produced?

For two weeks now, Roger has been an assiduous guest of the White Villa, and Madame Berjac seems visibly reborn. The presence of the "savior" has brought a little joy into that dwelling, which seemed consigned to desolation.

The charming woman chats, is agitated, is clutching on to life again, to hope.

And Roger has such a delicately exquisite fashion of paying court to her!

In his expressions, in his gaze, there is nothing of the misplaced levity of a flirtation. Nor is he playing the role of the tenebrous beau; he has been able to avoid the slightly ridiculous romanticism of the petrified lover. More simply, he has made himself a friend.

Beside the chaise-longue in the garden, where the still-plaintive convalescent is lying, he talks about frivolous or serious things; he is cheerful without extravagance, attentive without insistence. His stories are interesting, and stop in time not to become wearying.

With regard to Monsieur Thiérard-Leroy, Roger exhibits a deference, a modesty and an affability admirable in a scientist of his stripe—for everyone knows that two scientists in one another's presence quickly fall into controversy, which degenerates into dispute.

Here, nothing of the sort! To the slightly incredulous surprise of the director of the Observatoire, Roger offered to help him in his astronomical calculations—for the worthy man has not refrained from installing a telescope on the terrace of his villa in order to search the ever-pure sky at his leisure. And the astronomer's joy equaled his amazement when that unknown of the day before, not content with bringing hope to the soul of his dear invalid, set about resolving the most complicated problems as if they were child's play.

That amazement changed into profound admiration when, little by little, Roger revealed his theories to him, and his work on the Omega acid. A few laboratory experiments effected with the aid of the extraordinary acid ended up convincing the eminent astronomer of the immensity of the discovery.

The old man was so impressed that the following day, he opened up to me. "Oh, Monsieur, Monsieur, what a man your friend is! Once, he saved my daughter. Today, he seems to be restoring her to life as if he were pouring out a mysterious philter. Now, he's in a position—he has proved it to me—to revolutionize the face of the world."

He took his head in his hands. "You see, by virtue of living in the commerce of the stars, by virtue of scrutinizing Infinity, one becomes something of a visionary, and one acquire the soul of a mage. Now, your comrade causes me to marvel and frightens me by turns. I see in him an angel descended from Heaven, a supernatural being incarnating formidable forces unknown to our humanity. My God, may he protect my daughter!"

I calmed the old scientist's excitement by means of conventional words; I carefully refrained from identifying the terrible antecedents of the "angel." What was the point, now that "the Man of the Apocalypse" had become a man like others?

At the present moment, Roger was showing himself to be the absolute master of his will and his common sense.

I arrived at the conclusion that Roger had been subject last summer of a temporary crisis, of which no symptoms any longer subsisted. The cure might therefore be considered radical and definitive.

After that, nothing more remained for me to do but to associate myself wholeheartedly with my excellent friend's future projects, to sustain his joy and his confidence.

There is only one cloud on the horizon—decidedly, I shall never succeed in chasing them all away! Roger has made the acquaintance of the frightful Barnett.

The first contact was made by virtue of an absurd wager that we had unwittingly caused the American to lose. The maniac has an obsession with betting on anything, every time he encounters people stupid enough to take up his incoherent challenges. And he finds them! When he doesn't find them, he falls back, it seems, on his domestic and his bird doctor.

In brief, the third evening after our arrival, when we were at table, the Death's-Head approached us, and without any preamble, said: "I owe a thousand dollars, Messieurs."

Astonished, we waited for him to explain himself.

"I owe a thousand dollars, exactly—you've made me lose them."

What was he saying? I suspected that he was drunk.

"I owe a thousand dollars," the fellow repeated, for the third time, "because I bet the maître-d'hôtel that no traveler would consent to remain my neighbor for more than five meals…and I'm paying for it. The sixth meal is commencing now, and here you are. I've lost the bet. Thank you, Messieurs."

And, bowing with all the grace of which he was capable, he went back to his place.

"He's amusing!" Roger declared.

"You think so? Personally, I have a horror of drunkards."

He smiled indulgently.

"How severe you are! Perhaps the poor fellow is drowning in alcohol the chagrin he has at being so ugly."

In the meantime, whether I liked it or not, it was necessary for me to suffer the salutations and smiles of the Death's-Head, and exchange polite banalities with him. But when Roger was already an assiduous guest at the White Villa, a circumstance placed him in a more intimate relation with the American.

One evening, we were admiring the two marvelous hummingbirds that were in service at our strange neighbor's table.

In response to a compliment by my friend, Barnett said: "They please you, and you please me. I give them to you."

"I'll accept with gratitude, if you'll permit me to dispose of them in favor of a lady friend."

"I give them to you," he American repeated.

The next day, the two ravishing little birds drew cries of joy from Madame Berjac.

"Render him this justice," Roger said to me, when we returned to the hotel. "That Barnett, whom you can't abide, isn't a nasty fellow. Personally, I'm thinking of appropriate means to cure him of his suicidal mania."

"Try to stop him drinking," I muttered. "Yesterday evening he was dead drunk again."

"Come on! You're becoming as intractable as a member of the Temperance League. Personally, I'd be sorry if any misfortune overtook that inoffensive eccentric."

No, in spite of all arguments, Barnett remained deeply antipathetic to me; I could not accustom myself to his terrible visage. Unlike Roger, I was not going through a phase of universal tenderness.

367

"After all, you're neither malevolent nor stubborn," Roger conceded. "I've convinced you with regard to Jobert; in the end, I'll destroy your prejudices with regard to Barnett…"

How sensitive I still was, deep down! The name of the former laboratory assistant, dropped into the conversation, renewed my malaise.

At that moment, in any case, the inventor of the Omega acid was not thinking very much about Jobert. He was no longer living for anything but his amour. Losing sight of the earth, he was allowing himself to be carried away under full sail toward the land of Tendre.[65]

XIII. The Day of Joy

Oh, the beautiful, unforgettable day!

That morning, as was his habit, Roger had been to obtain news of Madame Berjac, a little after the daily visit of the physician.

Before lunch, he came to find me in the garden of the Casino.

"I've seen the doctor!" he shouted from a distance, as soon as he saw me. "He's lifted all detentions; henceforth, Hélène is no longer an invalid, so far as he's concerned, and scarcely a convalescent. He's only going to come twice a week in future. He's authorized tennis, the piano, walks in the town—in brief, all the distractions of which the poor child was deprived.

"From today onwards, she's resuming social life, and to begin with, we're going to the Biskra races."

I could only rejoice with my friend; the physician's indications dissipated my last anxieties. We were both able, therefore, to put our hearts in harmony with the echoes of the festival that as commencing—for in that Saharan city, the races have become a solemnity that agitates the whole of the surrounding desert.

Already, since the morning, the Arab chiefs have been performing caracoles in the city streets, followed by their *goums*. Trains are pouring out travelers coming from Constantine: white burnooses, and the uniforms of zouaves and riflemen are cutting cheerfully through the European crowd.

In the midst of the hubbub we head for lunch. We're dying of hunger.

At table, Livry is as joyful as a schoolboy on vacation. To give Barnett pleasure, he bets him that the first woman who comes into the restaurant will be blonde.

Damn! It's a negress!

With a burst of laughter, he pays his two thousand francs, and for the champagne as well.

---

[65] The reference is to the allegorical *Carte de Tendre* [Map of Tendre, or Tenderness] drawn up by several female hands in 17th century salon society, and printed in Madame de Scudéry's novel *Clélie* (1654-51). It represents the course of an amorous pilgrim's progress to the not-entirely-celestial abode of love.

I allow myself to be carried away by that child-like joy. I feel slightly intoxicated, drunk on intimate contentment, mental quietude and also deliverance. Perhaps egotistically, I think that Roger has no more need of me; soon, I shall be able to go back to my small abode on the Quai des Grands-Augustins, my dear books, my lycée! I can resume my life!

I am allowing myself to float among those sweet thoughts while a landau carries us away toward the White Villa, where we are going to pick up Monsieur Thiérard-Leroy and his daughter.

Madame Berjac appears on the threshold. She is a joy to behold.

The lily has become a rose. Her complexion has lost the waxy hue that squeezed my heart. This time, the blood is flowing beneath the transparency of the skin. The face is fuller, the lips are red, the eyes, finally, have the expression of wellbeing and vivacity that appears to certify a complete return to health.

Our carriage stops at the entrance to the passage. Roger offers his hand to the young woman to help her down, and then his arm, to lead her to the grandstand. They form a handsome couple, at whom everyone looks.

I abandon myself to the intoxication of the spectacle. How far the two of them are from the Biskra racecourse!

The races are over; the multicolored crowd breaks up in an indescribable confusion.

We climb back into the carriage and take the road of return.

But they do not want that first festival of their hearts to end yet.

"Father, what if these Messieurs were to give us the pleasure of dining with us this evening?"

Madame Berjac had uttered that remark with a spontaneous innocence that testified adorably to certain premeditation.

Roger played the worldly comedy of conventional protests, the fear of disturbance, the dread of imposing fatigue on the hostess; in the end, we accepted.

The dinner was all that a charmingly intimate repast can be.

Afterwards, we went on to the veranda to take coffee.

On the insistent plea of her father, Madame Berjac consented to remain in the drawing room; in spite of the mildness of the temperature, the old man was fearful on her behalf of the humidity of the evening.

While we were smoking a cigarette, the young woman sat down at the piano. Quietly, her fingers picked out a delightfully melancholy melody; I recognized a Chopin nocturne.

Roger has stopped talking, and then smoking. Perhaps without being aware of it, he has risen to his feet. He walks toward the drawing room at a somnambulistic pace; the music attracts him, hypnotizes him. Through the partly-open bay window, I see him lean his elbow on the corner of the piano.

Then the melody falls silent. Monsieur Thiérard-Leroy and I remain sunk in our rattan armchairs, contemplating he magnificent night. The astronomer seems happy.

In a low voice, he tells me about the immense, definitive relief that the day that has just gone by has brought him. He confides in me the fears and anguish he has passed through since his friend Destule, the great specialist in maladies of the lungs, had let him know the gravity of his child's condition, advising the voyage to Biskra as a last resort. Then, by way of excuse for the idyll that has been knotted so rapidly—too rapidly for the proprieties of society—he tells me the story of his daughter's marriage to Lieutenant Berjac. It was one of those unions arranged long before by the families, between childhood friends; a last wish expressed by his dead wife, who had died three years ago. Perhaps imprudent, that fashion of uniting two destinies with links formed by the passivity of mind and custom!

In my turn, I sing Roger's praises: his heart of gold. I touch lightly on the magnificent situation of his fortune. Then, on those mutual confidences, we return to the drawing room.

Roger and Hélène are no longer talking; they are holding hands.

They have the superb surprise of pure souls. On our arrival, they do not make a movement to release their clasp; they dispense with blushing and lowering their eyes.

Their two faces are radiant with a calm happiness, forged of certainties

"Come on, Roger," I say, in a tone of affable authority. "It's getting late. It's necessary not to abuse Madame Berjac's amiability."

He smiles benevolently.

"You're right, my Mentor."

With his usual correctness, without insipidity or foolishness, he takes his leave of the young woman.

"Until tomorrow!"

"Until tomorrow…!"

They were never to see one another again on this earth!

XIV. The Day of Woe

Alas, a day of tears was to follow the day of joy.

The next day, Roger was up early. Full of a juvenile ardor, he occupied himself with realizing a desire expressed the day before by Madame Berjac. We went to all the shops looking for equipment for a game of tennis.

It was in vain; the bazaars of Biskra possess many of the knick-knacks typical of Oriental countries—copper vases, carpets, embroidered gauzes and so on—which come directly from Lyon, but to procure tennis equipment, it is necessary to order it from Constantine, or even Algiers.

"That's annoying," said Roger. "Hélène would have been glad to play this afternoon."

"Bah!" I said. "Game postponed for forty-eight hours."

"At least I want to inform her. No disappointment, however slight, ought to be caused to her by me."

"Perfect!" I joked. "You'll be a model husband."

For want of tennis, he ravaged the greenhouses of a horticulturalist to put together a marvelous bouquet of camellias. Then, after having scribbled a few words on a card, shortly before lunch, he charged Étienne with taking the flowers and the note to the White Villa.

A quarter of an hour later, the boy came back. Roger had the impatience common to all those in love.

"Well, did Madame Hélène give you a good welcome? What did she say?"

"I didn't see her. She hasn't come down this morning. She's slightly indisposed."

As was appropriate, I calmed the keen annoyance experienced by my friend. "A little emotion and fatigue. After a day like yesterday, it's necessary to be expect that."

"Yes," Roger conceded. "It's a lesson."

Without allowing anything to show, I was anxious—and Tourte took advantage of a moment when I was alone to whisper some brief news into my ear that turned my anxiety to anguish.

"Oh, Monsieur Paul, it's not good at the Villa. At the end of the night Madame Hélène had a coughing fit. The doctor no longer leaves her..."

During lunch, Livery sought to mask the worry that was devouring him. I perceived it in the volubility of his conversation. He passed from one subject to another without transition, carried away by a flood of words, absent-mindedly, for he made no response to the few questions I asked him. When we left the table we went to the White Villa.

Monsieur Thiérard-Leroy came down to receive us. His head was shaky, his eyes haggard and his voice tremulous.

"Oh, my friends, my friends... She's not well...fever...coughing blood. The doctor doesn't understand it. All day yesterday she seemed so normal! I've telegraphed Algiers and Chanel for a specialist... and also Tunis, where Professor Maggio, the King of Italy's physician, is passing through, it seems. I've begged them to come. Let's hope that it's an alarm without consequence... let's hope!"

The old man held out his arms, with a tormented physiognomy that belied his appeal to hope.

Devastated, we left the Villa.

Until five o'clock Roger wanders around the town, with me by his side. That aimless course procures us the moral interval after which we can, without indecent insistence, return for news.

It is not good. The poor child has fallen unconscious; she has only emerged to fall into an ardent fever.

Roger says nothing, but his mute dolor is grim. Forgetting dinner time, we resume our aimless wandering through the streets that open before our feet. It would be impossible for us to wait at the hotel; walking is a means of expending our nervous energy.

Roger has violent impulses, fits of tension that recall the bad days of the last year. Sometimes, large tears emerge from beneath his eyelids. By the exasperation of his self-regard, however, he masters the despair that is gripping him.

Several times, I hear him murmur: "No, it's impossible...it can't be...I don't want it."

Twice more in the evening, at nine o'clock and midnight, we return to the Villa. Each time, on crossing the threshold, an indescribable anguish grips me, so keenly do I sense disaster suspended overhead.

If it were to fall...!

It does not. Madame Berjac is torpid, the fever having retreated before injections of quinine. That prostration, following the crisis, does not tell me anything worthwhile.

Roger has refused to go back to the hotel. He wants to sit on the edge of a ditch close to the White Villa.

With his head in his hands, he stays there.

He dreams and he weeps; sometimes, too—and that is more frightful—he laughs.

My God! What am I going to do with the poor fellow if fatality takes its course?

At dawn, he consents to follow me, on the assurance that nothing has changed in the young woman's condition.

Nothing has changed, except that she is growing weaker hour by hour, according to what Étienne reports, having remained in the servants' parlor at the Villa. But I don't add that detail.

The two practitioners summoned by Monsieur Thiérard-Leroy arrive that afternoon by the four o'clock train. Immediately, we run to the Villa.

In the drawing room, where the presence of the woman he loves floats everywhere, Roger awaits the result of the ultimate consultation.

Arms folded and head bowed, he marches back and forth like a beast in a cage.

He approaches the piano where the first oath was exchanged, and recoils, as if stuck in the heart. On the music-stand he has recognized the Chopin nocturne that she played two nights before.

He goes back to the door, which stands ajar; he recoils again, seized in the throat by the odor, insipid and bitter at the same time, of ether, camphorated alcohol and creosote: the odor of houses in which someone is dying.

Finally, a noise of footfalls is heard on the stairway.

In silence, the physicians descend, followed by Monsieur Thiérard-Leroy, who accompanies them to the door.

From where we are we witness a terrible mime, far more expressive than words. The doctors shake the father's hand effusively; they keep their eyes lowered, inclining their science before that heart-rending dolor.

They have gone, and the astronomer is still there, collapsed on the bench. He is sobbing convulsively. It is frightful to contemplate the affliction of that old man, weeping like a child.

It is necessary for us to approach, however. I take Roger by the arm and push him toward the vestibule.

Our presence stems the excess of tears. Monsieur Thiérard-Leroy shakes his head, and in a distant voice, murmurs as if speaking aside: "My dear child… a few more hours and it will be all over… a rapidly progressing pneumonia… she's just entered her death-throes."

And addressing Roger, he raises his voice, enclosing in his cry a rage, a blasphemy and a reproach: "And to think that nothing… no one can save her… not even God… not even you!"

Then, exhausted by that effort of violence, in a tone suddenly softened: "She loved you. Before losing consciousness, she wanted your flowers by her bed, close at hand. Do you want to see her?"

"No!"

Roger's exclamation emerges hoarse and brutal, and also heart-rending.

And without saluting the desolate father, without a word of condolence, he flees outside.

I addressed to the astronomer a gesture and a gaze that implored forgiveness and pity in favor of the distraught, and, quitting the lugubrious villa in my turn, I threw myself on Livry's trail.

I caught up with him at the hotel.

He had locked himself in his room, next to mine. Through the door, I heard the whistle of his labored respiration, and also the scratching of his pen running over the paper. Feverishly, he was writing letters.

I had the fearful thought that he was drawing up his last will, that he had formed the project this time of ending his existence. One fact reassured me: he did not have any weapon to hand, no razor, nothing that could procure him an immediate means of attempting to kill himself.

Close to the partition, I therefore remained on watch, prostrate in an armchair.

It was seven o'clock when there was a light tapping at my door.

I went to open it.

Little Tourte appeared before me, his eyes full of tears.

For a long moment, the child stood there without articulating a word, the sobs stuck in his throat. Finally, he stammered: "She's dead!"

I put a finger over my lips, designating Roger's room with a glance.

"Yes, Monsieur Paul, but… it's still necessary that he knows. Then, what will he do?"

Ah! I put off until later the examination of that terrible question. In my head, too, the ideas were clouded.

I threw myself back into my armchair and wept recklessly, all the tears I had. I wept for the poor little flower, scythed down, I wept for Livry and I wept for myself...

My chagrin was interrupted by the abrupt opening of the communicating door.

My friend was before me. His icy calm and his livid pallor seemed terrible to me. I thought my eyes were deceiving me... but no... he had put on his dinner-jacket!

He looked at me with an indefinable expression in which I read anger and scorn, and then said, in a curt voice: "You're weeping? What are you waiting for to get dressed? The dinner bell has rung."

Was I hearing correctly? Roger intended to go to dinner, in the glare of lights and flowers, to the music of violins, when nearby, his beloved, rigid on a white bed...

In spite of all the self-control that I had promised myself to maintain, I could not master a revolt.

"You're talking about dinner downstairs with everyone...but you don't know..."

He interrupted me with a furious snigger.

"Yes, I know... I knew before you. She died at exactly five-forty. At that precise moment, my heart burst, my terrestrial life stopped there. Imbeciles will tell you that it's telepathy—the donkeys! They know nothing but words... But if I no longer have a heart, I still have a stomach. For a little while, at least, I shall be obliged to satisfy it... This evening, I'm hungry!"

Those clashing words caused me to shudder. They opened my eyes to the verity that I had been simple enough, culpable enough, to cover up. Roger had never ceased to be mad.

For a few months the dementia had simply been dormant, manifest in another form. It still existed, and today, by virtue of a frightful shock, it had awoken again, more violently, like a volcano returning to activity after a long repose.

I knew what Roger, insane, was capable of doing. Fortunately, I had taken my precautions. His reign of terror was over.

Now, the Man of the Apocalypse gave way to a poor lunatic, neither more nor less dangerous than all the others, and worthy of an immense pity.

Unfortunate Roger, my pity would not fail him! But for the moment, my head and my heart were reeling. I did not feel strong enough to follow him to the restaurant.

"Excuse me this evening," I said to him, in a plaintive tone. "I have an atrocious headache."

"As you wish!"

With that brief remark, Roger left.

For some time afterwards, I remained slumped in my armchair.

Then, suddenly, the sentiment of a duty to fulfill brought me to my feet. It seemed to me to be appropriate to take my condolences to the old man who was weeping out there all alone. Similarly, it was a charity to put myself at his disposition in the cruel circumstances. Roger had the excuse of his madness. I had none.

I went downstairs in order to go to the White Villa. As I went past the restaurant I cast a glance through the windows. It was to collect a painful impression. Roger was finishing dinner at Barnett's table. The two men were exchanging words with an animation full of enthusiasm.

I fled.

At the sad house I fund Monsieur Thiérard-Leroy in conference with a man clad in black, who bore on his face the stereotyped conventional grief of undertakers.

Once, through tears, I had seen those faces gliding around me when my poor mother died.

As soon as he is free the astronomer comes toward me, his hands extended.

"Thank you, thank you! It's good of you…and Monsieur Livry?"

I represent my comrade devastated by such grief that he is under the threat of going mad, in no condition to accompany me. A pious lie!

"Poor fellow!" murmurs the old man, his shoulders drooping, crushed by his immense unhappiness. An in a soft, almost tender voice, he murmurs: "Would you like to see her?"

There are cruelties that one cannot avoid.

I see her again, the poor and charming creature. A further metamorphosis; the rose has become a lily again, a lily so white, so pure, that I fall to my knees. In smiling expression fixed by death, she seems to be asleep. Between her knotted hands, Roger Livry's bouquet of camellias has been disposed. Oh, those smiling lips, which will be veiled by a shroud tomorrow!

I withdrew, my head empty of sensation, my body exhausted as if in the wake of an immense effort. Like the dim-witted oxen that, abandoned to themselves, return to their stable, I found myself back on the threshold of the Imperial Hotel.

As I penetrated into the hall, though, I was offended by an unexpected, terrible and odious spectacle: Roger, his face illuminated and his voice loud, swilling champagne in the company of Barnett.

He perceived me, ran toward me, and, shoving me by the shoulders with a violence and a force that only hysterics, in their crises, possess, he said: "You're just in time…we're having a good laugh!"

And the other, the frightful Barnett, takes up the theme in his transatlantic jargon: "All right! No more perfectly joyful fellow than Master Livry! He's just bet me a million of your money that within a week, there'll be frost in Biskra!"

"A million!" I exclaimed, almost in spite of myself.

"Yes!" And with the insolent pride of those Americans parvenus, he added: "Oh, I could get more."

Imagine! Barnett of Cleveland, "worth" fifty million dollars!

The horrible individual uttered a demonic snigger, with which Roger mingled his strident laughter.

Between the two men I remained inert, enervated, impotent.

Then, Roger questions me in his turn: "You're not drinking?" And, as if traversed by a glimmer of light: "Oh...I get it...the dead woman. Do as I do, damn it—I'm not weeping!" His voice became muted, menacing and prophetic: "We'll give her, I swear to you, a beautiful funeral!"

XV. The Wind of Madness

For a long time, a very long time, I stand on the platform of Biskra railway station, watching the train draw away that is carrying Hélène Berjac's coffin.

Without any pomp and without any fuss, the young victim of pitiless destiny departs northwards, in accordance with her father's wishes. He has refused to display the spectacle of a cortege of mourning to the indifferent curiosity of strangers. How well I understand that! Alone, with a retired general, a comrade and Polytechnique classmate of Monsieur Thiérard-Leroy, I accompanied the old man on the first stage of his calvary.

Livry has not come!

And, my soul drowned in bitterness and sadness, I continue to follow with my eyes the black caterpillar of carriages crawling toward the darker confines of the sunlit plain.

The train has disappeared into the mist blurring the limit of the northern horizon.

I go away. I feel terribly alone and abandoned. This country, which had conquered and charmed me, now appears grim and hostile. How and when will I get out of it? What resolution is stopping Roger?

When I return to the hotel I find him hard at work.

"I'm busy setting up my batteries to win Barnett's million," he murmurs in my ear, in a confidential tone.

No allusion at all to the frightful drama that has just traversed his life: a complete indifference with regard to the last sad chapter that has closed the idyll of the White Villa. I can't hold it against him, any more than his scandalous attitude on the evening of Madame Berjac's death. He is irresponsible, alas, and if a respondent exists in this horrible adventure, it's me

Without appearing to perceive my presence, Roger is pursuing on the terrace manipulations analogous to those I witnessed in the building in Mourmelon. Fortunately, he only has a small quantity of radium at his disposal, too weak, in my opinion, to produce an appreciable result.

The first experiments, however, have proved to me that I ought to be ready for any eventuality. If necessary, I shall remove and hide the photographic baths in which he is mixing his terrible compound.

But in themselves, those suspicions and anxieties dictate my duty. The time has come to make it absolutely impossible for Roger to harm himself and others. Depriving him of the usage of his capital is only a palliative; complete assurance is necessary, and that assurance can only be obtained by the frightful but necessary extremity of his internment.

Is it not, in any case, the sole fashion of giving him the care that he needs?

At that moment, I make the dolorous decision.

Alas, Roger's attitude in the days that follow oblige me to hurry things.

He has lost his discretion as a man of good society. Now, he comes down to dinner in a flannel jacket spotted with acid-stains. Every evening, the poor fellow stays up late in the company of Barnett. The overstimulation of alcohol adding to that of madness might produce a furious crisis at any moment.

I could sense it rumbling, that crisis, in the rare words that my comrade addressed to me, for he now showed himself, with regard to me, suspicious, acerbic and almost coarse. In vain I tried to get him to tell me to whom he had addressed the numerous letters and no less numerous dispatches that he sent every day. With equal futility, I tried to discover the purpose of his frequent excursions. Several times, he instructed me brutally not to accompany him outside, arguing his desire to be alone.

In brief, I felt that he was barely tolerating my presence.

Almost in the same fashion, he began to keep Étienne at a distance. For that reason, the boy could only procure me very obscure information—for example, for several days Roger had a bunch of keys, which were certainly not those of his apartment at the hotel or his luggage. Also, in the course of his mysterious excursions, Roger often met an Arab in rags, who looked like a beggar, with whom he had long conversations.

"Poor Monsieur Roger," the child said, in reporting these incidents to me. "It's time to think of taking him away, or he's going to do something bad."

Yes, it was time.

One last blow came to spur my desire to act without losing any time. For two days, the temperature dropped in proportions absolutely abnormal for the hothouse that Biskra is. The winterers were buttoning their overcoats all the way to the collar, and the ladies were wearing furs to go out. The drop on temperature was explained by snowfalls in the nearby Aurès; there were precedents—but personally, I immediately gave the event its veritable and disquieting significance. The Man of the Apocalypse was on the march! Roger was setting out to win his bet.

Well, no, he wouldn't win it.

That same evening, while the lunatic was helping Barnett to empty bottles of gin and whisky, I went straight to the terrace where I had seen him set out the vats of acid. I was fully determined to remove the dangerous compound, to disperse it, to bury it in some corner of the desert.

But I searched for the containers in vain; they were no longer there.

Roger had certainly transported them outside to a location of which he alone was aware.

I swore that that would be his last experiment, but this time, I needed help. Incontinently, I wrote to the Public Prosecutor of Batna, the administrative center to which Biskra is attached. I explained Roger's case, recounted the lamentable story of his amour, insisted on the clear cerebral breakdown that had been manifest in him since Madame Berjac's death. A false shame prevented me from going to the end, of revealing the terrible and disconcerting things that might happen if Livry remained at liberty.

In addition, I would not have been understood.

By virtue of my own experience, I sensed clearly that ordinary minds were unable to accept such conjectures right away, without revolt. In the very interests of my request, it was better to keep quiet and not risk becoming a madman in the eyes of those I wanted to convince.

When I had finished my letter it was very late; I wanted nevertheless to put it into the box at the station myself.

When I got back, I had to submit to a furious scene on Roger's part.

"Ah, finally, there you are!" he roared, as soon as he heard me go into my room. Almost brutally, he dragged me into his, and stood before me, his features contracted, his gaze hostile.

"Look! Can you explain this letter that I've received from my stockbroker?"

He threw the piece of paper in my face rather than handing it to me.

I scanned the missive rapidly.

In substance, the stockbroker informed Livry that it was impossible for him to realize the six millions in cash demanded urgently, for the good reason that all his clients movable assets had been transformed into bonds with a long expiry date.

It had been necessary to expect that coup-de-théâtre one day or another, but it had arrived at a particularly deplorable moment.

Roger exploded. "So that's how you take care of my interests! By doing the opposite of my instructions and my desires!"

"Calm down, Roger," I replied, determined to weather the storm. "You knew in advance that I'm not a businessman. I did my best."

He threatened me with his fist, at the paroxysm of his fury. "You're lying! You're lying! You couldn't be unaware that I needed funds disposable at the end of February to pay for the delivery of fifty grams of radium. Your operations should have been limited to collecting that money. Instead of that you've lent yourself to I don't know what swindles..."

"Oh, Roger!"

The insult appeared to me to be so abominable, even in the mouth of a demented individual, that I did not have the strength to submit to it without protest.

Insensible to the cry of my offended soul, however, the poor fellow continued, with an atrocious snigger: "Of course! I can see your game clearly! You wanted to stop my arm, raised to accomplish an act of justice, an act of reason, an act of regeneration. You've attempted to preserve the rotten world, because you were afraid for yourself. Yes, afraid, afraid, afraid..."

He marched toward me, his arm raised, his eyes bulging. For a moment, I thought he was about to drive me into a corner, seize me by the throat, and strangle me in a fit of furious madness.

In that moment of anguish I felt so miserable, so bruised, that I almost wished for that frightful end. It would be a conclusion!

But his hoarse breath drew away from my face. He took a step backwards, and, pointing his finger at me, said: "Well, you won't succeed! You can do what you like, I shall have my radium. And instead of eighty grams, I'll buy the half-kilo that the Krafts of Nordlingen are offering me. Here, look at their letter! And I'll pay cash...

"Then, with the hundred and thirty liters of Omega acid I have, the Earth won't be so heavy!"

Mute with horror, I followed that rising tide of terrible arrogance. But Roger suddenly abandoned his comminatory tone, and with an accent full of bitterness, he expanded in reproaches.

"You have no backbone, little Paul. Instead of remaining my ally, you've taken it into your head to set ambushes for me. What do you expect? I've replaced you in my confidence and my affection. Today, I have other allies, more faithful, who have associated themselves more courageously, without a hidden agenda, with the goal I'm pursuing...

"I forgive you your treason, because the strong are ignorant of vengeance. But henceforth, I no longer know you. Go! You're free!"

His gesture was broader than the walls of the room—his gesture of expulsion.

That was too much.

Dejected, my head bowed, I head for the door. I'm about to reach it when I feel myself seized around the body. At the same time, I hear Roger's voice, imploring: "Paul, Paul... don't go! Don't abandon me!"

I turn round. Even more than the heart-rending timbre of his voice, the dolorous expression of his physiognomy stirs the very depths of my soul.

And the hands retain me.

"You don't see, then, that I'm mad...you don't sense my burning heart, my exploding head...oh, if you knew how I'm suffering!"

With his closed fist, he hammered his forehead.

"There, there, I feel something like a rasp passing back and forth through my brain. It's horrible..."

For a moment, I gazed into his eyes with a profound pity. "Why don't you want to let anyone care for you?" I said to him, in a very soft voice.

He smiled bitterly, and shook his head. "Care for me! My illness is incurable."

"Try anyway…I'll help you with all my might." I put the maximum of persuasive affection into the affirmation.

"What's the point?"

Roger let himself fall into a chair, wearily. In my turn, I had the impression that I was about to render myself the master of my friend, when I heard galloping footsteps in the neighboring corridor, and then a frantic hammering on the door.

"Hey, Master Livry! Gee up! Hurry!"

Without waiting for anyone to open the door, the odious Barnett shoved the batten. He stuck his horrible face through the gap. I had the sensation that behind the death's-head, madness and woe were mounting a triumphant offensive return.

"Hurrah!" the monster continued, his green eyes gleaming like those of an owl. "Hurrah! You've won the million! Outside in the Oasis, the seguias are frozen.[66] Ah, Monsieur friend of the Devil, tomorrow you're going to show me the little device…then I'll give you a check for as many millions as you please for the other affair, the great *chambardement* of the world, as you say in France."

At the first word, Roger had straightened up, his face blossoming. With an expression full of assurance and pride, he looked at me, and his gaze seemed to be saying: *You see!*

Oh yes, again I saw the gulf opening under our feet.

I was going to see many others. That frightful night had not yet tested me enough. After responding to Barnett's vigorous handshake, Roger made a proposition: "No need to wait until tomorrow to show you how I produce the cold. Would you like to see now, Barnett?"

"All right! You're expeditious, worthy of being born American."

"Let's go, then."

"Is it far?"

"A few steps."

"Right! I'll get Jim to follow with a basket of champagne. It's perfectly appropriate to celebrate an event as sensational as the end of the world, in fact!"

"Very true. Get Jim to bring a lantern too." Turning to me, he said, in the most natural tone in the world: "Are you coming with us, Paul?"

Since Barnett's irruption, Roger seemed to have lost the memory of the violent tirade he had just inflicted on me. In the same way, his mind no longer conserved any trace of the moment of sane reason during which my poor friend

---

[66] Author's note: "Seguias are little streams that are contrived in all directions around the feet of the palm trees, the cultivation of which requires irrigation."

had exhaled his dolorous plaint. In his brain on fire, the ideas and impressions were whirling like dead leaves whipped up by a storm wind.

For my part, I was ashamed of having abandoned myself to a momentary weakness. Before the immense peril that Barnett's intervention had just revealed to me, that weakness had become cowardice. Fortunately, Roger had not let me go!

Now we're outside, Roger, Barnett and I. A few paces behind, the negro Jim is following, with a basket full of bottles under his arm.

It's three o'clock in the morning. In spite of my overcoat, buttoned up to the neck, the cold penetrates me.

Where is Roger going to take us?

As soon as he takes the direction of the march, a suspicion invades me and causes me an indefinable malaise. A few paces more and the suspicion is confirmed. Another hundred meters, and it changes into a certainty.

We're outside the White Villa.

XVI. Trinity of Demons

Serenely, Roger has taken a bunch of keys out of his pocket—the keys glimpsed by Étienne. He opens the gate and goes into the garden. We follow him.

For my part, I have the impression that night-prowlers and grave-robbers must have. How powerful my friend's willpower or aberration must be, for him to dare to commit what I, personally, consider to be a sacrilegious violation.

Without slowing down he scales the six steps of the perron, and puts the key in the lock of the vestibule. On entering the house of the dead, instinct makes me remove my hat, as in a tomb.

This time, Roger wouldn't be lying if he accused me of being afraid. In spite of the people surrounding me, I can't rid myself of the grip of that nervous, irrational, stupid fear. It's the "nocturnal terror" classified by physicians, which attacks children neurasthenics, the weak and the expressed. It's the fear of noises and glimmers of light, the imprecise anxiety that evokes the abrupt intrusion of specters and phantoms, the expectation of *something*.

Now, the *something* is there!

Behind one of the doors that opens on to the vestibule—that of the kitchen—I can hear a slight rustling, a barely perceptible friction. Someone is there, moving with infinite precaution. Who can that someone by, if not a shade?

Now the handle of the door is turning, slowly, slowly...

A second, a century, and the door opens...

My blood freezes in my veins.

Through the gap, I white form presents itself, a head advancing with a feline prudence...a head...no, a fabric enveloping the appearance of a head. Can there be a material head within that white specter?

381

"Don't disturb yourself, it's me."

From the passage, Roger has just directed those words at the specter. Then, a ray of lantern-light projected in that direction completes the breaking of the detestable spell. What my unhealthy imagination has mistaken for a phantom is an Arab enveloped in a burnoose, coiffed with a hood that prevents his facial features from being discerned.

In any case, the Arab has stepped back, closing the door again.

Who can that indigene be, chosen by Roger to guard the dead woman's house? Undoubtedly, the one with whom the madman held the long conversations observed by Étienne. But where has Roger found that man of confidence?

Those questions, I pose without having the clarity of mind necessary to fathom them. The chemist is already going upstairs, bringing my thoughts back to the cruel memories that haunt this place.

On the first floor landing, he passes without pausing the door of the room where *she* died.

I breathe!

He continues going up to the door that gives access to the villa's roof-terrace. We set foot on that terrace.

On the concrete, the vats of acid that I saw being prepared are set out.

With a gesture, he indicates them to the American. "There!"

Barnett has the lantern moved closer. He gazes as the pale opaline substance formed by the mixture of the acid and the radium. A joyful grimace appears on his face; he puts out his hand...

"Go on! You're straight, Master Livry, and I'm your servant. I'll write the check..."

But the madman is able to resist that first success.

"One moment! I want your conviction to be entire, absolute. Before accepting your word and your money, I want to give you a tangible proof of the power of my Omega acid."

"The cold's falling on my shoulders; that's sufficient for me."

"No. Cold is felt, it isn't seen. I'm going to show you another application of my product, visible this time, and no less terrifying."

"All right! I'll open my eyes wide."

"Help me to take the basins down, then. You too, Paul, please."

Like Barnett, I obey without knowing what Roger is going to do."

We each take hold of one of the porcelain receptacles by the edges. Trembling, I considered the frightful substance. Apart from a few phosphorescent gleams that are escaping from it, it seems inert; one might have thought it the kind of paste used for making impressions, for low-cost molding.

On reflection, do not gun-cotton, melinite and all the most terrifying destructive agents offered to humankind by modern chemistry offer the same perfectly-inoffensive appearance?

The vague anxiety into which Roger's new determination has cast me at least has the effect of chasing away the specters prowling in my mind. We go back to the ground floor of the lugubrious house.

Having reached the vestibule, Roger knocks on the door that opened before, and the white silhouette appears again.

In a low voice, Roger exchanges a few words with the man in the burnoose. Afterwards he says to me: "Pass me the basin."

I still obey. He takes the object from my hands, hands it to the Arab, and does the same with the receptacle held by Barnett.

"Two will be enough. Let's keep the other two."

In a muffled voice, the Arab has murmured something.

That voice! It seems to me that I've heard it before. An illusion, no doubt. What common point can exist between my memories and that indigene? In any case, all my attention is now attracted by the Arab's maneuvers.

He has just lit a lamp. Then he places an oil-heater on the floor-tiles of the kitchen, lights the wick, and sets a saucepan on top of it. With the aid of a ladle, he transfers the contents of the two vats of acid into the saucepan.

What does this infernal cuisine signify?

"Let's go outside!" says Roger, who has thus far watched the strange preparations in silence.

Now we're in the garden.

The Arab has followed us there, but he stays in the shadows, outside the zone of the radiance projected by the lantern. He is beginning to intrigue me greatly, that individual who persists in hiding beneath the hood of his burnoose.

But Roger places a hand familiarly on Barnett's shoulder, and in a tone pierced by a grim bitterness, he says: "You see this house... well, I condemned it to disappear on the day of my departure from Biskra. To show you my power, I'm going to destroy it immediately...

Inside the house, a kind of sizzling is audible.

"It's starting," said the chemist, becomes more excited. And with the dramatic tone of an evil genie in a fairy tale, he proclaims: "One... two... three... accursed dwelling, return underground!"

That theatrical declamation might seem ridiculous but it sounded terrifying.

At Roger's invocation, a strange phenomenon occurred before our eyes. The white façade of the villa, made of stucco and molded plaster, suddenly vanished in the midst of a cascade of broken glass, and the noise of beams and furniture smashed to pieces.

There was scarcely anything to be seen but a light mist, like vapor rising toward the sky.

Abruptly, I understood. I had just seen a repetition of the terrible destructive process that hazard had delivered to Jobert. Thus had the millstone supports of the doorway of the Fontenay laboratory disappeared; thus had the calcareous foundations supporting the soil of Bouffarik and cemented the volcanic rocks of Messina disappeared.

It was frightening to think that such a power of subversion might fall into human hands—and what hands! Those of madmen.

With his arms, Roger indicated the formless heap of debris that lay on the ground. "Wood, a few bricks, a few bits of metal—not one stone! As soon as the Omega acid boiled, its vapors acted on the chalk like a spark on a powder-keg.

"And now that you've seen Monsieur Barnett, I await your decision."

Without saying a word, the phlegmatic American took out of his pocket a supple red morocco folder containing his check book.

Armed with a fountainpen, he filled in the blanks of the printed forms.

"First, the million of the bet. It's yours." He made as if to detach the check.

Roger stopped him. "No need. Add that million to the two hundred others that you're going to place at the disposal of the Kraft Company of Nordhausen for the first of March."

Barnett does not blink. "Time to cable New York, and the Krafts will be able to withdraw what they indicate from the Bank of Germany."

"I'll take charge of the rest."

Then the terrible man utters a snigger of joy. "I was right just now—you're the Devil."

"No, I'm the Man of the Apocalypse." That was like a roar, in which an exacerbated pride was mingled with an atrocious dolor and a furious overexcitement.

With a feverish movement, Roger takes hold of Barnett's hands and shakes them frenetically. Then, running to the Arab, he seizes him in his turn and draws him toward the Yankee. He unites the hands of the two men.

"Barnett, this is our other companion. We shall be three to work without fear and without weakness on the destruction of abominable terrestrial life.

Instinctively, I had retreated two spaces. I remained the mute, horrified witness of that diabolical pact.

And, the hood of the burnoose finally having been removed, by the faint light of the lantern, I discover the features of the third demon.

That emaciated face, bistre by virtue of being earthen, those eyes illuminated by the gleam of folly, that mouth contracted by a rictus of hate, all belonged to Jobert.

I had before me the murderer and thief of Fontenay, the irresponsible author of the catastrophes of Bouffarik and Messina.

I say "irresponsible" because it was not possible to be mistaken about the advanced degree of mental alienation that was eating the wretch away; it was only necessary to look at him.

And without difficulty, I explained his presence. He had come running in answer to the appeal launched by the advertisements placed by Roger in the newspapers. Hidden under that Arab disguise, he had arrived in Biskra at the very moment when my unfortunate friend was sinking into the crisis unleashed by the death of Madame Berjac.

He arrived in time to complete the frightful trinity of dementia.

Such is the truth that my reason imposes.

At least I have an advantage over Jobert!

As soon as possible, I'll notify the police of the location of the murderer of Fontenay. I'll put an end to his dangerous exploits.

Why not immediately? I'm now invisible, outside the circle of light.

In the crisis of excitement that has taken possession of them, the three madmen seem to have forgotten me. Without attracting their attention, I can reach the extremity of the garden and climb over the low wall that surrounds the villa.

Another step backwards and I can escape.

Involuntarily, however, a spectacle perhaps even more poignant than the collapse of the building nails me to the spot.

Roger brandishes his fist menacingly at the rubble. "Before leaving," he proclaims, "I want to leave nothing behind. Everything here belongs to me... even the memory." And, turning to Jobert: "Bring me the gasoline."

The fake Arab runs toward a shed that contains garden chairs and tools. A few seconds later, he comes back, his shoulders bending under the weight of six cans of gasoline.

"What are you going to do?" asks Barnett.

"Burn the last vestiges."

"Hurrah! A fire of joy!"

"Of joy!" Roger repeats, in a frightening voice. "That's right!"

Followed by Jobert, he runs toward the heap of beams, furniture, fabrics and the debris of household equipment. In order to proceed more rapidly, the two fanatics stave in the gas cans with a hatchet and spread the contents over the rubble.

A light shines, a flame shoots up as high as the treetops. In the blink of an eye, the conflagration is red, crowned by fuliginous smoke.

"Jim! Champagne!" cried Barnett, transported by delight.

The negro takes from his basket some of the enormous bottles knows as jeroboams, which only find grace with the clientele of Anglo-Saxon bars. Illuminated by the red glow of the conflagration, sometimes drowned by swirls of nauseating smoke, the three madmen and the negro gesticulate, sing, shout and drink in turn.

It is a demonic Sabbat, a vision of Hell!

Shivering with fear, I flee; I jump the wall, pursued by Roger's hoarse cry, which rises up like a war cry and drowns out Barnett's hurrahs:

"I am the Man of the Apocalypse!"

385

XVII. Alarm Call

The Marseille express has just passed through Villeneuve-Saint-Georges station with a thunderous din. Another twenty minutes and I shall be in Paris.

Oh, that return voyage lived in fever! It is always thus when one deplores lost time, time that one can never recover.

When I think of those two days, completely wasted, searching for Roger! When dawn broke, after the terrible night in Biskra, my poor friend had disappeared, in company with Barnett and Jobert. A rapid automobile had carried them away toward the coast.

I had an idea that the fugitive would head straight for his villa at Fontenay. That is why, as I approached Paris, my anguish bordered on sharp suffering.

As soon as I arrive, with Étienne, I leap into a taxi.

Finally, we're outside Roger's dwelling. Through the trees, I can see the closed shutters.

Trembling, I press the bell-push. A long wait, a minute, a century...

Obedient to my nerves, I ring again. Dragging footsteps are heard on the gravel; the little door opens cautiously, framing the head of old Philippe.

"Oh, it's you, Monsieur Paul."

"Roger has come back, hasn't he?" On my part, it's more of an affirmative cry than a question.

"Of course! Monsieur came back four days ago."

"Is he alone?"

"Yes."

"What is he doing?"

"That, I can't tell you, as Monsieur arrived at night and sent me to sleep at a hotel. Well, he is the master. This morning, when I came back here, he'd gone again. I only know that a large automobile must have come into the garden—I saw the tracks of its wheels in the gravel."

My anticipations were realized. I went pale.

"Philippe, go fetch a locksmith."

For a start, I was determined to get into the laboratory.

It took a full hour for workmen to reckon with the powerful locks replaced after Jobert's burglary. Guided by Étienne, I ran to the cupboards where Roger kept his provisions of Omega acid. The doors of the cupboards were wide open; the acid was no longer there.

One more confirmation of the impending danger!

One can, it appears now, telephone cities in Germany. Incontinently, I go to the central office at the Bourse. After extreme difficulty and a wait of more than seven hours, I eventually obtain communication with the Kraft Company of Nordhausen.

It's done! The Krafts have delivered the radium, a hundred grams—an enormous, extraordinary quantity that represents almost half of the stock existing in the world. And in the apparatus, the Teutonic accent of Kraft inflates with mocking joy and blissful pride to add that the settlement of forty million dollars has been made in cash, by Mr. Barnett, Monsieur Livry's authorized agent. Since the armistice, no industrialist has completed such a colossal deal..."

I left the Boches to their imbecilic satisfaction.

Oh, yes, they had done a wonderful dead! Thanks to them, humankind would be called upon to defend itself against circumstances that were doubtless unique in the history of the world. It would be far more devastating that the world war and its consequences.

To engage in that extraordinary struggle, it would be necessary to appeal to the united resources of all governments, all social organizations and all individual and collective energies.

Would even that be a sufficient guarantee? Where should the effort be applied? Where should the battle be joined? How could the point of the globe be discovered at which the trinity of monsters, Livry, Jobert and Barnett, intended to install the secret factory of death?

All that, others would determine. My own role was limited to sounding the alarm call.

But would that call be heeded?

Where is the man capable of accepting, coolly, the monstrous idea that the end of the world might be imminent?

That man, I believe I have found: it is Monsieur Thiérard-Leroy. The cruel loss of his only child disposes his soul more fully to envisage the worst eventualities with serenity. Then too, the great scientific worth of the astronomer eliminates any suspicion of folly or trickery. Finally, he knows the essence of Livry's discoveries, and has even determined their extreme consequences. Furthermore, his position as director of the Observatoire gives him the ear of the public powers. He will be heard where a teacher like myself would have every chance of being sent away, or even directed straight to the special infirmary of the remand prison.

My resolution is made; I shall place the fate of the world in the hands of Hélène's Berjac's father—and after that, to the grace of destiny.

The old scientist welcomed me with the affable mildness that is the foundation of his character. In addition, the bond of common dolor favored my bitter confidences.

I told him everything that he still did not know. I insisted particularly on the terrible results of Livry's procedures: the experiment at Mourmelon, confirmed by the experiment at Biskra. Then I revealed the no less troubling aspects of the problem revealed by Jobert: the crimes against humanity affirmed by the days of fear and mourning at Bouffarik and Messina.

The old man listened to me without interrupting. When I had finished, he headed toward a filing cabinet, pulled out a dossier, and brought it to me.

"My dear friend," he said, with a serene gravity, "on the basis of the data furnished by poor Livry, I calculated the effects of the Omega acid for myself; I did not know that these theoretical calculations had been anticipated by experiments." He shook his head. "The Earth is going to traverse a frightful crisis. I can even glimpse the means that might be employed to bring about the catastrophe...oh, this leaves far behind cometary collisions and other imaginative prophecies."

Then, tucking his dossier under his arm, he said: "It's necessary, even so, to seek advice."

We went together to see the President of the Council.

Monsieur Luissant, the head of the Government, was then the Minister of the Interior.

We met the Minister at the exit from a session in the Chambre that had been very stormy. There had, it seemed, been much verbal abuse with regard to a pending conflict between a gamekeeper and a mayor. How miserable those petty village squabbles were going to seem to Monsieur Luissant when he heard the extraordinary revelations that we were bringing him!

And what effect might those threats of total annihilation produce on the mind of that Statesman, still young, loving life for the satisfactions that it accorded him, and those greater still that the future seemed to reserve for the future of his powerful intelligence!

With an impressive coolness, he followed my explanations, corroborated by Monsieur Thiérard-Leroy's; he examined the evidence. After that, he showed the most magnificent kind of courage: that of credence. How many others in his place would have recoiled before the fear of ridicule by refusing to take the terrible prospect seriously?

I can still hear him pronouncing, in is calm but determined voice: "Well, Messieurs, we're going to act. But above all, I demand absolute secrecy from you. Think of the wind of terror, frenzy and dementia that would blow over the world if it knew...

"Against this trio of madmen we shall make use of the weapons given to us by the international entente regarding the anarchists. We shall track them everywhere without weakness, and without false sentimentality. It is no longer merely a matter of protecting a people, a race or a fatherland but humanity entire! This evening, my secret orders will be given, and the Sûreté Générale will commence the search."

With a pale smile he added: "The Sûreté Générale will never have better merited its title, will it?"

In the days that followed, the measures taken by the Government became more precise.

To begin with, Monsieur Thiérard-Leroy and I made a rapid journey to the abandoned house in Mourmelon. It was possible that Roger had passed that way in order to reactivate the acid disposed in the vats, or perhaps to remove the receptacles.

We were mistaken. The vats were found as the chemist had left them after his last trip. He had not returned to Mourmelon.

Our first concern was to bring the dangerous apparatus back to Paris.

Thanks to the indications that Roger had given the astronomer in a moment of expansion, it was possible to dissolve the unknown product that neutralized the Omega acid. The terrible substance became active again. A series of experiments with it could proceed, with which were associated Monsieur d'Arsaumont, the celebrated chemistry professor at the Collège de France and Dr. Manrichoff, the great biologist of the Institut Pasteur.

The President of the Council had judged it possible to share the secret of universal death with such men.

I remember those experiments as if it were yesterday, carried out in great mystery in the garden of the Observatoire and Professor d'Arsaumont's research laboratory behinds the Butte Montmartre.

Two events forgotten today relate to that exciting research: a powerful frost that descended unexpectedly in the middle of March 19** and a collapse of the ground that happened in the Rue Tourlaque in Montmartre and claimed a innocent victim, a poor woman surprised by the collapse of the roadway. To the terror of the three scientists, the vapor of an infinitesimal dose of the Omega acid had provoked the accident; no one apart from us ever knew the veritable cause.

After that, we had a clear comprehension of the role of Jobert, the evil genius of cataclysms, and we determined more exactly Livey's fantastic power.

It was terribly simple. With the quantities of acid and radium at his disposal, in less than three months, the drop in temperature would reach a hundred degrees below zero; another three months, and water vapor would no longer exist on our globe; the cold would be that of space.

It was a fortnight after our first visit that the scientists brought the terrifying results of their experiments to the Minister. I was there. I listened to those men of courage and science examining and rejecting means of preservation, one by one, like useless weapons.

"So," Professor d'Arsaumont summarized, "I can see nothing that can be done to prevent the diffusion of the cold. The action of the Omega acid spreads successively through the molecules of water vapor in the air. Very rapidly, the evaporation of the ocean will be nullified. Every day, the fissure through which the life of the earth is escaping will grow larger. First the oceans will freeze, and then the mountains of ice formed by the seas will flow over the continents. But well before that, all movement will be suspended; houses and stocks of combustibles will soon be impotent to defend humans against the bite of the freeze. The animals will perish first, then the plants. No more drinkable water, no more food. The soil, hardened by the frost, will even refuse to receive the bodies of those who succumb first. The others will follow soon after."

And with the most admirable stoicism, the great scientist added: "After all, the life of the humans who exist today in very little in space and time; if we make a leap of hundred years they will all have disappeared. What we have to preserve is the work of humans, the creation rather than the creature.

"Now, this Livry, holed up in some unknown corner of the globe—a forest, a mountain or a desert island—will suffice for that task of destruction if no one succeeds in stopping him in time."

At that point in the tragic conference, the President of the Council—I can still see him—shrugged his wrestler's shoulders in a movement of desperate impotence.

"We're searching, moving heaven and earth... we haven't found anything yet."

XVIII. Barnett's Hummingbirds

It was true.

Two weeks after the beginning of the search, the problem remained as obscure as it had been on the first day.

Only a few clues had been picked up, and they related to the American Barnett. Thus, it was known that he had embarked at Philippeville on a Spanish steamer. Several people had accompanied him; doubtless Livry and Jobert had been among them, but it had been impossible to establish that with certainty. Then Barnett had been seen in Paris at the Hôtel Majestic at a date that coincided with Roger's appearance at the villa in Fontenay, and the following day in Nordhausen, where the Krafts had placed the enormous consignment of radium in his hands.

Three weeks later the American had arrived in Biarritz in an immense automobile; there, all trace of him was definitively lost. What was certain was that neither Livry nor Jobert had accompanied him in those peregrinations.

Where were they hiding? A mystery!

At any rate, Monsieur Luissant estimated that the ten carboys of Omega acid—Étienne Tourte had given him that number, representing 250 liters, would have had difficulty escaping the investigations of the customs at terrestrial or maritime frontiers. Now, no chemical product of that kind had been identified in the frontier zones, where surveillance is particularly rigorous with respect to liquids. The Minister therefore found himself led to believe that the fatal carboys had not left French territory. That was, however, a theoretical deduction; did not Barnett's enormous fortune give him the means of purchasing a great deal of silence and complicity?

In brief, in spite of the efforts of all the police forces in the world—efforts stimulated by the promise of considerable rewards—nothing had come to dissipate the darkness. And those who knew expected from one day to the next to feel the first wave of cold passing over the Earth, the precursory sign of the terrible cataclysm.

Is it the heroic calm of the scientists surrounding me, or habituation to the terrible? In any case, the idea of the event no longer brings me the same terror.

I wish I could go to sleep one night and not wake up again, since there's nothing more to do.

In the mechanical life that was mine in those weeks of waiting, I could no longer even find the strength to devote myself to any kind of intellectual task. Every day I went either to the Tuileries or the Luxembourg, and mingled with the old rentiers, the retired, warming themselves in the early spring sunshine. Like them, I read the newspapers from the first line to the last—which is to say that my eyes scanned the printed symbols...but my mind was far away.

However!

It as the fourteenth of April in the Tuileries; my poor eyes abruptly pierced the fog through which, a absent reader floating in the unreal, I was scanning the text of my daily.

What news was capable of shaking my unhealthy apathy? Oh, nothing but, at first glance, an item of provincial gossip, one of the silly things that the occasional correspondents of small towns believe themselves to be obliged to send from time to time.

Tarbes, 12 April 19**. The fauna of our picturesque Pyrenean region has just been enriched by a rare species what has so far escaped the attention of naturalists. And when we say "fauna" it might be more appropriate to say "flora." Shepherds grazing their sheep on the edge of the Bois d'Astruc perceived marvelous birds flying through the low branches: dwarf birds with plumage iridescent with all the colors of the rainbow. They succeeded in capturing a few. The small birds, sent to Tarbes by courtesy of Monsieur Loubestal, a schoolteacher, were recognized as hummingbirds of the most delightful and purest species. How did these charming guests of the tropical forest been acclimatized to our woods? Such is the palpitating problem offered to the sagacity of the ornithologists of our region...

I uttered a cry, and bounded from my bench, offending the quietude of my placid neighbors.

"Barnett's birds! Barnett's birds!"

Like a leitmotiv I murmur that phrase, nothing more: by itself, it encloses the tyrannical suggestion that has imposed itself on my mind. At the same time, I run like a madman in the direction of the Concorde. I cross the Champs-Élysées and arrive at the Place Beauvau. I go into the Ministry of the Interior. I must have a troubling and bizarre appearance, because the Cabinet usher hesitates to pass on the request for an audience that I scribble in haste. Eventually, without having to wait too long, I am introduced into Monsieur Luissant's presence.

"Why, what is it?" the Minister says, benevolently. At the first glance, he has divined by emotion.

"Barnett's birds... there can be no question that they're Barnett's birds..."

I pass him the newspaper, indicating with my finger the article lost in the miscellaneous news on page three.

"We'll see!"

The Minister has pronounced those words with the serene tone of a man who effuses any hypothesis a priori; doubtless the frequentation of men and things has taught him that the negation of principle and he preconceived idea are the flaws of inferior minds.

In quick succession he demands telephonic communication with the Prefecture of Police in Tarbes, exchanges a few remarks with the director of the Sûreté and then with the Prefect of the Hautes-Pyrénées.

Turning back to me, he says: "No individual answering Barnett's description has been seen in the vicinity of Tarbes. There is a foreigner recently installed in a former Franciscan convent on the Montagne d'Ossat, close to the wood where the hummingbirds were found, but it's a matter of a South American by the name of Manuel Porfirias... so, no sign of the Yankee Barnett."

"Oh, if only I could see for myself!"

"Do that. Go down there, conduct an investigation yourself. To facilitate your actions, I'll attach an inspector from the Sûreté to you." And in a voice of infinite sadness, the Minister concludes: "In the present circumstances, we have a duty not to neglect anything, even mirages.

I depart the same evening, in the company of Étienne Tourte and the agent adjoined to me, a tall, modest and sympathetic fellow answering to the name of Martin.

As soon as we arrived in Tarbes we collected some initial information. The Franciscan convent of Ossat, the property of the Peruvian who excited my curiosity, has recently been put up for sale. It was a very old monastery dating from the fourteenth century, with the appearance of a fortified château. It was perched on the summit of the Montagne d'Ossat, an isolated hill four hundred meters high, which stands in the plain of Tarbes five kilometers from the first foothills of the Pyrenees. As for the new owner, according to rumor, he proposes to establish a sanitarium in the large buildings disposed for fresh air cures. Arrived three weeks before with his domestics and his luggage, he had proceeded with an initial summary installation. He had just departed on a journey to bring back the large furniture and other objects destined to complete the accommodation; he was expected that same evening at the Hôtel des Espagnes.

Those details were contrary to the entirely instinctive arguments that had brought me from the other end of France. Before returning to Paris, I wanted at least to follow the vain trail traced by my imagination to its end. Installed at the Hôtel des Espagnes I awaited the arrival of the Peruvian doctor.

He arrived at nightfall in an automobile truck laden with luggage. First, two negroes got down from the vehicle, in the midst of the wide-eyed admiration of the idlers of the sidewalk. My heart beat faster; in one of those negroes I seemed to recognize Jim!

But now the doctor gets down in his turn: a small thin man with stooped shoulders. He advances into the light of the electric bulb suspended above the portal. Then I utter a hoarse exclamation, repeated by Étienne beside me.

In the so-called Peruvian Manuelo Profirias, I have just recognized Barnett's mulatto veterinarian.

A pressure exerted on my arm by the agent Martin recalls me to prudence.

"Let's go," he whispers. "It's necessary that they don't see us."

Half an hour later, we held a meeting at the Prefecture, in which the Prefect, the Public Prosecutor, the Commissaire of Police and the Capitaine of the Gendarmerie take part.

The immediate arrest of the doctor and the negroes was decided.

At nine o'clock in the evening, as they were about to board a train for Bayonne, the mulatto and his two acolytes were apprehended.

At the first interrogation the individuals continued to lie; the mulatto claimed to be named Porfirias, was astonished when mention was made to him of Barnett and birds; he was visibly reciting a lesson learned. But the scene changed when I came into the Prosecutor's office.

At the sight of me, the frightened mulatto told everything he knew. Obedient to Barnett's orders, he had bought the convent of Ossat. He had arrived there three weeks before, coming from Spain in the company of his master and the two Frenchmen from Biskra. Rendered unrecognizable by make-up and wigs, they had passed for domestics. Since their arrival *the three* had been working night and day on chemical manipulations about which the mulatto knew absolutely nothing. Then, four days before, Barnett had given the order to set the birds free. Finally, the day before, the master had told him that he no longer had any need of his services. Well ballasted with money, he had intended to leave for America in the company of the two negro servants. Only *the three*, therefore, still occupied the monastery of Ossat.

That *coup-de-théâtre* left me stupefied. I glimpsed the incalculable consequences attached to the discovery of the three madmen. The others were bound to the supposition of an anarchist plot, but I knew the truth!

By virtue of the confidences extracted from Manuelo, it was learned that they possessed weapons, ammunition and food supplies for six months. Those precautions implied the idea of resistance, further encouraged by the very particular disposition of the location.

In that regard, the Prefect provided very curious details regarding the topography of the Mont d'Ossat, a kernel of granite embedded in a mass of marble. In eruptive eras, that granitic jet had traversed the calcareous sediments already formed and broken through the exterior to constitute the summit of a hill. It was on that needle of hard rock that the Franciscans had constructed the buildings of their monastery, extracting the materials from the granite itself, as people for whom time and trouble were of no account. The convent had thus been conceived as a fortress; it was, in fact, designed to withstand the assaults of the Saracens. It formed an ensemble of massive constructions, surrounded by a wall fifteen feet thick. Oak doors edged with iron and enormous grilles commanded the entrance to the various quarters established between the interior courtyards. In order to become masters of the ensemble, besiegers would therefore have to take those veritable redoubts successively.

But before thinking of taking it, it was necessary to reach it. Now, with the exception of a poor goat track traced by the monks, which the people of the region called "the marble staircase," the mountain rose up in a series of sheer escarpments.

The Prefect did not hide his perplexity. If the three men really had ideas of resistance, it would be necessary to expect a murderous combat, all the more terrible because the President of the Council, kept up to date from minute to minute, telephoned instructions to take possession of the Three no matter what the cost, and to employ extreme means if necessary: cannons and bombs.

Poor Roger! Now that the other danger seemed to be on the eve of being thwarted, my heart bled with fraternal pity. But how could I reach out a helping hand to that furious maniac?

So long as the diabolical trio had not been reduced to impotence, all compassion had to be effaced before the superior interest of humankind.

Finally, I extracted a little hope from the resolutions that were made. Before launching a frontal assault, a surprise attack would be attempted.

Two battalions from the garrison at Tarbes would leave in the dark of night in automobile trucks; a detachment of artillerymen would accompany them with a wagon of explosives. Those troops would surround the Mont d'Ossat; in all probability, they would be in place by three o'clock in the morning. Before daybreak, a group of volunteers, reinforced by artillerymen equipped with melinite petards would climb the marble staircase silently all the way to the door of the former convent. Without any preliminary warning, they would blow it up, and try to capture the three inhabitants as quickly as possible, taking advantage of the disturbance that the surprise attack was bound to cause.

The plan was wisely contrived to avoid bloodshed. But alas, this time, once again, wisdom was obliged to recoil before folly, and the surprise would be ours.

XIX. The War of Oblivion

Today, with the passage of years, the memory has almost been lost of the tragedy that unfolded around the Mont d'Ossat in the middle of April 19**.

At any rate, even rereading the newspapers of the epoch, it is very difficult to form a clear idea of those obscure and variously reported events. The imprecision of the accounts, the unexplained events—because they were inexplicable—and the malaise into which unsatisfied public curiosity was thrown, all contributed to thicken the mystery and favor the formidable secret, the prerogative of a handful of people.

One could not, however, cry to the crowd that, in that corner of land, the life or death of the world was in the balance.

But I shall resume my story at the moment when an automobile was carrying me through the black night in company with the Prefect, the Public Prosecutor and General de Lozières, commanding the garrison of Tarbes. By virtue of a special favor, young Étienne had been admitted to huddle next to me in a corner of the vehicle. It would have cost me dear to separate from that child, who, after all, was able to give useful information about Livry.

Following in a second vehicle were gendarmes escorting the mulatto Manuelo and the negro Jim; they had been brought along at hazard, even though it was understood that little help that could be expected from those accomplices, the first human rag sweating fear to the point of losing his memory and the second a colossal brute incapable of furnishing the slightest explanation.

We were heading for the Mont d'Ossat, a journey of some twenty-five kilometers.

It was two-thirds of the way along the route that a singular phenomenon occurred, of which we were to have the explanation a few hours later. I say "phenomenon," although the occurrence itself was perfect simple; in the very calm night, in which the absence of any wind contributed to the silence, a powerful gust passed by, agitating the trees that bordered the road: a whistling that seemed to be the result of a giant aspiration was audible in the higher layers of the atmosphere. Then, for the duration of a minute, the noise of a distant collapse was heard. And that was all; nature reentered into silence.

In the vehicle, the conversations stopped. All of us had shuddered, as if at the first clap of thunder presaging a storm.

"An avalanche in the high mountains!" murmured the Prefect.

No one replied. It might have been true, and yet, for my part, I had the intimate presentiment of something much more redoubtable.

The spectacle that was offered to us at first light justified that presentiment.

According to my companions, the panorama of the Mont d'Ossat had been completely modified, and in what a strange fashion!

Instead of the butte in the form of a pyramid with a wide base, a needle of granite with a vaguely triangular section stood up vertically above the plain. At the summit of that natural tower was the Franciscan convent, whose walls overhung the abyss at an altitude of four hundred meters. Only a granitic table bordered the enclosure toward the eastern apex of the triangle, forming a sort of esplanade, only a few meters across, literally suspended above the void, outside the entrance grille.

Around it, keeping a respectable distance from the base of the enormous monolith, the troops arrived during the night and peasants from the surrounding area were contemplating that fantastic décor with a stupor mingled with fear.

No more "marble stairway," no more escarpments, however steep: a smooth wall, without a ledge. The mountain of marble that wrapped the primitive rock had vanished without leaving a trace. At ground level, there was the alluvial terrain constituting the plain of Tarbes, but a chaotic terrain, pitted by potholes, sown with moraines and the debris of uprooted trees.

For educated individuals that change of view remained incomprehensible. An earthquake? An abrupt collapse of the subsoil? Nothing in familiar notions could help to construct an acceptable explanation. As for the others, the villagers and the soldiers, they were not far from attributing that magic to divine or diabolical intervention. Quite naturally, those simple souls cried either miracle or sorcery.

I alone was in possession of the truth. The strange upheaval was due to Roger's maneuvers. The Franciscan convent had not been chosen at random.

The curious geological particularity of the Montagne d'Ossat lent itself marvelously to the madman's frightful projects. Already very difficult, access to the convent became impracticable after the disappearance of the calcareous mass that constituted the mountain's slopes. Roger knew in advance that his acid gave him the means to upset nature by suppressing the marble at a stroke.

Then, a terrible deduction was imposed.

After Barnett's action in releasing his birds by virtue of one last incoherent impulse of pity, and the dismissal of the servants, the collapse of the mountain clearly indicated that the scientist was ready.

In effect, the scientist had cut the last bridge linking him to the earth. The Man of the Apocalypse was about to commence his work.

"Good," said General de Lozières, beside me. "At least this inexplicable phenomenon has the result of simplifying the phenomenon. If we can't climb up to the rogues, at least it's impossible for them to come down again. They're in prison." And, moved by a natural sentiment, he added: "At any rate, my brave soldiers won't have to risk their lives in an imbecilic struggle!"

Poor General! I did not take charge of dissipating his generous illusions. I did not have the right to divulge the terrible secret.

He would find out soon enough, alas.

I judged that there were better things to do than contemplate open-mouthed the eagle's nest from which death was about to spread over the world. As soon as possible, Monsieur Luissant needed to be brought up to date with the new situation, of which I alone possessed the key.

In haste, I had myself taken back to Tarbes. My head was so full of fearful thoughts that I was quite surprised when the auto deposited me outside the town's telephone office.

Addressing myself to the postmaster, I was able to obtain immediate communication with Luissant.

By the tremor of his voice in the receiver I sensed how distressed the Minister was by my revelations, even though, fearing the indiscretions of the telephone, I sought to filter the truth.

"I'm coming," Luissant said to me. "I'll bring the most eminent scientists engineers and army chiefs; I'll give immediate orders to have materiel of various sorts sent to Tarbes. We'll try everything that's humanly possible."

The President of the Council arrived at midnight on a special train. With him were the Minister of War, the Commander-in-Chief of the Artillery, the Chief Engineer of Explosives, the Director of the Meteorological Bureau and also, naturally, Messieurs Thiérard-Leroy, d'Arsaumont and Manrichoff.

Circumstances brought me, an obscure petty schoolteacher, to take my place in that cenacle of the highest notabilities of France.

The Council of War—and what a Council!—was held at daybreak before the somber mass of the Ossat.

"Messieurs," pronounced the Minister, with an anguishing gravity, "it's absolutely necessary that we find a means of reaching the summit of the peak and the people occupying it. Give me credit for the immense reasons that motivate the necessity; tell yourselves that they surpass reasons of State, that they concern, if you wish, what I shall call humanitarian reasons.

"And if you judge that my emotion, my efforts and my extreme determination are excessive and ridiculous by comparison with the goal to be attained, I beg Messieurs Thiérard-Leroy, d'Arsaumont and Manrichoff to contradict me. I make you the same plea, Monsieur Paul Lefort, who is sacrificing to these superior exigencies a close, quasi-fraternal friendship."

After the great scientists whose indisputable testimony the Minister had invoked, I nodded my head. Then, it seemed that a frisson stirred the epidermis of the others: those who did not yet know.

Then we debated. And in the course of the arguments exchanged, it was necessary to allow a few rays of extraordinary verity shine through. All the methods of scaling were examined in turn. None gave satisfaction. To climb up by means of ladders along the flanks of the rock was theoretically possible, but such work would require the establishment of successive landings. Even with the employment of the most advanced electric drilling equipment, the engineers judged that the enterprise would take more than a month, even supposing that the madmen at the summit would do nothing to oppose it.

In any case, the trenchant voice of the Minister put in: "It's necessary for us to be up there within a week, isn't it, Monsieur Thiérard-Leroy?"

"It's necessary," the astronomer repeated.

"I thought immediately of airplanes," Monsieur Luissant pronounced then, "but on the advice of the Commander-in-Chief of Aeronautics, it would be madness to think of landing on that pointed spur of rock or in that chaos of roofs. Dirigibles, on the other hand, floating above the Ossat, might be able to deposit a few resolute men in one of the interior courtyards."

The chief of military aeronautics made a sign of assent.

"Within forty-eight hours," the Minister continued, "our six available dirigibles must rally at Tarbes, whatever the weather." The statesman added: "But it goes without saying that before then, we'll have rendered the monsters incapable of doing any harm. That will be the task of our air force. General Hochtheim can explain that to you better than me."

The Chief of Aeronautics then set out a very simple plan for the employment of airplanes.

First of all, a few light aircraft would fly over the Ossat, for an initial reconnaissance that would permit photographs to be taken. Then a squadron of bombers would intervene, which would drop tons of explosives and gas shells on the building. We could count, on the one hand, of the destruction—or rather the dispersal—of the chemical substances produced by Livry, and on other, of the certain asphyxiation of the three wretches. Afterwards, a squad of specialists equipped with gas masks could be disembarked at leisure to verify the effects.

All that seemed very logically conceived.

An impression of immense relief ensued.

After the emotion of the first moment, it appeared to the most timorous eyes that perhaps we had exaggerated, if not the danger, at least the difficulty of warding it off in a manner as sure as it would be rapid.

I alone lowered my head; Roger's death sentence had just been pronounced. I would so much have liked to save the poor follow. But how could I have implored in his favor?

The orders can be launched immediately. An automobile radiotelegraphic apparatus has just arrived from Tarbes. It can easily communicate with the large station of the Croix d'Hins near Bordeaux; from there, the air force camp at Istre can be reached by telephone, where everything ought to be set in motion during the night.

However, the wireless telegraph apparatus, when switched on, does not work.

Is it a fault of attunement, or a breakdown in the transmission apparatus? At any rate, the waves are not transmitted.

After several fruitless attempts, the decision is made to send a dispatch by motorcycle to the nearest telegraph office.

"A bad start," murmurs Monsieur Luissant.

No one says a word.

The hours pass, with what slowness!

I'm cold.

Is it an unfortunate predisposition of my physical being, deprived of sleep, or a fallacious impression of my nerves by which I'm experiencing the expected sensation is advance?

No. Others than me seem to be suffering the uncomfortable effects of the atmospheric freshness. There is no doubt that it's accentuating. It contrasts strangely with the sun, which is rising over the horizon and ought to be better able to warm us with is rays.

At Monsieur Luissant's invitation, our group goes to seek shelter in a tawdry wagoners' inn at the intersection of two roads.

The common room has already been invaded by soldiers. We take refuge in a room with primitive furniture. An armful of vine-branches produces a bright flame in the fireplace and chases away the odor of mildew reigning in the room.

Eleven o'clock: our anxious impatience finally finds a diversion.

XX. Disappointment and Disaster

Three airplanes are spotted in a north-westerly direction. They are the reconnaissance aircraft.

They are flying at a low altitude, in spite of the sonorous purr of their engines. They pass over the needle of the Ossat and immediately veer away in order to land behind our position, a mound that overlooks the bifurcation of the two roads.

The aviators make their report.

They have fulfilled their mission. Several photographic views of the Ossat have been taken. They have not, however, distinguished any human being within the walls of the convent. They complain about the cold and the poor performance of their engines.

Another hour goes by.

Here comes the squadron of large bomber aircraft. The machines are flying very low, a hundred and fifty meters at the most; abrupt signals appear to be given by the squadron leader to regain altitude. Everyone divines that they want to pass over the needle.

But it seems to us that they cannot succeed in flying over the obstacle, because they disperse to the left and the right in order to go around the strange obelisk at mid-height, scarcely two hundred meters.

What does it mean? Machines that can normally reach seven thousand meters! That, at least, is the figure cited by the professionals that surround me.

Heavily, the large aircraft reach the neighboring landing-ground indicated to them by beacons.

Twenty minutes later, the commandant of the squadron, Capitaine Tenan, an ace among aces, presents himself to his chief, General Hochtheim.

"It's incomprehensible, General," he says. "About twenty kilometers from the place, our machines suffered a regular loss of altitude, as if they were falling along an inclined plane. If it had been a matter of one or two aircraft out of my six, I would have put the decline down to engine failure or a lack of fuel, but the whole squadron…!" He made a gesture of chagrin. "Explain it if you can! My planes have a ceiling of two hundred meters, and that with difficulty."

A disconcerting observation.

"Give me a report!" mutters the chief of aeronautics, deeply grieved to see the initial failure of the plan he had so judiciously explained that morning.

"You'll succeed better with your dirigibles," says Monsieur Luissant, to appease that disappointment.

"In the meantime, I want to ensure that the people up there sense our surveillance weighing upon them," says the General. "I'm waiting for observation balloons, and before our big dirigibles come on the scene this afternoon, we're going to be able to watch a captive ascent. The aerostatic fleet brought from Bordeaux is disembarking as we speak at the nearest railway station. Within an hour it will be in the vicinity of the Ossat."

We go to lunch.

Without waiting for the end of the meal, served with despairing slowness by the staff of the inn, the Minister gets up from the table. We all follow him

On foot, we go to the edge of a little wood. The ascent is to take place from there.

A captain who has come on ahead of his column examines the location. Nothing will be easier, he declares, than to float a "sausage" a hundred meters above the needle of the Ossat. Thus, we'll be able to complete the reconnaissance of the airplanes, and perhaps discover with binoculars the emplacement of Livry's "refrigerators."

That first ascent, therefore, promises very important results. Who can tell? Perhaps the solution vainly sought might suddenly appear.

Tenuous as the hope might be, it imposes itself even so; it brightens our expressions.

Now the captive aerostat appears; its baroque silhouette is bobbing a few meters above the vehicular winch around which the metallic cable is wound.

The "sausage" has been inflated on the way. Insufficiently, no doubt, for it seems flaccid; its ascensional force is very weak. That won't last! Behind comes the truck with cylinders of compressed hydrogen; in a quarter of an hour it can be reinflated properly.

The tubing is fitted, the taps opened—but the gas doesn't flow. Nothing! No pressure…"

"The hydrogen cylinders have been damaged," declares the vexed captain.

We are all nervous, disappointed by that further failure.

Fortunately, good news arrives to palliate the annoyance caused by that unfortunate incident. The Minister is summoned to the improvised telephone installed in a tent. After a brief conversation, Luissant returns to our group.

"A success, Messieurs," the Minister says, "The *Colonel Renard* and the *France* are floating over Tarbes. The Commandants of the dirigibles are requesting orders by optical signals, because it definitely seems that we'll have to go into mourning for wireless apparatus. It's no longer functioning."

General Hochtheim orders the *France* to press on to the Mont d'Ossat and carry out the reconnaissance that it has not been possible to effect. Within half an hour the airship is in sight.

We begin to hope again.

This time, nothing appears likely to trouble the dirigible's maneuvers.

As often happens at sunset, the breeze has dropped; the air is admirably calm. Already, the watchmen posted on a hill are agitating, sending signals in a northerly direction.

Preceded by Étienne, who is running as fast as he can, I climb up there.

Luissant joins us. He communicates the supplementary information he has just received about the large aerial units—for the alerted dirigibles have been taking off since the previous evening. With various fortunes, they are all attempting to reach the Pyrenees.

The *Ville de Paris*, departed from Toul, has come down in the Duchy of Bade. The *Ville de Nancy*, from Mayence, has been drawn north-eastwards; the balloon has been signaled passing over Utrecht; perhaps it is lost in the North Sea. The *Patrie* emerging brand new from the workshops of Moisson, has been obliged to turn back by an engine breakdown. The *République* has called in at Clermont-Ferrand; it will resume its south-westerly route in the evening.

In sum, only the *Colonel Renard* and the *France*, two navy dirigibles departed from Toulon that morning have been able to accomplish their aerial voyage without a hitch. In spite of the westerly wing blowing persistently, the two airships, traveling in convoy, have crossed the Cévennes and then continued their route as far as Tarbes, where the façade of the corn-market has been demolished in order to permit them to take temporary refuge there.

Already, the long gray spindle of the *France*, an ex-zeppelin, is a patch in the blue sky. The balloon is visibly increasing in size. But is it an illusion? As it gets closer, one might think that it were getting heavier.

Around me, comments underline the same impression: the balloon is losing speed, and losing altitude.

Now it's no more than two kilometers away, but its altitude must be less than a hundred and fifty meters. Is it a landing maneuver?

"No!" declares General de Lozières, who is following its movement with his binoculars. "The envelope is deforming; the balloon appears to be breaking in two..."

He utters a cry. "Damn! The balloon's falling."

That cry of anguish is repeated by all the spectators. With a vertiginous rapidity, the *France* spins on her axis and hurtles toward the ground.

My respiration halts. Instinctively, I close my eyes in order not to see.

A dull sound; that is the crash.

A horrified exclamation rises from the plain. Everyone runs toward the lamentable wreck. The immense envelope covers the nacelle and the martyrs enclosed therein like a shroud.

I don't have the courage to assist in the horrible recovery of the cadavers.

I retrace my steps as far as the inn. I collapse, prostrate, at a table, my head clasped in my hands.

The Minister has followed me, accompanied by his general staff. As if in a dream, I hear the plaints of General Hochtheim and the strange and despairing observation to which he has proceeded of his own accord.

Aircraft can no longer rise above the ground!

What incredible sorcery is retaining the aerial apparatus conceived by human genius, marvelous machines that have proved their worth?

The fact is there: those machines can no longer fly.

"No matter," says the Minister. "We'll try other means. Cannons, mines..."

We return to the terrain of the strange battle.

After the incredible failure of aviation and aerostatics, the floor is given to the artillery. Certainly, a bombardment of the convent is possible, on condition of bringing special engines. To make projectiles fall at an altitude of four hundred meters in a relatively narrow zone, one could not think of using field cannon; the projectiles would only produce insignificant scratches on the granite walls. At the very least, it would be necessary to employ much greater firepower: mortars capable of plunging fire, able to fire large explosive charges.

That operation will involve the transportation of extremely heavy materiel, the installation of platforms and, in sum, the extension of the railway line and the establishment of a spurs far as the location chosen for the establishment of the batteries—hence, extensive works and adaptations of the route. One would therefore run into the same inert factor, impossible to force: time.

The director of the artillery estimated at more than a week the necessary interval before the first cannon shot could be fired.

"And then," the General added, doubtless to the great mortification of his self-esteem, "thousands of shells might fall on the convent without producing appreciable results. Certainly, we could burn all the combustible materials—but what then?"

"It won't be sufficient to destroy!" Luissant interjected, almost violently. "The problem won't be solved is we don't succeed in setting foot up there!" He waved his fist at the abrupt summit. "Understand me well, my friends, we're engaged in a struggle for existence." Luissant emphasized the final phrase in a dramatic fashion. Full of grandeur, the gesture of his open hand ran around the entire horizon, encountered the sun and broadened out toward the sky.

As if in response to that mute invocation to the earth and the Universe, up above, on the accursed mountain, at the top of the squat bell tower that emerged from the crenellated walls of the monastery, a flag in the form of a pennant slowly unfurled.

"The black flag!" murmured General de Lozières, who had directed his binoculars toward the summit.

Then, at the moment when the sun disappeared behind the gold-rimmed mountains, a sudden cold breath descended from the sky, like an invisible cold shower.

On that splendid spring evening, the Man of the Apocalypse declared war on Life.

XXI. The Tide of Terror

Another late night of terror and tears.

The Minister, the generals, the scientists and I were entrenched in the low-ceilinged room of the inn. An infinite despair weighed upon us. In spite of the decent meal that the Prefect had summoned from Tarbes, the white tablecloth and the harsh light cast by two automobile headlights serving for illumination, our spirits could not overcome the prostration that was gripping us.

Never, even in the most critical hours of the war, on the eve of attacks, under bombardments, had I witnessed such depression.

After the semblance of a dinner in which the food was barely touched, everyone sought his corner in order to think or sink into torpor. The Minister refused the camp bed that had been prepared for him.

Vanquished by fatigue, I surrendered to a heavy slumber.

Abruptly, toward midnight, a loud detonation caused me to sit up, at the same time as all my companions.

The window panes had shattered into smithereens.

Most of us found ourselves hurled to the floor, struggling in a profound obscurity.

By the light of a pocket electric torch, we were able to look around. Those who had been knocked down among the overturned benches and chairs got up again.

Apart from a few cuts caused by broken glass, no one was wounded.

"What now?" asked the Minister.

"Undoubtedly an explosion nearby," General de Lozières supposed.

"In the direction of the air fleet!" exclaimed General Hochtheim, on the threshold of the door, partly open. "Oh! That light! Out there, everything's on fire!"

We race outside on the heels of the head of the air force, guided by the red smoke rising toward the sky.

Detachments camped in the vicinity come running, but imperative cries are heard dominating the tumult: "Stay back! Stay back! The gases!"

403

An officer, his eyes haggard and his clothing in tatters, gives us the explanation.

The bombs brought by the aircraft and sheltered under tarpaulins have suddenly exploded, setting fire to the airplanes and scything down the fleet's personnel.

Murder!

He does not form that thought precisely, but everyone understands, and with an instinctive movement, turned toward the mysterious Ossat.

Again, a profound silence reigns over the plain.

We go back to the inn in order to avoid the bite of the cold. As best we can, we block up the openings of the windows devoid of glass with the aid of bundles of straw and blankets.

Large log fires render the room a semblance of heat.

I continue to shiver until dawn, always expecting a further disaster.

Finally, daylight appears.

On reading the mental distress of those surrounding him in their dolorous faces, Luissant searches for words of comfort, which ring false.

Oh, Roger, Roger, if a vengeful God exists somewhere, will your dementia earn you forgiveness for your crime?

During those dolorous reflections, I walk instinctively toward the Ossat, my eyes fixed on the terrible mount.

But what is that white thing falling along the mass of black granite? Something draws away from the wall, gently pushed by the breeze, descending slowly toward the plain. One might think that it's one of those paper parachutes sold in bazaars as children's toys.

Soldiers run toward the object that arrives from the sky. They take possession of it, and assemble around it.

Then the circle breaks. A sergeant comes toward me. In his hand he holds an envelope of gummed cloth.

"A letter, Monsieur," says the sergeant. "It must have come from up there. Perhaps you'll take charge of giving it to Monsieur the President..."

"Give it to me, my friend."

I shiver. At the first glance, I've recognized the firm handwriting of Roger Livry.

The madman has traced the unusual inscription: *To the World's Heads of State.*

What can the nature be of that communication, whose address alone denounces the wretch's arrogant madness?

More than anyone else, Monsieur Luissant seems to me to be qualified to take cognizance of it.

I find the Minister at the inn at the intersection. He has taken refuge in a poor room that has been reserved for him In spite of all the power of self-possession that he has, the courage of the statesman is visibly under stress. His finger trembles as he indicates a poor wicker chair. Then he passes his hand over his brow.

"Excuse me, Monsieur Lefort, but what I've just seen is terrible. The explosion has torn some apart; others have been killed on the spot by the asphyxiating vapors. Oh, the poor fellows, the poor fellows!" He makes a effort to chase away the funereal scene that is haunting him. "Well, what is it?"

"A message from Livry."

In a few words, I tell him how the letter reached me.

The Minister breaks the seal. Frowning, he reads. A mask of dolor and resignation descends over his energetic face. He seizes my hands.

"Oh, my friend! This time, I believe we're doomed." The assured tone of his calm voice veils the superhuman anguish against which he is stiffening himself. "Here, read it for yourself."

I take the letter and read it in my turn.

I am neither a barbarian nor a torturer. As a scientist and a Frenchman I profoundly deplore the catastrophe of the dirigible that attempted to reach me, and similarly, last night's explosion, which must have claimed victims. I regret not having warned you that the radiations emitted by my acid attack hydrogen and modify its density within a radius of five thousand meters, which will increase by the hour.

In the same way, your aircraft can no longer fly in the vicinity of the Ossat. The air, the density of which is modified, will no longer support them.

Renounce, therefore, attempts to reach me with the aid of balloons. Similarly, do not count on destroying my frigorific installations by means of a bombardment. Firstly, they are shielded from your attacks; secondly, my radiations can decompose your explosives and provoke their deflagration. Do not bring explosive materials within fifty kilometers if you want to avoid further misfortunes. In any case, what could those means of attack achieve?

No power in the world can henceforth prevent the suspension of terrestrial life within a period that cannot surpass two full months. In consequence, your duty as governors is to avoid spreading alarm. Allow beings to sink slowly into a sleep that will be eternal.

After centuries, new life will flourish on the earth. By virtue of the law of progress, for the future humankind, that life will be adapted to an improved organism. The new beings will not have the terrible flaws that come from the lamentable imperfection of our organs and our rudimentary senses. Among those evils I will only cite those whose horror I know by virtue of having experienced or recognized them during my existence: war, tuberculosis, alcoholism, madness, and lovesickness, the greatest of them all.

Above all, I dream of a humankind that will only have one sex and no heart. From that will emerge the veritable superhuman.

In order that my work should be judged sanely, I am not a Power of Evil, and I am not a Maker of Oblivion. I am conscious of determining a leap in progress, for time is nothing, the centuries scarcely mark the hours of the history of the World. I am the Annunciator of the New Era. I am the Man of the Apocalypse.

Alas, I had been familiar with the lunatic's theory for a long time. But a nuance that struck me in that ultimate profession of faith was the bitterness and disenchantment that was visible beneath the superb declarations, and the need or self-justification that surfaced several times.

As or Monsieur Luissant, he shook his head sadly, his gaze lost in a distant dream. And in a low voice, he murmured: "From the philosophical point of view, this madman is perhaps a sage, preaching resignation for the present and hope for the future."

But in that poignant moment, it was me, the weakling, who drew from my sharp remorse the courage and the ardor necessary to bring the strong man round.

"Listen to me, Minister. I've penetrated the depths of the unfortunate Livry's soul. Well, in the tone of his letter I seem so glimpse a fissure through which a little pity has slipped into his sickness-exasperated brain. Oh, if only I could reach him, if only I could cry to him: *Have mercy on the World!*"

Luissant made a gesture indicating the extent to which he judged my desire illusory. In a dull voice, he said: "Haven't you read the newspapers, as I have? Haven't you seen the dispatches from the agencies?" And with is hand, he indicated a pile of printed papers scattered on the rickety table. "Well, in spite of all the means I have of imposing silence, within a few days, the terrible truth will burst forth. The press won't be content for long with the stories I allow to filter it, the rumors that my offices have refrained from denying.

"Quite naturally, people are beginning to get excited by the unusual movements taking place in the region of Tarbes. The opposition papers are talking about a vast anarchist plot, a kind of Mafia whose base of operations is situated on the Pyrenean frontier, receiving orders from Barcelona. The socialist papers are uttering loud protests, saying that the government is proceeding with a secret mobilization, denouncing our intention to declare war on Spain over Morocco..."

The Minister could not help shrugging his shoulders

"And our dirigibles dispersed to the four corners of the sky, one broken down, another lost! But what will the exasperation of opinion be on learning of the catastrophes of yesterday and last night? Already, correspondents from everywhere are laying siege to the press office that it's been necessary to set up in Tarbes. Tomorrow, In spite of my efforts, they'll be here, in our midst. What am I going to say to them?

"In Paris, the Chambre is becoming stormy; on the Bourse, the index has already fallen ten points." With a smile of bitterness and scorn, the Minister added: "If only it was just the stock prices!"

My resolution did not buckle before that profound and reasoned disenchantment. And an idea emerged, which had been sketched confusedly in mind since reading the letter.

"Minister, there might perhaps still be one means of reaching the summit, of which we haven't yet thought."

"What?"

"A glider."

Luissant recovered his bitter smile. "My God, Lefort, you heard General Hochtheim's declarations yesterday. If that man, the most audacious of all, has renounced employing that weapon, it's because your idea isn't practical."

"Look at the new Icaruses, though! They're now flying at heights that far surpass that of the Ossat! Hasn't Guy Mayrol reached fifteen hundred meters recently?"

"That's true—but those are exceptional exploits. Then again, it's not only a question of altitude. In the present case, where do you see the possibility of a landing for an alerion supported by the wind, which can't suspend its progress?"

"Mayrol accomplishes marvels of audacity and skill every day. Why shouldn't he be able to let himself down into one of the convent's three courtyards?

"Let's admit it—but do you believe that the madmen up there would let him land? They'd kill him."

"I'm still holding to the hypothesis of disembarking a passenger; I'm also assuming that the disembarkation would take place at night.

"Oh, my dear chap, you're straying into the implausible."

"At the point we've reached, as you've said yourself, everything ought to be attempted, even the impossible."

"I agree, but where is the audacious man ready to risk the adventure, without him needing to be brought into the terrible secret in order to convince him?"

"I believe that Guy Mayrol would accept. I know arguments capable of convincing him."

Rapidly, I retraced the scene at the Camp de Châlons in which Roger, by an impromptu stroke of genius, had so fortunately seconded the efforts of the young seeker.

"Summon Mayrol, then," said the Minister, in a disenchanted tone.

I ran to the telephone.

Within ten minutes, I had picked up Mayrol's trail. He was at Juvisy aerodrome, where he was trying out a new model of alerion. Within half an hour, my desire was on their way to realization. I did not have to say very much to decide the hero of unpowered flight; I simply told him that it was a matter of saving the mysterious unknown man, the Man of the Apocalypse, who had traversed his existence like a good genie never seen again. In giving him that reason I was sincere; while trying to save humankind, why should I not think also of saving one human being who was particularly dear to me?

I still have present in my memory the noble and simple words by which Mayrol made his acceptance known: "I owe your friend everything: my success and my fortune. Count me in!"

The details were quickly settled. At Juvisy, by order of the President of the Council, a special train was formed to bring Mayrol to Tarbes, with his crew of assistants and his best two machines. He would leave at four o'clock in the afternoon, and would reach the Mont d'Ossat the following morning.

In spite of the rapid success of my step, I was too agitated to savor the peace of any relief. Incapable of remaining in place, I had myself taken to Tarbes. I took Étienne Tourbe with me in order to take the child away from the sinister ambience of the Ossat.

I was able to get a few hours sleep in a hotel bed. Nevertheless, three hours before the arrival of the special train. I was at the station waiting for Mayrol.

XXII. The Savior

Mayrol arrived at eight o'clock. Immediately, the young man took care of unloading his alerions. Their long fuselages were carried on two trucks; with their wings folded, the marvelous gliders resembled, on a gigantic scale, the yellow dragonflies that pose on reeds in marshes.

A crowd had gathered along the barriers, in spite of the cold, to watch the maneuvers. I noticed that the people did not have the verbose and noisy agitation characteristic of southern idlers. What I read on those closed faces was an anxious curiosity and an ill-defined anguish. I remembered having once seen such a crowd near Douai, in the black country; its members were standing at the entrance to a mine to which the rumor of a firedamp explosion had brought them.

As the Minister feared, the comings and goings, the troop movements and the mystery that surrounded the Mont d'Ossat—the whole ensemble of occurrences—was beginning to excite public opinion.

Great God! What would they do if they knew? Mentally, I formed nightmarish scenes of the terror that the possible proximity of universal panic might evoke.

Yes, Luissant was right when he deployed all his energy to maintain silence. It there anything more pitiless and more cruel than to allow an invalid to understand that he is about to die?

And I admire the stoicism of little Étienne, who *knows*, and is nevertheless cheerful as he watches the disembarkation of the apparatus.

But the alerions have already been hoisted on to flat-bed motor-trucks, like those employed to transport tanks.

I take my place in an automobile with Mayrol.

The trucks and the mechanics follow.

In order not to give any warning to the madmen of the Ossat, it's agreed that we shall stop out of sight of the summit.

The alerions are garaged in two large barns on the edge of a large pastureland. Mayrol and I, still flanked by the boy, continue our route toward the granite needle.

Until now I have not given any elaborate explanations. I have understood that the imperturbably phlegmatic young man would first want to see and then judge with his own practical sense.

Without saying a word, smoking his cigarette, Mayrol makes a circuit of the tower of black rock. He examines it from different angles, and scrutinizes the bake-like rock that protrudes outside the convent wall. He compares the evidence of his eyes with those of a plan I have given him, labeled with altitudes and dimensions. He reflects for some time, and then comes back to me.

"Monsieur Lefort," he says, in his natural voice. "It's not a matter of a trial but a realization, isn't it?"

I make a sign of assent, and my features lit up with a sudden hope. "It's possible, then?"

"Yes thanks to the wind, which is steady, and the mountains that surround the lain of Tarbes. I'll find a point of departure in the foothills of the Pyrenees that will permit me to arrive above the needle. There, I can calculate my movements to descend on the convent in an ever-decreasing spiral, like a sparrowhawk. In the final circle the radius is so sort that the alerion turns on its axis and remains almost vertically above the landing-point."

"And you'll go down then into one of the interior courtyards?"

"No, because then I'd drop like a stone; it would be a mortal impact, which wouldn't get us any further forward. But a passenger cold take advantage of the precise moment of vertical descent to slide down a rope about...let's say fifteen meters long; He'd be able to reach the ground of the Ossat while giving me enough scope to reset my apparatus and take a tangential route, brushing the roof. The end of the descent toward the plain is nothing. Except..."

"Except?" I say, slightly dazed by the audacity of the maneuver so calmly explained.

"It's indispensable that my companion should be an accomplished gymnast, immune to vertigo. Finally, in order for me to retain full mastery of my controls, the passenger must be very light, fifty kilos at the maximum."

"No more?"

"Not is you desire a realization."

I am devastated. The hope, albeit vague, that I had forged since the previous day, collapses lamentably. And why? For a small difference of a few kilos! I weigh sixty-seven and Maytol cannot take more than fifty. Thus, the fate of the world depends on seventeen kilos, more or less.

Oh, it would be hilarious if it were not so frightful.

I shake the hand of the courageous pilot, with a desolate expression.

"Excuse me for having disturbed you unnecessarily, my dear Mayrol. Since, in fact, no one can reach the unfortunate Livry..."

"No one! What about me, M'sieur Paul? You're not counting me?"

Who said that?

It is little Tourte.

By voice of seeing him close by, an inseparable companion of these days of suffering, I had, in truth, forgotten him.

And I discover beneath me that little spindly figure, his intelligent and determined eyes gleaming.

"Me, I weigh forty-two kilos," he says, with assurance and pride.

Mayrol and I look at one another without saying a word. The gamin has stunned us with the unexpected proposition thrown into the midst of our impotence and distress.

Well, no, neither one of us had thought of him. And already, the idea of accepting the help of a child is causing us to shiver. But in a tone that seeks to be convincing, he now makes his generous offer precise. In order to argue, he recovers the mocking loquacity of a child of the slums.

"Monsieur Mayrol said fifty kilos, right? For that, only an anorexic or a kid like me is good for the stunt. It's almost as if I were made to measure. It needs someone agile—you know me, M'sieur Paul! I have the feet of a goat mounted on the body of a rubber doll. Me, who can leap down from a wooden horse on a steam-driven roundabout, I have what it needs to get down from the alerion. And vertigo—ha! Don't know it. What if I told you, Monsieur Mayrol, that I used to amuse myself sitting astride the pulley of a crane perched at the top of the scaffolding surrounding the church of Saint-Étienne-du-Mont? The roofers said that that was seventy-five meters high. You see, Monsieur Lefort, without wanting to offend you, that it isn't you who's learned to do as much."

And by way of conclusion, he brings out another argument: "Do you think that Monsieur Roger would seek to harm me, the little starveling he pulled out of the mud to make a Monsieur of me? Look, Monsieur Paul, without bragging, I've become a member of the family even more than you. Oh, I know what you're going to say; Jobert and Barnett, two dirty beasts. But then, lions don't eat rats. Then again, in that regard, Monsieur Roger must be something of a tamer: he'll protect me.

"And finally, it's necessary to tell you that it would amuse me a great deal to go up in an alerion."

What a flame of desire is shining in Étienne's eyes when he pronounces those final words! Then he blushes and murmurs a remark that shows us the depths of his soul: "One day, perhaps they'll talk about me in the newspapers."

The entire psychology of the Paris gamin is contained in that.

In spite of the poignancy of the situation, Mayrol and I can't help exchanging a smile. And by the play of his physiognomy, I sense that the aviator is leaving me the responsibility of making the decision.

In ordinary circumstances, the idea of discussing the child's heroic proposition would have seemed monstrous to me. But we are going through a crisis beyond the natural, in which questions of life and death cannot be posed from their habitual angle. Certainly, dangers will lie in wait for the boy at every step—but is not the other danger, the silent danger, affirming itself more terribly with every passing hour?

At midday, in April, in the middle of April, in that region, renowned for the mildness of its climate, the puddles formed in depressions are covered in a sheet of ice. Even more than the very judicious arguments put forward by Étienne, it was perhaps the abnormal sight of that frozen water that acted upon my decision.

"So," I said, in a grave voice, "you're sure you're not afraid?"

Astonished, Étienne affirms his bravery: "Afraid, Monsieur Paul! Of what and whom? Not Monsieur Mayrol, not Monsieur Roger. So?"

My only response is to seize the former pastry-cook in my arms, and say, after kissing him on both cheeks: "Well, go then, my brave lad!"

Emotion grips my throat, and I have to make an unusual effort in order not to weep.

Alas, I was later to shed the tears held back at that moment.

The decision taken, as a man of action, Mayrol does not lose a minute to make arrangements for the adventurous attempt.

I take him to Monsieur Luissant and General Hochtheim. When they know the plan as a whole and the role to be played by little Tourte, they accept it without objection, without a word of pity or affection. They simply give the accolade to the little fellow. For them, the child is a man, running to sacrifice.

Mayrol settles the details of the execution in concert with Hochtheim.

At first he thinks of taking off at dusk; then he decides to depart in complete darkness. At midnight, the moon will be low enough on the horizon to prevent the alerion being distinguished, while permitting the silhouette of the convent to be discerned in a perfectly sufficient fashion.

In any case, four powerful searchlights will concentrate their beams on the squat bell tower of the chapel. That will be the beacon that will guide Mayrol in his flight.

The choice of a launch-site for the apparatus is quickly made; various items of information coincide in indication an ideal terrain: a platform situated on the crests that rise up between Pierrefitte and Cauterets. It is seven hundred meters above the valley of Argelès and dominates the plain by about a thousand meters. From there the sliding skips departed that served for the exploitation of an abandoned mine.

That point of departure is twenty kilometers from the Ossat as a bird flies; the pilot thinks that he will arrive over the needle in half an hour.

Finally, one of the great advantages of the chosen point is that it is in the immediate vicinity of the electric railway line to Cauterets. Transportation of the alerions will thus be effected with ease.

A rapid reconnaissance permits Mayrol to take account himself of the excellent conditions offered by the platform of the mine.

Similarly, General Hochtheim will prepare him a landing-ground that will be illuminated from midnight on.

The material details having been duly settled, the pilot sets out to utilize the remaining hours of daylight to carry out a trial. A hillock masked from the Ossat by a pinewood is selected. Little Tourte takes his place on the saddle placed behind the pilot's seat. A rope fifteen meters long is solidly fixed to the framework of the apparatus.

Launched by the sandow, the alerion rises without difficulty. Lightly and easily, it rises above the plain, aided by the strong breeze.

Mayrol suggests to the child that he set down in a farmyard, on a heap of straw capable of deadening the shock in case of a fall.

And several times, the exercise, perilous in itself, is carried out with an ease that renews our hopes. At an agreed signal, emitted by Mayrol by means of a shrill whistle, Étienne lets himself slide down the cable at the precise moment when the apparatus passes over the heap of straw.

"It's nothing—less than nothing!" the boy says, when we congratulate him on his agility. "Like descending from a moving autobus."

After those encouraging trials, we go back to the inn for dinner: a sad meal that reminds me of those we had at the front, on the eve of an attack, when we and the chiefs were griped by the terrible responsibility. Risking one's own life is a little thing, once one gets used to it, but leading, *driving* others to death...

Isn't the present case similar in every point?

Mayrol is silent by temperament; I'm too emotional to talk; in any case, as soon as I attempt a remark, an interior thrill quivers within me and prevents me from continuing.

Fortunately, Étienne has coolness enough for two; his nose in his plate, he eats with a hearty appetite; he regales himself on a cream desert concocted by our hostess.

Oh, those hours of waiting that separate us from the supreme attempt! They seem all the more cruel to me because I'm alone now.

Luissant has been obliged to go back to Paris, recalled to the Council of Ministers; the Prefect is at his post in Tarbes; General de Lozières is supervising the installation of the railway track. The three scientists have gone to the observatory on the Pic du Midi to study the progress of the atmospheric refrigeration.

I have told Tourte to rest for a few hours before the great departure.

Mayrol has returned to his hangar to check the bodywork of his alerion one last time. In addition, he has given orders to paint the wings black, in order to render the apparatus invisible at night.

I am, therefore—I repeat—alone, horribly alone beside the smoky lamp.

Oh, that frightful vigil!

My apprehensions return in a host. Then night falls in my spirit and I fall back into my intellectual lethargy.

"Well, Monsieur Lefort," are you sleeping awake?"

Guy Mayrol is before me, shaking my shoulder.

It's true; I had seen him without seeing him.

"It's time," he says, simply.

I shudder. On the morning of his execution, a man condemned to death experiences what I'm experiencing at this moment. And yet, it isn't my life that is at stake,

I go to the next room, where the child is asleep. Before I wake him up, a sharp dolor traverses me. In the final analysis, it's necessary. Undoubtedly, there exists, beyond the immaterial wills that prowl around us in order to weigh upon us, if necessary, our own intimate will. I must be going through one of those psychological phases, because, when I shake the little sleeper gently, I am acting like the obedient subject of a hypnotist.

The gamin leaps out of bed, like a soldier hearing the alarm sounded.

I dress him in a fur jacket for which I've sent someone to search in Tarbes, because the cold outside is very sharp; the thermometer is marking seven degrees below. What a fall in three days!

We take our places in the automobile that will take us to Pierrefitte, a journey of thirty minutes. There, the electric train is waiting for us; a truck is carrying the glider. The train climbs the slope rapidly. Now we're at the alerion's launch-site.

The moon is due to disappear at about one o'clock. Mayrol will take off at about twenty past twelve. Everything is ready. The sandows are stretched by the aides.

In haste, I renew my instructions to Étienne. Once again, I hug the dear boy to my heart. Mayrol installs him on the saddle, and then seizes the controls.

The apparatus shudders, lifted by the winds but retained by the military engineers. My heart has stopped beating.

"Hup!"

That's the conventional "let go." The rubber bands contract. The black bird bounds into the void and disappears into the night. The die is cast.

XXIII. Life is Stronger than Death!

In haste, I make the return journey to Pierrefitte. The auto brings me back to the Ossat.

Followed by the engineers, I climb the wooded slope that masks us from the needle.

Now I'm at the crest. I stop dead; the soldiers accompanying me do likewise. The vision that is offered to our eyes breaks our momentum.

Illuminated by the white light of the electric projectors, the granite summit is outlined against the sky, an immense black tower with a bizarre crown formed by the tapering of the rock and the silhouette of the roofs, steeples and turrets of the Franciscan convent.

One might think it a fabulous animal crouched on the tower: a unicorn, dragon or chimera with trenchant claws and a crested spine.

Down below, all around, troubling glaucous glimmers rise from ground level, as if to prohibit any approach to that place of terror and mystery; they are low-lying pools of frozen water whose surface is iridescent in the moonlight.

The appearance is so fantastic that one can scarcely place it in the real world. It is a scene of Walpurgis Night, and one searches the air for phantasmal shadows, for deformed larvae.

I dig my fingernails into the palms of my hands in order to rid myself of the emprise of those hallucinations.

But now the moon has disappeared behind the western hills, plunging the plain and the base of the cyclopean giant into blackness. I fix my eyes on the darkness rising along the granite like a sea of ink. I prick up my ears. Will I discern the strident blast of a whistle that ought to mark the decisive moment? Or will I hear the racket of the fling machine crashing into the rocky wall?

My nerves are stretched to breaking point as the seconds succeed one another, as the tide of shadow gets closer to the summit.

A time elapses that must be quite short, but seems to me to be a century.

And through the night passes a light, distant sound that quavers like the call of a cricket in the hearth.

There is no doubt about it; it's Mayrol's signal.

Behind me, a bright light sets the curtain of trees masking the aviator's landing-ground ablaze; I divine that it is composed by acetylene beacons, lit at the agreed moment to facilitate Mayrol's return.

The lights go out abruptly. Perhaps Mayrol has already landed. Nevertheless I march a hundred meters and stop at the limit of the first potholes. With all my strength, I resume listening to the silence.

This time, toward the foot of the bluff, I hear a distinct sound. It recurs at regular intervals. One might think that it were the crystalline sound of glass breaking as it falls. What can it be?

I don't have time to forge hypotheses. From up above, I hear a cry.

In the muted echo, I rediscover the shrill, child-like timbre of a voice that has not yet broken, and also the heart-rending anguish of someone calling for help.

Horror! Only little Étienne could have uttered that cry.

414

I think I'm about to faint. My ears buzz, the blood beats in my temples with a staccato rhythm.

I truly think that at that moment, I was on the brink of collapsing under the sledgehammer blow of a cerebral congestion.

"Monsieur Lefort? Are you there?"

Perhaps it was that intervention by Mayrol that saved me, by provoking an instinctive reaction of my reflexes.

It is only at the third appeal, although the young man is almost within arm's length, that I can articulate: "Yes...I'm here."

I cling on to him, in order not to fall.

"Hey! Monsieur Lefort, you've allowed yourself to be gripped by the cold."

By the light of a lantern, I can vaguely distinguish other shadows moving around me. I feet a bottleneck introduced between my lips.

"Drink!"

I obey. A sensation of wellbeing invades me. Now, I've recovered my aplomb. I can now hear the pilot, who declares in his tranquil voice: "I succeeded. Little Étienne has set down up there. Before I prolonged my flight over the rooftops, the brave boy called: 'It's okay!' Except, it was time for me to come down to earth. I was gripped by the cold. Then I experienced a bizarre impression: the air was no longer supportive. When I reached the ground, I broke the machine...eh? What's that?"

A second apart, two detonations have just sounded on the summit of the Ossat: two gunshots.

I seize Mayrol's hands and in a breathless voice: "My fried, a frightful drama is in play up there. I'm a criminal, yes, criminal, for having let that child...to what? My God, what to do?"

I give signs of the most violent despair; I march, I totter, I weep with impotence and shame.

In vain, the pilot tries to calm me down.

I am obliged, however, to yield to the evidence of the arguments he enumerates. There is nothing we can do until daybreak.

How will the hours go by that separate us from the dawn?

I know nothing about them. There is nothing there in my memory but a dead time.

Except that, at the first light of morning, I have returned to a state of sluggishness, in much the same condition as when one emerges from a faint.

I can no longer feel much of anything, neither physical inconvenience nor mental anxiety. My bare hands are not suffering from the sharp cold that is powdering the earth with a white frost; my eyes rediscover the sinister stele of the Ossat indifferently.

My nerves are decidedly torpid.

Perhaps fatality wanted to have pity on me, by permitting me that anesthesia of my sensitive being, before pushing me toward the frightful calvary that still remained for me to climb.

Mechanically, I follow the officers and soldiers who are hastening toward the foot of the rick. They too are impatient to piece the mystery of the successive sounds that troubled the silence of the night of anguish. They have all heard the fall of broken glass, the supreme cry for help and the gunshots in the course of their guard duty—and also another sound, much duller and more muffled, that came from directly below the granitic spur, shortly before daybreak. That sound, I did not perceive.

With agility, those brave fellow run through the potholes and crevasses of collapsed earth. They give no thought to the possibility that the madmen might greet them with rifle fire from their lair.

As best I can, in follow on the heels of the nimble group—and suddenly, I see the soldiers stop, lean over toward the ground, step back, and then form a motionless circle.

I approach in my turn.

On the hardened ground, there is the cadaver of a man, a body folded in two, the limbs dislocated, the skull open.

Blood, the debris of viscera and cerebral matter have splashed the surrounding area.

At the exhortations of a lieutenant, the soldiers overcome their horror and lift up that miserable human wreck. They uncover the face, left almost intact. I throw my hands over my eyes; I have just recognized Roger Livry.

It's too much.

I move away a few paces in order to get further away from the abominable vision. I go around the granite base. There, other soldiers are considering curiously the debris of black glass that stews the ground, and also the gelatinous plaques extended here and there by splashes. The sight of those things forces my dolorous brain to think again.

That paste with the opaline tints is the terrible mixture of radium and the Omega aid.

In a host, question marks assail my mind. But I am decidedly empty, annihilated. The power of reasoning and the sense of observation have abandoned me.

By myself, I remain in no condition to untangle the tragic thread of events.

Someone has to come to my aid.

That aid, the dead man will bring me himself.

Before my distracted eyes the silhouette looms up of the lieutenant who substituted just now for my routed courage by occupying himself with the collection of Roger's mortal remains.

"Monsieur," the officer says, "this letter was found on the cadaver. I believe it's addressed to you."

I take the envelope that he hands to me. Indeed, the subscription, in which I recognize the handwriting of my childhood friend, is in my name.

I stammered a thank you.

Then, sitting on a large boulder at the foot of the sinister mountain, I took cognizance of the unfortunate's final missive.

Such as it is, I am copying that document, in which, in a flash of lucidity, the madman retraces the final act of the drama, crying his pain to the universe, imploring its pardon.

My dear Paul,

Have pity on me. I've suffered so much.

By virtue of the suffering of the last year of my life, more than my voluntary death, I have commenced the expiation of my crimes.

For a year I have lived in a fog of death and desolation, scarcely illuminated during the few days that you know. I have seen so many things that you could not see. Mad—I was mad!

That dream of the regeneration of the world by the destruction of present Life, I made in good faith, I swear to you. Never, at any moment, did I believe that I was yielding to an egotistical rage or an amorous despair. Never, before tonight, have I perceived the enormity of the sins of which I was the unconscious cause.

In order to remove the scales from my blind eyes, it has required one final sacrifice, that of an innocent, that of poor little Étienne.

By the time you read these lines, all those who were on the Mont d'Ossat will be dead. It is necessary, therefore, for me to tell you...

First of all, Barnett killed himself the other night. The wretch met a frightful end. Since our arrival in this convent he had not ceased drinking and getting drunk. In a fit of delirium tremens *he became fearful of the mortal cold that was increasing and wanted to protect himself from it. Soaking his garments in gin, he set fire to them. For a few minutes he ran, a living torch, uttering the cries of a damned soul. In an interior courtyard of the convent, a heap of calcined bones and black ashes will be found. That is what remains of Barnett.*

I remained alone with Jobert. As I got to know him better, the man filled me with horror: a sanguinary madman who exulted in the memory of his crimes. In the last few days, I have been obliged to use my authority to prevent him shooting with a rifle at the soldiers who appeared in the plain. Yesterday, he manifested a savage joy when the dirigible crashed.

This evening, he claimed to hear suspicious noises from the direction of our vats of acid—for my refrigerators are installed outside the convent, in an old vaulted cistern only receiving daylight from outside through long and narrow ventilation shafts; by that means, they were sheltered from the most powerful shells.

Alas, I judged it materially impossible for anyone to reach our eagle's nest by any means whatsoever. However, little Étienne was there. Guided by the radiation of the radium, the child had discovered the stone staircase leading to the cistern. He had had the idea of taking the sixty vats one by one—they only weigh fifteen kilos each—and throwing them to the foot of the rock.

He had reckoned without Jobert. Surprised by the wretch, Étienne tried to defend himself, but the other, like a coward, plunged a dagger into his heart.

Drawn by the martyred child's cries, I ran. I recognized Étienne, my pupil—almost my son—lying in a pool of blood, and standing over him, Jobert, his dagger red, laughing ferociously, uttering threats and insults.

Then, a veil was torn in my poor head. I discovered the abominable truth. I was horrified. Without saying a word, with two bullets from my revolver, I slew the monster.

After that execution, in my turn, I decided to die.

It is necessary for me to profit from that hour of temporary lucidity to protect the world from the inevitable return of my horrible folly. Before then, I wanted to write you this letter, certain that you would find it in the vicinity of the Ossat.

What more is there to say? Before disappearing, I want to beg forgiveness from my victims, from all those I have harmed.

First of all from you, my very dear friend, my brother, for the mental torture that I've imposed on you or more than a year. From Capitaine Berjac, whom I killed indirectly. From the people of Bouffarik and Messina. From the unfortunates who were manning the dirigible lost yesterday, the victims of last night's explosion. And above all from poor little Étienne. Was the blood of that child necessary, then, to redeem the supreme crime meditated against humankind? Finally, from the pure and gentle soul of Hélène Thiérard-Leroy.

A cruel punishment might await me in the afterlife: the reprobation of the woman in memory of whom I have perpetrated the most terrible of designs. That will be justice.

To you, Paul Lefort, I bequeath all my worldly goods; I know that you'll make noble use of them. May they serve, in the measure that is possible, to repair the damage I have done to others.

Before hurling myself into the void, I shall halt the effect of the mortal effluvia. I shall neutralize the vats of acid that still remain. You will find a formula included herewith; it will permit the separation of the radium from the Omega acid.

As for the formula of the acid itself, I shall take the secret with me. It is necessary that no madman or wretch can ever take up the destructive dream again.

May the world live in peace.

The Man of the Apocalypse is dead, killed by Eternal Life.